PENGUIN BOOKS

Casino Royale/ Live and Let Die/ Moonraker

Ian Fleming was born in 1908 and educated at Eton. After a brief period at the Royal Military Academy at Sandhurst he went abroad to further his education. In 1931, having failed to get an appointment in the Foreign Office, he joined Reuters News Agency. During the Second World War he was Personal Assistant to the Director of Naval Intelligence at the Admiralty, rising to the rank of Commander. His wartime experiences provided him with a first-hand knowledge of secret operations.

After the war he became Foreign Manager of Kemsley Newspapers. He built his house, Goldeneye, in Jamaica and there at the age of forty-four he wrote *Casino Royale*, the first of the novels featuring Commander James Bond. By the time of his death in 1964, the James Bond adventures had sold more than forty million copies. *Dr No*, the first film featuring James Bond and starring Sean Connery, was released in 1962 and the Bond films continue to be huge international successes. He is also the author of the magical children's book *Chitty Chitty Bang Bang*.

The novels of Ian Fleming were immediately recognized as classic thrillers by his contemporaries Kingsley Amis, Raymond Chandler and John Betjeman. With the invention of James Bond, Ian Fleming created the greatest British fictional icon of the late twentieth century.

THE JAMES BOND BOOKS

Casino Royale
Live and Let Die
Moonraker
Diamonds are Forever
From Russia with Love
Dr No
Goldfinger
For Your Eyes Only
Thunderball
The Spy Who Loved Me
On Her Majesty's Secret Service
You Only Live Twice
The Man with the Golden Gun
Octopussy/The Living Daylights

IAN FLEMING

Casino Royale

Live and Let Die

Moonraker

with an introduction by
Candia McWilliam

PENGUIN BOOKS

PENGUIN BOOKS

Published by the Penguin Group
Penguin Books Ltd, 80 Strand, London WC2R 0RL, England
Penguin Putnam Inc., 375 Hudson Street, New York, New York 10014, USA
Penguin Books Australia Ltd, 250 Camberwell Road, Camberwell, Victoria 3124, Australia
Penguin Books Canada Ltd, 10 Alcorn Avenue, Toronto, Ontario, Canada M4V 3B2
Penguin Books India (P) Ltd, 11, Community Centre, Panchsheel Park, New Delhi – 110 017, India
Penguin Books (NZ) Ltd, Cnr Rosedale and Airborne Roads, Albany, Auckland, New Zealand
Penguin Books (South Africa) (Pty) Ltd, 24 Sturdee Avenue, Rosebank 2196, South Africa

Penguin Books Ltd, Registered Offices: 80 Strand, London WC2R 0RL, England

www.penguin.com

Casino Royale first published in Great Britain by Jonathan Cape Ltd 1953
Published by Hodder and Stoughton 1988
Published in Penguin and Viking 2002
Live and Let Die first published in Great Britain by Jonathan Cape Ltd 1954
Published by Hodder and Stoughton 1988
Published in Penguin and Viking 2002
Moonraker first published in Great Britain by Jonathan Cape Ltd 1955
Published by Hodder and Stoughton 1989
Published in Penguin and Viking 2002
This omnibus edition published in Penguin Classics 2003
9

Casino Royale copyright © Glidrose Productions Ltd, 1953
Live and Let Die copyright © Glidrose Productions, 1954
Moonraker copyright © Glidrose Productions, 1955
Introduction copyright © Candia McWilliam, 2003
All rights reserved

The moral right of the author of the introduction has been asserted

Set in 10/12.5 pt Monotype Minion
Typeset by Rowland Phototypesetting Ltd, Bury St Edmunds, Suffolk
Printed in England by Clays Ltd, St Ives plc

ISBN-13: 978–0–141–18741–9
ISBN-10: 0–141–18741–7

Contents

Introduction

By Candia McWilliam

Most thrillers, many 'literary' novels indeed, may be read in one way only. This is not the case with the James Bond novels of Ian Fleming.

Why do the James Bond novels live on? Why is Bond himself immortal, inhabiting that particular literary Valhalla or Elysium where Sherlock Holmes and Count Dracula swap grooming tips? Why may these books be reread in a way almost mandatorily not the case with thrillers? What does the reader receive from the novelist that keeps tight what is most certainly a bond between the two, that bond essential for readerly satisfaction?

Short answers first, in order. It's the writing that makes the novels fresh.

Bond is immortal because he combines impossible panache and competence with essential isolation. Bond is wounded, we see it now. He is therefore fatally attractive – to both male and female readers. His exploits are impossibly masculine, his existential state that of an eagle, needing a mate and needing to drive her off.

The books deserve to be read again and again for their style; it is unlike any other. Heraldically decorative, the prose is seldom, until the author's last, bored, works, merely ornamental. There is a luscious clash of ostentation and restraint, and that always appealing trait in English prose, a willingness to go too far at the oddest times. The reader receives expensive thrills, is included in the many not particularly noble foibles and snobberies of Fleming's world, and achieves the simple satisfactions of plot resolution.

Perhaps most potently of all, the books repay close attention, yielding more on each reading, never mind that the stories are implausible and many of the habits of the author's mind and of his creation's mind pretty tricky to swallow. It simply does not matter that Bond has mores that would kill him were he made of less stern stuff than the fairy dust of romance (in the high chivalric sense). His seventy cigarettes a day are the breath of life to him. He is a hero particularly suited to our mock egalitarian times because he celebrates a world ungelded. He is a relief. James Bond arrived in the world at a drab time, when the feasts and excesses of his world brought brightness to readers starved of it by the necessary privations of the Second World War. He revives us now, in a jaded time of unpiquant plenty, with his rarefied treats and skills and taboos, his utterly non-Blairite attitudes, prejudices and appetites. He combines discrimination of appetite with an understanding of restraint and discipline.

Indeed – and the more I have thought about these books and reread them over the past months in order to write about them, the less avoidable this notion has become – these books are very considerably about control and the imposition of restraint, about discipline and the orgiastic instinct. They are certainly about being alone, if not about loneliness, and they are about forms of pain. Even Bond's name leads back to this.

Let's pass gently over what we all know about Fleming's mutually disciplinary marriage; after all, it seems to have been to some private benefit and is incontrovertibly to our benefit in the books. Hardly a chapter passes without an approving mention of a nicely-made belt, a prettily tied apron, an irresistible rear. The clothes in which he dresses his heroines have a pared-back chic and attention to fastenings worthy of Tom Ford. The jewellery is heavy, chaste, serious. Fetishism, of the sort that drives high-end glossy magazines, is everywhere.

The descriptions of food, of women and of what have come to be called commodities (cars, guns, belts, shoes, all the accessories of a hero) would not carry the weight they do were Bond not a man of discipline, of reined-in desire. He has the hunger-artist's mania for the perfect menu, the peach in season. His aversion to American food is an aversion to a substance that will not feed his hyperaesthetic hunger. His women are spoils of war, consoling artefacts. Bond is, like his creator, a Scot, a man of appetite trained to mistrust and suppress appetite. So sharp is this appetite, suppressed, that it will be assuaged only by fantastic, improbable, formalized menus or by ritualized customs of arcane habit (certain breakfasts for certain continents, the notorious unbruised Martini).

What does Bond fear? Boredom. Take this, from *Casino Royale*:

With most women his manner was a mixture of taciturnity and passion. The lengthy approaches to a seduction bored him almost as much as the subsequent mess of disentanglement. He found something grisly in the inevitability of the pattern of each affair. The conventional parabola – sentiment, the touch of the hand, the kiss, the passionate kiss, the feel of the body, the climax in bed, then more bed, then less bed, then the boredom, the tears and the final bitterness – was to him shameful and hypocritical. Even more he shunned the *mise en scène* for each of these acts in the play – the meeting at a party, the restaurant, the taxi, his flat, her flat, then the week-end by the sea, then the flats again, then the furtive alibis and the final angry farewell on some doorstep in the rain.

That is how Bond thinks he thinks. Actually, he sees that with Vesper there could be none of this. Later in the book it is she who says, 'People are islands. They don't really touch. However close they are, they're really quite separate. Even if they've been married for fifty years.'

Strawberries and champagne elide what Bond imagines to be Vesper's *vin triste*. But it is all sadder than that. Fleming equips Bond in this first book with another failsafe commodity, a broken heart.

Casino Royale established what would become a heroic roll call of absolutely apt, preposterous and symbolic names. It established too a fondness for high talk:

'So,' continued Bond, warming to his argument [this after being tortured with a carpet-beater to the balls], 'Le Chiffre was serving a wonderful purpose, a really vital purpose, perhaps the best and highest purpose of all. By his evil existence, which foolishly I have helped to destroy, he was creating a norm of badness by which, and by which alone, an opposite norm of goodness could exist. We were privileged, in our short knowledge of him, to see and estimate his wickedness and we emerge from the acquaintanceship better and more virtuous men.'

The conversation continues at this level, or perhaps pitch is the better word. The chapter ends:

Mathis opened the door and stopped on the threshold.

'Surround yourself with human beings, my dear James, they are easier to fight for than principles.'

He laughed. 'But don't let me down and become human yourself. We would lose such a wonderful machine.'

With a wave of his hand he shut the door.

'Hey,' shouted Bond.

But the footsteps went quickly off down the passage.

More than a thriller, certainly; more than a romance. A tale of chivalry for a pornographic century at its cusp, the old worlds falling to rubble and smoke, nostalgia, disdain and over-cultivation.

A final word on *Casino Royale*. Throughout, 'cold' and its derivatives and synonyms are terms of approval. Dissociation, distance, irony, poise, scrutiny, anathema, they all add to the layers of pleasure to be derived from reading these novels. They continue to produce the wonderful unease sent up when the genre's necessary humourlessness meets the author's bored wit. It's a refreshing *je m'en fichisme* now we all have to sound as though we mean what we say, especially when we don't.

Live and Let Die is even more decorated with emblems, motifs, literary references and distractions from tedium than its predecessor. It does offer an at-times squeamish glimpse of the superstitious inter-racial fear, and the prejudice it causes. Still, Bond is entirely prejudiced about his best (his only?) friend, Felix Leiter of the 'sort of liaison between the Central Intelligence Agency and our friends of the FBI', and that doesn't stop him being very fond of the poor fellow, especially when he is half-eaten in the pursuit of his calling. Leiter has a considerable wit. It is he who coins the verb 'hyphenate' for sexual intercourse. He is devoted to Bond, and well understands, as an American must, his own and his nation's second-rateness, especially in the matter of breakfast.

Fleming allows himself perhaps three particular treats, or antidotes to authorial *anomie*, in *Live and Let Die*. He lets rip his facility for horror. I find the voodoo passages almost too chilling to read, as though they will bring about harm. That is some authorial force. He has great fun with the arcana of ichthyology. In all the books, he sees off boredom with facts, but they are not ever there for padding. Facts with movement, that's hard to do, but Fleming does it, time and again. It's the adventurer in him, his brother Peter in him too, perhaps? The greatest treat the author offers himself is not even the glorious Solitaire, but Quarrel, the quasi-gillie, who trains Bond in the ways of nature and divests him, over drink- and tobacco-less days, of the sapping effects of civilization. Quarrel is, as it were, Fleming's nod to Robert Louis Stevenson and *Kidnapped*, most particularly to Alan Breck Stuart.

Ornament is extraneous to a central artistic structure, decoration integral, enhancing, heightening, a metaphor often for the central shape. The fish, great worms, sharks, faceless men are all echoes, dark and abidingly sinister, of the rites of voodoo.

'Why doesn't someone kill him?' asked Bond [of his enemy, Mr Big].

'You can't kill him,' she said. 'He's already dead. He's a Zombie.'

If Fleming came to feel a little like that about James Bond, we can understand perhaps, but we shall still be grateful that the author's own distaste was overcome by his creature's will to live – as well as possible.

Moonraker is a very peculiar book. Its charms, greeds, sentimentalities and better feelings remind me strongly of the diaries of the late Alan Clark, so charmingly or repellently (dependent on your view) wrong-headed on politics and sex, so wonderfully sound on nature observed and on love of landscape. Like all books starring wizard machinery, *Moonraker* has become touchingly risible. This adds to its great charm. It also continues to make us frightened, principally, I think, because of the threat to London, towards which the book demonstrates little less than love.

The villains are not, as in *Live and Let Die*, SMERSH, but old Nazis. Fleming is adept at describing bodies of men reduced to uniformity, a terrifying phenomenon in Fleming/Bond's (admittedly snobbish) individualistic world.

Even Krebs (evil German) is not immune to the loveliness of this country we poltroons of Englishmen mess up by living in it:

Krebs grinned happily to himself at the thought of the stupid English having to clean up all this mess. He settled himself back to enjoy the part of the drive he had always liked best, the spring woods full of bluebells and celandines on the way to Chilham.

They had made him particularly happy at night. Lit up amongst the green torches of the young trees by the great headlamps of the Mercedes, they made him think of the beautiful forests of the Ardennes and of the devoted little band with which he had served, and of driving along in a captured American jeep with, just like tonight, his adored leader at the wheel.

Krebs's 'adored leader' is Sir Hugo Drax. Of course this moustache-twirling name conceals a more Hunnish identity. The unmasking of Drax is beautifully paced, beginning with the great set piece of cards. The book is studded with set pieces, making it impossible to read slowly, desirable to read lingeringly. This paradox makes you want to reread it at once. There is the inestimable pleasure of spending some time with M, and the sentimental pleasure of seeing England through Fleming's eyes.

If we do not get to the bottom of 'this strange and cold profession with its tensions and hollow thrills' (being in the Secret Service, not writing novels, though they have much in common), we have time at the table, and at the tables, with Bond. Fleming's convinced, jewelled, thrillingly vulgar poetic gift is at its height in this book.

How, then, may these books be read? For plot, for sure. For a dislodging psychological unease that soaks them. For pleasingly retro tropes such as sexism. For cardiovascular threat by menu, wine list and tobacco. For a voluptuous sadness at the sure passing of certainties. For continual homeopathic doses of anti-Americanism, coupled with a kind of stars-&-stripestruck cousinhood. For the sense of an enemy who will be seen off, and the reassurance that offers, in a time of terror.

That is, for fun.

Casino Royale

Contents

1 The Secret Agent

The scent and smoke and sweat of a casino are nauseating at three in the morning. Then the soul-erosion produced by high gambling – a compost of greed and fear and nervous tension – becomes unbearable and the senses awake and revolt from it.

James Bond suddenly knew that he was tired. He always knew when his body or his mind had had enough and he always acted on the knowledge. This helped him to avoid staleness and the sensual bluntness that breeds mistakes.

He shifted himself unobtrusively away from the roulette he had been playing and went to stand for a moment at the brass rail which surrounded breast-high the top table in the *salle privée*.

Le Chiffre was still playing and still, apparently, winning. There was an untidy pile of flecked hundred-mille plaques in front of him. In the shadow of his thick left arm there nestled a discreet stack of the big yellow ones worth half a million francs each.

Bond watched the curious, impressive profile for a time, and then he shrugged his shoulders to lighten his thoughts and moved away.

The barrier surrounding the *caisse* comes as high as your chin and the *caissier*, who is generally nothing more than a minor bank clerk, sits on a stool and dips into his piles of notes and plaques. These are ranged on shelves. They are on a level, behind the protecting barrier, with your groin. The *caissier* has a cosh and a gun to protect him, and to heave over the barrier and steal some notes and then vault back and get out of the casino through the passages and doors would be impossible. And the *caissiers* generally work in pairs.

Bond reflected on the problem as he collected the sheaf of hundred thousand and then the sheaves of ten thousand franc notes. With another part of his mind, he had a vision of tomorrow's regular morning meeting of the casino committee.

'Monsieur Le Chiffre made two million. He played his usual game. Miss Fairchild made a million in an hour and then left. She executed three "bancos" of Monsieur Le Chiffre within an hour and then left. She played with coolness. Monsieur le Vicomte de Villorin made one million two at roulette. He was playing the maximum on the first and last dozens. He was lucky. Then the Englishman, Mister Bond, increased his winnings to exactly three million over the two days. He was playing a progressive system on red at table five. Duclos, the *chef de partie*, has the details. It seems that he is persevering and plays in maximums. He has luck. His nerves seem good. On the *soirée*, the chemin-de-fer won x, the baccarat won y and the roulette won z. The boule, which was again badly frequented, still makes its expenses.'

'*Merci, Monsieur Xavier.*'

'*Merci, Monsieur le Président.*'

Or something like that, thought Bond as he pushed his way through the swing doors of the *salle privée* and nodded to the bored man in evening clothes whose job it is to bar your entry and your exit with the electric foot-switch which can lock the doors at any hint of trouble.

And the casino committee would balance its books and break up to its homes or cafés for lunch.

As for robbing the *caisse*, in which Bond himself was not personally concerned, but only interested, he reflected that it would take ten good men, that they would certainly have to kill one or two employees, and that anyway you probably couldn't find ten non-squeal killers in France, or in any other country for the matter of that.

As he gave a thousand francs to the *vestiaire* and walked down the steps of the casino, Bond made up his mind that Le Chiffre would in no circumstances try to rob the *caisse* and he put the contingency out of his mind. Instead he explored his present physical sensations. He felt the dry, uncomfortable gravel under his evening shoes, the bad, harsh taste in his mouth and the slight sweat under his arms. He could feel his eyes filling their sockets. The front of his face, his nose and antrum, were congested. He breathed the sweet night air deeply and focused his senses and his wits. He wanted to know if anyone had searched his room since he had left it before dinner.

He walked across the broad boulevard and through the gardens to the Hôtel Splendide. He smiled at the concierge who gave him his key – No. 45 on the first floor – and took the cable.

It was from Jamaica and read:

KINGSTONJA XXXX XXXXXX XXXX XXX
BOND SPLENDIDE ROYALE-LES-EAUX SEINE INFERIEURE
HAVANA CIGAR PRODUCTION ALL CUBAN FACTORIES 1915
TEN MILLION REPEAT TEN MILLION STOP HOPE THIS FIGURE
YOU REQUIRE REGARDS.

DASILVA

This meant that ten million francs was on the way to him. It was the reply to a request Bond had sent that afternoon through Paris to his headquarters in London asking for more funds. Paris had spoken to London where Clements, the head of Bond's department, had spoken to M, who had smiled wryly and told 'The Broker' to fix it with the Treasury.

Bond had once worked in Jamaica and his cover on the Royale assignment was that of a very rich client of Messrs Caffery, the principal import and export firm of Jamaica. So he was being controlled through Jamaica, through a taciturn man who was head of the picture desk on the *Daily Gleaner*, the famous newspaper of the Caribbean.

This man on the *Gleaner*, whose name was Fawcett, had been book-keeper for one of the leading turtle-fisheries on the Cayman Islands. One of the men from the Caymans who had volunteered on the outbreak of war, he had ended up as a Paymaster's clerk in a small Naval Intelligence organization in Malta. At the end of the war, when, with a heavy heart, he was due to return to the Caymans, he was spotted by the section of the Secret Service concerned with the Caribbean. He was strenuously trained in photography and in some other arts and, with the quiet connivance of an influential man in Jamaica, found his way to the picture desk of the *Gleaner*.

In the intervals between sifting photographs submitted by the great agencies – Keystone, Wide-World, Universal, INP, and Reuter-Photo

– he would get peremptory instructions by telephone from a man he had never met to carry out certain simple operations requiring nothing but absolute discretion, speed, and accuracy. For these occasional services he received twenty pounds a month paid into his account with the Royal Bank of Canada by a fictitious relative in England.

Fawcett's present assignment was to relay immediately to Bond, full rates, the text of messages which he received at home by telephone from his anonymous contact. He had been told by this contact that nothing he would be asked to send would arouse the suspicion of the Jamaican post office. So he was not surprised to find himself suddenly appointed string correspondent for the 'Maritime Press and Photo Agency', with press-collect facilities to France and England, on a further monthly retainer of ten pounds.

He felt secure and encouraged, had visions of a BEM and made the first payment on a Morris Minor. He also bought a green eye-shade which he had long coveted and which helped him to impose his personality on the picture desk.

Some of this background to his cable passed through Bond's mind. He was used to oblique control and rather liked it. He felt it feather-bedded him a little, allowed him to give or take an hour or two in his communications with M. He knew that this was probably a fallacy, that probably there was another member of the Service at Royale-les-Eaux who was reporting independently, but it did give the illusion that he wasn't only 150 miles across the Channel from that deadly office building near Regent's Park, being watched and judged by those few cold brains that made the whole show work. Just as Fawcett, the Cayman Islander in Kingston, knew that if he bought that Morris Minor outright instead of signing the hire-purchase agreement, some-one in London would probably know and want to know where the money had come from.

Bond read the cable twice. He tore a telegram form off the pad on the desk (why give them carbon copies?) and wrote his reply in capital letters:

THANKS INFORMATION SHOULD SUFFICE – BOND

He handed this to the concierge and put the cable signed 'DaSilva' in his pocket. The employers (if any) of the concierge could bribe a copy out of the local post office, if the concierge hadn't already steamed the envelope open or read the cable upside down in Bond's hands.

He took his key and said good night and turned to the stairs, shaking his head at the liftman. Bond knew what an obliging danger-signal a lift could be. He didn't expect anyone to be moving on the first floor, but he preferred to be prudent.

Walking quietly up on the balls of his feet, he regretted the hubris of his reply to M via Jamaica. As a gambler he knew it was a mistake to rely on too small a capital. Anyway, M probably wouldn't let him have any more. He shrugged his shoulders and turned off the stairs into the corridor and walked softly to the door of his room.

Bond knew exactly where the switch was and it was with one flow of motion that he stood on the threshold with the door full open, the light on and a gun in his hand. The safe, empty room sneered at him. He ignored the half-open door of the bathroom and, locking himself in, he turned up the bed-light and the mirror-light and threw his gun on the settee beside the window. Then he bent down and inspected one of his own black hairs which still lay undisturbed where he had left it before dinner, wedged into the drawer of the writing-desk.

Next he examined a faint trace of talcum powder on the inner rim of the porcelain handle of the clothes cupboard. It appeared immaculate. He went into the bathroom, lifted the cover of the lavatory cistern and verified the level of the water against a small scratch on the copper ball-cock.

Doing all this, inspecting these minute burglar-alarms, did not make him feel foolish or self-conscious. He was a secret agent, and still alive thanks to his exact attention to the detail of his profession. Routine precautions were to him no more unreasonable than they would be to a deep-sea diver or a test pilot, or to any man earning danger-money.

Satisfied that his room had not been searched while he was at the casino, Bond undressed and took a cold shower. Then he lit his seventieth cigarette of the day and sat down at the writing-table with the thick wad of his stake money and winnings beside him and entered some figures in a small notebook. Over the two days' play, he was up exactly three million francs. In London he had been issued with ten million, and he had asked London for a further ten. With this on its way to the local branch of Crédit Lyonnais, his working capital amounted to twenty-three million francs, or some twenty-three thousand pounds.

For a few moments Bond sat motionless, gazing out of the window across the dark sea, then he shoved the bundle of banknotes under the pillow of the ornate single bed, cleaned his teeth, turned out the lights and climbed with relief between the harsh French sheets. For ten minutes he lay on his left side reflecting on the events of the day. Then he turned over and focused his mind towards the tunnel of sleep.

His last action was to slip his right hand under the pillow until it rested under the butt of the .38 Colt Police Positive with the sawn barrel. Then he slept, and with the warmth and humour of his eyes extinguished, his features relapsed into a taciturn mask, ironical, brutal, and cold.

2 Dossier for M

Two weeks before, this memorandum had gone from Station S of the Secret Service to M, who was then and is today head of this adjunct to the British Defence Ministries:

To: M.

From: Head of S.

Subject: A project for the destruction of Monsieur Le Chiffre (alias 'The Number', 'Herr Nummer', 'Herr Ziffer', etc.), one of the Opposition's chief agents in France and undercover Paymaster of the 'Syndicat des Ouvriers d'Alsace', the Communist-controlled trade union in the heavy and transport industries of Alsace, and as we know, an important fifth column in the event of war with Redland.

Documentation: Head of Archives' biography of Le Chiffre is attached at Appendix A. Also, Appendix B, a note on SMERSH.

We have been feeling for some time that Le Chiffre is getting into deep water. In nearly all respects he is an admirable agent of the USSR, but his gross physical habits and predilections are an Achilles heel of which we have been able to take advantage from time to time and one of his mistresses is a Eurasian (No. 1860) controlled by Station F, who has recently been able to obtain insight into his private affairs.

Briefly, it seems that Le Chiffre is on the brink of a financial crisis. Certain straws in the wind were noticed by 1860 – some discreet sales of jewellery, the disposal of a villa at Antibes, and a general tendency to check the loose spending which has always been a feature of his way of life. Further inquiries were made with the help of our friends of the Deuxième Bureau (with whom we have been working jointly on this case) and a curious story has come to light.

In January 1946, Le Chiffre bought control of a chain of brothels, known as the Cordon Jaune, operating in Normandy and Brittany. He was foolish enough to employ for this purpose some fifty million francs of the moneys entrusted to him by Leningrad Section III for the financing of SODA, the trade union mentioned above.

Normally the Cordon Jaune would have proved a most excellent investment and it is possible that Le Chiffre was motivated more by a desire to increase his union funds than by the hope of lining his own pocket by speculating with his employers' money. However that may be, it is clear that he could have found many investments more savoury than prostitution, if he had not been tempted by the by-product of unlimited women for his personal use.

Fate rebuked him with terrifying swiftness.

Barely three months later, on 13 April, there was passed in France Law No. 46685 entitled *Loi Tendant à la Fermeture des Maisons de Tolérance et au Renforcement de la Lutte contre le Proxénétisme*.

(When M came to this sentence he grunted and pressed a switch on the intercom.

'Head of S?'

'Sir.'

'What the hell does this word mean?' He spelt it out.

'Pimping, sir.'

'This is not the Berlitz School of Languages, Head of S. If you want to show off your knowledge of foreign jaw-breakers, be good enough to provide a crib. Better still, write in English.'

'Sorry, sir.'

M released the switch and turned back to the memorandum.

This law [he read] known popularly as 'La Loi Marthe Richard', closing all houses of ill-fame and forbidding the sale of pornographic books and films, knocked the bottom out of his investment almost overnight and suddenly Le Chiffre was faced with a serious deficit in his union funds. In desperation he turned his open houses into *maisons de passe*, where clandestine rendezvous could be arranged on the borderline of the law, and he continued to operate one or two *cinémas bleus* underground, but these shifts in no way served to cover his overheads, and all attempts to sell his investment, even at a heavy loss, failed dismally. Meanwhile the Police des Moeurs were on his trail and in a short while twenty or more of his establishments were closed down.

The police were, of course, only interested in this man as a big-time brothel-keeper and it was not until we expressed an interest in his finances that the Deuxième Bureau unearthed the parallel dossier which was running with their colleagues of the police department.

The significance of the situation became apparent to us and to our French friends and, in the past few months, a veritable rat-hunt has been operated by the police after the establishments of the Cordon Jaune, with the result that today nothing remains of Le Chiffre's original investment and any routine inquiry would reveal a deficit of around fifty million francs in the trade union funds of which he is the treasurer and paymaster.

It does not seem that the suspicions of Leningrad have been aroused yet but, unfortunately for Le Chiffre, it is possible that at any rate SMERSH is on the scent. Last week a high-grade source of Station P reported that a senior official of this efficient organ of Soviet vengeance had left Warsaw for Strasbourg via the Eastern sector of Berlin. There is no confirmation of this report from the Deuxième Bureau, nor from the authorities in Strasbourg (who are reliable and thorough) and there is also no news from Le Chiffre's headquarters there, which we have well covered by a double agent (in addition to 1860).

If Le Chiffre knew that SMERSH was on his tail or that they had the smallest suspicion of him, he would have no alternative but to commit suicide or attempt to escape, but his present plans suggest that while he is certainly desperate, he does not yet realize that his life may be at stake. It is these rather spectacular plans of his that have suggested to us a counter-operation which, though risky and unconventional, we submit at the end of this memorandum with confidence.

In brief, Le Chiffre plans, we believe, to follow the example of most other desperate till-robbers and make good the deficit in his accounts by gambling. The 'Bourse' is too slow. So are the various illicit traffics in drugs, or rare medicines, such as aureo- and streptomycin and cortisone. No race-tracks could carry the sort of stakes he will have to play and, if he wins, he would more likely be killed than paid off.

In any case, we know that he has withdrawn the final twenty-five million francs from the treasury of his union and that he has taken a small villa in the neighbourhood of Royale-les-Eaux, just north of Dieppe, for a week from a fortnight tomorrow.

Now, it is expected that the Casino at Royale will see the highest gambling in Europe this summer. In an effort to wrest the big money from Deauville and Le Touquet, the Société des Bains de Mers de Royale have leased the baccarat and the two top chemin-de-fer tables to the Mahomet Ali Syndicate, a group of émigré Egyptian bankers and businessmen with, it is said, a call on certain royal funds, who have for years been trying to cut in on the profits of Zographos and his Greek associates resulting from their monopoly of the highest French baccarat banks.

With the help of discreet publicity, a considerable number of the biggest operators in America and Europe have been encouraged to book at Royale this summer and it seems possible that this old-fashioned watering-place will regain some of its Victorian renown.

Be that as it may, it is here that Le Chiffre will, we are confident, endeavour on or after 15 June to make a profit at baccarat of fifty million francs on a working capital of twenty-five million. (And, incidentally, save his life.)

Proposed Counter-operation: It would be greatly in the interests of this country and of the other nations of the North Atlantic Treaty Organization that this powerful Soviet agent should be ridiculed and destroyed, that his Communist trade union should be bankrupted and brought into disrepute, and that this potential fifth column, with a strength of 50,000, capable in time of war of controlling a wide sector of France's northern frontier, should lose faith and cohesion. All this would result if Le Chiffre could be defeated at the tables. (NB Assassination is pointless. Leningrad would quickly cover up his defalcations and make him into a martyr.)

We therefore recommend that the finest gambler available to the Service should be given the necessary funds and endeavour to out-gamble this man.

The risks are obvious and the possible loss to the Secret funds is high, but other operations on which large sums have been hazarded have had fewer chances of success, often for a smaller objective.

If the decision is unfavourable, the only alternative would be to place our information and our recommendations in the hands of the Deuxième Bureau or of our American colleagues of the Central Intelligence Agency in Washington. Both of these organizations would doubtless be delighted to take over the scheme.

Signed: S.

Appendix A
Name: Le Chiffre.
Aliases: Variations on the words 'cypher' or 'number' in different languages; e.g. 'Herr Ziffer'.
Origin: Unknown.

First encountered as a displaced person, inmate of Dachau DP camp in the US Zone of Germany, June 1945. Apparently suffering from amnesia and paralysis of vocal cords (?both feigned). Dumbness succumbed to therapy, but subject continued to claim total loss of memory except associations with Alsace-Lorraine and Strasbourg whither he was transferred in September 1945, on Stateless Passport No. 304–596. Adopted the name 'Le Chiffre' ('since I am only a number on a passport'). No Christian names.

Age: About 45.

Description: Height 5 ft 8 ins. Weight 18 stones. Complexion very pale. Clean-shaven. Hair red-brown, 'en brosse'. Eyes very dark brown with whites showing all round iris. Small, rather feminine mouth. False teeth of expensive quality. Ears small, with large lobes, indicating some Jewish blood. Hands small, well-tended, hirsute. Feet small. Racially, subject is probably a mixture of Mediterranean with Prussian or Polish strains. Dresses well and meticulously, generally in dark double-breasted suits. Smokes incessantly Caporals, using a denicotinizing holder. At frequent intervals inhales from benzedrine inhale:. Voice soft and even. Bilingual in French and English. Good German. Traces of Marseilles accent. Smiles infrequently. Does not laugh.

Habits: Mostly expensive, but discreet. Large sexual appetites. Flagellant. Expert driver of fast cars. Adept with small arms and other forms of personal combat, including knives. Carries three Eversharp razor blades, in hat-band, heel of left shoe and cigarette-case. Knowledge of accountancy and mathematics. Fine gambler. Always accompanied by two armed guards, well-dressed, one French, one German (details available).

Comment: A formidable and dangerous agent of the USSR, controlled by Leningrad Section III through Paris.

Signed: Archivist

Appendix B
Subject: SMERSH
Sources: Own archives and scanty material made available by Deuxième Bureau and CIA Washington.

SMERSH is a conjunction of two Russian words: 'Smyert Shpionam', meaning roughly: 'Death to Spies'.

Ranks above MWD (formerly NKVD) and is believed to come under the personal direction of Beria.

Headquarters: Leningrad (sub-station at Moscow).

Its task is the elimination of all forms of treachery and back-sliding with the various branches of the Soviet Secret Service and Secret Police at home and abroad. It is the most powerful and feared organization in the USSR and is popularly believed never to have failed in a mission of vengeance.

It is thought that SMERSH was responsible for the assassination of Trotsky in Mexico (22 August 1940) and may indeed have made its name with this successful murder after attempts by other Russian individuals and organizations had failed.

SMERSH was next heard of when Hitler attacked Russia. It was then rapidly expanded to cope with treachery and double agents during the retreat of the Soviet forces in 1941. At that time it worked as an execution squad for the NKVD and its present selective mission was not so clearly defined.

The organization itself was thoroughly purged after the war and is now believed to consist of only a few hundred operatives of very high quality divided into five sections:

Department I: In charge of counter-intelligence among Soviet organizations at home and abroad.

Department II: Operations, including executions.

Department III: Administration and Finance.

Department IV: Investigations and legal work. Personnel.

Department V: Prosecutions: the section which passes final judgement on all victims.

Only one SMERSH operative has come into our hands since the war: Goytchev, alias Garrad-Jones. He shot Petchora, medical officer at the Yugoslav Embassy, in Hyde Park, 7 August 1948. During interrogation he committed suicide by swallowing a coat-button of compressed potassium cyanide. He revealed nothing beyond his membership of SMERSH, of which he was arrogantly boastful.

We believe that the following British double agents were victims of SMERSH: Donovan, Harthrop-Vane, Elizabeth Dumont, Ventnor, Mace, Savarin (For details see Morgue: Section Q).

Conclusion: Every effort should be made to improve our knowledge of this very powerful organization and destroy its operatives.

3 Number 007

Head of S (the section of the Secret Service concerned with the Soviet Union) was so keen on his plan for the destruction of Le Chiffre, and it was basically his own plan, that he took the memorandum himself and went up to the top floor of the gloomy building overlooking Regent's Park and through the green baize door and along the corridor to the end room.

He walked belligerently up to M's Chief of Staff, a young sapper who had earned his spurs as one of the secretariat to the Chiefs of Staff committee after having been wounded during a sabotage operation in 1944, and had kept his sense of humour in spite of both experiences.

'Now look here, Bill. I want to sell something to the Chief. Is this a good moment?'

'What do you think, Penny?' The Chief of Staff turned to M's private secretary, who shared the room with him.

Miss Moneypenny would have been desirable but for eyes which were cool and direct and quizzical.

'Should be all right. He won a bit of a victory at the FO this morning and he's not got anyone for the next half an hour.' She smiled encouragingly at Head of S whom she liked for himself and for the importance of his section.

'Well, here's the dope, Bill.' He handed over the black folder with the red star which stood for Top Secret. 'And for God's sake look enthusiastic when you give it him. And tell him I'll wait here and read a good code-book while he's considering it. He may want some more details, and anyway I want to see you two don't pester him with anything else until he's finished.'

'All right, sir.' The Chief of Staff pressed a switch and leant towards the intercom on his desk.

'Yes?' asked a quiet, flat voice.

'Head of S has an urgent docket for you, sir.'

There was a pause.

'Bring it in,' said a voice.

The Chief of Staff released the switch and stood up.

'Thanks, Bill. I'll be next door,' said Head of S.

The Chief of Staff crossed his office and went through the double doors leading into M's room. In a moment he came out and over the entrance a small blue light burned the warning that M was not to be disturbed.

Later, a triumphant Head of S said to his Number Two: 'We nearly cooked ourselves with that last paragraph. He said it was subversion and blackmail. He got pretty sharp about it. Anyway, he approves. Says the idea's crazy, but worth trying if the Treasury will play and he thinks they will. He's going to tell them it's a better gamble than the money we're putting into deserting Russian colonels who turn double after a few months' "asylum" here. And he's longing to get at Le Chiffre, and anyway he's got the right man and wants to try him out on the job.'

'Who is it?' asked Number Two.

'One of the Double Os – I guess 007. He's tough and M thinks there may be trouble with those gunmen of Le Chiffre's. He must be pretty good with the cards or he wouldn't have sat in the Casino in Monte Carlo for two months before the war watching that Roumanian team work their stuff with the invisible ink and the dark glasses. He and the Deuxième bowled them out in the end and 007 turned in a million francs he had won at shemmy. Good money in those days.'

James Bond's interview with M had been short.

'What about it, Bond?' asked M when Bond came back into his room after reading Head of S's memorandum and after gazing for ten minutes out of the waiting-room window at the distant trees in the park.

Bond looked across the desk into the shrewd, clear eyes.

'It's very kind of you, sir, I'd like to do it. But I can't promise to win. The odds at baccarat are the best after *trente-et-quarante* – evens except for the tiny *cagnotte* – but I might get a bad run against me and get cleaned out. Play's going to be pretty high – opening'll go up to half a million, I should think.'

Bond was stopped by the cold eyes. M knew all this already, knew the odds at baccarat as well as Bond. That was his job – knowing the odds at everything, and knowing men, his own and the opposition's. Bond wished he had kept quiet about his misgivings.

'He can have a bad run too,' said M. 'You'll have plenty of capital. Up to twenty-five million, the same as him. We'll start you on ten and send you another ten when you've had a look round. You can make the extra five yourself.' He smiled. 'Go over a few days before the big game starts and get your hand in. Have a talk to Q about rooms and trains, and any equipment you want. The Paymaster will fix the funds. I'm going to ask the Deuxième to stand by. It's their territory and as it is we shall be lucky if they don't kick up rough. I'll try and persuade them to send Mathis. You seemed to get on well with him in Monte Carlo on that other Casino job. And I'm going to tell Washington because of the NATO angle. CIA have got one or two good men at Fontainebleau with the joint intelligence chaps there. Anything else?'

Bond shook his head. 'I'd certainly like to have Mathis, sir.'

'Well, we'll see. Try and bring it off. We're going to look pretty fool-ish if you don't. And watch out. This sounds an amusing job, but I don't think it's going to be. Le Chiffre is a good man. Well, best of luck.'

'Thank you, sir,' said Bond and went to the door.

'Just a minute.'

Bond turned.

'I think I'll keep you covered, Bond. Two heads are better than one and you'll need someone to run your communications. I'll think it over. They'll get in touch with you at Royale. You needn't worry. It'll be someone good.'

Bond would have preferred to work alone, but one didn't argue with M. He left the room hoping that the man they sent would be loyal to him and neither stupid, nor, worse still, ambitious.

4 L'Ennemi Écoute

As two weeks later, James Bond awoke in his room at the Hôtel Splendide, some of this history passed through his mind.

He had arrived at Royale-les-Eaux in time for luncheon two days before. There had been no attempt to contact him and there had been no flicker of curiosity when he had signed the register 'James Bond, Port Maria, Jamaica'.

M had expressed no interest in his cover.

'Once you start to make a set at Le Chiffre at the tables, you'll have had it,' he said. 'But wear a cover that will stick with the general public.'

Bond knew Jamaica well, so he asked to be controlled from there and to pass as a Jamaican plantocrat whose father had made his pile in tobacco and sugar and whose son chose to play it away on the stock markets and in casinos. If inquiries were made, he would quote Charles DaSilva of Chaffery's, Kingston, as his attorney. Charles would make the story stick.

Bond had spent the last two afternoons and most of the nights at the Casino, playing complicated progression systems on the even chances at roulette. He made a high banco at chemin-de-fer whenever he heard one offered. If he lost, he would *suivi* once and not chase it further if he lost the second time.

In this way he had made some three million francs and had given his nerves and card-sense a thorough work-out. He had got the geography of the Casino clear in his mind. Above all, he had been able to observe Le Chiffre at the tables and to note ruefully that he was a faultless and lucky gambler.

Bond liked to make a good breakfast. After a cold shower, he sat at the writing-table in front of the window. He looked out at the beautiful day and consumed half a pint of iced orange juice, three scrambled eggs and bacon and a double portion of coffee without sugar. He lit his first cigarette, a Balkan and Turkish mixture made for him by Morlands of Grosvenor Street, and watched the small waves lick the long seashore and the fishing fleet from Dieppe string out towards the June heat haze followed by a paper-chase of herring-gulls.

He was lost in his thoughts when the telephone rang. It was the concierge announcing that a Director of Radio Stentor was waiting below with the wireless set he had ordered from Paris.

'Of course,' said Bond. 'Send him up.'

This was the cover fixed by the Deuxième Bureau for their liaison man with Bond. Bond watched the door, hoping that it would be Mathis.

When Mathis came in, a respectable businessman carrying a large square parcel by its leather handle, Bond smiled broadly and would have greeted him with warmth if Mathis had not frowned and held up his free hand after carefully closing the door.

'I have just arrived from Paris, monsieur, and here is the set you asked to have on approval – five valves, superhet, I think you call it in England, and you should be able to get most of the capitals of Europe from Royale. There are no mountains for forty miles in any direction.'

'It sounds all right,' said Bond, lifting his eyebrows at this mystery-making.

Mathis paid no attention. He placed the set, which he had un-wrapped, on the floor beside the unlit panel electric fire below the mantelpiece.

'It is just past eleven,' he said, 'and I see that the Compagnons de la Chanson should now be on the medium wave from Rome. They are touring Europe. Let us see what the reception is like. It should be a fair test.'

He winked. Bond noticed that he had turned the volume on to full and that the red light indicating the long waveband was illuminated, though the set was still silent.

Mathis fiddled at the back of the set. Suddenly an appalling roar of static filled the small room. Mathis gazed at the set for a few seconds with benevolence and then turned it off and his voice was full of dismay.

'My dear monsieur – forgive me please – badly tuned,' and he again bent to the dials. After a few adjustments the close harmony of the French came over the air and Mathis walked up and clapped Bond very hard on the back and wrang his hand until Bond's fingers ached.

Bond smiled back at him. 'Now, what the hell?' he asked.

'My dear friend,' Mathis was delighted, 'you are blown, blown, blown. Up there,' he pointed at the ceiling, 'at this moment, either Monsieur Muntz or his alleged wife, allegedly bedridden with the *grippe*, is deafened, absolutely deafened, and I hope in agony.' He grinned with pleasure at Bond's frown of disbelief.

Mathis sat down on the bed and ripped open a packet of Caporal with his thumbnail. Bond waited.

Mathis was satisfied with the sensation his words had caused. He became serious.

'How it has happened I don't know. They must have been on to you for several days before you arrived. The opposition is here in real strength. Above you is the Muntz family. He is German. She is from somewhere in Central Europe, perhaps a Czech. This is an old-fashioned hotel. There are disused chimneys behind these electric fires. Just here,' he pointed a few inches above the panel fire, 'is suspended a very powerful radio pick-up. The wires run up the chimney to behind the Muntzes' electric fire where there is an amplifier. In their room is a wire-recorder and a pair of earphones on which the Muntzes listen in turn. That is why Madame Muntz has the *grippe* and takes all her meals in bed and why Monsieur Muntz has to be constantly at her side instead of enjoying the sunshine and the gambling of this delightful resort.

'Some of this we knew because in France we are very clever. The rest we confirmed by unscrewing your electric fire a few hours before you got here.'

Suspiciously Bond walked over and examined the screws which secured the panel to the wall. Their grooves showed minute scratches.

'Now it is time for a little more play-acting,' said Mathis. He walked over to the radio, which was still transmitting close harmony to its audience of three, and switched it off.

'Are you satisfied, monsieur?' he asked. 'You notice how clearly they came over. Are they not a wonderful team?' He made a winding motion with his right hand and raised his eyebrows.

'They are so good,' said Bond, 'that I would like to hear the rest of the programme.' He grinned at the thought of the angry glances which the Muntzes must be exchanging overhead. 'The machine itself seems splendid. Just what I was looking for to take back to Jamaica.'

Mathis made a sarcastic grimace and switched back to the Rome programme.

'You and your Jamaica,' he said, and sat down again on the bed.

Bond frowned at him. 'Well, it's no good crying over spilt milk,' he said. 'We didn't expect the cover to stick for long, but it's worrying that they bowled it out so soon.' He searched his mind in vain for a clue. Could the Russians have broken one of our ciphers? If so, he might just as well pack up and go home. He and his job would have been stripped naked.

Mathis seemed to read his mind. 'It can't have been a cipher,' he said. 'Anyway, we told London at once and they will have changed them. A pretty flap we caused, I can tell you.' He smiled with the satisfaction of a friendly rival. 'And now to business, before our good "Compagnons" run out of breath.

'First of all,' and he inhaled a thick lungful of Caporal, 'you will be pleased with your Number Two. She is very beautiful' – Bond frowned – 'very beautiful indeed.' Satisfied with Bond's reaction, Mathis continued: 'She has black hair, blue eyes, and splendid . . . er . . . protuberances. Back and front,' he added. 'And she is a wireless expert which, though sexually less interesting, makes her a perfect employee of Radio Stentor and assistant to myself in my capacity as wireless salesman for this rich summer season down here.' He grinned. 'We are both staying in the hotel and my assistant will thus be on hand in case your new radio breaks down. All new machines, even French ones, are apt to have teething troubles in the first day or two. And occasionally at night,' he added with an exaggerated wink.

Bond was not amused. 'What the hell do they want to send me a woman for?' he said bitterly. 'Do they think this is a bloody picnic?'

Mathis interrupted. 'Calm yourself, my dear James. She is as serious as you could wish and as cold as an icicle. She speaks French like a native and knows her job backwards. Her cover's perfect and I have arranged for her to team up with you quite smoothly. What is more natural than that you should pick up a pretty girl here? As a Jamaican millionaire,' he coughed respectfully, 'what with your hot blood and all, you would look naked without one.'

Bond grunted dubiously.

'Any other surprises?' he asked suspiciously.

'Nothing very much,' answered Mathis. 'Le Chiffre is installed in his villa. It's about ten miles down the coast road. He has his two guards with him. They look pretty capable fellows. One of them has been seen visiting a little "pension" in the town where three mysterious and rather subhuman characters checked in two days ago. They may be part of the team. Their papers are in order – stateless Czechs apparently – but one of our men says the language they talk in their room is Bulgarian. We don't see many of those around. They're mostly used against the Turks and the Yugoslavs. They're stupid, but obedient. The Russians use them for simple killings or as fall-guys for more complicated ones.'

'Thanks very much. Which is mine to be?' asked Bond. 'Anything else?'

'No. Come to the bar of the Hermitage before lunch. I'll fix the introduction. Ask her to dinner this evening. Then it will be natural for her to come into the Casino with you. I'll be there too, but in the background. I've got one or two good chaps and we'll keep an eye on you. Oh, and there's an American called Leiter here, staying in the hotel. Felix Leiter. He's the CIA chap from Fontainebleau. London told me to tell you. He looks okay. May come in useful.'

A torrent of Italian burst from the wireless set on the floor. Mathis switched it off and they exchanged some phrases about the set and about how Bond should pay for it. Then with effusive farewells and a final wink Mathis bowed himself out.

Bond sat at the window and gathered his thoughts. Nothing that Mathis had told him was reassuring. He was completely blown and under really professional surveillance. An attempt might be made to put him away before he had a chance to pit himself against Le Chiffre at the tables. The Russians had no stupid prejudices about murder. And then there was this pest of a girl. He sighed. Women were for recreation. On a job, they got in the way and fogged things up with sex and hurt feelings and all the emotional baggage they carried around. One had to look out for them and take care of them.

'Bitch,' said Bond, and then remembering the Muntzes, he said 'bitch' again more loudly and walked out of the room.

5 The Girl From Headquarters

It was twelve o'clock when Bond left the Splendide and the clock on the *mairie* was stumbling through its midday carillon. There was a strong scent of pine and mimosa in the air and the freshly watered gardens of the Casino opposite, interspersed with neat gravel parterres and paths, lent the scene a pretty formalism more appropriate to ballet than to melodrama.

The sun shone and there was a gaiety and sparkle in the air which seemed to promise well for the new era of fashion and prosperity for which the little seaside town, after many vicissitudes, was making its gallant bid.

Royale-les-Eaux, which lies near the mouth of the Somme before the flat coastline soars up from the beaches of southern Picardy to the Brittany cliffs which run on to Le Havre, had experienced much the same fortunes as Trouville.

Royale (without the 'Eaux') also started as a small fishing village and its rise to fame as a fashionable watering-place during the Second Empire was as meteoric as that of Trouville. But as Deauville killed Trouville, so, after a long period of decline, did Le Touquet kill Royale.

At the turn of the century, when things were going badly for the little seaside town and when the fashion was to combine pleasure with a 'cure', a natural spring in the hills behind Royale was dis-covered to contain enough diluted sulphur to have a beneficent effect on the liver. Since all French people suffer from liver complaints, Royale quickly became 'Royale-les-Eaux', and 'Eau Royale', in a tor-pedo-shaped bottle, grafted itself demurely on to the tail of the mineral-water lists in hotels and restaurant cars.

It did not long withstand the powerful combines of Vichy and Perrier and Vittel. There came a series of lawsuits, a number of people lost a lot of money and very soon its sale was again entirely local. Royale fell back on the takings from the French and English families during the summer, on its fishing fleet in winter and on the crumbs which fell to its elegantly dilapidated Casino from the table at Le Touquet.

But there was something splendid about the Negresco baroque of the Casino Royale, a strong whiff of Victorian elegance and luxury, and in 1950 Royale caught the fancy of a syndicate in Paris which disposed of large funds belonging to a group of expatriate Vichyites.

Brighton had been revived since the war, and Nice. Nostalgia for more spacious, golden times might be a source of revenue.

The Casino was repainted in its original white and gilt and the rooms decorated in the palest grey with wine-red carpets and curtains. Vast chandeliers were suspended from the ceilings. The gardens were spruced and the fountains played again and the two main hotels, the Splendide and the Hermitage, were prinked and furbished and restaffed.

Even the small town and the *vieux-port* managed to fix welcoming smiles across their ravaged faces, and the main street became gay with the *vitrines* of great Paris jewellers and couturiers, tempted down for a butterfly season by rent-free sites and lavish promises.

Then the Mahomet Ali Syndicate was cajoled into starting a high game in the Casino and the Société des Bains de Mer de Royale felt that now at last Le Touquet would have to yield up some of the treasure stolen over the years from its parent *plage*.

Against the background of this luminous and sparkling stage Bond stood in the sunshine and felt his mission to be incongruous and remote and his dark profession an affront to his fellow actors.

He shrugged away the momentary feeling of unease and walked round the back of his hotel and down the ramp to the garage. Before his rendezvous at the Hermitage he decided to take his car down the coast road and have a quick look at Le Chiffre's villa and then drive back by the inland road until it crossed the *route nationale* to Paris.

Bond's car was his only personal hobby. One of the last of the 4½-litre Bentleys with the supercharger by Amherst-Villiers, he had bought it almost new in 1933 and had kept it in careful storage through the war. It was still serviced every year and, in London, a former Bentley mechanic, who worked in a garage near Bond's Chelsea flat, tended it with jealous care. Bond drove it hard and well and with an almost sensual pleasure. It was a battleship-grey convertible coupé, which really did convert, and it was capable of touring at ninety with thirty miles an hour in reserve.

Bond eased the car out of the garage and up the ramp and soon the loitering drum-beat of the two-inch exhaust was echoing down the tree-lined boulevard, through the crowded main street of the little town, and off through the sand dunes to the south.

An hour later, Bond walked into the Hermitage bar and chose a table near one of the broad windows.

The room was sumptuous with those over-masculine trappings which, together with briar pipes and wire-haired terriers, spell luxury in France. Everything was brass-studded leather and polished mahogany. The curtains and carpets were in royal blue. The waiters wore striped waistcoats and green baize aprons. Bond ordered an Americano and examined the sprinkling of over-dressed customers, mostly from Paris he guessed, who sat talking with focus and vivacity, creating that theatrically clubbable atmosphere of *l'heure de l'apéritif*.

The men were drinking inexhaustible quarter-bottles of champagne, the women dry martinis.

'*Moi, j'adore le "Dry",*' a bright-faced girl at the next table said to her companion, too neat in his unseasonable tweeds, who gazed at her with moist brown eyes over the top of an expensive shooting-stick from Hermes, '*fait avec du Gordon's, bien entendu.*'

'*D'accord, Daisy. Mais tu sais, un zeste de citron . . .*'

Bond's eye was caught by the tall figure of Mathis on the pavement outside, his face turned in animation to a dark-haired girl in grey. His arm was linked in hers, high up above the elbow, and yet there was a lack of intimacy in their appearance, an ironical chill in the girl's profile, which made them seem two separate people rather than a couple. Bond waited for them to come through the street door into the bar, but for appearances' sake continued to stare out of the window at the passers-by.

'But surely it is Monsieur Bond?' Mathis's voice behind him was full of surprised delight. Bond, appropriately flustered, rose to his feet. 'Can it be that you are alone? Are you awaiting someone? May I present my colleague, Mademoiselle Lynd? My dear, this is the gentleman from Jamaica with whom I had the pleasure of doing business this morning.'

Bond inclined himself with a reserved friendliness. 'It would be a great pleasure,' he addressed himself to the girl. 'I am alone. Would you both care to join me?' He pulled out a chair and while they sat down he beckoned to a waiter and despite Mathis's expostulations insisted on ordering the drinks – a *fine à l'eau* for Mathis and a Bacardi for the girl.

Mathis and Bond exchanged cheerful talk about the fine weather and the prospects of a revival in the fortunes of Royale-les-Eaux. The girl sat silent. She accepted one of Bond's cigarettes, examined it and then smoked it appreciatively and without affectation, drawing the smoke deeply into her lungs with a little sigh and then exhaling it casually through her lips and nostrils. Her movements were economical and precise with no trace of self-consciousness.

Bond felt her presence strongly. While he and Mathis talked, he turned from time to time towards her, politely including her in the conversation, but adding up the impressions recorded by each glance.

Her hair was very black and she wore it cut square and low on the nape of the neck, framing her face to below the clear and beautiful line of her jaw. Although it was heavy and moved with the movements of her head, she did not constantly pat it back into place, but let it alone. Her eyes were wide apart and deep blue and they gazed candidly back at Bond with a touch of ironical disinterest which, to his annoyance, he found he would like to shatter, roughly. Her skin was lightly suntanned and bore no trace of make-up except on her mouth which was wide and sensual. Her bare arms and hands had a quality of repose and the general impression of restraint in her appearance and movements was carried even to her fingernails which were unpainted and cut short. Round her neck she wore a plain gold chain of wide flat links and on the fourth finger of the right hand a broad topaz ring. Her medium-length dress was of grey *soie sauvage* with a square-cut bodice, lasciviously tight across her fine breasts. The skirt was closely pleated and flowered down from a narrow, but not a thin, waist. She wore a three-inch, handstitched black belt. A handstitched black *sabretache* rested on the chair beside her, together with a wide cart-wheel hat of gold straw, its crown encircled by a thin black velvet ribbon which tied at the back in a short bow. Her shoes were square-toed of plain black leather.

Bond was excited by her beauty and intrigued by her composure. The prospect of working with her stimulated him. At the same time he felt a vague disquiet. On an impulse he touched wood.

Mathis had noticed Bond's preoccupation. After a time he rose.

'Forgive me,' he said to the girl, 'while I telephone to the Dubernes. I must arrange my rendezvous for dinner tonight. Are you sure you won't mind being left to your own devices this evening?'

She shook her head.

Bond took the cue and, as Mathis crossed the room to the telephone booth beside the bar, he said: 'If you are going to be alone tonight, would you care to have dinner with me?'

She smiled with the first hint of conspiracy she had shown. 'I would like to very much,' she said, 'and then perhaps you would chaperon me to the Casino where Monsieur Mathis tells me you are very much at home. Perhaps I will bring you luck.'

With Mathis gone, her attitude towards him showed a sudden warmth. She seemed to acknowledge that they were a team and, as they discussed the time and place of their meeting, Bond realized that it would be quite easy after all to plan the details of his project with her. He felt that after all she was interested and excited by her role and that she would work willingly with him. He had imagined many hurdles before establishing a rapport, but now he felt he could get straight down to professional details. He was quite honest to himself about the hypocrisy of his attitude towards her. As a woman, he wanted to sleep with her but only when the job had been done.

When Mathis came back to the table Bond called for his bill. He explained that he was expected back at his hotel to have lunch with friends. When for a moment he held her hand in his he felt a warmth of affection and understanding pass between them that would have seemed impossible half an hour earlier.

The girl's eyes followed him out on to the boulevard.

Mathis moved his chair close to hers and said softly: 'That is a very good friend of mine. I am glad you have met each other. I can already feel the ice-floes on the two rivers breaking up.' He smiled, 'I don't think Bond has ever been melted. It will be a new experience for him. And for you.'

She did not answer him directly.

'He is very good-looking. He reminds me rather of Hoagy Carmichael, but there is something cold and ruthless in his . . .'

The sentence was never finished. Suddenly a few feet away the entire plate-glass window shivered into confetti. The blast of a terrific explosion, very near, hit them so that they were rocked back in their chairs. There was an instant of silence. Some objects pattered down on to the pavement outside. Bottles slowly toppled off the shelves behind the bar. Then there were screams and a stampede for the door.

'Stay there,' said Mathis.

He kicked back his chair and hurtled through the empty window-frame on to the pavement.

6 Two Men in Straw Hats

When Bond left the bar he walked purposefully along the pavement flanking the tree-lined boulevard towards his hotel a few hundred yards away. He was hungry.

The day was still beautiful, but by now the sun was very hot and the plane-trees, spaced about twenty feet apart on the grass verge between the pavement and the broad tarmac, gave a cool shade.

There were few people abroad and the two men standing quietly under a tree on the opposite side of the boulevard looked out of place.

Bond noticed them when he was still a hundred yards away and when the same distance separated them from the ornamental *porte cochère* of the Splendide.

There was something rather disquieting about their appearance. They were both small and they were dressed alike in dark and, Bond reflected, rather hot-looking suits. They had the appearance of a variety turn waiting for a bus on the way to the theatre. Each wore a straw hat with a thick black ribbon as a concession, perhaps, to the holiday atmosphere of the resort, and the brims of these and the shadow from the tree under which they stood obscured their faces. Incongruously, each dark, squat little figure was illuminated by a touch of bright colour. They were both carrying square camera-cases slung from the shoulder.

And one case was bright red and the other case bright blue.

By the time Bond had taken in these details, he had come to within fifty yards of the two men. He was reflecting on the ranges of various types of weapon and the possibilities of cover when an extraordinary and terrible scene was enacted.

Red-man seemed to give a short nod to Blue-man. With a quick movement Blue-man unslung his blue camera-case. Blue-man, and Bond could not see exactly as the trunk of a plane-tree beside him just then intervened to obscure his vision, bent forward and seemed to fiddle with the case. Then with a blinding flash of white light there was the ear-splitting crack of a monstrous explosion and Bond, despite the protection of the tree-trunk, was slammed down to the pavement by a bolt of hot air which dented his cheeks and stomach as if they had been made of paper. He lay, gazing up at the sun, while the air (or so it seemed to him) went on twanging with the explosion as if someone had hit the bass register of a piano with a sledgehammer.

When, dazed and half-conscious, he raised himself on one knee, a ghastly rain of pieces of flesh and shreds of blood-soaked clothing fell on him and around him, mingled with branches and gravel. Then a shower of small twigs and leaves. From all sides came the sharp tinkle of falling glass. Above in the sky hung a mushroom of black smoke which rose and dissolved as he drunkenly watched it. There was an obscene smell of high explosive, of burning wood, and of, yes, that was it – roast mutton. For fifty yards down the boulevard the trees were leafless and charred. Opposite, two of them had snapped off near the base and lay drunkenly across the road. Between them there was a still smoking crater. Of the two men in straw hats, there remained absolutely nothing. But there were red traces on the road, and on the pavements and against the trunks of the trees, and there were glittering shreds high up in the branches.

Bond felt himself starting to vomit.

It was Mathis who got to him first, and by that time Bond was standing with his arm round the tree which had saved his life.

Stupefied, but unharmed, he allowed Mathis to lead him off towards the Splendide from which guests and servants were pouring in chattering fright. As the distant clang of bells heralded the arrival of ambulances and fire-engines, they managed to push through the throng and up the short stairs and along the corridor to Bond's room.

Mathis paused only to turn on the radio in front of the fireplace, then, while Bond stripped off his blood-flecked clothes, Mathis sprayed him with questions.

When it came to the description of the two men, Mathis tore the telephone off its hook beside Bond's bed.

'. . . and tell the police,' he concluded, 'tell them that the Englishman from Jamaica who was knocked over by the blast is my affair. He is unhurt and they are not to worry him. I will explain to them in half an hour. They should tell the Press that it was apparently a vendetta between two Bulgarian Communists and that one killed the other

Casino Royale

with a bomb. They need say nothing of the third Bulgar who must have been hanging about somewhere, but they must get him at all costs. He will certainly head for Paris. Roadblocks everywhere. Understand? *Alors, bonne chance.*'

Mathis turned back to Bond and heard him to the end.

'*Merde*, but you were lucky,' he said when Bond had finished. 'Clearly the bomb was intended for you. It must have been faulty. They intended to throw it and then dodge behind their tree. But it all came out the other way round. Never mind. We will discover the facts.' He paused. 'But certainly it is a curious affair. And these people appear to be taking you seriously.' Mathis looked affronted. 'But how did these *sacré* Bulgars intend to escape capture? And what was the significance of the red and the blue cases? We must try and find some fragments of the red one.'

Mathis bit his nails. He was excited and his eyes glittered. This was becoming a formidable and dramatic affair, in many aspects of which he was now involved personally. Certainly it was no longer just a case of holding Bond's coat while he had his private battle with Le Chiffre in the Casino. Mathis jumped up.

'Now get a drink and some lunch and a rest,' he ordered Bond. 'For me, I must get my nose quickly into this affair before the police have muddied the trail with their big black boots.'

Mathis turned off the radio and waved an affectionate farewell. The door slammed and silence settled on the room. Bond sat for a while by the window and enjoyed being alive.

Later, as Bond was finishing his first straight whisky 'on the rocks' and was contemplating the pâté de foie gras and cold langouste which the waiter had just laid out for him, the telephone rang.

'This is Mademoiselle Lynd.'

The voice was low and anxious.

'Are you all right?'

'Yes, quite.'

'I'm glad. Please take care of yourself.'

She rang off.

Bond shook himself, then he picked up his knife and selected the thickest of the pieces of hot toast.

32

He suddenly thought: two of them are dead, and I have got one more on my side. It's a start.

He dipped the knife into the glass of very hot water which stood beside the pot of Strasbourg porcelain and reminded himself to tip the waiter doubly for this particular meal.

7 Rouge et Noir

Bond was determined to be completely fit and relaxed for a gambling session which might last most of the night. He ordered a masseur for three o'clock. After the remains of his luncheon had been removed, he sat at his window gazing out to sea until there came a knock on the door as the masseur, a Swede, presented himself.

Silently he got to work on Bond from his feet to his neck, melting the tensions in his body and calming his still twanging nerves. Even the long purpling bruises down Bond's left shoulder and side ceased to throb, and when the Swede had gone Bond fell into a dreamless sleep.

He awoke in the evening completely refreshed.

After a cold shower, Bond walked over to the Casino. Since the night before he had lost the mood of the tables. He needed to re-establish that focus which is half mathematical and half intuitive and which, with a slow pulse and a sanguine temperament, Bond knew to be the essential equipment of any gambler who was set on winning.

Bond had always been a gambler. He loved the dry riffle of the cards and the constant unemphatic drama of the quiet figures round the green tables. He liked the solid, studied comfort of card-rooms and casinos, the well-padded arms of the chairs, the glass of champagne or whisky at the elbow, the quiet unhurried attention of good servants. He was amused by the impartiality of the roulette ball and of the playing-cards – and their eternal bias. He liked being an actor and a spectator and from his chair to take part in other men's dramas and decisions, until it came to his own turn to say that vital 'yes' or 'no', generally on a fifty-fifty chance.

Above all, he liked it that everything was one's own fault. There was only oneself to praise or blame. Luck was a servant and not a master. Luck had to be accepted with a shrug or taken advantage of up to the hilt. But it had to be understood and recognized for what it was and not confused with a faulty appreciation of the odds, for, at gambling, the deadly sin is to mistake bad play for bad luck. And luck in all its moods had to be loved and not feared. Bond saw luck as a woman, to be softly wooed or brutally ravaged, never pandered to or pursued. But he was honest enough to admit that he had never yet been made to suffer by cards or by women. One day, and he accepted the fact, he would be brought to his knees by love or by luck. When that happened he knew that he too would be branded with the deadly question-mark he recognized so often in others, the promise to pay before you have lost: the acceptance of fallibility.

But on this June evening when Bond walked through the 'kitchen' into the *salle privée*, it was with a sensation of confidence and cheerful anticipation that he changed a million francs into plaques of fifty mille and took a seat next to the *chef de partie* at Roulette Table Number 1.

Bond borrowed the *chef*'s card and studied the run of the ball since the session had started at three o'clock that afternoon. He always did this although he knew that each turn of the wheel, each fall of the ball into a numbered slot, has absolutely no connexion with its predecessor. He accepted that the game begins afresh each time the croupier picks up the ivory ball with his right hand, gives one of the four spokes of the wheel a controlled twist clockwise with the same hand, and with a third motion, also with the right hand, flicks the ball round the outer rim of the wheel anticlockwise, against the spin.

It was obvious that all this ritual and all the mechanical minutiae of the wheel, of the numbered slots and the cylinder, had been devised and perfected over the years so that neither the skill of the croupier nor any bias in the wheel could affect the fall of the ball. And yet it is a convention among roulette players, and Bond rigidly adhered to it, to take careful note of the past history of each session and to be guided by any peculiarities in the run of the wheel. To note, for instance, and consider significant, sequences of more than two on a single number or of more than four at the other chances down to evens.

Bond didn't defend the practice. He simply maintained that the more effort and ingenuity you put into gambling, the more you took out.

On the record of that particular table, after about three hours' play, Bond could see little of interest except that the last dozen had been out of favour. It was his practice to play always with the wheel, and only to turn against its previous pattern and start on a new tack after a zero had turned up. So he decided to play one of his favourite gambits and back two – in this case the first two – dozens, each with the maximum – one hundred thousand francs. He thus had two-thirds of the board covered (less the zero) and, since the dozens pay odds of two to one, he stood to win a hundred thousand francs every time any number lower than twenty-five turned up.

After seven coups he had won six times. He lost on the seventh when thirty came up. His net profit was four hundred thousand francs. He kept off the table for the eighth throw. Zero turned up. This piece of luck cheered him further and, accepting the thirty as a finger-post to the last dozen, he decided to back the first and last dozens until he had lost twice. Ten throws later the middle dozen came up twice, costing him four hundred thousand francs, but he rose from the table one million francs to the good.

Directly Bond had started playing in maximums, his game had become the centre of interest at the table. As he seemed to be in luck, one or two pilot fish started to swim with the shark. Sitting directly opposite, one of these, whom Bond took to be an American, had shown more than the usual friendliness and pleasure at his share of the winning streak. He had smiled once or twice across the table, and there was something pointed in the way he duplicated Bond's movements, placing his two modest plaques of ten mille exactly opposite Bond's larger ones. When Bond rose, he too pushed back his chair and called cheerfully across the table:

'Thanks for the ride. Guess I owe you a drink. Will you join me?'

Bond had a feeling that this might be the CIA man. He knew he was right as they strolled off together towards the bar, after Bond had thrown a plaque of ten mille to the croupier and had given a mille to the *huissier* who drew back his chair.

'My name's Felix Leiter,' said the American. 'Glad to meet you.'

'Mine's Bond – James Bond.'

'Oh yes,' said his companion, 'and now let's see. What shall we have to celebrate?'

Bond insisted on ordering Leiter's Haig-and-Haig 'on the rocks' and then he looked carefully at the barman.

'A dry martini,' he said. 'One. In a deep champagne goblet.'

'*Oui, monsieur.*'

'Just a moment. Three measures of Gordon's, one of vodka, half a measure of Kina Lillet. Shake it very well until it's ice-cold, then add a large thin slice of lemon-peel. Got it?'

'Certainly, monsieur.' The barman seemed pleased with the idea.

'Gosh, that's certainly a drink,' said Leiter.

Bond laughed. 'When I'm . . . er . . . concentrating,' he explained, 'I never have more than one drink before dinner. But I do like that one to be large and very strong and very cold and very well-made. I hate small portions of anything, particularly when they taste bad. This drink's my own invention. I'm going to patent it when I can think of a good name.'

He watched carefully as the deep glass became frosted with the pale golden drink, slightly aerated by the bruising of the shaker. He reached for it and took a long sip.

'Excellent,' he said to the barman, 'but if you can get a vodka made with grain instead of potatoes, you will find it still better.'

'*Mais n'enculons pas des mouches,*' he added in an aside to the barman. The barman grinned.

'That's a vulgar way of saying "we won't split hairs",' explained Bond.

But Leiter was still interested in Bond's drink. 'You certainly think things out,' he said with amusement as they carried their glasses to a corner of the room. He lowered his voice.

'You'd better call it the "Molotov Cocktail" after the one you tasted this afternoon.'

They sat down. Bond laughed.

'I see that the spot marked "X" has been roped off and they're making cars take a detour over the pavement. I hope it hasn't frightened away any of the big money.'

'People are accepting the Communist story or else they think it was a burst gas-main. All the burnt trees are coming down tonight and if they work things here like they do at Monte Carlo, there won't be a trace of the mess left in the morning.'

Leiter shook a Chesterfield out of his pack. 'I'm glad to be working with you on this job,' he said, looking into his drink, 'so I'm particularly glad you didn't get blown to glory. Our people are definitely interested. They think it's just as important as your friends do and they don't think there's anything crazy about it at all. In fact, Washington's pretty sick we're not running the show, but you know what the big brass is like. I expect your fellows are much the same in London.'

Bond nodded. 'Apt to be a bit jealous of their scoops,' he admitted.

'Anyway, I'm under your orders and I'm to give you any help you ask for. With Mathis and his boys here, there may not be much that isn't taken care of already. But, anyway, here I am.'

'I'm delighted you are,' said Bond. 'The opposition has got me, and probably you and Mathis too, all weighed up and it seems no holds are going to be barred. I'm glad Le Chiffre seems as desperate as we thought he was. I'm afraid I haven't got anything very specific for you to do, but I'd be grateful if you'd stick around the Casino this evening. I've got an assistant, a Miss Lynd, and I'd like to hand her over to you when I start playing. You won't be ashamed of her. She's a good-looking girl.' He smiled at Leiter. 'And you might mark his two gunmen. I can't imagine he'll try a rough house, but you never know.'

'I may be able to help,' said Leiter. 'I was a regular in our Marine Corps before I joined this racket, if that means anything to you.' He looked at Bond with a hint of self-deprecation.

'It does,' said Bond.

It turned out that Leiter was from Texas. While he talked on about his job with the Joint Intelligence Staff of NATO and the difficulty of maintaining security in an organization where so many nationalities were represented, Bond reflected that good Americans were fine people and that most of them seemed to come from Texas.

Felix Leiter was about thirty-five. He was tall with a thin bony frame and his lightweight, tan-coloured suit hung loosely from his shoulders like the clothes of Frank Sinatra. His movements and speech were slow, but one had the feeling that there was plenty of speed and strength in him and that he would be a tough and cruel fighter. As he sat hunched over the table, he seemed to have some of the jack-knife quality of a falcon. There was this impression also in his face, in the sharpness of his chin and cheekbones and the wide wry mouth. His grey eyes had a feline slant which was increased by his habit of screwing them up against the smoke of the Chesterfields which he tapped out of the pack in a chain. The permanent wrinkles which this habit had etched at the corners gave the impression that he smiled more with his eyes than with his mouth. A mop of straw-coloured hair lent his face a boyish look which closer examination contradicted. Although he seemed to talk quite openly about his duties in Paris, Bond soon noticed that he never spoke of his American colleagues in Europe or in Washington and he guessed that Leiter held the interests of his own organization far above the mutual concerns of the North Atlantic Allies. Bond sympathized with him.

By the time Leiter had swallowed another whisky and Bond had told him about the Muntzes and his short reconnaissance trip down the coast that morning, it was seven-thirty, and they decided to stroll over to their hotel together. Before leaving the Casino, Bond deposited his total capital of twenty-four million at the *caisse*, keeping only a few notes of ten mille as pocket money.

As they walked across to the Splendide, they saw that a team of workmen was already busy at the scene of the explosion. Several trees were uprooted and hoses from three municipal tank cars were washing down the boulevard and pavements. The bomb-crater had disappeared and only a few passers-by had paused to gape. Bond assumed that similar face-lifting had already been carried out at the Hermitage and to the shops and frontages which had lost their windows.

In the warm blue dusk Royale-les-Eaux was once again orderly and peaceful.

'Who's the concierge working for?' asked Leiter as they approached the hotel. Bond was not sure, and said so.

Mathis had been unable to enlighten him. 'Unless you have bought him yourself,' he had said, 'you must assume that he has been bought by the other side. All concierges are venal. It is not their fault. They are trained to regard all hotel guests except maharajahs as potential cheats and thieves. They have as much concern for your comfort or well-being as crocodiles.'

Bond remembered Mathis's pronouncement when the concierge hurried up to inquire whether he had recovered from his most unfortunate experience of the afternoon. Bond thought it well to say that he still felt a little shaky. He hoped that if the intelligence were relayed, Le Chiffre would at any rate start playing that evening with a basic misinterpretation of his adversary's strength. The concierge proffered glycerine hopes for Bond's recovery.

Leiter's room was on one of the upper floors and they parted company at the lift after arranging to see each other at the Casino at around half past ten or eleven, the usual hour for the high tables to begin play.

8 Pink Lights and Champagne

Bond walked up to his room, which again showed no sign of trespass, threw off his clothes, took a long hot bath followed by an ice-cold shower and lay down on his bed. There remained an hour in which to rest and compose his thoughts before he met the girl in the Splendide bar, an hour to examine minutely the details of his plans for the game, and for after the game, in all the various circumstances of victory or defeat. He had to plan the attendant roles of Mathis, Leiter, and the girl and visualize the reactions of the enemy in various contingencies. He closed his eyes and his thoughts pursued his imagination through a series of carefully constructed scenes as if he was watching the tumbling chips of coloured glass in a kaleidoscope.

At twenty minutes to nine he had exhausted all the permutations which might result from his duel with Le Chiffre. He rose and dressed, dismissing the future completely from his mind.

As he tied his thin, double-ended, black satin tie, he paused for a moment and examined himself levelly in the mirror. His grey-blue eyes looked calmly back with a hint of ironical inquiry and the short lock of black hair which would never stay in place slowly subsided to form a thick comma above his right eyebrow. With the thin vertical scar down his right cheek the general effect was faintly piratical. Not much of Hoagy Carmichael there, thought Bond, as he filled a flat, light gunmetal box with fifty of the Morland cigarettes with the triple gold band. Mathis had told him of the girl's comment.

He slipped the case into his hip pocket and snapped his oxidized Ronson to see if it needed fuel. After pocketing the thin sheaf of ten-mille notes, he opened a drawer and took out a light chamois leather holster and slipped it over his left shoulder so that it hung about three inches below his arm-pit. He then took from under his shirts in another drawer a very flat .25 Beretta automatic with a skeleton grip, extracted the clip and the single round in the barrel and whipped the action to and fro several times, finally pulling the trigger on the empty chamber. He charged the weapon again, loaded it, put up the safety catch and dropped it into the shallow pouch of the shoulder-holster. He looked carefully round the room to see if anything had been forgotten and slipped his single-breasted dinner-jacket coat over his heavy silk evening shirt. He felt cool and comfortable. He verified in the mirror that there was absolutely no sign of the flat gun under his left arm, gave a final pull at his narrow tie and walked out of the door and locked it.

When he turned at the foot of the short stairs towards the bar he heard the lift-door open behind him and a cool voice call 'Good evening'.

It was the girl. She stood and waited for him to come up to her.

He had remembered her beauty exactly. He was not surprised to be thrilled by it again.

Her dress was of black velvet, simple and yet with the touch of splendour that only half a dozen couturiers in the world can achieve. There was a thin necklace of diamonds at her throat and a diamond clip in the low vee which just exposed the jutting swell of her breasts. She carried a plain black evening bag, a flat object which she now held, her arm akimbo, at her waist. Her jet black hair hung straight and simple to the final inward curl below the chin.

She looked quite superb and Bond's heart lifted.

'You look absolutely lovely. Business must be good in the radio world!'

She put her arm through his. 'Do you mind if we go straight into dinner?' she asked. 'I want to make a grand entrance and the truth is there's a horrible secret about black velvet. It marks when you sit down. And, by the way, if you hear me scream tonight, I shall have sat on a cane chair.'

Bond laughed. 'Of course, let's go straight in. We'll have a glass of vodka while we order our dinner.'

She gave him an amused glance and he corrected himself: 'Or a cocktail, of course, if you prefer it. The food here's the best in Royale.'

For an instant he felt nettled at the irony, the light shadow of a snub, with which she had met his decisiveness, and at the way he had risen to her quick glance.

But it was only an infinitesimal clink of foils and as the bowing maître d'hôtel led them through the crowded room, it was forgotten as Bond in her wake watched the heads of the diners turn to look at her.

The fashionable part of the restaurant was beside the wide crescent of window built out like the broad stern of a ship over the hotel gardens, but Bond had chosen a table in one of the mirrored alcoves at the back of the great room. These had survived from the Edwardian days and they were secluded and gay in white and gilt, with the red silk-shaded table and wall lights of the late Empire.

As they deciphered the maze of purple ink which covered the double folio menu, Bond beckoned to the sommelier. He turned to his companion.

'Have you decided?'

'I would love a glass of vodka,' she said simply, and went back to her study of the menu.

'A small carafe of vodka, very cold,' ordered Bond. He said to her abruptly: 'I can't drink the health of your new frock without knowing your Christian name.'

'Vesper,' she said. 'Vesper Lynd.'

Bond gave her a look of inquiry.

'It's rather a bore always having to explain, but I was born in the evening, on a very stormy evening according to my parents. Apparently they wanted to remember it.' She smiled. 'Some people like it, others don't. I'm just used to it.'

'I think it's a fine name,' said Bond. An idea struck him. 'Can I borrow it?' He explained about the special martini he had invented and his search for a name for it. 'The Vesper,' he said. 'It sounds perfect and it's very appropriate to the violet hour when my cocktail will now be drunk all over the world. Can I have it?'

'So long as I can try one first,' she promised. 'It sounds a drink to be proud of.'

'We'll have one together when all this is finished,' said Bond. 'Win or lose. And now have you decided what you would like to have for dinner? Please be expensive,' he added as he sensed her hesitation, 'or you'll let down that beautiful frock.'

'I'd made two choices,' she laughed, 'and either would have been delicious, but behaving like a millionaire occasionally is a wonderful treat and if you're sure . . . well, I'd like to start with caviar and then have a plain grilled *rognon de veau* with *pommes soufflés*. And then I'd like to have *fraises des bois* with a lot of cream. Is it very shameless to be so certain and so expensive?' She smiled at him inquiringly.

'It's a virtue, and anyway it's only a good plain wholesome meal.' He turned to the maître d'hôtel, 'And bring plenty of toast.'

'The trouble always is,' he explained to Vesper, 'not how to get enough caviar, but how to get enough toast with it.'

'Now,' he turned back to the menu, 'I myself will accompany Mademoiselle with the caviar, but then I would like a very small tournedos, underdone, with sauce Béarnaise and a *coeur d'artichaut*. While Mademoiselle is enjoying the strawberries, I will have half an avocado pear with a little French dressing. Do you approve?'

The maître d'hôtel bowed.

'My compliments, mademoiselle and monsieur. Monsieur George,' he turned to the sommelier and repeated the two dinners for his benefit.

'*Parfait*,' said the sommelier, proffering the leather-bound wine list.

'If you agree,' said Bond, 'I would prefer to drink champagne with you tonight. It is a cheerful wine and it suits the occasion – I hope,' he added.

'Yes I would like champagne,' she said.

With his finger on the page, Bond turned to the sommelier: 'The Taittinger 45?'

'A fine wine, monsieur,' said the sommelier. 'But if Monsieur will permit,' he pointed with his pencil, 'the Blanc de Blanc Brut 1943 of the same marque is without equal.'

Bond smiled. 'So be it,' he said.

'That is not a well-known brand,' Bond explained to his companion, 'but it is probably the finest champagne in the world.' He grinned suddenly at the touch of pretension in his remark.

'You must forgive me,' he said. 'I take a ridiculous pleasure in what I eat and drink. It comes partly from being a bachelor, but mostly from a habit of taking a lot of trouble over details. It's very pernickety and old-maidish really, but then when I'm working I generally have to eat my meals alone and it makes them more interesting when one takes trouble.'

Vesper smiled at him.

'I like it,' she said. 'I like doing everything fully, getting the most out of everything one does. I think that's the way to live. But it sounds rather schoolgirlish when one says it,' she added apologetically.

The little carafe of vodka had arrived in its bowl of crushed ice and Bond filled their glasses.

'Well, I agree with you anyway,' he said, 'and now, here's luck for tonight, Vesper.'

'Yes,' said the girl quietly, as she held up her small glass and looked at him with a curious directness straight in the eyes. 'I hope all will go well tonight.'

She seemed to Bond to give a quick involuntary shrug of the shoulders as she spoke, but then she leant impulsively towards him.

'I have some news for you from Mathis. He was longing to tell you himself. It's about the bomb. It's a fantastic story.'

9 The Game is Baccarat

Bond looked round, but there was no possibility of being overheard, and the caviar would be waiting for the hot toast from the kitchens.

'Tell me.' His eyes glittered with interest.

'They got the third Bulgar, on the road to Paris. He was in a Citroën and he had picked up two English hikers as protective colouring. At the roadblock his French was so bad that they asked for his papers and he brought out a gun and shot one of the motorcycle patrol. But the other man got him, I don't know how, and managed to stop him committing suicide. Then they took him down to Rouen and extracted the story – in the usual French fashion, I suppose.

'Apparently they were part of a pool held in France for this sort of job – saboteurs, thugs, and so on – and Mathis's friends are already trying to round up the rest. They were to get two million francs for killing you and the agent who briefed them told them there was absolutely no chance of being caught if they followed his instructions exactly.'

She took a sip of vodka. 'But this is the interesting part.'

'The agent gave them the two camera-cases you saw. He said the bright colours would make it easier for them. He told them that the blue case contained a very powerful smoke bomb. The red case was the explosive. As one of them threw the red case, the other was to press a switch on the blue case and they would escape under cover of the smoke. In fact, the smoke bomb was a pure invention to make the Bulgars think they could get away. Both cases contained an identical high-explosive bomb. There was no difference between the blue and the red cases. The idea was to destroy you and the bomb-throwers without trace. Presumably there were other plans for dealing with the third man.'

'Go on,' said Bond, full of admiration for the ingenuity of the double-cross.

'Well, apparently the Bulgars thought this sounded very fine, but cannily they decided to take no chances. It would be better, they thought, to touch off the smoke bomb first and, from inside the cloud of smoke, hurl the explosive bomb at you. What you saw was the assistant bomb-thrower pressing down the lever on the phoney smoke bomb and, of course, they both went up together.

'The third Bulgar was waiting behind the Splendide to pick his two friends up. When he saw what had happened, he assumed they had bungled. But the police picked up some fragments of the unexploded red bomb and he was confronted with them. When he saw that they had been tricked and that his two friends were meant to be murdered with you, he started to talk. I expect he's still talking now. But there's nothing to link all this with Le Chiffre. They were given the job by some intermediary, perhaps one of Le Chiffre's guards, and Le Chiffre's name means absolutely nothing to the one who survived.'

She finished her story just as the waiters arrived with the caviar, a mound of hot toast, and small dishes containing finely chopped onion and grated hard-boiled egg, the white in one dish and the yolk in another.

The caviar was heaped on to their plates and they ate for a time in silence.

After a while Bond said: 'It's very satisfactory to be a corpse who changes places with his murderers. For them it certainly was a case of being hoist with their own petard. Mathis must be very pleased with the day's work – five of the opposition neutralized in twenty-four hours,' and he told her how the Muntzes had been confounded.

'Incidentally,' he asked, 'how did you come to get mixed up in this affair? What section are you in?'

'I'm personal assistant to Head of S,' said Vesper. 'As it was his plan, he wanted his section to have a hand in the operation and he asked M if I could go. It seemed only to be a liaison job, so M said yes although he told my chief that you would be furious at being given a woman to work with.' She paused and when Bond said nothing continued: 'I had to meet Mathis in Paris and come down with him. I've got a friend who is a *vendeuse* with Dior and somehow she managed to borrow me this and the frock I was wearing this morning, otherwise I couldn't possibly have competed with all these people.' She made a gesture towards the room.

'The office was very jealous although they didn't know what the job was. All they knew was that I was to work with a Double O. Of course you're our heroes. I was enchanted.'

Bond frowned. 'It's not difficult to get a Double O number if you're prepared to kill people,' he said. 'That's all the meaning it has. It's nothing to be particularly proud of. I've got the corpses of a Japanese cipher expert in New York and a Norwegian double agent in Stockholm to thank for being a Double O. Probably quite decent people. They just got caught up in the gale of the world like that Yugoslav that Tito bumped off. It's a confusing business but if it's one's profession, one does what one's told. How do you like the grated egg with your caviar?'

'It's a wonderful combination,' she said. 'I'm loving my dinner. It seems a shame . . .' She stopped, warned by a cold look in Bond's eye.

'If it wasn't for the job, we wouldn't be here,' he said.

Suddenly he regretted the intimacy of their dinner and of their talk. He felt he had said too much and that what was only a working relationship had become confused.

'Let's consider what has to be done,' he said in a matter-of-fact voice. 'I'd better explain what I'm going to try and do and how you can help. Which isn't very much I'm afraid,' he added.

'Now these are the basic facts.' He proceeded to sketch out the plan and enumerate the various contingencies which faced them.

The maître d'hôtel supervised the serving of the second course and then as they ate the delicious food, Bond continued.

She listened to him coldly, but with attentive obedience. She felt thoroughly deflated by his harshness, while admitting to herself that she should have paid more heed to the warning of Head of S.

'He's a dedicated man,' her chief had said when he gave her the assignment. 'Don't imagine this is going to be any fun. He thinks of nothing but the job on hand and, while it's on, he's absolute hell to work for. But he's an expert and there aren't many about, so you won't be wasting your time. He's a good-looking chap, but don't fall for him. I don't think he's got much heart. Anyway, good luck and don't get hurt.'

All this had been something of a challenge and she was pleased when she felt she attracted and interested him, as she knew intuitively that she did. Then at a hint that they were finding pleasure together, a hint that was only the first words of a conventional phrase, he had suddenly turned to ice and had brutally veered away as if warmth were poison to him. She felt hurt and foolish. Then she gave a mental shrug and concentrated with all her attention on what he was saying. She would not make the same mistake again.

'. . . and the main hope is to pray for a run of luck for me, or against him.'

Bond was explaining just how baccarat is played.

'It's much the same as any other gambling game. The odds against the banker and the player are more or less even. Only a run against either can be decisive and "break the bank", or break the players.

'Tonight, Le Chiffre, we know, has bought the baccarat bank from the Egyptian syndicate which is running the high tables here. He paid a million francs for it and his capital has been reduced to twenty-four million. I have about the same. There will be ten players, I expect, and we sit round the banker at a kidney-shaped table.

'Generally, this table is divided into two tableaux. The banker plays two games, one against each of the tableaux to left and right of him. In the game that banker should be able to win by playing off one tableau against the other and by first-class accountancy. But there aren't enough baccarat players yet at Royale and Le Chiffre is just going to pit his luck against the other players at the single tableau. It's unusual because the odds in favour of the banker aren't so good, but they're a shade in his favour and, of course, he has control of the size of the stakes.

'Well, the banker sits there in the middle with a croupier to rake in the cards and call the amount of each bank and a *chef de partie* to umpire the game generally. I shall be sitting as near dead opposite Le Chiffre as I can get. In front of him he has a shoe containing six packs of cards, well shuffled. There's absolutely no chance of tampering with the shoe. The cards are shuffled by the croupier and cut by one of the players and put into the shoe in full view of the table. We've checked on the staff and they're all okay. It would be useful, but almost impossible, to mark all the cards, and it would mean the connivance at least of the croupier. Anyway, we shall be watching for that too.'

Bond drank some champagne and continued.

'Now what happens at the game is this. The banker announces an opening bank of five hundred thousand francs, of five hundred pounds as it is now. Each seat is numbered from the right of the banker and the player next to the banker, or Number 1, can accept this bet and push his money out on to the table, or pass it, if it is too much for him or he doesn't want to take it. Then Number 2 has the right to take it, and if he refuses, then Number 3, and so on round the table. If no single player takes it all, the bet is offered to the table as a whole and everyone chips in, including sometimes the spectators round the table, until the five hundred thousand is made up.

'That is a small bet which would immediately be met, but when it gets to a million or two it's often difficult to find a taker or even, if the bank seems to be in luck, a group of takers to cover the bet. At the moment I shall always try and step in and accept the bet – in fact, I shall attack Le Chiffre's bank whenever I get a chance until either I've bust his bank or he's bust me. It may take some time, but in the end one of us is bound to break the other, irrespective of the other players at the table, although they can, of course, make him richer or poorer in the meantime.

'Being the banker, he's got a slight advantage in the play, but knowing that I'm making a dead set at him and not knowing, I hope, my capital, is bound to play on his nerves a bit, so I'm hoping that we start about equal.'

He paused while the strawberries came and the avocado pear.

For a while they ate in silence, then they talked of other things while the coffee was served. They smoked. Neither of them drank brandy or a liqueur. Finally, Bond felt it was time to explain the actual mechanics of the game.

'It's a simple affair,' he said, 'and you'll understand it at once if you've ever played vingt-et-un, where the object is to get cards from the banker which add up more closely to a count of twenty-one than his do. In this game, I get two cards and the banker gets two, and unless anyone wins outright, either or both of us can get one more card. The object of the game is to hold two or three cards which together count nine points, or as nearly nine as possible. Court cards and tens count nothing; aces one each; any other card its face value.

It is only the last figure of your count that signifies. So nine plus seven equals six – not sixteen.

'The winner is the one whose count is nearest to nine. Draws are played over again.'

Vesper listened attentively, but she also watched the look of abstract passion on Bond's face.

'Now,' Bond continued, 'when the banker deals me my two cards, if they add up to eight or nine, they're a "natural" and I turn them up and I win, unless he has an equal or a better natural. If I haven't got a natural, I can stand on a seven or a six, perhaps ask for a card or perhaps not, on a five, and certainly ask for a card if my count is lower than five. Five is the turning point of the game. According to the odds, the chances of bettering or worsening your hand if you hold a five are exactly even.

'Only when I ask for a card or tap mine to signify that I stand on what I have, can the banker look at his. If he has a natural, he turns them up and wins. Otherwise he is faced with the same problems as I was. But he is helped in his decision to draw or not to draw a third card by my actions. If I have stood, he must assume that I have a five, six, or seven: if I have drawn, he will know that I had something less than a six and I may have improved my hand or not with the card he gave me. And this card was dealt to me face up. On its face value and a knowledge of the odds, he will know whether to take another card or to stand on his own.

'So he has a very slight advantage over me. He has a tiny help over his decision to draw or to stand. But there is always one problem card at this game – shall one draw or stand on a five and what will your opponent do with a five? Some players always draw or always stand. I follow my intuition.

'But in the end,' Bond stubbed out his cigarette and called for the bill, 'it's the natural eights and nines that matter, and I must just see that I get more of them than he does.'

10 The High Table

While telling the story of the game and anticipating the coming fight, Bond's face had lit up again. The prospect of at least getting to grips with Le Chiffre stimulated him and quickened his pulse. He seemed to have completely forgotten the brief coolness between them, and Vesper was relieved and entered into his mood.

He paid the bill and gave a handsome tip to the sommelier. Vesper rose and led the way out of the restaurant and out on to the steps of the hotel.

The big Bentley was waiting and Bond drove Vesper over, parking as close to the entrance as he could. As they walked through the ornate ante-rooms, he hardly spoke. She looked at him and saw that his nostrils were slightly flared. In other respects he seemed completely at ease, acknowledging cheerfully the greetings of the Casino functionaries. At the door to the *salle privée* they were not asked for their membership cards. Bond's high gambling had already made him a favoured client and any companion of his shared in the glory.

Before they had penetrated very far into the main room, Felix Leiter detached himself from one of the roulette tables and greeted Bond as an old friend. After being introduced to Vesper Lynd and exchanging a few remarks, Leiter said: 'Well, since you're playing baccarat this evening, will you allow me to show Miss Lynd how to break the bank at roulette? I've got three lucky numbers that are bound to show soon, and I expect Miss Lynd has some too. Then perhaps we could come and watch you when your game starts to warm up.'

Bond looked inquiringly at Vesper.

'I should love that,' she said, 'but will you give me one of your lucky numbers to play on?'

'I have no lucky numbers,' said Bond unsmilingly. 'I only bet on even chances, or as near them as I can get. Well, I shall leave you then.' He excused himself. 'You will be in excellent hands with my friend Felix Leiter.' He gave a short smile which embraced them both and walked with an unhurried gait towards the *caisse*.

Leiter sensed the rebuff.

'He's a very serious gambler, Miss Lynd,' he said. 'And I guess he has to be. Now come with me and watch Number 17 obey my extra-sensory perceptions. You'll find it quite a painless sensation being given plenty of money for nothing.'

Bond was relieved to be on his own again and to be able to clear his mind of everything but the task on hand. He stood at the *caisse* and took his twenty-four million francs against the receipt which had been given him that afternoon. He divided the notes into equal packets and put half the sum into his right-hand coat pocket and the other half into the left. Then he strolled slowly across the room between the thronged tables until he came to the top of the room where the broad baccarat table waited behind the brass rail.

The table was filling up and the cards were spread face down being stirred and mixed slowly in what is known as the 'croupiers' shuffle', supposedly the shuffle which is most effective and least susceptible to cheating.

The *chef de partie* lifted the velvet-covered chain which allowed entrance through the brass rail.

'I've kept Number 6 as you wished, Monsieur Bond.'

There were still three other empty places at the table. Bond moved inside the rail to where a *huissier* was holding out his chair. He sat down with a nod to the players on his right and left. He took out his wide gunmetal cigarette-case and his black lighter and placed them on the green baize at his right elbow. The *huissier* wiped a thick glass ash-tray with a cloth and put it beside them. Bond lit a cigarette and leant back in his chair.

Opposite him, the banker's chair was vacant. He glanced round the table. He knew most of the players by sight, but few of their names. At Number 7, on his right, there was a Monsieur Sixte, a wealthy Belgian with metal interests in the Congo. At Number 9 there was Lord Danvers, a distinguished but weak-looking man whose francs were presumably provided by his rich American wife, a middle-aged woman with the predatory mouth of a barracuda, who sat at Number 3. Bond reflected that they would probably play a pawky and nervous game and be amongst the early casualties. At Number 1, to the right of the bank was a well-known Greek gambler who owned, as in Bond's experience apparently everyone does in the Eastern Mediterranean, a profitable shipping line. He would play coldly and well and would be a stayer.

Bond asked the *huissier* for a card and wrote on it, under a neat question mark, the remaining numbers, 2, 4, 5, 8, 10, and asked the *huissier* to give it to the *chef de partie*.

Soon it came back with the names filled in.

Number 2, still empty, was to be Carmel Delane, the American film star with alimony from three husbands to burn and, Bond assumed, a call on still more from whoever her present companion at Royale might be. With her sanguine temperament she would play gaily and with panache and might run into a vein of luck.

Then came Lady Danvers at Number 3 and Numbers 4 and 5 were a Mr and Mrs Du Pont, rich-looking and might or might not have some of the real Du Pont money behind them. Bond guessed they would be stayers. They both had a businesslike look about them and were talking together easily and cheerfully as if they felt very much at home at the big game. Bond was quite happy to have them next to him – Mrs Du Pont sat at Number 5 – and he felt prepared to share with them or with Monsieur Sixte on his right, if they found themselves faced with too big a bank.

At Number 8 was the Maharajah of a small Indian state, probably with all his wartime sterling balances to play with. Bond's experience told him that few of the Asiatic races were courageous gamblers, even the much-vaunted Chinese being inclined to lose heart if the going was bad. But the Maharajah would probably stay in the game and stand some heavy losses if they were gradual.

Number 10 was a prosperous-looking young Italian, Signor Tomelli, who possibly had plenty of money from rackrents in Milan and would probably play a dashing and foolish game. He might lose his temper and make a scene.

Bond had just finished his sketchy summing-up of the players when Le Chiffre, with the silence and economy of movement of a big fish, came through the opening in the brass rail and, with a cold smile of welcome for the table, took his place directly opposite Bond in the banker's chair.

With the same economy of movement, he cut the thick slab of cards which the croupier had placed on the table squarely between his blunt relaxed hands. Then, as the croupier fitted the six packs with one swift exact motion into the metal and wooden shoe, Le Chiffre said something quietly to him.

'Messieurs, mesdames, les jeux sont faits. Un banco de cinq cent mille,' and as the Greek at Number 1 tapped the table in front of his fat pile of hundred-mille plaques, 'Le banco est fait.'

Le Chiffre crouched over the shoe. He gave it a short deliberate slap to settle the cards, the first of which showed its semicircular pale pink tongue through the slanting aluminium mouth of the shoe. Then, with a thick white fore-finger he pressed gently on the pink tongue and slipped out the first card six inches or a foot towards the Greek on his right hand. Then he slipped out a card for himself, then another for the Greek, then one more for himself.

He sat immobile, not touching his own cards.

He looked at the Greek's face.

With his flat wooden spatula, like a long bricklayer's trowel, the croupier delicately lifted up the Greek's two cards and dropped them with a quick movement an extra few inches to the right so that they lay just before the Greek's pale hairy hands which lay inert like two watchful pink crabs on the table.

The two pink crabs scuttled out together and the Greek gathered the cards into his wide left hand and cautiously bent his head so that he could see, in the shadow made by his cupped hand, the value of the bottom of the two cards. Then he slowly inserted the forefinger of his right hand and slipped the bottom card slightly sideways so that the value of the top card was also just perceptible.

His face was quite impassive. He flattened out his left hand on the table and then withdrew it, leaving the two pink cards face down before him, their secret unrevealed.

Then he lifted his head and looked Le Chiffre in the eye.

'Non,' said the Greek flatly.

From the decision to stand on his two cards and not ask for another, it was clear that the Greek had a five, or a six, or a seven. To be certain of winning, the banker had to reveal an eight or a nine. If the banker failed to show either figure, he also had the right to take another card which might or might not improve his count.

Le Chiffre's hands were clasped in front of him, his two cards three or four inches away. With his right hand he picked up the two cards and turned them face upwards on the table with a faint snap.

They were a four and a five, an undefeatable natural nine.

He had won.

'*Neuf à la banque*,' quietly said the croupier. With his spatula he faced the Greek's two cards, '*Et le sept*,' he said unemotionally, lifting up gently the corpses of the seven and queen and slipping them through the wide slot in the table near his chair which leads into the gib metal canister to which all dead cards are consigned. Le Chiffre's two cards followed them with a faint rattle which comes from the canister at the beginning of each session before the discards have made a cushion over the metal floor of their oubliette.

The Greek pushed forward five plaques of one hundred thousand and the croupier added these to Le Chiffre's half-million plaque which lay in the centre of the table. From each bet the Casino takes a tiny percentage, the *cagnotte*, but it is usual at a big game for the banker to subscribe this himself either in a prearranged lump or by contributions at the end of each hand, so that the amount of the bank's stake can always be a round figure. Le Chiffre had chosen the second course.

The croupier slipped some counters through the slot in the table which receives the *cagnotte* and announced quietly:

'*Un banco d'un million.*'

'*Suivi*,' murmured the Greek, meaning that he exercised his right to follow up his lost bet.

Bond lit a cigarette and settled himself in his chair. The long game was launched and the sequence of these gestures and the reiteration of this subdued litany would continue until the end came and the players dispersed. Then the enigmatic cards would be burnt or defaced, a shroud would be draped over the table and the grass-green baize battlefield would soak up the blood of its victims and refresh itself.

The Greek, after taking a third card, could achieve no better than a four to the bank's seven.

'*Un banco de deux millions,*' said the croupier.

The players on Bond's left remained silent.

'*Banco,*' said Bond.

11 *Moment of Truth*

Le Chiffre looked incuriously at him, the whites of his eyes, which showed all round the irises, lending something impassive and doll-like to his gaze.

He slowly removed one thick hand from the table and slipped it into the pocket of his dinner-jacket. The hand came out holding a small metal cylinder with a cap which Le Chiffre unscrewed. He inserted the nozzle of the cylinder, with an obscene deliberation, twice into each black nostril in turn, and luxuriously inhaled the benzedrine vapour.

Unhurriedly he pocketed the inhaler, then his hand came quickly back above the level of the table and gave the shoe its usual hard, sharp slap.

During this offensive pantomime Bond had coldly held the banker's gaze, taking in the wide expanse of white face surmounted by the short abrupt cliff of reddish-brown hair, the unsmiling wet red mouth and the impressive width of the shoulders, loosely draped in a massively cut dinner-jacket.

But for the highlights on the satin of the shawl-cut lapels, he might have been faced by the thick bust of a black-fleeced Minotaur rising out of a green grass field.

Bond slipped a packet of notes on to the table without counting them. If he lost, the croupier would extract what was necessary to cover the bet, but the easy gesture conveyed that Bond didn't expect to lose and that this was only a token display from the deep funds at Bond's disposal.

The other players sensed a tension between the two gamblers and there was silence as Le Chiffre fingered the four cards out of the shoe.

The croupier slipped Bond's two cards across to him with the tip of his spatula. Bond, still with his eyes holding Le Chiffre's, reached his right hand out a few inches, glanced down very swiftly, then as he looked up again impassively at Le Chiffre, with a disdainful gesture he tossed the cards face upwards on the table.

They were a four and a five – an unbeatable nine.

There was a little gasp of envy from the table and the players to the left of Bond exchanged rueful glances at their failure to accept the two million franc bet.

With a hint of a shrug, Le Chiffre slowly faced his own two cards and flicked them away with his fingernail. They were two valueless knaves.

'Le baccarat,' intoned the croupier as he spaded the thick chips over the table to Bond.

Bond slipped them into his right-hand pocket with the unused packet of notes. His face showed no emotion, but he was pleased with the success of his first coup and with the outcome of the silent clash of wills across the table.

The woman on his left, the American Mrs Du Pont, turned to him with a wry smile.

'I shouldn't have let it come to you,' she said. 'Directly the cards were dealt I kicked myself.'

'It's only the beginning of the game,' said Bond. 'You may be right the next time you pass it.'

Mr Du Pont leant forward from the other side of his wife: 'If one could be right every hand, none of us would be here,' he said philosophically.

'I would be,' his wife laughed. 'You don't think I do this for pleasure.'

As the game went on, Bond looked over the spectators leaning on the high brass rail round the table. He soon saw Le Chiffre's two gunmen. They stood behind and to either side of the banker. They looked respectable enough, but not sufficiently a part of the game to be unobtrusive.

The one more or less behind Le Chiffre's right arm was tall and funereal in his dinner-jacket. His face was wooden and grey, but his eyes flickered and gleamed like a conjurer's. His whole long body was restless and his hands shifted often on the brass rail. Bond guessed that he would kill without interest or concern for what he killed and that he would prefer strangling. He had something of Lennie in *Of Mice and Men*, but his inhumanity would not come from infantilism but from drugs. Marijuana, decided Bond.

The other man looked like a Corsican shopkeeper. He was short and very dark with a flat head covered with thickly greased hair. He seemed to be a cripple. A chunky malacca cane with a rubber tip hung on the rail beside him. He must have had permission to bring the cane into the Casino with him, reflected Bond, who knew that neither sticks nor any other objects were allowed in the rooms as a precaution against acts of violence. He looked sleek and well fed. His mouth hung vacantly half open and revealed very bad teeth. He wore a heavy black moustache and the backs of his hands on the rail were matted with black hair. Bond guessed that hair covered most of his squat body. Naked, Bond supposed, he would be an obscene object.

The game continued uneventfully, but with a slight bias against the bank.

The third coup is the 'sound barrier' at chemin-de-fer and baccarat. Your luck can defeat the first and second tests, but when the third deal comes along it most often spells disaster. Again and again at this point you find yourself being bounced back to earth. It was like that now. Neither the bank nor any of the players seemed to be able to get hot. But there was a steady and inexorable seepage against the bank, amounting after about two hours' play to ten million francs. Bond had no idea what profits Le Chiffre had made over the past two days. He estimated them at five million and guessed that now the banker's capital could not be more than twenty million.

In fact, Le Chiffre had lost heavily all that afternoon. At this moment he only had ten million left.

Bond, on the other hand, by one o'clock in the morning, had won four million, bringing his resources up to twenty-eight million.

Bond was cautiously pleased. Le Chiffre showed no trace of emotion. He continued to play like an automaton, never speaking except when he gave instructions in a low aside to the croupier at the opening of each new bank.

Outside the pool of silence round the high table, there was the constant hum of the other tables, chemin-de-fer, roulette, and trente-et-quarante, interspersed with the clear calls of the croupiers and occasional bursts of laughter or gasps of excitement from different corners of the huge *salle*.

In the background there thudded always the hidden metronome of the Casino, ticking up its little treasure of one-per-cents with each spin of a wheel and each turn of a card – a pulsing fat-cat with a zero for a heart.

It was at ten minutes past one by Bond's watch when, at the high table, the whole pattern of play suddenly altered.

The Greek at Number 1 was still having a bad time. He had lost the first coup of half a million francs and the second. He passed the third time, leaving a bank of two millions. Carmel Delane at Number 2 refused it. So did Lady Danvers at Number 3.

The Du Ponts looked at each other.

'*Banco*,' said Mrs Du Pont, and promptly lost to the banker's natural eight.

'*Un banco de quatre millions*,' said the croupier.

'*Banco*,' said Bond, pushing out a wad of notes.

Again he fixed Le Chiffre with his eye. Again he gave only a cursory look at his two cards.

'No,' he said. He held a marginal five. The position was dangerous.

Le Chiffre turned up a knave and a four. He gave the shoe another slap. He drew a three.

'*Sept à la banque*,' said the croupier, '*et cinq*,' he added as he tipped Bond's losing cards face upwards. He raked over Bond's money, extracted four million francs and returned the remainder to Bond.

'*Un banco de huit millions*.'

'*Suivi*,' said Bond.

And lost again, to a natural nine.

In two coups he had lost twelve million francs. By scraping the barrel, he had just sixteen million francs left, exactly the amount of the next banco.

Suddenly Bond felt the sweat on his palms. Like snow in sunshine his capital had melted. With the covetous deliberation of the winning gambler, Le Chiffre was tapping a light tattoo on the table with his right hand. Bond looked across into the eyes of murky basalt. They held an ironical question. 'Do you want the full treatment?' they seemed to ask.

'*Suivi*,' Bond said softly.

He took some notes and plaques out of his right-hand pocket and the entire stack of notes out of his left and pushed them forward. There was no hint in his movements that this would be his last stake.

His mouth felt suddenly as dry as flock wall-paper. He looked up and saw Vesper and Felix Leiter standing where the gunman with the stick had stood. He did not know how long they had been standing there. Leiter looked faintly worried, but Vesper smiled encouragement at him.

He heard a faint rattle on the rail behind him and turned his head. The battery of bad teeth under the black moustache gaped vacantly back at him.

'*Le jeu est fait*,' said the croupier, and the two cards came slithering towards him over the green baize – a green baize which was no longer smooth, but thick now, and furry and almost choking, its colour as livid as the grass on a fresh tomb.

The light from the broad satin-lined shades which had seemed so welcoming now seemed to take the colour out of his hand as he glanced at the cards. Then he looked again.

It was nearly as bad as it could have been – the king of hearts and an ace, the ace of spades. It squinted up at him like a black widow spider.

'A card.' He still kept all emotion out of his voice.

Le Chiffre faced his own two cards. He had a queen and a black five. He looked at Bond and pressed out another card with a wide forefinger. The table was absolutely silent. He faced it and flicked it away. The croupier lifted it delicately with his spatula and slipped it over to Bond. It was a good card, the five of hearts, but to Bond it was a difficult fingerprint in dried blood. He now had a count of six and Le Chiffre a count of five, but the banker, having a five and giving a five, would and must draw another card and try and improve with a one, two, three or four. Drawing any other card he would be defeated.

The odds were on Bond's side, but now it was Le Chiffre who

looked across into Bond's eyes and hardly glanced at the card as he flicked it face upwards on the table.

It was, unnecessarily, the best, a four, giving the bank a count of nine. He had won, almost slowing up.

Bond was beaten and cleaned out.

12 The Deadly Tube

Bond sat silent, frozen with defeat. He opened his wide black case and took out a cigarette. He snapped open the tiny jaws of the Ronson and lit the cigarette and put the lighter back on the table. He took a deep lungful of smoke and expelled it between his teeth with a faint hiss.

What now? Back to the hotel and bed, avoiding the commiserating eyes of Mathis and Leiter and Vesper. Back to the telephone call to London, and then tomorrow the plane home, the taxi up to Regent's Park, the walk up the stairs and along the corridor, and M's cold face across the table, his forced sympathy, his 'better luck next time' and, of course, there couldn't be one, not another chance like this.

He looked round the table and up at the spectators. Few were looking at him. They were waiting while the croupier counted the money and piled up the chips in a neat stack in front of the banker, waiting to see if anyone would conceivably challenge this huge bank of thirty-two million francs, this wonderful run of banker's luck.

Leiter had vanished, not wishing to look Bond in the eye after the knock-out, he supposed. Yet Vesper looked curiously unmoved, she gave him a smile of encouragement. But then, Bond reflected, she knew nothing of the game. Had no notion, probably, of the bitterness of his defeat.

The *huissier* was coming towards Bond inside the rail. He stopped beside him. Bent over him. Placed a squat envelope beside Bond on the table. It was as thick as a dictionary. Said something about the *caisse*. Moved away again.

Bond's heart thumped. He took the heavy anonymous envelope

below the level of the table and slit it open with his thumbnail, noticing that the gum was still wet on the flap.

Unbelieving and yet knowing it was true, he felt the broad wads of notes. He slipped them into his pockets, retaining the half-sheet of note-paper which was pinned to the topmost of them. He glanced at it in the shadow below the table. There was one line of writing in ink: 'Marshall Aid. Thirty-two million francs. With the compliments of the USA.'

Bond swallowed. He looked over towards Vesper. Felix Leiter was again standing beside her. He grinned slightly and Bond smiled back and raised his hand from the table in a small gesture of benediction. Then he set his mind to sweeping away all traces of the sense of complete defeat which had swamped him a few minutes before. This was a reprieve, but only a reprieve. There could be no more miracles. This time he had to win – if Le Chiffre had not already made his fifty million – if he was going to go on!

The croupier had completed his task of computing the *cagnotte*, changing Bond's notes into plaques and making a pile of the giant stake in the middle of the table.

There lay thirty-two thousand pounds. Perhaps, thought Bond, Le Chiffre needed just one more coup, even a minor one of a few million francs, to achieve his object. Then he would have made his fifty million francs and would leave the table. By tomorrow his deficits would be covered and his position secure.

He showed no signs of moving and Bond guessed with relief that somehow he must have overestimated Le Chiffre's resources.

The only hope, thought Bond, was to stamp on him now. Not to share the bank with the table, or to take some minor part of it, but to go the whole hog. This would really jolt Le Chiffre. He would hate to see more than ten or fifteen million of the stake covered, and he could not possibly expect anyone to banco the entire thirty-two millions. He might not know that Bond had been cleaned out, but he must imagine that Bond had by now only small reserves. He could not know of the contents of the envelope; if he did, he would probably withdraw the bank and start all over again on the wearisome journey up from the five hundred thousand franc opening bet.

The analysis was right.

Le Chiffre needed another eight million.

At last he nodded.

'*Un banco de trente-deux millions.*'

The croupier's voice rang out. A silence built itself up round the table.

'*Un banco de trente-deux millions.*'

In a louder, prouder voice the *chef de partie* took up the cry, hoping to draw big money away from the neighbouring chemin-de-fer tables. Besides, this was wonderful publicity. The stake had only once been reached in the history of baccarat – at Deauville in 1950. The rival Casino de la Forêt at Le Touquet had never got near it.

It was then that Bond leant slightly forward.

'*Suivi,*' he said quietly.

There was an excited buzz round the table. The word ran through the Casino. People crowded in. Thirty-two million! For most of them it was more than they had earned all their lives. It was their savings and the savings of their families. It was, literally, a small fortune.

One of the Casino directors consulted with the *chef de partie*. The *chef de partie* turned apologetically to Bond.

'*Excusez moi, monsieur. La mise?*'

It was an indication that Bond really must show he had the money to cover the bet. They knew, of course, that he was a very wealthy man, but after all, thirty-two millions! And it sometimes happened that desperate people would bet without a sou in the world and cheerfully go to prison if they lost.

'*Mes excuses, Monsieur Bond,*' added the *chef de partie* obsequiously.

It was when Bond shovelled the great wad of notes out on to the table and the croupier busied himself with the task of counting the pinned sheaves of ten thousand franc notes, the largest denomination issued in France, that he caught a swift exchange of glances between Le Chiffre and the gunman standing directly behind Bond.

Immediately he felt something hard press into the base of his spine, right into the cleft between his two buttocks on the padded chair.

At the same time a thick voice speaking southern French said softly, urgently, just behind his right ear:

'This is a gun, monsieur. It is absolutely silent. It can blow the base of your spine off without a sound. You will appear to have fainted. I shall be gone. Withdraw your bet before I count ten. If you call for help I shall fire.'

The voice was confident. Bond believed it. These people had shown they would unhesitatingly go the limit. The thick walking stick was explained. Bond knew the type of gun. The barrel a series of soft rubber baffles which absorbed the detonation, but allowed the passage of the bullet. They had been invented and used in the war for assassinations. Bond had tested them himself.

'*Un*,' said the voice.

Bond turned his head. There was the man, leaning forward close behind him, smiling broadly under his black moustache as if he was wishing Bond luck, completely secure in the noise and the crowd.

The discoloured teeth came together. '*Deux*,' said the grinning mouth.

Bond looked across. Le Chiffre was watching him. His eyes glittered back at Bond. His mouth was open and he was breathing fast. He was waiting, waiting for Bond's hand to gesture to the croupier, or else for Bond suddenly to slump backwards in his chair, his face grimacing with a scream.

'*Trois*.'

Bond looked over at Vesper and Felix Leiter. They were smiling and talking to each other. The fools. Where was Mathis? Where were those famous men of his?

'*Quatre*.'

And the other spectators. This crowd of jabbering idiots. Couldn't someone see what was happening? The *chef de partie*, the croupier, the *huissier*?

'*Cinq*.'

The croupier was tidying up the pile of notes. The *chef de partie* bowed smilingly towards Bond. Directly the stake was in order he would announce: '*Le jeux est fait*', and the gun would fire whether the gunman had reached ten or not.

'*Six*.'

Bond decided. It was a chance. He carefully moved his hands to the edge of the table, gripped it, edged his buttocks right back, feeling the sharp gun-sight grind into his coccyx.

'Sept.'

The *chef de partie* turned to Le Chiffre with his eyebrows lifted, waiting for the banker's nod that he was ready to play.

Suddenly Bond heaved backwards with all his strength. His momentum tipped the cross-bar of the chair-back down so quickly that it cracked across the malacca tube and wrenched it from the gunman's hand before he could pull the trigger.

Bond went head-over-heels on to the ground amongst the spectators' feet, his legs in the air. The back of the chair splintered with a sharp crack. There were cries of dismay. The spectators cringed away and then, reassured, clustered back. Hands helped him to his feet and brushed him down. The *huissier* bustled up with the *chef de partie*. At all costs a scandal must be avoided.

Bond held on to the brass rail. He looked confused and embarrassed. He brushed his hands across his forehead.

'A momentary faintness,' he said. 'It is nothing – the excitement, the heat.'

There were expressions of sympathy. Naturally, with this tremendous game. Would Monsieur prefer to withdraw, to lie down, to go home? Should a doctor be fetched?

Bond shook his head. He was perfectly all right now. His excuses to the table. To the banker also.

A new chair was brought and he sat down. He looked across at Le Chiffre. Through his relief at being alive, he felt a moment of triumph at what he saw – some fear in the fat, pale face.

There was a buzz of speculation round the table. Bond's neighbours on both sides of him bent forward and spoke solicitously about the heat and the lateness of the hour and the smoke and the lack of air.

Bond replied politely. He turned to examine the crowd behind him. There was no trace of the gunman, but the *huissier* was looking for someone to claim the malacca stick. It seemed undamaged. But it no longer carried a rubber tip. Bond beckoned to him.

'If you will give it to that gentleman over there,' he indicated Felix Leiter, 'he will return it. It belongs to an acquaintance of his.'

The *huissier* bowed.

Bond grimly reflected that a short examination would reveal to Leiter why he had made such an embarrassing public display of himself.

He turned back to the table and tapped the green cloth in front of him to show that he was ready.

13 'A Whisper of Love, a Whisper of Hate'

'La partie continue,' announced the *chef* impressively. *'Un banco de trente-deux millions.'*

The spectators craned forward. Le Chiffre hit the shoe with a flat-handed slap that made it rattle. As an afterthought he took out his benzedrine inhaler and sucked the vapour up his nose.

'Filthy brute,' said Mrs Du Pont on Bond's left.

Bond's mind was clear again. By a miracle he had survived a devastating wound. He could feel his armpits still wet with the fear of it. But the success of his gambit with the chair had wiped out all memories of the dreadful valley of defeat through which he had just passed.

He had made a fool of himself. The game had been interrupted for at least ten minutes, a delay unheard of in a respectable casino, but now the cards were waiting for him in the shoe. They must not fail him. He felt his heart lift at the prospect of what was to come.

It was two o'clock in the morning. Apart from the thick crowd round the big game, play was still going on at three of the chemin-de-fer games and at the same number of roulette tables.

In the silence round his own table, Bond suddenly heard a distant croupier intone: *'Neuf. Le rouge gagne, impair et manque.'*

Was this an omen for him or for Le Chiffre?

The two cards slithered towards him across the green sea.

Like an octopus under a rock, Le Chiffre watched him from the other side of the table.

Bond reached out a steady right hand and drew the cards towards him. Would it be the lift of the heart which a nine brings, or an eight brings?

He fanned the two cards under the curtain of his hand. The muscles of his jaw rippled as he clenched his teeth. His whole body stiffened in a reflex of self-defence.

He had two queens, two red queens.

They looked roguishly back at him from the shadows. They were the worst. They were nothing. Zero. Baccarat.

'A card,' said Bond fighting to keep hopelessness out of his voice. He felt Le Chiffre's eyes boring into his brain.

The banker slowly turned his own two cards face up.

He had a count of three – a king and a black three.

Bond softly exhaled a cloud of tobacco smoke. He still had a chance. Now he was really faced with the moment of truth. Le Chiffre slapped the shoe, slipped out a card, Bond's fate, and slowly turned it face up.

It was a nine, a wonderful nine of hearts, the card known in gipsy magic as 'a whisper of love, a whisper of hate', the card that meant almost certain victory for Bond.

The croupier slipped it delicately across. To Le Chiffre it meant nothing. Bond might have had a one, in which case he now had ten points, or nothing, or baccarat, as it is called. Or he might have had a two, three, four, or even five. In which case, with the nine, his maximum count would be four.

Holding a three and giving nine is one of the moot situations at the game. The odds are so nearly divided between to draw or not to draw. Bond let the banker sweat it out. Since his nine could only be equalled by the banker drawing a six, he would normally have shown his count if it had been a friendly game.

Bond's cards lay on the table before him, the two impersonal pale pink-patterned backs and the faced nine of hearts. To Le Chiffre the nine might be telling the truth or many variations of lies.

The whole secret lay in the reverse of the two pink backs where the pair of queens kissed the green cloth.

The sweat was running down either side of the banker's beaky nose. His thick tongue came out slyly and licked a drop out of the corner of his red gash of a mouth. He looked at Bond's cards, and then at his own, and then back at Bond's.

Then his whole body shrugged and he slipped out a card for himself from the lisping shoe.

He faced it. The table craned. It was a wonderful card, a five.

'*Huit à la banque*,' said the croupier.

As Bond sat silent, Le Chiffre suddenly grinned wolfishly. He must have won.

The croupier's spatula reached almost apologetically across the table. There was not a man at the table who did not believe Bond was defeated.

The spatula flicked the two pink cards over on their backs. The gay red queens smiled up at the lights.

'*Et le neuf*.'

A great gasp went up round the table, and then a hubbub of talk.

Bond's eyes were on Le Chiffre. The big man fell back in his chair as if slugged above the heart. His mouth opened and shut once or twice in protest and his right hand felt at his throat. Then he rocked back. His lips were grey.

As the huge stack of plaques was shunted across the table to Bond the banker reached into an inner pocket of his jacket and threw a wad of notes on to the table.

The croupier riffled through them.

'*Un banco de dix millions*,' he announced. He slapped down their equivalent in ten plaques of a million each.

This is the kill, thought Bond. This man has reached the point of no return. This is the last of his capital. He has come to where I stood an hour ago and he is making the last gesture that I made. But if this man loses, there is no one to come to his aid, no miracle to help him.

Bond sat back and lit a cigarette. On a small table beside him half a bottle of Clicquot and a glass had materialized. Without asking who the benefactor was, Bond filled the glass to the brim and drank it down in two long draughts.

Then he leant back with his arms curled forward on the table in front of him like the arms of a wrestler seeking a hold at the opening of a bout of ju-jitsu.

The players on his left remained silent.

'*Banco*,' he said, speaking straight at Le Chiffre.

Once more the two cards were borne over to him and this time the croupier slipped them into the green lagoon between the out-stretched arms.

Bond curled his right hand in, glanced briefly down and flipped the cards face up into the middle of the table.

'*Le neuf*,' said the croupier.

Le Chiffre was gazing down at his own two black kings.

'*Et le baccarat*,' and the croupier eased across the table the fat tide of plaques.

Le Chiffre watched them go to join the serried millions in the shadow of Bond's left arm, then he stood up slowly and without a word he brushed past the players to the break in the rail. He unhooked the velvet-covered chain and let it fall. The spectators opened a way for him. They looked at him curiously and rather fearfully as if he carried the smell of death on him. Then he vanished from Bond's sight.

Bond stood up. He took a hundred-mille plaque from the stacks beside him and slipped it across the table to the *chef de partie*. He cut short the effusive thanks and asked the croupier to have his winnings carried to the *caisse*. The other players were leaving their seats. With no banker, there could be no game, and by now it was half past two. He exchanged some pleasant words with his neighbours to right and left and then ducked under the rail to where Vesper and Felix Leiter were waiting for him.

Together they walked over to the *caisse*. Bond was invited to come into the private office of the Casino directors. On the desk lay his huge pile of chips. He added the contents of his pockets to it.

In all there was over seventy million francs.

Bond took Felix Leiter's money in notes and took a cheque to cash on the Crédit Lyonnais for the remaining forty-odd million. He was congratulated warmly on his winnings. The directors hoped that he would be playing again that evening.

Bond gave an evasive reply. He walked over to the bar and handed Leiter's money to him. For a few minutes they discussed the game over a bottle of champagne. Leiter took a .45 bullet out of his pocket and placed it on the table.

'I gave the gun to Mathis,' he said. 'He's taken it away. He was as puzzled as we were by the spill you took. He was standing at the back of the crowd with one of his men when it happened. The gunman got away without difficulty. You can imagine how they kicked themselves when they saw the gun. Mathis gave me this bullet to show you what you escaped. The nose has been cut with a dumdum cross. You'd have been in a terrible mess. But they can't tie it on to Le Chiffre. The man came in alone. They've got the form he filled up to get his entrance card. Of course, it'll all be phony. He got permission to bring the stick in with him. He had a certificate for a war-wound pension. These people certainly get themselves well organized. They've got his prints and they're on the Belinograph to Paris, so we may hear more about him in the morning.' Felix Leiter tapped out another cigarette. 'Anyway, all's well that ends well. You certainly took Le Chiffre for a ride at the end, though we had some bad moments. I expect you did too.'

Bond smiled. 'That envelope was the most wonderful thing that ever happened to me. I thought I was really finished. It wasn't at all a pleasant feeling. Talk about a friend in need. One day I'll try and return the compliment.'

He rose. 'I'll just go over to the hotel and put this away,' he said, tapping his pocket. 'I don't like wandering around with Le Chiffre's death-warrant on me. He might get ideas. Then I'd like to celebrate a bit. What do you think?'

He turned to Vesper. She had hardly said a word since the end of the game.

'Shall we have a glass of champagne in the nightclub before we go to bed? It's called the Roi Galant. You get to it through the public rooms. It looks quite cheerful.'

'I think I'd love to,' said Vesper. 'I'll tidy up while you put your winnings away. I'll meet you in the entrance hall.'

'What about you, Felix?' Bond hoped he could be alone with Vesper. Leiter looked at him and read his mind.

'I'd rather take a little rest before breakfast,' he said. 'It's been quite a day and I expect Paris will want me to do a bit of mopping-up tomorrow. There are several loose ends you won't have to worry about. I shall. I'll walk over to the hotel with you. Might as well convoy the treasure ship right into port.'

They strolled over through the shadows cast by the full moon. Both had their hands on their guns. It was three o'clock in the morning, but there were several people about and the courtyard of the Casino was still lined with motorcars.

The short walk was uneventful.

At the hotel, Leiter insisted on accompanying Bond to his room. It was as Bond had left it six hours before.

'No reception committee,' observed Leiter, 'but I wouldn't put it past them to try a last throw. Do you think I ought to stay up and keep you two company?'

'You get your sleep,' said Bond. 'Don't worry about us. They won't be interested in me without the money and I've got an idea for looking after that. Thanks for all you've done. I hope we get on a job again one day.'

'Suits me,' said Leiter, 'so long as you can draw a nine when it's needed – and bring Vesper along with you,' he added dryly. He went out and closed the door.

Bond turned back to the friendliness of his room.

After the crowded arena of the big table and the nervous strain of the three hours' play, he was glad to be alone for a moment and be welcomed by his pyjamas on the bed and his hairbrushes on the dressing-table. He went into the bathroom and dashed cold water over his face and gargled with a sharp mouthwash. He felt the bruises on the back of his head and on his right shoulder. He reflected cheerfully how narrowly he had twice that day escaped being murdered. Would he have to sit up all that night and wait for them to come again, or was Le Chiffre even now on his way to Le Havre or Bordeaux to pick up a boat for some corner of the world where he could escape the eyes and the guns of SMERSH?

Bond shrugged his shoulders. Sufficient unto that day had been its evil. He gazed for a moment into the mirror and wondered about Vesper's morals. He wanted her cold and arrogant body. He wanted to see tears and desire in her remote blue eyes and to take the ropes of her black hair in his hands and bend her long body back under his. Bond's eyes narrowed and his face in the mirror looked back at him with hunger.

He turned away and took out of his pocket the cheque for forty million francs. He folded this very small. Then he opened the door and looked up and down the corridor. He left the door wide open and with his ears cocked for footsteps or the sound of the lift, he set to work with a small screwdriver.

Five minutes later he gave a last-minute survey to his handiwork, put some fresh cigarettes in his case, closed and locked the door and went off down the corridor and across the hall and out into the moonlight.

14 'La Vie en Rose'?

The entrance to the Roi Galant was a seven-foot golden picture-frame which had once, perhaps, enclosed the vast portrait of a noble European. It was in a discreet corner of the 'kitchen' – the public roulette and boule room, where several tables were still busy. As Bond took Vesper's arm and led her over the gilded step, he fought back a hankering to borrow some money from the *caisse* and plaster maximums over the nearest table. But he knew that this would be a brash and cheap gesture *pour épater la bourgeoisie*. Whether he won or lost, it would be a kick in the teeth to the luck which had been given him.

The nightclub was small and dark, lit only by candles in gilded candelabra whose warm light was repeated in wall mirrors set in more gold picture-frames. The walls were covered in dark red satin and the chairs and *banquettes* in matching red plush. In the far corner, a trio, consisting of a piano, an electric guitar and drums, was playing 'La Vie en Rose' with muted sweetness. Seduction dripped on the quietly throbbing air. It seemed to Bond that every couple must be touching with passion under the tables.

They were given a corner table near the door. Bond ordered a bottle of Veuve Clicquot and scrambled eggs and bacon.

They sat for a time listening to the music and then Bond turned to Vesper: 'It's wonderful sitting here with you and knowing the job's finished. It's a lovely end to the day – the prize-giving.'

He expected her to smile. She said: 'Yes, isn't it,' in a rather brittle voice. She seemed to be listening carefully to the music. One elbow rested on the table and her hand supported her chin, but on the back of her hand and not on the palm, and Bond noticed that her knuckles showed white as if her fist was tightly clenched.

Between the thumb and first two fingers of her right hand she held one of Bond's cigarettes, as an artist holds a crayon, and though she smoked with composure, she tapped the cigarette occasionally into an ash-tray when the cigarette had no ash.

Bond noticed these small things because he felt intensely aware of her and because he wanted to draw her into his own feeling of warmth and relaxed sensuality. But he accepted her reserve. He thought it came from a desire to protect herself from him, or else it was her reaction to his coolness to her earlier in the evening, his deliberate coolness, which he knew had been taken as a rebuff.

He was patient. He drank champagne and talked a little about the happenings of the day and about the personalities of Mathis and Leiter and about the possible consequences for Le Chiffre. He was discreet and he only talked about the aspects of the case on which she must have been briefed by London.

She answered perfunctorily. She said that, of course, they had picked out the two gunmen, but had thought nothing of it when the man with the stick had gone to stand behind Bond's chair. They could not believe that anything would be attempted in the Casino itself. Directly Bond and Leiter had left to walk over to the hotel, she had telephoned Paris and told M's representative of the result of the game. She had had to speak guardedly and the agent had rung off without comment. She had been told to do this whatever the result. M had asked for the information to be passed on to him personally at any time of the day or night.

This was all she said. She sipped at her champagne and rarely glanced at Bond. She didn't smile. Bond felt frustrated. He drank a lot of champagne and ordered another bottle. The scrambled eggs came and they ate in silence.

At four o'clock Bond was about to call for the bill when the maître d'hôtel appeared at their table and inquired for Miss Lynd. He handed her a note which she took and read hastily.

'Oh, it's only Mathis,' she said. 'He says would I come to the entrance hall. He's got a message for you. Perhaps he's not in evening clothes or something. I won't be a minute. Then perhaps we could go home.'

She gave him a strained smile. 'I'm afraid I don't feel very good company this evening. It's been rather a nerve-racking day. I'm so sorry.'

Bond made a perfunctory reply and rose, pushing back the table. 'I'll get the bill,' he said, and watched her take the few steps to the entrance.

He sat down and lit a cigarette. He felt flat. He suddenly realized that he was tired. The stuffiness of the room hit him as it had hit him in the Casino in the early hours of the previous day. He called for the bill and took a last mouthful of champagne. It tasted bitter, as the first glass too many always does. He would have liked to have seen Mathis's cheerful face and heard his news, perhaps even a word of congratulation.

Suddenly the note to Vesper seemed odd to him. It was not the way Mathis would do things. He would have asked them both to join him at the bar of the Casino or he would have joined them in the nightclub, whatever his clothes. They would have laughed together and Mathis would have been excited. He had much to tell Bond, more than Bond had to tell him. The arrest of the Bulgarian, who had probably talked some more; the chase after the man with the stick; Le Chiffre's movements when he left the Casino.

Bond shook himself. He hastily paid the bill, not waiting for the change. He pushed back his table and walked quickly through the entrance without acknowledging the goodnights of the maître d'hôtel and the doorman.

He hurried through the gaming-room and looked carefully up and down the long entrance hall. He cursed and quickened his step. There were only one or two officials and two or three men and women in evening clothes getting their things at the *vestiaire*.

No Vesper. No Mathis.

He was almost running. He got to the entrance and looked along the steps to left and right down and amongst the few remaining cars.

The commissionaire came towards him.

'A taxi, monsieur?'

Bond waved him aside and started down the steps, his eyes staring into the shadows, the night air cold on his sweating temples.

He was half-way down when he heard a faint cry, then the slam of a door way to the right. With a harsh growl and stutter from the exhaust a beetle-browed Citroën shot out of the shadows into the light of the moon, its front-wheel drive dry-skidding through the loose pebbles of the forecourt.

Its tail rocked on its soft springs as if a violent struggle was taking place on the back seat.

With a snarl it raced out to the wide entrance gate in a spray of gravel. A small black object shot out of an open rear window and thudded into a flower-bed. There was a scream of tortured rubber as the tyres caught the boulevard in a harsh left-handed turn, the deafening echo of a Citroën's exhaust in second gear, a crash into top, then a swiftly diminishing crackle as the car hared off between the shops on the main street towards the coast road.

Bond knew he would find Vesper's evening bag among the flowers.

He ran back with it across the gravel to the brightly lit steps and scrabbled through its contents while the commissionaire hovered round him.

The crumpled note was there amongst the usual feminine baggage.

Can you come out to the entrance hall for a moment? I have news for your companion.

René Mathis

15 Black Hare and Grey Hound

It was the crudest possible forgery.

Bond leapt for the Bentley, blessing the impulse which had made him drive it over after dinner. With the choke full out, the engine answered at once to the starter and the roar drowned the faltering words of the commissionaire who jumped aside as the rear wheels whipped gravel at his piped trouser-legs.

As the car rocked to the left outside the gate, Bond ruefully longed for the front-wheel drive and low chassis of the Citroën. Then he went fast through the gears and settled himself for the pursuit, briefly savouring the echo of the huge exhaust as it came back at him from either side of the short main street through the town.

Soon he was out on the coast road, a broad highway through the sand-dunes which he knew from his morning's drive had an excellent surface and was well cat's-eyed on the bends. He pushed the revs up and up, hurrying the car to eighty then to ninety, his huge Marchal headlights boring a safe white tunnel, nearly half a mile long, between the walls of the night.

He knew the Citroën must have come this way. He had heard the exhaust penetrate beyond the town, and a little dust still hung on the bends. He hoped soon to see the distant shaft of its headlights. The night was still and clear. Only out at sea there must be a light summer mist for at intervals he could hear the fog-horns lowing like iron cattle down the coast.

As he drove, whipping the car faster and faster through the night, with the other half of his mind he cursed Vesper, and M for having sent her on the job.

This was just what he had been afraid of. These blithering women who thought they could do a man's work. Why the hell couldn't they stay at home and mind their pots and pans and stick to their frocks and gossip and leave men's work to the men. And now for this to happen to him, just when the job had come off so beautifully. For Vesper to fall for an old trick like that and get herself snatched and probably held to ranson like some bloody heroine in a strip cartoon. The silly bitch.

Bond boiled at the thought of the fix he was in.

Of course. The idea was a straight swop. The girl against his cheque for forty million. Well, he wouldn't play: wouldn't think of playing. She was in the Service and knew what she was up against. He wouldn't even ask M. This job was more important than her. It was just too bad. She was a fine girl, but he wasn't going to fall for this childish trick. No dice. He would try and catch the Citroën and shoot it out with them and if she got shot in the process, that was too bad too. He would have done his stuff – tried to rescue her before they got her off to some hideout – but if he didn't catch up with them he would get back to his hotel and go to sleep and say no more about it. The next morning he would ask Mathis what had happened to her and show him the note. If Le Chiffre put the touch on Bond for the money in exchange for the girl, Bond would do nothing and tell no one. The girl would just have to take it. If the commissionaire came along with the story of what he had seen, Bond would bluff it out by saying he had had a drunken row with the girl.

Bond's mind raged furiously on with the problem as he flung the great car down the coast road, automatically taking the curves and watching out for carts or cyclists on their way into Royale. On straight stretches the Amherst-Villiers supercharger dug spurs into the Bentley's twenty-five horses and the engine sent a high-pitched scream of pain into the night. Then the revolutions mounted until he was past 110 and on to the 120 mph mark on the speedometer.

He knew he must be gaining fast. Loaded as she was the Citroën could hardly better eighty even on this road. On an impulse he slowed down to seventy, turned on his foglights, and dowsed the twin Marchals. Sure enough, without the blinding curtain of his own lights, he could see the glow of another car a mile or two down the coast.

He felt under the dashboard and from a concealed holster took out a long-barrelled Colt Army Special .45 and laid it on the seat beside him. With this, if he was lucky with the surface of the road, he could hope to get their tyres or their petrol tank at anything up to a hundred yards.

Then he switched on the big lights again and screamed off in pursuit. He felt calm and at ease. The problem of Vesper's life was a problem no longer. His face in the blue light from the dashboard was grim but serene.

Ahead in the Citroën there were three men and the girl.

Le Chiffre was driving, his big fluid body hunched forward, his hands light and delicate on the wheel. Beside sat the squat man who had carried the stick in the Casino. In his left hand he grasped a thick lever which protruded beside him almost level with the floor. It might have been a lever to adjust the driving seat.

In the back seat was the tall thin gunman. He lay back relaxed, gazing at the ceiling, apparently uninterested in the wild speed of the car. His right hand lay caressingly on Vesper's left thigh which stretched out naked beside him.

Apart from her legs, which were naked to the hips, Vesper was only a parcel. Her long black velvet skirt had been lifted over her arms and head and tied above her head with a piece of rope. Where her face was, a small gap had been torn in the velvet so that she could breathe. She was not bound in any other way and she lay quiet, her body moving sluggishly with the swaying of the car.

Le Chiffre was concentrating half on the road ahead and half on the onrushing glare of Bond's headlights in the driving-mirror. He seemed undisturbed when not more than a mile separated the hare from the hounds and he even brought the car down from eighty to sixty miles an hour. Now, as he swept round a bend he slowed down still further. A few hundred yards ahead a Michelin post showed where a small parochial road crossed with the highway.

'*Attention*,' he said sharply to the man beside him.

The man's hand tightened on the lever.

A hundred yards from the crossroads he slowed to thirty. In the mirror Bond's great headlights were lighting up the bend.

Le Chiffre seemed to make up his mind.

'*Allez.*'

The man beside him pulled the lever sharply upwards. The boot at the back of the car yawned open like a whale's mouth. There was a tinkling clatter on the road and then a rhythmic jangling as if the car was towing lengths of chain behind it.

'*Coupez.*'

The man depressed the lever sharply and the jangling stopped with a final clatter.

Le Chiffre glanced again in the mirror. Bond's car was just entering the bend. Le Chiffre made a racing change and threw the Citroën left-handed down the narrow side-road, at the same time dowsing his lights.

He stopped the car with a jerk and all three men got swiftly out and doubled back under cover of a low hedge to the crossroads, now fiercely illuminated by the lights of the Bentley. Each of them carried a revolver and the thin man also had what looked like a large black egg in his right hand.

The Bentley screamed down towards them like an express train.

16 The Crawling of the Skin

As Bond hurtled round the bend, caressing the great car against the camber with an easy sway of body and hands, he was working out his plan of action when the distance between the two cars had narrowed still further. He imagined that the enemy driver would try to dodge off into a side-road if he got the chance. So when he got round the bend and saw no lights ahead, it was a normal reflex to ease up on the accelerator and, when he saw the Michelin post, to prepare to brake.

He was only doing about sixty as he approached the black patch across the right-hand crown of the road which he assumed to be the shadow cast by a wayside tree. Even so, there was no time to save himself. There was suddenly a small carpet of glinting steel spikes right under his off-side wing. Then he was on top of it.

Bond automatically slammed the brakes full on and braced all his sinews against the wheel to correct the inevitable slew to the left, but he only kept control for a split second. As the rubber was flayed from his off-side wheels and the rims for an instant tore up the tarmac, the heavy car whirled across the road in a tearing dry skid, slammed the left bank with a crash that knocked Bond out of the driving-seat on to the floor, and then, facing back up the road, it reared slowly up, its front wheels spinning and its great headlights searching the sky. For a split second, resting on the petrol tank, it seemed to paw at the heavens like a giant praying mantis. Then slowly it toppled over backwards and fell with a splintering crash of coachwork and glass.

In the deafening silence, the near-side front wheel whispered briefly on and then squeaked to a stop.

Le Chiffre and his two men only had to walk a few yards from their ambush.

'Put your guns away and get him out,' he ordered brusquely. 'I'll keep you covered. Be careful of him. I don't want a corpse. And hurry up, it's getting light.'

The two men got down on their knees. One of them took out a long knife and cut some of the fabric away from the side of the convertible hood and took hold of Bond's shoulders. He was unconscious and immovable. The other squeezed between the upturned car and the bank and forced his way through the crumpled window-frame. He eased Bond's legs, pinned between the steering-wheel and the fabric roof of the car. Then they inched him out through a hole in the hood.

They were sweating and filthy with dust and oil by the time they had him lying in the road.

The thin man felt his heart and then slapped his face hard on either side. Bond grunted and moved a hand. The thin man slapped him again.

'That's enough,' said Le Chiffre. 'Tie his arms and put him in the car. Here,' he threw a roll of flex to the man. 'Empty his pockets first and give me his gun. He may have got some other weapons, but we can get them later.'

He took the objects the thin man handed him and stuffed them and Bond's Beretta into his wide pockets without examining them. He left the men to it and walked back to the car. His face showed neither pleasure nor excitement.

It was the sharp bite of the wire flex into his wrists that brought

Bond to himself. He was aching all over as if he had been thrashed with a wooden club, but when he was yanked to his feet and pushed towards the narrow side-road where the engine of the Citroën was already running softly, he found that no bones were broken. But he felt in no mood for desperate attempts to escape and allowed himself to be dragged into the back seat of the car without resisting.

He felt thoroughly dispirited and weak in resolve as well as in his body. He had had to take too much in the past twenty-four hours and now this last stroke by the enemy seemed almost too final. This time there could be no miracles. No one knew where he was and no one would miss him until well on into the morning. The wreck of his car would be found before very long, but it would take hours to trace the ownership to him.

And Vesper. He looked to the right, past the thin man who was lying back with his eyes closed. His first reaction was one of scorn. Damn fool girl getting herself trussed up like a chicken, having her skirt pulled over her head as if the whole of this business was some kind of dormitory rag. But then he felt sorry for her. Her naked legs looked so childlike and defenceless.

'Vesper,' he said softly.

There was no answer from the bundle in the corner and Bond suddenly had a chill feeling, but then she stirred slightly.

At the same time the thin man caught him a hard backhanded blow over the heart.

'Silence.'

Bond doubled over with the pain and to shield himself from another blow, only to get a rabbit punch on the back of the neck which made him arch back again, the breath whistling through his teeth.

The thin man had hit him a hard professional cutting blow with the edge of the hand. There was something rather deadly about his accuracy and lack of effort. He was now again lying back, his eyes closed. He was a man to make you afraid, an evil man. Bond hoped he might get a chance of killing him.

Suddenly the boot of the car was thrown open and there was a clanking crash. Bond guessed that they had been waiting for the third man to retrieve the carpet of spiked chain-mail. He assumed it must be an adaptation of the nail-studded devices used by the Resistance against German staff-cars.

Again he reflected on the efficiency of these people and the ingenuity of the equipment they used. Had M underestimated their resourcefulness? He stifled a desire to place the blame on London. It was he who should have known; he who should have been warned by small signs and taken infinitely more precautions. He squirmed as he thought of himself washing down champagne in the Roi Galant while the enemy was busy preparing his counter-stroke. He cursed himself and cursed the hubris which had made him so sure the battle was won and the enemy in flight.

All this time Le Chiffre had said nothing. Directly the boot was shut, the third man, whom Bond at once recognized, climbed in beside him and Le Chiffre reversed furiously back on to the main road. Then he banged the gear lever through the gate and was soon doing seventy on down the coast.

By now it was dawn – about five o'clock, Bond guessed – and he reflected that a mile or two on was the turning to Le Chiffre's villa. He had not thought that they would take Vesper there. Now that he realized that Vesper had only been a sprat to catch a mackerel the whole picture became clear.

It was an extremely unpleasant picture. For the first time since his capture, fear came to Bond and crawled up his spine.

Ten minutes later the Citroën lurched to the left, ran on a hundred yards up a small side-road partly overgrown with grass and then between a pair of dilapidated stucco pillars into an unkempt forecourt surrounded by a high wall. They drew up in front of a peeling white door. Above a rusty bell-push in the door-frame, small zinc letters on a wooden base spelled out 'Les Noctambules' and, underneath, 'Sonnez SVP'.

From what Bond could see of the cement frontage, the villa was typical of the French seaside style. He could imagine the dead bluebottles being hastily swept out for the summer let and the stale rooms briefly aired by a cleaning woman sent by the estate agent in Royale. Every five years one coat of whitewash would be slapped over the rooms and the outside woodwork, and for a few weeks the villa would present a smiling front to the world. Then the winter rains would get to work, and the imprisoned flies, and quickly the villa would take on again its abandoned look.

But, Bond reflected, it would admirably serve Le Chiffre's purpose this morning, if he was right in assuming what that was to be. They had passed no other house since his capture and from his reconnaissance of the day before he knew there was only an occasional farm for several miles to the south.

As he was urged out of the car with a sharp crack in the ribs from the thin man's elbow, he knew that Le Chiffre could have them both to himself, undisturbed, for several hours. Again his skin crawled.

Le Chiffre opened the door with a key and disappeared inside. Vesper, looking incredibly indecent in the early light of day, was pushed in after him with a torrent of lewd French from the man whom Bond knew to himself as 'the Corsican'. Bond followed without giving the thin man a chance to urge him.

The key of the front door turned in the lock.

Le Chiffre was standing in the doorway of a room on the right. He crooked a finger at Bond in a silent, spidery summons.

Vesper was being led down a passage towards the back of the house. Bond suddenly decided.

With a wild backward kick which connected with the thin man's shins and brought a whistle of pain from him he hurled himself down the passage after her. With only his feet as weapons, there was no plan in his mind except to do as much damage as possible to the two gunmen and be able to exchange a few hurried words with the girl. No other plan was possible. He just wanted to tell her not to give in.

As the Corsican turned at the commotion Bond was on him and his right shoe was launched in a flying kick at the other man's groin.

Like lightning the Corsican slammed himself back against the wall of the passage and, as Bond's foot whistled past his hip, he very quickly, but somehow delicately, shot out his left hand, caught Bond's shoe at the top of its arch and twisted it sharply.

Completely off balance, Bond's other foot left the ground. In the air his whole body turned and with the momentum of his rush behind it crashed sideways and down on to the floor.

For a moment he lay there, all the breath knocked out of him. Then the thin man came and hauled him up against the wall by his collar. He had a gun in his hand. He looked Bond inquisitively in the eyes. Then unhurriedly he bent down and swiped the barrel viciously across Bond's shins. Bond grunted and caved at the knees.

'If there is a next time, it will be across your teeth,' said the thin man in bad French.

A door slammed. Vesper and the Corsican had disappeared. Bond turned his head to the right. Le Chiffre had moved a few feet out into the passage. He lifted his finger and crooked it again. Then for the first time he spoke.

'Come, my dear friend. We are wasting our time.'

He spoke in English with no accent. His voice was low and soft and unhurried. He showed no emotion. He might have been a doctor summoning the next patient from the waiting-room, a hysterical patient who had been expostulating feebly with a nurse.

Bond again felt puny and impotent. Nobody but an expert in ju-jitsu could have handled him with the Corsican's economy and lack of fuss. The cold precision with which the thin man had paid him back in his own coin had been equally unhurried, even artistic.

Almost docilely Bond walked back down the passage. He had nothing but a few more bruises to show for his clumsy gesture of resistance to these people.

As he preceded the thin man over the threshold he knew that he was utterly and absolutely in their power.

17 'My Dear Boy'

It was a large bare room, sparsely furnished in cheap French art nouveau style. It was difficult to say whether it was intended as a living- or dining-room for a flimsy-looking mirrored sideboard, sporting an orange crackleware fruit dish and two painted wooden candle-sticks, took up most of the wall opposite the door and contra-dicted the faded pink sofa ranged against the other side of the room.

There was no table in the centre under the alabasterine ceiling light, only a small square of stained carpet with a futurist design in contrasting browns.

Over by the window was an incongruous-looking throne-like chair in carved oak with a red velvet seat, a low table on which stood an empty water carafe and two glasses, and a light armchair with a round cane seat and no cushion.

Half-closed venetian blinds obscured the view from the window, but cast bars of early sunlight over the few pieces of furniture and over part of the brightly papered wall and the brown stained floorboards.

Le Chiffre pointed at the cane chair.

'That will do excellently,' he said to the thin man. 'Prepare him quickly. If he resists, damage him only a little.'

He turned to Bond. There was no expression on his large face and his round eyes were uninterested. 'Take off your clothes. For every effort to resist, Basil will break one of your fingers. We are serious people and your good health is of no interest to us. Whether you live or die depends on the outcome of the talk we are about to have.'

He made a gesture towards the thin man and left the room.

The thin man's first action was a curious one. He opened the clasp-knife he had used on the hood of Bond's car, took the small armchair and with a swift motion he cut out its cane seat.

Then he came back to Bond, sticking the still open knife, like a fountain-pen, in the vest pocket of his coat. He turned Bond round to the light and unwound the flex from his wrists. Then he stood quickly aside and the knife was back in his right hand.

'*Vite.*'

Bond stood chafing his swollen wrists and debating with himself how much time he could waste by resisting. He only delayed an instant. With a swift step and a downward sweep of his free hand, the thin man seized the collar of his dinner-jacket and dragged it down, pinning Bond's arms back. Bond made the traditional counter to this old policeman's hold by dropping down on one knee, but as he dropped the thin man dropped with him and at the same time brought his knife round and down behind Bond's back. Bond felt the back of the blade pass down his spine. There was the hiss of a sharp knife through cloth and his arms were suddenly free as the two halves of his coat fell forward.

He cursed and stood up. The thin man was back in his previous position, his knife again at the ready in his relaxed hand. Bond let the two halves of his dinner-jacket fall off his arms on to the floor.

'Allez,' said the thin man with a faint trace of impatience.

Bond looked him in the eye and then slowly started to take off his shirt.

Le Chiffre came quietly back into the room. He carried a pot of what smelt like coffee. He put it on the small table near the window. He also placed beside it on the table two other homely objects, a three-foot-long carpet-beater in twisted cane and a carving knife.

He settled himself comfortably on the throne-like chair and poured some of the coffee into one of the glasses. With one foot he hooked forward the small armchair, whose seat was now an empty circular frame of wood, until it was directly opposite him.

Bond stood stark naked in the middle of the room, bruises showing livid on his white body, his face a grey mask of exhaustion and knowledge of what was to come.

'Sit down there.' Le Chiffre nodded at the chair in front of him.

Bond walked over and sat down.

The thin man produced some flex. With this he bound Bond's wrists to the arms of the chair and his ankles to the front legs. He passed a double strand across his chest, under the arm-pits and through the chair-back. He made no mistakes with the knots and left no play in any of the bindings. All of them bit sharply into Bond's flesh. The legs of the chair were broadly spaced and Bond could not even rock it.

He was utterly a prisoner, naked and defenceless.

His buttocks and the underpart of his body protruded through the seat of the chair towards the floor.

Le Chiffre nodded to the thin man who quietly left the room and closed the door.

There was a packet of Gauloises on the table and a lighter. Le Chiffre lit a cigarette and swallowed a mouthful of coffee from the glass. Then he picked up the cane carpet-beater and, resting the handle comfortably on his knee, allowed the flat trefoil base to lie on the floor directly under Bond's chair.

He looked Bond carefully, almost caressingly, in the eyes. Then his wrists sprang suddenly upwards on his knee.

The result was startling.

Bond's whole body arched in an involuntary spasm. His face contracted in a soundless scream and his lips drew right away from his teeth. At the same time his head flew back with a jerk showing the taut sinews of his neck. For an instant, muscles stood out in knots all over his body and his toes and fingers clenched until they were quite white. Then his body sagged and perspiration started to bead all over his body. He uttered a deep groan.

Le Chiffre waited for his eyes to open.

'You see, dear boy?' He smiled a soft, fat smile. 'Is the position quite clear now?'

A drop of sweat fell off Bond's chin on to his naked chest.

'Now let us get down to business and see how soon we can be finished with this unfortunate mess you have got yourself into.' He puffed cheerfully at his cigarette and gave an admonitory tap on the floor beneath Bond's chair with his horrible and incongruous instrument.

'My dear boy,' Le Chiffre spoke like a father, 'the game of Red Indians is over, quite over. You have stumbled by mischance into a game for grown-ups and you have already found it a painful experience. You are not equipped, my dear boy, to play games with adults and it was very foolish of your nanny in London to have sent you out here with your spade and bucket. Very foolish indeed and most unfortunate for you.

'But we must stop joking, my dear fellow, although I am sure you would like to follow me in developing this amusing little cautionary tale.'

He suddenly dropped his bantering tone and looked at Bond sharply and venomously.

'Where is the money?'

Bond's bloodshot eyes looked emptily back at him.

Again the upward jerk of the wrist and again Bond's whole body writhed and contorted.

Le Chiffre waited until the tortured heart eased down its laboured pumping and until Bond's eyes dully opened again.

'Perhaps I should explain,' said Le Chiffre. 'I intend to continue attacking the sensitive parts of your body until you answer my question. I am without mercy and there will be no relenting. There is no one to stage a last-minute rescue and there is no possibility of escape for you. This is not a romantic adventure story in which the villain is finally routed and the hero is given a medal and marries the girl. Unfortunately these things don't happen in real life. If you continue to be obstinate, you will be tortured to the edge of madness and then the girl will be brought in and we will set about her in front of you. If that is still not enough, you will both be painfully killed and I shall reluctantly leave your bodies and make my way abroad to a comfortable house which is waiting for me. There I shall take up a useful and profitable career and live to a ripe and peaceful old age in the bosom of the family I shall doubtless create. So you see, my dear boy, that I stand to lose nothing. If you hand the money over, so much the better. If not, I shall shrug my shoulders and be on my way.'

He paused, and his wrist lifted slightly on his knee. Bond's flesh cringed as the cane surface just touched him.

'But you, my dear fellow, can only hope that I shall spare you further pain and spare your life. There is no other hope for you but that. Absolutely none.'

'Well?'

Bond closed his eyes and waited for the pain. He knew that the beginning of torture is the worst. There is a parabola of agony. A crescendo leading up to a peak and then the nerves are blunted and react progressively less until unconsciousness and death. All he could do was to pray for the peak, pray that his spirit would hold out so long and then accept the long free-wheel down to the final black-out.

He had been told by colleagues who had survived torture by the Germans and the Japanese that towards the end there came a wonderful period of warmth and languor leading into a sort of sexual twilight where pain turned to pleasure and where hatred and fear of the torturers turned to a masochistic infatuation. It was the supreme test of will, he had learnt, to avoid showing this form of punch-drunkenness.

Directly it was suspected they would either kill you at once and save themselves further useless effort, or let you recover sufficiently so that your nerves had crept back to the other side of the parabola. Then they would start again.

He opened his eyes a fraction.

Le Chiffre had been waiting for this and like a rattlesnake the cane instrument leapt from the floor. It struck again and again so that Bond screamed and his body jangled in the chair like a marionette.

Le Chiffre desisted only when Bond's tortured spasms showed a trace of sluggishness. He sat for a while sipping his coffee and frowning slightly like a surgeon watching a cardiograph during a difficult operation.

When Bond's eyes flickered and opened he addressed him again, but now with a trace of impatience.

'We know that the money is somewhere in your room,' he said. 'You drew a cheque to cash for forty million francs and I know that you went back to the hotel to hide it.'

For a moment Bond wondered how he had been so certain.

'Directly you left for the night club,' continued Le Chiffre, 'your room was searched by four of my people.'

The Muntzes must have helped, reflected Bond.

'We found a good deal in childish hiding-places. The ball-cock in the lavatory yielded an interesting little codebook and we found some more of your papers taped to the back of a drawer. All the furniture has been taken to pieces and your clothes and the curtains and bedclothes have been cut up. Every inch of the room has been searched and all the fittings removed. It is most unfortunate for you that we didn't find the cheque. If we had, you would now be comfortably in bed, perhaps with the beautiful Miss Lynd, instead of this.' He lashed upwards.

Through the red mist of pain, Bond thought of Vesper. He could imagine how she was being used by the two gunmen. They would be making the most of her before she was sent for by Le Chiffre. He thought of the fat wet lips of the Corsican and the slow cruelty of the thin man. Poor wretch to have been dragged into this. Poor little beast.

Le Chiffre was talking again.

88

'Torture is a terrible thing,' he was saying as he puffed at a fresh cigarette, 'but it is a simple matter for the torturer, particularly when the patient,' he smiled at the word, 'is a man. You see, my dear Bond, with a man it is quite unnecessary to indulge in refinements. With this simple instrument, or with almost any other object, one can cause a man as much pain as is possible or necessary. Do not believe what you read in novels or books about the war. There is nothing worse. It is not only the immediate agony, but also the thought that your manhood is being gradually destroyed and that at the end, if you will not yield, you will no longer be a man.

'That, my dear Bond, is a sad and terrible thought – a long chain of agony for the body and also for the mind, and then the final screaming moment when you will beg me to kill you. All that is inevitable unless you tell me where you hid the money.'

He poured some more coffee into the glass and drank it down leaving brown corners to his mouth.

Bond's lips were writhing. He was trying to say something. At last he got the word out in a harsh croak: 'Drink,' he said and his tongue came out and swilled across his dry lips.

'Of course, my dear boy, how thoughtless of me.' Le Chiffre poured some coffee into the other glass. There was a ring of sweat drops on the floor round Bond's chair.

'We must certainly keep your tongue lubricated.'

He laid the handle of the carpet-beater down on the floor between his thick legs and rose from his chair. He went behind Bond and taking a handful of his soaking hair in one hand, he wrenched Bond's head sharply back. He poured the coffee down Bond's throat in small mouthfuls so that he would not choke. Then he released his head so that it fell forward again on his chest. He went back to his chair and picked up the carpet-beater.

Bond raised his head and spoke thickly.

'Money no good to you.' His voice was a laborious croak. 'Police trace it to you.'

Exhausted by the effort, his head sank forward again. He was a little, but only a little, exaggerating the extent of his physical collapse. Anything to gain time and anything to defer the next searing pain.

'Ah, my dear fellow, I had forgotten to tell you.' Le Chiffre smiled wolfishly. 'We met after our little game at the Casino and you were such a sportsman that you agreed we would have one more run through the pack between the two of us. It was a gallant gesture. Typical of an English gentleman.

'Unfortunately you lost and this upset you so much that you decided to leave Royale immediately for an unknown destination. Like the gentleman you are, you very kindly gave me a note explaining the circumstances so that I would have no difficulty in cashing your cheque. You see, dear boy, everything has been thought of and you need have no fears on my account.' He chuckled fatly.

'Now shall we continue? I have all the time in the world and truth to tell I am rather interested to see how long a man can stand this particular form of ... er ... encouragement.' He rattled the harsh cane on the floor.

So that was the score, thought Bond, with a final sinking of the heart. The 'unknown destination' would be under the ground or under the sea, or perhaps, more simply, under the crashed Bentley. Well, if he had to die anyway, he might as well try it the hard way. He had no hope that Mathis or Leiter would get to him in time, but at least there was a chance that they would catch up with Le Chiffre before he could get away. It must be getting on for seven. The car might have been found by now. It was a choice of evils, but the longer Le Chiffre continued the torture the more likely he would be revenged.

Bond lifted his head and looked Le Chiffre in the eyes.

The china of the whites was now veined with red. It was like looking at two blackcurrants poached in blood. The rest of the wide face was yellowish except where a thick black stubble covered the moist skin. The upward edges of black coffee at the corners of the mouth gave his expression a false smile and the whole face was faintly striped by the light through the venetian blinds.

'No,' he said flatly, '... you ...'

Le Chiffre grunted and set to work again with savage fury. Occasionally he snarled like a wild beast.

After ten minutes Bond had fainted, blessedly.

Le Chiffre at once stopped. He wiped some sweat from his face with a circular motion of his disengaged hand. Then he looked at his watch and seemed to make up his mind.

He got up and stood behind the inert, dripping body. There was no colour in Bond's face or anywhere on his body above the waist. There was a faint flutter of his skin above the heart. Otherwise he might have been dead.

Le Chiffre seized Bond's ears and harshly twisted them. Then he leant forward and slapped his cheeks hard several times. Bond's head rolled from side to side with each blow. Slowly his breathing became deeper. An animal groan came from his lolling mouth.

Le Chiffre took a glass of coffee and poured some into Bond's mouth and threw the rest in his face. Bond's eyes slowly opened.

Le Chiffre returned to his chair and waited. He lit a cigarette and contemplated the spattered pool of blood on the floor beneath the inert body opposite.

Bond groaned again pitifully. It was an inhuman sound. His eyes opened and he gazed dully at his torturer.

Le Chiffre spoke.

'That is all, Bond. We will now finish with you. You understand? Not kill you, but finish with you. And then we will have in the girl and see if something can be got out of the remains of the two of you.'

He reached towards the table.

'Say goodbye to it, Bond.'

18 A Crag-like Face

It was extraordinary to hear the third voice. The hour's ritual had only demanded a duologue against the horrible noise of the torture. Bond's dimmed senses hardly took it in. Then suddenly he was half-way back to consciousness. He found he could see and hear again. He could hear the dead silence after the one quiet word from the doorway. He could see Le Chiffre's head slowly come up and the expression of blank astonishment, of innocent amazement, slowly give way to fear.

'Shtop,' had said the voice, quietly.

Bond heard slow steps approaching behind his chair.

'Dhrop it,' said the voice.

Bond saw Le Chiffre's hand open obediently and the knife fall with a clatter to the floor.

He tried desperately to read into Le Chiffre's face what was happening behind him, but all he saw was blind incomprehension and terror. Le Chiffre's mouth worked, but only a high-pitched 'eek' came from it. His heavy cheeks trembled as he tried to collect enough saliva in his mouth to say something, ask something. His hands fluttered vaguely in his lap. One of them made a slight movement towards his pocket, but instantly fell back. His round staring eyes had lowered for a split second and Bond guessed there was a gun trained on him.

There was a moment's silence.

'SMERSH.'

The word came almost with a sigh. It came with a downward cadence as if nothing else had to be said. It was the final explanation. The last word of all.

'No,' said Le Chiffre. 'No. I . . .' His voice tailed off.

Perhaps he was going to explain, to apologize, but what he must have seen in the other's face made it all useless.

'Your two men. Both dead. You are a fool and a thief and a traitor. I have been sent from the Soviet Union to eliminate you. You are fortunate that I have only time to shoot you. If it was possible, I was instructed that you should die most painfully. We cannot see the end of the trouble you have caused.'

The thick voice stopped. There was silence in the room save for the rasping breath of Le Chiffre.

Somewhere outside a bird began to sing and there were other small noises from the awakening countryside. The bands of sunlight were stronger and the sweat on Le Chiffre's face glistened brightly.

'Do you plead guilty?'

Bond wrestled with his consciousness. He screwed up his eyes and tried to shake his head to clear it, but his whole nervous system was numbed and no message was transmitted to his muscles. He could just keep his focus on the great pale face in front of him and on its bulging eyes.

A thin string of saliva crept from the open mouth and hung down from the chin.

'Yes,' said the mouth.

There was a sharp 'phut', no louder than a bubble of air escaping from a tube of toothpaste. No other noise at all, and suddenly Le Chiffre had grown another eye, a third eye on a level with the other two, right where the thick nose started to jut out below the forehead. It was a small black eye, without eyelashes or eyebrows.

For a second the three eyes looked out across the room and then the whole face seemed to slip and go down on one knee. The two outer eyes turned trembling up towards the ceiling. Then the heavy head fell sideways and the right shoulder and finally the whole upper part of the body lurched over the arm of the chair as if Le Chiffre were going to be sick. But there was only a short rattle of his heels on the ground and then no other movement.

The tall back of the chair looked impassively out across the dead body in its arms.

There was a faint movement behind Bond. A hand came from behind and grasped his chin and pulled it back.

For a moment Bond looked up into two glittering eyes behind a narrow black mask. There was the impression of a crag-like face under a hat-brim, the collar of a fawn mackintosh. He could take in nothing more before his head was pushed down again.

'You are fortunate,' said the voice. 'I have no orders to kill you. Your life has been saved twice in one day. But you can tell your organization that SMERSH is only merciful by chance or by mistake. In your case you were saved first by chance and now by mistake, for I should have had orders to kill any foreign spies who were hanging round this traitor like flies round a dog's mess.

'But I shall leave you my visiting-card. You are a gambler. You play at cards. One day perhaps you will play against one of us. It would be well that you should be known as a spy.'

Steps moved round to behind Bond's right shoulder. There was the click of a knife opening. An arm in some grey material came into Bond's line of vision. A broad hairy hand emerging from a dirty white shirt-cuff was holding a thin stiletto like a fountain-pen. It poised for

93

a moment above the back of Bond's right hand, immovably bound with flex to the arm of the chair. The point of the stiletto executed three quick straight slashes. A fourth slash crossed them where they ended, just short of the knuckles. Blood in the shape of an inverted 'M' welled out and slowly started to drip on to the floor.

The pain was nothing to what Bond was already suffering, but it was enough to plunge him again into unconsciousness.

The steps moved quietly away across the room. The door was softly closed.

In the silence, the cheerful small sounds of the summer's day crept through the closed window. High on the left-hand wall hung two small patches of pink light. They were reflections cast upwards from the floor by the zebra stripes of June sunshine, cast upwards from two separate pools of blood a few feet apart.

As the day progressed the pink patches marched slowly along the wall. And slowly they grew larger.

19 The White Tent

You are about to awake when you dream that you are dreaming.

During the next two days James Bond was permanently in this state without regaining consciousness. He watched the procession of his dreams go by without any effort to disturb their sequence, although many of them were terrifying and all were painful. He knew that he was in a bed and that he was lying on his back and could not move and in one of his twilight moments he thought there were people round him, but he made no effort to open his eyes and re-enter the world.

He felt safer in the darkness and he hugged it to him.

On the morning of the third day a bloody nightmare shook him awake, trembling and sweating. There was a hand on his forehead which he associated with his dream. He tried to lift an arm and smash it sideways into the owner of the hand, but his arms were immovable, secured to the sides of his bed. His whole body was strapped down and something like a large white coffin covered him from chest to feet and obscured his view of the end of the bed. He shouted a string of obscenities, but the effort took all his strength and the words tailed off into a sob. Tears of forlornness and self-pity welled out of his eyes.

A woman's voice was speaking and the words gradually penetrated to him. It seemed to be a kind voice and it slowly came to him that he was being comforted and that this was a friend and not an enemy. He could hardly believe it. He had been so certain that he was still a captive and that the torture was about to begin again. He felt his face being softly wiped with a cool cloth which smelt of lavender and then he sank back into his dreams.

When he awoke again some hours later all his terrors had gone and he felt warm and languorous. Sun was streaming into the bright room and garden sounds came through the window. In the background there was the noise of small waves on a beach. As he moved his head he heard a rustle, and a nurse who had been sitting beside his pillow rose and came into his line of vision. She was pretty and she smiled as she put her hand on his pulse.

'Well, I'm certainly glad you've woken up at last. I've never heard such dreadful language in my life.'

Bond smiled back at her.

'Where am I?' he asked and was surprised that his voice sounded firm and clear.

'You're in a nursing home at Royale and I've been sent over from England to look after you. There are two of us and I'm Nurse Gibson. Now just lie quiet and I'll go and tell the doctor you're awake. You've been unconscious since they brought you in and we've been quite worried.'

Bond closed his eyes and mentally explored his body. The worst pain was in his wrists and ankles and in his right hand where the Russian had cut him. In the centre of the body there was no feeling. He assumed that he had been given a local anaesthetic. The rest of his body ached dully as if he had been beaten all over. He could feel the pressure of bandages everywhere and his unshaven neck and chin prickled against the sheets. From the feel of the bristles he knew that he must have been at least three days without shaving. That meant two days since the morning of the torture.

He was preparing a short list of questions in his mind when the door opened and the doctor came in followed by the nurse and in the background the dear figure of Mathis, a Mathis looking anxious behind his broad smile, who put a finger to his lips and walked on tiptoe to the window and sat down.

The doctor, a Frenchman with a young and intelligent face, had been detached from his duties with the Deuxième Bureau to look after Bond's case. He came and stood beside Bond and put his hand on Bond's forehead while he looked at the temperature chart behind the bed.

When he spoke he was forthright.

'You have a lot of questions to ask, my dear Mr Bond,' he said in excellent English, 'and I can tell you most of the answers. I do not want you to waste your strength, so I will give you the salient facts and then you may have a few minutes with Monsieur Mathis who wishes to obtain one or two details from you. It is really too early for this talk, but I wish to set your mind at rest so that we can proceed with the task of repairing your body without bothering too much about your mind.'

Nurse Gibson pulled up a chair for the doctor and left the room.

'You have been here about two days,' continued the doctor. 'Your car was found by a farmer on the way to market in Royale and he informed the police. After some delay Monsieur Mathis heard that it was your car and he immediately went to Les Noctambules with his men. You and Le Chiffre were found and also your friend, Miss Lynd, who was unharmed and according to her account suffered no molestation. She was prostrated with shock, but is now fully recovered and is at her hotel. She has been instructed by her superiors in London to stay at Royale under your orders until you are sufficiently recovered to go back to England.

'Le Chiffre's two gunmen are dead, each killed by a single .35 bullet in the back of the skull. From the lack of expression on their faces, they evidently never saw or heard their assailant. They were found in the same room as Miss Lynd. Le Chiffre is dead, shot with a similar weapon between the eyes. Did you witness his death?'

'Yes,' said Bond.

'Your own injuries are serious, but your life is not in danger though you have lost a lot of blood. If all goes well, you will recover completely and none of the functions of your body will be impaired.' The doctor smiled grimly. 'But I fear that you will continue to be in pain for several days and it will be my endeavour to give you as much comfort as possible. Now that you have regained consciousness your arms will be freed, but you must not move your body and when you sleep the nurse has orders to secure your arms again. Above all, it is important that you rest and regain your strength. At the moment you are suffering from a grave condition of mental and physical shock.' The doctor paused. 'For how long were you maltreated?'

'About an hour,' said Bond.

'Then it is remarkable that you are alive and I congratulate you. Few men could have supported what you have been through. Perhaps that is some consolation. As Monsieur Mathis can tell you, I have had in my time to treat a number of patients who have suffered similar handling and not one has come through it as you have done.'

The doctor looked at Bond for a moment and then turned brusquely to Mathis.

'You may have ten minutes and then you will be forcibly ejected. If you put the patient's temperature up, you will answer for it.'

He gave them both a broad smile and left the room.

Mathis came over and took the doctor's chair.

'That's a good man,' said Bond. 'I like him.'

'He's attached to the Bureau,' said Mathis. 'He is a very good man and I will tell you about him one of these days. He thinks you are a prodigy – and so do I.

'However, that can wait. As you can imagine, there is much to clear up and I am being pestered by Paris and, of course, London, and even by Washington via our good friend Leiter. Incidentally,' he broke off, 'I have a personal message from M. He spoke to me himself on the telephone. He simply said to tell you that he is much impressed. I asked if that was all and he said: "Well, tell him that the Treasury is greatly relieved." Then he rang off.'

Bond grinned with pleasure. What most warmed him was that M

himself should have rung up Mathis. This was quite unheard of. The very existence of M, let alone his identity, was never admitted. He could imagine the flutter this must have caused in the ultra-security-minded organization in London.

'A tall thin man with one arm came over from London the same day we found you,' continued Mathis, knowing from his own experience that these shop details would interest Bond more than anything else and give him most pleasure, 'and he fixed up the nurses and looked after everything. Even your car's being repaired for you. He seemed to be Vesper's boss. He spent a lot of time with her and gave her strict instructions to look after you.'

Head of S, thought Bond. They're certainly giving me the red carpet treatment.

'Now,' said Mathis, 'to business. Who killed Le Chiffre?'

'SMERSH,' said Bond.

Mathis gave a low whistle.

'My God,' he said respectfully. 'So they *were* on to him. What did he look like?'

Bond explained briefly what had happened up to the moment of Le Chiffre's death, omitting all but the most essential details. It cost him an effort and he was glad when it was done. Casting his mind back to the scene awoke the whole nightmare and the sweat began to pour off his forehead and a deep throb of pain started up in his body.

Mathis realized that he was going too far. Bond's voice was getting feebler and his eyes were clouding. Mathis snapped shut his shorthand book and laid a hand on Bond's shoulder.

'Forgive me, my friend,' he said. 'It is all over now and you are in safe hands. All is well and the whole plan has gone splendidly. We have announced that Le Chiffre shot his two accomplices and then committed suicide because he could not face an inquiry into the union funds. Strasbourg and the north are in an uproar. He was considered a great hero there and a pillar of the Communist Party in France. This story of brothels and casinos has absolutely knocked the bottom out of his organization and they're all running around like scalded cats. At the moment the Communist Party is giving out that he was off his head. But that hasn't helped much after Thorez's breakdown not long ago. They're just making it look as if all their big shots were gaga. God knows how they're going to unscramble the whole business.'

Mathis saw that his enthusiasm had had the desired effect. Bond's eyes were brighter.

'One last mystery,' Mathis said, 'and then I promise I will go.' He looked at his watch. 'The doctor will be after my skin in a moment. Now, what about the money? Where is it? Where did you hide it? We too have been over your room with a toothcomb. It isn't there.'

Bond grinned.

'It is,' he said, 'more or less. On the door of each room there is a small square of black plastic with the number of the room on it. On the corridor side, of course. When Leiter left me that night, I simply opened the door and unscrewed my number plate and put the folded cheque underneath it and screwed the plate back. It'll still be there.' He smiled. 'I'm glad there's something the stupid English can teach the clever French.'

Mathis laughed delightedly.

'I suppose you think that's paid me back for knowing what the Muntzes were up to. Well, I'll call it quits. Incidentally, we've got them in the bag. They were just some minor fry hired for the occasion. We'll see they get a few years.'

He rose hastily as the doctor stormed into the room and took one look at Bond.

'Out,' he said to Mathis. 'Out and don't come back.'

Mathis just had time to wave cheerfully to Bond and call some hasty words of farewell before he was hustled through the door. Bond heard a torrent of heated French diminishing down the corridor. He lay back exhausted, but heartened by all he had heard. He found himself thinking of Vesper as he quickly drifted off into a troubled sleep.

There were still questions to be answered, but they could wait.

20 The Nature of Evil

Bond made good progress. When Mathis came to see him three days later he was propped up in bed and his arms were free. The lower half of his body was still shrouded in the oblong tent, but he looked cheerful and it was only occasionally that a twinge of pain narrowed his eyes.

Mathis looked crestfallen.

'Here's your cheque,' he said to Bond. 'I've rather enjoyed walking around with forty million francs in my pocket, but I suppose you'd better sign it and I'll put it to your account with the Crédit Lyonnais. There's no sign of our friend from SMERSH. Not a damn trace. He must have got to the villa on foot or on a bicycle because you heard nothing of his arrival and the two gunmen obviously didn't. It's pretty exasperating. We've got precious little on this SMERSH organization and neither has London. Washington said they had, but it turned out to be the usual waffle from refugee interrogation, and you know that's about as much good as interrogating an English man-in-the street about his own Secret Service, or a Frenchman about the Deuxième.'

'He probably came from Leningrad to Berlin via Warsaw,' said Bond. 'From Berlin they've got plenty of routes open to the rest of Europe. He's back home by now being told off for not shooting me too. I fancy they've got quite a file on me in view of one or two of the jobs M's given me since the war. He obviously thought he was being smart enough cutting his initial in my hand.'

'What's that?' asked Mathis. 'The doctor said the cuts looked like a square M with a tail to the top. He said they didn't mean anything.'

'Well, I only got a glimpse before I passed out, but I've seen the cuts several times while they were being dressed and I'm pretty certain they are the Russian letter for SH. It's rather like an inverted M with a tail. That would make sense; SMERSH is short for SMYERT SHPIONAM – Death to Spies – and he thinks he's labelled me as a SHPION. It's a nuisance because M will probably say I've got to go to hospital again when I get back to London and have new skin grafted over the whole of the back of my hand. It doesn't matter much. I've decided to resign.'

Mathis looked at him with his mouth open.

'Resign?' he asked incredulously. 'What the hell for?'

Bond looked away from Mathis. He studied his bandaged hands.

'When I was being beaten up,' he said, 'I suddenly liked the idea of being alive. Before Le Chiffre began, he used a phrase which stuck in my mind . . . "playing Red Indians". He said that's what I had been doing. Well, I suddenly thought he might be right.

'You see,' he said, still looking down at his bandages, 'when one's young, it seems very easy to distinguish between right and wrong, but as one gets older it becomes more difficult. At school it's easy to pick out one's own villains and heroes and one grows up wanting to be a hero and kill the villains.'

He looked obstinately at Mathis.

'Well, in the last few years I've killed two villains. The first was in New York – a Japanese cipher expert cracking our codes on the thirty-sixth floor of the RCA building in the Rockefeller centre, where the Japs had their consulate. I took a room on the fortieth floor of the next-door skyscraper and I could look across the street into his room and see him working. Then I got a colleague from our organization in New York and a couple of Remington thirty-thirty's with telescopic sights and silencers. We smuggled them up to my room and sat for days waiting for our chance. He shot at the man a second before me. His job was only to blast a hole through the windows so that I could shoot the Jap through it. They have tough windows at the Rockefeller centre to keep the noise out. It worked very well. As I expected, his bullet got deflected by the glass and went God knows where. But I shot immediately after him, through the hole he had made. I got the Jap in the mouth as he turned to gape at the broken window.'

Bond smoked for a minute.

'It was a pretty sound job. Nice and clean too. Three hundred yards away. No personal contact. The next time in Stockholm wasn't so pretty. I had to kill a Norwegian who was doubling against us for the Germans. He'd managed to get two of our men captured – probably bumped off for all I know. For various reasons it had to be an absolutely silent job. I chose the bedroom of his flat and a knife. And, well, he just didn't die very quickly.

'For those two jobs I was awarded a Double O number in the Service. Felt pretty clever and got a reputation for being good and tough. A Double O number in our Service means you've had to kill a chap in cold blood in the course of some job.

'Now,' he looked up again at Mathis, 'that's all very fine. The hero kills two villains, but when the hero Le Chiffre starts to kill the villain Bond and the villain Bond knows he isn't a villain at all, you see the other side of the medal. The villains and heroes get all mixed up.

'Of course,' he added, as Mathis started to expostulate, 'patriotism comes along and makes it seem fairly all right, but this country-right-or-wrong business is getting a little out-of-date. Today we are fighting Communism. Okay. If I'd been alive fifty years ago, the brand of Conservatism we have today would have been damn near called Communism and we should have been told to go and fight that. History is moving pretty quickly these days and the heroes and villains keep on changing parts.'

Mathis stared at him aghast. Then he tapped his head and put a calming hand on Bond's arm.

'You mean to say that this precious Le Chiffre who did his best to turn you into a eunuch doesn't qualify as a villain?' he asked. 'Anyone would think from the rot you talk that he had been battering your head instead of your . . .' He gestured down the bed. 'You wait till M tells you to get after another Le Chiffre. I bet you'll go after him all right. And what about SMERSH? I can tell you I don't like the idea of these chaps running around France killing anyone they feel has been a traitor to their precious political system. You're a bloody anarchist.'

He threw his arms in the air and let them fall helplessly to his sides. Bond laughed.

'All right,' he said. 'Take our friend Le Chiffre. It's simple enough to say he was an evil man, at least it's simple enough for me because he did evil things to me. If he was here now, I wouldn't hesitate to kill him, but out of personal revenge and not, I'm afraid, for some high moral reason or for the sake of my country.'

He looked up at Mathis to see how bored he was getting with these introspective refinements of what, to Mathis, was a simple question of duty.

Mathis smiled back at him.

'Continue, my dear friend. It is interesting for me to see this new Bond. Englishmen are so odd. They are like a nest of Chinese boxes. It takes a very long time to get to the centre of them. When one gets there the result is unrewarding, but the process is instructive and entertaining. Continue. Develop your arguments. There may be something I can use to my own chief the next time I want to get out of an unpleasant job.' He grinned maliciously.

Bond ignored him.

'Now in order to tell the difference between good and evil, we have manufactured two images representing the extremes – representing the deepest black and the purest white – and we call them God and the Devil. But in doing so we have cheated a bit. God is a clear image, you can see every hair on His beard. But the Devil. What does he look like?' Bond looked triumphantly at Mathis.

Mathis laughed ironically.

'A woman.'

'It's all very fine,' said Bond, 'but I've been thinking about these things and I'm wondering whose side I ought to be on. I'm getting very sorry for the Devil and his disciples such as the good Le Chiffre. The Devil has a rotten time and I always like to be on the side of the underdog. We don't give the poor chap a chance. There's a Good Book about goodness and how to be good and so forth, but there's no Evil Book about evil and how to be bad. The Devil has no prophets to write his Ten Commandments and no team of authors to write his biography. His case has gone completely by default. We know nothing about him but a lot of fairy stories from our parents and schoolmasters. He has no book from which we can learn the nature of evil in all its forms, with parables about evil people, proverbs about evil people, folk-lore about evil people. All we have is the living example of the people who are least good, or our own intuition.

'So,' continued Bond, warming to his argument, 'Le Chiffre was serving a wonderful purpose, a really vital purpose, perhaps the best and highest purpose of all. By his evil existence, which foolishly I have helped to destroy, he was creating a norm of badness by which, and by which alone, an opposite norm of goodness could exist. We were privileged, in our short knowledge of him, to see and estimate his wickedness and we emerge from the acquaintanceship better and more virtuous men.'

'Bravo,' said Mathis. 'I'm proud of you. You ought to be tortured every day. I really must remember to do something evil this evening. I must start at once. I have a few marks in my favour – only small ones, alas,' he added ruefully – 'but I shall work fast now that I have seen the light. What a splendid time I'm going to have. Now, let's see, where shall I start, murder, arson, rape? But no, these are peccadilloes. I must really consult the good Marquis de Sade. I am a child, an absolute child in these matters.'

His face fell.

'Ah, but our conscience, my dear Bond. What shall we do with him while we are committing some juicy sin? That is a problem. He is a crafty person this conscience and very old, as old as the first family of apes which gave birth to him. We must give that problem really careful thought or we shall spoil our enjoyment. Of course, we should murder him first, but he is a tough bird. It will be difficult, but if we succeed, we could be worse even than Le Chiffre.

'For you, dear James, it is easy. You can start off by resigning. That was a brilliant thought of yours, a splendid start to your new career. And so simple. Everyone has the revolver of resignation in his pocket. All you've got to do is pull the trigger and you will have made a big hole in your country and your conscience at the same time. A murder and a suicide with one bullet! Splendid! What a difficult and glorious profession. As for me, I must start embracing the new cause at once.'

He looked at his watch.

'Good. I've started already. I'm half an hour late for a meeting with the chief of police.'

He rose to his feet laughing.

'That was most enjoyable, my dear James. You really ought to go on the halls. Now about that little problem of yours, this business of not knowing good men from bad men and villains from heroes, and so forth. It is, of course, a difficult problem in the abstract. The secret lies in personal experience, whether you're a Chinaman or an Englishman.'

He paused at the door.

'You admit that Le Chiffre did you personal evil and that you would kill him if he appeared in front of you now?

'Well, when you get back to London you will find there are other Le Chiffres seeking to destroy you and your friends and your country. M will tell you about them. And now that you have seen a really evil man, you will know how evil they can be and you will go after them to destroy them in order to protect yourself and the people you love. You won't wait to argue about it. You know what they look like now and what they can do to people. You may be a bit more choosy about the jobs you take on. You may want to be certain that the target really is black, but there are plenty of really black targets around. There's still plenty for you to do. And you'll do it. And when you fall in love and have a mistress or a wife and children to look after, it will seem all the easier.'

Mathis opened the door and stopped on the threshold.

'Surround yourself with human beings, my dear James. They are easier to fight for than principles.'

He laughed. 'But don't let me down and become human yourself. We would lose such a wonderful machine.'

With a wave of the hand he shut the door.

'Hey,' shouted Bond.

But the footsteps went quickly off down the passage.

21 Vesper

It was on the next day that Bond asked to see Vesper.

He had not wanted to see her before. He was told that every day she came to the nursing home and asked after him. Flowers had arrived from her. Bond didn't like flowers and he told the nurse to give them to another patient. After this had happened twice, no more flowers came. Bond had not meant to offend her. He disliked having feminine things around him. Flowers seemed to ask for recognition of the person who had sent them, to be constantly transmitting a message of sympathy and affection. Bond found this irksome. He disliked being cosseted. It gave him claustrophobia.

Bond was bored at the idea of having to explain some of this to Vesper. And he was embarrassed at having to ask one or two questions which mystified him, questions about Vesper's behaviour. The answers would almost certainly make her out to be a fool. Then he had his full report to M to think about. In this he didn't want to have to criticize Vesper. It might easily cost her her job.

But above all, he admitted to himself, he shirked the answer to a more painful question.

The doctor had talked often to Bond about his injuries. He had always told him that there would be no evil effects from the terrible battering his body had received. He had said that Bond's full health would return and that none of his powers had been taken from him. But the evidence of Bond's eyes and his nerves refused these comforting assurances. He was still painfully swollen and bruised and whenever the injections wore off he was in agony. Above all, his imagination had suffered. For an hour in that room with Le Chiffre the certainty of impotence had been beaten into him and a scar had been left on his mind that could only be healed by experience.

From that day when Bond first met Vesper in the Hermitage bar, he had found her desirable and he knew that if things had been different in the night club, if Vesper had responded in any way and if there had been no kidnapping he would have tried to sleep with her that night. Even later, in the car and outside the villa when God knows he had had other things to think about, his eroticism had been hotly aroused by the sight of her indecent nakedness.

And now when he could see her again, he was afraid. Afraid that his senses and his body would not respond to her sensual beauty. Afraid that he would feel no stir of desire and that his blood would stay cool. In his mind he had made this first meeting into a test and he was shirking the answer. That was the real reason, he admitted, why he had waited to give his body a chance to respond, why he had put off their first meeting for over a week. He would like to have put off the meeting still further, but he explained to himself that his report must be written, that any day an emissary from London would come over and want to hear the full story, that today was as good as tomorrow, that anyway he might as well know the worst.

So on the eighth day he asked for her, for the early morning when he was feeling refreshed and strong after the night's rest.

For no reason at all, he had expected that she would show some sign of her experiences, that she would look pale and even ill. He was not prepared for the tall bronzed girl in a cream tussore frock with a black belt who came happily through the door and stood smiling at him.

'Good heavens, Vesper,' he said with a wry gesture of welcome, 'you look absolutely splendid. You must thrive on disaster. How have you managed to get such a wonderful sunburn?'

'I feel very guilty,' she said sitting down beside him. 'But I've been bathing every day while you've been lying here. The doctor said I was to and Head of S said I was to, so, well, I just thought it wouldn't help you for me to be moping away all day long in my room. I've found a wonderful stretch of sand down the coast and I take my lunch and go there every day with a book and I don't come back till the evening. There's a bus that takes me there and back with only a short walk over the dunes, and I've managed to get over the fact that it's on the way down that road to the villa.'

Her voice faltered.

The mention of the villa had made Bond's eyes flicker.

She continued bravely, refusing to be defeated by Bond's lack of response.

'The doctor says it won't be long before you're allowed up. I thought perhaps . . . I thought perhaps I could take you down to this beach later on. The doctor says that bathing would be very good for you.'

Bond grunted.

'God knows when I'll be able to bathe,' he said. 'The doctor's talking through his hat. And when I can bathe it would probably be better for me to bathe alone for a bit. I don't want to frighten anybody. Apart from anything else,' he glanced pointedly down the bed, 'my body's a mass of scars and bruises. But you enjoy yourself. There's no reason why you shouldn't enjoy yourself.'

Vesper was stung by the bitterness and injustice in his voice.

'I'm sorry,' she said, 'I just thought . . . I was just trying . . .'

Suddenly her eyes filled with tears. She swallowed.

'I wanted . . . I wanted to help you get well.'

Her voice strangled. She looked piteously at him, facing the accusation in his eyes and in his manner.

Then she broke down and buried her face in her hands and sobbed.

'I'm sorry,' she said in a muffled voice. 'I'm really sorry.' With one hand she searched for a handkerchief in her bag. 'It's all my fault,' she dabbed at her eyes. 'I know it's all my fault.'

Bond at once relented. He put out a bandaged hand and laid it on her knee.

'It's all right, Vesper. I'm sorry I was so rough. It's just that I was jealous of you in the sunshine while I'm stuck here. Directly I'm well enough I'll come with you and you must show me your beach. Of course it's just what I want. It'll be wonderful to get out again.'

She pressed his hand and stood up and walked over to the window. After a moment she busied herself with her make-up. Then she came back to the bed.

Bond looked at her tenderly. Like all harsh, cold men, he was easily tipped over into sentiment. She was very beautiful and he felt warm towards her. He decided to make his questions as easy as possible.

He gave her a cigarette and for a time they talked of the visit of Head of S and of the reactions in London to the rout of Le Chiffre.

From what she said it was clear that the final object of the plan had been more than fulfilled. The story was still being splashed all over the world and correspondents of most of the English and American papers had been at Royale trying to trace the Jamaican millionaire who had defeated Le Chiffre at the tables. They had got on to Vesper, but she had covered up well. Her story was that Bond had told her he was going on to Cannes and Monte Carlo to gamble with his winnings. The hunt had moved down to the South of France. Mathis and the police had obliterated all other traces and the papers were forced to concentrate on the Strasbourg angles and the chaos in the ranks of the French Communists.

'By the way, Vesper,' said Bond after a time. 'What really happened to you after you left me in the night-club? All I saw was the actual kidnapping.' He told her briefly of the scene outside the Casino.

'I'm afraid I must have lost my head,' said Vesper, avoiding Bond's eyes. 'When I couldn't see Mathis anywhere in the entrance hall I went outside and the commissionaire asked me if I was Miss Lynd, and then told me the man who had sent in the note was waiting in a car down on the right of the steps. Somehow I wasn't particularly surprised. I'd only known Mathis for a day or two and I didn't know how he worked, so I just walked down towards the car. It was away on the right and more or less in the shadows. Just as I was coming up to it, Le Chiffre's two men jumped out from behind one of the other cars in the row and simply scooped my skirt over my head.'

Vesper blushed.

'It sounds a childish trick,' she looked penitently at Bond, 'but it's really frightfully effective. One's a complete prisoner and although I screamed I don't expect any sound came out from under my skirt. I kicked out as hard as I could, but that was no use as I couldn't see and my arms were absolutely helpless. I was just a trussed chicken.

'They picked me up between them and shoved me into the back of the car. I went on struggling, of course, and when the car started and while they were trying to tie a rope or something round the top of my skirt over my head, I managed to get an arm free and throw my bag through the window. I hope it was some use.'

Bond nodded.

'It was rather instinctive. I just thought you'd have no idea what had happened to me and I was terrified. I did the first thing I could think of.'

Bond knew that it was him they had been after and that if Vesper hadn't thrown her bag out, they would probably have thrown it out themselves directly they saw him appear on the steps.

'It certainly helped,' said Bond, 'but why didn't you make any sign when they finally got me after the car smash, when I spoke to you? I was dreadfully worried. I thought they might have knocked you out or something.'

'I'm afraid I must have been unconscious,' said Vesper. 'I fainted once from lack of air and when I came to they had cut a hole in front of my face. I must have fainted again. I don't remember much until we got to the villa. I really only gathered you had been captured when I heard you try and come after me in the passage.'

'And they didn't touch you?' asked Bond. 'They didn't try and mess about with you while I was being beaten up?'

'No,' said Vesper. 'They just left me in an armchair. They drank and played cards – "belotte" I think it was from what I heard – and then they went to sleep. I suppose that was how SMERSH got them. They bound my legs and put me on a chair in a corner facing the wall and I saw nothing of SMERSH. I heard some odd noises. I expect they woke me up. And then what sounded like one of them falling off his chair. Then there were some soft footsteps and a door closed and then nothing happened until Mathis and the police burst in hours later. I slept most of the time. I had no idea what had happened to you, but,' she faltered, 'I did once hear a terrible scream. It sounded very far away. At least, I think it must have been a scream. At the time I thought it might have been a nightmare.'

'I'm afraid that must have been me,' said Bond.

Vesper put out a hand and touched one of his. Her eyes filled with tears.

'It's horrible,' she said. 'The things they did to you. And it was all my fault. If only . . .'

She buried her face in her hands.

'That's all right,' said Bond comfortingly. 'It's no good crying over spilt milk. It's all over now and thank heavens they let you alone.' He patted her knee. 'They were going to start on you when they'd got me really softened up,' (softened up is good, he thought to himself). 'We've got a lot to thank SMERSH for. Now, come on, let's forget about it. It certainly wasn't anything to do with you. Anybody could have fallen for that note. Anyway, it's all water over the dam,' he added cheerfully.

Vesper looked at him gratefully through her tears. 'You really promise?' she asked. 'I thought you would never forgive me. I . . . I'll try and make it up to you. Somehow.' She looked at him.

Somehow? thought Bond to himself. He looked at her. She was smiling at him. He smiled back.

'You'd better look out,' he said. 'I may hold you to that.'

She looked into his eyes and said nothing, but the enigmatic challenge was back. She pressed his hand and rose. 'A promise is a promise,' she said.

This time they both knew what the promise was.

She picked up her bag from the bed and walked to the door.

'Shall I come tomorrow?' She looked at Bond gravely.

'Yes, please, Vesper,' said Bond. 'I'd like that. Please do some more exploring. It will be fun to think of what we can do when I get up. Will you think of some things?'

'Yes,' said Vesper. 'Please get well quickly.'

They gazed at each other for a second. Then she went out and closed the door and Bond listened until the sound of her footsteps had disappeared.

22 The Hastening Saloon

From that day Bond's recovery was rapid.

He sat up in bed and wrote his report to M. He made light of what he still considered amateurish behaviour on the part of Vesper. By juggling with the emphasis, he made the kidnapping sound much more Machiavellian than it had been. He praised Vesper's coolness and composure throughout the whole episode without saying that he had found some of her actions unaccountable.

Every day Vesper came to see him and he looked forward to these visits with excitement. She talked happily of her adventures of the day before, her explorations down the coast and the restaurants where she had eaten. She had made friends with the chief of police and with one of the directors of the Casino and it was they who took her out in the evening and occasionally lent her a car during the day. She kept an eye on the repairs to the Bentley which had been towed down to coachbuilders at Rouen, and she even arranged for some new clothes to be sent out from Bond's London flat. Nothing survived from his original wardrobe. Every stitch had been cut to ribbons in the search for the forty million francs.

The Le Chiffre affair was never mentioned between them. She occasionally told Bond amusing stories of Head of S's office. She had apparently transferred there from the WRNS. And he told her of some of his adventures in the Service.

He found he could speak to her easily and he was surprised.

With most women his manner was a mixture of taciturnity and passion. The lengthy approaches to a seduction bored him almost as much as the subsequent mess of disentanglement. He found something grisly in the inevitability of the pattern of each affair. The conventional parabola – sentiment, the touch of the hand, the kiss, the passionate kiss, the feel of the body, the climax in the bed, then more bed, then less bed, then the boredom, the tears and the final bitterness – was to him shameful and hypocritical. Even more he shunned the *mise en scène* for each of these acts in the play – the meeting at a party, the restaurant, the taxi, his flat, her flat, then the week-end by the sea, then the flats again, then the furtive alibis and the final angry farewell on some doorstep in the rain.

But with Vesper there could be none of this.

In the dull room and the boredom of his treatment her presence was each day an oasis of pleasure, something to look forward to. In their talk there was nothing but companionship with a distant undertone of passion. In the background there was the unspoken zest of the promise which, in due course and in their own time, would be met. Over all there brooded the shadow of his injuries and the tantalus of their slow healing.

Whether Bond liked it or not, the branch had already escaped his knife and was ready to burst into flower.

With enjoyable steps Bond recovered. He was allowed up. Then he was allowed to sit in the garden. Then he could go for a short walk, then for a long drive. And then the afternoon came when the doctor appeared on a flying visit from Paris and pronounced him well again.

His clothes were brought round by Vesper, farewells were exchanged with the nurses, and a hired car drove them away.

It was three weeks from the day when he had been on the edge of death, and now it was July and the hot summer shimmered down the coast and out to sea. Bond clasped the moment to him.

Their destination was to be a surprise for him. He had not wanted to go back to one of the big hotels in Royale and Vesper said she would find somewhere away from the town. But she insisted on being mysterious about it and only said that she had found a place he would like. He was happy to be in her hands, but he covered up his surrender by referring to their destination as 'Trou sur Mer' (she admitted it was by the sea), and lauding the rustic delights of outside lavatories, bed-bugs, and cockroaches.

Their drive was spoiled by a curious incident.

While they followed the coast road in the direction of Les Noctambules, Bond described to her his wild chase in the Bentley, finally pointing out the curve he had taken before the crash and the exact place where the vicious carpet of spikes had been laid. He slowed the car down and leant out to show her the deep cuts in the tarmac made by the rims of the wheels and the broken branches in the hedge and the patch of oil where the car had come to rest.

But all the time she was distrait and fidgety and commented only in monosyllables. Once or twice he caught her glancing in the driving-mirror, but when he had a chance to look back through the rear window, they had just rounded a bend and he could see nothing.

Finally he took her hand.

'Something's on your mind, Vesper,' he said.

She gave him a taut, bright smile. 'It's nothing. Absolutely nothing. I had a silly idea we were being followed. It's just nerves, I suppose. This road is full of ghosts.'

Under cover of a short laugh she looked back again.

'Look.' There was an edge of panic in her voice.

Obediently Bond turned his head. Sure enough, a quarter of a mile away, a black saloon was coming after them at a good pace.

Bond laughed.

'We can't be the only people using this road,' he said. 'Anyway, who wants to follow us? We've done nothing wrong.' He patted her hand. 'It's a middle-aged commercial traveller in car-polish on his way to Le Havre. He's probably thinking of his lunch and his mistress in Paris. Really, Vesper, you mustn't think evil of the innocent.'

'I expect you're right,' she said nervously. 'Anyway, we're nearly there.'

She relapsed into silence and gazed out of the window.

Bond could still feel her tenseness. He smiled to himself at what he took to be simply a hangover from their recent adventures. But he decided to humour her and when they came to a small lane leading towards the sea and slowed to turn down it, he told the driver to stop directly they were off the main road.

Hidden by the tall hedge, they watched together through the rear window.

Through the quiet hum of summer noises they could hear the car approaching. Vesper dug her fingers into his arm. The pace of the car did not alter as it approached their hiding-place and they had only a brief glimpse of a man's profile as a black saloon tore by.

It was true that he seemed to glance quickly towards them, but above them in the hedge there was a gaily painted sign pointing down the lane and announcing 'L'Auberge du Fruit Défendu, crustaces, fritures'. It was obvious to Bond that it was this that had caught the driver's eye.

As the rattle of the car's exhaust diminished down the road, Vesper sank back into her corner. Her face was pale.

'He looked at us,' she said, 'I told you so. I knew we were being followed. Now they know where we are.'

Bond could not contain his impatience. 'Bunkum,' he said. 'He was looking at that sign.' He pointed it out to Vesper.

She looked slightly relieved. 'Do you really think so?' she asked. 'Yes. I see. Of course, you must be right. Come on. I'm sorry to be so stupid. I don't know what came over me.'

She leant forward and talked to the driver through the partition, and the car moved on. She sank back and turned a bright face towards Bond. The colour had almost come back to her cheeks. 'I really am sorry. It's just that . . . it's that I can't believe everything's over and there's no one to be frightened of any more.' She pressed his hand. 'You must think me very stupid.'

'Of course not,' said Bond. 'But really nobody could be interested in us now. Forget it all. The whole job's finished, wiped up. This is our holiday and there's not a cloud in the sky. Is there?' he persisted.

'No, of course not.' She shook herself slightly. 'I'm mad. Now we'll be there in a second. I do hope you're going to like it.'

They both leant forward. Animation was back in her face and the incident left only the smallest question-mark hanging in the air. Even that faded as they came through the dunes and saw the sea and the modest little inn amongst the pines.

'It's not very grand, I'm afraid,' said Vesper. 'But it's very clean and the food's wonderful.' She looked at him anxiously.

She need not have worried. Bond loved the place at first sight – the terrace leading almost to the high-tide mark, the low two-storied house with gay brick-red awnings over the windows and the crescent-shaped bay of blue water and golden sands. How many times in his life would he have given anything to have turned off a main road to find a lost corner like this where he could let the world go by and live in the sea from dawn to dusk? And now he was to have a whole week of this. And of Vesper. In his mind he fingered the necklace of the days to come.

They drew up in the courtyard behind the house and the proprietor and his wife came out to greet them.

Monsieur Versoix was a middle-aged man with one arm. The other he had lost fighting with the Free French in Madagascar. He was a friend of the chief of police of Royale and it was the Commissaire who had suggested the place to Vesper and had spoken to the proprietor on the telephone. As a result, nothing was going to be too good for them.

Madame Versoix had been interrupted in the middle of preparing dinner. She wore an apron and held a wooden spoon in one hand. She was younger than her husband, chubby and handsome and warm-eyed. Instinctively Bond guessed that they had no children and that they gave their thwarted affection to their friends and some regular customers, and probably to some pets. He thought that their life was probably something of a struggle and that the inn must be very lonely in winter time with the big seas and the noise of the wind in the pines.

The proprietor showed them to their rooms.

Vesper's was a double room and Bond was next door, at the corner of the house, with one window looking out to sea and another with a view of the distant arm of the bay. There was a bathroom between them. Everything was spotless, and sparsely comfortable.

The proprietor was pleased when they both showed their delight. He said that dinner would be at seven-thirty and that *Madame la patronne* was preparing broiled lobsters with melted butter. He was sorry that they were so quiet just then. It was Tuesday. There would be more people at the weekend. The season had not been good. Generally they had plenty of English people staying, but times were difficult over there and the English just came for a weekend at Royale and then went home after losing their money at the Casino. It was not like the old days. He shrugged his shoulders philosophically. But then no day was like the day before, and no century like the previous one, and . . .

'Quite so,' said Bond.

23 Tide of Passion

They were talking on the threshold of Vesper's room. When the proprietor left them, Bond pushed her inside and closed the door. Then he put his hands on her shoulders and kissed her on both cheeks.

'This is heaven,' he said.

Then he saw that her eyes were shining. Her hands came up and rested on his forearms. He stepped right up against her and his arms dropped round her waist. Her head went back and her mouth opened beneath his.

'My darling,' he said. He plunged his mouth down on to hers, forcing her teeth apart with his tongue and feeling her own tongue working at first shyly then more passionately. He slipped his hands down to her swelling buttocks and gripped them fiercely, pressing the centres of their bodies together. Panting, she slipped her mouth away from his and they clung together while he rubbed his cheek against hers and felt her hard breasts pressing into him. Then he reached up and seized her hair and bent her head back until he could kiss her again. She pushed him away and sank back exhausted on to the bed. For a moment they looked at each other hungrily.

'I'm sorry, Vesper,' he said. 'I didn't mean to then.'

She shook her head, dumb with the storm which had passed through her.

He came and sat beside her and they looked at each other with lingering tenderness as the tide of passion ebbed in their veins.

She leant over and kissed him on the corner of the mouth, then she brushed the black comma of hair back from his damp forehead.

'My darling,' she said. 'Give me a cigarette. I don't know where my bag is.' She looked vaguely round the room.

Bond lit one for her and put it between her lips. She took a deep lungful of smoke and let it pour out through her mouth with a slow sigh.

Bond put his arm round her, but she got up and walked over to the window. She stood there with her back to him.

Bond looked down at his hands and saw they were still trembling.

'It's going to take some time to get ready for dinner,' said Vesper still not looking at him. 'Why don't you go and bathe? I'll unpack for you.'

Bond left the bed and came and stood close against her. He put his arms round her and put a hand over each breast. They filled his hands and the nipples were hard against his fingers. She put her hands over his and pressed them into her, but still she looked away from him out of the window.

'Not now,' she said in a low voice.

Bond bent and burrowed his lips into the nape of her neck. For a moment he strained her hard to him, then he let her go.

'All right, Vesper,' he said.

He walked over to the door and looked back. She had not moved. For some reason he thought she was crying. He took a step towards her and then realized that there was nothing to say between them then.

'My love,' he said.

Then he went out and shut the door.

Bond walked along to his room and sat down on the bed.

He felt weak from the passion which had swept through his body. He was torn between the desire to fall back full-length on the bed and his longing to be cooled and revived by the sea. He played with the choice for a moment, then he went over to his suitcase and took out white linen bathing-drawers and a dark blue pyjama-coat.

Bond had always disliked pyjamas and had slept naked until in Hong Kong at the end of the war he came across the perfect compromise. This was a pyjama-coat which came almost down to the knees. It had no buttons, but there was a loose belt round the waist. The sleeves were wide and short, ending just above the elbow. The result was cool and comfortable and now when he slipped the coat on over his trunks, all his bruises and scars were hidden except the thin white bracelets on wrists and ankles and the mark of SMERSH on his right hand.

He slipped his feet into a pair of dark-blue leather sandals and went downstairs and out of the house and across the terrace to the beach. As he passed across the front of the house he thought of Vesper, but he refrained from looking up to see if she was still standing at the window. If she saw him, she gave no sign.

He walked along the waterline on the hard golden sand until he was out of sight of the inn. Then he threw off his pyjama-coat and took a short run and a quick flat dive into the small waves. The beach shelved quickly and he kept underwater as long as he could, swimming with powerful strokes and feeling the soft coolness all over him. Then he surfaced and brushed the hair out of his eyes. It was nearly seven and the sun had lost much of its heat. Before long it would sink beneath the further arm of the bay, but now it was straight in his eyes and he turned on his back and swam away from it so that he could keep it with him as long as possible.

When he came ashore nearly a mile down the bay the shadows had already engulfed his distant pyjamas but he knew he had time to lie on the hard sand and dry before the tide of dusk reached him.

He took off his bathing-trunks and looked down at his body. There were only a few traces left of his injuries. He shrugged his shoulders and lay down with his limbs spread out in a star and gazed up at the empty blue sky and thought of Vesper.

His feelings for her were confused and he was impatient with the confusion. They had been so simple. He had intended to sleep with her as soon as he could, because he desired her and also because, and he admitted it to himself, he wanted coldly to put the repairs to his body to the final test. He thought they would sleep together for a few days and then he might see something of her in London. Then would come the inevitable disengagement which would be all the easier because of their positions in the Service. If it was not easy, he could go off on an assignment abroad or, which was also in his mind, he could resign and travel to different parts of the world as he had always wanted.

But somehow she had crept under his skin and over the last two weeks his feelings had gradually changed.

He found her companionship easy and unexacting. There was something enigmatic about her which was a constant stimulus. She gave little of her real personality away and he felt that however long they were together there would always be a private room inside her which he could never invade. She was thoughtful and full of consideration without being slavish and without compromising her arrogant spirit. And now he knew that she was profoundly, excitingly sensual, but that the conquest of her body, because of the central privacy in her, would each time have the sweet tang of rape. Loving her physically would each time be a thrilling voyage without the anticlimax of arrival. She would surrender herself avidly, he thought, and greedily enjoy all the intimacies of the bed without ever allowing herself to be possessed.

Naked, Bond lay and tried to push away the conclusions he read in the sky. He turned his head and looked down the beach and saw that the shadows of the headland were almost reaching for him.

He stood up and brushed off as much of the sand as he could reach. He reflected that he would have a bath when he got in and he absent-mindedly picked up his trunks and started walking back along the beach. It was only when he reached his pyjama-coat and bent to pick it up that he realized he was still naked. Without bothering about the trunks, he slipped on the light coat and walked on to the hotel.

At that moment his mind was made up.

24 Fruit Défendu

When he got back to his room he was touched to find all his belongings put away and in the bathroom his toothbrush and shaving things neatly arranged at one end of the glass shelf over the wash-basin. At the other end was Vesper's toothbrush and one or two small bottles and a jar of face-cream.

He glanced at the bottles and was surprised to see that one contained nembutal sleeping-pills. Perhaps her nerves had been more shaken by the events at the villa than he had imagined.

The bath had been filled for him and there was a new flask of some expensive pine bath-essence on a chair beside it with his towel.

'Vesper,' he called.

'Yes?'

'You really are the limit. You make me feel like an expensive gigolo.'

'I was told to look after you. I'm only doing what I was told.'

'Darling, the bath's absolutely right. Will you marry me?'

She snorted. 'You need a slave, not a wife.'

'I want you.'

'Well, I want my lobster and champagne, so hurry up.'

'All right, all right,' said Bond.

He dried himself and dressed in a white shirt and dark blue slacks. He hoped that she would be dressed as simply and he was pleased when, without knocking, she appeared in the doorway wearing a blue linen shirt which had faded to the colour of her eyes and a dark red skirt in pleated cotton.

'I couldn't wait. I was famished. My room's over the kitchen and I've been tortured by the wonderful smells.'

He came over and put his arm round her.

She took his hand and together they went downstairs out on to the terrace where their table had been laid in the light cast by the empty dining-room.

The champagne which Bond had ordered on their arrival stood on a plated wine-cooler beside their table and Bond poured out two full glasses. Vesper busied herself with a delicious home-made liver pâté and helped them both to the crisp French bread and the thick square of deep yellow butter set in chips of ice.

They looked at each other and drank deeply and Bond filled their glasses again to the rim.

While they ate Bond told her of his bathe and they talked of what they would do in the morning. All through the meal they left unspoken their feelings for each other, but in Vesper's eyes as much as in Bond's there was excited anticipation of the night. They let their hands and their feet touch from time to time as if to ease the tension in their bodies.

When the lobster had come and gone and the second bottle of champagne was half-empty and they had just ladled thick cream over their *fraises des bois*, Vesper gave a deep sigh of contentment.

'I'm behaving like a pig,' she said happily. 'You always give me all the things I like best. I've never been so spoiled before.' She gazed across the terrace at the moonlit bay. 'I wish I deserved it.' Her voice had a wry undertone.

'What do you mean?' asked Bond surprised.

'Oh, I don't know. I suppose people get what they deserve, so perhaps I do deserve it.'

She looked at him and smiled. Her eyes narrowed quizzically.

'You really don't know much about me,' she said suddenly.

Bond was surprised by the undertone of seriousness in her voice.

'Quite enough,' he said laughing. 'All I need until tomorrow and the next day and the next. You don't know much about me for the matter of that.' He poured out more champagne.

Vesper looked at him thoughtfully.

'People are islands,' she said. 'They don't really touch. However close they are, they're really quite separate. Even if they've been married for fifty years.'

Bond thought with dismay that she must be going into a *vin triste*. Too much champagne had made her melancholy. But suddenly she gave a happy laugh. 'Don't look so worried.' She leaned forward and put her hand over his. 'I was only being sentimental. Anyway, my island feels very close to your island tonight.' She took a sip of champagne.

Bond laughed, relieved. 'Let's join up and make a peninsula,' he said. 'Now, directly we've finished the strawberries.'

'No,' she said, flirting. 'I must have coffee.'

'And brandy,' countered Bond.

The small shadow had passed. The second small shadow. This too left a tiny question-mark hanging in the air. It quickly dissolved as warmth and intimacy enclosed them again.

When they had had their coffee and Bond was sipping his brandy, Vesper picked up her bag and came and stood behind him.

'I'm tired,' she said, resting a hand on his shoulder.

He reached up and held it there and they stayed motionless for a moment. She bent down and lightly brushed his hair with her lips. Then she was gone and a few seconds later the light came on in her room.

Bond smoked and waited until it had gone out. Then he followed her, pausing only to say good night to the proprietor and his wife and thank them for the dinner. They exchanged compliments and he went upstairs.

It was only half past nine when he stepped into her room from the bathroom and closed the door behind him.

The moonlight shone through the half-closed shutters and lapped at the secret shadows in the snow of her body on the broad bed.

Bond awoke in his own room at dawn and for a time he lay and stroked his memories.

Then he got quietly out of bed and in his pyjama-coat he crept past Vesper's door and out of the house to the beach.

The sea was smooth and quiet in the sunrise. The small pink waves idly licked the sand. It was cold, but he took off his jacket and wandered naked along the edge of the sea to the point where he had bathed the evening before, then he walked slowly and deliberately into the water until it was just below his chin. He took his feet off the bottom and sank, holding his nose with one hand and shutting his eyes, feeling the cold water comb his body and his hair.

The mirror of the bay was unbroken except where it seemed a fish had jumped. Under the water he imagined the tranquil scene and wished that Vesper could just then come through the pines and be astonished to see him suddenly erupt from the empty seascape.

When after a full minute he came to the surface in a froth of spray, he was disappointed. There was no one in sight. For a time he swam and drifted and then when the sun seemed hot enough, he came in to the beach and lay on his back and revelled in the body which the night had given back to him.

As on the evening before, he stared up into the empty sky and saw the same answer there.

After a while he rose and walked back slowly along the beach to his pyjama-coat.

That day he would ask Vesper to marry him. He was quite certain. It was only a question of choosing the right moment.

25 'Black-Patch'

As he walked quietly from the terrace into the half-darkness of the still shuttered dining-room, he was surprised to see Vesper emerge from the glass-fronted telephone booth near the front door and softly turn up the stairs towards their rooms.

'Vesper,' he called, thinking she must have had some urgent message which might concern them both.

She turned quickly, a hand up to her mouth.

For a moment longer than necessary she stared at him, her eyes wide.

'What is it, darling?' he asked, vaguely troubled and fearing some crisis in their lives.

'Oh,' she said breathlessly, 'you made me jump. It was only . . . I was just telephoning to Mathis. To Mathis,' she repeated. 'I wondered if he could get me another frock. You know, from that girlfriend I told you about. The *vendeuse*. You see,' she talked quickly, her words coming out in a persuasive jumble, 'I've really got nothing to wear. I thought I'd catch him at home before he went to the office. I don't know my friend's telephone number and I thought it would be a surprise for you. I didn't want you to hear me moving and wake you up. Is the water nice? Have you bathed? You ought to have waited for me.'

'It's wonderful,' said Bond, deciding to relieve her mind, though irritated with her obvious guilt over this childish mystery. 'You must go in and we'll have breakfast on the terrace. I'm ravenous. I'm sorry I made you jump. I was just startled to see anyone about at this hour of the morning.'

He put his arm round her, but she disengaged herself, and moved quickly on up the stairs.

'It was such a surprise to see you,' she said, trying to cover the incident up with a light touch. 'You looked like a ghost, a drowned man, with the hair down over your eyes like that.' She laughed harshly. Hearing the harshness, she turned the laugh into a cough.

'I hope I haven't caught cold,' she said.

She kept on patching up the edifice of her deceit until Bond wanted to spank her and tell her to relax and tell the truth. Instead he just gave her a reassuring pat on the back outside her room and told her to hurry up and have her bathe.

Then he went on to his room.

That was the end of the integrity of their love. The succeeding days were a shambles of falseness and hypocrisy, mingled with her tears and moments of animal passion to which she abandoned herself with a greed made indecent by the hollowness of their days.

Several times Bond tried to break down the dreadful walls of mistrust. Again and again he brought up the subject of the telephone call, but she obstinately bolstered up her story with embellishments which Bond knew she had thought out afterwards. She even accused Bond of thinking she had another lover.

These scenes always ended in her bitter tears and in moments almost of hysteria.

Each day the atmosphere became more hateful.

It seemed fantastic to Bond that human relationships could collapse into dust overnight and he searched his mind again and again for a reason.

He felt that Vesper was just as horrified as he was and, if anything, her misery seemed greater than his. But the mystery of the telephone conversation which Vesper angrily, almost fearfully it seemed to Bond, refused to explain was a shadow which grew darker with other small mysteries and reticences.

Already at luncheon on that day things got worse.

After a breakfast which was an effort for both of them, Vesper said she had a headache and would stay in her room out of the sun. Bond took a book and walked for miles down the beach. By the time he returned he had argued to himself that they would be able to sort the problem out over lunch.

Directly they sat down, he apologized gaily for having startled her at the telephone booth and then he dismissed the subject and went on to describe what he had seen on his walk. But Vesper was distrait and commented only in monosyllables. She toyed with her food and she avoided Bond's eyes and gazed past him with an air of preoccupation.

When she had failed once or twice to respond to some conversational gambit or other, Bond also relapsed into silence and occupied himself with his own gloomy thoughts.

All of a sudden she stiffened. Her fork fell with a clatter on to the edge of her plate and then noisily off the table on to the terrace.

Bond looked up. She had gone as white as a sheet and she was looking over his shoulder with terror in her face.

Bond turned his head and saw that a man had just taken his place at a table on the opposite side of the terrace, well away from them. He seemed ordinary enough, perhaps rather sombrely dressed, but in his first quick glance Bond put him down as some businessman on his way along the coast who had just happened on the inn or had picked it out of the Michelin.

'What is it, darling?' he asked anxiously.

Vesper's eyes never moved from the distant figure.

'It's the man in the car,' she said in a stifled voice. 'The man who was following us. I know it is.'

Bond looked again over his shoulder. The *patron* was discussing the menu with the new customer. It was a perfectly normal scene. They exchanged smiles over some item on the menu and apparently agreed that it would suit for the *patron* took the card and with, Bond guessed, a final exchange about the wine, he withdrew.

The man seemed to realize that he was being watched. He looked up and gazed incuriously at them for a moment. Then he reached for a briefcase on the chair beside him, extracted a newspaper and started to read it, his elbows propped up on the table.

When the man had turned his face towards them, Bond noticed that he had a black patch over one eye. It was not tied with a tape across the eye, but screwed in like a monocle. Otherwise he seemed a friendly middle-aged man, with dark brown hair brushed straight back, and, as Bond had seen while he was talking to the *patron*, particularly large, white teeth.

He turned back to Vesper. 'Really, darling. He looks very innocent. Are you sure he's the same man? We can't expect to have this place entirely to ourselves.'

Vesper's face was still a white mask. She was clutching the edge of the table with both hands. He thought she was going to faint and almost rose to come round to her, but she made a gesture to stop him. Then she reached for a glass of wine and took a deep draught. The glass rattled on her teeth and she brought up her other hand to help. Then she put the glass down.

She looked at him with dull eyes.

'I know it's the same.'

He tried to reason with her, but she paid no attention. After glancing once or twice over his shoulder with eyes that held a curious submissiveness, she said that her headache was still bad and that she would spend the afternoon in her room. She left the table and walked indoors without a backward glance.

Bond was determined to set her mind at rest. He ordered coffee to be brought to the table and then he rose and walked swiftly to the courtyard. The black Peugeot which stood there might indeed have been the saloon they had seen, but it might equally have been one of a million others on the French roads. He took a quick glance inside, but the interior was empty and when he tried the boot, it was locked. He made a note of the Paris number-plate then he went quickly to the lavatory adjoining the dining-room, pulled the chain and walked out on to the terrace.

The man was eating and didn't look up.

Bond sat down in Vesper's chair so that he could watch the other table.

A few minutes later the man asked for the bill, paid it and left. Bond heard the Peugeot start up and soon the noise of its exhaust had disappeared in the direction of the road to Royale.

When the *patron* came back to his table, Bond explained that Madame had unfortunately a slight touch of sunstroke. After the *patron* had expressed his regret and enlarged on the dangers of going out of doors in almost any weather, Bond casually asked about the other customer. 'He reminds me of a friend who also lost an eye. They wear similar black patches.'

The *patron* answered that the man was a stranger. He had been pleased with his lunch and had said that he would be passing that way again in a day or two and would take another meal at the *auberge*. Apparently he was Swiss, which could also be seen from his accent. He was a traveller in watches. It was shocking to have only one eye. The strain of keeping that patch in place all day long. He supposed one got used to it.

'It is indeed very sad,' said Bond. 'You also have been unlucky,' he gestured to the proprietor's empty sleeve. 'I myself was very fortunate.'

For a time they talked about the war. Then Bond rose.

'By the way,' he said, 'Madame had an early telephone call which I must remember to pay for. Paris. An Elysée number I think,' he added, remembering that that was Mathis's exchange.

'Thank you, monsieur, but the matter is regulated. I was speaking to Royale this morning and the exchange mentioned that one of my guests had put through a call to Paris and that there had been no answer. They wanted to know if Madame would like the call kept in. I'm afraid the matter escaped my mind. Perhaps Monsieur would mention it to Madame. But, let me see, it was an Invalides number the exchange referred to.'

26 'Sleep Well, My Darling'

The next two days were much the same.

On the fourth day of their stay Vesper went off early to Royale. A taxi came and fetched her and brought her back. She said she needed some medicine.

That night she made a special effort to be gay. She drank a lot and when they went upstairs, she led him into her bedroom and made passionate love to him. Bond's body responded, but afterwards she cried bitterly into her pillow and Bond went to his room in grim despair.

He could hardly sleep and in the early hours he heard her door open softly. Some small sounds came from downstairs. He was sure she was in the telephone booth. Very soon he heard her door softly close and he guessed that again there had been no reply from Paris.

This was Saturday.

On Sunday the man with the black patch was back again. Bond knew it directly he looked up from his lunch and saw her face. He had told her all that the *patron* had told him, withholding only the man's statement that he might be back. He had thought it would worry her.

He had also telephoned Mathis in Paris and checked on the Peugeot. It had been hired from a respectable firm two weeks before. The customer had had a Swiss triptyque. His name was Adolph Gettler. He had given a bank in Zurich as his address.

Mathis had got on to the Swiss police. Yes, the bank had an account in this name. It was little used. Herr Gettler was understood to be connected with the watch industry. Inquiries could be pursued if there was a charge against him.

Vesper had shrugged her shoulders at the information. This time when the man appeared she left her lunch in the middle and went straight up to her room.

Bond made up his mind. When he had finished, he followed her. Both her doors were locked and when he made her let him in, he saw that she had been sitting in the shadows by the window, watching, he presumed.

Her face was of cold stone. He led her to the bed and drew her down beside him. They sat stiffly, like people in a railway carriage.

'Vesper,' he said, holding her cold hands in his, 'we can't go on like this. We must finish with it. We are torturing each other and there is only one way of stopping it. Either you must tell me what all this is about or we must leave. At once.'

She said nothing and her hands were lifeless in his.

'My darling,' he said. 'Won't you tell me? Do you know, that first morning I was coming back to ask you to marry me. Can't we go back to the beginning again? What is this dreadful nightmare that is killing us?'

At first she said nothing, then a tear rolled slowly down her cheek.

'You mean you would have married me?'

Bond nodded.

'Oh my God,' she said. 'My God.' She turned and clutched him, pressing her face against his chest.

He held her closely to him. 'Tell me, my love,' he said. 'Tell me what's hurting you.'

Her sobs became quieter.

'Leave me for a little,' she said and a new note had come into her voice. A note of resignation. 'Let me think for a little.' She kissed his face and held it between her hands. She looked at him with yearning. 'Darling, I'm trying to do what's best for us. Please believe me. But it's terrible. I'm in a frightful . . .' She wept again, clutching him like a child with nightmares.

He soothed her, stroking the long black hair and kissing her softly.

'Go away now,' she said. 'I must have time to think. We've got to do something.'

She took his handkerchief and dried her eyes.

She led him to the door and there they held tightly to each other. Then he kissed her again and she shut the door behind him.

That evening most of the gayness and intimacy of their first night came back. She was excited and some of her laughter sounded brittle, but Bond was determined to fall in with her new mood and it was only at the end of dinner that he made a passing remark which made her pause.

She put her hand over his.

'Don't talk about it now,' she said. 'Forget it now. It's all past. I'll tell you about it in the morning.'

She looked at him and suddenly her eyes were full of tears. She found a handkerchief in her bag and dabbed at them.

'Give me some more champagne,' she said. She gave a queer little laugh. 'I want a lot more. You drink much more than me. It's not fair.'

They sat and drank together until the bottle was finished. Then she got to her feet. She knocked against her chair and giggled.

'I do believe I'm tight,' she said, 'how disgraceful. Please, James, don't be ashamed of me. I did so want to be gay. And I am gay.'

She stood behind him and ran her fingers through his black hair.

'Come up quickly,' she said. 'I want you badly tonight.'

She blew a kiss at him and was gone.

For two hours they made slow, sweet love in a mood of happy passion which the day before Bond would never have thought they could regain. The barriers of self-consciousness and mistrust seemed to have vanished and the words they spoke to each other were innocent and true again and there was no shadow between them.

'You must go now,' said Vesper when Bond had slept for a while in her arms.

As if to take back her words she held him more closely to her, murmuring endearments and pressing her body down the whole length of his.

When he finally rose and bent to smooth back her hair and finally kiss her eyes and her mouth good night, she reached out and turned on the light.

'Look at me,' she said, 'and let me look at you.'

He knelt beside her.

She examined every line on his face as if she was seeing him for the first time. Then she reached up and put an arm round his neck. Her deep blue eyes were swimming with tears as she drew his head slowly towards her and kissed him gently on the lips. Then she let him go and turned off the light.

'Good night, my dearest love,' she said.

Bond bent and kissed her. He tasted the tears on her cheek.

He went to the door and looked back.

'Sleep well, my darling,' he said. 'Don't worry, everything's all right now.'

He closed the door softly and walked to his room with a full heart.

27 The Bleeding Heart

The *patron* brought him the letter in the morning.

He burst into Bond's room holding the envelope in front of him as if it was on fire.

'There has been a terrible accident. Madame . . .'

Bond hurled himself out of bed and through the bathroom, but the communicating door was locked. He dashed back and through his room and down the corridor past a shrinking, terrified maid.

Vesper's door was open. The sunlight through the shutters lit up the room. Only her black hair showed above the sheet and her body under the bedclothes was straight and moulded like a stone effigy on a tomb.

Bond fell on his knees beside her and drew back the sheet.

She was asleep. She must be. Her eyes were closed. There was no change in the dear face. She was just as she would look and yet, and yet she was so still, no movement, no pulse, no breath. That was it. There was no breath.

Later the *patron* came and touched him on the shoulder. He pointed at the empty glass on the table beside her. There were white dregs in the bottom of it. It stood beside her book and her cigarettes and matches and the small pathetic litter of her mirror and lipstick and handkerchief. And on the floor the empty bottle of sleeping-pills, the pills Bond had seen in the bathroom that first evening.

Bond rose to his feet and shook himself. The *patron* was holding out the letter towards him. He took it.

'Please notify the Commissaire,' said Bond. 'I will be in my room when he wants me.'

He walked blindly away without a backward glance.

He sat on the edge of his bed and gazed out of the window at the peaceful sea. Then he stared dully at the envelope. It was addressed simply in a large round hand 'Pour Lui'.

The thought passed through Bond's mind that she must have left orders to be called early, so that it would not be he who found her.

He turned the envelope over. Not long ago it was her warm tongue which had sealed the flap.

He gave a sudden shrug and opened it.

It was not long. After the first few words he read it quickly, the breath coming harshly through his nostrils.

Then he threw it down on the bed as if it had been a scorpion.

My darling James [the letter opened],

I love you with all my heart and while you read these words I hope you still love me because, now, with these words, this is the last moment that your love will last. So goodbye, my sweet love, while we still love each other. Goodbye, my darling.

I am an agent of the MWD. Yes, I am a double agent for the Russians. I was taken on a year after the war and I have worked for them ever since. I was in love with a Pole in the RAF. Until you, I still was. You can find out who he was. He had two DSOs and after the war he was trained by M and dropped back into Poland. They caught him and by torturing him they found out a lot and also about me. They came after me and told me he could live if I would work for them. He knew nothing of this, but he was allowed to write to me. The letter arrived on the fifteenth of each month. I found I couldn't stop. I couldn't bear the idea of a fifteenth coming round without his letter. It would mean that I had killed him. I tried to give them as little as possible. You must believe me about this. Then it came to you. I told them you had been given this job at Royale, what your cover was and so on. That was why they knew about you before you arrived and why they had time to put the microphones in. They suspected Le Chiffre, but they didn't know what your assignment was except that it was something to do with him. That was all I told them.

Then I was told not to stand behind you in the Casino and to see that neither Mathis nor Leiter did. That was why the gunman was nearly able to shoot you. Then I had to stage that kidnapping. You may have wondered why I was so quiet in the night-club. They didn't hurt me because I was working for MWD.

But when I found out what had been done to you, even though it was Le Chiffre who did it and he turned out to be a traitor, I decided I couldn't go on. By that time I had begun to fall in love with you. They wanted me to find out things from you while you were recovering, but I refused. I was controlled from Paris. I had to ring up an Invalides number twice a day. They threatened me, and finally they withdrew my control and I knew my lover in Poland would have to die. But they were afraid I would talk, I suppose, and I got a final warning that SMERSH would come for me if I didn't obey them. I took no notice. I was in love with you. Then I saw the man with the black patch in the Splendide and I found he had been making inquiries about my movements. This was the day before we came down here. I hoped I could shake him off. I decided that we would have an affair and I would escape to South America from Le Havre. I hoped I would have a baby of yours and be able to start again somewhere. But they followed us. You can't get away from them.

I knew it would be the end of our love if I told you. I realized that I could either wait to be killed by SMERSH, would perhaps get you killed too, or I could kill myself.

There it is, my darling love. You can't stop me calling you that or saying that I love you. I am taking that with me and the memories of you.

I can't tell you much to help you. The Paris number was Invalides 55200. I never met any of them in London. Everything was done through an accommodation address, a newsagent's at 450 Charing Cross Place.

At our first dinner together you talked about that man in Yugoslavia who was found guilty of treason. He said: 'I was carried away by the gale of the world.' That's my only excuse. That, and for love of the man whose life I tried to save.

It's late now and I'm tired, and you're just through two doors. But I've got to be brave. You might save my life, but I couldn't bear the look in your dear eyes.

My love, my love.

V.

Bond threw the letter down. Mechanically he brushed his fingers together. Suddenly he banged his temples with his fists and stood up. For a moment he looked out towards the quiet sea, then he cursed aloud, one harsh obscenity.

His eyes were wet and he dried them.

He pulled on a shirt and trousers and with a set cold face he walked down and shut himself in the telephone booth.

While he was getting through to London, he calmly reviewed the facts of Vesper's letter. They all fitted. The little shadows and question-marks of the past four weeks, which his instinct had noted but his mind rejected, all stood out now like signposts.

He saw her now only as a spy. Their love and his grief were relegated to the boxroom of his mind. Later, perhaps they would be dragged out, dispassionately examined, and then bitterly thrust back with other sentimental baggage he would rather forget. Now he could only think of her treachery to the Service and to her country and of the damage it had done. His professional mind was completely absorbed with the consequences – the covers which must have been blown over the years, the codes which the enemy must have broken, the secrets which must have leaked from the centre of the very section devoted to penetrating the Soviet Union.

It was ghastly. God knew how the mess would be cleared up.

He ground his teeth. Suddenly Mathis's words came back to him: 'There are plenty of really black targets around,' and, earlier, 'What about SMERSH? I don't like the idea of these chaps running around France killing anyone they feel has been a traitor to their precious political system.'

How soon Mathis had been proved right and how soon his own little sophistries had been exploded in his face!

While he, Bond, had been playing Red Indians through the years (yes, Le Chiffre's description was perfectly accurate), the real enemy had been working quietly, coldly, without heroics, right there at his elbow.

He suddenly had a vision of Vesper walking down a corridor with documents in her hand. On a tray. They just got it on a tray while the cool secret agent with a Double O number was gallivanting round the world – playing Red Indians.

His fingernails dug into the palms of his hands and his body sweated with shame.

Well, it was not too late. Here was a target for him, right to hand. He would take on SMERSH and hunt it down. Without SMERSH, without this cold weapon of death and revenge, the MWD would be just another bunch of civil servant spies, no better and no worse than any of the western services.

SMERSH was the spur. Be faithful, spy well, or you die. Inevitably and without any question, you will be hunted down and killed.

It was the same with the whole Russian machine. Fear was the impulse. For them it was always safer to advance than to retreat. Advance against the enemy and the bullet might miss you. Retreat, evade, betray, and the bullet would never miss.

But now he would attack the arm that held the whip and the gun. The business of espionage could be left to the white-collar boys. They could spy, and catch the spies. He would go after the threat behind the spies, the threat that made them spy.

The telephone rang and Bond snatched up the receiver.

He was on to 'the Link', the outside liaison officer who was the only man in London he might telephone from abroad. Then only in dire necessity.

'This is 007 speaking. This is an open line. It's an emergency. Can you hear me? Pass this on at once. 3030 was a double, working for Redland.

'Yes, dammit, I said "was". The bitch is dead now.'

Live and
Let Die

Contents

1 The Red Carpet

There are moments of great luxury in the life of a secret agent. There are assignments on which he is required to act the part of a very rich man; occasions when he takes refuge in good living to efface the memory of danger and the shadow of death; and times when, as was now the case, he is a guest in the territory of an allied Secret Service.

From the moment the BOAC Stratocruiser taxied up to the International Air Terminal at Idlewild, James Bond was treated like royalty.

When he left the aircraft with the other passengers he had resigned himself to the notorious purgatory of the US Health, Immigration and Customs machinery. At least an hour, he thought, of overheated, drab-green rooms smelling of last year's air and stale sweat and guilt and the fear that hangs round all frontiers, fear of those closed doors marked PRIVATE that hide the careful men, the files, the teleprinters chattering urgently to Washington, to the Bureau of Narcotics, Counter Espionage, the Treasury, the FBI.

As he walked across the tarmac in the bitter January wind he saw his own name going over the network: BOND, JAMES. BRITISH DIPLOMATIC PASSPORT 0094567, the short wait and the replies coming back on the different machines: NEGATIVE, NEGATIVE, NEGATIVE. And then, from the FBI: POSITIVE AWAIT CHECK. There would be some hasty traffic on the FBI circuit with the Central Intelligence Agency and then: FBI TO IDLEWILD: BOND OKAY OKAY, and the bland official out front would hand him back his passport with a 'Hope you enjoy your stay, Mr Bond.'

Bond shrugged his shoulders and followed the other passengers through the wire fence towards the door marked US HEALTH SERVICE.

141

In his case it was only a boring routine, of course, but he disliked the idea of his dossier being in the possession of any foreign power. Anonymity was the chief tool of his trade. Every thread of his real identity that went on record in any file diminished his value and, ultimately, was a threat to his life. Here in America, where they knew all about him, he felt like a negro whose shadow has been stolen by the witch-doctor. A vital part of himself was in pawn, in the hands of others. Friends, of course, in this instance, but still . . .

'Mr Bond?'

A pleasant-looking nondescript man in plain clothes had stepped forward from the shadow of the Health Service building.

'My name's Halloran. Pleased to meet you!'

They shook hands.

'Hope you had a pleasant trip. Would you follow me, please?'

He turned to the officer of the Airport police on guard at the door.

'Okay, Sergeant.'

'Okay, Mr Halloran. Be seeing you.'

The other passengers had passed inside. Halloran turned to the left, away from the building. Another policeman held open a small gate in the high boundary fence.

' 'Bye, Mr Halloran.'

' 'Bye, Officer. Thanks.'

Directly outside a black Buick waited, its engine sighing quietly. They climbed in. Bond's two light suitcases were in front next to the driver. Bond couldn't imagine how they had been extracted so quickly from the mound of passengers' luggage he had seen only minutes before being trolleyed over to Customs.

'Okay, Grady. Let's go.'

Bond sank back luxuriously as the big limousine surged forward, slipping quickly into top through the Dynaflow gears.

He turned to Halloran.

'Well, that's certainly one of the reddest carpets I've ever seen. I expected to be at least an hour getting through Immigration. Who laid it on? I'm not used to VIP treatment. Anyway, thanks very much for your part in it all.'

'You're very welcome, Mr Bond.' Halloran smiled and offered him a cigarette from a fresh pack of Luckies. 'We want to make your stay comfortable. Anything you want, just say so and it's yours. You've got some good friends in Washington. I don't myself know why you're here but it seems the authorities are keen that you should be a privileged guest of the Government. It's my job to see you get to your hotel as quickly and as comfortably as possible and then I'll hand over and be on my way. May I have your passport a moment, please.'

Bond gave it to him. Halloran opened a brief-case on the seat beside him and took out a heavy metal stamp. He turned the pages of Bond's passport until he came to the US Visa, stamped it, scribbled his signature over the dark blue circle of the Department of Justice cypher and gave it back to him. Then he took out his pocket-book and extracted a thick white envelope which he gave to Bond.

'There's a thousand dollars in there, Mr Bond.' He held up his hand as Bond started to speak. 'And it's Communist money we took in the Schmidt–Kinaski haul. We're using it back at them and you are asked to co-operate and spend this in any way you like on your present assignment. I am advised that it will be considered a very unfriendly act if you refuse. Let's please say no more about it and,' he added, as Bond continued to hold the envelope dubiously in his hand, 'I am also to say that the disposal of this money through your hands has the knowledge and approval of your own Chief.'

Bond eyed him narrowly and then grinned. He put the envelope away in his notecase.

'All right,' he said. 'And thanks. I'll try and spend it where it does most harm. I'm glad to have some working capital. It's certainly good to know it's been provided by the opposition.'

'Fine,' said Halloran; 'and now, if you'll forgive me, I'll just write up my notes for the report I'll have to put in. Have to remember to get a letter of thanks sent to Immigration and Customs and so forth for their co-operation. Routine.'

'Go ahead,' said Bond. He was glad to keep silent and gaze out at his first sight of America since the war. It was no waste of time to start picking up the American idiom again: the advertisements, the new car models and the prices of second-hand ones in the used-car lots; the exotic pungency of the road signs: SOFT SHOULDERS – SHARP

143

CURVES – SQUEEZE AHEAD – SLIPPERY WHEN WET; the standard of driving; the number of women at the wheel, their menfolk docilely beside them; the men's clothes; the way the women were doing their hair; the Civil Defence warnings: IN CASE OF ENEMY ATTACK – KEEP MOVING – GET OFF BRIDGE; the thick rash of television aerials and the impact of TV on hoardings and shop windows; the occasional helicopter; the public appeals for cancer and polio funds: THE MARCH OF DIMES – all the small, fleeting impressions that were as important to his trade as are broken bark and bent twigs to the trapper in the jungle.

The driver chose the Triborough Bridge and they soared across the breath-taking span into the heart of up-town Manhattan, the beautiful prospect of New York hastening towards them until they were down amongst the hooting, teeming, petrol-smelling roots of the stressed-concrete jungle.

Bond turned to his companion.

'I hate to say it,' he said, 'but this must be the fattest atomic-bomb target on the whole face of the globe.'

'Nothing to touch it,' agreed Halloran. 'Keeps me awake nights thinking what would happen.'

They drew up at the best hotel in New York, the St Regis, at the corner of Fifth Avenue and 55th Street. A saturnine middle-aged man in a dark blue overcoat and black homburg came forward behind the commissionaire. On the sidewalk, Halloran introduced him.

'Mr Bond, meet Captain Dexter.' He was deferential. 'Can I pass him along to you now, Captain?'

'Sure, sure. Just have his bags sent up. Room 2100. Top floor. I'll go ahead with Mr Bond and see he has everything he wants.'

Bond turned to say good-bye to Halloran and thank him. For a moment Halloran had his back to him as he said something about Bond's luggage to the commissionaire. Bond looked past him across 55th Street. His eyes narrowed. A black sedan, a Chevrolet, was pulling sharply out into the thick traffic, right in front of a Checker cab that braked hard, its driver banging his fist down on the horn and holding it there. The sedan kept going, just caught the tail of the green light, and disappeared north up Fifth Avenue.

It was a smart, decisive bit of driving, but what startled Bond was that it had been a negress at the wheel, a fine-looking negress in a black chauffeur's uniform, and through the rear window he had caught a glimpse of the single passenger – a huge grey-black face which had turned slowly towards him and looked directly back at him, Bond was sure of it, as the car accelerated towards the Avenue.

Bond shook Halloran by the hand. Dexter touched his elbow impatiently.

'We'll go straight in and through the lobby to the elevators. Half-right across the lobby. And would you please keep your hat on, Mr Bond.'

As Bond followed Dexter up the steps into the hotel he reflected that it was almost certainly too late for these precautions. Hardly anywhere in the world will you find a negress driving a car. A negress acting as a chauffeur is still more extraordinary. Barely conceivable even in Harlem, but that was certainly where the car was from.

And the giant shape in the back seat? That grey-black face? Mister Big?

'Hm,' said Bond to himself as he followed the slim back of Captain Dexter into the elevator.

The elevator slowed up for the twenty-first floor.

'We've got a little surprise ready for you, Mr Bond,' said Captain Dexter, without, Bond thought, much enthusiasm.

They walked down the corridor to the corner room.

The wind sighed outside the passage windows and Bond had a fleeting view of the tops of other skyscrapers and, beyond, the stark fingers of the trees in Central Park. He felt far out of touch with the ground and for a moment a strange feeling of loneliness and empty space gripped his heart.

Dexter unlocked the door of No. 2100 and shut it behind them. They were in a small lighted lobby. They left their hats and coats on a chair and Dexter opened the door in front of them and held it for Bond to go through.

He walked into an attractive sitting-room decorated in Third Avenue 'Empire' – comfortable chairs and a broad sofa in pale yellow silk, a fair copy of an Aubusson on the floor, pale grey walls and ceiling, a bow-fronted French sideboard with bottles and glasses and a plated ice-bucket, a wide window through which the winter sun poured out of a Swiss-clear sky. The central heating was just bearable.

The communicating door with the bedroom opened.

'Arranging the flowers by your bed. Part of the famous CIA "Service With a Smile".' The tall thin young man came forward with a wide grin, his hand outstretched, to where Bond stood rooted with astonishment.

'Felix Leiter! What the hell are you doing here?' Bond grasped the hard hand and shook it warmly. 'And what the hell are you doing in my bedroom, anyway? God! it's good to see you. Why aren't you in Paris? Don't tell me they've put you on this job?'

Leiter examined the Englishman affectionately.

'You've said it. That's just exactly what they have done. What a break! At least, it is for me. CIA, thought we did all right together on the Casino job* so they hauled me away from the Joint Intelligence chaps in Paris, put me through the works in Washington and here I am. I'm sort of liaison between the Central Intelligence Agency and our friends of the FBI.' He waved towards Captain Dexter, who was watching this unprofessional ebullience without enthusiasm. 'It's their case, of course, at least the American end of it is, but as you know there are some big overseas angles which are CIA's territory, so we're running it joint. Now you're here to handle the Jamaican end for the British and the team's complete. How does it look to you? Sit down and let's have a drink. I ordered lunch directly I got the word you were downstairs and it'll be on its way.' He went over to the sideboard and started mixing a Martini.

'Well, I'm damned,' said Bond. 'Of course that old devil M never told me. He just gives one the facts. Never tells one any good news. I suppose he thinks it might influence one's decision to take a case or not. Anyway, it's grand.'

Bond suddenly felt the silence of Captain Dexter. He turned to him.

'I shall be very glad to be under your orders here, Captain,' he said tactfully. 'As I understand it, the case breaks pretty neatly into two

---

* This terrifying gambling case is described in the author's *Casino Royale*.

halves. The first half lies wholly on American territory. Your jurisdiction, of course. Then it looks as if we shall have to follow it into the Caribbean. Jamaica. And I understand I am to take over outside United States territorial waters. Felix here will marry up the two halves so far as your government is concerned. I shall report to London through CIA while I'm here, and direct to London, keeping CIA informed, when I move to the Caribbean. Is that how you see it?'

Dexter smiled thinly. 'That's just about it, Mr Bond. Mr Hoover instructs me to say that he's very pleased to have you along. As our guest,' he added. 'Naturally we are not in any way concerned with the British end of the case and we're very happy that CIA will be handling that with you and your people in London. Guess everything should go fine. Here's luck,' and he lifted the cocktail Leiter had put into his hand.

They drank the cold hard drink appreciatively, Leiter with a faintly quizzical expression on his hawk-like face.

There was a knock on the door. Leiter opened it to let in the bellboy with Bond's suitcases. He was followed by two waiters pushing trolleys loaded with covered dishes, cutlery and snow-white linen, which they proceeded to lay out on a folding table.

'Soft-shell crabs with tartare sauce, flat beef Hamburgers, medium-rare, from the charcoal grill, french-fried potatoes, broccoli, mixed salad with thousand-island dressing, ice-cream with melted butterscotch and as good a Liebfraumilch as you can get in America. Okay?'

'It sounds fine,' said Bond with a mental reservation about the melted butterscotch.

They sat down and ate steadily through each delicious course of American cooking at its rare best.

They said little, and it was only when the coffee had been brought and the table cleared away that Captain Dexter took the fifty-cent cigar from his mouth and cleared his throat decisively.

'Mr Bond,' he said, 'now perhaps you would tell us what you know about this case.'

Bond slit open a fresh pack of King Size Chesterfields with his thumb-nail and, as he settled back in his comfortable chair in the warm luxurious room, his mind went back two weeks to the bitter

raw day in early January when he had walked out of his Chelsea flat
into the dreary half-light of a London fog.

2 Interview with M

The grey Bentley convertible, the 1933 4½-litre with the Amherst-
Villiers supercharger, had been brought round a few minutes earlier
from the garage where he kept it and the engine had kicked directly
he pressed the self-starter. He had turned on the twin fog lights and
had driven gingerly along King's Road and then up Sloane Street into
Hyde Park.

M's Chief of Staff had telephoned at midnight to say that M wanted
to see Bond at nine the next morning. 'Bit early in the day,' he had
apologized, 'but he seems to want some action from somebody. Been
brooding for weeks. Suppose he's made up his mind at last.'

'Any line you can give me over the telephone?'

'A for Apple and C for Charlie,' said the Chief of Staff, and rang off.

That meant that the case concerned Stations A and C, the sections
of the Secret Service dealing respectively with the United States and
the Caribbean. Bond had worked for a time under Station A during
the war, but he knew little of C or its problems.

As he crawled beside the kerb up through Hyde Park, the slow
drumbeat of his two-inch exhaust keeping him company, he felt
excited at the prospect of his interview with M, the remarkable man
who was then, and still is, head of the Secret Service. He had not
looked into those cold, shrewd eyes since the end of the summer. On
that occasion M had been pleased.

'Take some leave,' he had said. 'Plenty of leave. Then get some new
skin grafted over the back of that hand. "Q" will put you on to the
best man and fix a date. Can't have you going round with that damn
Russian trade-mark on you. See if I can find you a good target when
you've got cleaned up. Good luck.'

The hand had been fixed, painlessly but slowly. The thin scars, the
single Russian letter which stands for SCH, the first letter of *Spion*, a

spy, had been removed and as Bond thought of the man with the stiletto who had cut them he clenched his hands on the wheel.

What was happening to the brilliant organization of which the man with the knife had been an agent, the Soviet organ of vengeance, SMERSH, short for *Smyert Spionam* – Death to Spies? Was it still as powerful, still as efficient? Who controlled it now that Beria was gone? After the great gambling case in which he had been involved at Royale-les-Eaux, Bond had sworn to get back at them. He had told M as much at that last interview. Was this appointment with M to start him on his trail of revenge?

Bond's eyes narrowed as he gazed into the murk of Regent's Park and his face in the faint dashlight was cruel and hard.

He drew up in the mews behind the gaunt high building, handed his car over to one of the plain-clothes drivers from the pool and walked round to the main entrance. He was taken up in the lift to the top floor and along the thickly carpeted corridor he knew so well to the door next to M's. The Chief of Staff was waiting for him and at once spoke to M on the intercom.

'007's here now, Sir.'

'Send him in.'

The desirable Miss Moneypenny, M's all-powerful private secretary, gave him an encouraging smile and he walked through the double doors. At once the green light came on, high on the wall in the room he had left. M was not to be disturbed as long as it burned.

A reading lamp with a green glass shade made a pool of light across the red leather top of the broad desk. The rest of the room was darkened by the fog outside the windows.

'Morning, 007. Let's have a look at the hand. Not a bad job. Where did they take the skin from?'

'High up on the forearm, Sir.'

'Hm. Hairs'll grow a bit thick. Crooked too. However. Can't be helped. Looks all right for the time being. Sit down.'

Bond walked round to the single chair which faced M across the desk. The grey eyes looked at him, through him.

'Had a good rest?'

'Yes thank you, Sir.'

'Ever seen one of these?' M abruptly fished something out of his waistcoat pocket. He tossed it half way across the desk towards Bond. It fell with a faint clang on the red leather and lay, gleaming richly, an inch-wide, hammered gold coin.

Bond picked it up, turned it over, weighed it in his hand.

'No, Sir. Worth about five pounds, perhaps.'

'Fifteen to a collector. It's a Rose Noble of Edward IV.'

M fished again in his waistcoat pocket and tossed more magnificent gold coins on to the table in front of Bond. As he did so, he glanced at each one and identified it.

'Double Excellente, Spanish, Ferdinand and Isabella, 1510; Ecu au Soleil, French, Charles IX, 1574; Double Ecu d'or, French, Henry IV, 1600; Double Ducat, Spanish, Philip II, 1560; Ryder, Dutch, Charles d'Egmond, 1538; Quadruple, Genoa, 1617; Double louis, à la mèche courte, French, Louis XIV, 1644. Worth a lot of money melted down. Much more to collectors, ten to twenty pounds each. Notice anything common to them all?'

Bond reflected. 'No, Sir.'

'All minted before 1650. Bloody Morgan, the pirate, was Governor and Commander-in-Chief of Jamaica from 1675 to 1688. The English coin is the joker in the pack. Probably shipped out to pay the Jamaica garrison. But for that and the dates, these could have come from any other treasure-trove put together by the great pirates – L'Ollonais, Pierre le Grand, Sharp, Sawkins, Blackbeard. As it is, and both Spinks and the British Museum agree, this is almost certainly part of Bloody Morgan's treasure.'

M paused to fill his pipe and light it. He didn't invite Bond to smoke and Bond would not have thought of doing so uninvited.

'And the hell of a treasure it must be. So far nearly a thousand of these and similar coins have turned up in the United States in the last few months. And if the Special Branch of the Treasury, and the FBI, have traced a thousand, how many more have been melted down or disappeared into private collections? And they keep on coming in, turning up in banks, bullion merchants, curio shops, but mostly pawnbrokers of course. The FBI are in a proper fix. If they put these on the police notices of stolen property they know the source will dry up. They'd be melted down into gold bars and channelled straight into the black bullion market. Have to sacrifice the rarity value of the coins, but the gold would go straight underground. As it is, someone's using the negroes – porters, sleeping-car attendants, truck-drivers – and getting the money well spread over the States. Quite innocent people. Here's a typical case.' M opened a brown folder bearing the Top Secret red star and selected a single sheet of paper. Through the reverse side, as M held it up, Bond could see the engraved heading: 'Department of Justice. Federal Bureau of Investigations.' M read from it:

'Zachary Smith, 35, Negro, Member of the Sleeping Car Porters Brotherhood, address 90b West 126th Street, New York City.' (M looked up: 'Harlem,' he said.) 'Subject was identified by Arthur Fein of Fein Jewels Inc., 870 Lenox Avenue, as having offered for sale on November 21st last four gold coins of the sixteenth and seventeenth century (details attached). Fein offered a hundred dollars which was accepted. Interrogated later, Smith said they had been sold to him in Seventh Heaven Bar-B-Q (a well-known Harlem bar) for twenty dollars each by a negro he had never seen before or since. Vendor had said they were worth fifty dollars each at Tiffany's, but that he, the vendor, wanted ready cash and Tiffany's was too far anyway. Smith bought one for twenty dollars and on finding that a neighbouring pawnbroker would offer him twenty-five dollars for it, returned to the bar and purchased the remaining three for sixty dollars. The next morning he took them to Fein's. Subject has no criminal record.'

M returned the paper to the brown folder.

'That's typical,' he said. 'Several times they've caught up with the next link, the middle man who bought them a bit cheaper and they find that he bought a handful, in one case a hundred of them, from some man who presumably got them cheaper still. All these larger transactions have taken place in Harlem or Florida. Always the next man in the link was an unknown negro, in all cases a white-collar man, prosperous, educated, who said he guessed they were treasure-trove, Blackbeard's treasure.

'This Blackbeard story would stand up to most investigations,' continued M, 'because there is reason to believe that part of his hoard was dug up around Christmas Day, 1928, at a place called Plum Point. It's a narrow neck of land in Beaufort County, North Carolina, where a stream called Bath Creek flows into the Pamlico River. Don't think I'm an expert,' he smiled, 'you can read all about this in the dossier. So, in theory, it would be quite reasonable for those lucky treasure-hunters to have hidden the loot until everyone had forgotten the story and then thrown it fast on the market. Or else they could have sold it en bloc at the time, or later, and the purchaser has just decided to cash in. Anyway it's a good enough cover except on two counts.'

M paused and relit his pipe.

'Firstly, Blackbeard operated from about 1690 to 1710 and it's improbable that none of his coin should have been minted later than 1650. Also, as I said before, it's very unlikely that his treasure would contain Edward IV Rose Nobles, since there's no record of an English treasure-ship being captured on its way to Jamaica. The Brethren of the Coast wouldn't take them on. Too heavily escorted. There were much easier pickings if you were sailing in those days "on the plundering account" as they called it.

'Secondly,' and M looked at the ceiling and then back at Bond, 'I know where the treasure is. At least I'm pretty sure I do. And it's not in America. It's in Jamaica, and it is Bloody Morgan's, and I guess it's one of the most valuable treasure-troves in history.'

'Good Lord,' said Bond. 'How . . . where do we come into it?'

M held up his hand. 'You'll find all the details in here,' he let his hand come down on the brown folder. 'Briefly, Station C has been interested in a Diesel yacht, the *Secatur*, which has been running from a small island on the North Coast of Jamaica through the Florida Keys into the Gulf of Mexico, to a place called St Petersburg. Sort of pleasure resort, near Tampa. West Coast of Florida. With the help of the FBI we've traced the ownership of this boat and of the island to a man called Mr Big, a negro gangster. Lives in Harlem. Ever heard of him?'

'No,' said Bond.

'And curiously enough,' M's voice was softer and quieter, 'a twenty-dollar bill which one of these casual negroes had paid for a gold coin and whose number he had noted for Peaka Peow, the Numbers game, was paid out by one of Mr Big's lieutenants. And it was paid,' M pointed the stem of his pipe at Bond, 'for information received, to an FBI double-agent who is a member of the Communist Party.'

Bond whistled softly.

'In short,' continued M, 'we suspect that this Jamaican treasure is being used to finance the Soviet espionage system, or an important part of it, in America. And our suspicion becomes a certainty when I tell you who this Mr Big is.'

Bond waited, his eyes fixed on M's.

'Mr Big,' said M, weighing his words, 'is probably the most powerful negro criminal in the world. He is,' and he enumerated carefully, 'the head of the Black Widow Voodoo cult and believed by that cult to be the Baron Samedi himself. (You'll find all about that here,' he tapped the folder, 'and it'll frighten the daylights out of you.) He is also a Soviet agent. And finally he is, and this will particularly interest you, Bond, a known member of SMERSH.'

'Yes,' said Bond slowly, 'I see now.'

'Quite a case,' said M, looking keenly at him. 'And quite a man, this Mr Big.'

'I don't think I've ever heard of a great negro criminal before,' said Bond, 'Chinamen, of course, the men behind the opium trade. There've been some big-time Japs, mostly in pearls and drugs. Plenty of negroes mixed up in diamonds and gold in Africa, but always in a small way. They don't seem to take to big business. Pretty law-abiding chaps I should have thought except when they've drunk too much.'

'Our man's a bit of an exception,' said M. 'He's not pure negro. Born in Haiti. Good dose of French blood. Trained in Moscow, too, as you'll see from the file. And the negro races are just beginning to throw up geniuses in all the professions – scientists, doctors, writers. It's about time they turned out a great criminal. After all, there are 250,000,000 of them in the world. Nearly a third of the white population. They've got plenty of brains and ability and guts. And now Moscow's taught one of them the technique.'

'I'd like to meet him,' said Bond. Then he added, mildly, 'I'd like to meet any member of SMERSH.'

'All right then, Bond. Take it away.' M handed him the thick brown folder. 'Talk it over with Plender and Damon. Be ready to start in a week. It's a joint CIA and FBI job. For God's sake don't step on the FBI's toes. Covered with corns. Good luck.'

Bond had gone straight down to Commander Damon, Head of Station A, an alert Canadian who controlled the link with the Central Intelligence Agency, America's Secret Service.

Damon looked up from his desk. 'I see you've bought it,' he said, looking at the folder. 'Thought you would. Sit down,' he waved to an armchair beside the electric fire. 'When you've waded through it all, I'll fill in the gaps.'

3 A Visiting-Card

And now it was ten days later and the talk with Dexter and Leiter had not added much, reflected Bond as he awoke slowly and luxuriously in his bedroom at the St Regis the morning after his arrival in New York.

Dexter had had plenty of detail on Mr Big, but nothing that threw any new light on the case. Mr Big was forty-five years old, born in Haiti, half negro and half French. Because of the initial letters of his fanciful name, Buonaparte Ignace Gallia, and because of his huge height and bulk, he came to be called, even as a youth, 'Big Boy' or just 'Big'. Later this became 'The Big Man' or 'Mr Big', and his real names lingered only on a parish register in Haiti and on his dossier with the FBI. He had no known vices except women, whom he consumed in quantities. He didn't drink or smoke and his only Achilles heel appeared to be a chronic heart disease which had, in recent years, imparted a greyish tinge to his skin.

The Big Boy had been initiated into Voodoo as a child, earned his living as a truck-driver in Port au Prince, then emigrated to America and worked successfully for a hi-jacking team in the Legs Diamond gang. With the end of Prohibition he had moved to Harlem and bought half-shares in a small nightclub and a string of coloured call-girls. His partner was found in a barrel of cement in the Harlem River in 1938 and Mr Big automatically became sole proprietor of the business. He was called up in 1943 and, because of his excellent French, came to the notice of the Office of Strategic Services, the wartime secret service of America, who trained him with great thoroughness and put him into Marseilles as an agent against the Pétain collaborationists. He merged easily with African negro dock-hands, and worked well, providing good and accurate naval intelligence. He operated closely with a Soviet spy who was doing a similar job for the Russians. At the end of the war he was demobilized in France (and decorated by the Americans and the French) and then he disappeared for five years, probably to Moscow. He returned to Harlem in 1950 and soon came to the notice of the FBI as a suspected Soviet agent. But he never incriminated himself or fell into any of the traps laid by the FBI. He bought up three nightclubs and a prosperous chain of Harlem brothels. He seemed to have unlimited funds and paid all his lieutenants a flat rate of twenty thousand dollars a year. Accordingly, and as a result of weeding by murder, he was expertly and diligently served. He was known to have originated an underground Voodoo temple in Harlem and to have established a link between it and the main cult in Haiti. The rumour had started that he was the Zombie or living corpse of Baron Samedi himself, the dreaded Prince of Darkness, and he fostered the story so that now it was accepted through all the lower strata of the negro world. As a result, he commanded real fear, strongly substantiated by the immediate and often mysterious deaths of anyone who crossed him or disobeyed his orders.

Bond had questioned Dexter and Leiter very closely on the evidence connecting the giant negro with SMERSH. It certainly seemed conclusive.

In 1951, by the promise of one million dollars in gold and a safe refuge after six months' work for them, the FBI had at last persuaded a known Soviet agent of the MWD to turn double. All went well for a month and the results exceeded the highest expectations. The Russian spy held the appointment of an economic expert on the Soviet delegation to the United Nations. One Saturday, he had gone to take the subway to Pennsylvania Station en route for the Soviet weekend rest camp at Glen Cove, the former Morgan estate on Long Island.

A huge negro, positively identified from photographs as The Big Man, had stood beside him on the platform as the train came in and was seen walking towards the exit even before the first coach had come to a standstill over the bloody vestiges of the Russian. He had not been seen to push the man, but in the crowd it would not have been difficult. Spectators said it could not have been suicide. The man screamed horribly as he fell and he had had (melancholy touch!) a bag of golf clubs over his shoulder. The Big Man, of course, had had an alibi as solid as Fort Knox. He had been held and questioned, but was quickly sprung by the best lawyer in Harlem.

The evidence was good enough for Bond. He was just the man for SMERSH, with just the training. A real, hard weapon of fear and death. And what a brilliant set-up for dealing with the smaller fry of the negro underworld and for keeping a coloured information network well up to the mark! – the fear of Voodoo and the supernatural, still deeply, primevally ingrained in the negro subconscious! And what genius to have, as a beginning, the whole transport system of America under surveillance, the trains, the porters, the truck-drivers, the steve-dores! To have at his disposal a host of key men who would have no idea that the questions they answered had been asked by Russia. Small-time professional men who, if they thought at all, would guess that the information on freights and schedules was being sold to rival transport concerns.

Not for the first time, Bond felt his spine crawl at the cold, brilliant efficiency of the Soviet machine, and at the fear of death and torture which made it work and of which the supreme engine was SMERSH – SMERSH, the very whisper of death.

Now, in his bedroom at the St Regis, Bond shook away his thoughts and jumped impatiently out of bed. Well, there was one of them at hand, ready for the crushing. At Royale he had only caught a glimpse of his man. This time it would be face to face. Big Man? Then let it be a giant, a homeric slaying.

Bond walked over to the window and pulled back the curtains. His room faced north, towards Harlem. Bond gazed for a moment towards the northern horizon, where another man would be in his bedroom asleep, or perhaps awake and thinking conceivably of him, Bond, whom he had seen with Dexter on the steps of the hotel. Bond looked at the beautiful day and smiled. And no man, not even Mr Big, would have liked the expression on his face.

Bond shrugged his shoulders and walked quickly to the telephone.

'St Regis Hotel. Good morning,' said a voice.

'Room Service, please,' said Bond.

'Room Service? I'd like to order breakfast. Half a pint of orange juice, three eggs, lightly scrambled, with bacon, a double portion of café Espresso with cream. Toast. Marmalade. Got it?'

The order was repeated back to him. Bond walked out into the lobby and picked up the five pounds' weight of newspapers which had been placed quietly inside the door earlier in the morning. There was also a pile of parcels on the hall table which Bond disregarded.

The afternoon before he had had to submit to a certain degree of Americanization at the hands of the FBI. A tailor had come and measured him for two single-breasted suits in dark blue light-weight worsted (Bond had firmly refused anything more dashing) and a haberdasher had brought chilly white nylon shirts with long points to the collars. He had had to accept half a dozen unusually patterned foulard ties, dark socks with fancy clocks, two or three 'display kerchiefs' for his breast pocket, nylon vests and pants (called T-shirts and shorts), a comfortable light-weight camel-hair overcoat with over-buttressed shoulders, a plain grey snap-brim Fedora with a thin black ribbon and two pairs of hand-stitched and very comfortable black Moccasin 'casuals'.

He also acquired a 'Swank' tie-clip in the shape of a whip, an alligator-skin billfold from Mark Cross, a plain Zippo lighter, a plastic 'Travel-Pak' containing razor, hairbrush and toothbrush, a pair of horn-rimmed glasses with plain lenses, various other oddments and, finally, a light-weight Hartmann 'Skymate' suitcase to contain all these things.

He was allowed to retain his own Beretta .25 with the skeleton grip and the chamois leather shoulder-holster, but all his other possessions were to be collected at midday and forwarded down to Jamaica to await him.

He was given a military haircut and was told that he was a New

157

Englander from Boston and that he was on holiday from his job with the London office of the Guaranty Trust Company. He was reminded to ask for the 'check' rather than the 'bill', to say 'cab' instead of 'taxi' and (this from Leiter) to avoid words of more than two syllables. ('You can get through any American conversation,' advised Leiter, 'with "Yeah", "Nope" and "Sure".') The English word to be avoided at all costs, added Leiter, was 'Ectually'. Bond had said that this word was not part of his vocabulary.

Bond looked grimly at the pile of parcels which contained his new identity, stripped off his pyjamas for the last time ('We mostly sleep in the raw in America, Mr Bond') and gave himself a sizzling cold shower. As he shaved he examined his face in the glass. The thick comma of black hair above his right eyebrow had lost some of its tail and his hair was trimmed close across the temples. Nothing could be done about the thin vertical scar down his right cheek, although the FBI had experimented with 'Cover-Mark', or about the coldness and hint of anger in his grey-blue eyes, but there was the mixed blood of America in the black hair and high cheekbones and Bond thought he might get by – except, perhaps, with women.

Naked, Bond walked out into the lobby and tore open some of the packages. Later, in white shirt and dark blue trousers, he went into the sitting-room, pulled a chair up to the writing-desk near the window and opened *The Traveller's Tree*, by Patrick Leigh Fermor.

This extraordinary book had been recommended to him by M.

'It's by a chap who knows what he's talking about,' he said, 'and don't forget that he was writing about what was happening in Haiti in 1950. This isn't medieval black-magic stuff. It's being practised every day.'

Bond was half way through the section on Haiti.

The next step [he read] is the invocation of evil denizens of the Voodoo pantheon – such as Don Pedro, Kitta, Mondongue, Bakalou and Zandor – for harmful purposes, for the reputed practice (which is of Congolese origin) of turning people into zombies in order to use them as slaves, the casting of maleficent spells, and the destruction of enemies. The effects of the spell, of which the outward form may be an image of the intended victim, a miniature coffin or a toad, are frequently stiffened by the separate use of poison. Father Cosme enlarged on the superstitions that maintain that men with certain powers change themselves into snakes; on the 'Loups-Garoups' that fly at night in the form of vampire bats and suck the blood of children; on men who reduce themselves to infinitesimal size and roll about the countryside in calabashes. What sounded far more sinister were a number of mystico-criminal secret societies of wizards, with nightmarish titles – 'les Mackanda', named after the poison campaign of the Haitian hero; 'les Zobop', who were also robbers; the 'Mazanxa', the 'Caporelata' and the 'Vlinbindingue'. These, he said, were the mysterious groups whose gods demand – instead of a cock, a pigeon, a goat, a dog, or a pig, as in the normal rites of Voodoo – the sacrifice of a 'cabrit sans cornes'. This hornless goat, of course, means a human being . . .

Bond turned over the pages, occasional passages combining to form an extraordinary picture in his mind of a dark religion and its terrible rites.

. . . Slowly, out of the turmoil and the smoke and the shattering noise of the drums, which, for a time, drove everything except their impact from the mind, the details began to detach themselves . . .

. . . Backwards and forwards, very slowly, the dancers shuffled, and at each step their chins shot out and their buttocks jerked upwards, while their shoulders shook in double time. Their eyes were half closed and from their mouths came again and again the same incomprehensible words, the same short line of chanted song, repeated after each iteration, half an octave lower. At a change in the beat of the drums, they straightened their bodies, and flinging their arms in the air while their eyes rolled upwards, spun round and round . . .

. . . At the edge of the crowd we came upon a little hut, scarcely larger than a dog kennel: 'Le caye Zombi'. The beam of a torch revealed a black cross inside and some rags and chains and shackles and whips: adjuncts used at the Ghédé ceremonies, which Haitian ethnologists connect with the rejuvenation rites of Osiris recorded in the Book of the Dead. A fire was burning, in which two sabres and a large pair of pincers were standing, their lower parts red with the heat: 'le Feu Marinette', dedicated to a goddess who is the evil obverse of the bland and amorous Maîtresse Erzulie Fréda Dahomin, the Goddess of Love.

Beyond, with its base held fast in a socket of stone, stood a large black wooden cross. A white death's head was painted near the base, and over the crossbar were pulled the sleeves of a very old morning coat. Here also rested the brim of a battered bowler hat, through the torn crown of which the top of the cross projected. This totem, with which every peristyle must be equipped, is not a lampoon of the central event of the Christian faith, but represents the God of the Cemeteries and the Chief of the Legion of the Dead, Baron Samedi. The Baron is paramount in all matters immediately beyond the tomb. He is Cerberus and Charon as well as Aeacus, Rhadamanthus and Pluto . . .

. . . The drums changed and the Houngenikon came dancing on to the floor, holding a vessel filled with some burning liquid from which sprang blue and yellow flames. As he circled the pillar and spilt three flaming libations, his steps began to falter. Then, lurching backwards with the same symptoms of delirium that had manifested themselves in his forerunner, he flung down the whole blazing mass. The houncis caught him as he reeled, and removed his sandals and rolled his trousers up, while the kerchief fell from his head and laid bare his young woolly skull. The other houncis knelt to put their hands in the flaming mud, and rub it over their hands and elbows and faces. The Houngan's bell and 'açon' rattled officiously and the young priest was left by himself, reeling and colliding against the pillar, helplessly catapulting across the floor, and falling among the drums. His eyes were shut, his forehead screwed up and his chin hung loose. Then, as though an invisible fist had dealt him a heavy blow, he fell to the ground and lay there, with his head stretching backwards in a rictus of anguish until the tendons of his neck and shoulders projected like roots. One hand clutched at the other elbow behind his hollowed back as though he were striving to break his own arm, and his whole body, from which the sweat was streaming, trembled and shuddered like a dog in a dream. Only the whites of his eyes were visible as, although his eye-sockets were now wide open, the pupils had vanished under the lids. Foam collected on his lips . . .

. . . Now the Houngan, dancing a slow step and brandishing a cutlass, advanced from the fireside, flinging the weapon again and again into the air, and catching it by the hilt. In a few minutes he was holding it by the blunted end of the blade. Dancing slowly towards him, the Houngenikon reached out and grasped the hilt. The priest retired, and the young man, twirling and leaping, spun from side to side of the 'tonnelle'. The ring of spectators rocked backwards as he bore down upon them whirling the blade over his head, with the gaps in his bared teeth lending to his mandril face a still more feral aspect. The 'tonnelle' was filled for a few seconds with genuine and unmitigated terror. The singing had turned to a universal howl and the drummers, rolling and lolling with the furious and invisible motion of their hands, were lost in a transport of noise.

Flinging back his head, the novice drove the blunt end of the cutlass into his stomach. His knees sagged, and his head fell forward . . .

There came a knock on the door and a waiter came in with breakfast. Bond was glad to put the dreadful tale aside and re-enter the world of normality. But it took him minutes to forget the atmosphere, heavy with terror and the occult, that had surrounded him as he read.

With breakfast came another parcel, about a foot square, expensive-looking, which Bond told the waiter to put on the sideboard. Some afterthought of Leiter's, he supposed. He ate his breakfast with enjoyment. Between mouthfuls he looked out of the wide window and reflected on what he had just read.

It was only when he had swallowed his last mouthful of coffee and had lit his first cigarette of the day that he suddenly became aware of the tiny noise in the room behind him.

It was a soft, muffled ticking, unhurried, metallic. And it came from the direction of the sideboard.

'Tick-tock . . . tick-tock . . . tick-tock.'

Without a moment's hesitation, without caring that he looked a fool, he dived to the floor behind his armchair and crouched, all his senses focused on the noise from the square parcel. 'Steady,' he said to himself. 'Don't be an idiot. It's just a clock.' But why a clock? Why should he be given a clock? Who by?

'Tick-tock . . . tick-tock . . . tick-tock.'

It had become a huge noise against the silence of the room. It seemed to be keeping time with the thumping of Bond's heart. 'Don't be ridiculous. That Voodoo stuff of Leigh Fermor's has put your nerves on edge. Those drums . . .'

'Tick-tock . . . tick-tock . . . tick –'

And then, suddenly, the alarm went off with a deep, melodious, urgent summons.

'Tongtongtongtongtongtong . . .'

Bond's muscles relaxed. His cigarette was burning a hole in the carpet. He picked it up and put it in his mouth. Bombs in alarm clocks go off when the hammer first comes down on the alarm. The hammer hits a pin in a detonator, the detonator fires the explosive and WHAM . . .

Bond raised his head above the back of the chair and watched the parcel.

'Tongtongtongtongtong . . .'

The muffled gonging went on for half a minute, then it started to slow down.

'tong . . tong . . . tong . . . . tong . . . . . tong . . . .

'C-R-A-C-K . . .'

It was not louder than a 12-bore cartridge, but in the confined space it was an impressive explosion.

The parcel, in tatters, had fallen to the ground. The glasses and bottles on the sideboard were smashed and there was a black smudge of smoke on the grey wall behind them. Some pieces of glass tinkled on to the floor. There was a strong smell of gunpowder in the room.

Bond got slowly to his feet. He went to the window and opened it. Then he dialled Dexter's number. He spoke levelly.

'Pineapple . . . No, a small one . . . only some glasses . . . okay, thanks . . . of course not . . .'bye.'

He skirted the debris, walked through the small lobby to the door leading into the passage, opened it, hung the DON'T DISTURB sign outside, locked it, and went through into his bedroom.

By the time he had finished dressing there was a knock on the door.

'Who is it?' he called.

'Okay. Dexter.'

Dexter hustled in, followed by a sallow young man with a black box under his arm.

'Trippe, from Sabotage,' announced Dexter.

They shook hands and the young man at once went on his knees beside the charred remnants of the parcel.

He opened his box and took out some rubber gloves and a handful of dentist's forceps. With his tools he painstakingly extracted small bits of metal and glass from the charred parcel and laid them out on a broad sheet of blotting paper from the writing-desk.

While he worked, he asked Bond what had happened.

'About a half-minute alarm? I see. Hullo, what's this?' He delicately extracted a small aluminium container such as is used for exposed film. He put it aside.

After a few minutes he sat up on his haunches.

'Half-minute acid capsule,' he announced. 'Broken by the first hammer-stroke of the alarm. Acid eats through thin copper wire. Thirty seconds later wire breaks, releases plunger on to cap of this.' He held up the base of a cartridge. '4-bore elephant gun. Black powder. Blank. No shot. Lucky it wasn't a grenade. Plenty of room in the parcel. You'd have been damaged. Now let's have a look at this.' He picked up the aluminium cylinder, unscrewed it, extracted a small roll of paper, and unravelled it with his forceps.

He carefully flattened it out on the carpet, holding its corners down with four tools from his black box. It contained three typewritten sentences. Bond and Dexter bent forward.

'THE HEART OF THIS CLOCK HAS STOPPED TICKING,' they read. 'THE BEATS OF YOUR OWN HEART ARE NUMBERED. I KNOW THAT NUMBER AND I HAVE STARTED TO COUNT.'

The message was signed '1234567 . . . ?'

They stood up.

'Hm,' said Bond. 'Bogeyman stuff.'

'But how the hell did he know you were here?' asked Dexter.

Bond told him of the black sedan on 55th Street.

'But the point is,' said Bond, 'how did he know what I was here *for*? Shows he's got Washington pretty well sewn up. Must be a leak the size of the Grand Canyon somewhere.'

'Why should it be Washington?' asked Dexter testily. 'Anyway,' he controlled himself with a forced laugh, 'Hell and damnation. Have to make a report to Headquarters on this. So long, Mr Bond. Glad you came to no harm.'

'Thanks,' said Bond. 'It was just a visiting-card. I must return the compliment.'

4 The Big Switchboard

When Dexter and his colleague had gone, taking the remains of the bomb with them, Bond took a damp towel and rubbed the smoke-mark off the wall. Then he rang for the waiter and, without explanation, told him to put the broken glass on his check and clear away the breakfast things. Then he took his hat and coat and went out on the street.

He spent the morning on Fifth Avenue and on Broadway, wandering aimlessly, gazing into the shop windows and watching the passing crowds. He gradually assimilated the casual gait and manners of a visitor from out of town, and when he tested himself out in a few shops and asked the way of several people he found that nobody looked at him twice.

He had a typical American meal at an eating house called 'Glory-fried Ham-N-Eggs' ('The Eggs We Serve Tomorrow Are Still in the Hens') on Lexington Avenue and then took a cab downtown to police headquarters, where he was due to meet Leiter and Dexter at 2.30.

A Lieutenant Binswanger of Homicide, a suspicious and crusty officer in his late forties, announced that Commissioner Monahan had said that they were to have complete co-operation from the Police Department. What could he do for them? They examined Mr Big's police record, which more or less duplicated Dexter's information, and they were shown the records and photographs of most of his known associates.

They went over the reports of the US Coastguard Service on the comings and goings of the yacht *Secatur* and also the comments of the US Customs Service, who had kept a close watch on the boat each time she had docked at St Petersburg.

These confirmed that the yacht had put in at irregular intervals over the previous six months and that she always tied up in the Port of St Petersburg at the wharf of the Ourobouros Worm and Bait Shippers Inc., an apparently innocent concern whose main business was to sell live bait to fishing clubs throughout Florida, the Gulf of Mexico and further afield. The company also had a profitable sideline in sea-shells and coral for interior decoration, and a further sideline in tropical aquarium fish – particularly rare poisonous species for the research departments of medical and chemical foundations.

According to the proprietor, a Greek sponge-fisher from the neighbouring Tarpon Springs, the *Secatur* did big business with his company, bringing in cargoes of queen conchs and other shells from Jamaica and also highly prized varieties of tropical fish. These were purchased by Ourobouros Inc., stored in their warehouse and sold in bulk to wholesalers and retailers up and down the coast. The name of the Greek was Papagos. No criminal record.

The FBI, with the help of Naval Intelligence, had tried listening in to the *Secatur*'s wireless. But she kept off the air except for short messages before she sailed from Cuba or Jamaica and then transmitted *en clair* in a language which was unknown and completely indecipherable. The last notation on the file was to the effect that the operator was talking in 'Language', the secret Voodoo speech only used by initiates, and that every effort would be made to hire an expert from Haiti before the next sailing.

'More gold been turning up lately,' announced Lieutenant Binswanger as they walked back to his office from the Identification Bureau across the street. ''Bout a hundred coins a week in Harlem and New York alone. Want us to do anything about it? If you're right and these are Commie funds, they must be pulling it in pretty fast while we sit on our asses doin' nothing.'

'Chief says to lay off,' said Dexter. 'Hope we'll see some action before long.'

'Well, the case is all yours,' said Binswanger grudgingly. 'But the Commissioner sure don't like having this bastard crappin' away on his own front doorstep while Mr Hoover sits down in Washington well to leeward of the stink. Why don't we pull him in on tax evasion or misuse of the mails or parkin' in front of a hydrant or sumpn? Take him down to the Tombs and give 'em the works? If the Feds won't do it, we'd be glad to oblige.'

'D'you want a race riot?' objected Dexter sourly. 'There's nothing against him and you know it, and we know it. If he wasn't sprung in half an hour by that black mouthpiece of his, those Voodoo drums would start beating from here to the Deep South. When they're full of that stuff we all know what happens. Remember '35 and '43? You'd have to call out the Militia. We didn't ask for the case. The President gave it us and we've got to stick with it.'

They were back in Binswanger's drab office. They picked up their coats and hats.

'Anyway, thanks for the help, Lootenant,' said Dexter with forced cordiality, as they made their farewells. 'Been most valuable.'

'You're welcome,' said Binswanger stonily. 'Elevator's to your right.' He closed the door firmly behind them.

Leiter winked at Bond behind Dexter's back. They rode down to the main entrance on Center Street in silence.

On the sidewalk, Dexter turned to them.

'Had some instructions from Washington this morning,' he said unemotionally. 'Seems I'm to look after the Harlem end, and you two are to go down to St Petersburg tomorrow. Leiter's to find out what he can there and then move right on to Jamaica with you, Mr Bond. That is,' he added, 'if you'd care to have him along. It's your territory.'

'Of course,' said Bond. 'I was going to ask if he could come anyway.'

'Fine,' said Dexter. 'Then I'll tell Washington everything's fixed. Anything else I can do for you? All communications with FBI, Washington, of course. Leiter's got the names of our men in Florida, knows the Signals routine and so forth.'

'If Leiter's interested and if you don't mind,' said Bond, 'I'd like very much to get up to Harlem this evening and have a look round. Might help to have some idea of what it looks like in Mr Big's back yard.'

Dexter reflected.

'Okay,' he said finally. 'Probably no harm. But don't show yourselves too much. And don't get hurt,' he added. 'There's no one to help you up there. And don't go stirring up a lot of trouble for us. This case isn't ripe yet. Until it is, our policy with Mr Big is "live and let live".'

Bond looked quizzically at Captain Dexter.

'In my job,' he said, 'when I come up against a man like this one, I have another motto. It's "live and let die".'

Dexter shrugged his shoulders. 'Maybe,' he said, 'but you're under my orders here, Mr Bond, and I'd be glad if you'd accept them.'

'Of course,' said Bond, 'and thanks for all your help. Hope you have luck with your end of the job.'

Dexter flagged a cab. They shook hands.

''Bye, fellers,' said Dexter briefly. 'Stay alive.' His cab pulled out into the uptown traffic.

Bond and Leiter smiled at each other.

'Able guy, I should say,' said Bond.

'They're all that in his show,' said Leiter. 'Bit inclined to be stuffed shirts. Very touchy about their rights. Always bickering with us or with the police. But I guess you have much the same problem in England.'

'Oh of course,' said Bond. 'We're always rubbing MI5 up the wrong way. And they're always stepping on the corns of the Special Branch. Scotland Yard,' he explained. 'Well, how about going up to Harlem tonight?'

'Suits me,' said Leiter. 'I'll drop you at the St Regis and pick you up again about six-thirty. Meet you in the King Cole Bar, on the ground floor. Guess you want to take a look at Mr Big,' he grinned. 'Well, so do I, but it wouldn't have done to tell Dexter so.' He flagged a Yellow Cab.

'St Regis Hotel. Fifth at 55th.'

They climbed into the overheated tin box reeking of last week's cigar-smoke.

Leiter wound down a window.

'Whaddya want ter do?' asked the driver over his shoulder. 'Gimme pneumony?'

'Just that,' said Leiter, 'if it means saving us from this gas chamber.'

'Wise guy, hn?' said the driver, crashing tinnily through his gears. He took the chewed end of a cigar from behind his ear and held it up. 'Two bits for three,' he said in a hurt voice.

'Twenty-four cents too much,' said Leiter. The rest of the drive was passed in silence.

They parted at the hotel and Bond went up to his room. It was four o'clock. He asked the telephone operator to call him at six. For a while he looked out of the window of his bedroom. To his left, the sun was setting in a blaze of colour. In the skyscrapers the lights were coming on, turning the whole town into a golden honeycomb. Far below the streets were rivers of neon lighting, crimson, blue, green. The wind sighed sadly outside in the velvet dusk, lending his room still more warmth and security and luxury. He drew the curtains and turned on the soft lights over his bed. Then he took off his clothes and climbed between the fine percale sheets. He thought of the bitter weather in the London streets, the grudging warmth of the hissing gas-fire in his office at Headquarters, the chalked-up menu on the pub he had passed on his last day in London: 'Giant Toad & 2 Veg.'

He stretched luxuriously. Very soon he was asleep.

Up in Harlem, at the big switchboard, 'The Whisper' was dozing over his racing form. All his lines were quiet. Suddenly a light shone on the right of the board – an important light.

'Yes, Boss,' he said softly into his headphone. He couldn't have spoken any louder if he had wished to. He had been born on 'Lung Block', on Seventh Avenue, at 142nd Street, where death from TB is twice as high as anywhere in New York. Now, he only had part of one lung left.

'Tell all "Eyes",' said a slow, deep voice, 'to watch out from now on. Three men.' A brief description of Leiter, Bond and Dexter followed. 'May be coming in this evening or tomorrow. Tell them to watch particularly on First to Eight and the other Avenues. The night spots too, in case they're missed coming in. They're not to be molested. Call me when you get a sure fix. Got it?'

'Yes, Sir, Boss,' said The Whisper, breathing fast. The voice went quiet. The operator took the whole handful of plugs, and soon the big switchboard was alive with winking lights. Softly, urgently, he whispered on into the evening.

At six o'clock Bond was awakened by the soft burr of the telephone. He took a cold shower and dressed carefully. He put on a garishly striped tie and allowed a broad wedge of bandana to protrude from his breast pocket. He slipped the chamois leather holster over his shirt so that it hung three inches below his left armpit. He whipped at the mechanism of the Beretta until all eight bullets lay on the bed. Then he packed them back into the magazine, loaded the gun, put up the safety-catch and slipped it into the holster.

He picked up the pair of Moccasin casuals, felt their toes and weighed them in his hand. Then he reached under the bed and pulled out a pair of his own shoes he had carefully kept out of the suitcase full of his belongings the FBI had taken away from him that morning.

He put them on and felt better equipped to face the evening.

Under the leather, the toe-caps were lined with steel.

At six twenty-five he went down to the King Cole Bar and chose a table near the entrance and against the wall. A few minutes later Felix Leiter came in. Bond hardly recognized him. His mop of straw-coloured hair was now jet black and he wore a dazzling blue suit with a white shirt and a black-and-white polka-dot tie.

Leiter sat down with a broad grin.

'I suddenly decided to take these people seriously,' he explained. 'This stuff's only a rinse. It'll come off in the morning. I hope,' he added.

Leiter ordered medium-dry Martinis with a slice of lemon peel. He stipulated House of Lords gin and Martini Rossi. The American gin, a much higher proof than English gin, tasted harsh to Bond. He reflected that he would have to be careful what he drank that evening.

'We'll have to keep on our toes, where we're going,' said Felix Leiter, echoing his thoughts. 'Harlem's a bit of a jungle these days. People don't go up there any more like they used to. Before the war, at the end of an evening, one used to go to Harlem just as one goes to Montmartre in Paris. They were glad to take one's money. One used to go to the Savoy Ballroom and watch the dancing. Perhaps pick up a high-yaller and risk the doctor's bills afterwards. Now that's all changed. Harlem doesn't like being stared at any more. Most of the places have closed and you go to the others strictly on sufferance. Often you get tossed out on your ear, simply because you're white. And you don't get any sympathy from the police either.'

Leiter extracted the lemon peel from his Martini and chewed it reflectively. The bar was filling up. It was warm and companionable – a far cry, Leiter reflected, from the inimical, electric climate of the negro pleasure-spots they would be drinking in later.

'Fortunately,' continued Leiter, 'I like the negroes and they know it somehow. I used to be a bit of an aficionado of Harlem. Wrote a few pieces on Dixieland Jazz for the *Amsterdam News*, one of the local papers. Did a series for the North American Newspaper Alliance on the negro theatre about the time Orson Welles put on his *Macbeth* with an all-negro cast at the Lafayette. So I know my way about up there. And I admire the way they're getting on in the world, though God knows I can't see the end of it.'

They finished their drinks and Leiter called for the check.

'Of course there are some bad ones,' he said. 'Some of the worst anywhere. Harlem's the capital of the negro world. In any half a million people of any race you'll get plenty of stinkeroos. The trouble with our friend Mr Big is that he's the hell of a good technician, thanks to his OSS and Moscow training. And he must be pretty well organized up there.'

Leiter paid. He shrugged his shoulders.

'Let's go,' he said. 'We'll have ourselves some fun and try and get back in one piece. After all, this is what we're paid for. We'll take a bus on Fifth Avenue. You won't find many cabs that want to go up there after dark.'

They walked out of the warm hotel and took the few steps to the bus stop on the Avenue.

It was raining. Bond turned up the collar of his coat and gazed up the Avenue to his right, towards Central Park, towards the dark citadel that housed The Big Man.

Bond's nostrils flared slightly. He longed to get in there after him. He felt strong and compact and confident. The evening awaited him, to be opened and read, page by page, word by word.

In front of his eyes, the rain came down in swift, slanting strokes – italic script across the unopened black cover that hid the secret hours that lay ahead.

5 *Nigger Heaven*

At the bus stop at the corner of Fifth and Cathedral Parkway three negroes stood quietly under the light of a street lamp. They looked wet and bored. They were. They had been watching the traffic on Fifth since the call went out at four-thirty.

'Yo next, Fatso,' said one of them as the bus came up out of the rain and stopped with a sigh from the great vacuum brakes.

'Ahm tahd,' said the thick-set man in the mackintosh. But he pulled his hat down over his eyes and climbed aboard, slotted his coins and moved down the bus, scanning the occupants. He blinked as he saw the two white men, walked on and took the seat directly behind them.

He examined the backs of their necks, their coats and hats and their profiles. Bond sat next to the window. The negro saw the reflection of his scar in the dark glass.

He got up and moved to the front of the bus without looking back. At the next stop he got off the bus and made straight for the nearest drugstore. He shut himself into the paybox.

Whisper questioned him urgently, then broke the connection.

He plugged in on the right of the board.

'Yes?' said the deep voice.

'Boss, one of them's just come in on Fifth. The Limey with the scar. Got a friend with him, but he don't seem to fit the dope on the other two.' Whisper passed on an accurate description of Leiter. 'Coming north, both of them,' he gave the number and probable timing of the bus.

There was a pause.

'Right,' said the quiet voice. 'Call off all Eyes on the other avenues. Warn the night spots that one of them's inside and get this to Tee-Hee Johnson, McThing, Blabbermouth Foley, Sam Miami and The Flannel . . .'

The voice spoke for five minutes.

'Got that? Repeat.'

'Yes, Sir, Boss,' said The Whisper. He glanced at his shorthand pad and whispered fluently and without a pause into the mouthpiece.

'Right.' The line went dead.

His eyes bright, The Whisper took up a fistful of plugs and started talking to the town.

From the moment that Bond and Leiter walked under the canopy of Sugar Ray's on Seventh Avenue at 123rd Street there was a team of men and women watching them or waiting to watch them, speaking softly to The Whisper at the big switchboard on the Riverside Exchange, handing them on towards the rendezvous. In a world where they were naturally the focus of attention, neither Bond nor Leiter felt the hidden machine nor sensed the tension around them.

In the famous night-spot the stools against the long bar were crowded, but one of the small booths against the wall was empty and Bond and Leiter slipped into the two seats with the narrow table between them.

They ordered scotch-and-soda – Haig and Haig Pinchbottle. Bond looked the crowd over. It was nearly all men. There were two or three whites, boxing fans or reporters for the New York sports columns, Bond decided. The atmosphere was warmer, louder than downtown. The walls were covered with boxing photographs, mostly of Sugar Ray Robinson and of scenes from his great fights. It was a cheerful place, doing great business.

'He was a wise guy, Sugar Ray,' said Leiter. 'Let's hope we both know when to stop when the time comes. He stashed plenty away and now he's adding to his pile on the music halls. His percentage of this place must be worth a packet and he owns a lot of real estate around here. He works hard still, but it's not the sort of work that sends you blind or gives you a haemorrhage of the brain. He quit while he was still alive.'

'He'll probably back a Broadway show and lose it all,' said Bond. 'If I quit now and went in for fruit-farming in Kent, I'd most likely hit the worst weather since the Thames froze over, and be cleaned out. One can't plan for everything.'

'One can try,' said Leiter. 'But I know what you mean – better the frying-pan you know than the fire you don't. It isn't a bad life when it consists of sitting in a comfortable bar drinking good whisky. How do you like this corner of the jungle?' He leant forward. 'Just listen in to the couple behind you. From what I've heard they're straight out of "Nigger Heaven".'

Bond glanced carefully over his shoulder.

The booth behind him contained a handsome young negro in an expensive fawn suit with exaggerated shoulders. He was lolling back against the wall with one foot up on the bench beside him. He was paring the nails of his left hand with a small silver pocket-knife, occasionally glancing in bored fashion towards the animation at the bar. His head rested on the back of the booth just behind Bond and a whiff of expensive hair-straightener came from him. Bond took in the artificial parting traced with a razor across the left side of the scalp, through the almost straight hair which was a tribute to his mother's constant application of the hot comb since childhood. The plain black silk tie and the white shirt were in good taste.

Opposite him, leaning forward with concern on her pretty face, was a sexy little negress with a touch of white blood in her. Her jet-black hair, as sleek as the best permanent wave, framed a sweet almond-shaped face with rather slanting eyes under finely drawn eyebrows. The deep purple of her parted, sensual lips was thrilling against the bronze skin. All that Bond could see of her clothes was the bodice of a black satin evening dress, tight and revealing across the firm, small breasts. She wore a plain gold chain round her neck and a plain gold band round each thin wrist.

She was pleading anxiously and paid no heed to Bond's quick embracing glance.

'Listen and see if you can get the hang of it,' said Leiter. 'It's straight Harlem – Deep South with a lot of New York thrown in.'

Bond picked up the menu and leant back in the booth, studying the Special Fried Chicken Dinner at $3.75.

'Cmon, honey,' wheedled the girl. 'How come yuh-all's actin' so tahd tonight?'

'Guess ah jist nacherlly gits tahd listenin' at yuh,' said the man languidly. 'Why'nt yuh hush yo' mouff'n let me 'joy mahself 'n peace 'n qui-yet.'

'Is yuh wan' me tuh go 'way, honey?'

'Yuh kin suit yo sweet self.'

'Aw, honey,' pleaded the girl. 'Don' ack mad at me, honey. Ah was fixin' tuh treat yuh tonight. Take yuh tuh Smalls Par'dise, mebbe. See dem high-yallers shakin' 'n truckin'. Dat Birdie Johnson, da maitre d', he permis me a ringside whenebber Ah come nex'.'

The man's voice suddenly sharpened. 'Wha' dat Birdie he mean tuh yuh, hey?' he asked suspiciously. 'Perzackly,' he paused to let the big word sink in, 'perzackly wha' goes 'tween yuh 'n dat lowdown ornery wuthless Nigguh? Yuh sleepin' wid him mebbe? Guess Ah gotta study 'bout dat little situayshun 'tween yuh an' Birdie Johnson. Mebbe git mahself a betterer gal. Ah jist don' lak gals which runs off ever' which way when Ah jist happen be busticated temporaneously. Yesmam. Ah gotta study 'bout dat little situayshun.' He paused threateningly. 'Sure have,' he added.

'Aw, honey,' the girl was anxious. ''dey ain't no use tryin' tuh git mad at me. Ah done nuthen tuh give yuh recasion tuh ack dat way. Ah jist thunk you mebbe preshiate a ringside at da Par'dise 'nstead of settin' hyah countin' yo troubles. Why, honey, yuh all knows Ah wudden fall fo' dat richcrat ack' of Birdie Johnson. No sir. He don' mean nuthen tuh me. Him duh wusstes' man 'n Harlem, dawg bite me effn he ain't. All da same, he permis me da bestess seats 'nda house 'n Ah sez let's us go set 'n dem, 'n have us a beer 'n a good time. Cmon, honey. Let's git out of hyah. Yuh done look so swell 'n Ah jist wan' mah frens tuh see usn together.'

'Yuh done look okay yoself, honeychile,' said the man, mollified by the tribute to his elegance, 'an' dat's da troof. But Ah mus' spressify dat yuh stays close up tuh me an keeps yo eyes off'n dat lowdown trash 'n his hot pants. 'N Ah may say,' he added threateningly, 'dat ef Ah ketches yuh makin' up tuh dat dope Ah'll jist nachrally whup da hide off'n yo sweet ass.'

'Shoh ting, honey,' whispered the girl excitedly.

Bond heard the man's foot scrape off the seat to the ground.

'Cmon, baby, lessgo. Waiduh!'

Bond put down the menu. 'Got the gist of it,' he said. 'Seems they're interested in much the same things as everyone else – sex, having fun, and keeping up with the Jones's. Thank God they're not genteel about it.'

'Some of them are,' said Leiter. 'Tea-cups, aspidistras and tut-tutting all over the place. The Methodists are almost their strongest sect. Harlem's riddled with social distinctions, the same as any other big city, but with all the colour variations added. Come on,' he suggested, 'let's go and get ourselves something to eat.'

They finished their drinks and Bond called for the check.

'All this evening's on me,' he said. 'I've got a lot of money to get rid of and I've brought three hundred dollars of it along with me.'

'Suits me,' said Leiter, who knew about Bond's thousand dollars.

As the waiter was picking up the change, Leiter suddenly said, 'Know where The Big Man's operating tonight?'

The waiter showed the whites of his eyes.

He leant forward and flicked the table down with his napkin.

'I've got a wife'n kids, Boss,' he muttered out of the corner of his mouth. He stacked the glasses on his tray and went back to the bar.

'Mr Big's got the best protection of all,' said Leiter. 'Fear.'

They went out on to Seventh Avenue. The rain had stopped, but 'Hawkins', the bone-chilling wind from the north which the negroes greet with a reverent 'Hawkins is here', had come instead to keep the streets free of their usual crowds. Leiter and Bond moved with the trickle of couples on the sidewalk. The looks they got were mostly contemptuous or frankly hostile. One or two men spat in the gutter when they had passed.

Bond suddenly felt the force of what Leiter had told him. They were trespassing. They just weren't wanted. Bond felt the uneasiness that he had known so well during the war, when he had been working for a time behind the enemy lines. He shrugged the feeling away.

'We'll go to Ma Frazier's, further up the Avenue,' said Leiter. 'Best food in Harlem, or at any rate it used to be.'

As they went along Bond gazed into the shop windows.

He was struck by the number of barbers' saloons and 'beauticians'. They all advertised various forms of hair-straightener – 'Apex Glossatina, for use with the hot comb', 'Silky Strate. Leaves no redness, no burn' – or nostrums for bleaching the skin. Next in frequency were the haberdashers and clothes shops, with fantastic men's snakeskin shoes, shirts with small aeroplanes as a pattern, peg-top trousers with inch-wide stripes, zoot suits. All the book shops were full of educational literature – how to learn this, how to do that – and comics. There were several shops devoted to lucky charms and various occultisms – *Seven Keys to Power*, 'The Strangest book ever written', with sub-titles such as: 'If you are CROSSED, shows you how to remove and cast it back.' 'Chant your desires in the Silent Tongue.' 'Cast a Spell on Anyone, no matter where.' 'Make any person Love you.' Among the charms were 'High John the Conqueror Root', 'Money Drawing Brand Oil', 'Sachet Powders, Uncrossing Brand', 'Incense, Jinx removing Brand', and the 'Lucky Whamie Hand Charm, giving Protection from Evil. Confuses and Baffles Enemies'.

Bond reflected it was no wonder that the Big Man found Voodooism such a powerful weapon on minds that still recoiled at a white chicken's feather or crossed sticks in the road – right in the middle of the shining capital city of the Western world.

'I'm glad we came up here,' said Bond. 'I'm beginning to get the hang of Mr Big. One just doesn't catch the smell of all this in a country like England. We're a superstitious lot there of course – particularly the Celts – but here one can almost hear the drums.'

Leiter grunted. 'I'll be glad to get back to my bed,' he said. 'But we need to size up this guy before we decide how to get at him.'

Ma Frazier's was a cheerful contrast to the bitter streets. They had an excellent meal of Little Neck Clams and Fried Chicken Maryland with bacon and sweet corn. 'We've got to have it,' said Leiter. 'It's the national dish.'

It was very civilized in the warm restaurant. Their waiter seemed glad to see them and pointed out various celebrities, but when Leiter slipped in a question about Mr Big the waiter seemed not to hear. He kept away from them until they called for their bill.

Leiter repeated the question.

'Sorry, Sah,' said the waiter briefly. 'Ah cain't recall a gemmun of dat name.'

By the time they left the restaurant it was ten-thirty and the Avenue was almost deserted. They took a cab to the Savoy Ballroom, had a scotch-and-soda, and watched the dancers.

'Most modern dances were invented here,' said Leiter. 'That's how good it is. The Lindy Hop, Truckin', the Susie Q, the Shag. All started on that floor. Every big American band you've ever heard of is proud that it once played here – Duke Ellington, Louis Armstrong, Cab Calloway, Noble Sissle, Fletcher Henderson. It's the Mecca of jazz and jive.'

They had a table near the rail round the huge floor. Bond was spellbound. He found many of the girls very beautiful. The music hammered its way into his pulse until he almost forgot what he was there for.

'Gets you, doesn't it?' said Leiter at last. 'I could stay here all night. Better move along. We'll miss out Small's Paradise. Much the same as this, but not quite in the same class. Think I'll take you to "Yeah Man", back on Seventh. After that we must get moving to one of Mr Big's own joints. Trouble is, they don't open till midnight. I'll pay a visit to the washroom while you get the check. See if I can get a line on where we're likely to find him tonight. We don't want to have to go to all his places.'

Bond paid the check and met Leiter downstairs in the narrow entrance hall.

Leiter drew him outside and they walked up the street looking for a cab.

'Cost me twenty bucks,' said Leiter, 'but the word is he'll be at The Boneyard. Small place on Lenox Avenue. Quite close to his headquarters. Hottest strip in town. Girl called G-G Sumatra. We'll have another drink at "Yeah Man" and hear the piano. Move on at about twelve-thirty.'

The big switchboard, now only a few blocks away, was almost quiet. The two men had been checked in and out of Sugar Ray's, Ma Frazier's and the Savoy Ballroom. Midnight had them entering 'Yeah Man'. At twelve-thirty the final call came and then the board was silent.

Mr Big spoke on the house-phone. First to the head waiter.

'Two white men coming in in five minutes. Give them the Z table.'

'Yes, Sir, Boss,' said the head waiter. He hurried across the dance-floor to a table away on the right, obscured from most of the room by a wide pillar. It was next to the Service entrance but with a good view of the floor and the band opposite.

It was occupied by a party of four, two men and two girls.

'Sorry folks,' said the head waiter. 'Been a mistake. Table's reserved. Newspaper men from downtown.'

One of the men began to argue.

'Move, Bud,' said the head waiter crisply. 'Lofty, show these folks to table F. Drinks is on the house. Sam,' he beckoned to another waiter, 'clear the table. Two covers.' The party of four moved docilely away, mollified by the prospect of free liquor. The head waiter put a Reserved sign on table Z, surveyed it and returned to his post at his table-plan on the high desk beside the curtained entrance.

Meanwhile Mr Big had made two more calls on the house-phone. One to the Master of Ceremonies.

'Lights out at the end of G-G's act.'

'Yes, Sir, Boss,' said the MC with alacrity.

The other call was to four men who were playing craps in the basement. It was a long call, and very detailed.

6 Table Z

At twelve forty-five Bond and Leiter paid off their cab and walked in under the sign which announced 'The Boneyard' in violet and green neon.

The thudding rhythm and the sour-sweet smell rocked them as they pushed through the heavy curtains inside the swing door. The eyes of the hat-check girls glowed and beckoned.

'Have you reserved, Sir?' asked the head waiter.

'No,' said Leiter. 'We don't mind sitting at the bar.'

The head waiter consulted his table-plan. He seemed to decide. He put his pencil firmly through a space at the end of the card.

'Party hasn't shown. Guess Ah cain't hold their res'vation all night. This way, please.' He held his card high over his head and led them round the small crowded dance-floor. He pulled out one of the two chairs and removed the 'Reserved' sign.

'Sam,' he called a waiter over. 'Look after these gemmums order.' He moved away.

They ordered scotch-and-soda and chicken sandwiches.

Bond sniffed. 'Marijuana,' he commented.

'Most of the real hep-cats smoke reefers,' explained Leiter. 'Wouldn't be allowed most places.'

Bond looked round. The music had stopped. The small four-piece band, clarinet, double-bass, electric guitar and drums, was moving out of the corner opposite. The dozen or so couples were walking and jiving to their tables and the crimson light was turned off under the glass dance-floor. Instead, pencil-thin lights in the roof came on and hit coloured glass witch-balls, larger than footballs, that hung at intervals round the wall. They were of different hues, golden, blue, green, violet, red. As the beams of light hit them, they glowed like coloured suns. The walls, varnished black, mirrored their reflections as did the sweat on the ebony faces of the men. Sometimes a man sitting between two lights showed cheeks of different colour, green on one side, perhaps, and red on the other. The lighting made it impossible to distinguish features unless they were only a few feet away. Some of the lights turned the girls' lipstick black, others lit their whole faces in a warm glow on one side and gave the other profile the luminosity of a drowned corpse.

The whole scene was macabre and livid, as if El Greco had done a painting by moonlight of an exhumed graveyard in a burning town.

It was not a large room, perhaps sixty foot square. There were about fifty tables and the customers were packed in like black olives in a jar. It was hot and the air was thick with smoke and the sweet, feral smell of two hundred negro bodies. The noise was terrific – an undertone of the jabber of negroes enjoying themselves without restraint, punctuated by sharp bursts of noise, shouts and high giggles, as loud voices called to each other across the room.

'Sweet Jeessus, look who's hyar . . .'

'Where you been keepin yoself, baby . . .'

'Gawd's troof. It's Pinkus . . . Hi Pinkus . . .'

'Cmon over . . .'

'Lemme be . . . Lemme be, I'se telling ya . . .' (The noise of a slap.)

'Where's G-G. Cmon G-G. Strut yo stuff . . .'

From time to time a man or girl would erupt on to the dance-floor and start a wild solo jive. Friends would clap the rhythm. There would be a burst of catcalls and whistles. If it was a girl, there would be cries of 'Strip, strip, strip,' 'Get hot, baby!' 'Shake it, shake it,' and the MC would come out and clear the floor amidst groans and shouts of derision.

The sweat began to bead on Bond's forehead. Leiter leant over and cupped his hands. 'Three exits. Front. Service behind us. Behind the band.' Bond nodded. At that moment he felt it didn't matter. This was nothing new to Leiter, but for Bond it was a close-up of the raw material on which The Big Man worked, the clay in his hands. The evening was gradually putting flesh on the dossiers he had read in London and New York. If the evening ended now, without any closer sight of Mr Big himself, Bond still felt his education in the case would be almost complete. He took a deep draught of his whisky. There was a burst of applause. The MC had come out on to the dance-floor, a tall negro in immaculate tails with a red carnation in his button hole. He stood, holding up his hands. A single white spotlight caught him. The rest of the room went dark.

There was silence.

'Folks,' announced the MC with a broad flash of gold and white teeth. 'This is it.'

There was excited clapping.

He turned to the left of the floor, directly across from Leiter and Bond.

He flung out his right hand. Another spot came on.

'Mistah Jungles Japhet 'n his drums.'

A crash of applause, catcalls, whistles.

Four grinning negroes in flame-coloured shirts and peg-top white trousers were revealed, squatting astride four tapering barrels with rawhide membranes. The drums were of different sizes. The negroes were all gaunt and stringy. The one sitting astride the bass drum rose briefly and shook clasped hands at the spectators.

'Voodoo drummers from Haiti,' whispered Leiter.

There was silence. With the tips of their fingers the drummers began a slow, broken beat, a soft rumba shuffle.

'And now, friends,' announced the MC, still turned towards the drums, 'G-G . . .' he paused, 'SUMATRA.'

The last word was a yell. He began to clap. There was pandemonium in the room, a frenzy of applause. The door behind the drums burst open and two huge negroes, naked except for gold loincloths, ran out on to the floor carrying between them, her arms round their necks, a tiny figure, swathed completely in black ostrich feathers, a black domino across her eyes.

They put her down in the middle of the floor. They bowed down on either side of her until their foreheads met the ground. She took two paces forward. With the spotlight off them, the two negroes melted away into the shadows and through the door.

The MC had disappeared. There was absolute silence save for the soft thud of the drums.

The girl put her hand up to her throat and the cloak of black feathers came away from the front of her body and spread out into a five-foot black fan. She swirled it slowly behind her until it stood up like a peacock's tail. She was naked except for a brief vee of black lace and a black sequin star in the centre of each breast and the thin black domino across her eyes. Her body was small, hard, bronze, beautiful. It was slightly oiled and glinted in the white light.

The audience was silent. The drums began to step up the tempo. The bass drum kept its beat dead on the timing of the human pulse.

The girl's naked stomach started slowly to revolve in time with the rhythm. She swept the black feathers across and behind her again, and her hips started to grind in time with the bass drum. The upper part of her body was motionless. The black feathers swirled again, and now her feet were shifting and her shoulders. The drums beat louder. Each part of her body seemed to be keeping a different time. Her lips were bared slightly from her teeth. Her nostrils began to flare. Her eyes glinted hotly through the diamond slits. It was a sexy, pug-like face – *chienne* was the only word Bond could think of.

The drums thudded faster, a complexity of interlaced rhythms. The girl tossed the big fan off the floor, held her arms up above her head. Her whole body began to shiver. Her belly moved faster. Round and round, in and out. Her legs straddled. Her hips began to revolve in a wide circle. Suddenly she plucked the sequin star off her right breast and threw it into the audience. The first noise came from the spectators, a quiet growl. Then they were silent again. She plucked off the other star. Again the growl and then silence. The drums began to crash and roll. Sweat poured off the drummers. Their hands fluttered like grey flannel on the pale membranes. Their eyes were bulging, distant. Their heads were slightly bent to one side as if they were listening. They hardly glanced at the girl. The audience panted softly, liquid eyes bulging and rolling.

The sweat was shining all over her now. Her breasts and stomach glistened with it. She broke into great shuddering jerks. Her mouth opened and she screamed softly. Her hands snaked down to her sides and suddenly she had torn away the strip of lace. She threw it into the audience. There was nothing now but a single black G-string. The drums went into a hurricane of sexual rhythm. She screamed softly again and then, her arms stretched before her as a balance, she started to lower her body down to the floor and up again. Faster and faster. Bond could hear the audience panting and grunting like pigs at the trough. He felt his own hands gripping the tablecloth. His mouth was dry.

The audience began to shout at her. 'Cmon, G-G. Take it away, Baby. Cmon. Grind Baby, grind.'

She sank to her knees and as the rhythm slowly died so she too went into a last series of juddering spasms, mewing softly.

The drums came down to a slow tom-tom beat and shuffle. The audience howled for her body. Harsh obscenities came from different corners of the room.

The MC came on to the floor. A spot went on him.

'Okay, folks, okay.' The sweat was pouring off his chin. He spread his arms in surrender.

'Da G-G AGREES!'

There was a delighted howl from the audience. Now she would be quite naked. 'Take it off, G-G. Show yoself Baby. Cmon, cmon.'

The drums growled and stuttered softly.

'But, mah friends,' yelled the MC, 'she stipperlates – With da lights OUT!'

There was a frustrated groan from the audience. The whole room was plunged in darkness.

Must be an old gag, thought Bond to himself.

Suddenly all his senses were alert.

The howling of the mob was disappearing, rapidly. At the same time he felt cold air on his face. He felt as if he was sinking.

'Hey,' shouted Leiter. His voice was close but it sounded hollow.

Christ! thought Bond.

Something snapped shut above his head. He put his hand out behind him. It touched a moving wall a foot from his back.

'Lights,' said a voice, quietly.

At the same time both his arms were gripped. He was pressed down in his chair.

Opposite him, still at the table, sat Leiter, a huge negro grasping his elbows. They were in a tiny square cell. To right and left were two more negroes in plain clothes with guns trained on them.

There was the sharp hiss of a hydraulic garage lift and the table settled quietly to the floor. Bond glanced up. There was the faint join of a broad trap-door a few feet above their heads. No sound came through it.

One of the negroes grinned.

'Take it easy, folks. Enjoy da ride?'

Leiter let out one single harsh obscenity. Bond relaxed his muscles, waiting.

'Which is da Limey?' asked the negro who had spoken. He seemed to be in charge. The pistol he held trained lazily on Bond's heart was very fancy. There was a glint of mother-of-pearl between his black fingers on the stock and the long octagonal barrel was finely chased.

'Dis one, Ah guess,' said the negro who was holding Bond's arm. 'He got da scar.'

The negro's grip on Bond's arm was terrific. It was as if he had two fierce tourniquets applied above the elbows. His hands were beginning to go numb.

The man with the fancy gun came round the corner of the table. He shoved the muzzle of his gun into Bond's stomach. The hammer was back.

'You oughtn't to miss at that range,' said Bond.

'Shaddap,' said the negro. He frisked Bond expertly with his left hand – legs, thighs, back, sides. He dug out Bond's gun and handed it to the other armed man.

'Give dat to da Boss, Tee-Hee,' he said. 'Take da Limey up. Yuh go 'long wid em. Da other guy stays wid me.'

'Yassuh,' said the man called Tee-Hee, a paunchy negro in a chocolate shirt and lavender-coloured peg-top trousers.

Bond was hauled to his feet. He had one foot hooked under a leg of the table. He yanked hard. There was a crash of glass and silverware. At the same moment, Leiter kicked out backwards round the leg of his chair. There was a satisfactory 'klonk' as his heel caught his guard's shin. Bond did the same but missed. There was a moment of chaos, but neither of the guards slackened his grip. Leiter's guard picked him bodily out of the chair as if he had been a child, faced him to the wall and slammed him into it. It nearly smashed Leiter's nose. The guard swung him round. Blood was streaming down over his mouth.

The two guns were still trained unwaveringly on them. It had been a futile effort, but for a split second they had regained the initiative and effaced the sudden shock of capture.

'Don' waste yo breff,' said the negro who had been giving the orders. 'Take da Limey away.' He addressed Bond's guard. 'Mr Big's waiten.' He turned to Leiter. 'Yo kin tell yo fren' goodbye,' he said. 'Yo is unlikely be seein' yoselves agin.'

Bond smiled at Leiter. 'Lucky we made a date for the police to meet us here at two,' he said. 'See you at the line-up.'

Leiter grinned back. His teeth were red with blood. 'Commissioner Monahan's going to be pleased with this bunch. Be seeing you.'

'Crap,' said the negro with conviction. 'Get goin'.'

Bond's guard whipped him round and shoved him against a section of the wall. It opened on a pivot into a long bare passage. The man called Tee-Hee pushed past them and led the way.

The door swung to behind them.

7 Mister Big

Their footsteps echoed down the stone passage. At the end there was a door. They went through into another long passage lit by an occasional bare bulb in the roof. Another door and they found themselves in a large warehouse. Cases and bales were stacked in neat piles. There were runways for overhead cranes. From the markings on the crates it seemed to be a liquor store. They followed an aisle across to an iron door. The man called Tee-Hee rang a bell. There was absolute silence. Bond guessed they must have walked at least a block away from the night club.

There was a clang of bolts and the door opened. A negro in evening dress with a gun in his hand stepped aside and they went through into a carpeted hallway.

'Yo kin go on in, Tee-Hee,' said the man in evening dress.

Tee-Hee knocked on a door facing them, opened it and led the way through.

In a high-backed chair, behind an expensive desk, Mr Big sat looking quietly at them.

'Good morning, Mister James Bond.' The voice was deep and soft. 'Sit down.'

Bond's guard led him across the thick carpet to a low armchair in leather and tubular steel. He released Bond's arms and Bond sat down and faced The Big Man across the wide desk.

It was a blessed relief to be rid of the two vice-like hands. All sensation had left Bond's forearms. He let them hang beside him and welcomed the dull pain as the blood started to flow again.

Mr Big sat looking at him, his huge head resting against the back of the tall chair. He said nothing.

Bond at once realized that the photographs had conveyed nothing of this man, nothing of the power and the intellect which seemed to radiate from him, nothing of the oversize features.

It was a great football of a head, twice the normal size and very nearly round. The skin was grey-black, taut and shining like the face of a week-old corpse in the river. It was hairless, except for some grey-brown fluff above the ears. There were no eyebrows and no eyelashes and the eyes were extraordinarily far apart so that one could not focus on them both, but only on one at a time. Their gaze was very steady and penetrating. When they rested on something, they seemed to devour it, to encompass the whole of it. They bulged slightly and the irises were golden round black pupils which were now wide. They were animal eyes, not human, and they seemed to blaze.

The nose was wide without being particularly negroid. The nostrils did not gape at you. The lips were only slightly everted, but thick and dark. They opened only when the man spoke and then they opened wide and drew back from the teeth and the pale pink gums.

There were few wrinkles or creases on the face, but there were two deep clefts above the nose, the clefts of concentration. Above them the forehead bulged slightly before merging with the polished, hairless crown.

Curiously, there was nothing disproportionate about the monstrous head. It was carried on a wide, short neck supported by the shoulders of a giant. Bond knew from the records that he was six and a half foot tall and weighed twenty stone, and that little of it was fat. But the total impression was awe-inspiring, even terrifying, and Bond could imagine that so ghastly a misfit must have been bent since childhood on revenge against fate and against the world that hated because it feared him.

The Big Man was draped in a dinner-jacket. There was a hint of vanity in the diamonds that blazed on his shirt-front and at his cuffs. His huge flat hands rested half-curled on the table in front of him. There were no signs of cigarettes or an ash-tray and the smell of the room was neutral. There was nothing on the desk save a large intercom with about twenty switches and, incongruously, a very small ivory riding-crop with a long thin white lash.

Mr Big gazed with silent and deep concentration across the table at Bond.

After inspecting him carefully in return, Bond glanced round the room.

It was full of books, spacious and restful and very quiet, like the library of a millionaire.

There was one high window above Mr Big's head but otherwise the walls were solid with bookshelves. Bond turned round in his chair. More bookshelves, packed with books. There was no sign of a door, but there might have been any number of doors faced with dummy books. The two negroes who had brought him to the room stood rather uneasily against the wall behind his chair. The whites of their eyes showed. They were not looking at Mr Big, but at a curious effigy which stood on a table in an open space of floor to the right, and slightly behind Mr Big.

Even with his slight knowledge of Voodoo, Bond recognized it at once from Leigh Fermor's description.

A five-foot white wooden cross stood on a raised white pedestal. The arms of the cross were thrust into the sleeves of a dusty black frock-coat whose tails hung down behind the table towards the floor. Above the neck of the coat a battered bowler hat gaped at him, its crown pierced by the vertical bar of the cross. A few inches below the rim, round the neck of the cross, resting on the crossbar, was a deep starched clergyman's collar.

At the base of the white pedestal, on the table, lay an old pair of lemon-coloured gloves. A short malacca stick with a gold knob, its ferrule resting beside the gloves, rose against the left shoulder of the effigy. Also on the table was a battered black top hat.

This evil scarecrow gazed out across the room – God of the Cemeteries and Chief of the Legion of the Dead – Baron Samedi. Even to Bond it seemed to carry a dreadful gaping message.

Bond looked away, back to the great grey-black face across the desk. Mr Big spoke.

'I want you, Tee-Hee.' His eyes shifted. 'You can go, Miami.'

'Yes, Sir, Boss,' they both said together.

Bond heard a door open and close.

Silence fell again. At first, Mr Big's eyes had been focused sharply on Bond. They had examined him minutely. Now, Bond noticed that though the eyes rested on him they had become slightly opaque. They gazed upon Bond without perception. Bond had the impression that the brain behind them was occupied elsewhere.

Bond was determined not to be disconcerted. Feeling had returned to his hands and he moved them towards his body to reach for his cigarettes and lighter.

Mr Big spoke.

'You may smoke, Mister Bond. In case you have any other intentions you may care to lean forward and inspect the keyhole of the drawer in this desk facing your chair. I shall be ready for you in a moment.'

Bond leant forward. It was a large keyhole. In fact, Bond estimated, .45 of an inch in diameter. Fired, Bond supposed, by a foot-switch under the desk. What a bunch of tricks this man was. Puerile. Puerile? Perhaps, after all, not to be dismissed so easily. The tricks – the bomb, the disappearing table – had worked neatly, efficiently. They had not been just empty conceits, designed to impress. Again, there was nothing absurd about this gun. Rather painstaking, perhaps, but, he had to admit, technically sound.

He lit a cigarette and gratefully drew the smoke deep into his lungs. He did not feel particularly worried by his position. He refused to believe he would come to any harm. It would be a clumsy affair to have him disappear a couple of days after he arrived from England unless a very expert accident could be contrived. And Leiter would have to be disposed of at the same time. That would be altogether too much for their two Services and Mr Big must know it. But he was worried about Leiter in the hands of those clumsy black apes.

The Big Man's lips rolled slowly back from his teeth.

'I have not seen a member of the Secret Service for many years, Mister Bond. Not since the war. Your Service did well in the war. You have some able men. I learn from my friends that you are high up in your Service. You have a double-0 number, I believe – 007, if I remember right. The significance of that double-0 number, they tell me, is that you have had to kill a man in the course of some assignment. There cannot be many double-0 numbers in a Service which does not use assassination as a weapon. Whom have you been sent over to kill here, Mister Bond? Not me by any chance?'

The voice was soft and even, without expression. There was a slight mixture of accents, American and French, but the English was almost pedantically accurate, without a trace of slang.

Bond remained silent. He assumed that Moscow had signalled his description.

'It is necessary for you to reply, Mister Bond. The fate of both of you depends upon your doing so. I have confidence in the sources of my information. I know much more than I have said. I shall easily detect a lie.'

Bond believed him. He chose a story he could support and which would cover the facts.

'There are English gold coins circulating in America. Edward IV Rose Nobles,' he said. 'Some have been sold in Harlem. The American Treasury asked for assistance in tracing them since they must come from a British source. I came up to Harlem to see for myself, with a representative of the American Treasury, who I hope is now safely on his way back to his hotel.'

'Mr Leiter is a representative of the Central Intelligence Agency, not of the Treasury,' said Mr Big without emotion. 'His position at this moment is extremely precarious.'

He paused and seemed to reflect. He looked past Bond.

'Tee-Hee.'

'Yassuh, Boss.'

'Tie Mister Bond to his chair.'

Bond half rose to his feet.

'Don't move, Mister Bond,' said the voice softly. 'You have a bare chance of survival if you stay where you are.'

Bond looked at The Big Man, at the golden, impassive eyes.

He lowered himself back into his chair. Immediately a broad strap was passed round his body and buckled tight. Two short straps went round his wrists and tied them to the leather and metal arms. Two more went round his ankles. He could hurl himself and the chair to the floor, but otherwise he was powerless.

Mr Big pressed down a switch on the intercom.

'Send in Miss Solitaire,' he said and centred the switch again.

There was a moment's pause and then a section of the bookcase to the right of the desk swung open.

One of the most beautiful women Bond had ever seen came slowly in and closed the door behind her. She stood just inside the room and

189

stood looking at Bond, taking him in slowly inch by inch, from his head to his feet. When she had completed her detailed inspection, she turned to Mr Big.

'Yes?' she inquired flatly.

Mr Big had not moved his head. He addressed Bond.

'This is an extraordinary woman, Mister Bond,' he said in the same quiet soft voice, 'and I am going to marry her because she is unique. I found her in a cabaret, in Haiti, where she was born. She was doing a telepathic act which I could not understand. I looked into it and I still could not understand. There was nothing to understand. It was telepathy.'

Mr Big paused.

'I tell you this to warn you. She is my inquisitor. Torture is messy and inconclusive. People tell you what will ease the pain. With this girl it is not necessary to use clumsy methods. She can divine the truth in people. That is why she is to be my wife. She is too valuable to remain at liberty. And,' he continued blandly, 'it will be interesting to see our children.'

Mr Big turned towards her and gazed at her impassively.

'For the time being she is difficult. She will have nothing to do with men. That is why, in Haiti, she was called "Solitaire".'

'Draw up a chair,' he said quietly to her. 'Tell me if this man lies. Keep clear of the gun,' he added.

The girl said nothing but took a chair similar to Bond's from beside the wall and pushed it towards him. She sat down almost touching his right knee. She looked into his eyes.

Her face was pale, with the pallor of white families that have lived long in the tropics. But it contained no trace of the usual exhaustion which the tropics impart to the skin and hair. The eyes were blue, alight and disdainful, but, as they gazed into his with a touch of humour, he realized they contained some message for him personally. It quickly vanished as his own eyes answered. Her hair was blue-black and fell heavily to her shoulders. She had high cheekbones and a wide, sensual mouth which held a hint of cruelty. Her jawline was delicate and finely cut. It showed decision and an iron will which were repeated in the straight, pointed nose. Part of the beauty of the face lay in its lack of compromise. It was a face born to command. The face of the daughter of a French Colonial slave-owner.

She wore a long evening dress of heavy white matt silk whose classical line was broken by the deep folds which fell from her shoulders and revealed the upper half of her breasts. She wore diamond earrings, square-cut in broken bands, and a thin diamond bracelet on her left wrist. She wore no rings. Her nails were short and without enamel.

She watched his eyes on her and nonchalantly drew her forearms together in her lap so that the valley between her breasts deepened.

The message was unmistakable and an answering warmth must have showed on Bond's cold, drawn face, for suddenly The Big Man picked up the small ivory whip from the desk beside him and lashed across at her, the thong whistling through the air and landing with a cruel bite across her shoulders.

Bond winced even more than she did. Her eyes blazed for an instant and then went opaque.

'Sit up,' said The Big Man softly, 'you forget yourself.'

She sat slowly more upright. She had a pack of cards in her hands and she started to shuffle them. Then, out of bravado perhaps, she sent him yet another message – of complicity and of more than complicity.

Between her hands, she faced the knave of hearts. Then the queen of spades. She held the two halves of the pack in her lap so that the two court cards looked at each other. She brought the two halves of the pack together until they kissed. Then she riffled the cards and shuffled them again.

At no moment of this dumb show did she look at Bond and it was all over in an instant. But Bond felt a glow of excitement and a quickening of the pulse. He had a friend in the enemy's camp.

'Are you ready, Solitaire?' asked The Big Man.

'Yes, the cards are ready,' said the girl, in a low, cool voice.

'Mister Bond, look into the eyes of this girl and repeat the reason for your presence here which you gave me just now.'

Bond looked into her eyes. There was no message. They were not focused on his. They looked through him.

He repeated what he had said.

For a moment he felt an uncanny thrill. Could this girl tell? If she could tell, would she speak for him or against him?

For a moment there was dead silence in the room. Bond tried to look indifferent. He gazed up at the ceiling – then back at her.

Her eyes came back into focus. She turned away from him and looked at Mr Big.

'He speaks the truth,' she said coldly.

8 No Sensayuma

Mr Big reflected for a moment. He seemed to decide. He pressed a switch on the intercom.

'Blabbermouth?'

'Yassuh, Boss.'

'You're holding that American, Leiter.'

'Yassuh.'

'Hurt him considerably. Ride him down to Bellevue Hospital and dump him nearby. Got that?'

'Yassuh.'

'Don't be seen.'

'Nossuh.'

Mr Big centred the switch.

'God damn your bloody eyes,' said Bond viciously. 'The CIA won't let you get away with this!'

'You forget, Mister Bond. They have no jurisdiction in America. The American Secret Service has no power in America – only abroad. And the FBI are no friends of theirs. Tee-Hee, come here.'

'Yassuh, Boss.' Tee-Hee came and stood beside the desk.

Mr Big looked across at Bond.

'Which finger do you use least, Mister Bond?'

Bond was startled by the question. His mind raced.

'On reflection, I expect you will say the little finger of the left hand,' continued the soft voice. 'Tee-Hee, break the little finger of Mr Bond's left hand.'

The negro showed the reason for his nickname.

'Hee-hee,' he gave a falsetto giggle. 'Hee-hee.'

He walked jauntily over to Bond. Bond clutched madly at the arms of his chair. Sweat started to break out on his forehead. He tried to imagine the pain so that he could control it.

The negro slowly unhinged the little finger of Bond's left hand, immovably bound to the arm of his chair.

He held the tip between finger and thumb and very deliberately started to bend it back, giggling inanely to himself.

Bond rolled and heaved, trying to upset the chair, but Tee-Hee put his other hand on the chair-back and held it there. The sweat poured off Bond's face. His teeth started to bare in an involuntary rictus. Through the increasing pain he could just see the girl's eyes wide upon him, her red lips slightly parted.

The finger stood upright, away from the hand. Started to bend slowly backwards towards his wrist. Suddenly it gave. There was a sharp crack.

'That will do,' said Mr Big.

Tee-Hee released the mangled finger with reluctance.

Bond uttered a soft animal groan and fainted.

'Da guy ain't got no sensayuma,' commented Tee-Hee.

Solitaire sat limply back in her chair and closed her eyes.

'Did he have a gun?' asked Mr Big.

'Yassuh.' Tee-Hee took Bond's Beretta out of his pocket and slipped it across the desk. The Big Man picked it up and looked at it expertly. He weighed it in his hand, testing the feel of the skeleton grip. Then he pumped the shells out on to the desk, verified that he had also emptied the chamber and slid it over towards Bond.

'Wake him up,' he said, looking at his watch. It said three o'clock.

Tee-Hee went behind Bond's chair and dug his nails into the lobes of Bond's ears.

Bond groaned and lifted his head.

His eyes focused on Mr Big and he uttered a string of obscenities.

'Be thankful you're not dead,' said Mr Big without emotion. 'Any pain is preferable to death. Here is your gun. I have the shells. Tee-Hee, give it back to him.'

Tee-Hee took it off the desk and slipped it back into Bond's holster.

'I will explain to you briefly,' continued The Big Man, 'why it is that you are not dead; why you have been permitted to enjoy the sensation of pain instead of adding to the pollution of the Harlem River from the folds of what is jocularly known as a cement overcoat.'

He paused for a moment and then spoke.

'Mister Bond, I suffer from boredom. I am a prey to what the early Christians called "accidie", the deadly lethargy that envelops those who are sated, those who have no more desires. I am absolutely pre-eminent in my chosen profession, trusted by those who occasionally employ my talents, feared and instantly obeyed by those whom I myself employ. I have, literally, no more worlds to conquer within my chosen orbit. Alas, it is too late in my life to change that orbit for another one, and since power is the goal of all ambition, it is unlikely that I could possibly acquire more power in another sphere than I already possess in this one.'

Bond listened with part of his mind. With the other half he was already planning. He sensed the presence of Solitaire, but he kept his eyes off her. He gazed steadily across the table at the great grey face with its unwinking golden eyes.

The soft voice continued.

'Mister Bond, I take pleasure now only in artistry, in the polish and finesse which I can bring to my operations. It has become almost a mania with me to impart an absolute rightness, a high elegance, to the execution of my affairs. Each day, Mister Bond, I try and set myself still higher standards of subtlety and technical polish so that each of my proceedings may be a work of art, bearing my signature as clearly as the creations of, let us say, Benvenuto Cellini. I am content, for the time being, to be my only judge, but I sincerely believe, Mister Bond, that the approach to perfection which I am steadily achieving in my operations will ultimately win recognition in the history of our times.'

Mr Big paused. Bond saw that his great yellow eyes were wide, as if he saw visions. He's a raving megalomaniac, thought Bond. And all the more dangerous because of it. The fault in most criminal minds was that greed was their only impulse. A dedicated mind was quite another matter. This man was no gangster. He was a menace. Bond was fascinated and slightly awestruck.

'I accept anonymity for two reasons,' continued the low voice. 'Because the nature of my operations demands it and because I admire the self-negation of the anonymous artist. If you will allow the conceit, I see myself sometimes as one of those great Egyptian fresco painters who devoted their lives to producing masterpieces in the tombs of kings, knowing that no living eye would ever see them.'

The great eyes closed for a moment.

'However, let us return to the particular. The reason, Mister Bond, why I have not killed you this morning is because it would give me no aesthetic pleasure to blow a hole in your stomach. With this engine,' he gestured towards the gun trained on Bond through the desk drawer, 'I have already blown many holes in many stomachs, so I am quite satisfied that my little mechanical toy is a sound technical achievement. Moreover, as no doubt you rightly surmise, it would be a nuisance for me to have a lot of busybodies around here asking questions about the disappearance of yourself and your friend Mr Leiter. Not more than a nuisance; but for various reasons I wish to concentrate on other matters at the present time.

'So,' Mr Big looked at his watch, 'I decided to leave my card upon each of you and to give you one more solemn warning. You must leave the country today, and Mr Leiter must transfer to another assignment. I have quite enough to bother me without having a lot of agents from Europe added to the considerable strength of local busybodies with which I have to contend.

'That is all,' he concluded. 'If I see you again, you will die in a manner as ingenious and appropriate as I can devise on that day.

'Tee-Hee, take Mister Bond to the garage. Tell two of the men to take him to Central Park and throw him in the ornamental water. He may be damaged but not killed if he resists. Understood?'

'Yassuh, Boss,' said Tee-Hee, giggling in a high falsetto.

He undid Bond's ankles, then his wrists. He took Bond's injured hand and twisted it right up his back. Then with his other hand he undid the strap round his waist. He yanked Bond to his feet.

'Giddap,' said Tee-Hee.

Bond gazed once more into the great grey face.

'Those who deserve to die,' he paused, 'die the death they deserve. Write that down,' he added. 'It's an original thought.'

Then he glanced at Solitaire. Her eyes were bent on the hands in her lap. She didn't look up.

'Git goin,' said Tee-Hee. He turned Bond round towards the wall and pushed him forward, twisting Bond's wrist up his back until his forearm was almost dislocated. Bond uttered a realistic groan and his footsteps faltered. He wanted Tee-Hee to believe that he was cowed and docile. He wanted the torturing grip to ease just a little on his left arm. As it was, any sudden movement would only result in his arm being broken.

Tee-Hee reached over Bond's shoulder and pressed on one of the books in the serried shelves. A large section opened on a central pivot. Bond was pushed through and the negro kicked the heavy section back into place. It closed with a double click. From the thickness of the door, Bond guessed it would be soundproof. They were faced by a short carpeted passage ending in some stairs that led downwards. Bond groaned.

'You're breaking my arm,' he said. 'Look out. I'm going to faint.'

He stumbled again, trying to measure exactly the negro's position behind him. He remembered Leiter's injunction: 'Shins, groin, stomach, throat. Hit 'em anywhere else and you'll just break your hand.'

'Shut yo mouf,' said the negro, but he pulled Bond's hand an inch or two down his back.

This was all Bond needed.

They were half way down the passage with only a few feet more to the top of the stairs. Bond faltered again, so that the negro's body bumped into his. This gave him all the range and direction he needed.

He bent a little and his right hand, straight and flat as a board, whipped round and inwards. He felt it thud hard into the target. The negro screamed shrilly like a wounded rabbit. Bond felt his left arm come free. He whirled round, pulling out his empty gun with his right hand. The negro was bent double, his hands between his legs, uttering little panting screams. Bond whipped the gun down hard on the back of the woolly skull. It gave back a dull klonk as if he had hammered on a door, but the negro groaned and fell forward on his knees, throwing out his hands for support. Bond got behind him and with all the force he could put behind the steel-capped shoe, he gave one mighty kick below the lavender-coloured seat of the negro's pants.

A final short scream was driven out of the man as he sailed the few feet to the stairs. His head hit the side of the iron banisters and then, a twisting wheel of arms and legs, he disappeared over the edge, down into the well. There was a short crash as he caromed off some obstacle, then a pause, then a mingled thud and crack as he hit the ground. Then silence.

Bond wiped the sweat out of his eyes and stood listening. He thrust his wounded left hand into his coat. It was throbbing with pain and swollen to almost twice its normal size. Holding his gun in his right hand, he walked to the head of the stairs and slowly down, moving softly on the balls of his feet.

There was only one floor between him and the spread-eagled body below. When he reached the landing, he stopped again and listened. Quite close, he could hear the high-pitched whine of some form of fast wireless transmitter. He verified that it came from behind one of the two doors on the landing. This must be Mr Big's communications centre. He longed to carry out a quick raid. But his gun was empty and he had no idea how many men he would find in the room. It could only have been the earphones on their ears that had prevented the operators from hearing the sounds of Tee-Hee's fall. He crept on down.

Tee-Hee was either dead or dying. He lay spreadeagled on his back. His striped tie lay across his face like a squashed adder. Bond felt no remorse. He frisked the body for a gun and found one stuck in the waistband of the lavender trousers, now stained with blood. It was a Colt .38 Detective Special with a sawn barrel. All chambers were loaded. Bond slipped the useless Beretta back in its holster. He nestled the big gun into his palm and smiled grimly.

A small door faced him, bolted on the inside. Bond put his ear to it. The muffled sound of an engine reached him. This must be the garage. But the running engine? At that time of the morning? Bond ground his teeth. Of course. Mr Big would have spoken on the intercom and warned them that Tee-Hee was bringing him down. They must be wondering what was holding him. They were probably watching the door for the negro to emerge.

Bond thought for a moment. He had the advantage of surprise. If only the bolts were well-oiled.

His left hand was almost useless. With the Colt in his right, he tested the first bolt with the edge of his damaged hand. It slipped easily back. So did the second. There remained only a press-down handle. He eased it down and pulled the door softly towards him.

It was a thick door and the noise of the engine got louder as the crack widened. The car must be just outside. Any further movement of the door would betray him. He whipped it open and stood facing sideways like a fencer so as to offer as small a target as possible. The hammer lay back on his gun.

A few feet away stood a black sedan, its engine running. It faced the open double doors of the garage. Bright arc-lights lit up the shining bodywork of several other cars. There was a big negro at the wheel of the sedan and another stood near him, leaning against the rear door. No one else was in view.

At sight of Bond the negroes' mouths fell open in astonishment. A cigarette dropped from the mouth of the man at the wheel. Then they both dived for their guns.

Instinctively, Bond shot first at the man standing, knowing he would be quickest on the draw.

The heavy gun roared hollowly in the garage.

The negro clutched his stomach with both hands, staggered two steps towards Bond, and collapsed on his face, his gun clattering on to the concrete.

The man at the wheel screamed as Bond's gun swung on to him. Hampered by the wheel the negro's shooting hand was still inside his coat.

Bond shot straight into the screaming mouth and the man's head crashed against the side window.

Bond ran round the car and opened the door. The negro sprawled horribly out. Bond threw his revolver on to the driving-seat and yanked the body out on to the ground. He tried to avoid the blood. He got into the seat and blessed the running engine and the steering-wheel gear-lever. He slammed the door, rested his injured hand on the left of the wheel and crashed the lever forward.

The hand-brake was still on. He had to lean under the wheel to release it with his right hand.

It was a dangerous pause. As the heavy car surged forward out of the wide doors there was the boom of a gun and a bullet hammered into the bodywork. He tore the wheel round right-handed and there was another shot that missed high. Across the street a window splintered.

The flash came from low down near the floor and Bond guessed that the first negro had somehow managed to reach his gun.

There were no other shots and no sound came from the blank faces of the buildings behind him. As he went through the gears he could see nothing in the driving-mirror except the broad bar of light from the garage shining out across the dark empty street.

Bond had no idea where he was or where he was heading. It was a wide featureless street and he kept going. He found himself driving on the left-hand side and quickly swerved over to the right. His hand hurt terribly but the thumb and forefinger helped to steady the wheel. He tried to remember to keep his left side away from the blood on the door and window. The endless street was populated only by the little ghosts of steam that wavered up out of the gratings in the asphalt that gave access to the piped heat system of the city. The ugly bonnet of the car mowed them down one by one, but in the driving-mirror Bond could see them rising again behind him in a diminishing vista of mildly gesticulating white wraiths.

He kept the big car at fifty. He came to some red traffic lights and jumped them. Several more dark blocks and then there was a lighted avenue. There was traffic and he paused until the lights went green. He turned left and was rewarded by a succession of green lights, each one sweeping him on and further away from the enemy. He checked at an intersection and read the signs. He was on Park Avenue and 116th Street. He slowed again at the next street. It was 115th. He was heading downtown, away from Harlem, back into the City. He kept going. He turned off at 60th Street. It was deserted. He switched off the engine and left the car opposite a fire hydrant. He took the gun off the seat, shoved it down the waistband of his trousers and walked back to Park Avenue.

A few minutes later he flagged a prowling cab and then suddenly he was walking up the steps of the St Regis.

'Message for you, Mr Bond,' said the night porter. Bond kept his left side away from him. He opened the message with his right hand. It was from Felix Leiter, timed at four a.m. 'Call me at once,' it said.

Bond walked to the elevator and was carried up to his floor. He let himself into 2100 and went through into the sitting-room.

So both of them were alive. Bond fell into a chair beside the telephone.

'God Almighty,' said Bond with deep gratitude. 'What a break.'

9 True or False?

Bond looked at the telephone, then he got up and walked over to the sideboard. He put a handful of wilted ice-cubes into a tall glass, poured in three inches of Haig and Haig and swilled the mixture round in the glass to cool and dilute it. Then he drank down half the glass in one long swallow. He put the glass down and eased himself out of his coat. His left hand was so swollen that he could only just get it through the sleeve. His little finger was still crooked back and the pain was vicious as it scraped against the cloth. The finger was nearly black. He pulled down his tie and undid the top of his shirt. Then he picked up his glass, took another deep swallow, and walked back to the telephone.

Leiter answered at once.

'Thank God,' said Leiter with real feeling. 'What's the damage?'

'Broken finger,' said Bond. 'How about you?'

'Blackjack. Knocked out. Nothing serious. They started off by considering all sorts of ingenious things. Wanted to couple me to the compressed-air pump in the garage. Start on the ears and then proceed elsewhere. When no instructions came from The Big Man they got bored and I got to arguing the finer points of Jazz with Blabbermouth, the man with the fancy six-shooter. We got on to Duke Ellington and agreed that we liked our band-leaders to be percussion men, not wind. We agreed the piano or the drums held the band together better than any other solo instrument – Jellyroll Morton, for instance. Apropos the Duke, I told him the crack about the clarinet – "an ill woodwind that nobody blows good". That made him laugh fit to bust. Suddenly we were friends. The other man – The Flannel, he was called – got sour and Blabbermouth told him he could go off duty, he'd look after me. Then The Big Man rang down.'

'I was there,' said Bond. 'It didn't sound so hot.'

'Blabbermouth was worried as hell. He wandered round the room talking to himself. Suddenly he used the blackjack, hard, and I went out. Next thing I knew we were outside Bellevue Hospital. About half after three. Blabbermouth was very apologetic, said it was the least he could have done. I believe him. He begged me not to give him away. Said he was going to report that he'd left me half dead. Of course I promised to leak back some very lurid details. We parted on the best of terms. I got some treatment at the Emergency ward and came home. I was worried to Hell an' gone about you, but after a while the telephone started ringing. Police and FBI. Seems The Big Man has complained that some fool Limey went berserk at The Boneyard early this morning, shot three of his men – two chauffeurs and a waiter, if you please – stole one of his cars and got away, leaving his overcoat and hat in the cloakroom. The Big Man's yelling for action. Of course I warned off the dicks and the FBI, but they're madder'n hell and we've got to get out of town at once. It'll miss the mornings but it'll be splashed all over the afternoon blatts and Radio and TV'll have it. Apart from all that, Mr Big will be after you like a nest of hornets. Anyway, I've got some plans fixed. Now you tell, and God, am I glad to hear your voice!'

Bond gave a detailed account of all that had happened. He forgot nothing. When he had finished, Leiter gave a low whistle.

'Boy,' he said with admiration. 'You certainly made a dent in The

Big Man's machine. But were you lucky. That Solitaire dame certainly seems to have saved your bacon. D'you think we can use her?'

'Could if we could get near her,' said Bond. 'I should think he keeps her pretty close.'

'We'll have to think about that another day,' said Leiter. 'Now we'd better get moving. I'll hang up and call you back in a few minutes. First I'll get the police surgeon round to you right away. Be along in a quarter of an hour or so. Then I'll talk to the Commissioner myself and sort out some of the police angles. They can stall a bit by discovering the car. The FBI'll have to tip off the radio and newspaper boys so that at least we can keep your name out of it and all this Limey talk. Otherwise we shall have the British Ambassador being hauled out of bed and parades by the National Association for the Advancement of Coloured People and God knows what all.' Leiter chuckled down the telephone. 'Better have a word with your chief in London. It's about half after ten their time. You'll need a bit of protection. I can look after the CIA, but the FBI have got a bad attack of "see-here-young-man" this morning. You'll need some more clothes. I'll see to that. Keep awake. We'll get plenty of sleep in the grave. Be calling you.'

He hung up. Bond smiled to himself. Hearing Leiter's cheerful voice and knowing everything was being taken care of had wiped away his exhaustion and his black memories.

He picked up the telephone and talked to the overseas operator. Ten minutes' delay, she said.

Bond walked into his bedroom and somehow got out of his clothes. He gave himself a very hot shower and then an ice-cold one. He shaved and managed to pull on a clean shirt and trousers. He put a fresh clip in his Beretta and wrapped the Colt in his discarded shirt and put it in his suitcase. He was half way through his packing when the telephone rang.

He listened to the zing and echo on the line, the chatter of distant operators, the patches of Morse from aircraft and ships at sea, quickly suppressed. He could see the big, grey building near Regent's Park and imagine the busy switchboard and the cups of tea and a girl saying, 'Yes, this is Universal Export,' the address Bond had asked for, one of the covers used by agents for emergency calls on open lines from abroad. She would tell the Supervisor, who would take the call over.

'You're connected, caller,' said the overseas operator. 'Go ahead, please. New York calling London.'

Bond heard the calm English voice. 'Universal Export. Who's speaking, please?'

'Can I speak to the Managing Director,' said Bond. 'This is his nephew James speaking from New York.'

'Just a moment, please.' Bond could follow the call to Miss Moneypenny and see her press the switch on the intercom. 'It's New York, Sir,' she would say. 'I think it's 007.' 'Put him through,' M would say.

'Yes?' said the cold voice that Bond loved and obeyed.

'It's James, Sir,' said Bond. 'I may need a bit of help over a difficult consignment.'

'Go ahead,' said the voice.

'I went uptown to see our chief customer last night,' said Bond. 'Three of his best men went sick while I was there.'

'How sick?' asked the voice.

'As sick as can be, Sir,' said Bond. 'There's a lot of 'flu about.'

'Hope you didn't catch any.'

'I've got a slight chill, Sir,' said Bond, 'but absolutely nothing to worry about. I'll write to you about it. The trouble is that with all this 'flu about Federated think I will do better out of town.' (Bond chuckled to himself at the thought of M's grin.) 'So I'm off right away with Felicia.'

'Who?' asked M.

'Felicia,' Bond spelled it out. 'My new secretary from Washington.'

'Oh, yes.'

'Thought I'd try that factory you advised at San Pedro.'

'Good idea.'

'But Federated may have other ideas and I hoped you'd give me your support.'

'I quite understand,' said M. 'How's business?'

'Rather promising, Sir. But tough going. Felicia will be typing my full report today.'

'Good,' said M. 'Anything else?'

'No, that's all, Sir. Thanks for your support.'

'That's all right. Keep fit. Goodbye.'

'Goodbye, Sir.'

Bond put down the telephone. He grinned. He could imagine M calling in the Chief of Staff. '007's already tangled up with the FBI. Dam' fool went up to Harlem last night and bumped off three of Mr Big's men. Got hurt himself, apparently, but not much. Got to get out of town with Leiter, the CIA man. Going down to St Petersburg. Better warn A and C. Expect we'll have Washington round our ears before the day's over. Tell A to say I fully sympathize, but that 007 has my full confidence and I'm sure he acted in self-defence. Won't happen again, and so forth. Got that?' Bond grinned again as he thought of Damon's exasperation at having to dish out a lot of soft soap to Washington when he probably had plenty of other Anglo-American snarls to disentangle.

The telephone rang. It was Leiter again.

'Now listen,' he said. 'Everybody's calming down somewhat. Seems the men you got were a pretty nasty trio – Tee-Hee Johnson, Sam Miami and a man called McThing. All wanted on various counts. The FBI's covering up for you. Reluctantly of course, and the Police are stalling like mad. The FBI big brass had already asked my Chief for you to be sent home – got him out of bed, if you please – mostly jealousy, I guess – but we've killed all that. Same time, we've both got to quit town at once. That's all fixed too. We can't go together, so you're taking the train and I'll fly. Jot this down.'

Bond cradled the telephone against his shoulder and reached for a pencil and paper. 'Go ahead,' he said.

'Pennsylvania Station. Track 14. Ten-thirty this morning. "The Silver Phantom". Through train to St Petersburg via Washington, Jacksonville and Tampa. I've got you a compartment. Very luxurious. Car 245, Compartment H. Ticket'll be on the train. Conductor will have it. In the name of Bryce. Just go to Gate 14 and down to the train. Then straight to your compartment and lock yourself in till the train starts. I'm flying down in an hour by Eastern, so you'll be alone from now on. If you get stuck call Dexter, but don't be surprised if he bites your head off. Train gets in around midday tomorrow. Take a cab and go to the Everglades Cabanas, Gulf Boulevard West, on Sunset Beach. That's on a place called Treasure Island where all the beach hotels are. Connected with St Petersburg by a causeway. Cabby'll know it.

'I'll be waiting for you. Got all that? And for God's sake watch out. And I mean it. The Big Man'll get you if he possibly can and a police escort to the train would only put the finger on you. Take a cab and keep out of sight. I'm sending you up another hat and a fawn raincoat. The check's taken care of at the St Regis. That's the lot. Any questions?'

'Sounds fine,' said Bond. 'I've talked to M and he'll square Washington if there's any trouble. Look after yourself too,' he added. 'You'll be next on the list after me. See you tomorrow. So long.'

'I'll watch out,' said Leiter. ''Bye.'

It was half-past six and Bond pulled back the curtains in the sitting-room and watched the dawn come up over the city. It was still dark down in the caverns below but the tips of the great concrete stalagmites were pink and the sun lit up the windows floor by floor as if an army of descending janitors was at work in the buildings.

The police surgeon came, stayed for a painful quarter of an hour and left.

'Clean fracture,' he had said. 'Take a few days to heal. How did you come by it?'

'Caught it in a door,' said Bond.

'You ought to keep away from doors,' commented the surgeon. 'They're dangerous things. Ought to be forbidden by law. Lucky you didn't catch your neck in this one.'

When he had gone, Bond finished packing. He was wondering how soon he could order breakfast when the telephone rang.

Bond was expecting a harsh voice from the Police or the FBI. Instead, a girl's voice, low and urgent, asked for Mr Bond.

'Who's calling?' asked Bond, gaining time. He knew the answer.

'I know it's you,' said the voice, and Bond could feel that it was right up against the mouthpiece. 'This is Solitaire.' The name was scarcely breathed into the telephone.

Bond waited, all his senses pricked to what might be the scene at the other end of the line. Was she alone? Was she speaking foolishly on a house-phone with extensions to which other listeners were now coldly, intently glued? Or was she in a room with only Mr Big's eyes bent carefully on her, a pencil and pad beside him so that he could prompt the next question?

'Listen,' said the voice. 'I've got to be quick. You must trust me. I'm in a drugstore, but I must get back at once to my room. Please believe me.'

Bond had his handkerchief out. He spoke into it. 'If I can reach Mr Bond what shall I tell him?'

'Oh damn you,' said the girl with what sounded like a genuine touch of hysteria. 'I swear by my mother, by my unborn children. I've got to get away. And so have you. You've got to take me. I'll help you. I know a lot of his secrets. But be quick. I'm risking my life here talking to you.' She gave a sob of exasperation and panic. 'For God's sake trust me. You must. You must!'

Bond still paused, his mind working furiously.

'Listen,' she spoke again, but this time dully, almost hopelessly. 'If you don't take me, I shall kill myself. Now will you? Do you want to murder me?'

If it was acting, it was too good acting. It was still an unpardonable gamble, but Bond decided. He spoke directly into the telephone, his voice low.

'If this is a double-cross, Solitaire, I'll get at you and kill you if it's the last thing I do. Have you got a pencil and paper?'

'Wait,' said the girl, excitedly. 'Yes, yes.'

If it had been a plant, reflected Bond, all that would have been ready.

'Be at Pennsylvania Station at ten-twenty exactly. The Silver Phantom to . . .' he hesitated. '. . . to Washington. Car 245, Compartment H. Say you're Mrs Bryce. Conductor has the ticket in case I'm not there already. Go straight to the compartment and wait for me. Got that?'

'Yes,' said the girl, 'and thank you, thank you.'

'Don't be seen,' said Bond. 'Wear a veil or something.'

'Of course,' said the girl. 'I promise. I really promise. I must go.' She rang off.

Bond looked at the dead receiver, then put it down on the cradle. 'Well,' he said aloud. 'That's torn it.'

He got up and stretched. He walked to the window and looked out, seeing nothing. His thoughts raced. Then he shrugged and turned back to the telephone. He looked at his watch. It was seven-thirty.

'Room Service, good morning,' said the golden voice.

'Breakfast, please,' said Bond. 'Pineapple juice, double. Cornflakes and cream. Shirred eggs with bacon. Double portion of Café Espresso. Toast and marmalade.'

'Yes, Sir,' said the girl. She repeated the order. 'Right away.'

'Thank you.'

'You're welcome.'

Bond grinned to himself.

'The condemned man made a hearty breakfast,' he reflected. He sat down by the window and gazed up at the clear sky, into the future.

Up in Harlem, at the big switchboard, The Whisper was talking to the town again, passing Bond's description again to all Eyes: 'All de railroads, all de airports. Fifth Avenue an' 55th Street doors of da San Regis. Mr Big sez we gotta chance da highways. Pass it down da line. All de railroads, all de airports . . .'

10 The Silver Phantom

Bond, the collar of his new raincoat up round his ears, was missed as he came out of the entrance of the St Regis Drugstore on 55th Street, which has a connecting door into the hotel.

He waited in the entrance and leaped at a cruising cab, hooking the door open with the thumb of his injured hand and throwing his light suitcase in ahead of him. The cab hardly checked. The negro with the collecting-box for the Coloured Veterans of Korea and his colleague fumbling under the bonnet of his stalled car stayed on the job until, much later, they were called off by a man who drove past and sounded two shorts and a long on his horn.

But Bond was immediately spotted as he left his cab at the drive-in to the Pennsylvania Station. A lounging negro with a wicker basket walked quickly into a call-box. It was ten-fifteen.

Only fifteen minutes to go and yet, just before the train started, one of the waiters in the diner reported sick and was hurriedly replaced by a man who had received a full and careful briefing on the telephone. The chef swore there was something fishy, but the new man said a word or two to him and the chef showed the whites of his eyes and went silent, surreptitiously touching the lucky bean that hung round his neck on a string.

Bond had walked quickly through the great glass-covered concourse and through Gate 14 down to his train.

It lay, a quarter of a mile of silver carriages, quietly in the dusk of the underground station. Up front, the auxiliary generators of the 4000 horsepower twin Diesel electric units ticked busily. Under the bare electric bulbs the horizontal purple and gold bands, the colours of the Seaboard Railroad, glowed regally on the streamlined locomotives. The engineman and fireman who would take the great train on the first two hundred mile lap into the south lolled in the spotless aluminium cabin, twelve feet above the track, watching the ammeter and the air-pressure dial, ready to go.

It was quiet in the great concrete cavern below the city and every noise threw an echo.

There were not many passengers. More would be taken on at Newark, Philadelphia, Baltimore and Washington. Bond walked a hundred yards, his feet ringing on the empty platform, before he found Car 245, towards the rear of the train. A Pullman porter stood at the door. He wore spectacles. His black face was bored but friendly. Below the windows of the carriage, in broad letters of brown and gold, was written 'Richmond, Fredericksburg and Potomac', and below that 'Bellesylvania', the name of the Pullman car. A thin wisp of steam rose from the couplings of the central heating near the door.

'Compartment H,' said Bond.

'Mr Bryce, Suh? Yassuh. Mrs Bryce just come aboard. Straight down da cyar.'

Bond stepped on to the train and turned down the drab olive

green corridor. The carpet was thick. There was the usual American train-smell of old cigar-smoke. A notice said 'Need a second pillow? For any extra comfort ring for your Pullman Attendant. His name is,' then a printed card, slipped in: 'Samuel D. Baldwin.'

H was more than half-way down the car. There was a respectable-looking American couple in E, otherwise the rooms were empty. The door of H was closed. He tried it and it was locked.

'Who's that?' asked a girl's voice, anxiously.

'It's me,' said Bond.

The door opened. Bond walked through, put down his bag and locked the door behind him.

She was in a black tailor-made. A wide-mesh veil came down from the rim of a small black straw hat. One gloved hand was up to her throat and through the veil Bond could see that her face was pale and her eyes were wide with fear. She looked rather French and very beautiful.

'Thank God,' she said.

Bond gave a quick glance round the room. He opened the lavatory door and looked in. It was empty.

A voice on the platform outside called 'Board!' There was a clang as the attendant pulled up the folding iron step and shut the door and then the train was rolling quietly down the track. A bell clanged monotonously as they passed the automatic signals. There was a slight clatter from the wheels as they crossed some points and then the train began to accelerate. For better or for worse, they were on their way.

'Which seat would you like?' asked Bond.

'I don't mind,' she said anxiously. 'You choose.'

Bond shrugged and sat down with his back to the engine. He preferred to face forwards.

She sat down nervously facing him. They were still in the long tunnel that takes the Philadelphia lines out of the city.

She took off her hat and unpinned the broad-mesh veil and put them on the seat beside her. She took some hairpins out of the back of her hair and shook her head so that the heavy black hair fell forward. There were blue shadows under her eyes and Bond reflected that she too must have gone without sleep that night.

There was a table between them. Suddenly she reached forward and pulled his right hand towards her on the table. She held it in both her hands and bent forward and kissed it. Bond frowned and tried to pull his hand away, but for a moment she held it tight in both of hers.

She looked up and her wide blue eyes looked candidly into his.

'Thank you,' she said. 'Thank you for trusting me. It was difficult for you.' She released his hand and sat back.

'I'm glad I did,' said Bond inadequately, his mind trying to grapple with the mystery of this woman. He dug in his pocket for his cigarettes and lighter. It was a new pack of Chesterfields and with his right hand he scrabbled at the cellophane wrapper.

She reached over and took the pack from him. She slit it with her thumb-nail, took out a cigarette, lit it and handed it to him. Bond took it from her and smiled into her eyes, tasting the hint of lipstick from her mouth.

'I smoke about three packs a day,' he said. 'You're going to be busy.'

'I'll just help with the new packs,' she said. 'Don't be afraid I'm going to fuss over you the whole way to St Petersburg.'

Bond's eyes narrowed and the smile went out of them.

'You don't believe I thought we were only going as far as Washington,' she said. 'You weren't very quick on the telephone this morning. And anyway, Mr Big was certain you would make for Florida. I heard him warning his people down there about you. He spoke to a man called "The Robber", long distance. Said to watch the airport at Tampa and the trains. Perhaps we ought to get off the train earlier, at Tarpon Springs or one of the small stations up the coast. Did they see you getting on the train?'

'Not that I know of,' said Bond. His eyes had relaxed again. 'How about you? Have any trouble getting away?'

'It was my day for a singing lesson. He's trying to make a torch singer out of me. Wants me to go on at The Boneyard. One of his men took me to my teacher as usual and was due to pick me up again at midday. He wasn't surprised I was having a lesson so early. I often have breakfast with my teacher so as to get away from Mr Big. He expects me to have all my meals with him.' She looked at her watch. He noted cynically that it was an expensive one – diamonds and platinum, Bond guessed. 'They'll be missing me in about an hour. I waited until the car had gone, then I walked straight out again and called you. Then I took a cab downtown. I bought a toothbrush and a few other things at a drugstore. Otherwise I've got nothing except my jewellery and the mad money I've always kept hidden from him. About five thousand dollars. So I won't be a financial burden.' She smiled. 'I thought I'd get my chance one day.' She gestured towards the window. 'You've given me a new life. I've been shut up with him and his nigger gangsters for nearly a year. This is heaven.'

The train was running through the unkempt barren plains and swamps between New York and Trenton. It wasn't an attractive prospect. It reminded Bond of some of the stretches on the pre-war Trans-Siberian Railway except for the huge lonely hoardings advertising the current Broadway shows and the occasional dumps of scrap-iron and old motor cars.

'I hope I can find you something better than that,' he said smiling. 'But don't thank me. We're quits now. You saved my life last night. That is,' he added looking at her curiously, 'if you really have got second sight.'

'Yes,' she said, 'I have. Or something very like it. I can often see what's going to happen, particularly to other people. Of course I embroider on it and when I was earning my living doing it in Haiti it was easy to turn it into a good cabaret act. They're riddled with Voodoo and superstitions there and they were quite certain I was a witch. But I promise that when I first saw you in that room I knew you had been sent to save me. I,' she blushed, 'I saw all sorts of things.'

'What sort of things?'

'Oh I don't know,' she said, her eyes dancing. 'Just things. Anyway, we'll see. But it's going to be difficult,' she added seriously, 'and dangerous. For both of us.' She paused. 'So will you please take good care of us?'

'I'll do my best,' said Bond. 'The first thing is for us both to get some sleep. Let's have a drink and some chicken sandwiches and then we'll get the porter to put our beds down. You mustn't be embarrassed,' he added, seeing her eyes recoil. 'We're in this together. We have to spend twenty-four hours in a double bedroom together, and it's no good being squeamish. Anyway, you're Mrs Bryce,' he grinned, 'and you must just act like her. Up to a point anyway,' he added.

She laughed. Her eyes speculated. She said nothing but rang the bell below the window.

The conductor arrived at the same time as the Pullman attendant. Bond ordered Old Fashioneds, and stipulated 'Old Grandad' Bourbon, chicken sandwiches, and decaffeined 'Sanka' coffee so that their sleep would not be spoilt.

'I have to collect another fare from you, Mr Bryce,' said the conductor.

'Of course,' said Bond. Solitaire made a movement towards her handbag. 'It's all right, darling,' said Bond, pulling out his notecase. 'You've forgotten you gave me your money to look after before we left the house.'

'Guess the lady'll need plenty for her summer frocks,' said the conductor. 'Shops is plenty expensive in St Pete. Plenty hot down there too. You folks been to Florida before?'

'We always go at this time of year,' said Bond.

'Hope you have a pleasant trip,' said the conductor.

When the door shut behind him, Solitaire laughed delightedly.

'You can't embarrass me,' she said. 'I'll think up something really fierce if you're not careful. To begin with, I'm going in there,' she gestured towards the door behind Bond's head. 'I must look terrible.'

'Go ahead, darling,' laughed Bond as she disappeared.

Bond turned to the window and watched the pretty clapboard houses slip by as they approached Trenton. He loved trains and he looked forward with excitement to the rest of the journey.

The train was slowing down. They slid past sidings full of empty freight cars bearing names from all over the States – 'Lackawanna', 'Chesapeake and Ohio', 'Lehigh Valley', 'Seaboard Fruit Express', and the lilting 'Acheson, Topeka and Santa Fe' – names that held all the romance of the American railroads.

'British Railways?' thought Bond. He sighed and turned his thoughts back to the present adventure.

For better or worse he had decided to accept Solitaire, or rather, in his cold way, to make the most of her. There were many questions to be answered but now was not the time to ask them. All that immediately concerned him was that another blow had been struck at Mr Big – where it would hurt most, in his vanity.

As for the girl, as a girl, he reflected that it was going to be fun teasing her and being teased back and he was glad that they had already crossed the frontiers into comradeship and even intimacy.

Was it true what The Big Man had said, that she would have nothing to do with men? He doubted it. She seemed open to love and to desire. At any rate he knew she was not closed to him. He wanted her to come back and sit down opposite him again so that he could look at her and play with her and slowly discover her. Solitaire. It was an attractive name. No wonder they had christened her that in the sleazy nightclubs of Port au Prince. Even in her present promise of warmth towards him there was much that was withdrawn and mysterious. He sensed a lonely childhood on some great decaying plantation, an echoing 'Great House' slowly falling into disrepair and being encroached on by the luxuriance of the tropics. The parents dying, and the property being sold. The companionship of a servant or two and an equivocal life in lodgings in the capital. The beauty which was her only asset and the struggle against the shady propositions to be a 'governess', a 'companion', a 'secretary', all of which meant respectable prostitution. Then the dubious, unknown steps into the world of entertainment. The evening stint at the nightclub with the mysterious act which, among people dominated by magic, must have kept many away from her and made her a person to be feared. And then, one evening, the huge man with the grey face sitting at a table by himself. The promise that he would put her on Broadway. The chance of a new life, of an escape from the heat and the dirt and the solitude.

Bond turned brusquely away from the window. A romantic picture, perhaps. But it must have been something like that.

He heard the door unlock. The girl came back and slid into the seat opposite him. She looked fresh and gay. She examined him carefully.

'You have been wondering about me,' she said. 'I felt it. Don't worry. There is nothing very bad to know. I will tell you all about it some day. When we have time. Now I want to forget about the past. I will just tell you my real name. It is Simone Latrelle, but you can call me what you like. I am twenty-five. And now I am happy. I like this little room. But I am hungry and sleepy. Which bed will you have?'

Bond smiled at the question. He reflected.

'It's not very gallant,' he said, 'but I think I'd better have the bottom one. I'd rather be close to the floor – just in case. Not that there's anything to worry about,' he added, seeing her frown, 'but Mr Big seems to have a pretty long arm, particularly in the negro world. And that includes the railroads. Do you mind?'

'Of course not,' she said. 'I was going to suggest it. And you couldn't climb into the top one with your poor hand.'

Their lunch arrived, brought from the diner by a preoccupied negro waiter. He seemed anxious to be paid and get back to his work.

When they had finished and Bond rang for the Pullman porter, he also seemed distrait and avoided looking at Bond. He took his time getting the beds made up. He made much show of not having enough room to move around in.

Finally, he seemed to pluck up courage.

'Praps Mistress Bryce like set down nex' door while Ah git the room fixed,' he said, looking over Bond's head. 'Nex' room goin' to be empty all way to St Pete.' He took out a key and unlocked the communicating door without waiting for Bond's reply.

At a gesture from Bond, Solitaire took the hint. He heard her lock the door into the corridor. The negro bumped the communicating door shut.

Bond waited for a moment. He remembered the negro's name.

'Got something on your mind, Baldwin?' he asked.

Relieved, the attendant turned and looked straight at him.

'Sho' have, Mister Bryce. Yassuh.' Once started, the words came in a torment. 'Shouldn be tellin' yuh this, Mister Bryce, but dere's plenty trouble 'n this train this trip. Yuh gotten yoself a henemy 'n dis train, Mister Bryce. Yassuh. Ah hears tings which Ah don' like at all. Cain't say much. Get mahself 'n plenty trouble. But yuh all want to watch yo step plenty good. Yassuh. Certain party got da finger 'n yuh, Mister Bryce, 'n dat man is bad news. Better take dese hyah,' he reached in his pocket and brought out two wooden window wedges. 'Push dem under the doors,' he said. 'Ah cain't do nuthen else. Git mah throat cut. But Ah don' like any foolin' aroun' wid da customers 'n my cyar. Nossuh.'

Bond took the wedges from him. 'But . . .'

'Cain't help yuh no more, Sah,' said the negro with finality, his hand on the door. 'Ef yuh ring fo me dis evenin', Ah'll fetch yo dinner. Doan yuh go lettin' any person else in the room.'

His hand came out to take the twenty-dollar bill. He crumpled it into his pocket.

'Ah'll do all Ah can, Sah,' he said. 'But dey'll git me ef Ah don' watch it. Sho will.' He went out and quickly shut the door behind him.

Bond thought for a moment then he opened the communicating door. Solitaire was reading.

'He's fixed everything,' he said. 'Took a long time about it. Wanted to tell me all his life-story as well. I'll keep out of your way until you've climbed up to your nest. Call me when you're ready.'

He sat down next door in the seat she had left and watched the grim suburbs of Philadelphia showing their sores, like beggars, to the rich train.

No object in frightening her until it had to be. But the new threat had come sooner than he expected, and her danger if the watcher on the train discovered her identity would be as great as his.

She called and he went in.

The room was in darkness save for his bed-light, which she had turned on.

'Sleep well,' she said.

Bond got out of his coat. He quietly slipped the wedges firmly under both doors. Then he lay down carefully on his right side on the comfortable bed and without a thought for the future fell into a deep sleep, lulled by the pounding gallop of the train.

A few cars away, in the deserted diner, a negro waiter read again what he had written on a telegraph blank and waited for the ten-minute stop at Philadelphia.

11 Allumeuse

The crack train thundered on through the bright afternoon towards the south. They left Pennsylvania behind, and Maryland. There came a long halt at Washington, where Bond heard through his dreams the measured clang of the warning bells on the shunting engines and the soft think-speak of the public-address system on the station. Then on into Virginia. Here the air was already softer and the dusk, only five hours away from the bright frosty breath of New York, smelled almost of spring.

An occasional group of negroes, walking home from the fields, would hear the distant rumble on the silent sighing silver rails and one would pull out his watch and consult it and announce, 'Hyah comes da Phantom. Six o'clock. Guess ma watch is right on time.' 'Sho nuff,' one of the others would say as the great beat of the Diesels came nearer and the lighted coaches streaked past and on towards North Carolina.

They awoke around seven to the hasty ting of a grade-crossing alarm bell as the big train nosed its way out of the fields into the suburbs of Raleigh. Bond pulled the wedges from under the doors before he turned on the lights and rang for the attendant.

He ordered dry Martinis and when the two little 'personalized' bottles appeared with the glasses and the ice they seemed so inadequate that he at once ordered four more.

They argued over the menu. The fish was described as being 'Made From Flaky Tender Boneless Filets' and the chicken as 'Delicious French Fried to a Golden Brown, Served Disjointed'.

'Eyewash,' said Bond, and they finally ordered scrambled eggs and bacon and sausages, a salad, and some of the domestic Camembert that is one of the most welcome surprises on American menus.

It was nine o'clock when Baldwin came to clear the dishes away. He asked if there was anything else they wanted.

Bond had been thinking. 'What time do we get into Jacksonville?' he asked.

'Aroun' five 'n the morning, Suh.'

'Is there a subway on the platform?'

'Yassuh. Dis cyar stops right alongside.'

'Could you have the door open and the steps down pretty quick?'

The negro smiled. 'Yassuh. Ah kin take good care of that.'

Bond slipped him a ten-dollar bill. 'Just in case I miss you when we arrive in St Petersburg,' he said.

The negro grinned. 'Ah greatly preeshiate yo kindness, Suh. Good night, Suh. Good night, Mam.'

He went out and closed the door.

Bond got up and pushed the wedges firmly under the two doors.

'I see,' said Solitaire. 'So it's like that.'

'Yes,' said Bond. 'I'm afraid so.' He told her of the warning he had had from Baldwin.

'I'm not surprised,' said the girl when he had finished. 'They must have seen you coming into the station. He's got a whole team of spies called "The Eyes" and when they're put out on a job it's almost impossible to get by them. I wonder who he's got on the train. You can be certain it's a negro, either a Pullman attendant or someone in the diner. He can make these people do absolutely anything he likes.'

'So it seems,' said Bond. 'But how does it work? What's he got on them?'

She looked out of the window into the tunnel of darkness through which the lighted train was burning its thundering path. Then she looked back across the table into the cool wide grey-blue eyes of the English agent. She thought: how can one explain to someone with that certainty of spirit, with that background of common sense, brought up with clothes and shoes among the warm houses and the lighted streets? How can one explain to someone who hasn't lived close to the secret heart of the tropics, at the mercy of their anger and stealth and poison; who hasn't experienced the mystery of the drums, seen the quick workings of magic and the mortal dread it inspires? What can he know of catalepsy, and thought-transference and the sixth sense of fish, of birds, of negroes; the deadly meaning of a white chicken's feather, a crossed stick in the road, a little leather bag of bones and herbs? What of Mialism, of shadow-taking, of the death by swelling and the death by wasting?

She shivered and a whole host of dark memories clustered round her. Above all, she remembered that first time in the Houmfor where her black nurse had once taken her as a child. 'It do yuh no harm, Missy. Dis powerful good juju. Care fe yuh res 'f yo life.' And the disgusting old man and the filthy drink he had given her. How her nurse had held her jaws open until she had drunk the last drop and how she had lain awake screaming every night for a week. And how her nurse had been worried and then suddenly she had slept all right until, weeks later, shifting on her pillow, she had felt something hard and had dug it out from the pillow-case, a dirty little packet of muck. She had thrown it out of the window, but in the morning she could not find it. She had continued to sleep well and she knew it must have been found by the nurse and secreted somewhere under the floorboards.

Years later, she had found out about the Voodoo drink – a concoction of rum, gunpowder, grave-dirt and human blood. She almost retched as the taste came back to her mouth.

What could this man know of these things or of her half-belief in them?

She looked up and found Bond's eyes fixed quizzically on her.

'You're thinking I shan't understand,' he said. 'And you're right up to a point. But I know what fear can do to people and I know that fear can be caused by many things. I've read most of the books on Voodoo and I believe that it works. I don't think it would work on me because I stopped being afraid of the dark when I was a child and I'm not a good subject for suggestion or hypnotism. But I know the jargon and you needn't think I shall laugh at it. The scientists and doctors who wrote the books don't laugh at it.'

Solitaire smiled. 'All right,' she said. 'Then all I need tell you is that they believe The Big Man is the Zombie of Baron Samedi. Zombies are bad enough by themselves. They're animated corpses that have been made to rise from the dead and obey the commands of the person who controls them. Baron Samedi is the most dreadful spirit in the whole of Voodooism. He is the spirit of darkness and death. So for Baron Samedi to be in control of his own Zombie is a very dreadful conception. You know what Mr Big looks like. He is huge and grey and he has great psychic power. It is not difficult for a negro to believe that he is a Zombie and a very bad one at that. The step to Baron Samedi is simple. Mr Big encourages the idea by having the Baron's fetish at his elbow. You saw it in his room.'

She paused. She went on quickly, almost breathlessly: 'And I can tell you that it works and that there's hardly a negro who has seen him and heard the story who doesn't believe it and who doesn't regard him with complete and absolute dread. And they are right,' she added. 'And you would say so too if you knew the way he deals with those who haven't obeyed him completely, the way they are tortured and killed.'

'Where does Moscow come in?' asked Bond. 'Is it true he's an agent of SMERSH?'

'I don't know what SMERSH is,' said the girl, 'but I know he works for Russia, at least I've heard him talking Russian to people who come from time to time. Occasionally he's had me in to that room and asked me afterwards what I thought of his visitors. Generally it seemed to me they were telling the truth although I couldn't understand what they said. But don't forget I've only known him for a year and he's fantastically secretive. If Moscow does use him they've got hold of one of the most powerful men in America. He can find out almost anything he wants to and if he doesn't get what he wants somebody gets killed.'

'Why doesn't someone kill him?' asked Bond.

'You can't kill him,' she said. 'He's already dead. He's a Zombie.'

'Yes, I see,' said Bond slowly. 'It's quite an impressive arrangement. Would you try?'

She looked out of the window, then back at him.

'As a last resort,' she admitted unwillingly. 'But don't forget I come from Haiti. My brain tells me I could kill him, but . . .' She made a helpless gesture with her hands. '. . . my instinct tells me I couldn't.'

She smiled at him docilely. 'You must think me a hopeless fool,' she said.

Bond reflected. 'Not after reading all those books,' he admitted. He put his hand across the table and covered hers with it. 'When the time comes,' he said, smiling, 'I'll cut a cross in my bullet. That used to work in the old days.'

She looked thoughtful. 'I believe that if anybody can do it, you can,' she said. 'You hit him hard last night in exchange for what he did to you.' She took his hand in hers and pressed it. 'Now tell me what I must do.'

'Bed,' said Bond. He looked at his watch. It was ten o'clock. 'Might as well get as much sleep as we can. We'll slip off the train at Jacksonville and chance being spotted. Find another way down to the Coast.'

They got up. They stood facing each other in the swaying train.

Suddenly Bond reached out and took her in his right arm. Her arms went round his neck and they kissed passionately. He pressed her up against the swaying wall and held her there. She took his face between her two hands and held it away, panting. Her eyes were bright and hot. Then she brought his lips against hers again and kissed him long and lasciviously, as if she was the man and he the woman.

Bond cursed the broken hand that prevented him exploring her body, taking her. He freed his right hand and put it between their bodies, feeling her hard breasts, each with its pointed stigma of desire. He slipped it down her back until it came to the cleft at the base of her spine and he let it rest there, holding the centre of her body hard against him until they had kissed enough.

She took her arms away from around his neck and pushed him away.

'I hoped I would one day kiss a man like that,' she said. 'And when I first saw you, I knew it would be you.'

Her arms were down by her sides and her body stood there, open to him, ready for him.

'You're very beautiful,' said Bond. 'You kiss more wonderfully than any girl I have ever known.' He looked down at the bandages on his left hand. 'Curse this arm,' he said. 'I can't hold you properly or make love to you. It hurts too much. That's something else Mr Big's got to pay for.'

She laughed.

She took a handkerchief out of her bag and wiped the lipstick off his mouth. Then she brushed the hair away from his forehead, and kissed him again, lightly and tenderly.

'It's just as well,' she said. 'There are too many other things on our minds.'

The train rocked him back against her.

He put his hand on her left breast and kissed her white throat. Then he kissed her mouth.

He felt the pounding of his blood softening. He took her by the hand and drew her out into the middle of the little swaying room.

He smiled. 'Perhaps you're right,' he said. 'When the time comes I want to be alone with you, with all the time in the world. Here there is at least one man who will probably disturb our night. And we'll have to be up at four in the morning anyway. So there simply isn't time to begin making love to you now. You get ready for bed and I'll climb up after you and kiss you good night.'

They kissed once more, slowly, then he stepped away.

'We'll just see if we have company next door,' he said.

He softly pulled the wedge away from under the communicating door and gently turned the lock. He took the Beretta out of its holster, thumbed back the safety-catch and gestured to her to pull open the door so that she was behind it. He gave the signal and she wrenched it quickly open. The empty compartment yawned sarcastically at them.

Bond smiled at her and shrugged his shoulders.

'Call me when you're ready,' he said and went in and closed the door.

The door to the corridor was locked. The room was identical with theirs. Bond went over it very carefully for vulnerable points. There was only the airconditioning vent in the ceiling and Bond, who was prepared to consider any possibility, dismissed the employment of gas in the system. It would slay all the other occupants of the car. There only remained the waste pipes in the small lavatory and while these certainly could be used to insert some death-dealing medium from the underbelly of the train, the operator would have to be a daring and skilled acrobat. There was no ventilating grill into the corridor.

Bond shrugged his shoulders. If anyone came, it would be through the doors. He would just have to stay awake.

Solitaire called for him. The room smelled of Balmain's 'Vent Vert'.

She was leaning on her elbow and looking down at him from the upper berth.

The bedclothes were pulled up round her shoulder. Bond guessed that she was naked. Her black hair fell away from her head in a dark cascade. With only the reading-lamp on behind her, her face was in shadow. Bond climbed up the little aluminium ladder and leant towards her. She reached towards him and suddenly the bedclothes fell away from her shoulders.

'Damn you,' said Bond. 'You . . .'

She put her hand over his mouth.

'"Allumeuse" is the nice word for it,' she said. 'It is fun for me to be able to tease such a strong silent man. You burn with such an angry flame. It is the only game I have to play with you and I shan't be able to play it for long. How many days until your hand is well again?'

Bond bit hard into the soft hand over his mouth. She gave a little scream.

'Not many,' said Bond. 'And then one day when you're playing your little game you'll suddenly find yourself pinned down like a butterfly.'

She put her arms round him and they kissed, long and passionately.

Finally she sank back among the pillows.

'Hurry up and get well,' she said. 'I'm tired of my game already.'

Bond climbed down to the floor and pulled her curtains across the berth.

'Try and get some sleep now,' he said. 'We've got a long day tomorrow.'

She murmured something and he heard her turn over. She switched off the light.

Bond verified that the wedges were in place under the doors. Then he took off his coat and tie and lay down on the bottom berth. He turned off his own light and lay thinking of Solitaire and listening to the steady gallop of the wheels beneath his head and the comfortable small noises in the room, the gentle rattles and squeaks and murmurs in the coachwork that bring sleep so quickly on a train at night-time.

It was eleven o'clock and the train was on the long stretch between Columbia and Savannah, Georgia. There were another six hours or so to Jacksonville, another six hours of darkness during which The

Big Man would almost certainly have instructed his agent to make some move, while the whole train was asleep and while a man could use the corridors without interference.

The great train snaked on through the dark, pounding out the miles through the empty plains and mingy hamlets of Georgia, the 'Peach State', the angry moan of its four-toned wind-horn soughing over the wide savannah and the long shaft of its single searchlight ripping the black calico of the night.

Bond turned on his light again and read for a while, but his thoughts were too insistent and he soon gave up and switched the light off. Instead, he thought of Solitaire and of the future and of the more immediate prospects of Jacksonville and St Petersburg and of seeing Leiter again.

Much later, around one o'clock in the morning, he was dozing and on the edge of sleep, when a soft metallic noise quite close to his head brought him wide awake with his hand on his gun.

There was someone at the passage door and the lock was being softly tried.

Bond was immediately on the floor and moving silently on his bare feet. He gently pulled the wedge away from under the door to the next compartment and as gently pulled the bolt and opened the door. He crossed the next compartment and softly began to open the door to the corridor.

There was a deafening click as the bolt came back. He tore the door open and threw himself into the corridor, only to see a flying figure already nearing the forward end of the car.

If his two hands had been free he could have shot the man, but to open the doors he had to tuck his gun into the waistband of his trousers. Bond knew that pursuit would be hopeless. There were too many empty compartments into which the man could dodge and quietly close the door. Bond had worked all this out beforehand. He knew his only chance would be surprise and either a quick shot or the man's surrender.

He walked a few steps to Compartment H. A tiny diamond of paper protruded into the corridor.

He went back and into their room, locking the doors behind him.

He softly turned on his reading light. Solitaire was still asleep. The rest of the paper, a single sheet, lay on the carpet against the passage door. He picked it up and sat on the edge of his bed.

It was a sheet of cheap ruled notepaper. It was covered with irregular lines of writing in rough capitals, in red ink. Bond handled it gingerly, without much hope that it would yield any prints. These people weren't like that.

> *Oh Witch* [he read] *do not slay me,*
> *Spare me. His is the body.*
>
> *The divine drummer declares that*
> *When he rises with the dawn*
> *He will sound his drums for* YOU *in the morning*
> *Very early, very early, very early, very early.*
> *Oh Witch that slays the children of men before they are fully matured*
> *Oh Witch that slays the children of men before they are fully matured*
> *The divine drummer declares that*
> *When he rises with the dawn*
> *He will sound his drums for* YOU *in the morning*
> *Very early, very early, very early, very early.*
> *We are addressing* YOU
> *And* YOU *will understand.*

Bond lay down on his bed and thought.

Then he folded the paper and put it in his pocket-book.

He lay on his back and looked at nothing, waiting for daybreak.

12 The Everglades

It was around five o'clock in the morning when they slipped off the train at Jacksonville.

It was still dark and the naked platforms of the great Florida junction were sparsely lit. The entrance to the subway was only a few yards from Car 245 and there was no sign of life on the sleeping train

224

as they dived down the steps. Bond had told the attendant to keep the door of their compartment locked after they had gone and the blinds drawn and he thought there was quite a chance they would not be missed until the train reached St Petersburg.

They came out of the subway into the booking-hall. Bond verified that the next express for St Petersburg would be the Silver Meteor, the sister train of the Phantom, due at about nine o'clock, and he booked two Pullman seats on it. Then he took Solitaire's arm and they walked out of the station into the warm dark street.

There were two or three all-night diners to choose from and they pushed through the door that announced 'Good Eats' in the brightest neon. It was the usual sleazy food-machine – two tired waitresses behind a zinc counter loaded with cigarettes and candy and paper-backs and comics. There was a big coffee percolator and a row of butane gas-rings. A door marked 'Restroom' concealed its dreadful secrets next to a door marked 'Private' which was probably the back entrance. A group of overalled men at one of the dozen stained crueted tables looked up briefly as they came in and then resumed their low conversation. Relief crews for the Diesels, Bond guessed.

There were four narrow booths on the right of the entrance and Bond and Solitaire slipped into one of them. They looked dully at the stained menu card.

After a time, one of the waitresses sauntered over and stood leaning against the partition, running her eyes over Solitaire's clothes.

'Orange juice, coffee, scrambled eggs, twice,' said Bond briefly.

' 'Kay,' said the girl. Her shoes lethargically scuffed the floor as she sauntered away.

'The scrambled eggs'll be cooked with milk,' said Bond. 'But one can't eat boiled eggs in America. They look so disgusting without their shells, mixed up in a tea-cup the way they do them here. God knows where they learned the trick. From Germany, I suppose. And bad American coffee's the worst in the world, worse even than in England. I suppose they can't do much harm to the orange juice. After all we are in Florida now.' He suddenly felt depressed by the thought of their four-hour wait in this unwashed, dog-eared atmosphere.

'Everybody's making easy money in America these days,' said

Solitaire. 'That's always bad for the customer. All they want is to strip a quick dollar off you and toss you out. Wait till you get down to the coast. At this time of the year, Florida's the biggest sucker-trap on earth. On the East Coast they fleece the millionaires. Where we're going they just take it off the little man. Serves him right, of course. He goes there to die. He can't take it with him.'

'For heaven's sake,' said Bond, 'what sort of a place are we going to?'

'Everybody's nearly dead in St Petersburg,' explained Solitaire. 'It's the Great American Graveyard. When the bank clerk or the post-office worker or the railroad conductor reaches sixty he collects his pension or his annuity and goes to St Petersburg to get a few years' sunshine before he dies. It's called "The Sunshine City". The weather's so good that the evening paper there, the *Independent*, is given away free any day the sun hasn't shone by edition time. It only happens three or four times a year and it's a fine advertisement. Everybody goes to bed around nine o'clock in the evening and during the day the old folks play shuffleboard and bridge, herds of them. There's a couple of baseball teams down there, the "Kids" and the "Kubs", all over seventy-five! Then they play bowls, but most of the time they sit squashed together in droves on things called "Sidewalk Davenports", rows of benches up and down the sidewalks of the main streets. They just sit in the sun and gossip and doze. It's a terrifying sight, all these old people with their spectacles and hearing-aids and clicking false-teeth.'

'Sounds pretty grim,' said Bond. 'Why the hell did Mr Big choose this place to operate from?'

'It's perfect for him,' said Solitaire seriously. 'There's practically no crime, except cheating at bridge and Canasta. So there's a very small police force. There's quite a big Coastguard Station but it's mainly concerned with smuggling between Tampa and Cuba, and sponge-fishing out of season at Tarpon Springs. I don't really know what he does there except that he's got a big agent called "The Robber". Something to do with Cuba, I expect,' she added thoughtfully. 'Probably mixed up with Communism. I believe Cuba comes under Harlem and runs red agents all through the Caribbean.

'Anyway,' she went on, 'St Petersburg is probably the most innocent town in America. Everything's very "folksy" and "gracious". It's true there's a place called "The Restorium", a hospital for alcoholics. But very old ones, I suppose,' she laughed, 'and I expect they're past doing anyone any harm. You'll love it,' she smiled maliciously at Bond. 'You'll probably want to settle down there for life and be an "Oldster" too. That's the great word down there . . . "oldster".'

'God forbid,' said Bond fervently. 'It sounds rather like Bourne-mouth or Torquay. But a million times worse. I hope we don't get into a shooting match with "The Robber" and his friends. We'd probably hurry a few hundred oldsters off to the cemetery with heart-failure. But isn't there anyone young in this place?'

'Oh yes,' laughed Solitaire. 'Plenty of them. All the local inhabitants who take the money off the oldsters, for instance. The people who own the motels and the trailer-camps. You could make plenty of money running the bingo tournaments. I'll be your "barker" – the girl outside who gets the suckers in. Dear Mr Bond,' she reached over and pressed his hand, 'will you settle down with me and grow old gracefully in St Petersburg?'

Bond sat back and looked at her critically. 'I want a long time of disgraceful living with you first,' he said with a grin. 'I'm probably better at that. But it suits me that they go to bed at nine down there.'

Her eyes smiled back at him. She took her hand away from his as their breakfast arrived. 'Yes,' she said. 'You go to bed at nine. Then I shall slip out by the back door and go on the tiles with the Kids and the Kubs.'

The breakfast was as bad as Bond had prophesied.

When they had paid they wandered over to the station waiting-room.

The sun had risen and the light swarmed in dusty bars into the vaulted, empty hall. They sat together in a corner and until the Silver Meteor came in Bond plied her with questions about The Big Man and all she could tell him about his operations.

Occasionally he made a note of a date or a name but there was little she could add to what he knew. She had an apartment to herself in the same Harlem block as Mr Big and she had been kept virtually a prisoner there for the past year. She had two tough negresses as 'companions' and was never allowed out without a guard.

From time to time Mr Big would have her brought over to the room where Bond had seen him. There she would be told to divine whether some man or woman, generally bound to the chair, was lying or not. She varied her replies according to whether she sensed these people were good or evil. She knew that her verdict might often be a death sentence but she felt indifferent to the fate of those she judged to be evil. Very few of them were white.

Bond jotted down the dates and details of all these occasions.

Everything she told him added to the picture of a very powerful and active man, ruthless and cruel, commanding a huge network of operations.

All she knew of the gold coins was that she had several times had to question men on how many they had passed and the price they had been paid for them. Very often, she said, they were lying on both counts.

Bond was careful to divulge very little of what he himself knew or guessed. His growing warmth towards Solitaire and his desire for her body were in a compartment which had no communicating door with his professional life.

The Silver Meteor came in on time and they were both relieved to be on their way again and to get away from the dreary world of the big junction.

The train sped on down through Florida, through the forests and swamps, stark and bewitched with Spanish moss, and through the mile upon mile of citrus groves.

All through the centre of the state the moss lent a dead, spectral feeling to the landscape. Even the little townships through which they passed had a grey skeletal aspect with their dried-up, sun-sucked clapboard houses. Only the citrus groves laden with fruit looked green and alive. Everything else seemed baked and desiccated with the heat.

Looking out at the gloomy silent withered forests, Bond thought that nothing could be living in them except bats and scorpions, horned toads and black widow spiders.

They had lunch and then suddenly the train was running along the Gulf of Mexico, through the mangrove swamps and palm groves, endless motels and caravan sites, and Bond caught the smell of the other Florida, the Florida of the advertisements, the land of 'Miss Orange Blossom 1954'.

They left the train at Clearwater, the last station before St Petersburg. Bond took a cab and gave the address on Treasure Island, half an hour's drive away. It was two o'clock and the sun blazed down out of a cloudless sky. Solitaire insisted on taking off her hat and veil. 'It's sticking to my face,' she said. 'Hardly a soul has ever seen me down here.'

A big negro with a face pitted with ancient smallpox was held up in his cab at the same time as they were checked at the intersection of Park Street and Central Avenue, where the Avenue runs on to the long Treasure Island causeway across the shallow waters of Boca Ciega Bay.

When the negro saw Solitaire's profile his mouth fell open. He pulled his cab into the kerb and dived into a drugstore. He called a St Petersburg number.

'Dis is Poxy,' he said urgently into the mouthpiece. 'Gimme da Robber 'n step on it. Dat you, Robber? Lissen, Da Big Man muss be n'town. Whaddya mean yuh jes talked wit him 'n New York? Ah jes seen his gal 'n a Clearwater cab, one of da Stassen Company's. Headin' over da Causeway. Sho Ahm sartin. Cross ma heart. Couldn mistake dat eyeful. Wid a man 'n a blue suit, grey Stetson. Seemed like a scar down his face. Whaddya mean, follow 'em? Ah jes couldn believe yuh wouldn tell me da Big Man wuz 'n town ef he wuz. Thought mebbe Ahd better check 'n make sho. Okay, okay. Ah'll ketch da cab when he comes back over da Causeway, else at Clearwater. Okay, okay. Keep yo shirt on. Ah ain't done nuthen wrong.'

The man called 'The Robber' was through to New York in five minutes. He had been warned about Bond but he couldn't understand where Solitaire tied in to the picture. When he had finished talking to The Big Man he still didn't know, but his instructions were quite definite.

He rang off and sat for a while drumming his fingers on his desk. Ten Grand for the job. He'd need two men. That would leave eight Grand for him. He licked his lips and called a poolroom in a downtown bar in Tampa.

Bond paid off the cab at The Everglades, a group of neat white-and-yellow clapboard cottages set on three sides of a square of Bahama grass which ran fifty yards down to a bone-white beach and then to the sea. From there, the whole Gulf of Mexico stretched away, as calm as a mirror, until the heat-haze on the horizon married it into the cloudless sky.

After London, after New York, after Jacksonville, it was a sparkling transition.

Bond went through a door marked 'Office' with Solitaire demurely at his heels. He rang a bell that said, 'Manageress: Mrs Stuyvesant', and a withered shrimp of a woman with blue-rinsed hair appeared and smiled with her pinched lips. 'Yes?'

'Mr Leiter?'

'Oh yes, you're Mr Bryce. Cabana Number One, right down on the beach. Mr Leiter's been expecting you since lunchtime. And . . . ?' She heliographed with her pince-nez towards Solitaire.

'Mrs Bryce,' said Bond.

'Ah yes,' said Mrs Stuyvesant, wishing to disbelieve. 'Well, if you'd care to sign the register, I'm sure you and Mrs Bryce would like to freshen up after the journey. The full address, please. Thank you.'

She led them out and down the cement path to the end cottage on the left. She knocked and Leiter appeared. Bond had looked forward to a warm welcome, but Leiter seemed staggered to see him. His mouth hung open. His straw-coloured hair, still faintly black at the roots, looked like a haystack.

'You haven't met my wife, I think,' said Bond.

'No, no, I mean, yes. How do you do?'

The whole situation was beyond him. Forgetting Solitaire, he almost dragged Bond through the door. At the last moment he remembered the girl and seized her with his other hand and pulled her in too, banging the door shut with his heel so that Mrs Stuyvesant's 'I hope you have a happy . . .' was guillotined before the 'stay'.

Once inside, Leiter could still not take them in. He stood and gaped from one to the other.

Bond dropped his suitcase on the floor of the little lobby. There were two doors. He pushed open the one on his right and held it for Solitaire. It was a small living-room that ran the width of the cottage and faced across the beach to the sea. It was pleasantly furnished with bamboo beach chairs upholstered in foam rubber covered with a red-and-green hibiscus chintz. Palm-leaf matting covered the floor. The walls were duck's-egg blue and in the centre of each was a colour print of tropical flowers in a bamboo frame. There was a large drum-shaped table in bamboo with a glass top. It held a bowl of flowers and a white telephone. There were broad windows facing the sea and to the right of them a door leading on to the beach. White plastic jalousies were drawn half up the windows to cut the glare from the sand.

Bond and Solitaire sat down. Bond lit a cigarette and threw the pack and his lighter on to the table.

Suddenly the telephone rang. Leiter came out of his trance and walked over from the door and picked up the receiver.

'Speaking,' he said. 'Put the Lieutenant on. That you, Lieutenant? He's here. Just walked in. No, all in one piece.' He listened for a moment, then turned to Bond. 'Where did you leave the Phantom?' he asked. Bond told him. 'Jacksonville,' said Leiter into the telephone. 'Yeah, I'll say. Sure. I'll get the details from him and call you back. Will you call off Homicide? I'd sure appreciate it. And New York. Much obliged, Lieutenant. Orlando 9000. Okay. And thanks again. 'Bye.' He put down the receiver. He wiped the sweat off his forehead and sat down opposite Bond.

Suddenly he looked at Solitaire and grinned apologetically. 'I guess you're Solitaire,' he said. 'Sorry for the rough welcome. It's been quite a day. For the second time in around twenty-four hours I didn't expect to see this guy again.' He turned back to Bond. 'Okay to go ahead?' he asked.

'Yes,' said Bond. 'Solitaire's on our side now.'

'That's a break,' said Leiter. 'Well, you won't have seen the papers or heard the radio, so I'll give you the headlines first. The Phantom was stopped soon after Jacksonville. Between Waldo and Ocala. Your compartment was tommy-gunned and bombed. Blown to bits. Killed the Pullman porter who was in the corridor at the time. No other casualties. Bloody uproar going on. Who did it? Who's Mr Bryce and who's Mrs Bryce? Where are they? Of course we were sure you'd been snatched. The police at Orlando are in charge. Traced the bookings back to New York. Found the FBI had made them. Everyone comes down on me like a load of bricks. Then you walk in with a pretty girl on your arm looking as happy as a clam.'

Leiter burst out laughing. 'Boy! You should have heard Washington a while back. Anybody would have thought it was me that bombed the goddam train.'

He reached for one of Bond's cigarettes and lit it.

'Well,' he said. 'That's the synopsis. I'll hand over the shooting script when I've heard your end. Give.'

Bond described in detail what had happened since he had spoken to Leiter from the St Regis. When he came to the night on the train he took the piece of paper out of his pocket-book and pushed it across the table.

Leiter whistled. 'Voodoo,' he said. 'This was meant to be found on the corpse, I guess. Ritual murder by friends of the men you bumped in Harlem. That's how it was supposed to look. Take the heat right away from The Big Man. They certainly think out all the angles. We'll get after that thug they had on the train. Probably one of the help in the diner. He must have been the man who put the finger on your compartment. You finish. Then I'll tell you how he did it.'

'Let me see,' said Solitaire. She reached across for the paper.

'Yes,' she said quietly. 'It's an *ouanga*, a Voodoo fetish. It's the invocation to the Drum Witch. It's used by the Ashanti tribe in Africa when they want to kill someone. They use something like it in Haiti.' She handed it back to Bond. 'It was lucky you didn't tell me about it,' she said seriously. 'I would still be having hysterics.'

'I didn't care for it myself,' said Bond. 'I felt it was bad news. Lucky we got off at Jacksonville. Poor Baldwin. We owe him a lot.'

He finished the story of the rest of their trip.

'Anyone spot you when you left the train?' asked Leiter.

'Shouldn't think so,' said Bond. 'But we'd better keep Solitaire under cover until we can get her out. Thought we ought to fly her over to Jamaica tomorrow. I can get her looked after there till we come on.'

'Sure,' agreed Leiter. 'We'll put her in a charter plane at Tampa. Get her down to Miami by tomorrow lunchtime and she can take one of the afternoon services – KLM or Panam. Get her in by dinner time tomorrow. Too late to do anything this afternoon.'

'Is that all right, Solitaire?' Bond asked her.

The girl was staring out of the window. Her eyes had the faraway look that Bond had seen before.

Suddenly she shivered.

Her eyes came back to Bond. She put out a hand and touched his sleeve.

'Yes,' she said. She hesitated. 'Yes, I guess so.'

13 Death of a Pelican

Solitaire stood up.

'I must go and tidy myself,' she said. 'I expect you've both got plenty to talk about.'

'Of course,' said Leiter, jumping up. 'Crazy of me! You must be dead beat. Guess you'd better take James's room and he can bed down with me.'

Solitaire followed him out into the little hall and Bond heard Leiter explaining the arrangement of the rooms.

In a moment Leiter came back with a bottle of Haig and Haig and some ice.

'I'm forgetting my manners,' he said. 'We could both do with a drink. There's a small pantry next to the bathroom and I've stocked it with all we're likely to need!'

He fetched some soda-water and they both took a long drink.

'Let's have the details,' said Bond, sitting back. 'Must have been the hell of a fine job.'

'Sure was,' agreed Leiter, 'except for the shortage of corpses.'

He put his feet on the table and lit a cigarette.

'Phantom left Jacksonville around five,' he began. 'Got to Waldo around six. Just after leaving Waldo – and here I'm guessing – Mr

Big's man comes along to your car, gets into the next compartment to yours and hangs a towel between the drawn blind and the window, meaning – and he must have done a good deal of telephoning at stations on the way down – meaning "the window to the right of this towel is it".

'There's a long stretch of straight track between Waldo and Ocala,' continued Leiter, 'running through forest and swamp land. State highway right alongside the track. About twenty minutes outside Waldo, Wham! goes a dynamite emergency signal under the leading Diesel. Driver comes down to forty. Wham! And another Wham! Three in line! Emergency! Halt at once! He halts the train wondering what the hell. Straight track. Last signal green over green. Nothing in sight. It's around quarter after six and just getting light. There's a sedan, clouted heap I expect [Bond raised an eyebrow. 'Stolen car,' explained Leiter], grey, thought to have been a Buick, no lights, engine running, waiting on the highway opposite the centre of the train. Three men get out. Coloured. Probably negro. They walk slowly in line abreast along the grass verge between the road and the track. Two on the outside carry rippers – tommy-guns. Man in the centre has something in his hand. Twenty yards and they stop outside Car 245. Men with the rippers give a double squirt at your window. Open it up for the pineapple. Centre man tosses in the pineapple and all three run back to the car. Two seconds fuse. As they reach the car, BOOM! Fricassee of Compartment H. Fricassee, presumably, of Mr and Mrs Bryce. In fact fricassee of your Baldwin who runs out and crouches in corridor directly he sees men approaching his car. No other casualties except multiple shock and hysterics throughout train. Car drives away very fast towards limbo where it still is and will probably remain. Silence, mingled with screams, falls. People run to and fro. Train limps gingerly into Ocala. Drops Car 245. Is allowed to proceed three hours later. Scene II. Leiter sits alone in cottage, hoping he has never said an unkind word to his friend James, and wondering how Mr Hoover will have Mr Leiter served for his dinner tonight. That's all, folks.'

Bond laughed. 'What an organization!' he said. 'I'm sure it's all beautifully covered up and alibied. What a man! He certainly seems to have the run of this country. Just shows how one can push a democracy around, what with *habeas corpus* and human rights and all the rest. Glad we haven't got him on our hands in England. Wooden truncheons wouldn't make much of a dent in him. Well,' he concluded, 'that's three times I've managed to get away with it. The pace is beginning to get a bit hot.'

'Yes,' said Leiter thoughtfully. 'Before you arrived over here you could have counted the mistakes Mr Big has ever made on one thumb. Now he's made three all in a row. He won't like that. We've got to put the heat on him while he's still groggy and then get out, quick. Tell you what I've got in mind. There's no doubt that gold gets into the States through this place. We've tracked the *Secatur* again and again and she just comes straight over from Jamaica to St Petersburg and docks at that worm-and-bait factory – Rubberus or whatever it's called.'

'Ourobouros,' said Bond. 'The Great Worm of mythology. Good name for a worm-and-bait factory.' Suddenly a thought struck him. He hit the glass table-top with the flat of his hand. 'Felix! Of course. Ourobouros – "The Robber" – don't you see? Mr Big's man down here. It must be the same.'

Leiter's face lit up. 'Christ Almighty,' he exclaimed. 'Of course it's the same. That Greek who's supposed to own it, the man in Tarpon Springs that figures in the reports that blockhead showed us in New York, Binswanger. He's probably just a figurehead. Probably doesn't even know there's anything phoney about it. It's his manager here we've got to get after. "The Robber." Of course that's who it is.'

Leiter jumped up.

'C'mon. Let's get going. We'll go right along and look the place over. I was going to suggest it anyway, seeing the *Secatur* always docks at their wharf. She's in Cuba now, by the way,' he added, 'Havana. Cleared from here a week ago. They searched her good and proper when she came in and when she left. Didn't find a thing, of course. Thought she might have a false keel. Almost tore it off. She had to go into dock before she could sail again. Nix. Not a shadow of anything wrong. Let alone a stack of gold coins. Anyway, we'll go and smell around. See if we can get a look at our Robber friend. I'll just have to talk to Orlando and Washington. Tell 'em all we know. They must catch up quick with the Big Man's fellow on the train. Probably too late by now. You go and see how Solitaire's getting on. Tell her she's not to move till we get back. Lock her in. We'll take her out to dinner in Tampa. They've got the best restaurant on the whole coast, Cuban, "Los Novedades". We'll stop at the airport on the way and fix her flight for tomorrow.'

Leiter reached for the telephone and asked for Long Distance. Bond left him to it.

Ten minutes later they were on their way.

Solitaire had not wanted to be left. She had clung to Bond. 'I want to get away from here,' she said, her eyes frightened. 'I have a feeling . . .' She didn't end the sentence. Bond kissed her.

'It's all right,' he said. 'We'll be back in an hour or so. Nothing can happen to you here. Then I shan't leave you until you're on the plane. We can even stay the night in Tampa and get you off at first light.'

'Yes, please,' said Solitaire anxiously. 'I'd rather do that. I'm frightened here. I feel in danger.' She put her arms round his neck. 'Don't think I'm being hysterical.' She kissed him. 'Now you can go. I just wanted to see you. Come back quickly.'

Leiter had called and Bond had closed the door on her and locked it.

He followed Leiter to his car on the Parkway feeling vaguely troubled. He couldn't imagine that the girl could come to any harm in this peaceful, law-abiding place, or that the Big Man could conceivably have traced her to The Everglades, which was only one of a hundred similar beach establishments on Treasure Island. But he respected the extraordinary power of her intuitions and her attack of nerves made him uneasy.

The sight of Leiter's car put these thoughts out of his mind.

Bond liked fast cars and he liked driving them. Most American cars bored him. They lacked personality and the patina of individual craftsmanship that European cars have. They were just 'vehicles', similar in shape and in colour, and even in the tone of their horns. Designed to serve for a year and then be turned in in part exchange for the next year's model. All the fun of driving had been taken out of them with the abolition of a gear-change, with hydraulic-assisted steering and spongy suspension. All effort had been smoothed away and all of that close contact with the machine and the road that extracts skill and nerve from the European driver. To Bond, American cars were just beetle-shaped Dodgems in which you motored along with one hand on the wheel, the radio full on, and the power-operated windows closed to keep out the draughts.

But Leiter had got hold of an old Cord, one of the few American cars with a personality, and it cheered Bond to climb into the low-hung saloon, to hear the solid bite of the gears and the masculine tone of the wide exhaust. Fifteen years old, he reflected, yet still one of the most modern-looking cars in the world.

They swung on to the causeway and across the wide expanse of unrippled water that separates the twenty miles of narrow island from the broad peninsula sprawling with St Petersburg and its suburbs.

Already as they idled up Central Avenue on their way across the town to the Yacht Basin and the main harbour and the big hotels, Bond caught a whiff of the atmosphere that makes the town the 'Old Folks Home' of America. Everyone on the sidewalks had white hair, white or blue, and the famous Sidewalk Davenports that Solitaire had described were thick with oldsters sitting in rows like the starlings in Trafalgar Square.

Bond noted the small grudging mouths of the women, the sun gleaming on their pince-nez; the stringy, collapsed chests and arms of the men displayed to the sunshine in Truman shirts. The fluffy, sparse balls of hair on the women showing the pink scalp. The bony bald heads of the men. And, everywhere, a prattling camaraderie, a swapping of news and gossip, a making of folksy dates for the shuffle-board and the bridge-table, a handing round of letters from children and grandchildren, a tut-tutting about prices in the shops and the motels.

You didn't have to be amongst them to hear it all. It was all in the nodding and twittering of the balls of blue fluff, the back-slapping and hawk-an-spitting of the little old baldheads.

'It makes you want to climb right into the tomb and pull the lid down,' said Leiter at Bond's exclamations of horror. 'You wait till we get out and walk. If they see your shadow coming up the sidewalk behind them they jump out of the way as if you were the Chief Cashier coming to look over their shoulders in the bank. It's ghastly. Makes me think of the bank clerk who went home unexpectedly at midday and found the President of the bank sleeping with his wife. He went back and told his pals in the ledger department and said, "Gosh, fellers, he nearly caught me!"'

Bond laughed.

'You can hear all the presentation gold watches ticking in their pockets,' said Leiter. 'Place is full of undertakers, and pawnshops stuffed with gold watches and masonic rings and bits of jet and lockets full of hair. Makes you shiver to think of it all. Wait till you go to "Aunt Milly's Place" and see them all in droves mumbling over their corn-beef hash and cheeseburgers, trying to keep alive till ninety. It'll frighten the life out of you. But they're not all old down here. Take a look at that ad over there.' He pointed towards a big hoarding on a deserted lot.

It was an advertisement for maternity clothes. 'STUTZHEIMER & BLOCK,' it said, 'IT'S NEW! OUR ANTICIPATION DEPART-MENT, AND AFTER! CLOTHES FOR CHIPS (1–4) AND TWIGS (4–8).'

Bond groaned. 'Let's get away from here,' he said. 'This is really beyond the call of duty.'

They came down to the waterfront and turned right until they came to the seaplane base and the coastguard station. The streets were free of oldsters and here there was the normal life of a harbour – wharves, warehouses, a ship's chandler, some up-turned boats, nets drying, the cry of seagulls, the rather fetid smell coming in off the bay. After the teeming boneyard of the town the sign over the garage: 'Drive-ur-Self. Pat Grady. The Smiling Irishman. Used cars,' was a cheerful reminder of a livelier, bustling world.

'Better get out and walk,' said Leiter. 'The Robber's place is in the next block.'

They left the car beside the harbour and sauntered along past a timber warehouse and some oil-storage tanks. Then they turned left again towards the sea.

The side-road ended at a small weather-beaten wooden jetty that reached out twenty feet on barnacled piles into the bay. Right up against its open gate was a long low corrugated-iron warehouse. Over its wide double doors was painted, black on white, 'Ourobouros Inc. Live Worm and Bait Merchants. Coral, Shells, Tropical Fish. Wholesale only.' In one of the double doors there was a smaller door with a gleaming Yale lock. On the door was a sign: 'Private. Keep Out.'

Against this a man sat on a kitchen chair, its back tilted so that the door supported his weight. He was cleaning a rifle, a Remington 30 it looked like to Bond. He had a wooden toothpick sticking out of his mouth and a battered baseball cap on the back of his head. He was wearing a stained white singlet that revealed tufts of black hair under his arms, and slept-in white canvas trousers and rubber-soled sneakers. He was around forty and his face was as knotted and seamed as the mooring posts on the jetty. It was a thin, hatchet face, and the lips were thin too, and bloodless. His complexion was the colour of tobacco dust, a sort of yellowy-beige. He looked cruel and cold, like the bad man in a film about poker-players and gold mines.

Bond and Leiter walked past him and on to the pier. He didn't look up from his rifle as they went past but Bond sensed that his eyes were following them.

'If that isn't the Robber,' said Leiter, 'it's a blood relation.'

A pelican, grey with a pale yellow head, was hunched on one of the mooring posts at the end of the jetty. He let them get very close, then reluctantly gave a few heavy beats of his wings and planed down towards the water. The two men stood and watched him flying slowly along just above the surface of the harbour. Suddenly he crashed clumsily down, his long bill snaking out and down in front of him. It came up clutching a small fish which he moodily swallowed. Then the heavy bird got up again and went on fishing, flying mostly into the sun so that its big shadow would give no warning. When Bond and Leiter turned to walk back down the jetty it gave up fishing and glided back to its post. It settled with a clatter of wings and resumed its thoughtful consideration of the late afternoon.

The man was still bent over his gun, wiping the mechanism with an oily rag.

'Good afternoon,' said Leiter. 'You the manager of this wharf?'

'Yep,' said the man without looking up.

'Wondered if there was any chance of mooring my boat here. Basin's pretty crowded.'

'Nope.'

Leiter took out his notecase. 'Would twenty talk?'

'Nope.' The man gave a rattling hawk in his throat and spat directly between Bond and Leiter.

'Hey,' said Leiter. 'You want to watch your manners.'

The man deliberated. He looked up at Leiter. He had small, close-set eyes as cruel as a painless dentist's.

'What's a name of your boat?'

'The *Sybil*,' said Leiter.

'Ain't no sich boat in the Basin,' said the man. He clicked the breech shut on his rifle. It lay casually on his lap pointing down the approach to the warehouse, away from the sea.

'You're blind,' said Leiter. 'Been there a week. Sixty-foot twin-screw Diesel. White with a green awning. Rigged for fishing.'

The rifle started to move lazily in a low arc. The man's left hand was at the trigger, his right just in front of the trigger-guard, pivoting the gun.

They stood still.

The man sat lazily looking down at the breech, his chair still tilted against the small door with the yellow Yale lock.

The gun slowly traversed Leiter's stomach, then Bond's. The two men stood like statues, not risking a move of the hand. The gun stopped pivoting. It was pointing down the wharf. The Robber looked briefly up, narrowed his eyes and pulled the trigger. The pelican gave a faint squawk and they heard its heavy body crash into the water. The echo of the shot boomed across the harbour.

'What the hell d'you do that for?' asked Bond furiously.

'Practice,' said the man, pumping another bullet into the breech.

'Guess there's a branch of the ASPCA in this town,' said Leiter. 'Let's get along there and report this guy.'

'Want to be prosecuted for trespass?' asked the Robber, getting slowly up and shifting the gun under his arm. 'This is private property. Now,' he spat the words out, 'git the hell out of here.' He turned and yanked the chair away from the door, opened the door with a key and turned with one foot on the threshold, 'You both got guns,' he said. 'I kin smell 'em. You come aroun' here again and you follow the boid 'n I plead self-defence. I've had a bellyful of you lousy dicks aroun' here lately breathin' down my neck. *Sybil* my ass!' He turned contemptuously through the door and slammed it so that the frame rattled.

They looked at each other. Leiter grinned ruefully and shrugged his shoulders.

'Round One to the Robber,' he said.

They moved off down the dusty sideroad. The sun was setting and the sea behind them was a pool of blood. When they got to the main road. Bond looked back. A big arc light had come on over the door and the approach to the warehouse was stripped of shadows.

'No good trying anything from the front,' said Bond. 'But there's never been a warehouse with only one entrance.'

'Just what I was thinking,' said Leiter. 'We'll save that for the next visit.'

They got into the car and drove slowly home across Central Avenue.

On their way home Leiter asked a string of questions about Solitaire. Finally he said casually: 'By the way, hope I fixed the rooms like you want them.'

'Couldn't be better,' said Bond cheerfully.

'Fine,' said Leiter. 'Just occurred to me you two might be hyphenating.'

'You read too much Winchell,' said Bond.

'It's just a delicate way of putting it,' said Leiter. 'Don't forget the walls of those cottages are pretty thin. I use my ears for hearing with – not for collecting lipstick.'

Bond grabbed for a handkerchief. 'You lousy, goddam sleuth,' he said furiously.

Leiter watched him scrubbing at himself out of the corner of his eye. 'What are you doing?' he asked innocently. 'I wasn't for a moment suggesting the colour of your ears was anything but a natural red. However . . .' He put a wealth of meaning into the word.

'If you find yourself dead in your bed tonight,' laughed Bond, 'you'll know who did it.'

They were still chaffing each other when they arrived at The Everglades and they were laughing when the grim Mrs Stuyvesant greeted them on the lawn.

'Pardon me, Mr Leiter,' she said. 'But I'm afraid we can't allow music here. I can't have the other guests disturbed at all hours.'

They looked at her in astonishment. 'I'm sorry, Mrs Stuyvesant,' said Leiter. 'I don't quite get you.'

'That big radiogram you had sent round,' said Mrs Stuyvesant. 'The men could hardly get the packing-case through the door.'

14 'He Disagreed with Something that Ate Him'

The girl had not put up much of a struggle.

When Leiter and Bond, leaving the manageress gaping on the lawn, raced down to the end cottage, they found her room untouched and the bedclothes barely rumpled.

The lock of her room had been forced with one swift wrench of a jemmy and then the two men must have just stood there with guns in their hands.

'Get going, Lady. Get your clothes on. Try any tricks and we'll let the fresh air into you.'

Then they must have gagged her or knocked her out and doubled her into the packing-case and nailed it up. There were tyre-marks at the back of the cottage where the truck had stood. Almost blocking the entrance hall was a huge old-fashioned radiogram. Second-hand it must have cost them under fifty bucks.

Bond could see the expression of blind terror on Solitaire's face as if she was standing before him. He cursed himself bitterly for leaving her alone. He couldn't guess how she had been traced so quickly. It was just another example of the Big Man's machine.

Leiter was talking to the FBI headquarters at Tampa. 'Airports, railroad terminals and the highways,' he was saying. 'You'll get blanket orders from Washington just as soon as I've spoken to them. I guarantee they'll give this top priority. Thanks a lot. Much appreciated. I'll be around. Okay.'

He hung up. 'Thank God they're co-operating,' he said to Bond, who was standing gazing with hard blank eyes out to sea. 'Sending a couple of their men round right away and throwing as wide a net as they can. While I sew this up with Washington and New York, get what you can from that old battle-axe. Exact time, descriptions, etc. Better make out it was a burglary and that Solitaire has skipped with the men. She'll understand that. It'll keep the whole thing on the level of the usual hotel crimes. Say the police are on the way and that we don't blame the Everglades. She'll want to avoid a scandal. Say we feel the same way.'

Bond nodded. 'Skipped with the men?' That was possible too. But somehow he didn't think so. He went back to Solitaire's room and searched it minutely. It still smelled of her, of the 'Vent Vert' that reminded him of their journey together. Her hat and veil were in the cupboard and her few toilet articles on the shelf in the bathroom. He soon found her bag and knew that he was right to have trusted her. It was under the bed and he visualized her kicking it there as she got up with the guns trained on her. He emptied it out on the bed and felt the lining. Then he took out a small knife and carefully cut a few threads. He took out the five thousand dollars and slipped them into his pocket-book. They would be safe with him. If she was killed by Mr Big, he would spend them on avenging her. He covered up the torn lining as best he could, replaced the other contents of the bag and kicked it back under the bed.

Then he went up to the office.

It was eight o'clock by the time the routine work was finished. They had a stiff drink together and then went to the central dining-room, where the handful of other guests were just finishing their dinner. Everyone looked curiously and rather fearfully at them. What were these two rather dangerous-looking young men doing in this place? Where was the woman who had come with them? Whose wife was she? What had all those goings on meant that evening? Poor Mrs Stuyvesant running about looking quite distracted. And didn't they realize that dinner was at seven o'clock? The kitchen staff would be just going home. Serve them right if their food was quite cold. People must have consideration for others. Mrs Stuyvesant had said she thought they were government men, from Washington. Well, what did that mean?

The consensus of opinion was that they were bad news and no credit to the carefully restricted clientele of The Everglades.

Bond and Leiter were shown to a bad table near the service door. The set dinner was a string of inflated English and pidgin French. What it came down to was tomato juice, boiled fish with a white sauce, a strip of frozen turkey with a dab of cranberry, and a wedge of lemon curd surmounted by a whorl of stiff cream substitute. They munched it down gloomily while the dining-room emptied of its oldster couples and the table lights went out one by one. Fingerbowls, in which floated one hibiscus petal, was the final gracious touch to their meal.

Bond ate silently and when they had finished Leiter made a determined effort to be cheerful.

'Come and get drunk,' he said. 'This is the bad end to a worse day. Or do you want to play bingo with the oldsters? It says there's a bingo tournament in the "romp room" this evening.'

Bond shrugged his shoulders and they went back to their sitting-room and sat gloomily for a while, drinking and staring out across the sand, bonewhite in the light of the moon, towards the endless dark sea.

When Bond had drunk enough to drown his thoughts he said good night and went off to Solitaire's room, which he had now taken over as his bedroom. He climbed between the sheets where her warm body had lain and, before he slept, he had made up his mind. He would go after the Robber as soon as it was light and strangle the truth out of him. He had been too preoccupied to discuss the case with Leiter but he was certain that the Robber must have had a big hand in the kidnapping of Solitaire. He thought of the man's little cruel eyes and the pale thin lips. Then he thought of the scrawny neck rising like a turtle's out of the dirty sweat-shirt. Under the bedclothes the muscles of his arms went taut. Then, his mind made up, he relaxed his body into sleep.

He slept until eight. When he saw the time on his watch he cursed.

He quickly took a shower, holding his eyes open into the needles of water until they smarted. Then he put a towel round his waist and went into Leiter's room. The slats of the jalousies were still down but there was light enough to see that neither bed had been slept in.

He smiled, thinking that Leiter had probably finished the bottle of whisky and fallen asleep on the couch in the living-room. He walked through. The room was empty. The bottle of whisky, still half full, was on the table and a pile of cigarette butts overflowed the ashtray.

Bond went to the window, pulled up the jalousies and opened it. He caught a glimpse of a beautiful clear morning before he turned back into the room.

Then he saw the envelope. It was on a chair in front of the door through which he had come. He picked it up. It contained a note scribbled in pencil.

Got to thinking and don't feel like sleep. It's about five a.m. Going to visit the worm-and-bait store. All same early bird. Odd that trick-shot artist was sitting there while S. was being snatched. As if he knew we were in town and was ready for trouble in case the snatch went wrong. If I'm not back by ten, call out the militia. Tampa 88. *Felix*

Bond didn't wait. While he shaved and dressed he ordered some coffee and rolls and a cab. In just over ten minutes he had got them all and had scalded himself with the coffee. He was leaving the cottage when he heard the telephone ring in the living-room. He ran back.

'Mr Bryce? Mound Park Hospital speaking,' said a voice. 'Emergency ward. Doctor Roberts. We have a Mr Leiter here who's asking for you. Can you come right over?'

'God Almighty,' said Bond, gripped with fear. 'What's the matter with him. Is he bad?'

'Nothing to worry about,' said the voice. 'Automobile accident. Looks like a hit-and-run job. Slight concussion. Can you come over? He seems to want you.'

'Of course,' said Bond, relieved. 'Be there right away.'

Now what the hell, he wondered as he hurried across the lawn. Must have been beaten up and left in the road. On the whole, Bond was glad it was no worse.

As they turned across Treasure Island Causeway an ambulance passed them, its bell clanging.

More trouble, thought Bond. Don't seem to be able to move without running into it.

They crossed St Petersburg by Central Avenue and turned right down the road he and Leiter had taken the day before. Bond's suspicions seemed to be confirmed when he found the hospital was only a couple of blocks from Ourobouros Inc.

Bond paid off the cab and ran up the steps of the impressive building. There was a reception desk in the spacious entrance hall. A pretty nurse sat at the desk reading the ads in the *St Petersburg Times*.

'Dr Roberts?' inquired Bond.

'Dr which?' asked the girl looking at him with approval.

'Dr Roberts, Emergency ward,' said Bond impatiently, 'Patient called Leiter, Felix Leiter. Brought in this morning.'

'No doctor called Roberts here,' said the girl. She ran a finger down a list on the desk. 'And no patient called Leiter. Just a moment and I'll call the ward. What did you say your name was?'

'Bryce,' said Bond. 'John Bryce.' He started to sweat profusely although it was quite cool in the hall. He wiped his wet hands on his trousers, fighting to keep from panic. The damn girl just didn't know her job. Too pretty to be a nurse. Ought to have someone competent on the desk. He ground his teeth as she talked cheerfully into the telephone.

She put down the receiver. 'I'm sorry, Mr Bryce. Must be some mistake. No cases during the night and they've never heard of a Dr Roberts or a Mr Leiter. Sure you've got the right hospital?'

Bond turned away without answering her. Wiping the sweat from his forehead, he made for the exit.

The girl made a face at his back and picked up her paper.

Mercifully, a cab was just drawing up with some other visitors. Bond took it and told the driver to get him back quick to the Everglades. All he knew was that they had got Leiter and had wanted to draw Bond away from the cottage. Bond couldn't make it out, but he knew that suddenly everything was going bad on them and that the initiative was back in the hands of Mr Big and his machine.

Mrs Stuyvesant hurried out when she saw him leave the cab.

'Your poor friend,' she said without sympathy. 'Really he should be more careful.'

'Yes, Mrs Stuyvesant. What is it?' said Bond impatiently.

'The ambulance came just after you left.' The woman's eyes were gleaming with the bad news. 'Seems Mr Leiter was in an accident with his car. They had to carry him to the cottage on a stretcher. Such a nice coloured man was in charge. He said Mr Leiter would be quite all right but he mustn't be disturbed on any account. Poor boy! Face all covered with bandages. They said they'd make him comfortable and a doctor would be coming later. If there's anything I can . .'

Bond didn't wait for more. He ran down the lawn to the cottage and dashed through the lobby into Leiter's room.

There was the shape of a body on Leiter's bed. It was covered with a sheet. Over the face, the sheet seemed to be motionless.

Bond gritted his teeth as he leant over the bed. Was there a tiny flutter of movement?

Bond snatched the shroud down from the face. There was no face. Just something wrapped round and round with dirty bandages, like a white wasps' nest.

He softly pulled the sheet down further. More bandages, still more roughly wound, with wet blood seeping through. Then the top of a sack which covered the lower half of the body. Everything soaked in blood.

There was a piece of paper protruding from a gap in the bandages where the mouth should have been.

Bond pulled it away and leant down. There was the faintest whisper of breath against his cheek. He snatched up the bedside telephone. It took minutes before he could make Tampa understand. Then the urgency in his voice got through. They would get to him in twenty minutes.

He put down the receiver and looked vaguely at the paper in his hand. It was a rough piece of white wrapping paper. Scrawled in pencil in ragged block letters were the words:

HE DISAGREED WITH SOMETHING THAT ATE HIM

And underneath in brackets:

(P.S. WE HAVE PLENTY MORE JOKES
AS GOOD AS THIS)

With the movements of a sleepwalker, Bond put the piece of paper down on the bedside table. Then he turned back to the body on the bed. He hardly dared touch it for fear that the tiny fluttering breath would suddenly cease. But he had to find out something. His fingers worked softly at the bandages on top of the head. Soon he uncovered some of the strands of hair. The hair was wet and he put his fingers to his mouth. There was a salt taste. He pulled out some strands of hair and looked closely at them. There was no more doubt.

He saw again the pale straw-coloured mop that used to hang down in disarray over the right eye, grey and humorous, and below it the wry, hawk-like face of the Texan with whom he had shared so many adventures. He thought of him for a moment, as he had been. Then he tucked the lock of hair back into the bandages and sat on the edge of the other bed and quietly watched over the body of his friend and wondered how much of it could be saved.

When the two detectives and the police surgeon arrived he told them all he knew in a quiet flat voice. Acting on what Bond had already told them on the telephone they had sent a squad car down to The Robber's place and they waited for a report while the surgeon worked next door.

He was finished first. He came back into the sitting-room looking anxious. Bond jumped to his feet. The police surgeon slumped into a chair and looked up at him.

'I think he'll live,' he said. 'But it's fifty-fifty. They certainly did a job on the poor guy. One arm gone. Half the left leg. Face in a mess, but only superficial. Darned if I know what did it. Only thing I can think of is an animal or a big fish. Something's been tearing at him. Know a bit more when I can get him to the hospital. There'll be traces left from the teeth of whatever it was. Ambulance should be along any time.'

They sat in gloomy silence. The telephone rang intermittently. New York, Washington. The St Petersburg Police Department wanted to know what the hell was going on down at the wharf and were told to keep out of the case. It was a Federal job. Finally, from a call-box, there was the lieutenant in charge of the squad car reporting.

They had been over The Robber's place with a toothcomb. Nothing but tanks of fish and bait and cases of coral and shells. The Robber and two men who were down there in charge of the pumps and the water-heating had been taken in custody and grilled for an hour. Their alibis had been checked and found to be solid as the Empire State. The Robber had angrily demanded his mouthpiece and when the lawyer had finally been allowed to get to them they had been automatically sprung. No charge and no evidence to base one on. Dead-ends everywhere except that Leiter's car had been found the other side of the yacht basin, a mile away from the wharf. A mass of fingerprints, but none that fitted the three men. Any suggestions?

'Keep with it,' said the senior man in the cottage who had introduced himself as Captain Franks. 'Be along presently. Washington says we've got to get these men if it's the last thing we do. Two top operatives flying down tonight. Time to get co-operation from the police. I'll tell 'em to get their stoolies working in Tampa. This isn't only a St Petersburg job. 'Bye now.'

It was three o'clock. The police ambulance came and left again with the surgeon and the body that was so near to death. The two men left. They promised to keep in touch. They were anxious to know Bond's plans. Bond was evasive. Said he'd have to talk to Washington. Meanwhile, could he have Leiter's car? Yes, it would be brought round directly Records had finished with it.

When they had gone, Bond sat lost in thought. They had made sandwiches from the well-stocked pantry and Bond now finished these and had a stiff drink.

The telephone rang. Long-distance. Bond found himself speaking to the head of Leiter's Section of the Central Intelligence Agency. The gist of it was that they'd be very glad if Bond would move on to Jamaica at once. All very polite. They had spoken to London, who had agreed. When should they tell London that Bond would arrive in Jamaica?

Bond knew there was a Transcarib plane via Nassau due out next day. He said he'd be taking it. Any other news? Oh yes, said the CIA. The gentleman from Harlem and his girl friend had left by plane for Havana, Cuba, during the night. Private charter from a little place up the East coast called Vero Beach. Papers were in order and charter company was such a small one the FBI had not bothered to include them when they put the watch on all airports. Arrival had been reported by the CIA man in Cuba. Yes, too bad. Yes, the *Secatur* was still there. No sailing date. Well, too bad about Leiter. Fine man. Hope he makes out. So Bond would be in Jamaica tomorrow? Okay. Sorry things been so hectic. 'Bye.

Bond thought for a while, then he picked up the telephone and spoke briefly to a man at the Eastern Garden Aquarium at Miami and consulted him about buying a live shark to keep in an ornamental lagoon.

'Only place I ever heard of is right near you now, Mr Bryce,' said the helpful voice. '"Ourobouros Worm and Bait." They got sharks. Big ones. Do business with foreign zoos and suchlike. White, Tiger, even Hammerheads. They'll be glad to help you. Costs a lot to feed 'em. You're welcome. Any time you're passing. 'Bye.'

Bond took out his gun and cleaned it, waiting for the night.

15 Midnight Among the Worms

Around six Bond packed his bag and paid the check. Mrs Stuyvesant was glad to see the last of him. The Everglades hadn't experienced such alarums since the last hurricane.

Leiter's car was back on the Boulevard and he drove it over to the town. He visited a hardware store and made various purchases. Then he had the biggest steak, rare, with French fries, he had ever seen. It was a small grill called Pete's, dark and friendly. He drank a quarter of a pint of Old Grandad with the steak and had two cups of very strong coffee. With all this under his belt he began to feel more sanguine.

He spun out the meal and the drinks until nine o'clock. Then he studied a map of the city and took the car and made a wide detour that brought him within a block of the Robber's wharf from the south. He ran the car down to the sea and got out.

It was a bright moonlit night and the buildings and warehouses threw great blocks of indigo shadow. The whole section seemed deserted and there was no sound except the quiet lapping of the small waves against the sea-wall and water gurgling under the empty wharves.

The top of the low sea-wall was about three feet wide. It was in shadow for the hundred yards or more that separated him from the long black outline of the Ourobouros warehouse.

Bond climbed on to it and walked carefully and silently along between the buildings and the sea. As he got nearer a steady, high-pitched whine became louder, and by the time he dropped down on the wide cement parking space at the back of the building it was a muted scream. Bond had expected something of the sort. The noise came from the air-pumps and heating systems which he knew would be necessary to keep the fish healthy through the chill of the night hours. He had also relied on the fact that most of the roof would certainly be of glass to admit sunlight during the day. Also that there would be good ventilation.

He was not disappointed. The whole of the south wall of the warehouse, from just above the level of his head, was of plate glass, and through it he could see the moonlight shining down through half an acre of glass roofing. High up above him, and well out of reach, broad windows were open to the night air. There was, as he and Leiter had expected, a small door low down, but it was locked and bolted and leaded wires near the hinges suggested some form of burglar-alarm.

Bond was not interested in the door. Following his hunch, he had come equipped for an entry through glass. He cast about for something that would raise him an extra two feet. In a land where litter and junk are so much a part of the landscape he soon found what he wanted.

It was a discarded heavy gauge tyre. He rolled it to the wall of the warehouse away from the door and took off his shoes.

He put bricks against the bottom edges of the tyre to hold it steady and hoisted himself up. The steady scream of the pumps gave him protection and he at once set to work with a small glass-cutter which he had bought, together with a hunk of putty, on his way to dinner. When he had cut down the two vertical sides of one of the yard-square panes, he pressed the putty against the centre of the glass and worked it to a protruding knob. He then went to work on the lateral edges of the pane.

While he worked he gazed through into the moonlit vistas of the huge repository. The endless rows of tanks stood on wooden trestles with narrow passages between. Down the centre of the building there was a wider passage. Under the trestles Bond could see long tanks and trays let into the floor. Just below him, broad racks covered with regiments of seashells jutted out from the walls. Most of the tanks were dark but in some a tiny strip of electric light glimmered spectrally and glinted on little fountains of bubbles rising from the weeds and sand. There was a light metal runway suspended from the roof over each row of tanks and Bond guessed that any individual tank could be lifted out and brought to the exit for shipment or to extract sick fish for quarantine. It was a window into a queer world and into a queer business. It was odd to think of all the worms and eels and fish stirring quietly in the night, the thousands of gills sighing and the multitude of antennae waving and pointing and transmitting their tiny radar signals to the dozing nerve-centres.

After a quarter of an hour's meticulous work there was a slight cracking noise and the pane came away attached to the putty knob in his hand.

He climbed down and put the pane carefully on the ground away from the tyre. Then he stuffed his shoes inside his shirt. With only one good hand they might be vital weapons. He listened. There was no sound but the unfaltering whine of the pumps. He looked up to see if by chance there were any clouds about to cross the moon but the sky was empty save for its canopy of brightly burning stars. He got back on top of the tyre and with an easy heave half of his body was through the wide hole he had made.

He turned and grasped the metal frame above his head and putting all his weight on his arms he jack-knifed his legs through and down so that they were hanging a few inches above the racks full of shells. He lowered himself until he could feel the backs of the shells with his stockinged toes, then he softly separated them with his toes until he had exposed a width of board. Then he let his whole weight subside softly on to the tray. It held, and in a moment he was down on the floor listening with all his senses for any noise behind the whine of the machinery.

But there was none. He took his steel-tipped shoes out of his shirt and left them on the cleared board, then he moved off on the concrete floor with a pencil flashlight in his hand.

He was in the aquarium-fish section, and as he examined the labels he caught flashes of coloured light from the deep tanks and occasionally a piece of living jewellery would materialize and briefly goggle at him before he moved on.

There were all kinds – Swordtails, Guppies, Platys, Terras, Neons, Cichlids, Labyrinth and Paradise fish, and every variety of exotic Goldfish. Underneath, sunk in the floor, and most of them covered with chicken wire, there were tray upon tray swarming and heaving with worms and baits: white worms, micro worms, Daphnia, shrimp, and thick slimy clam worms. From these ground tanks, forests of tiny eyes looked up at his torch.

There was the foetid smell of a mangrove swamp in the air and the temperature was in the high seventies. Soon Bond began to sweat slightly and to long for the clean night air.

He had moved to the central passageway before he found the poison fish which were one of his objectives. When he had read about them in the files of the police headquarters in New York, he had made a mental note that he would like to know more about this sideline of the peculiar business of Ourobouros Inc.

Here the tanks were smaller and there was generally only one specimen in each. Here the eyes that looked sluggishly at Bond were cold and hooded and an occasional fang was bared at the torch or a spined backbone slowly swelled.

Each tank bore an ominous skull-and-crossbones in chalk and there were large labels that said VERY DANGEROUS and KEEP OFF.

There must have been at least a hundred tanks of various sizes, from the large ones to hold Torpedo Skates and the sinister Guitar Fish, to smaller ones for the Horse-killer Eel, Mud Fish from the Pacific, and the monstrous West Indian Scorpion Fish, each of whose spines has a poison sac as powerful as a rattlesnake's.

Bond's eyes narrowed as he noticed that in all the dangerous tanks the mud or sand on the bottom occupied nearly half the tank.

He chose a tank containing a six-inch Scorpion Fish. He knew something of the habits of this deadly species and in particular that they do not strike, but poison only on contact.

The top of the tank was on a level with his waist. He took out a strong pocket-knife he had purchased and opened the longest blade. Then he leant over the tank and with his sleeve rolled up he deliberately aimed his knife at the centre of the craggy head between the overhung grottoes of the eye-sockets. As his hand broke the surface of the water the white dinosaur spines stood threateningly erect and the mottled stripes of the fish turned to a uniform muddy brown. Its broad, wing-like pectorals rose slightly, poised for flight.

Bond lunged swiftly, correcting his aim for the refraction from the surface of the tank. He pinned the bulging head down as the tail threshed wildly and slowly drew the fish towards him and up the glass side of the tank. He stood aside and whipped it out on to the floor, where it continued flapping and jumping despite its shattered skull.

He leant over the tank and plunged his hand deep into the centre of the mud and sand.

Yes, they were there. His hunch about the poison fish had been right. His fingers felt the close rows of coin deep under the mud, like counters in a box. They were in a flat tray. He could feel the wooden partitions. He pulled out a coin, rinsing it and his hand in the cleaner surface water as he did so. He shone his torch on it. It was as big as a modern five-shilling piece and nearly as thick and it was gold. It bore the arms of Spain and the head of Philip II.

He looked at the tank, measuring it. There must be a thousand coins in this one tank that no customs officer would think of disturbing. Ten to twenty thousand dollars' worth, guarded by one poison-fanged

Cerberus. These must be the cargo brought in by the *Secatur* on her last trip a week ago. A hundred tanks. Say one hundred and fifty thousand dollars' worth of gold per trip. Soon the trucks would be coming for the tanks and somewhere down the road men with rubber-coated tongs would extract the deadly fish and throw them back in the sea or burn them. The water and the mud would be emptied out and the gold coin washed and poured into bags. Then the bags would go to agents and the coins would trickle out on the market, each one strictly accounted for by Mr Big's machine.

It was a scheme after Mr Big's philosophy, effective, technically brilliant, almost foolproof.

Bond was full of admiration as he bent to the floor and speared the Scorpion Fish in the side. He dropped it back in the tank. There was no point in divulging his knowledge to the enemy.

It was as he turned away from the tank that all the lights in the warehouse suddenly blazed on and a voice of sharp authority said, 'Don't move an inch. Stick 'em up.'

As Bond took a rolling dive under the tank he caught a glimpse of the lank figure of the Robber squinting down the sights of his rifle about twenty yards away, up against the main entrance. As he dived he prayed that the Robber would miss, but also he prayed that the floor tank which was to take his dive would be one of the covered ones. It was. It was covered with chicken wire. Something snapped up at him as he hit the wire and sprawled clear in the next passageway. As he dived, the rifle cracked and the Scorpion Fish tank above his head splintered sharply and water gushed down.

Bond sprinted fast between the tanks back towards his only means of retreat. Just as he turned the corner there was a shot and a tank of angel fish exploded like a bomb just beside his ear.

He was now at his end of the warehouse with the Robber at the other, fifty yards away. There was no possible chance of jumping for his window on the other side of the central passageway. He stood for a moment gaining his breath and thinking. He realized that the lines of tanks would only protect him to the knees and that between the tanks he would be in full view down the narrow passages. Either way, he could not stand still. He was reminded of the fact as a shot whammed between his legs into a pile of conchs, sending splinters of their hard china buzzing round him like wasps. He ran to his right and another shot came at his legs. It hit the floor and zoomed into a huge carboy of clams that split in half and emptied a hundred shell-fish over the floor. Bond raced back, taking long quick strides. He had his Beretta out and loosed off two shots as he crossed the central passageway. He saw the Robber jump for shelter as a tank shattered above his head.

Bond grinned as he heard a shout drowned by the crash of glass and water.

He immediately dropped to one knee and fired two shots at the Robber's legs, but fifty yards for his small-calibre pistol was too much. There was the crash of another tank but the second shot clanged emptily into the iron entrance gates.

Then the Robber was shooting again and Bond could only dodge to and fro behind the cases and wait to be caught in the kneecap. Occasionally he fired a shot in return to make the Robber keep his distance, but he knew the battle was lost. The other man seemed to have endless ammunition. Bond had only two shots left in his gun and one fresh clip in his pocket.

As he shuttled to and fro, slipping on the rare fish that flapped wildly on the concrete, he even stooped to snatching up heavy queen conchs and helmet shells and hurling them towards the enemy. Often they burst impressively on top of some tank at the Robber's end and added to the appalling racket inside the corrugated-iron shed. But they were quite ineffective. He thought of shooting out the lights, but there were at least twenty of them in two rows.

Finally Bond decided to give up. He had one ruse to fall back on, and any change in the battle was better than exhausting himself at the wrong end of this deadly coconut-shy.

As he passed a row of cases of which the one near him was shattered, he pushed it on to the floor. It was still half full of rare Siamese Fighting Fish, and Bond was pleased with the expensive crash as the remains of the tank burst in fragments on the floor. A wide space was cleared on the trestle table, and after making two quick darts to pick up his shoes he dashed back to the table and jumped up.

With no target for the Robber to shoot at there was a moment's silence save for the whine of the pumps, the sound of water dripping out of broken tanks and the flapping of dying fish. Bond slipped his shoes on and laced them tight.

'Hey, Limey,' called the Robber patiently. 'Come on out or I start using pineapples. I been expectin' you an' I got plenty ammo.'

'Guess I got to give up,' answered Bond through cupped hands. 'But only because you smashed one of my ankles.'

'I'll not shoot,' called the Robber. 'Drop your gun on the floor and come down the central passage with your hands up. We'll have a quiet little talk.'

'Guess I got no option,' said Bond, putting hopelessness into his voice. He dropped his Beretta with a clatter on to the cement floor. He took the gold coin out of his pocket and clenched it in his bandaged left hand.

Bond groaned as he put his feet to the floor. He dragged his left leg behind him as he limped heavily up the central passage, his hands held level with his shoulders. He stopped half way up the passage.

The Robber came slowly towards him, half-crouching, his rifle pointed at Bond's stomach. Bond was glad to see that his shirt was soaked and that he had a cut over the left eye.

The Robber walked well to the left of the passageway. When he was about ten yards away from Bond he paused with one stockinged foot casually resting on a small obstruction in the cement floor.

He gestured with his rifle. 'Higher,' he said harshly.

Bond groaned and lifted his hands a few inches so that they were almost across his face, as if in defence.

Between the fingers he saw the Robber's toes kick something sharply sideways and there was a faint clang as if a bolt had been drawn. Bond's eyes glinted behind his hands and his jaw tightened. He knew now what had happened to Leiter.

The Robber came on, his hard, thin frame obscuring the spot where he had paused.

'Christ,' said Bond, 'I gotta sit down. My leg won't hold me.'

The Robber stopped a few feet away. 'Go ahead and stand while I ask you a few questions, Limey.' He bared his tobacco-stained teeth.

'You'll soon be lying down, and for keeps.' The Robber stood and looked him over. Bond sagged. Behind the defeat in his face his brain was measuring in inches.

'Nosey bastard,' said the Robber . . .

At that moment Bond dropped the gold coin out of his left hand. It clanged on the cement floor and started to roll.

In the fraction of a second that the Robber's eyes flickered down, Bond's right foot in its steel-capped shoe lashed out to its full length. It kicked the rifle almost out of the Robber's hands. At the same moment that the Robber pulled the trigger and the bullet crashed harmlessly through the glass ceiling, Bond launched himself in a dive at the man's stomach, his two arms flailing.

Both hands connected with something soft and brought a grunt of agony. Pain shot through Bond's left hand and he winced as the rifle crashed down across his back. He bore on into the man, blind to pain, hitting with both hands, his head down between hunched shoulders, forcing the man back and off his balance. As he felt the balance yield he straightened himself slightly and lashed out again with his steel-capped foot. It connected with the Robber's kneecap. There was a scream of agony and the rifle clattered to the ground as the Robber tried to save himself. He was half way to the floor when Bond's uppercut hit him and projected the body another few feet.

The Robber fell in the centre of the passage just opposite what Bond could now see was a drawn bolt in the floor.

As the body hit the ground a section of the floor turned swiftly on a central pivot and the body almost disappeared down the black opening of a wide trapdoor in the concrete.

As he felt the floor give under his weight the Robber gave a shrill scream of terror and his hands scrabbled for a hold. They caught the edge of the floor and clutched it just as his whole body slid into space and the six-foot panel of reinforced concrete revolved smoothly until it rested upright on its pivot, a black rectangle yawning on either side.

Bond gasped for air. He put his hands on his hips and got back some of his breath. Then he walked to the edge of the right-hand hole and looked down.

The Robber's terrified face, the lips drawn back from the teeth and the eyes madly distended, jabbered up at him.

Looking beyond him, Bond could see nothing, but he heard the lapping of water against the foundations of the building and there was a faint luminescence on the seaward side. Bond guessed that there was access to the sea through wire or narrow bars.

As the Robber's voice died down to a whimper, Bond could hear something stirring down there, awoken by the light. A Hammerhead or a Tiger Shark, he guessed, with their sharper reactions.

'Pull me out, friend. Give me a break. Pull me out. I can't hold much longer. I'll do anything you want. Tell you anything.' The Robber's voice was a hoarse whisper of supplication.

'What happened to Solitaire?' Bond stared down into the frenzied eyes.

'The Big Man did it. Told me to fix a snatch. Two men in Tampa. Ask for Butch and The Lifer. Poolroom behind the "Oasis". She came to no harm. Lemme out, pal.'

'And the American, Leiter?'

The agonized face pleaded. 'It was his fault. Called me out early this mornin'. Said the place was on fire. Seen it passing in his car. Held me up and brought me back in here. Wanted to search the place. Just fell through the trap. Accident. I swear it was his fault. We pulled him out before he was finished. He'll be okay.'

Bond looked down coldly at the white fingers desperately clinging to the sharp edge of concrete. He knew that the Robber must have got the bolt back and somehow engineered Leiter over the trap. He could hear the man's laugh of triumph as the floor swung open, could see the cruel smile as he pencilled the note and stuck it into the bandages when they had fished the half-eaten body out.

For a moment blind rage seized him.

He kicked out sharply, twice.

One short scream came up out of the depths. There was a splash and then a great commotion in the water.

Bond walked to the side of the trapdoor and pushed the upright concrete slab. It revolved easily on its central pivot.

Just before its edges shut out the blackness below, Bond heard one terrible snuffling grunt as if a great pig was getting its mouth full. He knew it for the grunt that a shark makes as its hideous flat nose comes up out of the water and its sickle-shaped mouth closes on a floating carcass. He shuddered and kicked the bolt home with his foot.

Bond collected the gold coin off the floor and picked up his Beretta. He went to the main entrance and looked back for a moment at the shambles of the battlefield.

He reflected that there was nothing to show that the secret of the treasure had been discovered. The top had been shot off the Scorpion Fish tank under which Bond had dived, and when the other men came in the morning they would not be surprised to find the fish dead in the tank. They would get the remains of the Robber out of the Shark tank and report to Mr Big that he'd been worsted in a gun battle and that there were X thousand dollars' worth of damage which would have to be repaired before the *Secatur* could bring over its next cargo. They would find some of Bond's bullets and soon guess that it was his work.

Bond grimly shut his mind to the horror beneath the floor of the warehouse. He turned off the lights and let himself out by the main entrance.

A small payment had been made on account of Solitaire and Leiter.

16 The Jamaica Version

It was two o'clock in the morning. Bond eased his car away from the sea-wall and moved off through the town on to 4th Street, the highway to Tampa.

He dawdled along down the four-lane concrete highway through the endless gauntlet of motels, trailer camps and roadside emporia selling beach furniture, sea-shells and concrete gnomes.

He stopped at the 'Gulf Winds Bar and Snacks' and ordered a double Old Grandad on the rocks. While the barman poured it he went into the washroom and cleaned himself up. The bandages on his left hand were covered with dirt and the hand throbbed painfully. The splint had broken on the Robber's stomach. There was nothing Bond could do about it. His eyes were red with strain and lack of sleep. He went back to the bar, drank down the Bourbon and ordered another one. The barman looked like a college kid spending his holidays the hard way. He wanted to talk but there was no talk left in Bond. Bond sat and looked into his glass and thought about Leiter and the Robber and heard the sickening grunt of the feeding shark.

He paid and went out and on again over the Gandy Bridge, and the air of the Bay was cool on his face. At the end of the bridge he turned left towards the airport and stopped at the first motel that looked awake.

The middle-aged couple that owned the place were listening to late rhumba music from Cuba with a bottle of rye between them. Bond told a story of a blowout on his way from Sarasota to Silver Springs. They weren't interested. They were just glad to take his ten dollars. He drove his car up to the door of Room 5 and the man unlocked the door and turned on the light. There was a double bed and a shower and a chest-of-drawers and two chairs. The motif was white and blue. It looked clean and Bond put his bag down thankfully and said good night. He stripped and threw his clothes unfolded on to a chair. Then he took a quick shower, cleaned his teeth and gargled with a sharp mouthwash and climbed into bed.

He plunged at once into a calm untroubled sleep. It was the first night since he had arrived in America that did not threaten a fresh battle with his stars on the morrow.

He awoke at midday and walked down the road to a cafeteria where the short-order cook fixed him a delicious three-decker western sandwich and coffee. Then he came back to his room and wrote a detailed report to the FBI at Tampa. He omitted all reference to the gold in the poison tanks for fear that the Big Man would close down his operations in Jamaica. The nature of these had still to be discovered. Bond knew that the damage he had done to the machine in America had no bearing on the heart of his assignment – the discovery of the source of the gold, its seizure, and the destruction, if possible, of Mr Big himself.

He drove to the airport and caught the silver, four-engined plane

261

with a few minutes to spare. He left Leiter's car in the parking space as in his report he had told the FBI he would. He guessed that he need not have mentioned it to the FBI when he saw a man in an unnecessary raincoat hanging round the souvenir shop, buying nothing. Raincoats seemed almost the badge of office of the FBI. Bond was certain they wanted to see he caught the plane. They would be glad to see the last of him. Wherever he had gone in America he had left dead bodies. Before he boarded the plane he called the hospital in St Petersburg. He wished he hadn't; Leiter was still unconscious and there was no news. Yes, they would cable him when they had something definite.

It was five in the evening when they circled over Tampa Bay and headed East. The sun was low on the horizon. A big jet from Pensacola swept by, well to port, leaving four trails of vapour that hung almost motionless in the still air. Soon it would complete its training circuit and go in to land, back to the Gulf Coast packed with oldsters in Truman shirts. Bond was glad to be on his way to the soft green flanks of Jamaica and to be leaving behind the great hard continent of Eldollarado.

The plane swept on across the waist of Florida, across the acres of jungle and swamp without sign of human habitation, its wing-lights blinking green and red in the gathering dark. Soon they were over Miami and the monster chump-traps of the Eastern Seaboard, their arteries ablaze with Neon. Away to port, State Highway No. 1 disappeared up the coast in a golden ribbon of motels, gas stations and fruit-juice stands, up through Palm Beach and Daytona to Jacksonville, three hundred miles away. Bond thought of the breakfast he had had at Jacksonville not three days before and of all that had happened since. Soon, after a short stop at Nassau, he would be flying over Cuba, perhaps over the hideout where Mr Big had put her away. She would hear the noise of the plane and perhaps her instincts would make her look up towards the sky and feel that for a moment he was nearby.

Bond wondered if they would ever meet again and finish what they had begun. But that would have to come later, when his work was over – the prize at the end of the dangerous road that had started three weeks before in the fog of London.

After a cocktail and an early dinner they came in to Nassau and spent half an hour on the richest island in the world, the sandy patch where a thousand million pounds of frightened sterling lies buried beneath the Canasta tables and where bungalows surrounded by a thin surf of screwpine and casuarina change hands at fifty thousand pounds a piece.

They left the platinum whistle-stop behind and were soon crossing the twinkling mother-of-pearl lights of Havana, so different in their pastel modesty from the harsh primary colours of American cities at night.

They were flying at fifteen thousand feet when, just after crossing Cuba, they ran into one of those violent tropical storms that suddenly turn aircraft from comfortable drawing-rooms into bucketing death-traps. The great plane staggered and plunged, its screws now roaring in vacuum and now biting harshly into walls of solid air. The thin tube shuddered and swung. Crockery crashed in the pantry and huge rain hammered on the perspex windows.

Bond gripped the arms of his chair so that his left hand hurt and cursed softly to himself.

He looked at the racks of magazines and thought: they won't help much when the steel tires at fifteen thousand feet, nor will the eau-de-cologne in the washroom, nor the personalized meals, the free razor, the 'orchid for your lady' now trembling in the ice-box. Least of all the safety-belts and the life-jackets with the whistle that the steward demonstrates will really blow, nor the cute little rescue-lamp that glows red.

No, when the stresses are too great for the tired metal, when the ground mechanic who checks the de-icing equipment is crossed in love and skimps his job, way back in London, Idlewild, Gander, Montreal; when those or many things happen, then the little warm room with propellers in front falls straight down out of the sky into the sea or on to the land, heavier than air, fallible, vain. And the forty little heavier-than-air people, fallible within the plane's fallibility, vain within its larger vanity, fall down with it and make little holes in the land or little splashes in the sea. Which is anyway their destiny, so why worry? You are linked to the ground mechanic's careless fingers in

Nassau just as you are linked to the weak head of the little man in the family saloon who mistakes the red light for the green and meets you head-on, for the first and last time, as you are motoring quietly home from some private sin. There's nothing to do about it. You start to die the moment you are born. The whole of life is cutting through the pack with death. So take it easy. Light a cigarette and be grateful you are still alive as you suck the smoke deep into your lungs. Your stars have already let you come quite a long way since you left your mother's womb and whimpered at the cold air of the world. Perhaps they'll even let you get to Jamaica tonight. Can't you hear those cheerful voices in the control tower that have said quietly all day long, 'Come in BOAC. Come in Panam. Come in KLM'? Can't you hear them calling you down too: 'Come in Transcarib. Come in Transcarib'? Don't lose faith in your stars. Remember that hot stitch of time when you faced death from the Robber's gun last night. You're still alive, aren't you? There, we're out of it already. It was just to remind you that being quick with a gun doesn't mean you're really tough. Just don't forget it. This happy landing at Palisadoes Airport comes to you by courtesy of your stars. Better thank them.

Bond unfastened his seatbelt and wiped the sweat off his face.

To hell with it, he thought, as he stepped down out of the huge strong plane.

Strangways, the chief Secret Service agent for the Caribbean, was at the airport to meet him and he was quickly through the Customs and Immigration and Finance Control.

It was nearly eleven and the night was quiet and hot. There was the shrill sound of crickets from the dildo cactus on both sides of the airport road and Bond gratefully drank in the sounds and smells of the tropics as the military pick-up cut across the corner of Kingston and took them up towards the gleaming, moonlit foothills of the Blue Mountains.

They talked in monosyllables until they were settled on the comfortable veranda of Strangways's neat white house on the Junction Road below Stony Hill.

Strangways poured a strong whisky-and-soda for both of them and then gave a concise account of the whole of the Jamaica end of the case.

He was a lean, humorous man of about thirty-five, a former Lieuten-ant-Commander in the Special Branch of the RNVR. He had a black patch over one eye and the sort of aquiline good looks that are associated with the bridges of destroyers. But his face was heavily lined under its tan and Bond sensed from his quick gestures and clipped sentences that he was nervous and highly strung. He was certainly efficient and he had a sense of humour, and he showed no signs of jealousy at someone from headquarters butting in on his territory. Bond felt that they would get on well together and he looked forward to the partnership.

This was the story that Strangways had to tell.

It had always been rumoured that there was treasure on the Isle of Surprise and everything that was known about Bloody Morgan supported the rumour.

The tiny island lay in the exact centre of Shark Bay, a small harbour that lies at the end of the Junction Road that runs across the thin waist of Jamaica from Kingston to the north coast.

The great buccaneer had made Shark Bay his headquarters. He liked to have the whole width of the island between himself and the Governor at Port Royal so that he could slip in and out of Jamaican waters in complete secrecy. The Governor also liked the arrangement. The Crown wished a blind eye to be turned on Morgan's piracy until the Spaniards had been cleared out of the Caribbean. When this was accomplished, Morgan was rewarded with a Knighthood and the Governorship of Jamaica. Till then, his actions had to be disavowed to avoid a European war with Spain.

So, for the long period before the poacher turned gamekeeper, Morgan used Shark Bay as his sallyport. He built three houses on the neighbouring estate, christened Llanrumney after his birthplace in Wales. These houses were called 'Morgan's', 'The Doctor's' and 'The Lady's'. Buckles and coins are still turned up in the ruins of them.

His ships always anchored in Shark Bay and he careened them in the lee of the Isle of Surprise, a precipitous lump of coral and limestone that surges straight up out of the centre of the bay and is surmounted by a jungly plateau of about an acre.

When, in 1683, he left Jamaica for the last time, it was under open arrest to be tried by his peers for flouting the Crown. His treasure was left behind somewhere in Jamaica and he died in penury without revealing its whereabouts. It must have been a vast hoard, the fruits of countless raids on Hispaniola, of the capture of innumerable treasure-ships sailing for The Plate, of the sacking of Panama and the looting of Maracaibo. But it vanished without trace.

It was always thought that the secret lay somewhere on the Isle of Surprise, but for two hundred years the diving and digging of treasure-hunters yielded nothing. Then, said Strangways, just six months before, two things had happened within a few weeks. A young fisherman disappeared from the village of Shark Bay, and had not been heard of since, and an anonymous New York syndicate purchased the island for a thousand pounds from the present owner of the Llanrumney Estate, which was now a rich banana and cattle property.

A few weeks after the sale, the yacht *Secatur* put in to Shark Bay and dropped anchor in Morgan's old anchorage in the lee of the island. It was manned entirely by negroes. They went to work and cut a stairway in the rock face of the island and erected on the summit a number of low-lying shacks in the fashion known in Jamaica as 'wattle-and-daub'.

They appeared to be completely equipped with provisions, and all they purchased from the fishermen of the bay was fresh fruit and water.

They were a taciturn and orderly lot who gave no trouble. They explained to the Customs which they had cleared in the neighbouring Port Maria that they were there to catch tropical fish, especially the poisonous varieties, and collect rare shells for Ourobouros Inc. in St Petersburg. When they had established themselves they purchased large quantities of these from the Shark Bay, Port Maria and Oracabessa fishermen.

For a week they carried out blasting operations on the island and it was given out that these were for the purpose of excavating a large fish-tank.

The *Secatur* began a fortnightly shuttle-service with the Gulf of Mexico and watchers with binoculars confirmed that, before each sailing, consignments of portable fish-tanks were taken aboard. Always half a dozen men were left behind. Canoes approaching the island were warned off by a watchman, at the base of the steps in the cliff, who fished all day from a narrow jetty alongside which the *Secatur* on her visits moored with two anchors out, well sheltered from the prevailing north-easterly winds.

No one succeeded in landing on the island by daylight and, after two tragic attempts, nobody tried to gain access by night.

The first attempt was made by a local fisherman spurred on by the rumours of buried treasure that no talk of tropical fish could suppress. He had swum out one dark night and his body had been washed back over the reef next day. Sharks and barracuda had left nothing but the trunk and the remains of a thigh.

At about the time he should have reached the island the whole village of Shark Bay was awakened by the most horrible drumming noise. It seemed to come from inside the island. It was recognized as the beating of Voodoo drums. It started softly and rose slowly to a thunderous crescendo. Then it died down again and stopped. It lasted about five minutes.

From that moment the island was ju-ju, or obeah, as it is called in Jamaica, and even in daylight canoes kept at a safe distance.

By this time Strangways was interested and he made a full report to London. Since 1950 Jamaica had become an important strategic target, thanks to the development by Reynolds Metal and the Kaiser Corporation of huge bauxite deposits found on the island. So far as Strangways was concerned, the activities on Surprise might easily be the erection of a base for one-man submarines in the event of war, particularly since Shark Bay was within range of the route followed by the Reynolds ships to the new bauxite harbour at Ocho Rios, a few miles down the coast.

London followed the report up with Washington and it came to light that the New York syndicate that had purchased the island was wholly owned by Mr Big.

This was three months ago. Strangways was ordered to penetrate the island at all costs and find out what was going on. He mounted quite an operation. He rented a property on the western arm of Shark Bay called Beau Desert. It contained the ruins of one of the famous

Jamaican Great Houses of the early nineteenth century and also a modern beach-house directly across from the *Secatur*'s anchorage up against Surprise.

He brought down two very fine swimmers from the naval base at Bermuda and set up a permanent watch on the island through day- and night-glasses. Nothing of a suspicious nature was seen and on a dark calm night he sent out the two swimmers with instructions to make an underwater survey of the foundations of the island.

Strangways described his horror when, an hour after they had left to swim across the three hundred yards of water, the terrible drumming had started up somewhere inside the cliffs of the island.

That night the two men did not return.

On the next day they were both washed up at different parts of the bay. Or rather, the remains left by the shark and barracuda.

At this point in Strangways's narrative, Bond interrupted him.

'Just a minute,' he said. 'What's all this about shark and barracuda? They're not generally savage in these waters. There aren't very many of them round Jamaica and they don't often feed at night. Anyway, I don't believe either of them attack humans unless there's blood in the water. Occasionally they might snap at a white foot out of curiosity. Have they ever behaved like this round Jamaica before?'

'Never been a case since a girl got a foot bitten off in Kingston harbour in 1942,' said Strangways. 'She was being towed by a speed-boat, flipping her feet up and down. The white feet must have looked particularly appetising. Travelling at just the right speed too. Everyone agrees with your theory. And my men had harpoons and knives. I thought I'd done everything to protect them. Dreadful business. You can imagine how I felt about it. Since then we've done nothing except try to get legitimate access to the island via the Colonial Office and Washington. You see, it belongs to an American now. Damn slow business, particularly as there's nothing against these people. They seem to have pretty good protection in Washington and some smart international lawyers. We're absolutely stuck. London told me to hang on until you came.' Strangways took a pull at his whisky and looked expectantly at Bond.

'What are the *Secatur*'s movements?' asked Bond.

'Still in Cuba. Sailing in about a week, according to the CIA.'

'How many trips has she done?'

'About twenty.'

Bond multiplied one hundred and fifty thousand dollars by twenty. If his guess was right, Mr Big had already taken a million pounds in gold out of the island.

'I've made some provisional arrangements for you,' said Strangways. 'There's the house at Beau Desert. I've got you a car, Sunbeam Talbot coupé. New tyres. Fast. Right car for these roads. I've got a good man to act as your factotum. A Cayman Islander called Quarrel. Best swimmer and fisherman in the Caribbean. Terribly keen. Nice chap. And I've borrowed the West Indian Citrus Company's rest-house at Manatee Bay. It's the other end of the island. You could rest up there for a week and get in a bit of training until the *Secatur* comes in. You'll need to be fit if you're going to try to get over to Surprise, and I honestly believe that's the only answer. Anything else I can do? I'll be about, of course, but I'll have to stay around Kingston to keep up communications with London and Washington. They'll want to know everything we do. Anything else you'd like me to fix up?'

Bond had been making up his mind.

'Yes,' he said. 'You might ask London to get the Admiralty to lend us one of their frogmen suits complete with compressed-air bottles. Plenty of spares. And a couple of good underwater harpoon guns. The French ones called "Champion" are the best. Good underwater torch. A commando dagger. All the dope they can get from the Natural History Museum on barracuda and shark. And some of that shark-repellent stuff the Americans used in the Pacific. Ask BOAC to fly it all out on their direct service.'

Bond paused. 'Oh yes,' he said. 'And one of those things our saboteurs used against ships in the war. Limpet mine, with assorted fuses.'

17 The Undertaker's Wind

Paw-paw with a slice of green lime, a dish piled with red bananas, purple star-apples and tangerines, scrambled eggs and bacon, Blue Mountain coffee – the most delicious in the world – Jamaican marmalade, almost black, and guava jelly.

As Bond, wearing shorts and sandals, had his breakfast on the veranda and gazed down on the sunlit panorama of Kingston and Port Royal, he thought how lucky he was and what wonderful moments of consolation there were for the darkness and danger of his profession.

Bond knew Jamaica well. He had been there on a long assignment just after the war when the Communist headquarters in Cuba was trying to infiltrate the Jamaican labour unions. It had been an untidy and inconclusive job but he had grown to love the great green island and its staunch, humorous people. Now he was glad to be back and to have a whole week of respite before the grim work began again.

After breakfast, Strangways appeared on the veranda with a tall brown-skinned man in a faded blue shirt and old brown twill trousers.

This was Quarrel, the Cayman Islander, and Bond liked him immediately. There was the blood of Cromwellian soldiers and buccaneers in him and his face was strong and angular and his mouth was almost severe. His eyes were grey. It was only the spatulate nose and the pale palms of his hands that were negroid.

Bond shook him by the hand.

'Good morning, Captain,' said Quarrel. Coming from the most famous race of seamen in the world, this was the highest title he knew. But there was no desire to please, or humility, in his voice. He was speaking as mate of the ship and his manner was straightforward and candid.

That moment defined their relationship. It remained that of a Scots laird with his head stalker; authority was unspoken and there was no room for servility.

After discussing their plans, Bond took the wheel of the little car

Quarrel had brought up from Kingston and they started on up the Junction Road, leaving Strangways to busy himself with Bond's requirements.

They had got off before nine and it was still cool as they crossed the mountains that run along Jamaica's back like the central ridges of a crocodile's armour. The road wound down towards the northern plains through some of the most beautiful scenery in the world, the tropical vegetation changing with the altitude. The green flanks of the uplands, all feathered with bamboo interspersed with the dark, glinting green of breadfruit and the sudden Bengal fire of Flame of the Forest, gave way to the lower forests of ebony, mahogany, mahoe and logwood. And when they reached the plains of Agualta Vale the green sea of sugarcane and bananas stretched away to where the distant fringe of glittering shrapnel bursts marked the palm-groves along the north coast.

Quarrel was a good companion on the drive and a wonderful guide. He talked about the trapdoor spiders as they passed through the famous palm-gardens of Castleton, he told about a fight he had witnessed between a giant centipede and a scorpion and he explained the difference between the male and female paw-paw. He described the poisons of the forest and the healing properties of tropical herbs, the pressure the palm kernel develops to break open its coconut, the length of a humming-bird's tongue, and how crocodiles carry their young in their mouths laid lengthways like sardines in a tin.

He spoke exactly but without expertise, using Jamaican language in which plants 'strive' or 'quail', moths are 'bats', and 'love' is used instead of 'like'. As he talked he would raise his hand in greeting to the people on the road and they would wave back and shout his name.

'You seem to know a lot of people,' said Bond as the driver of a bulging bus with ROMANCE in large letters over the windshield gave him a couple of welcoming blasts on his wind-horn.

'I bin watching Surprise for tree muns, Cap'n,' answered Quarrel, ''n I been travelling this road twice a week. Everyone soon know you in Jamaica. They got good eyes.'

By half-past ten they had passed through Port Maria and branched off along the little parochial road that runs down to Shark Bay. Round a turning they suddenly came on it below them and Bond stopped the car and they got out.

The bay was crescent shaped, perhaps three-quarters of a mile wide at its arms. Its blue surface was ruffled by a light breeze blowing from the north-east, the edge of the Trade Winds that are born five hundred miles away in the Gulf of Mexico and then go on their long journey round the world.

A mile from where they stood, a long line of breakers showed the reef just outside the bay and the narrow untroubled waters of the passage which was the only entrance to the anchorage. In the centre of the crescent, the Isle of Surprise rose a hundred feet sheer out of the water, small waves creaming against its easterly base, calm waters in its lee.

It was nearly round, and it looked like a tall grey cake topped with green icing on a blue china plate.

They had stopped about a hundred feet above the little cluster of fishermen's huts behind the palm-fringed beach of the bay and they were level with the flat green top of the island, half a mile away. Quarrel pointed out the thatched roofs of the wattle-and-daub shanties among the trees in the centre of the island. Bond examined them through Quarrel's binoculars. There was no sign of life except a thin wisp of smoke blowing away with the breeze.

Below them, the water of the bay was pale green on the white sand. Then it deepened to dark blue just before the broken brown of a submerged fringe of inner reef that made a wide semicircle a hundred yards from the island. Then it was dark blue again with patches of lighter blue and aquamarine. Quarrel said that the depth of the *Secatur*'s anchorage was about thirty feet.

To their left, in the middle of the western arms of the bay, deep among the trees behind a tiny white sand beach, was their base of operations, Beau Desert. Quarrel described its layout and Bond stood for ten minutes examining the three-hundred-yard stretch of sea between it and the *Secatur*'s anchorage up against the island.

In all, Bond spent an hour reconnoitring the place, then, without going near their house or the village, they turned the car and got back on the main coast road.

They drove on through the beautiful little banana port of Oraca-bessa and Ocho Rios with its huge new bauxite plant, along the north shore to Montego Bay, two hours away. It was now February and the season was in full swing. The little village and the straggle of large hotels were bathed in the four-month gold-rush that sees them through the whole year. They stopped at a rest-house on the other side of the wide bay and had lunch and then drove on through the heat of the afternoon to the western tip of the island, two hours further on.

Here, because of the huge coastal swamps, nothing has happened since Columbus used Manatee Bay as a casual anchorage. Jamaican fishermen have taken the place of the Arawak Indians, but otherwise there is the impression that time has stood still.

Bond thought it the most beautiful beach he had ever seen, five miles of white sand sloping easily into the breakers and, behind, the palm trees marching in graceful disarray to the horizon. Under them, the grey canoes were pulled up beside pink mounds of discarded conch shells, and among them smoke rose from the palm thatch cabins of the fishermen in the shade between the swamp-lands and the sea.

In a clearing among the cabins, set on a rough lawn of Bahama grass, was the house on stilts built as a weekend cottage for the employees of the West Indian Citrus Company. It was built on stilts to keep the termites at bay and it was closely wired against mosquito and sandfly. Bond drove off the rough track and parked under the house. While Quarrel chose two rooms and made them comfortable Bond put a towel round his waist and walked through the palm trees to the sea, twenty yards away.

For an hour he swam and lazed in the warm buoyant water, thinking of Surprise and its secret, fixing these three hundred yards in his mind, wondering about the shark and barracuda and the other hazards of the sea, that great library of books one cannot read.

Walking back to the little wooden bungalow, Bond picked up his first sandfly bites. Quarrel chuckled when he saw the flat bumps on his back that would soon start to itch maddeningly.

'Can't do nuthen to keep them away, Cap'n,' he said. 'But Ah kin stop them ticklin'. You best take a shower first to git the salt off. They only bites hard for an hour in the evenin' and then they likes salt with their dinner.'

When Bond came out of the shower Quarrel produced an old medicine bottle and swabbed the bites with a brown liquid that smelled of creosote.

'We get more skeeters and sandfly in the Caymans than anywheres else in the world,' he said, 'but we gives them no attention so long as we got this medicine.'

The ten minutes of tropical twilight brought its quick melancholy and then the stars and the three-quarter moon blazed down and the sea died to a whisper. There was the short lull between the two great winds of Jamaica, and then the palms began to whisper again.

Quarrel jerked his head towards the window.

'De "Undertaker's Wind",' he commented.

'How's that?' asked Bond, startled.

'On-and-off shore breeze de sailors call it,' said Quarrel. 'De Undertaker blow de bad air out of de Island night-times from six till six. Then every morning de "Doctor's Wind" come and blow de sweet air in from de sea. Leastwise dat's what we calls dem in Jamaica.'

Quarrel looked quizzically at Bond.

'Guess you and de Undertaker's Wind got much de same job, Cap'n,' he said half-seriously.

Bond laughed shortly. 'Glad I don't have to keep the same hours,' he said.

Outside, the crickets and the tree-frogs started to zing and tinkle and the great hawkmoths came to the wire-netting across the windows and clutched it, gazing with trembling ecstasy at the two oil lamps that hung from the cross-beams inside.

Occasionally a pair of fishermen, or a group of giggling girls, would walk by down the beach on their way to the single tiny rum-shop at the point of the bay. No man walked alone for fear of the duppies under the trees, or the rolling calf, the ghastly animal that comes rolling towards you along the ground, its legs in chains and flames coming out of its nostrils.

While Quarrel prepared one of the succulent meals of fish and eggs and vegetables that were to be their staple diet, Bond sat under the light and pored over the books that Strangways had borrowed from the Jamaica Institute, books on the tropical sea and its denizens by Beebe and Allyn and others, and on sub-marine hunting by Cousteau and Hass. When he set out to cross those three hundred yards of sea, he was determined to do it expertly and to leave nothing to chance. He knew the calibre of Mr Big and he guessed that the defences of Surprise would be technically brilliant. He thought they would not involve simple weapons like guns and high explosives. Mr Big needed to work undisturbed by the police. He had to keep out of reach of the law. He guessed that somehow the forces of the sea had been harnessed to do the Big Man's work for him and it was on these that he concentrated, on murder by shark and barracuda, perhaps by Manta Ray and octopus.

The facts set out by the naturalists were chilling and awe-inspiring, but the experiences of Cousteau in the Mediterranean and of Hass in the Red Sea and Caribbean were more encouraging.

That night Bond's dreams were full of terrifying encounters with giant squids and sting rays, hammerheads and the saw-teeth of barracuda, so that he whimpered and sweated in his sleep.

On the next day he started his training under the critical, appraising eyes of Quarrel. Every morning he swam a mile up the beach before breakfast and then ran back along the firm sand to the bungalow. At about nine they would set out in a canoe, the single triangular sail taking them fast through the water up the coast to Bloody Bay and Orange Bay where the sand ends in cliffs and small coves and the reef is close in against the coast.

Here they would beach the canoe and Quarrel would take him out with spears and masks and an old underwater harpoon gun on breathtaking expeditions in the sort of waters he would encounter in Shark Bay.

They hunted quietly, a few yards apart, Quarrel moving effortlessly in an element in which he was almost at home.

Soon Bond too learned not to fight the sea but always to give and take with the currents and eddies and not to struggle against them, to use judo tactics in the water.

On the first day he came home cut and poisoned by the coral and with a dozen sea-egg spines in his side. Quarrel grinned and treated the wounds with merthiolate and Milton. Then, as every evening, he massaged Bond for half an hour with palm oil, talking quietly the while about the fish they had seen that day, explaining the habits of the carnivores and the ground-feeders, the camouflage of fish and their machinery for changing colour through the blood stream.

He also had never known fish to attack a man except in desperation or because there was blood in the water. He explained that fish are rarely hungry in tropical waters and that most of their weapons are for defence and not for attack. The only exception, he admitted, was the barracuda. 'Mean fish,' he called them, fearless since they knew no enemy except disease, capable of fifty miles an hour over short distances, and with the worst battery of teeth of any fish in the sea.

One day they shot a ten-pounder that had been hanging round them, melting into the grey distances and then reappearing, silent, motionless in the upper water, its angry tiger's eyes glaring at them so close that they could see its gills working softly and the teeth glinting like a wolf's along its cruel underslung jaw.

Quarrel finally took the harpoon gun from Bond and shot it, badly, through the streamlined belly. It came straight for them, its jaws on their great hinges wide open like a striking rattlesnake. Bond made a wild lunge at it with his spear just as it was on to Quarrel. He missed but the spear went between its jaws. They immediately snapped shut on the steel shaft, and as the fish tore the spear out of Bond's hand, Quarrel stabbed at it with his knife and it went mad, dashing through the water with its entrails hanging out, the spear clenched between its teeth, and the harpoon dangling from its body. Quarrel could scarcely hold the line as the fish tried to tear the wide barb through the walls of its stomach, but he moved with it towards a piece of submerged reef and climbed on to it and slowly pulled the fish in.

When Quarrel had cut its throat and they twisted the spear out of its jaws they found bright, deep scratches in the steel.

They took the fish ashore and Quarrel cut its head off and opened the jaws with a piece of wood. The upper jaw rose in an enormous gape, almost at right angles to the lower, and revealed a fantastic battery of razor-sharp teeth, so crowded that they overlapped like shingles on a roof. Even the tongue had several runs of small pointed recurved teeth and, in front, there were two huge fangs that projected forward like a snake's.

Although it only weighed just over ten pounds, it was over four feet long, a nickel bullet of muscle and hard flesh.

'We shoot no more cudas,' said Quarrel. 'But for you I been in hospital for a month and mebbe lost ma face. It was foolish of me. If we swim towards it, it gone away. Dey always do. Dey cowards like all fish. Doan you worry bout those,' he pointed at the teeth. 'You never see dem again.'

'I hope not,' said Bond. 'I haven't got a face to spare.'

By the end of the week, Bond was sunburned and hard. He had cut his cigarettes down to ten a day and had not had a single drink. He could swim two miles without tiring, his hand was completely healed and all the scales of big city life had fallen from him.

Quarrel was pleased. 'You ready for Surprise, Cap'n,' he said, 'and I not like be de fish what tries to eat you.'

Towards nightfall on the eighth day they came back to the rest-house to find Strangways waiting for them.

'I've got some good news for you,' he said: 'your friend Felix Leiter's going to be all right. At all events he's not going to die. They've had to amputate the remains of an arm and a leg. Now the plastic surgery chaps have started building up his face. They called me up from St Petersburg yesterday. Apparently he insisted on getting a message to you. First thing he thought of when he could think at all. Says he's sorry not to be with you and to tell you not to get your feet wet – or at any rate, not as wet as he did.'

Bond's heart was full. He looked out of the window. 'Tell him to get well quickly,' he said abruptly. 'Tell him I miss him.' He looked back into the room. 'Now what about the gear? Everything okay?'

'I've got it all,' said Strangways, 'and the *Secatur* sails tomorrow for Surprise. After clearing at Port Maria, they should anchor before nightfall. Mr Big's on board – only the second time he's been down here. Oh and they've got a woman with them. Girl called Solitaire, according to the CIA. Know anything about her?'

277

'Not much,' said Bond. 'But I'd like to get her away from him. She's not one of his team.'

'Sort of damsel in distress,' said the romantic Strangways. 'Good show. According to the CIA she's a corker.'

But Bond had gone out on the veranda and was gazing up at his stars. Never before in his life had there been so much to play for. The secret of the treasure, the defeat of a great criminal, the smashing of a Communist spy ring, and the destruction of a tentacle of SMERSH, the cruel machine that was his own private target. And now Solitaire, the ultimate personal prize.

The stars winked down their cryptic morse and he had no key to their cipher.

18 Beau Desert

Strangways went back alone after dinner and Bond agreed that they would follow at first light. Strangways left him a fresh pile of books and pamphlets on shark and barracuda and Bond went through them with rapt attention.

They added little to the practical lore he had picked up from Quarrel. They were all by scientists and much of the data on attacks was from the beaches of the Pacific where a flashing body in the thick surf would excite any inquisitive fish.

But there seemed to be general agreement that the danger to underwater swimmers with breathing equipment was far less than to surface swimmers. They might be attacked by almost any of the shark family, particularly when the shark was stimulated and excited by blood in the water, by the smell of a swimmer or by the sensory vibration set up by an injured person in the water. But they could sometimes be frightened off, he read, by loud noises in the water – even by shouting below the surface, and they would often flee if a swimmer chased them.

The most successful form of shark repellent, according to US Naval Research Laboratory tests, was a combination of copper acetate and a dark nigrosine dye, and cakes of this mixture were apparently now attached to the Mae Wests of all the US Armed Forces.

Bond called in Quarrel. The Cayman Islander was scornful until Bond read out to him what the Navy Department had to say about their researches at the end of the war among packs of sharks stimulated by what was described as 'extreme mob behaviour conditions': '. . . Sharks were attracted to the back of the shrimp boat with trash fish,' read out Bond. 'Sharks appeared as a slashing, splashing shoal. We prepared a tub of fresh fish and another tub of fish mixed with repellent powder. We got up to the shoal of sharks and the photographer started his camera. I shovelled over the plain fish for 30 seconds while the sharks, with much splashing, ate them. Then I started on the repellent fish and shovelled for 30 seconds repeating the procedure 3 times. On the first trial the sharks were quite ferocious in feeding on plain fish right at the stern of the boat. They cut fish for only about 5 seconds after the repellent mixture was thrown over. A few came back when the plain fish were put out immediately following the repellent. On a second trial 30 minutes later, a ferocious school fed for the 30 seconds that plain fish were supplied, but left as soon as the repellent struck the water. There were no attacks on fish while the repellent was in the water. On the third trial we could not get the sharks nearer than 20 yards of the stern of the boat.'

'What do you make of that?' asked Bond.

'You better have some of dat stuff,' said Quarrel, impressed against his will.

Bond was inclined to agree with him. Washington had cabled that cakes of the stuff were on the way. But they had not yet arrived and were not expected for another forty-eight hours. If the repellent did not arrive, Bond was not dismayed. He could not imagine that he would encounter such dangerous conditions in his underwater swim to the island.

Before he went to bed, he finally decided that nothing would attack him unless there was blood in the water or unless he communicated fear to a fish that threatened. As for octopus, scorpion fish and morays, he would just have to watch where he put his feet. To his mind, the three-inch spines of the black sea-eggs were the greatest hazard to normal underwater swimming in the tropics and the pain they caused would not be enough to interfere with his plans.

They left before six in the morning and were at Beau Desert by half-past ten.

The property was a beautiful old plantation of about a thousand acres with the ruins of a fine Great House commanding the bay. It was given over to pimento and citrus inside a fringe of hardwoods and palms and had a history dating back to the time of Cromwell. The romantic name was in the fashion of the eighteenth century, when Jamaican properties were called Bellair, Bellevue, Boscobel, Harmony, Nymphenburg or had names like Prospect, Content or Repose.

A track, out of sight of the island in the bay, led them among the trees down to the little beach-house. After the week's picnic at Manatee Bay, the bathrooms and comfortable bamboo furniture seemed very luxurious and the brightly coloured rugs were like velvet under Bond's hardened feet.

Through the slats of the jalousies Bond looked across the little garden, aflame with hibiscus, bougainvillea and roses, which ended in the tiny crescent of white sand half obscured by the trunks of the palms. He sat on the arm of a chair and let his eyes go on, inch by inch, across the different blues and browns of sea and reef until they met the base of the island. The upper half of it was obscured by the dipping feathers of the palm trees in the foreground, but the stretch of vertical cliff within his vision looked grey and formidable in the half-shadow cast by the hot sun.

Quarrel cooked lunch on a primus stove so that no smoke would betray them, and in the afternoon Bond slept and then went over the gear from London that had been sent across from Kingston by Strangways. He tried on the thin black rubber frogman's suit that covered him from the skull-tight helmet with the perspex window to the long black flippers over his feet. It fitted like a glove and Bond blessed the efficiency of M's 'Q' Branch.

They tested the twin cylinders each containing a thousand litres of free air compressed to two hundred atmospheres and Bond found the manipulation of the demand valve and the reserve mechanism simple and fool-proof. At the depth he would be working the supply of air would last him for nearly two hours under water.

There was a new and powerful Champion harpoon gun and a commando dagger of the type devised by Wilkinsons during the war. Finally, in a box covered with danger-labels, there was the heavy limpet mine, a flat cone of explosive on a base, studded with wide copper bosses, so powerfully magnetized that the mine would stick like a clam to any metal hull. There were a dozen pencil-shaped metal and glass fuses set for ten minutes to eight hours and a careful memorandum of instructions that were as simple as the rest of the gear. There was even a box of benzedrine tablets to give endurance and heightened perception during the operation and an assortment of underwater torches, including one that threw only a tiny pencil-thin beam.

Bond and Quarrel went through everything, testing joints and contacts until they were satisfied that nothing further remained to be done, then Bond went down among the trees and gazed and gazed at the waters of the bay, guessing at depths, tracing routes through the broken reef and estimating the path of the moon, which would be his only point of reckoning on the tortuous journey.

At five o'clock, Strangways arrived with news of the *Secatur*.

'They've cleared Port Maria,' he said. 'They'll be here in ten minutes at the outside. Mr Big had a passport in the name of Gallia and the girl in the name of Latrelle, Simone Latrelle. She was in her cabin, prostrate with what the negro captain of the *Secatur* described as seasickness. It may have been. Scores of empty fish-tanks on board. More than a hundred. Otherwise nothing suspicious and they were given a clean bill. I wanted to go on board as one of the Customs team but I thought it best that the show should be absolutely normal. Mr Big stuck to his cabin. He was reading when they went to see his papers. How's the gear?'

'Perfect,' said Bond. 'Guess we'll operate tomorrow night. Hope there's a bit of a wind. If the air-bubbles are spotted we shall be in a mess.'

Quarrel came in. 'She's coming through the reef now, Cap'n.'

They went down as close to the shore as they dared and put their glasses on her.

She was a handsome craft, black with a grey superstructure, seventy foot long and built for speed – at least twenty knots, Bond guessed. He knew her history, built for a millionaire in 1947 and powered with twin General Motors Diesels, steel hull and all the latest wireless gadgets, including ship-to-shore telephone and Decca navigator. She was wearing the Red Ensign at her cross-trees and the Stars and Stripes aft and she was making about three knots through the twenty-foot opening of the reef.

She turned sharply inside the reef and came down to seaward of the island. When she was below it, she put her helm hard over and came up with the island to port. At the same time three negroes in white ducks came running down the cliff steps to the narrow jetty and stood by to catch lines. There was a minimum of backing and filling before she was made fast just opposite to the watchers ashore, and the two anchors roared down among the rocks and coral scattered round the island's foundations in the sand. She lay well secured even against a 'Norther'. Bond estimated there would be about twenty feet of water below her keel.

As they watched, the huge figure of Mr Big appeared on deck. He stepped on to the jetty and started slowly to climb the steep cliff steps. He paused often, and Bond thought of the diseased heart pumping laboriously in the great grey-black body.

He was followed by two negro members of the crew hauling up a light stretcher on which a body was strapped. Through his glasses Bond could see Solitaire's black hair. Bond was worried and puzzled and he felt a tightening of the heart at her nearness. He prayed the stretcher was only a precaution to prevent Solitaire from being recognized from the shore.

Then a chain of twelve men was established up the steps and the fish-tanks were handed up one by one. Quarrel counted a hundred and twenty of them.

Then some stores went up by the same method.

'Not taking much up this time,' commented Strangways when the operation ceased. 'Only half a dozen cases gone up. Generally about fifty. Can't be staying long.'

He had hardly finished speaking before a fish-tank, which their glasses showed was half full of water and sand, was being gingerly passed back to the ship, down the human ladder of hands. Then another and another, at about five-minute intervals.

'My God,' said Strangways. 'They're loading her up already. That means they'll be sailing in the morning. Wonder if it means they've decided to clean the place out and that this is the last cargo.'

Bond watched carefully for a while and then they walked quietly up through the trees, leaving Quarrel to report developments.

They sat down in the living-room, and while Strangways mixed himself a whisky-and-soda, Bond gazed out of the window and marshalled his thoughts.

It was six o'clock and the fireflies were beginning to show in the shadows. The pale primrose moon was already high up in the eastern sky and the day was dying swiftly at their backs. A light breeze was ruffling the bay and the scrolls of small waves were unfurling on the white beach across the lawn. A few small clouds, pink and orange in the sunset, were meandering by overhead and the palm trees clashed softly in the cool Undertaker's Wind.

'Undertaker's Wind,' thought Bond and smiled wryly. So it would have to be tonight. The only chance, and the conditions were so nearly perfect. Except that the shark-repellent stuff would not arrive in time. And that was only a refinement. There was no excuse. This was what he had travelled two thousand miles and five deaths to do. And yet he shivered at the prospect of the dark adventure under the sea that he had already put off in his mind until tomorrow. Suddenly he loathed and feared the sea and everything in it. The millions of tiny antennae that would stir and point as he went by that night, the eyes that would wake and watch him, the pulses that would miss for the hundredth of a second and then go beating quietly on, the jelly tendrils that would grope and reach for him, as blind in the light as in the dark.

He would be walking through thousands of millions of secrets. In three hundred yards, alone and cold, he would be blundering through a forest of mystery towards a deadly citadel whose guardians had already killed three men. He, Bond, after a week's paddling with his nanny beside him in the sunshine, was going out tonight, in a few hours, to walk alone under that black sheet of water. It was crazy, unthinkable. Bond's flesh cringed and his fingers dug into his wet palms.

There was a knock on the door and Quarrel came in. Bond was glad to get up and move away from the window to where Strangways was enjoying his drink under a shaded reading light.

'They're working with lights now, Cap'n,' Quarrel said with a grin. 'Still a tank every five minutes. I figure that'll be ten hours' work. Be through about four in the morning. Won't sail before six. Too dangerous to try the passage without plenty light.'

Quarrel's warm grey eyes in the splendid mahogany face were looking into Bond's, waiting for orders.

'I'll start at ten sharp,' Bond found himself saying. 'From the rocks to the left of the beach. Can you get us some dinner and then get the gear out on to the lawn? Conditions are perfect. I'll be over there in half an hour.' He counted on his fingers. 'Give me fuses for five to eight hours. And the quarter-hour one in reserve in case anything goes wrong. Okay?'

'Aye aye, Cap'n,' said Quarrel. 'You jes leave 'em all to me.'

He went out.

Bond looked at the whisky bottle, then he made up his mind and poured half a glass on top of three ice cubes. He took the box of benzedrine tablets out of his pocket and slipped a tablet between his teeth.

'Here's luck,' he said to Strangways and took a deep swallow. He sat down and enjoyed the tough hot taste of his first drink for more than a week. 'Now,' he said, 'tell me exactly what they do when they're ready to sail. How long it takes them to clear the island and get through the reef. If it's the last time, don't forget they'll be taking off an extra six men and some stores. Let's try to work it out as closely as we can.'

In a moment Bond was immersed in a sea of practical details and the shadow of fear had fled back to the dark pools under the palm trees.

Exactly at ten o'clock, with nothing but anticipation and excitement in him, the shimmering black bat-like figure slipped off the rocks into ten feet of water and vanished under the sea.

'Go safely,' said Quarrel to the spot where Bond had disappeared. He crossed himself. Then he and Strangways moved back through the shadows to the house to sleep uneasily in watches and wait fearfully for what might come.

19 Valley of Shadows

Bond was carried straight to the bottom by the weight of the limpet mine that he had secured to his chest with tapes and by the leaded belt which he wore round his waist to correct the buoyancy of the compressed-air cylinders.

He didn't pause for an instant but immediately streaked across the first fifty yards of open sand in a fast crawl, his face just above the sand. The long webbed feet would almost have doubled his normal speed if he had not been hampered by the weight he was carrying and by the light harpoon gun in his left hand, but he travelled fast and in under a minute he came to rest in the shadow of a mass of sprawling coral.

He paused and examined his sensations.

He was warm in the rubber suit, warmer than he would have been swimming in the sunshine. He found his movements very easy and breathing perfectly simple so long as his breath was even and re-laxed. He watched the tell-tale bubbles streaming up against the coral in a fountain of silver pearls and prayed that the small waves were hiding them.

In the open he had been able to see perfectly. The light was soft and milky but not strong enough to melt the mackerel shadows of the surface waves that chequered the sand. Now, up against the reef, there was no reflection from the bottom, and the shadows under the rocks were black and impenetrable.

He risked a quick glance with his pencil torch and immediately the underbelly of the mass of brown tree-coral came alive. Anemones with crimson centres waved their velvet tentacles at him, a colony of black sea-eggs moved their toledo-steel spines in sudden alarm and a hairy sea-centipede halted in its hundred strides and questioned with its eyeless head. In the sand at the base of the tree a toad-fish softly drew its hideous warty head back into its funnel and a number of flower-like sea-worms whisked out of sight down their gelatinous tubes. A covey of bejewelled butterfly and angel fish flirted into the light and he marked the flat spiral of a Long-spined Star Shell.

Bond tucked the light back in his belt.

Above him the surface of the sea was a canopy of quicksilver. It crackled softly like fat frying in a saucepan. Ahead the moonlight glinted down into the deep crooked valley that sloped down and away on the route he had to follow. He left his sheltering tree of coral and walked softly forward. Now it was not so easy. The light was tricky and bad and the petrified forest of the coral reef was full of culs-de-sac and tempting but misleading avenues.

Sometimes he had to climb almost to the surface to get over a tangled scrub of tree- and antler-coral and when this happened he profited by it to check his position with the moon that glowed like a huge pale rocket-burst through the broken water. Sometimes the hourglass waist of a niggerhead gave him shelter and he rested for a few moments knowing that the small froth of his air-bubbles would be hidden by the jagged knob protruding above the surface. Then he would focus his eyes on the phosphorescent scribbles of the minute underwater night-life and perceive whole colonies and populations about their microscopic business.

There were no big fish about, but many lobsters were out of their holes looking huge and prehistoric in the magnifying lens of the water. Their stalk-like eyes glared redly at him and their foot-long spined antennae asked him for the password. Occasionally they scuttled nervously backwards into their shelters, their powerful tails kicking up the sand, and crouched on the tips of their eight hairy feet, waiting for the danger to pass. Once the great streamers of a portuguese man-of-war floated slowly by. They almost reached his head from the surface, fifteen feet away, and he remembered the whiplash of a sting from the contact of one of their tendrils that had burned for three of his days at Manatee Bay. If they caught a man across the heart they could kill him. He saw several green and speckled moray eels, the latter moving like big yellow and black snakes along patches of sand, the green ones baring their teeth from some hole in the rock, and several West Indian blowfish, like brown owls with huge soft green eyes. He poked at one with the end of his gun and it swelled out to the size of a football and became a mass of dangerous white spines. Wide sea fans swayed and beckoned in the eddies, and in the grey valleys they caught the light of the moon and waved spectrally, like fragments of the shrouds of men buried at sea. Often in the shadows there were unexplained, heavy movements and swirls in the water and the sudden glare of large eyes at once extinguished. Then Bond would whirl round, thumbing up the safety-catch on his harpoon gun, and stare back into the darkness. But he shot at nothing and nothing attacked him as he scrambled and slithered through the reef.

The hundred yards of coral took him a quarter of an hour. When he got through and rested on a round lump of brain-coral under the shelter of a last niggerhead, he was glad that nothing but a hundred yards of grey-white water lay in front of him. He still felt perfectly fresh and the elation and clarity of mind produced by the benzedrine were still with him, but the gauntlet of hazards through the reef had been a constant fret, with the risk of tearing his rubber skin always on his mind. Now the forest of razor-blade coral was behind, to be exchanged for shark and barracuda or perhaps a sudden stick of dynamite dropped into the centre of the little flower of his bubbles on the surface.

It was while he was measuring the dangers ahead that the octopus got him. Round both ankles.

He had been sitting with his feet on the sand and suddenly they were manacled to the base of the round toadstool of coral on which he was resting. Even as he realized what had happened a tentacle began to snake up his leg and another one, purple in the dim light, wandered down his webbed left foot.

He gave a start of fear and disgust and at once he was on his feet, shuffling and straining to get away. But there was no inch of yield and his movements only gave the octopus an opportunity to pull his heels tighter under the overhang of the round rock. The strength of the brute was prodigious and Bond could feel his balance going fast. In a moment he would be pulled down flat on his face and then, hampered by the mine on his chest and the cylinders on his back, it might be almost impossible to get at the beast.

Bond snatched his dagger out of his belt and jabbed down between his legs. But the overhang of the rock impeded him and he was terrified of cutting his rubber skin. Suddenly he was toppled over, lying on the sand. At once his feet began to be drawn into a wide lateral cleft under the rock. He scrabbled at the sand and tried to curl round to get within range with the dagger. But the thick hump of the mine protruding from his chest prevented him. On the edge of panic, he remembered the harpoon gun. Before, he had dismissed it as being a hopeless weapon at that short range, but now it was the only chance. It lay on the sand where he had left it. He reached for it and put up the safety-catch. The mine prevented him from aiming. He slid the barrel along his legs and probed each of his feet with the tip of the harpoon to find the gap between them. At once a tentacle seized the steel tip and began tugging. The gun slipped between his manacled feet and he pulled the trigger blindly.

Immediately a great cloud of viscous, stringy ink rolled out of the cleft towards his face. But one leg was free and then the other and he whipped them round and under him and seized the haft of the three-foot harpoon where it disappeared under the rock. He pulled and strained until, with a rending of flesh, it came away from the black fog that hung over the hole. Panting, he got up and stood away from the rock, the sweat pouring down his face under the mask. Above him, the tell-tale stream of silver bubbles rose straight to the surface and he cursed the wounded 'pusfeller' in its lair.

But there was no time to worry further with it and he re-loaded his gun and struck out with the moon over his right shoulder.

Now he made good going through the misty grey water and he concentrated only on keeping his face a few inches above the sand and his head well down to streamline his body. Once, out of the corner of his eye, he saw a stingray as big as a ping-pong table shuffle out of his path, the tip of its great speckled wings beating like a bird's, its long horned tail streaming out behind it. But he paid it no attention, remembering that Quarrel had said that rays never attack except in self-defence. He reflected that it had probably come in over the outer reef to lay its eggs, or 'Mermaids' Purses' as the fishermen call them, because they are shaped like a pillow with a stiff black string at each corner. on the sheltered sandy bottom.

Many shadows of big fish lazed across the moonlit sand, some as long as himself. When one followed beside him for at least a minute he looked up to see the white belly of a shark ten feet above him like a glaucous tapering airship. Its blunt nose was buried inquisitively in his stream of air-bubbles. The wide sickle slit of its mouth looked like a puckered scar. It leant sideways and glanced down at him out of one hard pink naked eye, then it wobbled its great scythe-shaped tail and moved slowly into the wall of grey mist.

He frightened a family of squids, ranging from about six pounds down to an infant of six ounces, frail and luminous in the half-light, hanging almost vertical in a diminishing chorus-line. They righted themselves and shot off with streamlined jet propulsion.

Bond rested for a moment about half way and then went on. Now there were barracuda about, big ones of up to twenty pounds. They looked just as deadly as he had remembered them. They glided above him like silver submarines, looking down out of their angry tigers' eyes. They were curious about him and about his bubbles and they followed him, around and above him, like a pack of silent wolves. By the time Bond met the first bit of coral that meant he was coming up with the island there must have been twenty of them moving quietly, watchfully in and out of the opaque wall that enclosed him.

Bond's skin cringed under the black rubber but he could do nothing about them and he concentrated on his objective.

Suddenly there was a long metallic shape hanging in the water above him. Behind it there was a jumble of broken rock leading steeply upwards.

It was the keel of the *Secatur* and Bond's heart thumped in his chest.

He looked at the Rolex watch on his wrist. It was three minutes past eleven o'clock. He selected the seven-hour fuse from the handful he extracted from a zipped side-pocket and inserted it in the fuse pocket of the mine and pushed it home. The rest of the fuses he buried in the sand so that if he was captured the mine would not be betrayed.

As he swam up, carrying the mine between his hands, bottom upwards, he was aware of a commotion in the water behind him. A barracuda flashed by, its jaws half open, almost hitting him, its eyes fixed on something at his back. But Bond was intent only on the centre of the ship's keel and on a point about three feet above it.

The mine almost dragged him the last few feet, its huge magnets straining for the metallic kiss with the hull. Bond had to pull hard against it to prevent the clang of contact. Then it was silently in place and with its weight removed Bond had to swim strongly to counter his new buoyancy and get down again and away from the surface.

It was as he turned to swim towards the twin propellers on his way to the shelter of the rocks that he suddenly saw the terrible things that had been going on behind him.

The great pack of barracudas seemed to have gone mad. They were whirling and snapping in the water like hysterical dogs. Three sharks that had joined them were charging through the water with a clumsier frenzy. The water was boiling with the dreadful fish and Bond was slammed in the face and buffeted again and again within a few yards. At any moment he knew his rubber skin would be torn with the flesh below it and then the pack would be on him.

'Extreme mob behaviour conditions.' The Navy Department's phrase flashed into his mind. This was just when he might have saved himself with the shark-repellent stuff. Without it he might only have a few more minutes to live.

In desperation he threshed through the water along the ship's keel, the safety-catch up on the harpoon gun that was now only a toy in the face of this drove of maddened cannibal fish.

He reached the two big copper screws and clung to one of them, panting, his lips drawn back from his teeth in a snarl of fear, his eyes distended as he faced the frenzy of the boiling sea around him.

He at once saw that the mouths of the hurtling, darting fish were half open and that they were plunging in and out of a brownish cloud, spreading downwards from the surface. Close to him a barracuda hung for an instant, something brown and glittering in its jaws. It gave a great swallow and then swirled back into the mêlée.

At the same time he noticed that it was getting darker. He looked up and saw with dawning comprehension that the quicksilver surface of the sea had turned red, a horrible glinting crimson.

Threads of the stuff drifted within his reach. He hooked some towards him with the end of his gun. Held the end close up against his glass mask.

There was no doubt about it.

Up above, someone was spraying the surface of the sea with blood and offal.

20 Bloody Morgan's Cave

Immediately Bond understood why all these barracuda and shark were lurking round the island, how they were kept frenzied with bloodlust by this nightly banquet, why, against all reason, the three men had been washed up half-eaten by the fish.

Mr Big had just harnessed the forces of the sea for his protection. It was a typical invention – imaginative, technically foolproof and very easy to operate.

Even as Bond's mind grasped it all, something hit him a terrific blow in the shoulder and a twenty-pound barracuda backed away, black rubber and flesh hanging from its jaws. Bond felt no pain as he let go of the bronze propeller and threshed wildly for the rocks, only a horrible sickness in the pit of his stomach at the thought of part of himself between those hundred razor-sharp teeth. Water started to ooze between the close-fitting rubber and his skin. It would not be long before it penetrated up his neck and into the mask.

He was just going to give up and shoot the twenty feet to the surface when he saw a wide fissure in the rocks in front of him. Beside it a great boulder lay on its side and somehow he got behind it. He turned from the partial shelter it gave just in time to see the same barracuda coming at him again, its upper jaw held at right angles to the lower for its infamous gaping strike.

Bond fired almost blind with the harpoon gun. The rubber thongs whammed down the barrel and the barbed harpoon caught the big

fish in the centre of its raised upper jaw, pierced it and stuck with half
the shaft and the line still free.

The barracuda stopped dead in its tracks, three feet from Bond's
stomach. It tried to get its jaws together and then gave a mighty shake
of its long reptile's head. Then it shot away, zigzagging madly, the gun
and line, jerked from Bond's hand, streaming behind it. Bond knew
that the other fish would be on to it, tearing it to bits, before it had
gone a hundred yards.

Bond thanked God for the diversion. His shoulder was now surrounded by a cloud of blood. In a matter of seconds the other fish
would catch the scent. He slipped round the boulder with the thought
that he would scramble up under the shelter of the jetty and somehow
hide himself above the level of the sea until he had made a fresh plan.

Then he saw the cave that the boulder had hidden.

It was really almost a door into the base of the island. If Bond had
not been swimming for his life he could have walked in. As it was, he
dived straight through the opening and only stopped when several
yards separated him from the glimmering entrance.

Then he stood upright on the soft sand and switched on his torch.
A shark might conceivably come in after him but in the confined space
it would be almost impossible for it to bring its underslung mouth to
bear on him. It would certainly not come in with a rush for even the
shark is frightened of hazarding its tough skin among rocks, and he
would have plenty of chance of going for its eyes with his dagger.

Bond shone his torch on the ceiling and sides of the cave. It had
certainly been fashioned or finished by man. Bond guessed that it had
been dug outwards from somewhere in the centre of the island.

'At least another twenty yards to go, men,' Bloody Morgan must
have said to the slave overseers. And then the picks would have burst
suddenly through to the sea and a welter of arms and legs and
screaming mouths, gagged for ever with water, would have hurtled
back into the rock to join the bodies of other witnesses.

The great boulder at the entrance would have been put in position
to seal the seaward exit. The Shark Bay fisherman who suddenly
disappeared six months before must have one day found it rolled
away by a storm or by the tidal wave following a hurricane. Then he had

found the treasure and had known he would need help to dispose of it. A white man would cheat him. Better go to the great negro gangster in Harlem and make the best terms he could. The gold belonged to the black men who had died to hide it. It should go back to the black men.

Standing there, swaying in the slight current in the tunnel, Bond guessed that one more barrel of cement had splashed into the mud of the Harlem River.

It was then that he heard the drums.

Out amongst the big fish he had heard a soft thunder in the water that had grown as he entered the cave. But he had thought it was only the waves against the base of the island, and anyway he had had other things to think about.

But now he could distinguish a definite rhythm and the sound boomed and swelled around him in a muffled roar as if he himself was imprisoned inside a vast kettle-drum. The water seemed to tremble with it. He guessed its double purpose. It was a great fish-call used, when intruders were about, to attract and excite the fish still further. Quarrel had told him how the fishermen at night beat the sides of their canoes with the paddle to wake and bring the fish. This must be the same idea. And at the same time it would be a sinister Voodoo warning to the people on shore, made doubly effective when the dead body was washed up on the following day.

Another of Mr Big's refinements, thought Bond. Another spark thrown off by that extraordinary mind.

Well, at least he knew where he was now. The drums meant that he had been spotted. What would Strangways and Quarrel think as they heard them? They would just have to sit and sweat it out. Bond had guessed the drums were some sort of trick and he had made them promise not to interfere unless the *Secatur* got safely away. That would mean that all Bond's plans had failed. He had told Strangways where the gold was hidden and the ship would have to be intercepted on the high seas.

Now the enemy was alerted, but would not know who he was nor that he was still alive. He would have to go on if only to stop Solitaire at all costs from sailing in the doomed ship.

Bond looked at his watch. It was half an hour after midnight. So far as Bond was concerned, it might have been a week since he started his lonely voyage through the sea of dangers.

He felt the Beretta under his rubber skin and wondered if it was already ruined by the water that had got in through the rent made by the barracuda's teeth.

Then, the roar of the drums getting louder every moment, he moved on into the cave, his torch throwing a tiny pinpoint of light ahead of him.

He had gone about ten yards when a faint glimmer showed in the water ahead of him. He dowsed the torch and went cautiously towards it. The sandy floor of the cave started to move upwards and with every yard the light grew brighter. Now he could see dozens of small fish playing around him and ahead the water seemed full of them, attracted into the cave by the light. Crabs peered from the small crevices in the rocks and a baby octopus flattened itself into a phosphorescent star against the ceiling.

Then he could make out the end of the cave and a wide shining pool beyond it, the white sandy bottom as bright as day. The throb of the drums was very loud. He stopped in the shadow of the entrance and saw that the surface was only a few inches away and that lights were shining down into the pool.

Bond was in a quandary. Any further step and he would be in full view of anyone looking at the pool. As he stood, debating with himself, he was horrified to see a thin red cloud of blood spreading beyond the entrance from his shoulder. He had forgotten the wound, but now it began to throb, and when he moved his arm the pain shot through it. There was also the thin stream of bubbles from the cylinders, but he hoped these were just creeping up to burst unnoticed at the lip of the entrance.

Even as he drew back a few inches into his hole, his future was settled for him.

Above his head there was a single huge splash and two negroes, naked except for the glass masks over their faces, were on to him, long daggers held like lances in their left hands.

Before his hand reached the knife at his belt they had seized both his arms and were hauling him to the surface.

Hopelessly, helplessly, Bond let himself be man-handled out of the pool on to flat sand. He was pulled to his feet and the zips of his rubber suit were torn open. His helmet was snatched off his head and his holster from his shoulder and suddenly he was standing among the debris of his black skin, like a flayed snake, naked except for his brief swimming-trunks. Blood oozed down from the jagged hole in his left shoulder.

When his helmet came off Bond was almost deafened by the shattering boom and stutter of the drums. The noise was in him and all around him. The hastening syncopated rhythm galloped and throbbed in his blood. It seemed enough to wake all Jamaica. Bond grimaced and clenched his senses against the buffeting tempest of noise. Then his guards turned him round and he was faced with a scene so extraordinary that the sound of the drums receded and all his consciousness was focused through his eyes.

In the foreground, at a green baize card-table, littered with papers, in a folding chair, sat Mr Big, a pen in his hand, looking incuriously at him. A Mr Big in a well-cut fawn tropical suit, with a white shirt and black knitted silk tie. His broad chin rested on his left hand and he looked up at Bond as if he had been disturbed in his office by a member of the staff asking for a raise in salary. He looked polite but faintly bored.

A few steps away from him, sinister and incongruous, the scarecrow effigy of Baron Samedi, erect on a rock, gaped at Bond from under its bowler hat.

Mr Big took his hand off his chin, and his great golden eyes looked Bond over from top to toe.

'Good morning, Mister James Bond,' he said at last, throwing his flat voice against the dying crescendo of the drums. 'The fly has indeed been a long time coming to the spider, or perhaps I should say "the minnow to the whale". You left a pretty wake of bubbles after the reef.'

He leant back in his chair and was silent. The drums softly thudded and boomed.

So it was the fight with the octopus that had betrayed him. Bond's mind automatically registered the fact as his eyes moved on past the man at the table.

He was in a rock chamber as big as a church. Half the floor was taken up with the clear white pool from which he had come and which verged into aquamarine and then blue near the black hole of the underwater entrance. Then there was the narrow strip of sand on which he was standing and the rest of the floor was smooth flat rock dotted with a few grey and white stalagmites.

Some way behind Mr Big, steep steps mounted towards a vaulted ceiling from which short limestone stalactites hung down. From their white nipples water dripped intermittently into the pool or on to the points of the young stalagmites that rose towards them from the floor.

A dozen bright arc lights were fixed high up on the walls and reflected golden highlights from the naked chests of a group of negroes standing to his left on the stone floor rolling their eyes and watching Bond, their teeth showing in delighted cruel grins.

Round their black and pink feet, in a debris of broken timber and rusty iron hoops, mildewed strips of leather and disintegrating canvas, was a blazing sea of gold coin – yards, piles, cascades of round golden specie from which the black legs rose as if they had been halted in the middle of a walk through flame.

Beside them were piled row upon row of shallow wooden trays. There were some on the floor partly filled with gold coin, and at the bottom of the steps a single negro had stopped on his way up and he was holding one of the trays in his hands and it was full of gold coin, four cylindrical rows of it, held out as if for sale between his hands.

Further to the left, in a corner of the chamber, two negroes stood by a bellying iron cauldron suspended over three hissing blow-lamps, its base glowing red. They held iron skimmers in their hands and these were splashed with gold half way up the long handles. Beside them was a towering jumble of gold objects, plate, altar pieces, drinking vessels, crosses, and a stack of gold ingots of various sizes. Along the wall near them were ranged rows of metal cooling trays, their segmented surfaces gleaming yellow, and there was an empty tray on the floor near the cauldron and a long gold-spattered ladle, its handle bound with cloth.

Squatting on the floor not far from Mr Big, a single negro had a knife in one hand and a jewelled goblet in the other. Beside him on a tin plate was a pile of gems that winked dully, red and blue and green, in the glare of the arcs.

It was warm and airless in the great rock chamber and yet Bond shivered as his eyes took in the whole splendid scene, the blazing violet-white lights, the shimmering bronze of the sweating bodies, the bright glare of the gold, the rainbow pool of jewels and the milk and aquamarine of the pool. He shivered at the beauty of it all, at this fabulous petrified ballet in the great treasure-house of Bloody Morgan.

His eyes came back to the square of green baize and the great zombie face and he looked at the face and into the wide yellow eyes with awe, almost with reverence.

'Stop the drums,' said The Big Man to no one in particular. They had died almost to a whisper, a lisping beat right on the pulse of the blood. One of the negroes took two softly clanging steps amongst the gold coin and bent down. There was a portable phonograph on the floor and a powerful amplifier leant beside it against the rock wall. There was a click and the drums stopped. The negro shut the lid of the machine and went back to his place.

'Get on with the work,' said Mr Big, and at once all the figures started moving as if a penny had been put in a slot. The cauldron was stirred, the gold was picked up and clicked into the boxes, the man picked busily at his jewelled goblet and the negro with the tray of gold moved on up the stairs.

Bond stood and dripped sweat and blood.

The Big Man bent over the lists on his table and wrote one or two figures with his pen.

Bond stirred and felt the prick of a dagger over his kidneys.

The Big Man put down his pen and got slowly to his feet. He moved away from the table.

'Take over,' he said to one of Bond's guards and the naked man walked round the table and sat down in Mr Big's chair and picked up the pen.

'Bring him up.' Mr Big walked over to the steps in the rock and started to climb them slowly.

Bond felt a prick in his side. He stepped out of the debris of his black skin and followed the slowly climbing figure.

No one looked up from his work. No one would slacken when Mr Big was out of sight. No one would put a jewel or a coin in his mouth.

Baron Samedi was left in charge.

Only his Zombie had gone from the cave.

21 'Good Night to You Both'

They climbed slowly up, past an open door near the ceiling, for about forty feet and then paused on a wide landing in the rock. Here a single negro with an acetylene light beside him was fitting trays full of gold coin into the centre of the fish-tanks, scores of which were stacked against the wall.

As they waited, two negroes came down the steps from the surface, picked up one of the prepared tanks and went back up the steps with it.

Bond guessed the tanks were stocked with sand and weed and fish somewhere up above and then passed to the human chain that stretched down the cliff face.

Bond noticed that some of the waiting tanks had gold ingots fitted in the centre, and others a gravel of jewels, and he revised his estimate of the treasure, quadrupling it to around four million sterling.

Mr Big stood for a few moments with his eyes on the stone floor. His breathing was deep but controlled. Then they went on up.

Twenty steps higher there was another landing, smaller and with a door leading off it. The door had a new chain and padlock on it. The door itself was made of platted iron slats, brown and corroded with rust.

Mr Big paused again and they stood side by side on the small platform of rock.

For a moment Bond thought of escape, but, as if reading his mind, the negro guard crowded him up against the stone wall away from The Big Man. And Bond knew his first duty was to stay alive and get to Solitaire and somehow keep her away from the doomed ship where the acid was slowly eating through the copper of the time-fuse.

From above, a strong draught of cold air was coming down the shaft and Bond felt the sweat drying on him. He put his right hand up to the wound in his shoulder, undeterred by the prick of the guard's dagger in his side. The blood was dry and caked and most of the arm was numb. It ached viciously.

Mr Big spoke.

'That wind, Mister Bond,' he pointed up the shaft, 'is known in Jamaica as "The Undertaker's Wind".'

Bond shrugged his right shoulder and saved his breath.

Mr Big turned to the iron door, took a key from his pocket and unlocked it. He went through and Bond and his guard followed.

It was a long, narrow passage of a room with rusty shackles low down in the walls at less than yard intervals.

At the far end, where a hurricane light hung from the stone roof, there was a motionless figure under a blanket on the floor. There was one more hurricane light over their heads near the door, otherwise nothing but a smell of damp rock, and ancient torture, and death.

'Solitaire,' said Mr Big softly.

Bond's heart leapt and he started forward. At once a huge hand grasped him by the arm.

'Hold it, white man,' snapped his guard and twisted his wrist up between his shoulder-blades, hefting it higher until Bond lashed out with his left heel. It hit the other man's shin, and hurt Bond more than the guard.

Mr Big turned round. He had a small gun almost covered by his huge hand.

'Let him go,' he said, quietly. 'If you want an extra navel, Mister Bond, you can have one. I have six of them in this gun.'

Bond brushed past The Big Man. Solitaire was on her feet, coming towards him. When she saw his face she broke into a run, holding out her two hands.

'James,' she sobbed. 'James.'

She almost fell at his feet. Their hands clutched at each other.

'Get me some rope,' said Mr Big in the doorway.

'It's all right, Solitaire,' said Bond, knowing that it wasn't. 'It's all right. I'm here now.'

He picked her up and held her at arm's length. It hurt his left arm. She was pale and dishevelled. There was a bruise on her forehead and black circles under her eyes. Her face was grimy and tears had made streaks down the pale skin. She had no make-up. She wore a dirty white linen suit and sandals. She looked thin.

'What's the bastard been doing to you?' said Bond. He suddenly held her tightly to him. She clung to him, her face buried in his neck.

Then she drew away and looked at her hand.

'But you're bleeding,' she said. 'What is it?'

She turned him half round and saw the black blood on his shoulder and down his arm.

'Oh my darling, what is it?'

She started to cry again, forlornly, hopelessly, realizing suddenly that they were both lost.

'Tie them up,' said The Big Man from the door. 'Here under the light. I have things to say to them.'

The negro came towards them and Bond turned. Was it worth a gamble? The negro had nothing but rope in his hands. But The Big Man had stepped sideways and was watching him, the gun held loosely, half pointing at the floor.

'No, Mister Bond,' he said simply.

Bond eyed the big negro and thought of Solitaire and his own wounded arm.

The negro came up and Bond allowed his arms to be tied behind his back. They were good knots. There was no play in them. They hurt.

Bond smiled at Solitaire. He half closed one eye. It was nothing but bravado, but he saw a hopeful awareness dawn through her tears.

The negro led him back to the doorway.

'There,' said The Big Man, pointing at one of the shackles.

The negro cut Bond's legs from under him with a sudden sweep of his shin. Bond fell on his wounded shoulder. The negro pulled him by the rope up to the shackle, tested it, and put the rope through and then down to Bond's ankles which he bound securely. He had stuck his dagger in a crevice in the rock. He pulled it out and cut the rope and went back to where Solitaire was standing.

Bond was left sitting on the stone floor, his legs straight out in front, his arms hoisted up and secured behind him. Blood dripped down from his freshly opened wound. Only the remains of the benzedrine in his system kept him from fainting.

Solitaire was bound and placed almost opposite him. There was a yard between their feet.

When it was done, The Big Man looked at his watch.

'Go,' he said to the guard. He closed the iron door behind the man and leant against it.

Bond and the girl looked at each other and The Big Man gazed down on both of them.

After one of his long silences he addressed Bond. Bond looked up at him. The great grey football of a head under the hurricane lamp looked like an elemental, a malignant spectre from the centre of the earth, as it hung in mid air, the golden eyes blazing steadily, the great body in shadow. Bond had to remind himself that he had heard its heart pumping in its chest, had heard it breathe, had seen sweat on the grey skin. It was only a man, of the same species as himself, a big man, with a brilliant brain, but still a man who walked and defecated, a mortal man with a diseased heart.

The wide rubbery mouth split open and the flat slightly everted lips drew back from the big white teeth.

'You are the best of those that have been sent against me,' said Mr Big. His quiet flat voice was thoughtful, measured. 'And you have achieved the death of four of my assistants. My followers find this incredible. It was fully time that accounts should be squared. What happened to the American was not sufficient. The treachery of this girl,' he still looked at Bond, 'whom I found in the gutter and whom I was prepared to put on my right hand, has also brought my infallibility in question. I was wondering how she should die, when providence, or Baron Samedi as my followers will believe, brought you also to the altar with your head bowed ready for the axe.'

The mouth paused, with the lips parted. Bond saw the teeth come together to form the next word.

'So it is convenient that you should die together. That will happen, in an appropriate fashion,' The Big Man looked at his watch, 'in two and a half hours' time. At six o'clock, give or take,' he added, 'a few minutes.'

'Let's give those minutes,' said Bond. 'I enjoy my life.'

'In the history of negro emancipation,' Mr Big continued in an easy conversational tone, 'there have already appeared great athletes, great musicians, great writers, great doctors and scientists. In due course, as in the developing history of other races, there will appear negroes great and famous in every other walk of life.' He paused. 'It is unfortunate for you, Mister Bond, and for this girl, that you have encountered the first of the great negro criminals. I use a vulgar word, Mister Bond, because it is the one you, as a form of policeman, would yourself use. But I prefer to regard myself as one who has the ability and the mental and nervous equipment to make his own laws and act according to them rather than accept the laws that suit the lowest common denominator of the people. You have doubtless read Trotter's *Instincts of the Herd in War and Peace*, Mister Bond. Well, I am by nature and predilection a wolf and I live by a wolf's laws. Naturally the sheep describe such a person as a "criminal".

'The fact, Mister Bond,' The Big Man continued after a pause, 'that I survive and indeed enjoy limitless success, although I am alone against countless millions of sheep, is attributable to the modern techniques I described to you on the occasion of our last talk, and to an infinite capacity for taking pains. Not dull, plodding pains, but artistic, subtle pains. And I find, Mister Bond, that it is not difficult to outwit sheep, however many of them there may be, if one is dedicated to the task and if one is by nature an extremely well-equipped wolf.

'Let me illustrate to you, by an example, how my mind works. We will take the method I have decided upon by which you are both to die. It is a modern variation on the method used in the time of my kind patron, Sir Henry Morgan. In those days it was known as "keel-hauling".'

'Pray continue,' said Bond, not looking at Solitaire.

'We have a paravane on board the yacht,' continued Mr Big as if he was a surgeon describing a delicate operation to a body of students, 'which we use for trawling for shark and other big fish. This paravane, as you know, is a large buoyant torpedo-shaped device, which rides on the end of a cable, away from the side of a ship, and which can be used for sustaining the end of a net, and drawing it through the water when the ship is in motion, or if fitted with a cutting device, for severing the cables of moored mines in time of war.

'I intend,' said Mr Big, in a matter-of-fact discursive tone of voice, 'to bind you together to a line streamed from this paravane and to tow you through the sea until you are eaten by sharks.'

He paused, and his eyes looked from one to the other. Solitaire was gazing wide-eyed at Bond and Bond was thinking hard, his eyes blank and his mind boring into the future. He felt he ought to say something.

'You are a big man,' he said, 'and one day you will die a big, horrible death. If you kill us, that death will come soon. I have arranged for it. You are going mad very fast or you would see what our murder will bring down on you.'

Even as he spoke Bond's mind was working fast, counting hours and minutes, knowing that The Big Man's own death was creeping, with the acid in the fuse, round the minute hand towards his personal hour of final rendezvous. But would he and Solitaire be dead before that hour struck? There would not be more than minutes, perhaps seconds in it. The sweat poured off his face on to his chest. He smiled across at Solitaire. She looked back at him opaquely, her eyes not seeing him.

Suddenly she gave an agonized cry that made Bond's nerves jerk.

'I don't know,' she cried. 'I can't see. It's so near, so close. There is much death. But . . .'

'Solitaire,' shouted Bond, terrified that whatever strange things she saw in the future might give a warning to The Big Man. 'Pull yourself together.'

There was an angry bite in his voice.

Her eyes cleared. She looked dumbly at him, without comprehension.

The Big Man spoke again.

'I am not going mad, Mister Bond,' he said evenly, 'and nothing you have arranged will affect me. You will die beyond the reef and there will be no evidence. I shall tow the remains of your bodies until there is nothing left. That is part of the dexterity of my intentions. You may also know that shark and barracuda play a role in Voodooism. They will have their sacrifice and Baron Samedi will be appeased. That will satisfy my followers. I wish also to continue my experiments with carnivorous fish. I believe they only attack when there is blood in the water. So your bodies will be towed from the island. The paravane will take them over the reef. I believe you will not be harmed inside the reef. The blood and offal that is thrown into these waters every night will have dispersed or been consumed. But when your bodies have been dragged over the reef, then I'm afraid you will bleed, your bodies will be very raw. And then we will see if my theories are correct.'

The Big Man put his hand behind him and pulled the door open.

'I will leave you now,' he said, 'to reflect on the excellence of the method I have invented for your death together. Two necessary deaths are achieved. No evidence is left behind. Superstition is satisfied. My followers pleased. The bodies are used for scientific research.

'That is what I meant, Mister James Bond, by an infinite capacity for taking artistic pains.'

He stood in the doorway and looked at them.

'A short, but very good night to you both.'

22 Terror by Sea

It was not yet light when their guards came for them. Their leg ropes were cut and with their arms still pinioned they were led up the remaining stone stairs to the surface.

They stood amongst the sparse trees and Bond sniffed the cool morning air. He gazed through the trees towards the east and saw that there the stars were paler and the horizon luminous with the breaking dawn. The night-song of the crickets was almost done and somewhere on the island a mocking bird bubbled its first notes.

He guessed that it was either side of half-past five.

They stood there for several minutes. Negroes brushed past them carrying bundles and jippa-jippa holdalls, talking in cheerful whispers.

The doors of the handful of thatched huts among the trees had been left swinging open. The men filed to the edge of the cliff to the right of where Bond and Solitaire were standing and disappeared over the edge. They didn't come back. It was evacuation. The whole garrison of the island was decamping.

Bond rubbed his naked shoulder against Solitaire and she pressed against him. It was cold after the stuffy dungeon and Bond shivered. But it was better to be on the move than for the suspense down below to be prolonged.

They both knew what had to be done, the nature of the gamble.

When The Big Man had left them, Bond had wasted no time. In a whisper, he had told the girl of the limpet mine against the side of the ship timed to explode a few minutes after six o'clock and he had explained the factors that would decide who would die that morning.

First, he gambled on Mr Big's mania for exactitude and efficiency. The *Secatur* must sail on the dot of six o'clock. Then there must be no cloud, or visibility in the half-light of dawn would not be sufficient for the ship to make the passage through the reef and Mr Big would postpone the sailing. If Bond and Solitaire were on the jetty alongside the ship, they would then be killed with Mr Big.

Supposing the ship sailed dead on time, how far behind and to one side of her would their bodies be towed? It would have to be on the port side for the paravane to clear the island. Bond guessed the cable to the paravane would be fifty yards and that they would be towed twenty or thirty yards behind the paravane.

If he was right, they would be hauled over the outer reef about fifty yards after the *Secatur* had cleared the passage. She would probably approach the passage at about three knots and then put on speed to ten or even twenty. At first their bodies would be swept away from the island in a slow arc, twisting and turning at the end of the tow-rope. Then the paravane would straighten out and when the ship had got through the reef, they would still be approaching it. The paravane would then cross the reef when the ship was about forty yards outside it and they would follow.

Bond shuddered to think of the mauling their bodies would suffer being dragged at any speed over the razor-sharp ten yards of coral

305

rocks and trees. The skin on their backs and legs would be flayed off.

Once over the reef they would be just a huge bleeding bait and it would be only a matter of minutes before the first shark or barracuda was on to them.

And Mr Big would sit comfortably in the stern sheets, watching the bloody show, perhaps with glasses, and ticking off the seconds and minutes as the living bait got smaller and smaller and finally the fish snapped at the bloodstained rope.

Until there was nothing left.

Then the paravane would be hoisted inboard and the yacht would plough gracefully on towards the distant Florida Keys, Cape Sable and the sun-soaked wharf in St Petersburg Harbour.

And if the mine exploded while they were still in the water, only fifty yards away from the ship? What would be the effect of the shock-waves on their bodies? It might not be deadly. The hull of the ship should absorb most of it. The reef might protect them.

Bond could only guess and hope.

Above all they must stay alive to the last possible second. They must keep breathing as they were hauled, a living bundle, through the sea. Much depended on how they would be bound together. Mr Big would want them to stay alive. He would not be interested in dead bait.

If they were still alive when the first shark's fin showed on the surface behind them Bond had coldly decided to drown Solitaire. Drown her by twisting her body under his and holding her there. Then he would try and drown himself by twisting her dead body back over his to keep him under.

There was nightmare at every turn of his thoughts, sickening horror in every grisly aspect of the monstrous torture and death this man had invented for them. But Bond knew he must remain cold and absolutely resolved to fight for their lives to the end. There was at least warmth in the knowledge that Mr Big and most of his men would also die. And there was a glimmer of hope that he and Solitaire would survive. Unless the mine failed, there was no such hope for the enemy.

All this, and a hundred other details and plans went through Bond's mind in the last hour before they were brought up the shaft to the surface. He shared all his hopes with Solitaire. None of his fears.

She had lain opposite him, her tired blue eyes fixed on him, obedient, trusting, drinking in his face and his words, pliant, loving.

'Don't worry about me, my darling,' she had said when the men came for them. 'I am happy to be with you again. My heart is full of it. For some reason I am not afraid although there is much death very close. Do you love me a little?'

'Yes,' said Bond. 'And we shall have our love.'

'Giddap,' said one of the men.

And now, on the surface, it was getting lighter, and from below the cliff Bond heard the great twin Diesels stutter and roar. There was a light flutter of breeze to windward, but to leeward, where the ship lay, the bay was a gunmetal mirror.

Mr Big appeared up the shaft, a businessman's leather briefcase in his hand. He stood for a moment looking round, gaining his breath. He paid no attention to Bond and Solitaire nor to the two guards standing beside them with revolvers in their hands.

He looked up at the sky, and suddenly called out, in a loud clear voice, towards the rim of the sun:

'Thank you, Sir Henry Morgan. Your treasure will be well spent. Give us a fair wind.'

The negro guards showed the whites of their eyes.

'The Undertaker's Wind it is,' said Bond.

The Big Man looked at him.

'All down?' he asked the guards.

'Yassuh, Boss,' answered one of them.

'Take them along,' said The Big Man.

They went to the edge of the cliff and down the steep steps, one guard in front, one behind. Mr Big followed.

The engines of the long graceful yacht were turning over quietly, the exhaust bubbling glutinously, a thread of blue vapour rising astern.

There were two men on the jetty at the guide ropes. There were only three men on deck besides the Captain and the navigator on the grey streamlined bridge. There was no room for more. All the available deckspace, save for a fishing chair rigged right aft, was covered with fish-tanks. The Red Ensign had been struck and only the Stars and Stripes hung motionless at the stern.

A few yards clear of the ship the red torpedo-shaped paravane, about six foot long, lay quietly on the water, now aquamarine in the early dawn. It was attached to a thick pile of wire cable, coiled up on the deck aft. To Bond there looked to be a good fifty yards of it. The water was crystal clear and there were no fish about.

The Undertaker's Wind was almost dead. Soon the Doctor's Wind would start to breathe in from the sea. How soon? wondered Bond. Was it an omen?

Away beyond the ship he could see the roof of Beau Desert among the trees, but the jetty and the ship and the cliff path were still in deep shadow. Bond wondered if night-glasses would be able to pick them out. And if they could, what Strangways would be thinking.

Mr Big stood on the jetty and supervised the process of binding them together.

'Strip her,' he said to Solitaire's guard.

Bond flinched. He stole a glance at Mr Big's wrist watch. It said ten minutes to six. Bond kept silence. There must not be even a minute's delay.

'Throw the clothes on board,' said Mr Big. 'Tie some strips round his shoulder. I don't want any blood in the water, yet.'

Solitaire's clothes were cut off her with a knife. She stood pale and naked. She hung her head and the heavy black hair fell forward over her face. Bond's shoulder was roughly bound with strips of her linen skirt.

'You bastard,' said Bond through his teeth.

Under Mr Big's direction, their hands were freed. Their bodies were pressed together, face to face, and their arms held round each other's waists and then bound tightly again.

Bond felt Solitaire's soft breasts pressed against him. She leant her chin on his right shoulder.

'I didn't want it to be like this,' she whispered tremulously.

Bond didn't answer. He hardly felt her body. He was counting seconds.

On the jetty there was a pile of rope to the paravane. It hung down off the jetty and Bond could see it lying along the sand until it rose to meet the belly of the red torpedo.

The free end was tied under their armpits and knotted tightly between them in the space between their necks. It was all very carefully done. There was no possible escape.

Bond was counting the seconds. He made it five minutes to six.

Mr Big had a last look at them.

'Their legs can stay free,' he said. 'They'll make appetizing bait.' He stepped off the jetty on to the deck of the yacht.

The two guards went aboard. The two men on the jetty unhitched their lines and followed. The screws churned up the still water and with the engines at half speed ahead the *Secatur* slid swiftly away from the island.

Mr Big went aft and sat down in the fishing chair. They could see his eyes fixed on them. He said nothing. Made no gesture. He just watched.

The *Secatur* cut through the water towards the reef. Bond could see the cable to the paravane snaking over the side. The paravane started to move softly after the ship. Suddenly it put its nose down, then righted itself and sped away, its rudder pulling out and away from the wake of the ship.

The coil of rope beside them leapt into life.

'Look out,' said Bond urgently, holding tighter to the girl.

Their arms were pulled almost out of their sockets as they were jerked together off the jetty into the sea.

For a second they both went under, then they were on the surface, their joined bodies smashing through the water.

Bond gasped for breath amongst the waves and spray that dashed past his twisted mouth. He could hear the rasping of Solitaire's breath next to his ear.

'Breathe, breathe,' he shouted through the rushing of the water. 'Lock your legs against mine.'

She heard him and he felt her knees pressing between his thighs. She had a paroxysm of coughing, then her breath became more even against his ear and the thumping of her heart eased against his breast. At the same time their speed slackened.

'Hold your breath,' shouted Bond. 'I've got to have a look. Ready?'

A pressure of her arms answered him. He felt her chest heave as she filled her lungs.

With the weight of his body he swung her round so that his head was now quite out of water.

They were ploughing along at about three knots. He twisted his head above the small bow-wave they were throwing up.

The *Secatur* was entering the passage through the reef, about eighty yards away, he guessed. The paravane was skimming slowly along almost at right angles to her. Another thirty yards and the red torpedo would be crossing the broken water over the reef. A further thirty yards behind, they were riding slowly across the surface of the bay.

Sixty yards to go to the reef.

Bond twisted his body and Solitaire came up, gasping.

Still they moved slowly along through the water.

Five yards, ten, fifteen, twenty.

Only forty yards to go before they hit the coral.

The *Secatur* would be just through: Bond gathered his breath. It must be past six now. What had happened to the blasted mine? Bond thought a quick fervent prayer. God save us, he said into the water.

Suddenly he felt the rope tighten under his arms.

'Breathe, Solitaire, breathe,' he shouted as they got under way and the water started to hiss past them.

Now they were flying over the sea towards the crouching reef.

There was a slight check. Bond guessed that the paravane had fouled a niggerhead or a piece of surface coral. Then their bodies hurtled on again in their deadly embrace.

Thirty yards to go, twenty, ten.

Jesus Christ, thought Bond. We're for it. He braced his muscles to take the crashing, searing pain, edged Solitaire further above him to protect her from the worst of it.

Suddenly the breath whistled out of his body and a giant fist thumped him into Solitaire so that she rose right out of the sea above him and then fell back. A split second later lightning flashed across the sky and there was the thunder of an explosion.

They stopped dead in the water and Bond felt the weight of the slack rope pulling them under.

His legs sank down beneath his stunned body and water rushed into his mouth.

It was this that brought him back to consciousness. His legs pounded under him and brought their mouths to the surface. The girl was a dead weight in his arms. He trod water desperately and looked round him, holding Solitaire's lolling head on his shoulder above the surface.

The first thing he saw was the swirling waters of the reef not five yards away. Without its protection they would both have been crushed by the shock-wave of the explosion. He felt the tug and eddy of its currents round his legs. He backed desperately towards it, catching gulps of air when he could. His chest was bursting with the strain and he saw the sky through a red film. The rope dragged him down and the girl's hair filled his mouth and tried to choke him.

Suddenly he felt the sharp scrape of the coral against the back of his legs. He kicked and felt frantically with his feet for a foothold, flaying the skin off with every movement.

He hardly felt the pain.

Now his back was being scraped and his arms. He floundered clumsily, his lungs burning in his chest. Then there was a bed of needles under his feet. He put all his weight on it, leaning back against the strong eddies that tried to dislodge him. His feet held and there was rock at his back. He leant back panting, blood streaming up around him in the water, holding the girl's cold, scarcely breathing body against him.

For a minute he rested, blessedly, his eyes shut and the blood pounding through his limbs, coughing painfully, waiting for his senses to focus again. His first thought was for the blood in the water around him. But he guessed the big fish would not venture into the reef. Anyway there was nothing he could do about it.

Then he looked out to sea.

There was no sign of the *Secatur*.

High up in the still sky there was a mushroom of smoke, beginning to trail, with the Doctor's Wind, in towards the land.

There were things strewn all over the water and a few heads bobbing up and down and the whole sea was glinting with the white stomachs of fish stunned or killed by the explosion. There was a strong smell of

311

explosive in the air. On the fringe of the debris, the red paravane lay quietly, hull down, anchored by the cable whose other end must lie somewhere on the bottom. Fountains of bubbles were erupting on the glassy surface of the sea.

On the edge of the circle of bobbing heads and dead fish a few triangular fins were cutting fast through the water. More appeared as Bond watched. Once he saw a great snout come out of the water and smash down on something. The fins threw up spray as they flashed among the tidbits. Two black arms suddenly stuck up in the air and then disappeared. There were screams. Two or three pairs of arms started to flail the water towards the reef. One man stopped to bang the water in front of him with the flat of his hand. Then his hands disappeared under the surface. Then he too began to scream and his body jerked to and fro in the water. Barracuda hitting into him, said Bond's dazed mind.

But one of the heads was getting nearer, making for the bit of reef where Bond stood, the small waves breaking under his armpits, the girl's black hair hanging down his back.

It was a large head and a veil of blood streamed down over the face from a wound in the great bald skull.

Bond watched it come on.

The Big Man was executing a blundering breaststroke, making enough flurry in the water to attract any fish that wasn't already occupied.

Bond wondered whether he would make it. Bond's eyes narrowed and his breath became calmer as he watched the cruel sea for its decision.

The surging head came nearer. Bond could see the teeth showing in a rictus of agony and frenzied endeavour. Blood half veiled the eyes that Bond knew would be bulging in their sockets. He could almost hear the great diseased heart thumping under the grey-black skin. Would it give out before the bait was taken?

The Big Man came on. His shoulders were naked, his clothes stripped off him by the explosion, Bond supposed, but the black silk tie had remained and it showed round the thick neck and streamed behind the head like a Chinaman's pigtail.

A splash of water cleared some blood away from the eyes. They were wide open, staring madly towards Bond. They held no appeal for help, only a fixed glare of physical exertion.

Even as Bond looked into them, now only ten yards away, they suddenly shut and the great face contorted in a grimace of pain.

'Aarrh,' said the distorted mouth.

Both arms stopped flailing the water and the head went under and came up again. A cloud of blood welled up and darkened the sea. Two six-foot thin brown shadows backed out of the cloud and then dashed back into it. The body in the water jerked sideways. Half of The Big Man's left arm came out of the water. It had no hand, no wrist, no wrist watch.

But the great turnip head, the drawn-back mouth full of white teeth almost splitting it in half, was still alive. And now it was screaming, a long gurgling scream that only broke each time a barracuda hit into the dangling body.

There was a distant shout from the bay behind Bond. He paid no attention. All his senses were focused on the horror in the water in front of him.

A fin split the surface a few yards away and stopped.

Bond could feel the shark pointing like a dog, the short-sighted pink button eyes trying to pierce the cloud of blood and weigh up the prey. Then it shot in towards the chest and the screaming head went under as sharply as a fisherman's float.

Some bubbles burst on the surface.

There was the swirl of a sharp brown-spotted tail as the huge Leopard shark backed out to swallow and attack again.

The head floated back to the surface. The mouth was closed. The yellow eyes seemed still to look at Bond.

Then the shark's snout came right out of the water and it drove in towards the head, the lower curved jaw open so that light glinted on the teeth. There was a horrible grunting scrunch and a great swirl of water. Then silence.

Bond's dilated eyes went on staring at the brown stain that spread wider and wider across the sea.

Then the girl moaned and Bond came to his senses.

There was another shout from behind him and he turned his head towards the bay.

It was Quarrel, his brown gleaming chest towering above the slim hull of a canoe, his arms flailing at the paddle, and a long way behind him all the other canoes of Shark Bay skimming like water-boatmen across the small waves that had started to ripple the surface.

The fresh north-east trade winds had started to blow and the sun was shining down on the blue water and on the soft green flanks of Jamaica.

The first tears since his childhood came into James Bond's blue-grey eyes and ran down his drawn cheeks into the bloodstained sea.

23 Passionate Leave

Like dangling emerald pendants the two humming-birds were making their last rounds of the hibiscus and a mocking bird had started on its evening song, sweeter than a nightingale's, from the summit of a bush of night-scented jasmine.

The jagged shadow of a man-of-war bird floated across the green Bahama grass of the lawn as it sailed on the air currents up the coast to some distant colony, and a slate-blue kingfisher chattered angrily as it saw the man sitting in the chair in the garden. It changed its flight and swerved off across the sea to the island. A brimstone butterfly flirted among the purple shadows under the palms.

The graded blue waters of the bay were quite still. The cliffs of the island were a deep rose in the light of the setting sun behind the house.

There was a smell of evening and of coolness after a hot day and a slight scent of peat-smoke that came from cassava being roasted in one of the fishermen's huts in the village away to the right.

Solitaire came out of the house and walked on naked feet across the lawn. She was carrying a tray with a cocktail shaker and two glasses. She put it down on a bamboo table beside Bond's chair.

'I hope I've made it right,' she said. 'Six to one sounds terribly strong. I've never had Vodka Martinis before.'

Bond looked up at her. She was wearing a pair of his white silk pyjamas. They were far too large for her. She looked absurdly childish.

She laughed. 'How do you like my Port Maria lipstick?' she asked, 'and the eyebrows made up with an HB pencil. I couldn't do anything with the rest of me except wash it.'

'You look wonderful,' said Bond. 'You're far the prettiest girl in the whole of Shark Bay. If I had some legs and arms I'd get up and kiss you.'

Solitaire bent down and kissed him long on the lips, one arm tightly round his neck. She stood up and smoothed back the comma of black hair that had fallen down over his forehead.

They looked at each other for a moment, then she turned to the table and poured him out a cocktail. She poured half a glass for herself and sat down on the warm grass and put her head against his knee. He played with her hair with his right hand and they sat for a while looking out between the trunks of the palm trees at the sea and the light fading on the island.

The day had been given over to licking wounds and cleaning up the remains of the mess.

When Quarrel had landed them on the little beach at Beau Desert, Bond had half carried Solitaire across the lawn and into the bathroom. He had filled the bath full of warm water. Without her knowing what was happening he had soaped and washed her whole body and her hair. When he had cleaned away all the salt and coral slime he helped her out, dried her and put merthiolate on the coral cuts that striped her back and thighs. Then he gave her a sleeping draught and put her naked between the sheets in his own bed. He kissed her. Before he had finished closing the jalousies she was asleep.

Then he got into the bath and Strangways soaped him down and almost bathed his body in merthiolate. He was raw and bleeding in a hundred places and his left arm was numb from the barracuda bite. He had lost a mouthful of muscle at the shoulder. The sting of the merthiolate made him grind his teeth.

He put on a dressing-gown and Quarrel drove him to the hospital at Port Maria. Before he left he had a Lucullian breakfast and a blessed first cigarette. He fell asleep in the car and he slept on the operating table and in the cot where they finally put him, a mass of bandages and surgical tape.

Quarrel brought him back in the early afternoon. By that time Strangways had acted on the information Bond had given him. There was a police detachment on the Isle of Surprise, the wreck of the *Secatur*, lying in about twenty fathoms, was buoyed and the position being patrolled by the Customs launch from Port Maria. The salvage tug and divers were on their way from Kingston. Reporters from the local press had been given a brief statement and there was a police guard on the entrance to Beau Desert prepared to repel the flood of newspapermen who would arrive in Jamaica when the full story got out to the world. Meanwhile a detailed report had gone to M, and to Washington, so that The Big Man's team in Harlem and St Petersburg could be rounded up and provisionally held on a blanket gold-smuggling charge.

There were no survivors from the *Secatur*, but the local fishermen had brought in nearly a ton of dead fish that morning.

Jamaica was aflame with rumours. There were serried ranks of cars on the cliffs above the bay and along the beach below. Word had got out about Bloody Morgan's treasure, but also about the packs of shark and barracuda that had defended it, and because of them there was not a swimmer who was planning to get out to the scene of the wreck under cover of darkness.

A doctor had been to visit Solitaire but had found her chiefly concerned about getting some clothes and the right shade of lipstick. Strangways had arranged for a selection to be sent over from Kingston next day. For the time being she was experimenting with the contents of Bond's suitcase and a bowl of hibiscus.

Strangways got back from Kingston shortly after Bond's return from hospital. He had a signal for Bond from M. It read:

PRESUME YOU HAVE FILED CLAIM TO TREASURE IN YOUR NAME BEHALF UNIVERSAL EXPORT STOP PROCEED

IMMEDIATELY WITH SALVAGE STOP HAVE ENGAGED
COUNSEL TO PRESS OUR RIGHTS WITH TREASURY AND
COLONIAL OFFICE STOP MEANWHILE VERY WELL DONE
STOP FORTNIGHT'S PASSIONATE LEAVE GRANTED ENDIT

'I suppose he means "Compassionate", said Bond.

Strangways looked solemn. 'I expect so,' he said. 'I made a full
report of the damage to you. And to the girl,' he added.

'Hm,' said Bond. 'M's cipherenes don't often pick a wrong group.
However.'

Strangways looked carefully out of the window with his one eye.

'It's so like the old devil to think of the gold first,' said Bond.
'Suppose he thinks he can get away with it and somehow dodge a
reduction in the Secret Fund when the next parliamentary estimates
come round. I expect half his life is taken up with arguing with the
Treasury. But still he's been pretty quick off the mark.'

'I filed your claim at Government House directly I got the signal,'
said Strangways. 'But it's going to be tricky. The Crown will be after
it and America will come in somewhere as he was an American citizen.
It'll be a long business.'

They had talked some more and then Strangways had left and Bond
had walked painfully out into the garden to sit for a while in the
sunshine with his thoughts.

In his mind he ran once more the gauntlet of dangers he had
entered on his long chase after The Big Man and the fabulous treasure,
and he lived again through the searing flashes of time when he had
looked various deaths in the face.

And now it was over and he sat in the sunshine among the flowers
with the prize at his feet and his hand in her long black hair. He
clasped the moment to him and thought of the fourteen tomorrows
that would be theirs between them.

There was a crash of broken crockery from the kitchen at the back
of the house and the sound of Quarrel's voice thundering at someone.

'Poor Quarrel,' said Solitaire. 'He's borrowed the best cook in the
village and ransacked the markets for surprises for us. He's even found
some black crabs, the first of the season. Then he's roasting a pitiful

little sucking pig and making an avocado pear salad and we're to finish up with guavas and coconut cream. And Commander Strangways has left a case of the best champagne in Jamaica. My mouth's watering already. But don't forget it's supposed to be a secret. I wandered into the kitchen and found he had almost reduced the cook to tears.'

'He's coming with us on our passionate holiday,' said Bond. He told her of M's cable. 'We're going to a house on stilts with palm trees and five miles of golden sand. And you'll have to look after me very well because I shan't be able to make love with only one arm.'

There was open sensuality in Solitaire's eyes as she looked up at him. She smiled innocently.

'What about my back?' she said.

Moonraker

Contents

Part 1: Monday

Part 2: Tuesday, Wednesday

Part 3: Thursday, Friday

Part 1: Monday

1 Secret Paper-Work

The two thirty-eights roared simultaneously.

The walls of the underground room took the crash of sound and batted it to and fro between them until there was silence. James Bond watched the smoke being sucked from each end of the room towards the central Ventaxia fan. The memory in his right hand of how he had drawn and fired with one sweep from the left made him confident. He broke the chamber sideways out of the Colt Detective Special and waited, his gun pointing at the floor, while the Instructor walked the twenty yards towards him through the half-light of the gallery.

Bond saw that the Instructor was grinning. 'I don't believe it,' he said. 'I got you that time.'

The Instructor came up with him. 'I'm in hospital, but you're dead, sir,' he said. In one hand he held the silhouette target of the upper body of a man. In the other a polaroid film, postcard size. He handed this to Bond and they turned to a table behind them on which there was a green-shaded desk-light and a large magnifying glass.

Bond picked up the glass and bent over the photograph. It was a flash-light photograph of him. Around his right hand there was a blurred burst of white flame. He focused the glass carefully on the left side of his dark jacket. In the centre of his heart there was a tiny pinpoint of light.

Without speaking, the Instructor laid the big white man-shaped target under the lamp. Its heart was a black bull's-eye, about three inches across. Just below and half an inch to the right was the rent made by Bond's bullet.

'Through the left wall of the stomach and out at the back,' said the

Instructor, with satisfaction. He took out a pencil and scribbled an addition on the side of the target. 'Twenty rounds and I make it you owe me seven-and-six, sir,' he said impassively.

Bond laughed. He counted out some silver. 'Double the stakes next Monday,' he said.

'That's all right with me,' said the Instructor. 'But you can't beat the machine, sir. And if you want to get into the team for the Dewar Trophy we ought to give the thirty-eights a rest and spend some time on the Remington. That new long twenty-two cartridge they've just brought out is going to mean at least 7900 out of a possible 8000 to win. Most of your bullets have got to be in the X-ring and that's only as big as a shilling when it's under your nose. At a hundred yards it isn't there at all.'

'To hell with the Dewar Trophy,' said Bond. 'It's your money I'm after.' He shook the unfired bullets in the chamber of his gun into his cupped hand and laid them and the gun on the table. 'See you Monday. Same time?'

'Ten o'clock'll be fine, sir,' said the Instructor, jerking down the two handles on the iron door. He smiled at Bond's back as it disappeared up the steep concrete stairs leading to the ground floor. He was pleased with Bond's shooting, but he wouldn't have thought of telling him that he was the best shot in the Service. Only M was allowed to know that, and his Chief of Staff, who would be told to enter the scores of that day's shoot on Bond's Confidential Record.

Bond pushed through the green baize door at the top of the basement steps and walked over to the lift that would take him up to the eighth floor of the tall, grey building near Regent's Park that is the headquarters of the Secret Service. He was satisfied with his score but not proud of it. His trigger finger twitched in his pocket as he wondered how to conjure up that little extra flash of speed that would beat the machine, the complicated box of tricks that sprung the target for just three seconds, fired back at him with a blank .38, and shot a pencil of light aimed at him and photographed it as he stood and fired from the circle of chalk on the floor.

The lift doors sighed open and Bond got in. The liftman could smell the cordite on him. They always smelled like that when they came up from the shooting gallery. He liked it. It reminded him of the Army. He pressed the button for the eighth and rested the stump of his left arm against the control handle.

If only the light was better, thought Bond. But M insisted that all shooting should be done in averagely bad conditions. A dim light and a target that shot back at you was as close as he could get to copying the real thing. 'Shooting hell out of a piece of cardboard doesn't prove anything' was his single-line introduction to the Small-arms Defence Manual.

The lift eased to a stop and as Bond stepped out into the drab Ministry-of-Works-green corridor and into the bustling world of girls carrying files, doors opening and shutting, and muted telephone bells, he emptied his mind of all thoughts of his shoot and prepared himself for the normal business of a routine day at Headquarters.

He walked along to the end door on the right. It was as anonymous as all the others he had passed. No numbers. If you had any business on the eighth floor, and your office was not on that floor, someone would come and fetch you to the room you needed and see you back into the lift when you were through.

Bond knocked and waited. He looked at his watch. Eleven o'clock. Mondays were hell. Two days of dockets and files to plough through. And weekends were generally busy times abroad. Empty flats got burgled. People were photographed in compromising positions. Motorcar 'accidents' looked better, got a more cursory handling, amidst the weekend slaughter on the roads. The weekly bags from Washington, Istanbul, and Tokyo would have come in and been sorted. They might hold something for him.

The door opened and he had his daily moment of pleasure at having a beautiful secretary. 'Morning, Lil,' he said.

The careful warmth of her smile of welcome dropped about ten degrees.

'Give me that coat,' she said. 'It stinks of cordite. And don't call me Lil. You know I hate it.'

Bond took off his coat and handed it to her. 'Anyone who gets christened Loelia Ponsonby ought to get used to pet names.'

He stood beside her desk in the little anteroom which she had somehow made to seem a little more human than an office and watched her hang his coat on the iron frame of the open window.

She was tall and dark with a reserved, unbroken beauty to which the war and five years in the Service had lent a touch of sternness. Unless she married soon, Bond thought for the hundredth time, or had a lover, her cool air of authority might easily become spinsterish and she would join the army of women who had married a career.

Bond had told her as much, often, and he and the two other members of the 00 Section had at various times made determined assaults on her virtue. She had handled them all with the same cool motherliness (which, to salve their egos, they privately defined as frigidity) and, the day after, she treated them with small attentions and kindnesses to show that it was really her fault and that she forgave them.

What they didn't know was that she worried herself almost to death when they were in danger and that she loved them equally; but that she had no intention of becoming emotionally involved with any man who might be dead next week. And it was true that an appointment in the Secret Service was a form of peonage. If you were a woman there wasn't much of you left for other relationships. It was easier for the men. They had an excuse for fragmentary affairs. For them marriage and children and a home were out of the question if they were to be of any use 'in the field' as it was cosily termed. But, for the women, an affair outside the Service automatically made you a 'security risk' and in the last analysis you had a choice of resignation from the Service and a normal life, or of perpetual concubinage to your King and Country.

Loelia Ponsonby knew that she had almost reached the time for decision and all her instincts told her to get out. But every day the drama and romance of her Cavell-Nightingale world locked her more securely into the company of the other girls at Headquarters and every day it seemed more difficult to betray by resignation the father-figure which the Service had become.

Meanwhile she was one of the most envied girls in the building, and a member of the small company of Principal Secretaries who had access to the innermost secrets of the Service – 'The Pearls and

Twin-set' as they were called behind their backs by the other girls, with ironical reference to their supposedly 'County' and 'Kensington' backgrounds – and, so far as the Personnel Branch was concerned, her destiny in twenty years' time would be that single golden line right at the end of a New Year's Honours List, among the medals for officials of the Fishery Board, of the Post Office, of the Women's Institute, towards the bottom of the OBEs: 'Miss Loelia Ponsonby, Principal Secretary in the Ministry of Defence.'

She turned away from the window. She was dressed in a sugar-pink and white striped shirt and a plain dark blue skirt.

Bond smiled into her grey eyes. 'I only call you Lil on Mondays,' he said. 'Miss Ponsonby the rest of the week. But I'll never call you Loelia. It sounds like somebody in an indecent limerick. Any messages?'

'No,' she said shortly. She relented. 'But there's piles of stuff on your desk. Nothing urgent. But there's an awful lot of it. Oh, and the powder-vine says that 008's got out. He's in Berlin, resting. Isn't it wonderful!'

Bond looked quickly at her. 'When did you hear that?'

'About half an hour ago,' she said.

Bond opened the inner door to the big office with the three desks and shut it behind him. He went and stood by the window, looking out at the late spring green of the trees in Regent's Park. So Bill had made it after all. Peenemunde and back. Resting in Berlin sounded bad. Must be in pretty poor shape. Well, he'd just have to wait for news from the only leak in the building – the girls' rest-room, known to the impotent fury of the Security staff as 'The powder-vine'.

Bond sighed and sat down at his desk, pulling towards him the tray of brown folders bearing the top-secret red star. And what about 0011? It was two months since he had vanished into the 'Dirty Half-mile' in Singapore. Not a word since. While he, Bond, No. 007, the senior of the three men in the Service who had earned the double 0 number, sat at his comfortable desk doing paper-work and flirting with their secretary.

He shrugged his shoulders and resolutely opened the top folder. Inside there was a detailed map of southern Poland and north-eastern Germany. Its feature was a straggling red line connecting Warsaw and Berlin. There was also a long typewritten memorandum headed *Mainline: A well-established Escape Route from East to West.*

Bond took out his black gunmetal cigarette-box and his black-oxidized Ronson lighter and put them on the desk beside him. He lit a cigarette, one of the Macedonian blend with the three gold rings round the butt that Morlands of Grosvenor Street made for him, then he settled himself forward in the padded swivel chair and began to read.

It was the beginning of a typical routine day for Bond. It was only two or three times a year that an assignment came along requiring his particular abilities. For the rest of the year he had the duties of an easy-going senior civil servant – elastic office hours from around ten to six; lunch, generally in the canteen; evenings spent playing cards in the company of a few close friends, or at Crockford's; or making love, with rather cold passion, to one of three similarly disposed married women; weekends playing golf for high stakes at one of the clubs near London.

He took no holidays, but was generally given a fortnight's leave at the end of each assignment – in addition to any sick-leave that might be necessary. He earned £1500 a year, the salary of a Principal Officer in the Civil Service, and he had a thousand a year free of tax of his own. When he was on a job he could spend as much as he liked, so for the other months of the year he could live very well on his £2000 a year net.

He had a small but comfortable flat off the King's Road, an elderly Scottish housekeeper – a treasure called May – and a 1930 4½-litre Bentley coupé, super-charged, which he kept expertly tuned so that he could do a hundred when he wanted to.

On these things he spent all his money and it was his ambition to have as little as possible in his banking account when he was killed, as, when he was depressed, he knew he would be, before the statutory age of forty-five.

Eight years to go before he was automatically taken off the 00 list and given a staff job at Headquarters. At least eight tough assignments. Probably sixteen. Perhaps twenty-four. Too many.

There were five cigarette-ends in the big glass ashtray by the time

Bond had finished memorizing the details of 'Mainline'. He picked up a red pencil and ran his eye down the distribution list on the cover. The list started with 'M', then 'CoS.', then a dozen or so letters and numbers and then, at the end '00'. Against this he put a neat tick, signed it with the figure 7, and tossed the file into his OUT tray.

It was twelve o'clock. Bond took the next folder off the pile and opened it. It was from the Radio Intelligence Division of NATO, 'For Information Only' and it was headed 'Radio Signatures'.

Bond pulled the rest of the pile towards him and glanced at the first page of each. These were their titles:

The Inspectoscope – a machine for the detection of contraband.
Philopon – A Japanese murder-drug.
Possible points of concealment on trains. No. II. Germany.
The methods of SMERSH. No. 6. Kidnapping.
Route five to Pekin.
Vladivostock. A photographic Reconnaissance by US Thunderjet.

Bond was not surprised by the curious mixture he was supposed to digest. The 00 Section of the Secret Service was not concerned with the current operations of other sections and stations, only with background information which might be useful or instructive to the only three men in the Service whose duties included assassination – who might be ordered to kill. There was no urgency about these files. No action was required by him or his two colleagues except that each of them jotted down the numbers of dockets which he considered the other two should also read when they were next attached to Headquarters. When the 00 Section had finished with this lot they would go down to their final destination in 'Records'.

Bond turned back to the NATO paper.

'The almost inevitable manner', he read, 'in which individuality is revealed by minute patterns of behaviour, is demonstrated by the indelible characteristics of the "fist" of each radio operator. This "fist", or manner of tapping out messages, is distinctive and recognizable by those who are practised in receiving messages. It can also be measured by very sensitive mechanisms. To illustrate, in 1943 the United States Radio Intelligence Bureau made use of this fact in tracing an enemy station in Chile operated by "Pedro", a young German. When the Chilean police closed in on the station, "Pedro" escaped. A year later, expert listeners spotted a new illegal transmitter and were able to recognize "Pedro" as the operator. In order to disguise his "fist" he was transmitting left-handed, but the disguise was not effective and he was captured.

'NATO Radio Research has recently been experimenting with a form of "scrambler" which can be attached to the wrist of operators with the object of interfering minutely with the nerve centres which control the muscles of the hand. However . . .'

There were three telephones on Bond's desk. A black one for outside calls, a green office telephone, and a red one which went only to M and his Chief of Staff. It was the familiar burr of the red one that broke the silence of the room.

It was M's Chief of Staff.

'Can you come up?' asked the pleasant voice.

'M?' asked Bond.

'Yes.'

'Any clue?'

'Simply said if you were about he'd like to see you.'

'Right,' said Bond, and put down the receiver.

He collected his coat, told his secretary he would be with M and not to wait for him, left his office and walked along the corridor to the lift.

While he waited for it, he thought of those other times, when, in the middle of an empty day, the red telephone had suddenly broken the silence and taken him out of one world and set him down in another. He shrugged his shoulders – Monday! He might have expected trouble.

The lift came. 'Ninth,' said Bond, and stepped in.

2 The Columbite King

The ninth was the top floor of the building. Most of it was occupied by Communications, the hand-picked inter-services team of operators whose only interest was the world of microwaves, sunspots, and the 'heaviside layer'. Above them, on the flat roof, were the three squat masts of one of the most powerful transmitters in England, explained on the bold bronze list of occupants in the entrance hall of the building by the words 'Radio Tests Ltd'. The other tenants were declared to be 'Universal Export Co.', 'Delaney Bros. (1940) Ltd', 'The Omnium Corporation', and 'Enquiries (Miss E. Twining, OBE)'.

Miss Twining was a real person. Forty years earlier she had been a Loelia Ponsonby. Now, in retirement, she sat in a small office on the ground floor and spent her days tearing up circulars, paying the rates and taxes of her ghostly tenants, and politely brushing off salesmen and people who wanted to export something or have their radios mended.

It was always very quiet on the ninth floor. As Bond turned to the left outside the lift and walked along the softly carpeted corridor to the green baize door that led to the offices of M and his personal staff, the only sound he heard was a thin high-pitched whine that was so faint that you almost had to listen for it.

Without knocking he pushed through the green door and walked into the last room but one along the passage.

Miss Moneypenny, M's private secretary, looked up from her type-writer and smiled at him. They liked each other and she knew that Bond admired her looks. She was wearing the same model shirt as his own secretary, but with blue stripes.

'New uniform, Penny?' said Bond.

She laughed. 'Loelia and I share the same little woman,' she said. 'We tossed and I got blue.'

A snort came through the open door of the adjoining room. The Chief of Staff, a man of about Bond's age, came out, a sardonic grin on his pale, overworked face.

'Break it up,' he said. 'M's waiting. Lunch afterwards?'

'Fine,' said Bond. He turned to the door beside Miss Moneypenny, walked through and shut it after him. Above it, a green light went on. Miss Moneypenny raised her eyebrows at the Chief of Staff. He shook his head.

'I don't think it's business, Penny,' he said. 'Just sent for him out of the blue.' He went back into his own room and got on with the day's work.

When Bond came through the door, M was sitting at his broad desk, lighting a pipe. He made a vague gesture with the lighted match towards the chair on the other side of the desk and Bond walked over and sat down. M glanced at him sharply through the smoke and then threw the box of matches on to the empty expanse of red leather in front of him.

'Have a good leave?' he asked abruptly.

'Yes, thank you, sir,' said Bond.

'Still sunburned, I see.' M looked his disapproval. He didn't really begrudge Bond a holiday which had been partly convalescence. The hint of criticism came from the Puritan and the Jesuit who live in all leaders of men.

'Yes, sir,' said Bond noncommittally. 'It's very hot near the equator.'

'Quite,' said M. 'Well-deserved rest.' He screwed up his eyes without humour. 'Hope the colour won't last too long. Always suspicious of sunburned men in England. Either they've not got a job of work to do or they put it on with a sun-lamp.' He dismissed the subject with a short sideways jerk of his pipe.

He put the pipe back in his mouth and pulled at it absent-mindedly. It had gone out. He reached for the matches and wasted some time getting it going again.

'Looks as if we'll get that gold after all,' he said finally. 'There's been some talk of the Hague Court, but Ashenheim's a fine lawyer.'*

'Good,' said Bond.

There was silence for a moment. M gazed into the bowl of his pipe. Through the open windows came the distant roar of London's traffic.

---

* This refers to Bond's previous assignment, described in *Live and Let Die*.

A pigeon landed on one of the window-sills with a clatter of wings and quickly took off again.

Bond tried to read something in the weatherbeaten face he knew so well and which held so much of his loyalty. But the grey eyes were quiet and the little pulse that always beat high up on the right temple when M was tense showed no sign of life.

Suddenly Bond suspected that M was embarrassed. He had the feeling that M didn't know where to begin. Bond wanted to help. He shifted in his chair and took his eyes off M. He looked down at his hands and idly picked at a rough nail.

M lifted his eyes from his pipe and cleared his throat.

'Got anything particular on at the moment, James?' he asked in a neutral voice.

'James.' That was unusual. It was rare for M to use a Christian name in this room.

'Only paperwork and the usual courses,' said Bond. 'Anything you want me for, sir?'

'As a matter of fact there is,' said M. He frowned at Bond. 'But it's really got nothing to do with the Service. Almost a personal matter. Thought you might give me a hand.'

'Of course, sir,' said Bond. He was relieved for M's sake that the ice had been broken. Probably one of the old man's relations had got into trouble and M didn't want to ask a favour of Scotland Yard. Blackmail, perhaps. Or drugs. He was pleased that M should have chosen him. Of course he would take care of it. M was such a desperate stickler about Government property and personnel. Using Bond on a personal matter must have seemed to him like stealing the Government's money.

'Thought you'd say so,' said M, gruffly. 'Won't take up much of your time. An evening ought to be enough.' He paused. 'Well now, you've heard of this man Sir Hugo Drax?'

'Of course, sir,' said Bond, surprised at the name. 'You can't open a paper without reading something about him. *Sunday Express* is running his life. Extraordinary story.'

'I know,' said M shortly. 'Just give me the facts as you see them. I'd like to know if your version tallies with mine.'

Bond gazed out of the window for a moment to marshal his thoughts. M didn't like haphazard talk. He liked a fully detailed story with no um-ing and er-ing. No afterthoughts or hedging.

'Well, sir,' said Bond finally. 'For one thing the man's a national hero. The public have taken to him. I suppose he's in much the same class as Jack Hobbs or Gordon Richards. They've got a real feeling for him. They consider he's one of them, but a glorified version. A sort of superman. He's not much to look at, with all those scars from his war injuries, and he's a bit loud-mouthed and ostentatious. But they rather like that. Makes him a sort of Lonsdale figure, but more in their class. They like his friends calling him "Hugger" Drax. It makes him a bit of a card and I expect it gives the women a thrill. And then when you think what he's doing for the country, out of his own pocket and far beyond what any government seems to be able to do, it's really extraordinary that they don't insist on making him Prime Minister.'

Bond saw the cold eyes getting chillier, but he was determined not to let his admiration for Drax's achievements be dampened by the older man. 'After all, sir,' he continued reasonably, 'it looks as if he's made this country safe from war for years. And he can't be much over forty. I feel the same as most people about him. And then there's all this mystery about his real identity. I'm not surprised people feel rather sorry for him, although he is a multimillionaire. He seems to be a lonely sort of man in spite of his gay life.'

M smiled drily. 'All that sounds rather like a trailer for the *Express* story. He's certainly an extrordinary man. But what's your version of the facts? I don't expect I know much more than you do. Probably less. Don't read the papers very carefully, and there are no files on him except at the War Office and they're not very illuminating. Now then. What's the gist of the *Express* story?'

'Sorry, sir,' said Bond. 'But the facts are pretty slim. Well,' he looked out of the window again and concentrated, 'in the German breakthrough in the Ardennes in the winter of '44, the Germans made a lot of use of guerrillas and saboteurs. Gave them the rather spooky name of Werewolves. They did quite a lot of damage of one sort or another. Very good at camouflage and stay-behind tricks of all sorts and some of them went on operating long after Ardennes had failed and we had crossed the Rhine. They were supposed to carry on even when we had overrun the country. But they packed up pretty quickly when things got really bad.

'One of their best coups was to blow up one of the rear liaison HQs between the American and British armies. Reinforcement Holding Units I think they're called. It was a mixed affair, all kinds of Allied personnel – American signals, British ambulance drivers – a rather shifting group from every sort of unit. The Werewolves somehow managed to mine the mess-hall and, when it blew, it took with it quite a lot of the field hospital as well. Killed or wounded over a hundred. Sorting out all the bodies was the hell of a business. One of the English bodies was Drax. Half his face was blown away. Total amnesia that lasted a year and at the end of that time they didn't know who he was and nor did he. There were about twenty-five other unidentified bodies that neither we nor the Americans could sort out. Either not enough bits, or perhaps people in transit, or there without authorization. It was that sort of a unit. Two commanding officers, of course. Sloppy staff work. Lousy records. So after a year in various hospitals they took Drax through the War Office file of Missing Men. When they came to the papers of a no-next-of-kin called Hugo Drax, an orphan who had been working in the Liverpool docks before the war, he showed signs of interest, and the photograph and physical description seemed to tally more or less with what our man must have looked like before he was blown up. From that time he began to mend. He started to talk a bit about simple things he remembered, and the doctors got very proud of him. The War Office found a man who had served in the same Pioneer unit as this Hugo Drax and he came along to the hospital and said he was sure the man was Drax. That settled it. Advertising didn't produce another Hugo Drax and he was finally discharged late in 1945 in that name with back pay and a full disability pension.'

'But he still says he doesn't really know who he is,' interrupted M. 'He's a member of Blades. I've often played cards with him and talked to him afterwards at dinner. He says he sometimes gets a strong feeling of "having been there before". Often goes to Liverpool to try and hunt up his past. Anyway, what else?'

Bond's eyes were turned inwards, remembering. 'He seems to have disappeared for about three years after the war,' he said. 'Then the City started to hear about him from all over the world. The Metal Market heard about him first. Seems he'd cornered a very valuable ore called Columbite. Everybody was wanting the stuff. It's got an extraordinarily high melting point. Jet engines can't be made without it. There's very little of it in the world, only a few thousand tons are produced every year, mostly as a by-product of the Nigerian tin mines. Drax must have looked at the Jet Age and somehow put his finger on its main scarcity. He must have got hold of about £10,000 from somewhere because the *Express* says that in 1946 he'd bought three tons of Columbite, which cost him around £3,000 a ton. He got a £5,000 premium on this lot from an American aircraft firm who wanted it in a hurry. Then he started buying futures in the stuff, six months, nine months, a year forward. In three years he'd made a corner. Anyone who wanted Columbite went to Drax Metals for it. All this time he'd been playing about with futures in other small commodities – shellac, sisal, black pepper – anything where you could build up a big position on margin. Of course he gambled on a rising commodity market but he had the guts to keep his foot right down on the pedal even when the pace got hot as hell. And whenever he took a profit he ploughed the money back again. For instance, he was one of the first men to buy up used ore-dumps in South Africa. Now they're being re-mined for their uranium content. Another fortune there.'

M's quiet eyes were fixed on Bond. He puffed at his pipe, listening.

'Of course,' continued Bond, lost in his story, 'all this made the City wonder what the hell was going on. The commodity brokers kept on coming across the name of Drax. Whatever they wanted Drax had got it and was holding out for a much higher price than they were prepared to pay. He operated from Tangier – free port, no taxes, no currency restrictions. By 1950 he was a multimillionaire. Then he came back to England and started spending it. He simply threw it about. Best houses, best cars, best women. Boxes at the Opera, at Goodwood. Prize-winning Jersey herds. Prize-winning carnations. Prize-winning two-year-olds. Two yachts; money for the Walker Cup team; £100,000 for the Flood Disaster Fund; Coronation Ball for Nurses at the Albert Hall – there wasn't a week when he wasn't hitting the headlines with some splash or other. And all the time he went on getting richer and the people simply loved it. It was the Arabian Nights. It lit up their lives. If a wounded soldier from Liverpool could get there in five years, why shouldn't they or their sons? It sounded almost as easy as winning a gigantic football pool.

'And then came his astonishing letter to the Queen: "Your Majesty, may I have the temerity . . ." and the typical genius of the single banner-line across the *Express* next day: TEMERITY DRAX, and the story of how he had given to Britain his entire holding in Columbite to build a super atomic rocket with a range that would cover nearly every capital in Europe – the immediate answer to anyone who tried to atom-bomb London. £10,000,000 he was going to put up out of his own pocket, and he had the design of the thing and was prepared to find the staff to build it.

'And then there were months of delay and everyone got impatient. Questions in the House. The Opposition nearly forced a vote of Confidence. And then the announcement by the Prime Minister that the design had been approved by the Woomera Range experts of the Ministry of Supply, and that the Queen had been graciously pleased to accept the gift on behalf of the people of Britain and had conferred a knighthood on the donor.'

Bond paused, almost carried away by the story of this extraordinary man.

'Yes,' said M. 'Peace in Our Time – This Time. I remember the headline. A year ago. And now the rocket's nearly ready. "The Moonraker". And from all I hear it really should do what he says. It's very odd.' He relapsed into silence, gazing out of the window.

He turned back and faced Bond across the desk.

'That's about it,' he said slowly. 'I don't know much more than you do. A wonderful story. Extraordinary man.' He paused, reflecting. 'There's only one thing . . .' M tapped the stem of his pipe against his teeth.

'What's that, sir?' asked Bond.

M seemed to make up his mind. He looked mildly across at Bond.

'Sir Hugo Drax cheats at cards.'

337

3 'Belly Strippers', etc.

'Cheats at cards?'

M frowned. 'That's what I said,' he commented drily. 'It doesn't seem to you odd that a multimillionaire should cheat at cards?'

Bond grinned apologetically. 'Not as odd as all that, sir,' he said. 'I've known very rich people cheat themselves at Patience. But it just didn't fit in with my picture of Drax. Bit of an anticlimax.'

'That's the point,' said M. 'Why does he do it? And don't forget that cheating at cards can still smash a man. In so-called Society, it's about the only crime that can still finish you, whoever you are. Drax does it so well that nobody's caught him yet. As a matter of fact I doubt if anyone has begun to suspect him except Basildon. He's the Chairman of Blades. He came to me. He's got a vague idea I've got something to do with Intelligence and I've given him a hand over one or two little troubles in the past. Asked my advice. Said he didn't want a fuss at the club, of course, but above all he wants to save Drax from making a fool of himself. He admires him as much as we all do and he's terrified of an incident. You couldn't stop a scandal like that getting out. A lot of MPs are members and it would soon get talked about in the Lobby. Then the gossip-writers would get hold of it. Drax would have to resign from Blades and the next thing there'd be a libel action brought in his defence by one of his friends. Tranby Croft all over again. At least, that's how Basildon's mind is working and I must say I can see it that way too. Anyway,' said M with finality, 'I've agreed to help and', he looked levelly at Bond, 'that's where you come in. You're the best card-player in the Service, or,' he smiled ironically, 'you should be after the casino jobs you've been on, and I remembered that we'd spent quite a lot of money putting you through a course in card-sharping before you went after those Roumanians in Monte Carlo before the war.'

Bond smiled grimly. 'Steffi Esposito,' he said softly. 'That was the chap. American. Made me work ten hours a day for a week learning a thing called the Riffle Stack and how to deal Seconds and Bottoms and Middles. I wrote a long report about it at the time. Must be buried in Records. He knew every trick in the game. How to wax the aces so that the pack will break at them; Edge Work and Line Work with a razor on the backs of the high cards; Trimming; Arm Pressure Holdouts – mechanical gadgets up your sleeve that feed you cards. Belly Strippers – trimming a whole pack less than a millimetre down both sides, but leaving a slight belly on the cards you're interested in – the aces, for instance. Shiners, tiny mirrors built into rings, or fitted into the bottom of a pipe-bowl. Actually,' Bond admitted, 'it was his tip about Luminous Readers that helped me on that Monte Carlo job. A croupier was using an invisible ink the team could pick out with special glasses. But Steffi was a wonderful chap. Scotland Yard found him for us. He could shuffle the pack once and then cut the four aces out of it. Absolute magic.'

'Sounds a bit too professional for our man,' commented M. 'That sort of work needs hours of practice every day, or an accomplice, and I can't believe he'd find that at Blades. No, there's nothing sensational about his cheating and for all I know it might be a fantastic run of luck. It's odd. He's not a particularly good player – he only plays bridge, by the way – but quite often he brings off bids or doubles or finesses that are absolutely phenomenal – quite against the odds. Or the conventions. But they come off. He's always a big winner and they play high at Blades. He hasn't lost on a weekly settlement since he joined a year ago. We've got two or three of the finest players in the world in the Club and none of them has ever had a record like that over twelve months. It's getting talked about in a sort of joking way and I think Basildon's right to do something about it. What system do you suppose Drax has got?'

Bond was longing for his lunch. The Chief of Staff must have given him up half an hour ago. He could have talked to M about cheating for hours, and M, who never seemed to be interested in food or sleep, would have listened to everything and remembered it afterwards. But Bond was hungry.

'Assuming he's not a professional, sir, and can't doctor the cards in any way, there are only two answers. He's either looking, or else he's got a system of signals with his partner. Does he often play with the same man?'

'We always cut for partners after each rubber,' said M. 'Unless there's a challenge. And on guest nights, Mondays and Thursdays, you stick to your guest. Drax nearly always brings a man called Meyer, his metal broker. Nice chap. Jew. Very fine player.'

'I might be able to tell if I watched,' said Bond.

'That's what I was going to say,' said M. 'How about coming along tonight? At any rate you'll get a good dinner. Meet you there about six. I'll take some money off you at piquet and we'll watch the bridge for a little. After dinner we'll have a rubber or two with Drax and his friend. They're always there on Monday. All right? Sure I'm not taking you away from your work?'

'No, sir,' said Bond with a grin. 'And I'd like to come very much. Bit of a busman's holiday. And if Drax is cheating, I'll show him I've spotted it and that should be enough to warn him off. I wouldn't like to see him get into a mess. That all, sir?'

'Yes, James,' said M. 'And thank you for your help. Drax must be a bloody fool. Obviously a bit of a crank. But it isn't the man I'm worried about. I wouldn't like to chance anything going wrong with this rocket of his. And Drax more or less *is* the Moonraker. Well, see you at six. Don't bother about dressing. Some of us do for dinner and some of us don't. Tonight we won't. Better go along now and sandpaper your fingertips or whatever you sharpers do.'

Bond smiled back at M and got to his feet. It sounded a promising evening. As he walked over to the door and let himself out he reflected that here at last was an interview with M that didn't cast a shadow.

M's secretary was still at her desk. There was a plate of sandwiches and a glass of milk beside her typewriter. She looked sharply at Bond, but there was nothing to be read in his expression.

'I suppose he gave up,' said Bond.

'Nearly an hour ago,' said Miss Moneypenny reproachfully. 'It's half-past two. He'll be back any minute now.'

'I'll go down to the canteen before it closes,' he said. 'Tell him I'll pay for his lunch next time.' He smiled at her and walked out into the corridor and along to the lift.

There were only a few people left in the officers' canteen. Bond sat by himself and ate a grilled sole, a large mixed salad with his own dressing laced with mustard, some Brie cheese and toast, and half a carafe of white Bordeaux. He had two cups of black coffee and was back in his office by three. With half his mind preoccupied with M's problem, he hurried through the rest of the NATO file, said goodbye to his secretary after telling her where he would be that evening, and at four-thirty was collecting his car from the staff garage at the back of the building.

'Supercharger's whining a bit, sir,' said the ex-RAF mechanic who regarded Bond's Bentley as his own property. 'Take it down tomorrow if you won't be needing her at lunch-time.'

'Thanks,' said Bond, 'that'll be fine.' He took the car quietly out into the park and over to Baker Street, the two-inch exhaust bubbling fatly in his wake.

He was home in fifteen minutes. He left the car under the plane trees in the little square and let himself into the ground floor of the converted Regency house, went into the book-lined sitting-room and, after a moment's search, pulled *Scarne on Cards* out of its shelf and dropped it on the ornate Empire desk near the broad window.

He walked through into the smallish bedroom with the white and gold Cole wallpaper and the deep red curtains, undressed and threw his clothes, more or less tidily, on the dark blue counterpane of the double bed. Then he went into the bathroom and had a quick shower. Before leaving the bathroom he examined his face in the glass and decided that he had no intention of sacrificing a lifetime prejudice by shaving twice in one day.

In the glass, the grey-blue eyes looked back at him with the extra light they held when his mind was focused on a problem that interested him. The lean, hard face had a hungry, competitive edge to it. There was something swift and intent in the way he ran his fingers along his jaw and in the impatient stroke of the hairbrush to put back the comma of black hair that fell down an inch above his right eyebrow. It crossed his mind that, with the fading of his sunburn, the scar down the right cheek that had shown so white was beginning to be less prominent, and automatically he glanced down his naked body and registered that the almost indecent white area left by his bathing

341

trunks was less sharply defined. He smiled at some memory and went through into the bedroom.

Ten minutes later, in a heavy white silk shirt, dark blue trousers of Navy serge, dark blue socks, and well-polished black moccasin shoes, he was sitting at his desk with a pack of cards in one hand and Scarne's wonderful guide to cheating open in front of him.

For half an hour, as he ran quickly through the section on Methods, he practised the vital Mechanic's Grip (three fingers curled round the long edge of the cards, and the index finger at the short upper edge away from him), Palming and Nullifying the Cut. His hands worked automatically at these basic manoeuvres, while his eyes read, and he was glad to find that his fingers were supple and assured and that there was no noise from the cards even with the very difficult single-handed Annulment.

At five-thirty he slapped the cards on the table and shut the book.

He went into his bedroom, filled the wide black case with cigarettes and slipped it into his hip pocket, put on a black knitted silk tie and his coat and verified that his cheque book was in his notecase.

He stood for a moment, thinking. Then he selected two white silk handkerchiefs, carefully rumpled them, and put one into each side-pocket of his coat.

He lit a cigarette and walked back into the sitting-room and sat down at his desk again and relaxed for ten minutes, gazing out of the window at the empty square and thinking about the evening that was just going to begin and about Blades, probably the most famous private card club in the world.

The exact date of the foundation of Blades is uncertain. The second half of the eighteenth century saw the opening of many coffee houses and gaming rooms, and premises and proprietors shifted often with changing fashions and fortunes. White's was founded in 1755, Almack's in 1764, and Brooks's in 1774, and it was in that year that the Scavoir Vivre, which was to be the cradle of Blades, opened its doors on to Park Street, a quiet backwater off St James's.

The Scavoir Vivre was too exclusive to live and it blackballed itself to death within a year. Then, in 1776, Horace Walpole wrote: 'A new club is opened off St James's Street that piques itself in surpassing all its predecessors' and in 1778 'Blades' first occurs in a letter from Gibbon, the historian, who coupled it with the name of its founder, a German called Longchamp at that time conducting the Jockey Club at Newmarket.

From the outset Blades seems to have been a success, and in 1782 we find the Duke of Wirtemberg writing excitedly home to his younger brother: 'This is indeed the "Ace of Clubs"! There have been four or five quinze tables going in the room at the same time, with whist and piquet, after which a full Hazard table. I have known two at the same time. Two chests each containing 4000 guinea rouleaus were scarce sufficient for the night's circulation.'

Mention of Hazard perhaps provides a clue to the club's prosperity. Permission to play this dangerous but popular game must have been given by the Committee in contravention of its own rules which laid down that 'No game is to be admitted to the House of the Society but Chess, Whist, Picket, Cribbage, Quadrille, Ombre and Tredville'.

In any event the club continued to flourish and remains to this day the home of some of the highest 'polite' gambling in the world. It is not as aristocratic as it was, the redistribution of wealth has seen to that, but it is still the most exclusive club in London. The membership is restricted to two hundred and each candidate must have two qualifications for election; he must behave like a gentleman and he must be able to 'show' £100,000 in cash or gilt-edged securities.

The amenities of Blades, apart from the gambling, are so desirable that the Committee has had to rule that every member is required to win or lose £500 a year on the club premises, or pay an annual fine of £250. The food and wine are the best in London and no bills are presented, the cost of all meals being deducted at the end of each week *pro rata* from the profits of the winners. Seeing that about £5000 changes hands each week at the tables the impost is not too painful and the losers have the satisfaction of saving something from the wreck; and the custom explains the fairness of the levy on infrequent gamblers.

Club servants are the making or breaking of any club and the servants of Blades have no equal. The half-dozen waitresses in the dining-room are of such a high standard of beauty that some of the younger members have been known to smuggle them undetected into débutante balls, and if, at night, one or other of the girls is persuaded to stray into one of the twelve members' bedrooms at the back of the club, that is regarded as the members' private concern.

There are one or two other small refinements which contribute to the luxury of the place. Only brand-new currency notes and silver are paid out on the premises and, if a member is staying overnight, his notes and small change are taken away by the valet who brings the early morning tea and *The Times* and are replaced with new money. No newspaper comes to the reading room before it has been ironed. Floris provides the soaps and lotions in the lavatories and bedrooms; there is a direct wire to Ladbroke's from the porter's lodge; the club has the finest tents and boxes at the principal race-meetings, at Lord's, Henley, and Wimbledon, and members travelling abroad have automatic membership of the leading club in every foreign capital.

In short, membership of Blades, in return for the £100 entrance fee and the £50 a year subscription, provides the standard of luxury of the Victorian age together with the opportunity to win or lose, in great comfort, anything up to £20,000 a year.

Bond, reflecting on all this, decided that he was going to enjoy his evening. He had only played at Blades a dozen times in his life, and on the last occasion he had burnt his fingers badly in a high poker game, but the prospect of some expensive bridge and of the swing of a few, to him, not unimportant hundred pounds made his muscles taut with anticipation.

And then, of course, there was the little business of Sir Hugo Drax, which might bring an additional touch of drama to the evening.

He was not even disturbed by a curious portent he encountered while he was driving along King's Road into Sloane Square with half his mind on the traffic and the other half exploring the evening ahead.

It was a few minutes to six and there was thunder about. The sky threatened rain and it had become suddenly dark. Across the square from him, high up in the air, a bold electric sign started to flash on and off. The fading light-waves had caused the cathode tube to start the mechanism which would keep the sign flashing through the dark hours until, around six in the morning, the early light of day would again sensitize the tube and cause the circuit to close.

Startled at the great crimson words. Bond pulled in to the curb, got out of the car and crossed to the other side of the street to get a better view of the big skysign.

Ah! That was it. Some of the letters had been hidden by a neighbouring building. It was only one of those Shell advertisements. 'SUMMER SHELL IS HERE' was what it said.

Bond smiled to himself and walked back to his car and drove on.

When he had first seen the sign, half-hidden by the building, great crimson letters across the evening sky had flashed a different message. They had said: 'HELL IS HERE . . . HELL IS HERE . . . HELL IS HERE.'

4 The 'Shiner'

Bond left the Bentley outside Brooks's and walked round the corner into Park Street.

The Adam frontage of Blades, recessed a yard or so back from its neighbours, was elegant in the soft dusk. The dark red curtains had been drawn across the ground-floor bow-windows on either side of the entrance and a uniformed servant showed for a moment as he drew them across the three windows of the floor above. In the centre of the three, Bond could see the heads and shoulders of two men bent over a game, probably backgammon he thought, and he caught a glimpse of the spangled fire of one of the three great chandeliers that illuminate the famous gambling room.

Bond pushed through the swing doors and walked up to the old-fashioned porter's lodge ruled over by Brevett, the guardian of Blades and the counsellor and family friend of half the members.

'Evening, Brevett. Is the Admiral in?'

'Good evening, sir,' said Brevett, who knew Bond as an occasional guest at the club. 'The Admiral's waiting for you in the card room. Page, take Commander Bond up to the Admiral. Lively now!'

As Bond followed the uniformed page-boy across the worn black and white marble floor of the hall and up the wide staircase with its fine mahogany balustrade, he remembered the story of how, at one election, nine blackballs had been found in the box when there were only eight members of the committee present. Brevett, who had handed the box from member to member, was said to have confessed to the Chairman that he was so afraid the candidate would be elected that he had put in a blackball himself. No one had objected. The committee would rather have lost its chairman than the porter whose family had held the same post at Blades for a hundred years.

The page pushed open one wing of the tall doors at the top of the stairs and held it for Bond to go through. The long room was not crowded and Bond saw M sitting by himself playing patience in the alcove formed by the left hand of the three bow windows. He dismissed the page and walked across the heavy carpet, noticing the rich background smell of cigar-smoke, the quiet voices that came from the three tables of bridge, and the sharp rattle of dice across an unseen backgammon board.

'There you are,' said M as Bond came up. He waved to the chair that faced him across the card table. 'Just let me finish this. I haven't cracked this man Canfield for months. Drink?'

'No, thanks,' said Bond. He sat down and lit a cigarette and watched with amusement the concentration M was putting into his game.

'Admiral Sir M – M – : something at the Ministry of Defence.' M looked like any member of any of the clubs in St James's Street. Dark grey suit, stiff white collar, the favourite dark blue bow-tie with spots, rather loosely tied, the thin black cord of the rimless eyeglass that M seemed only to use to read menus, the keen sailor's face, with the clear, sharp sailor's eyes. It was difficult to believe that an hour before he had been playing with a thousand live chessmen against the enemies of England; that there might be, this evening, fresh blood on his hands, or a successful burglary, or the hideous knowledge of a disgusting blackmail case.

And what could the casual observer think of him, 'Commander James Bond, GMG, RNVSR', also 'something at the Ministry of Defence', the rather saturnine young man in his middle thirties sitting opposite the Admiral? Something a bit cold and dangerous in that face. Looks pretty fit. May have been attached to Templer in Malaya.

Or Nairobi. Mau Mau work. Tough-looking customer. Doesn't look the sort of chap one usually sees in Blades.

Bond knew that there was something alien and un-English about himself. He knew that he was a difficult man to cover up. Particularly in England. He shrugged his shoulders. Abroad was what mattered. He would never have a job to do in England. Outside the jurisdiction of the Service. Anyway, he didn't need a cover this evening. This was recreation.

M snorted and threw his cards down. Bond automatically gathered in the pack and as automatically gave it the Scarne shuffle, marrying the two halves with the quick downward riffle that never brings the cards off the table. He squared off the pack and pushed it away.

M beckoned to a passing waiter. 'Piquet cards, please, Tanner,' he said.

The waiter went away and came back a moment later with the two thin packs. He stripped off the wrapping and placed them, with two markers, on the table. He stood waiting.

'Bring me a whisky and soda,' said M. 'Sure you won't have anything?'

Bond looked at his watch. It was half past six. 'Could I have a dry Martini?' he said. 'Made with Vodka. Large slice of lemon peel.'

'Rot-gut,' commented M briefly as the waiter went away. 'Now I'll just take a pound or two off you and then we'll go and have a look at the bridge. Our friend hasn't turned up yet.'

For half an hour they played the game at which the expert player can nearly always win even with the cards running slightly against him. At the end of the game Bond laughed and counted out three pound-notes.

'One of these days I'm going to take some trouble and really learn piquet,' he said. 'I've never won against you yet.'

'It's all memory and knowing the odds,' said M with satisfaction. He finished his whisky and soda. 'Let's go over and see what's going on at the bridge. Our man's playing at Basildon's table. Came in about ten minutes ago. If you notice anything, just give me a nod and we'll go downstairs and talk about it.'

He stood up and Bond followed suit.

The far end of the room had begun to fill up and half a dozen tables of bridge were going. At the round poker table under the centre chandelier three players were counting out chips into five stacks, waiting for two more players to come in. The kidney-shaped baccarat table was still shrouded and would probably remain so until after dinner, when it would be used for chemin-de-fer.

Bond followed M out of their alcove, relishing the scene down the long room, the oases of green, the tinkle of glasses as the waiters moved amongst the tables, the hum of talk punctuated by sudden exclamations and warm laughter, the haze of blue smoke rising up through the dark red lamp shades that hung over the centre of each table. His pulses quickened with the smell of it all and his nostrils flared slightly as the two men came down the long room and joined the company.

M, with Bond beside him, wandered casually from table to table, exchanging greetings with the players until they reached the last table beneath the fine Lawrence of Beau Brummel over the wide Adam fireplace.

'Double, damn you,' said the loud, cheerful voice of the player with his back to Bond. Bond thoughtfully noted the head of tight reddish hair that was all he could see of the speaker, then he looked to the left at the rather studious profile of Lord Basildon. The Chairman of Blades was leaning back, looking critically down his nose at the hand of cards which he held out and away from him as if it were a rare object.

'My hand is so exquisite that I am forced to redouble, my dear Drax,' he said. He looked across at his partner. 'Tommy,' he said. 'Charge this to me if it goes wrong.'

'Rot,' said his partner. 'Meyer? Better take Drax out.'

'Too frightened,' said the middle-aged florid man who was playing with Drax. 'No bid.' He picked up his cigar from the brass ashtray and put it carefully into the middle of his mouth.

'No bid here,' said Basildon's partner.

'And nothing here,' came Drax's voice.

'Five clubs redoubled,' said Basildon. 'Your lead, Meyer.'

Bond looked over Drax's shoulder. Drax had the ace of spades and the ace of hearts. He promptly made them both and led another heart which Basildon took on the table with the king.

'Well,' said Basildon. 'There are four trumps against me including the queen. I shall play Drax to have her.' He finessed against Drax. Meyer took the trick with the queen.

'Hell and damnation,' said Basildon. 'What's the queen doing in Meyer's hand? Well, I'm damned. Anyway the rest are mine.' He fanned his cards down on the table. He looked defensively at his partner. 'Can you beat it, Tommy? Drax doubles and Meyer has the queen.' There was not more than a natural exasperation in his voice.

Drax chuckled. 'Didn't expect my partner to have a Yarborough did you?' he said cheerfully to Basildon. 'Well, that's just the four hundred above the line. Your deal.' He cut the cards to Basildon and the game went on.

So it had been Drax's deal the hand before. That might be important. Bond lit a cigarette and reflectively examined the back of Drax's head.

M's voice cut in on Bond's thoughts. 'You remember my friend Commander Bond, Basil? Thought we'd come along and play some bridge this evening.'

Basildon smiled up at Bond. 'Evening,' he said. He waved a hand round the table from the left to right. 'Meyer, Dangerfield, Drax.' The three men looked up briefly and Bond nodded a greeting to the table in general. 'You all know the Admiral,' added the Chairman, starting to deal.

Drax half turned in his chair. 'Ah, the Admiral,' he said boisterously. 'Glad to have you aboard, Admiral. Drink?'

'No, thanks,' said M with a thin smile. 'Just had one.'

Drax turned and glanced up at Bond, who caught a glimpse of a tuft of reddish moustache and a rather chilly blue eye. 'What about you?' asked Drax perfunctorily.

'No, thanks,' said Bond.

Drax swivelled back to the table and picked up his cards. Bond watched the big blunt hands sort them.

Then he moved round the table with a second clue to ponder.

Drax didn't sort his cards into suits as most players do, but only into reds and blacks, ungraded, making his hand very difficult to kibitz and almost impossible for one of his neighbours, if they were so inclined, to decipher.

Bond knew it for the way people hold their hands who are very careful card-players indeed.

Bond went and stood beside the chimneypiece. He took out a cigarette and lit it at the flame from a small gas-jet enclosed in a silver grille – a relic of the days before the use of matches – that protruded from the wall beside him.

From where he stood he could see the hand of Meyer, and by moving a pace to the right, of Basildon. His view of Sir Hugo Drax was uninterrupted and he inspected him carefully while appearing to interest himself only in the game.

Drax gave the impression of being a little larger than life. He was physically big – about six foot tall, Bond guessed – and his shoulders were exceptionally broad. He had a big square head and the tight reddish hair was parted in the middle. On either side of the parting the hair dipped down in a curve towards the temples with the object, Bond assumed, of hiding as much as possible of the tissue of shining puckered skin that covered most of the right half of his face. Other relics of plastic surgery could be detected in the man's right ear, which was not a perfect match with its companion on the left, and the right eye, which had been a surgical failure. It was considerably larger than the left eye, because of a contraction of the borrowed skin used to rebuild the upper and lower eyelids, and it looked painfully bloodshot. Bond doubted if it was capable of closing completely and he guessed that Drax covered it with a patch at night.

To conceal as much as possible of the unsightly taut skin that covered half his face, Drax had grown a bushy reddish moustache and had allowed his whiskers to grow down to the level of the lobes of his ears. He also had patches of hair on his cheek-bones.

The heavy moustache served another purpose. It helped to hide a naturally prognathous upper jaw and a marked protrusion of the upper row of teeth. Bond reflected that this was probably due to sucking his thumb as a child, and it had resulted in an ugly splaying, or diastema, of what Bond had heard his dentist call 'the centrals'. The moustache helped to hide these 'ogre's teeth' and it was only when

Drax uttered, as he frequently did, his short braying laugh that the splay could be seen.

The general effect of the face – the riot of red-brown hair, the powerful nose and jaw, the florid skin – was flamboyant. It put Bond in mind of a ring-master at a circus. The contrasting sharpness and coldness of the left eye supported the likeness.

A bullying, boorish, loud-mouthed vulgarian. That would have been Bond's verdict if he had not known something of Drax's abilities. As it was, it crossed his mind that much of the effect might be Drax's idea of a latter-day Regency buck – the harmless disguise of a man with a smashed face who was also a snob.

Looking for further clues, Bond noticed that Drax was sweating rather freely. Despite the occasional growl of thunder outside it was a cool evening, and yet Drax was constantly mopping his face and neck with a huge bandana handkerchief. He smoked incessantly, stubbing out the cork-tipped Virginia cigarettes after a dozen lungfuls of smoke and almost immediately lighting another from a box of fifty in his coat pocket. His big hands, their backs thickly covered with reddish hair, were always on the move, fiddling with his cards, handling the cigarette lighter that stood beside a plain flat silver cigarette-case in front of him, twisting a lock of hair on the side of his head, using the handkerchief on his face and neck. Occasionally he put a finger greedily to his mouth and worried a nail. Even at a distance Bond could see that every finger-nail was bitten down to the quick.

The hands themselves were strong and capable but the thumbs had something ungainly about them which it took Bond a moment or two to define. He finally detected that they were unnaturally long and reached level with the top joint of the index finger.

Bond concluded his inspection with Drax's clothes which were expensive and in excellent taste – a dark blue pinstripe in lightweight flannel, double-breasted with turnback cuffs, a heavy white silk shirt with a stiff collar, an unobtrusive tie with a small grey and white check, modest cufflinks, which looked like Cartier, and a plain gold Patek Philippe watch with a black leather strap.

Bond lit another cigarette and concentrated on the game, leaving his subconscious to digest the details of Drax's appearance and manner that had seemed to him significant and that might help to explain the riddle of his cheating, the nature of which had still to be discovered.

Half an hour later the cards had completed the circle.

'My deal,' said Drax with authority. 'Game all and we have a satisfactory inflation above the line. Now then, Max, see if you can't pick up a few aces. I'm tired of doing all the work.' He dealt smoothly and slowly round the table, keeping up a running fire of rather heavy-handed banter with the company. 'Long rubber,' he said to M who was sitting smoking his pipe between Drax and Basildon. 'Sorry to have kept you out so long. How about a challenge after dinner? Max and I'll take on you and Commander Thingummy. What did you say his name was? Good player?'

'Bond,' said M. 'James Bond. Yes, I think we'd like that very much. What do you say, James?'

Bond's eyes were glued to the bent head and slowly moving hands of the dealer. Yes, that was it! Got you, you bastard. A Shiner. A simple, bloody Shiner that wouldn't have lasted five minutes in a pro's game. M saw the glint of assurance in Bond's eyes as they met across the table.

'Fine,' said Bond cheerfully. 'Couldn't be better.' He made an imperceptible movement of the head. 'How about showing me the Betting Book before dinner? You always say it'll amuse me.'

M nodded. 'Yes. Come along. It's in the Secretary's office. Then Basildon can come down and give us a cocktail and tell us the result of this death-struggle.' He got up.

'Order what you want,' said Basildon with a sharp glance at M. 'I'll be down directly we've polished them off.'

'Around nine then,' said Drax, glancing from M to Bond. 'Show him the bet about the girl in the balloon.' He picked up his hand. 'Looks like I shall have the Casino's money to play with,' he said after a rapid glance at his cards. 'Three No Trumps.' He shot a triumphant glance at Basildon. 'Put that in your pipe and smoke it.'

Bond, following M out of the room, missed Basildon's reply.

They walked down the stairs and along to the Secretary's office in silence. The room was in darkness. M switched on the light and went and sat down in the swivel chair in front of the busy-looking desk. He turned the chair to face Bond who had walked over to the empty fireplace and was taking out a cigarette.

'Any luck?' he asked looking up at him.

'Yes,' said Bond. 'He cheats all right.'

'Ah,' said M unemotionally. 'How does he do it?'

'Only on the deal,' said Bond. 'You know that silver cigarette-case he has in front of him, with his lighter? He never takes cigarettes from it. Doesn't want to get fingermarks on the surface. It's plain silver and very highly polished. When he deals, it's almost concealed by the cards and his big hands. And he doesn't move his hands away from it. Deals four piles quite close to him. Every card is reflected in the top of the case. It's just as good as a mirror although it looks perfectly innocent lying there. As he's such a good businessman it would be normal for him to have a first-class memory. You remember I told you about "Shiners"? Well, that's just a version of one. No wonder he brings off these miraculous finesses every once in a while. That double we watched was easy. He knew his partner had the guarded queen. With his two aces the double was a certainty. The rest of the time he just plays his average game. But knowing all the cards on every fourth deal is a terrific edge. It's not surprising he always shows a profit.'

'But one doesn't notice him doing it,' protested M.

'It's quite natural to look down when one's dealing,' said Bond. 'Everybody does. And he covers up with a lot of banter, much more than he produces when someone else is dealing. I expect he's got very good peripheral vision – the thing they mark us so highly for when we take our medical for the Service. Very wide angle of sight.'

The door opened and Basildon came in. He was bristling. He shut the door behind him. 'That dam' shut-out bid of Drax's,' he exploded. 'Tommy and I could have made four hearts if we could have got around to bidding it. Between them they had the ace of hearts, six club tricks, and the ace, king of diamonds and a bare guard in spades. Made nine tricks straight off. How he had the face to open Three No Trumps I can't imagine.' He calmed down a little. 'Well, Miles,' he said, 'has your friend got the answer?'

M gestured to Bond, who repeated what he had told M. Lord Basildon's face got angrier as Bond talked.

'Damn the man,' he exploded when Bond had finished. 'What the hell does he want to do that for? Bloody millionaire. Rolling in money. Fine scandal we're in for. I'll simply have to tell the Committee. Haven't had a cheating case since the 'fourteen-eighteen war.' He paced up and down the room. The club was quickly forgotten as he remembered the significance of Drax himself. 'And they say this rocket of his is going to be ready before long. Only comes up here once or twice a week for a bit of relaxation. Why, the man's a public hero! this is terrible.'

Basildon's anger was chilled by the thought of his responsibility. He turned to M for help. 'Now, Miles, what am I to do? He's won thousands of pounds in this club and others have lost it. Take this evening. It doesn't matter about my losses, of course. But what about Dangerfield? I happen to know he's been having a bad time on the stock market lately. I don't see how I can avoid telling the Committee. Can't shirk it – whoever Drax is. And you know what that'll mean. There are ten on the Committee. Bound to be a leak. And then look at the scandal. They tell me the Moonraker can't exist without Drax and the papers say the whole future of the country depends on the thing. This is a damned serious business.' He paused and shot a hopeful glance at M and then at Bond. 'Is there any alternative?'

Bond stubbed out his cigarette. 'He could be stopped,' he said quietly. 'That is,' he added with a thin smile, 'if you don't mind paying him out in his own coin.'

'Do anything you bloody well like,' said Basildon emphatically. 'What are you thinking of?' Hope dawned in his eyes at Bond's assurance.

'Well,' said Bond. 'I could show him I'd spotted him and at the same time flay the hide off him at his own game. Of course Meyer'd get hurt in the process. Might lose a lot of money as Drax's partner. Would that matter?'

'Serve him right,' said Basildon, overcome with relief and ready to grasp at any solution. 'He's been riding along on Drax's back. Making plenty of money playing with him. You don't think . . .'

'No,' said Bond. 'I'm sure he doesn't know what's going on. Although some of Drax's bids must come as a bit of a shock. Well,' he turned to M, 'is it all right with you, sir?'

M reflected. He looked at Basildon. There was no doubt of his view.

He looked at Bond. 'All right,' he said. 'What must be, must be. Don't like the idea, but I can see Basildon's point. So long as you can bring it off and,' he smiled, 'as long as you don't want me to palm any cards or anything of that sort. No talent for it.'

'No,' said Bond. He put his hands in his coat pockets and touched the two silk handkerchiefs. 'And I think it should work. All I need is a couple of packs of used cards, one of each colour, and ten minutes in here alone.'

5 Dinner at Blades

It was eight o'clock as Bond followed M through the tall doors, across the well of the staircase from the card room, that opened into the beautiful white and gold Regency dining-room of Blades.

M chose not to hear a call from Basildon who was presiding over the big centre table where there were still two places vacant. Instead, he walked firmly across the room to the end one of a row of six smaller tables, waved Bond into the comfortable armed chair that faced outwards into the room, and himself took the one on Bond's left so that his back was to the company.

The head steward was already behind Bond's chair. He placed a broad menu card beside his plate and handed another to M. 'Blades' was written in fine gold script across the top. Below there was a forest of print.

'Don't bother to read through all that,' said M, 'unless you've got no ideas. One of the first rules of the club, and one of the best, was that any member may speak for any dish, cheap or dear, but he must pay for it. The same's true today, only the odds are one doesn't have to pay for it. Just order what you feel like.' He looked up at the steward. 'Any of that Beluga caviar left, Porterfield?'

'Yes, sir. There was a new delivery last week.'

'Well,' said M. 'Caviar for me. Devilled kidney and a slice of your excellent bacon. Peas and new potatoes. Strawberries in kirsch. What about you, James?'

'I've got a mania for really good smoked salmon,' said Bond. Then he pointed down the menu. 'Lamb cutlets. The same vegetables as you, as it's May. Asparagus with Béarnaise sauce sounds wonderful. And perhaps a slice of pineapple.' He sat back and pushed the menu away.

'Thank heaven for a man who makes up his mind,' said M. He looked up at the steward. 'Have you got all that, Porterfield?'

'Yes, sir.' The steward smiled. 'You wouldn't care for a marrow bone after the strawberries, sir? We got half a dozen in today from the country, and I'd specially kept one in case you came in.'

'Of course. You know I can't resist them. Bad for me but it can't be helped. God knows what I'm celebrating this evening. But it doesn't often happen. Ask Grimley to come over, would you.'

'He's here now, sir,' said the steward, making way for the wine-waiter.

'Ah, Grimley, some vodka, please.' He turned to Bond. 'Not the stuff you had in your cocktail. This is real pre-war Wolfschmidt from Riga. Like some with your smoked salmon?'

'Very much,' said Bond.

'Then what?' asked M. 'Champagne? Personally I'm going to have a half-bottle of claret. The Mouton Rothschild '34, please, Grimley. But don't pay any attention to me, James. I'm an old man. Champagne's no good for me. We've got some good champagnes, haven't we, Grimley? None of that stuff you're always telling me about, I'm afraid, James. Don't often see it in England. Taittinger, wasn't it?'

Bond smiled at M's memory. 'Yes,' he said, 'but it's only a fad of mine. As a matter of fact, for various reasons I believe I would like to drink champagne this evening. Perhaps I could leave it to Grimley.'

The wine-waiter was pleased. 'If I may suggest it, sir, the Dom Perignon '46. I understand that France only sells it for dollars, sir, so you don't often see it in London. I believe it was a gift from the Regency Club in New York, sir. I have some on ice at the moment. It's the Chairman's favourite and he's told me to have it ready every evening in case he needs it.'

Bond smiled his agreement.

'So be it, Grimley,' said M. 'The Dom Perignon. Bring it straight away, would you?'

A waitress appeared and put racks of fresh toast on the table and a silver dish of Jersey butter. As she bent over the table her black skirt brushed Bond's arm and he looked up into two pert, sparkling eyes under a soft fringe of hair. The eyes held his for a fraction of a second and then she whisked away. Bond's eyes followed the white bow at her waist and the starched collar and cuffs of her uniform as she went down the long room. His eyes narrowed. He recalled a pre-war establishment in Paris where the girls were dressed with the same exciting severity. Until they turned round and showed their backs.

He smiled to himself. The Marthe Richards law had changed all that.

M turned from studying their neighbours behind him. 'Why were you so cryptic about drinking champagne?'

'Well, if you don't mind, sir,' Bond explained, 'I've got to get a bit tight tonight. I'll have to seem very drunk when the time comes. It's not an easy thing to act unless you do it with a good deal of conviction. I hope you won't get worried if I seem to get frayed at the edges later on.'

M shrugged his shoulders. 'You've got a head like a rock, James,' he said. 'Drink as much as you like if it's going to help. Ah, here's the vodka.'

When M poured him three fingers from the frosted carafe Bond took a pinch of black pepper and dropped it on the surface of the vodka. The pepper slowly settled to the bottom of the glass leaving a few grains on the surface which Bond dabbed up with the tip of a finger. Then he tossed the cold liquor well to the back of his throat and put his glass, with the dregs of the pepper at the bottom, back on the table.

M gave him a glance of rather ironical inquiry.

'It's a trick the Russians taught me that time you attached me to the Embassy in Moscow,' apologized Bond. 'There's often quite a lot of fusel oil on the surface of this stuff – at least there used to be when it was badly distilled. Poisonous. In Russia, where you get a lot of

357

bath-tub liquor, it's an understood thing to sprinkle a little pepper in your glass. It takes the fusel oil to the bottom. I got to like the taste and now it's a habit. But I shouldn't have insulted the club Wolfschmidt,' he added with a grin.

M grunted. 'So long as you don't put pepper in Basildon's favourite champagne,' he said drily.

A harsh bray of laughter came from a table at the far end of the room. M looked over his shoulder and then turned back to his caviar.

'What do you think of this man Drax?' he said through a mouthful of buttered toast.

Bond helped himself to another slice of smoked salmon from the silver dish beside him. It had the delicate glutinous texture only achieved by Highland curers – very different from the desiccated products of Scandinavia. He rolled a wafer-thin slice of brown bread-and-butter into a cylinder and contemplated it thoughtfully.

'One can't like his manner much. At first I was rather surprised that you tolerate him here.' He glanced at M, who shrugged his shoulders. 'But that's none of my business and anyway clubs would be very dull without a sprinkling of eccentrics. And in any case he's a national hero and a millionaire and obviously an adequate card-player. Even when he isn't helping himself to the odds,' he added. 'But I can see he's the sort of man I always imagined. Full-blooded, ruthless, shrewd. Plenty of guts. I'm not surprised he's managed to get where he is. What I don't understand is why he should be quite happy to throw it all away. This cheating of his. It's really beyond belief. What's he trying to prove with it? That he can beat everyone at everything? He seems to put so much passion into his cards – as if it wasn't a game at all, but some sort of trial of strength. You've only got to look at his finger-nails. Bitten to the quick. And he sweats too much. There's a lot of tension there somewhere. It comes out in those ghastly jokes of his. They're harsh. There's no light touch about them. He seemed to want to squash Basildon like a fly. Hope I shall be able to keep my temper. That manner of his is pretty riling. He even treats his partner as if he was muck. He hasn't quite got under my skin, but I shan't at all mind sticking a very sharp pin in him tonight.' He smiled at M. 'If it comes off, that is.'

'I know what you mean,' said M. 'But you may be being a bit hard on the man. After all, it's a big step from the Liverpool docks, or wherever he came from, to where he is now. And he's one of those people who was born with naturally hairy heels. Nothing to do with snobbery. I expect his mates in Liverpool found him just as loud-mouthed as Blades does. As for his cheating, there's probably a crooked streak in him somewhere. I dare say he took plenty of short cuts on his way up. Somebody said that to become very rich you have to be helped by a combination of remarkable circumstances and an unbroken run of luck. It certainly isn't only the qualities of people that make them rich. At least that's my experience. At the beginning, getting together the first ten thousand, or the first hundred thousand, things have got to go damn right. And in that commodity business after the war, with all the regulations and restrictions, I expect it was often a case of being able to drop a thousand pounds in the right pocket. Officials. The ones who understand nothing but addition, division – and silence. The useful ones.'

M paused while the next course came. With it arrived the champagne in a silver ice-bucket, and the small wicker-basket containing M's half-bottle of claret.

The wine-steward waited until they had delivered a favourable judgement on the wines and then moved away. As he did so a page came up to their table. 'Commander Bond?' he asked.

Bond took the envelope that was handed to him and slit it open. He took out a thin paper packet and carefully opened it under the level of the table. It contained a white powder. He took a silver fruit knife off the table and dipped the tip of the blade into the packet so that about half its contents were transferred to the knife. He reached for his glass of champagne and tipped the powder into it.

'Now what?' said M with a trace of impatience.

There was no hint of apology in Bond's face. It wasn't M who was going to have to do the work that evening. Bond knew what he was doing. Whenever he had a job of work to do he would take infinite pains beforehand and leave as little as possible to chance. Then if something went wrong it was the unforeseeable. For that he accepted no responsibility.

'Benzedrine,' he said. 'I rang up my secretary before dinner and asked her to wangle some out of the surgery at Headquarters. It's what I shall need if I'm going to keep my wits about me tonight. It's apt to make one a bit overconfident, but that'll be a help too.' He stirred the champagne with a scrap of toast so that the white powder whirled among the bubbles. Then he drank the mixture down with one long swallow. 'It doesn't taste,' said Bond, 'and the champagne is quite excellent.'

M smiled at him indulgently. 'It's your funeral,' he said. 'Now we'd better get on with our dinner. How were the cutlets?'

'Superb,' said Bond. 'I could cut them with a fork. The best English cooking is the best in the world – particularly at this time of the year. By the way, what stakes will we be playing for this evening? I don't mind very much. We ought to end up the winners. But I'd like to know how much it will cost Drax.'

'Drax likes to play for what he calls "One and One",' said M, helping himself from the strawberries that had just been put on the table. 'Modest sounding stake, if you don't know what it stands for. In fact it's one tenner a hundred and one hundred pounds on the rubber.'

'Oh,' said Bond respectfully. 'I see.'

'But he's perfectly happy to play for Two and Two or even Three and Three. Mounts up at those figures. The average rubber of bridge at Blades is about ten points. That's £200 at One and One. And the bridge here makes for big rubbers. There are no conventions so there's plenty of gambling and bluffing. Sometimes it's more like poker. They're a mixed lot of players. Some of them are the best in England, but others are terribly wild. Don't seem to mind how much they lose. General Bealey, just behind us.' M made a gesture with his head, 'Doesn't know the reds from the blacks. Nearly always a few hundred down at the end of the week. Doesn't seem to care. Bad heart. No dependants. Stacks of money from jute. But Duff Sutherland, the scruffy-looking chap next to the chairman, is an absolute killer. Makes a regular ten thousand a year out of the club. Nice chap. Wonderful card manners. Used to play chess for England.'

M was interrupted by the arrival of his marrow bone. It was placed upright in a spotless lace napkin on the silver plate. An ornate silver marrow-scoop was laid beside it.

After the asparagus, Bond had little appetite for the thin slivers of pineapple. He tipped the last of the ice-cold champagne into his glass. He felt wonderful. The effects of the benzedrine and champagne had more than offset the splendour of the food. For the first time he took his mind away from the dinner and his conversation with M and glanced round the room.

It was a sparkling scene. There were perhaps fifty men in the room, the majority in dinner jackets, all at ease with themselves and their surroundings, all stimulated by the peerless food and drink, all animated by a common interest – the prospect of high gambling, the grand slam, the ace pot, the key-throw in a 64 game at backgammon. There might be cheats or possible cheats amongst them, men who beat their wives, men with perverse instincts, greedy men, cowardly men, lying men; but the elegance of the room invested each one with a kind of aristocracy.

At the far end, above the cold table, laden with lobsters, pies, joints and delicacies in aspic, Romney's unfinished full-length portrait of Mrs Fitzherbert gazed provocatively across at Fragonard's *Jeu de Cartes*, the broad conversation-piece which half-filled the opposite wall above the Adam fireplace. Along the lateral walls, in the centre of each gilt-edged panel, was one of the rare engravings of the Hell-Fire Club in which each figure is shown making a minute gesture of scatological or magical significance. Above, marrying the walls into the ceiling, ran a frieze in plaster relief of carved urns and swags interrupted at intervals by the capitals of the fluted pilasters which framed the windows and the tall double doors, the latter delicately carved with a design showing the Tudor Rose interwoven with a ribbon effect.

The central chandelier, a cascade of crystal ropes terminating in a broad basket of strung quartz, sparkled warmly above the white damask tablecloths and George IV silver. Below, in the centre of each table, branched candlesticks distributed the golden light of three candles, each surmounted by a red silk shade, so that the faces of the diners shone with a convivial warmth which glossed over the occasional chill of an eye or cruel twist of a mouth.

Even as Bond drank in the warm elegance of the scene, some of the groups began to break up. There was a drift towards the door accompanied by an exchange of challenges, side-bets, and exhortations to hurry up and get down to business. Sir Hugo Drax, his hairy red face shining with cheerful anticipation, came towards them with Meyer in his wake.

'Well, gentlemen,' he said jovially as he reached their table. 'Are the lambs ready for the slaughter and the geese for the plucking?' He grinned and in wolfish pantomime drew a finger across his throat. 'We'll go ahead and lay out the axe and the basket. Made your wills?'

'Be with you in a moment,' said M edgily. 'You go along and stack the cards.'

Drax laughed. 'We shan't need any artificial aids,' he said. 'Don't be long.' He turned and made for the door. Meyer enveloped them in an uncertain smile and followed him.

M grunted. 'We'll have coffee and brandy in the card room,' he said to Bond. 'Can't smoke here. Now then. Any final plans?'

'I'll have to fatten him up for the kill, so please don't worry if I seem to be getting high,' said Bond. 'We'll just have to play our normal game till the time comes. When it's his deal, we'll have to be careful. Of course, he can't alter the cards and there's no reason why he shouldn't deal us good hands, but he's bound to bring off some pretty remarkable coups. Do you mind if I sit on his left?'

'No,' said M. 'Anything else?'

Bond reflected for a moment. 'Only one thing, sir,' he said. 'When the time comes, I shall take a white handerchief out of my coat pocket. That will mean that you are about to be dealt a Yarborough. Would you please leave the bidding of that hand to me?'

6 Cards with a Stranger

Drax and Meyer were waiting for them. They were leaning back in their chairs, smoking Cabinet Havanas.

On the small tables beside them there was coffee and large balloons of brandy. As M and Bond came up, Drax was tearing the paper cover off a new pack of cards. The other pack was fanned out across the green baize in front of him.

'Ah, there you are,' said Drax. He leant forward and cut a card. They all followed suit. Drax won the cut and elected to stay where he was and take the red cards.

Bond sat down on Drax's left.

M beckoned to a passing waiter. 'Coffee and the club brandy,' he said. He took out a thin black cheroot and offered one to Bond who accepted it. Then he picked up the red cards and started to shuffle them.

'Stakes?' asked Drax, looking at M. 'One and One? Or more? I'll be glad to accommodate you up to Five and Five.'

'One and One'll be enough for me,' said M. 'James?'

Drax cut in, 'I suppose your guest knows what he's in for?' he asked sharply.

Bond answered for M. 'Yes,' he said briefly. He smiled at Drax. 'And I feel rather generous tonight. What would you like to take off me?'

'Every penny you've got,' said Drax cheerfully. 'How much can you afford?'

'I'll tell you when there's none left,' said Bond. He suddenly decided to be ruthless. 'I'm told that Five and Five is your limit. Let's play for that.'

Almost before the words were out of his mouth he regretted them. £50 a hundred! £500 side-bets! Four bad rubbers would be double his income for a year. If something went wrong he'd look pretty stupid. Have to borrow from M. And M wasn't a particularly rich man. Suddenly he saw that this ridiculous game might end in a very nasty mess. He felt the prickle of sweat on his forehead. That damned benzedrine. And, for him of all people to allow himself to be needled by a blustering loud-mouthed bastard like Drax. And he wasn't even on a job. The whole evening was a bit of a social pantomime that meant less than nothing to him. Even M had only been dragged into it by chance. And all of a sudden he'd let himself be swept up into a duel with this multimillionaire, into a gamble for literally all Bond possessed, for the simple reason that the man had got filthy manners and he'd wanted to teach him a lesson. And supposing the lesson

363

didn't come off? Bond cursed himself for an impulse that earlier in the day would have seemed unthinkable. Champagne and benzedrine! Never again.

Drax was looking at him in sarcastic disbelief. He turned to M who was still unconcernedly shuffling the cards. 'I suppose your guest is good for his commitments,' he said. Unforgivably.

Bond saw the blood rush up M's neck and into his face. M paused for an instant in his shuffling. When he continued Bond noticed that his hands were quite calm. M looked up and took the cheroot very deliberately out from between his teeth. His voice was perfectly controlled. 'If you mean "Am I good for my guest's commitments",' he said coldly, 'the answer is yes.'

He cut the cards to Drax with his left hand and with his right knocked the ash off his cheroot into the copper ashtray in the corner of the table. Bond heard the faint hiss as the burning ash hit the water.

Drax squinted sideways at M. He picked up the cards. 'Of course, of course,' he said hastily. 'I didn't mean . . .' He left the sentence unfinished and turned to Bond. 'Right, then,' he said, looking rather curiously at Bond. 'Five and Five it is. Meyer,' he turned to his partner, 'how much would you like to take? There's Six and Six to cut up.'

'One and One's enough for me, Hugger,' said Meyer apologetically. 'Unless you'd like me to take some more.'

He looked anxiously at his partner.

'Of course not,' said Drax. 'I like a high game. Never get enough on, generally. Now then,' he started to deal. 'Off we go.'

And suddenly Bond didn't care about the high stakes. Suddenly all he wanted to do was to give this hairy ape the lesson of his life, give him a shock which would make him remember this evening for ever, remember Bond, remember M, remember the last time he would cheat at Blades, remember the time of day, the weather outside, what he had had for dinner.

For all its importance, Bond had forgotten the Moonraker. This was a private affair between two men.

As he watched the casual downward glance at the cigarette-case between the two hands and felt the cool memory ticking up the card values as they passed over its surface, Bond cleared his mind of all regrets, absolved himself of all blame for what was about to happen, and focused his attention on the game. He settled himself more comfortably into his chair and rested his hands on the padded leather arms. Then he took the thin cheroot from between his teeth, laid it on the burnished copper surround of the ashtray beside him and reached for his coffee. It was very black and strong. He emptied the cup and picked up the balloon glass with its fat measure of pale brandy. As he sipped it and then drank again, more deeply, he looked over the rim at M. M met his eye and smiled briefly.

'Hope you like it,' he said. 'Comes from one of the Rothschild estates at Cognac. About a hundred years ago one of the family bequeathed us a barrel of it every year in perpetuity. During the war they hid a barrel for us every year and then sent us over the whole lot in 1945. Ever since then we've been drinking doubles. And,' he gathered up his cards, 'now we shall have to concentrate.'

Bond picked up his hand. It was average. A bare two-and-a-half quick tricks, the suits evenly distributed. He reached for his cheroot and gave it a final draw, then killed it in the ashtray.

'Three clubs,' said Drax.

No bid from Bond.

Four clubs from Meyer.

No bid from M.

Hm, thought Bond. He's not quite got the cards for a game call this time. Shut-out call – knows that his partner has got a bare raise. M may have got a perfectly good bid. We may have all the hearts between us, for instance. But M never gets a bid. Presumably they'll make four clubs.

They did, with the help of one finesse through Bond. M turned out not to have had hearts, but a long string of diamonds, missing only the king, which was in Meyer's hand and would have been caught. Drax didn't have nearly enough length for a three call. Meyer had the rest of the clubs.

Anyway, thought Bond as he dealt the next hand, we were lucky to escape without a game call.

Their good luck continued. Bond opened a No Trump, was put up to three by M, and they made it with an over-trick. On Meyer's deal

365

they went one down in five diamonds, but on the next hand M opened four spades and Bond's three small trumps and an outside king, queen were all M needed for the contract.

First rubber to M and Bond. Drax looked annoyed. He had lost £900 on the rubber and the cards seemed to be running against them.

'Shall we go straight on?' he asked. 'No point in cutting.'

M smiled across at Bond. The same thought was in both their minds. So Drax wanted to keep the deal. Bond shrugged his shoulders.

'No objection,' said M. 'These seats seem to be doing their best for us.'

'Up to now,' said Drax, looking more cheerful.

And with reason. On the next hand he and Meyer bid and made a small slam in spades that required two hair-raising finesses, both of which Drax, after a good deal of pantomime and hemming and hawing, negotiated smoothly, each time commenting loudly on his good fortune.

'Hugger, you're wonderful,' said Meyer fulsomely. 'How the devil do you do it?'

Bond thought it time to sow a tiny seed. 'Memory,' he said.

Drax looked at him, sharply. 'What do you mean, memory?' he said. 'What's that got to do with taking a finesse?'

'I was going to add "and card sense",' said Bond smoothly. 'They're the two qualities that make great card-players.'

'Oh,' said Drax slowly. 'Yes, I see.' He cut the cards to Bond and as Bond dealt he felt the other man's eyes examining him carefully.

The game proceeded at an even pace. The cards refused to get hot and no one seemed inclined to take chances. M doubled Meyer in an incautious four-spade bid and got him two down vulnerable, but on the next hand Drax went out with a lay down three No Trumps. Bond's win on the first rubber was wiped out and a bit more besides.

'Anyone care for a drink?' asked M as he cut the cards to Drax for the third rubber. 'James. A little more champagne. The second bottle always tastes better.'

'I'd like that very much,' said Bond.

The waiter came. The others ordered whiskies and sodas.

Drax turned to Bond. 'This game needs livening up,' he said. 'A hundred we win this hand.' He had completed the deal and the cards lay in neat piles in the centre of the table.

Bond looked at him. The damaged eye glared at him redly. The other was cold and hard and scornful. There were beads of sweat on either side of the large, beaky nose.

Bond wondered if he was having a fly thrown over him to see if he was suspicious of the deal. He decided to leave the man in doubt. It was a hundred down the drain, but it would give him an excuse for increasing the stakes later.

'On your deal?' he said with a smile. 'Well,' he weighed imaginary chances. 'Yes. All right.' An idea seemed to come to him. 'And the same on the next hand. If you like,' he added.

'All right, all right,' said Drax impatiently. 'If you want to throw good money after bad.'

'You seem very certain about this hand,' said Bond indifferently, picking up his cards. They were a poor lot and he had no answer to Drax's opening No Trump except to double it. The bluff had no effect on Drax's partner. Meyer said 'Two No Trumps' and Bond was relieved when M, with no long suit, said 'No bid'. Drax left it in two No Trumps and made the contract.

'Thanks,' he said with relish, and wrote carefully on his score. 'Now let's see if you can get it back.'

Much to his annoyance, Bond couldn't. The cards still ran for Meyer and Drax and they made three hearts and the game.

Drax was pleased with himself. He took a long swallow at his whisky and soda and wiped down his face with his bandana handkerchief.

'God is with the big battalions,' he said jovially. 'Got to have the cards as well as play them. Coming back for more or had enough?'

Bond's champagne had come and was standing beside him in its silver bucket. There was a glass goblet three-quarters full beside it on the side table. Bond picked it up and drained it, as if to give himself Dutch courage. Then he filled it again.

'All right,' he said thickly, 'a hundred on the next two hands.'

And promptly lost them both, and the rubber.

Bond suddenly realized that he was nearly £1500 down. He drank

367

another glass of champagne. 'Save trouble if we just double the stakes on this rubber,' he said rather wildly. 'All right with you?'

Drax had dealt and was looking at his cards. His lips were wet with anticipation. He looked at Bond who seemed to be having difficulty lighting his cigarette. 'Taken,' he said quickly. 'A hundred pounds a hundred and a thousand on the rubber.' Then he felt he could risk a touch of sportsmanship. Bond could hardly cancel the bet now. 'But I seem to have got some good tickets here,' he added. 'Are you still on?'

'Of course, of course,' said Bond, clumsily picking up his hand. 'I made the bet, didn't I?'

'All right, then,' said Drax with satisfaction. 'Three No Trumps here.'

He made four.

Then, to Bond's relief, the cards turned. Bond bid and made a small slam in hearts and on the next hand M ran out in three No Trumps.

Bond grinned cheerfully into the sweating face. Drax was picking angrily at his nails. 'Big battalions,' said Bond, rubbing it in.

Drax growled something and busied himself with the score. Bond looked across at M, who was putting a match, with evident satisfaction at the way the game had gone, to his second cheroot of the evening, an almost unheard of indulgence.

''Fraid this'll have to be my last rubber,' said Bond. 'Got to get up early. Hope you'll forgive me.'

M looked at his watch. 'It's past midnight,' he said. 'What about you, Meyer?'

Meyer, who had been a silent passenger for most of the evening and who had the look of a man caught in a cage with a couple of tigers, seemed relieved at being offered a chance of making his escape. He leapt at the idea of getting back to his quiet flat in Albany and the soothing companionship of his collection of Battersea snuff-boxes.

'Quite all right with me, Admiral,' he said quickly. 'What about you, Hugger? Nearly ready for bed?'

Drax ignored him. He looked up from his score-sheet at Bond. He noticed the signs of intoxication. The moist forehead, the black comma of hair that hung untidily over the right eyebrow, the sheen of alcohol in the grey-blue eyes.

'Pretty miserable balance so far,' he said. 'I make it you win a couple of hundred or so. Of course if you want to run out of the game you can. But how about some fireworks to finish up with? Treble the stakes on the last rubber? Fifteen and fifteen? Historic match. Am I on?'

Bond looked up at him. He paused before answering. He wanted Drax to remember every detail of this last rubber, every word that had been spoken, every gesture.

'Well,' said Drax impatiently. 'What about it?'

Bond looked into the cold left eye in the flushed face. He spoke to it alone.

'One hundred and fifty pounds a hundred, and £1500 on the rubber,' he said distinctly. 'You're on.'

7 The Quickness of the Hand

There was a moment's silence at the table. It was broken by the agitated voice of Meyer.

'Here I say,' he said anxiously. 'Don't include me in on this, Hugger.' He knew it was a private bet with Bond, but he wanted to show Drax that he was thoroughly nervous about the whole affair. He saw himself making some ghastly mistake that would cost his partner a lot of money.

'Don't be ridiculous, Max,' said Drax harshly. 'You play your hand. This is nothing to do with you. Just an enjoyable little bet with our rash friend here. Come along, come along. My deal, Admiral.'

M cut the cards and the game began.

Bond lit a cigarette with hands that had suddenly become quite steady. His mind was clear. He knew exactly what he had to do, and when, and he was glad that the moment of decision had come.

He sat back in his chair and for a moment he had the impression that there was a crowd behind him at each elbow, and that faces were peering over his shoulder, waiting to see his cards. He somehow felt that the ghosts were friendly, that they approved of the rough justice that was about to be done.

He smiled as he caught himself sending this company of dead gamblers a message, that they should see that all went well.

The background noise of the famous gaming room broke in on his thoughts. He looked round. In the middle of the long room, under the central chandelier, there were several onlookers round the poker game. 'Raise you a hundred.' 'And a hundred.' 'And a hundred.' 'Damn you. I'll look', and a shout of triumph followed by a hubbub of comment. In the distance he could hear the rattle of a croupier's rake against the counters at the Shemmy game. Nearer at hand, at his end of the room, there were three other tables of bridge over which the smoke of cigars and cigarettes rose towards the barrelled ceiling.

Nearly every night for more than a hundred and fifty years there had been just such a scene, he reflected, in this famous room. The same cries of victory and defeat, the same dedicated faces, the same smell of tobacco and drama. For Bond, who loved gambling, it was the most exciting spectacle in the world. He gave it a last glance to fix it all in his mind and then he turned back to his table.

He picked up his cards and his eyes glittered. For once, on Drax's deal, he had a cast-iron game hand; seven spades with the four top honours, the ace of hearts, and the ace, king of diamonds. He looked at Drax. Had he and Meyer got the clubs? Even so Bond could overbid. Would Drax try and force him too high and risk a double? Bond waited.

'No bid,' said Drax, unable to keep the bitterness of his private knowledge of Bond's hand out of his voice.

'Four spades,' said Bond.

No bid from Meyer; from M; reluctantly from Drax.

M provided some help, and they made five.

One hundred and fifty points below the line. A hundred above for honours.

'Humph,' said a voice at Bond's elbow. He looked up. It was Basildon. His game had finished and he had strolled over to see what was happening on this separate battlefield.

He picked up Bond's score-sheet and looked at it.

'That was a bit of a beetle-crusher,' he said cheerfully. 'Seems you're holding the champions. What are the stakes?'

Bond left the answer to Drax. He was glad of the diversion. It could not have been better timed. Drax had cut the blue cards to him. He married the two halves and put the pack just in front of him, near the edge of the table.

'Fifteen and fifteen. On my left,' said Drax.

Bond heard Basildon draw in his breath.

'Chap seemed to want to gamble, so I accommodated him. Now he goes and gets all the cards . . .'

Drax grumbled on.

Across the table, M saw a white handkerchief materialize in Bond's right hand. M's eyes narrowed. Bond seemed to wipe his face with it. M saw him glance sharply at Drax and Meyer, then the handkerchief was back in his pocket.

A blue pack was in Bond's hands and he had started to deal.

'That's the hell of a stake,' said Basildon. 'We once had a thousand-pound side-bet on a game of bridge. But that was in the rubber boom before the fourteen-eighteen war. Hope nobody's going to get hurt.' He meant it. Very high stakes in a private game generally led to trouble. He walked round and stood between M and Drax.

Bond completed the deal. With a touch of anxiety he picked up his cards.

He had nothing but five clubs to the ace, queen, ten, and eight small diamonds to the queen.

It was all right. The trap was set.

He almost felt Drax stiffen as the big man thumbed through his cards, and then, unbelieving, thumbed them through again. Bond knew that Drax had an incredibly good hand. Ten certain tricks, the ace, king of diamonds, the four top honours in spades, the four top honours in hearts, and the king, knave, nine of clubs.

Bond had dealt them to him – in the Secretary's room before dinner.

Bond waited, wondering how Drax would react to the huge hand. He took an almost cruel interest in watching the greedy fish come to the lure.

Drax exceeded his expectations.

Casually he folded his hand and laid it on the table. Nonchalantly he took the flat carton out of his pocket, selected a cigarette and lit it. He didn't look at Bond. He glanced up at Basildon.

'Yes,' he said, continuing the conversation about their stakes. 'It's a high game, but not the highest I've ever played. Once played for two thousand a rubber in Cairo. At the Mahomet Ali as a matter of fact. They've really got guts there. Often bet on every trick as well as on the game and rubber. 'Now,' he picked up his hand and looked slyly at Bond. 'I've got some good tickets here. I'll admit it. But then you may have too, for all I know.' (Unlikely, you old shark, thought Bond, with three of the ace-kings in your own hand.) 'Care to have something extra just on this hand?'

Bond made a show of studying his cards with the minuteness of someone who is nearly very drunk. 'I've got a promising lot too,' he said thickly. 'If my partner fits and the cards lie right I might make a lot of tricks myself. What are you suggesting?'

'Sounds as if we're pretty evenly matched,' lied Drax. 'What do you say to a hundred a trick on the side? From what you say it shouldn't be too painful.'

Bond looked thoughtful and rather fuddled. He took another careful look at his hand, running through the cards one by one. 'All right,' he said. 'You're on. And frankly you've made me gamble. You've obviously got a big hand, so I must shut you out and chance it.'

Bond looked blearily across at M. 'Pay your losses on this one, partner,' he said. 'Here we go. Er – seven clubs.'

In the dead silence that followed, Basildon, who had seen Drax's hand, was so startled that he dropped his whisky and soda on the floor. He looked dazedly down at the broken glass and let it lie.

Drax said 'What?' in a startled voice and hastily ran through his cards again for reassurance.

'Did you say grand slam in clubs?' he asked, looking curiously at his obviously drunken opponent. 'Well, it's your funeral. What do you say, Max?'

'No bid,' said Meyer, feeling in the air the electricity of just that crisis he had hoped to avoid. Why the hell hadn't he gone home before this last rubber? He groaned inwardly.

'No bid,' said M apparently unperturbed. 'Double.' The word came viciously out of Drax's mouth. He put down his hand and looked cruelly, scornfully at this tipsy oaf who had at last, inexplicably, fallen into his hands.

'That mean you double the side-bets too?' asked Bond.

'Yes,' said Drax greedily. 'Yes. That's what I meant.'

'All right,' said Bond. He paused. He looked at Drax and not at his hand. 'Redouble. The contract and the side-bets. £400 a trick on the side.'

It was at that moment that the first hint of a dreadful, incredible doubt entered Drax's mind. But again he looked at his hand, and again he was reassured. At the very worst he couldn't fail to make two tricks.

A muttered 'No bid' from Meyer. A rather strangled 'No bid' from M. An impatient shake of the head from Drax.

Basildon stood, his face very pale, looking intently across the table at Bond.

Then he walked slowly round the table, scrutinizing all the hands. What he saw was this:

BOND

◇ Queen, 8, 7, 6, 5, 4, 3, 2

♣ Ace, queen, 10, 8, 4

DRAX

♠ Ace, king, queen, knave

♡ Ace, king, queen, knave

◇ Ace, king

♣ King, knave, 9

MEYER

♠ 6, 5, 4, 3, 2

♡ 10, 9, 8, 7, 2

◇ Knave, 10, 9

M

♠ 10, 9, 8, 7

♡ 6, 5, 4, 3

♣ 7, 6, 5, 3, 2

And suddenly Basildon understood. It was a laydown Grand Slam for Bond against any defence. Whatever Meyer led, Bond must get in with a trump in his own hand or on the table. Then, in between clearing trumps, finessing of course against Drax, he would play two rounds of diamonds, trumping them in dummy and catching Drax's ace and king in the process. After five plays he would be left with the remaining trumps and six winning diamonds. Drax's aces and kings would be totally valueless.

It was sheer murder.

Basildon, almost in a trance, continued round the table and stood between M and Meyer so that he could watch Drax's face, and Bond's. His own face was impassive, but his hands, which he had stuffed into his trouser pockets so that they would not betray him, were sweating. He waited, almost fearfully, for the terrible punishment that Drax was about to receive – thirteen separate lashes whose scars no card-player would ever lose.

'Come along, come along,' said Drax impatiently. 'Lead something. Max. Can't be here all night.'

You poor fool, thought Basildon. In ten minutes you'll wish that Meyer had died in his chair before he could pull out that first card.

In fact, Meyer looked as if at any moment he might have a stroke. He was deathly pale, and the perspiration was dropping off his chin on to his shirt front. For all he knew, his first card might be a disaster.

At last, reasoning that Bond might be void in his own long suits, spades and hearts, he led the knave of diamonds.

It made no difference what he led, but when M's hand went down showing chicane in diamonds, Drax snarled across at his partner. 'Haven't you got anything else, you dam' fool? Want to hand it to him on a plate? Whose side are you on, anyway?'

Meyer cringed into his clothes. 'Best I could do, Hugger,' he said miserably, wiping his face with his handkerchief.

But by this time Drax had got his own worries.

Bond trumped on the table, catching Drax's king of diamonds, and promptly led a club. Drax put up his nine. Bond took it with his ten and led a diamond, trumping it on the table. Drax's ace fell. Another club from the table, catching Drax's knave.

Then the ace of clubs.

As Drax surrendered his king, for the first time he saw what might be happening. His eyes squinted anxiously at Bond, waiting fearfully for the next card. Had Bond got the diamonds? Hadn't Meyer got them guarded? After all, he had opened with them. Drax waited, his cards slippery with sweat.

Morphy, the great chess player, had a terrible habit. He would never raise his eyes from the game until he knew his opponent could not escape defeat. Then he would slowly lift his great head and gaze curiously at the man across the board. His opponent would feel the gaze and would slowly, humbly raise his eyes to meet Morphy's. At that moment he would know that it was no good continuing the game. The eyes of Morphy said so. There was nothing left but surrender.

Now, like Morphy, Bond lifted his head and looked straight into Drax's eyes. Then he slowly drew out the queen of diamonds and placed it on the table. Without waiting for Meyer to play he followed it, deliberately, with the 8, 7, 6, 5, 4, and the two winning clubs.

Then he spoke. 'That's all, Drax,' he said quietly, and sat slowly back in his chair.

Drax's first reaction was to lurch forward and tear Meyer's cards out of his hand. He faced them on the table, scrabbling feverishly among them for a possible winner.

Then he flung them back across the baize.

His face was dead white, but his eyes blazed redly at Bond. Suddenly he raised one clenched fist and crashed it on the table among the pile of impotent aces and kings and queens in front of him.

Very low, he spat the words at Bond. 'You're a che . . .'

'That's enough, Drax.' Basildon's voice came across the table like a whiplash. 'None of that talk here. I've been watching the whole game. Settle up. If you've got any complaints, put them in writing to the Committee.'

Drax got slowly to his feet. He stood away from his chair and ran a hand through his wet red hair. The colour came slowly back into his face and with it an expression of cunning. He glanced down at Bond and there was in his good eye a contemptuous triumph which Bond found curiously disturbing.

He turned to the table. 'Good night, gentlemen,' he said, looking at each of them with the same oddly scornful expression. 'I owe about £15,000. I will accept Meyer's addition.'

He leant forward and picked up his cigarette-case and lighter.

Then he looked again at Bond and spoke very quietly, the red moustache lifting slowly from the splayed upper teeth.

'I should spend the money quickly, Commander Bond,' he said.

Then he turned away from the table and walked swiftly out of the room.

Part 2: Tuesday, Wednesday

8 The Red Telephone

Although he had not got to bed until two, Bond walked into his headquarters punctually at ten the next morning. He was feeling dreadful. As well as acidity and liver as a result of drinking nearly two whole bottles of champagne, he had a touch of the melancholy and spiritual deflation that were partly the after-effects of the benzedrine and partly reaction to the drama of the night before.

When he went up in the lift towards another routine day, the bitter taste of the midnight hours was still with him.

After Meyer had scuttled thankfully off to bed, Bond had taken the two packs of cards out of the pockets of his coat and had put them on the table in front of Basildon and M. One was the blue pack that Drax had cut to him and that he had pocketed, substituting instead, under cover of his handkerchief, the stacked blue pack in his right-hand pocket. The other was the stacked red pack in his left-hand pocket which had not been needed.

He fanned the red pack out on the table and showed M and Basildon that it would have produced the same freak grand slam that had defeated Drax.

'It's a famous Culbertson hand,' he explained. 'He used it to spoof his own quick-trick conventions. I had to doctor a red and a blue pack. Couldn't know which colour I would be dealing with.'

'Well, it certainly went with a bang,' said Basildon gratefully. 'I expect he'll put two and two together and either stay away or play straight in future. Expensive evening for him. Don't let's have any arguments about your winnings,' he added. 'You've done everyone –

and particularly Drax – a good turn tonight. Things might have gone wrong. Then it would have been your fingers that would have got burned. Cheque will reach you on Saturday.'

They had said goodnight and Bond, in a mood of anticlimax, had gone off to bed. He had taken a mild sleeping pill to try and clear his mind of the bizarre events of the evening and prepare himself for the morning and the office. Before he slept he reflected, as he had often reflected in other moments of triumph at the card table, that the gain to the winner is, in some odd way, always less than the loss to the loser.

When he closed the door behind him Loelia Ponsonby looked curiously at the dark shadows under his eyes. He noticed the glance, as she had intended.

He grinned. 'Partly work and partly play,' he explained. 'In strictly masculine company,' he added. 'And thanks very much for the benze-drine. It really was badly needed. Hope I didn't interfere with your evening?'

'Of course not,' she said, thinking of the dinner and the library book she had abandoned when Bond telephoned. She looked down at her shorthand pad. 'The Chief of Staff telephoned half an hour ago. He said that M would be wanting you today. He couldn't say when. I told him that you've got Unarmed Combat at three and he said to cancel it. That's all, except the dockets left over from yesterday.'

'Thank heavens,' said Bond. 'I couldn't have stood being thrown about by that dam' Commando chap today. Any news of 008?'

'Yes,' she said. 'They say he's all right. He's been moved to the military hospital at Wahnerheide. Apparently it's only shock.'

Bond knew what 'shock' might mean in his profession. 'Good,' he said without conviction. He smiled at her and went into his office and closed the door.

He walked decisively round his desk to the chair, sat down, and pulled the top file towards him. Monday was gone. This was Tuesday. A new day. Closing his mind to his headache and to thoughts about the night, he lit a cigarette and opened the brown folder with the Top Secret red star on it. It was a memorandum from the Office of the

Chief Preventive Officer of the United States Customs Branch and it was headed *The Inspectoscope*.

He focused his eyes.

'The Inspectoscope,' he read, 'is an instrument using fluoroscopic principles for the detection of contraband. It is manufactured by the Sicular Inspectoscope Company of San Francisco and is widely used in American prisons for the secret detection of metal objects concealed in the clothing or on the person of criminals and prison visitors. It is also used in the detection of IDB (Illicit Diamond Buying) and diamond smuggling in the diamond fields of Africa and Brazil. The instrument costs seven thousand dollars, is approximately eight feet long by seven feet high and weighs nearly three tons. It requires two trained operators. Experiments have been made with this instrument in the customs hall of the International Airport at Idlewild with the following results . . .'

Bond skipped two pages containing details of a number of petty smuggling cases and studied the 'Summary of Conclusions' from which he deduced, with some irritation, that he would have to think of some place other than his armpit for carrying his .25 Beretta the next time he travelled abroad. He made a mental note to discuss the problem with the Technical Devices Section.

He ticked and initialled the distribution slip and automatically reached for the next folder entitled *Philopon. A Japanese murder-drug*.

'Philopon', his mind was trying to wander and he dragged it sharply back to the typewritten pages.

'Philopon is the chief factor in the increase in crime in Japan. According to the Welfare Ministry there are now 1,500,000 addicts in the country, of whom one million are under the age of 20, and the Tokyo Metropolitan Police attribute 70 per cent of juvenile crime to the influences of the drug.

'Addiction, as in the case of marijuana in the United States, begins with one "shot". The effect is "stimulating" and the drug is habit-forming. It is also cheap – about ten yen (sixpence) a shot – and the addict rapidly increases his shots to the neighbourhood of one hundred a day. In these quantities the addiction becomes expensive and the victim automatically turns to crime to pay for the drug. That the crime often includes physical assault and murder is due to a peculiar property of the drug. It induces an acute persecution complex in the addict who becomes prey to the illusion that people want to kill him and that he is always being followed with harmful intent. He will turn with his feet and fists, or with a razor, on a stranger in the streets who he thinks has scrutinized him offensively. Less advanced addicts tend to avoid an old friend who has reached the one hundred shots a day dosage, and this of course merely increases his feeling of persecution.

'In this way murder becomes an act of self-defence, virtuous and justified, and it will readily be seen what a dangerous weapon it can become in the handling and direction of organized crime by a "master-mind".

'Philopon has been traced as the motive power behind the notorious Bar Mecca murder case and as a result of that unpleasant affair the police rounded up more than 5000 purveyors of the drug in a matter of weeks.

'As usual Korean nationals are being blamed . . .'

Suddenly Bond rebelled. What the hell was he doing reading all this stuff? When would he conceivably require to know about a Japanese murder-drug called Philopon?

Inattentively he skimmed through the remaining pages, ticked himself off the distribution slip, and threw the docket into his out-tray.

His headache was still sitting over his right eye as if it had been nailed there. He opened one of the drawers of his desk and took out a bottle of Phensic. He considered asking his secretary for a glass of water, but he disliked being cosseted. With distaste he crunched two tablets between his teeth and swallowed down the harsh powder.

Then he lit a cigarette and got up and stood by the window. He looked across the green panorama far below him and, without seeing it, let his eyes wander aimlessly along the jagged horizon of London while his mind focused on the strange events of the night before.

And the more he thought about it, the stranger it all seemed.

Why should Drax, a millionaire, a public hero, a man with a unique position in the country, why should this remarkable man cheat at cards? What could he achieve by it? What could he prove to himself? Did he think that he was so much a law unto himself, so far above the common herd and their puny canons of behaviour that he could spit in the face of public opinion?

Bond's mind paused. Spit in their faces. That just about described his manner at Blades. The combination of superiority and scorn. As if he was dealing with human muck so far beneath contempt that there was no need to put up even a pretence of decent behaviour in its company.

Presumably Drax enjoyed gambling. Perhaps it eased the tensions in him, the tensions that showed in his harsh voice, his nail-biting, the constant sweating. But he musn't lose. It would be contemptible to lose to these inferior people. So, at whatever risk, he must cheat his way to victory. As for the possibility of detection, presumably he thought that he could bluster his way out of any corner. If he thought about it at all. And people with obsessions, reflected Bond, were blind to danger. They even courted it in a perverse way. Kleptomaniacs would try to steal more and more difficult objects. Sex maniacs would parade their importunities as if they were longing to be arrested. Pyromaniacs often made no attempt to avoid being linked with their fire-raising.

But what obsession was it that was consuming this man? What was the origin of the compulsive urge that was driving him down the steep hill into the sea?

All the signs pointed to paranoia. Delusions of grandeur and, behind that, of persecution. The contempt in his face. The bullying voice. The expression of secret triumph with which he had met defeat after a moment of bitter collapse. The triumph of the maniac who knows that whatever the facts may say he is right. Whoever may try to thwart him he can overcome. For him there is no defeat because of his secret power. He knows how to make gold. He can fly like a bird. He is almighty – the man in the padded cell who is God.

Yes, thought Bond, gazing blindly out over Regent's Park. That is the solution. Sir Hugo Drax is a raving paranoiac. That is the power which has driven him on, by devious routes, to make his millions. That is the mainspring of the gift to England of this giant rocket that will annihilate our enemies. Thanks to the all-powerful Drax.

But who can tell how near to breaking-point this man is? Who has penetrated behind that bluster, behind all that red hair on his face, who has read the signs as more than the effect of his humble origins or of sensitivity about his war wounds?

Apparently no one. Then was he, Bond, right in his analysis? What was it based on? Was this glimpse through a shuttered window into a man's soul sufficient evidence? Perhaps others had caught such a glimpse. Perhaps there had been other moments of supreme tension in Singapore, Hong Kong, Nigeria, Tangier, when some merchant sitting across a table from Drax had noticed the sweat and the bitten nails and the red blaze of the eyes in the face from which all the blood had suddenly been drained.

If one had time, thought Bond, one ought to seek those people out, if they existed, and really find out about this man, perhaps get him in the killing-bottle before it was too late.

Too late? Bond smiled to himself. What was he being so dramatic about? What had this man done to him? Made him a present of £15,000. Bond shrugged. It was none of his business anyway. But that last remark of his, 'Spend it quickly, Commander Bond.' What had he meant by that? It must be those words, Bond reflected, that had stayed in the back of his mind and made him ponder so carefully over the problem of Drax.

Bond turned brusquely away from the window. To hell with it, he thought. I'm getting obsessed myself. Now then. Fifteen thousand pounds. A miraculous windfall. All right then, he *would* spend it quickly. He sat down at his desk and picked up a pencil. He thought for a moment and then wrote carefully on a memorandum pad headed 'Top Secret':

(1) Rolls-Bentley Convertible, say £5000.

(2) Three diamond clips at £250 each, £750.

He paused. That still left nearly £10,000. Some clothes, paint the flat, a set of the new Henry Cotton irons, a few dozen of the Taittinger champagne. But those could wait. He would go that afternoon and buy the clips and talk to Bentley's. Put all the rest into gold shares. Make a fortune. Retire.

In angry protest the red telephone splintered the silence. 'Can you come up? M wants you.' It was the Chief of Staff, speaking urgently.

'Coming,' said Bond, suddenly alert. 'Any clue?'

'Search me,' said the Chief of Staff. 'Hasn't touched his signals yet. Been over at the Yard and the Ministry of Supply all the morning.'

He rang off.

9 Take it From Here

A few minutes later Bond was walking through the familiar door and the green light had gone on over the entrance. M looked sharply at him. 'You look pretty dreadful, 007,' he said. 'Sit down.'

It's business, thought Bond, his pulse quickening. No Christian names today. He sat down. M was studying some pencilled notes on a scratch-pad. He looked up. His eyes were no longer interested in Bond.

'Trouble down at Drax's plant last night,' he said. 'Double killing. Police tried to get hold of Drax. Didn't think of Blades apparently. Caught up with him when he got back to the Ritz about half-past one this morning. Two men from the Moonraker got shot in a public house near the plant. Both dead. Drax told the police he couldn't care less and then hung up. Typical of the man. He's down there now. Taking the thing a bit more seriously, I gather.'

'Curious coincidence,' said Bond thoughtfully. 'But where do we come in, sir? Isn't it a police job?'

'Partly,' said M, 'but it happens that we're responsible for a lot of the key personnel down there. Germans,' he added. 'I'd better explain.' He looked down at his pad. 'It's an RAF establishment and the cover-plan is that it's part of the big radar network along the East Coast. The RAF are responsible for guarding the perimeter and the Ministry of Supply only has authority at the centre where the work is going on. It's on the edge of the cliffs between Dover and Deal. The whole area covers about a thousand acres, but the site itself is about two hundred. On the site there are only Drax and fifty-two others left. All the construction team have gone.'

Pack of cards and a joker, reflected Bond.

'Fifty of these are Germans,' continued M. 'More or less all the guided missile experts the Russians didn't get. Drax paid for them to come over here and work on the Moonraker. Nobody was very happy with the arrangement but there was no alternative. The Ministry of Supply couldn't spare any of their experts from Woomera. Drax had to find his men where he could. To strengthen the RAF security people, the Ministry of Supply appointed their own security officer to live on the site. Man called Major Tallon.'

M paused and looked up at the ceiling.

'He was one of the two who got killed last night. Shot by one of the Germans, who then shot himself.'

M lowered his eyes and looked at Bond. Bond said nothing, waiting for the rest of the story.

'It happened in a public house near the site. Plenty of witnesses. Apparently it's an inn on the edge of the site that is in bounds to the men. Must have somewhere to go to, I suppose.' M paused. He kept his eyes on Bond. 'Now you asked where we come in on all this. We come in because we cleared this particular German, and all the others, before they were allowed to come over here. We've got the dossiers of all of them. So when this happened the first thing RAF Security and Scotland Yard wanted was the dossier of the dead man. They got on to the Duty Officer last night and he dug the papers out of Records and sent them over to the Yard. Routine job. He noted it in the log. When I got here this morning and saw the entry in the log I suddenly got interested.' M spoke quietly. 'After spending the evening with Drax, it was, as you remarked, a curious coincidence.'

'Very curious, sir,' said Bond, still waiting.

'And there's one more thing,' concluded M. 'And this is the real reason why I've let myself get involved instead of keeping clear of the whole business. This has got to take priority over everything.' M's voice was very quiet. 'They're going to fire the Moonraker on Friday. Less than four days' time. Practice shoot.'

M paused and reached for his pipe and busied himself lighting it.

Bond said nothing. He still couldn't see what all this had to do with the Secret Service whose jurisdiction runs only outside the United Kingdom. It seemed a job for the Special Branch of Scotland Yard, or conceivably for MI5. He waited. He looked at his watch. It was noon.

M got his pipe going and continued.

'But quite apart from that,' said M, 'I got interested because last night I got interested in Drax.'

'So did I, sir,' said Bond.

'So when I read the log,' said M, ignoring Bond's comment, 'I telephoned Vallance at the Yard and asked him what it was all about. He was rather worried and asked me to come over. I said I didn't want to tread on Five's corns but he said he had already spoken to them. They maintained it was a matter between my department and the police since it was we who had cleared the German who did the killing. So I went along.'

M paused and looked down at his notes.

'The place is on the coast about three miles north of Dover,' he said. 'There's this inn nearby on the main coast road, the "World Without Want", and the men from the site go there in the evening. Last night, about seven-thirty, the Security man from the Ministry, this man Tallon, went along there and was having a whisky and soda and chatting away with some of the Germans when the murderer, if you like to call him that, came in and walked straight up to Tallon. He pulled out a Luger – no serial numbers by the way – out of his shirt and said,' M looked up, ' "I love Gala Brand. You shall not have her." Then he shot Tallon through the heart and put the smoking gun in his own mouth and pulled the trigger.'

'What a ghastly business,' said Bond. He could see every detail of the shambles in the crowded taproom of a typical English public house. 'Who's the girl?'

'That's another complication,' said M. 'She's an agent of the Special Branch. Bilingual in German. One of Vallance's best girls. She and Tallon were the only two non-Germans Drax had with him on the site. Vallance is a suspicious chap. Has to be. This Moonraker plan is obviously the most important thing happening in England. Without telling anyone and acting more or less on instinct, he planted this Brand girl on Drax and somehow fixed for her to be taken on as his private secretary. Been on the site since the beginning. She's had absolutely nothing to report. Says that Drax is an excellent chief, except for his manners, and drives his men like hell. Apparently he started by making passes at her, even after she'd spun the usual yarn about being engaged, but after she'd shown she could defend herself, which of course she can, he gave up and she says they're perfectly good friends. Naturally she knew Tallon, but he was old enough to be her father, besides being happily married with four children, and she told Vallance's man who got a word with her this morning that he's taken her to the cinema in a paternal sort of way twice in eighteen months. As for the killer, man called Egon Bartsch, he was an electronics expert whom she barely knew by sight.'

'What do his friends say about all this?' asked Bond.

'The man who shared his room with him backs up Bartsch. Says he was madly in love with the Brand woman and put his whole lack of success down to "The Englishman". He says Bartsch had been getting very moody and reserved lately and that he wasn't a bit surprised to hear of the shooting.'

'Sounds pretty corroborative,' said Bond. 'Somehow one can see the picture. One of those highly strung nervous chaps with the usual German chip on the shoulder. What does Vallance think?'

'He's not sure,' said M. 'He's mainly concerned with protecting his girl from the Press and seeing that her cover doesn't get blown. All the papers are on to it, of course. It'll be in the midday editions. And they're all howling for a picture of the girl. Vallance is having one cooked up and got down to her that'll look more or less like any girl, but just sufficiently like her. She'll send it out this evening. Fortunately the reporters can't get near the place. She's refusing to talk and Vallance is praying that some friend or relation won't blow the gaff. They're holding the inquest today and Vallance is hoping that the case will be officially closed by this evening and that the papers will have to let it die for lack of material.'

'What about this practice shoot?' asked Bond.

'They're sticking to the schedule,' said M. 'Noon on Friday. They're using a dummy warhead and firing her vertically with only three-quarter tanks. They're clearing about a hundred square miles of the North Sea from about Latitude 52 up. That's north of a line joining

The Hague and the Wash. Full details are going to be given out by the PM on Thursday night.'

M stopped talking. He swivelled his chair round so that he could look out of the window. Bond heard a distant clock chime the four quarters. One o'clock. Was he going to miss his lunch again? If M would stop ferreting about in the business of other Departments he could have a quick lunch and get round to Bentley's. Bond shifted slightly in his chair.

M turned back and faced him again across the desk.

'The people who are most worried about all this,' he said, 'are the Ministry of Supply. Tallon was one of their best men. His reports had been completely negative all along. Then he suddenly rang up the Assistant Under-Secretary yesterday afternoon and said he thought something fishy was going on at the site and he asked to see the Minister personally at ten o'clock this morning. Wouldn't say anything more on the telephone. And a few hours later he gets shot. Another funny coincidence, wasn't it?'

'Very funny,' said Bond. 'But why don't they close down the site and have a wholesale inquiry? After all, this thing's too big to take a chance on.'

'The Cabinet met early this morning,' said M, 'and the Prime Minister asked the obvious question. What evidence was there of any attempt, or even of any intention, to sabotage the Moonraker? The answer was none. There were only fears which had been brought to the surface in the last twenty-four hours by Tallon's vague message and the double murder. Everyone agreed that unless there was a grain of evidence, which so far hasn't turned up, both these incidents could be put down to the terrific nervous tension on the site. The way things are in the world at the moment it was decided that the sooner the Moonraker could give us an independent say in world affairs the better for us and,' M shrugged his shoulders, 'quite possibly for the world. And it was agreed that for a thousand reasons why the Moonraker should be fired the reasons against didn't stand up. The Minister of Supply had to agree, but he knows as well as you or I that, whatever the facts, it would be a colossal victory for the Russians to sabotage the Moonraker on the eve of her practice shoot. If they did it well enough they might easily get the whole project shelved. There are fifty Germans working on the thing. Any one of them could have relatives still being held in Russia whose lives could be used as a lever.' M paused. He looked up at the ceiling. Then his eyes came down and rested thoughtfully on Bond.

'The Minister asked me to go and see him after the Cabinet. He said that the least he could do was replace Tallon at once. The new man must be bilingual in German, a sabotage expert, and have had plenty of experience of our Russian friends. MI5 have put up three candidates. They're all on cases at the moment, but they could be extricated in a few hours. But then the Minister asked my opinion. I gave it. He talked to the Prime Minister and a lot of red tape got cut very quickly.'

Bond looked sharply, resentfully, into the grey, uncompromising eyes.

'So,' said M flatly, 'Sir Hugo Drax has been notified of your appointment and he expects you down at his headquarters in time for dinner this evening.'

10 Special Branch Agent

At six o'clock that Tuesday evening towards the end of May, James Bond was thrashing the big Bentley down the Dover road along the straight stretch that runs into Maidstone.

Although he was driving fast and with concentration, part of his mind was going back over his movements since he had left M's office four and a half hours earlier.

After giving a brief outline of the case to his secretary and eating a quick lunch at a table to himself in the canteen, he had told the garage for God's sake to hurry up with his car and deliver it, filled up, to his flat not later than four o'clock. Then he had taken a taxi down to Scotland Yard where he had an appointment with Assistant Commissioner Vallance at a quarter to three.

The courtyards and cul-de-sacs of the Yard had reminded him as usual of a prison without roofs. The overhead strip lighting in the cold corridor took the colour out of the cheeks of the police sergeant who asked his business and watched him sign the apple-green chit. It did the same for the face of the constable who led him up the short steps and along the bleak passage between the rows of anonymous doors to the waiting-room.

A quiet, middle-aged woman with the resigned eyes of someone who had seen everything came in and said the Assistant Commissioner would be free in five minutes. Bond had gone to the window and had looked out into the grey courtyard below. A constable, looking naked without his helmet, had come out of a building and walked across the yard munching a split roll with something pink between the two halves. It had been very quiet and the noise of the traffic on Whitehall and on the Embankment had sounded far away. Bond had felt dispirited. He was getting tangled up with strange departments. He would be out of touch with his own people and his own Service routines. Already, in this waiting-room, he felt out of his element. Only criminals or informers came and waited here, or influential people vainly trying to get out of a dangerous driving charge or desperately hoping to persuade Vallance that their sons were not really homosexuals. You could not be in the waiting-room of the Special Branch for any innocent purpose. You were either prosecuting or defending.

At last the woman came for him. He stubbed out his cigarette in the top of the Player's cigarette tin that serves as an ashtray in the waiting-rooms of government departments, and followed her across the corridor.

After the gloom of the waiting-room the unseasonable fire in the hearth of the large cheerful room had seemed like a trick, like the cigarette offered you by the Gestapo.

It had taken Bond a full five minutes to shake off his depression and realize that Ronnie Vallance was relieved to see him, that he was not interested in interdepartmental jealousies and that he was only looking to Bond to protect the Moonraker and get one of his best officers out of what might be a bad mess.

Vallance was a man of great tact. For the first few minutes he had spoken only of M. And he had spoken with inside knowledge and with sincerity. Without even mentioning the case he had gained Bond's friendship and co-operation.

As Bond swung the Bentley through the crowded streets of Maidstone he reflected that Vallance's gift had come from twenty years of avoiding the corns of MI5, of working in with the uniformed branch of the police, and of handling ignorant politicians and affronted foreign diplomats.

When Bond had left him after a quarter of an hour's hard talking, each man knew that he had acquired an ally. Vallance had sized up Bond and knew that Gala Brand would get all Bond's help and whatever protection she needed. He also respected Bond's professional approach to the assignment and his absence of departmental rivalry with the Special Branch. As for Bond, he was full of admiration for what he had learned about Vallance's agent, and he felt that he was no longer naked and that he had Vallance and the whole of Vallance's department behind him.

Bond had left Scotland Yard with the feeling that he had achieved Clausewitz's first principle. He had made his base secure.

His visit to the Ministry of Supply had added nothing to his knowledge of the case. He had studied Tallon's record and his reports. The former was quite straightforward – a lifetime in Army Intelligence and Field Security – and the latter painted a picture of a very lively and well-managed technical establishment – one or two cases of drunkenness, one of petty theft, several personal vendettas leading to fights and mild bloodshed but otherwise a loyal and hardworking team of men.

Then he had had an inadequate half-hour in the Operations Room of the Ministry with Professor Train, a fat, scruffy, undistinguished-looking man who had been runner-up for the Physics Division of the Nobel Prize the year before and who was one of the greatest experts on guided missiles in the world.

Professor Train had walked up to a row of huge wall maps and had pulled down the cord of one of them. Bond was faced with a ten-foot horizontal scale diagram of something that looked like a V2 with big fins.

'Now,' said Professor Train, 'you know nothing about rockets so

I'm going to put this in simple terms and not fill you up with a lot of stuff about Nozzle Expansion Ratios, Exhaust Velocity, and the Keplerian Ellipse. The Moonraker, as Drax chooses to call it, is a single-stage rocket. It uses up all its fuel shooting itself into the air and then it homes on to the objective. The V2's trajectory was more like a shell fired from a gun. At the top of its 200-mile flight it had climbed to about 70 miles. It was fuelled with a very combustible mixture of alcohol and liquid oxygen which was watered down so as not to burn out the mild steel which was all they were allocated for the engine. There are far more powerful fuels available but until now we hadn't been able to achieve very much with them for the same reason, their combustion temperature is so high that they would burn out the toughest engine.'

The professor paused and stuck a finger in Bond's chest. 'All you, my dear sir, have to remember about this rocket is that, thanks to Drax's Columbite, which has a melting point of about 3500 degrees Centigrade, compared with 1300 in the V2 engines, we can use one of the super fuels without burning out the engine. In fact,' he looked at Bond as if Bond should be impressed, 'we are using fluorine and hydrogen.'

'Oh, really,' said Bond reverently.

The Professor looked at him sharply. 'So we hope to achieve a speed in the neighbourhood of 1500 miles an hour and a vertical range of about 1000 miles. This should produce an operational range of about 4000 miles, bringing every European capital within reach of England. Very useful,' he added drily, 'in certain circumstances. But, for the scientists, chiefly desirable as a step towards escape from the earth. Any questions?'

'How does it work?' asked Bond dutifully.

The Professor gestured brusquely towards the diagram.

'Let's start from the nose,' he said. 'First comes the warhead. For the practice shoot this will contain upper-atmosphere instruments, radar and suchlike. Then the gyro compasses to make it fly straight – pitch-and-yaw gyro and roll gyro. Then various minor instruments, servo motors, power supply. And then the big fuel tanks – 30,000 pounds of the stuff.

'At the stern you get two small tanks to drive the turbine. Four hundred pounds of hydrogen peroxide mixes with forty pounds of potassium permanganate and makes steam which drives the turbines underneath them. These drive a set of centrifugal pumps which force the main fuel into the rocket motor. Under terrific pressure. Do you follow me?' He cocked a dubious eyebrow at Bond.

'Sounds much the same principle as a jet plane,' said Bond.

The Professor seemed pleased. 'More or less,' he said. 'But the rocket carries all its fuel inside it, instead of sucking in oxygen from outside like the Comet. Well then,' he continued, 'the fuel gets ignited in the motor and squirts out at the end in a continuous blast. Rather like a continuous recoil from a gun. And this blast forces the rocket into the air like any other firework. Of course it's at the stern that the Columbite comes in. It's allowed us to make a motor that won't be melted by the fantastic heat. And then,' he pointed, 'those are the tail fins to keep it steady at the beginning of its flight. Also made of Columbite alloy or they'd break away with the colossal air pressure. Anything else?'

'How can you be certain it'll come down where you mean it to?' asked Bond. 'What's to prevent it falling on The Hague next Friday?'

'The gyros will see to that. But as a matter of fact we're taking no chances on Friday and we're using a radar homing device on a raft in the middle of the sea. There'll be a radar transmitter in the nose of the rocket which will pick up an echo from our gadget in the sea and home on to it automatically. Of course,' the Professor grinned, 'if we ever had to use the thing in wartime it would be a great help to have a homing device transmitting energy from the middle of Moscow or Warsaw or Prague or Monte Carlo or wherever we might be shooting at. It'll probably be up to you chaps to get one there. Good luck to you.'

Bond smiled non-committally. 'One more question,' he said. 'If you wanted to sabotage the rocket what would be the easiest way?'

'Any number,' said the Professor cheerfully. 'Sand in the fuel. Grit in the pumps. A small hole anywhere on the fuselage or the fins. With that power and at those speeds the smallest fault would finish it.'

'Thanks very much,' said Bond. 'It seems you've got fewer worries about the Moonraker than I have.'

'It's a wonderful machine,' said the Professor. 'She'll fly all right if nobody interferes with her. Drax has done a sound job. Wonderful organizer. That's a brilliant team he put together. And they'll do anything for him. We've got a lot to thank him for.'

Bond did a racing change and swung the big car left at the Charing fork, preferring the clear road by Chilham and Canterbury to the bottlenecks of Ashford and Folkestone. The car howled up to eighty in third and he held it in the same gear to negotiate the hairpin at the top of the long gradient leading up to the Molash road.

And, he wondered, going back into top and listening with satisfaction to the relaxed thunder of the exhaust, and what about Drax? What sort of a reception was Drax going to give him this evening? According to M, when his name had been suggested over the telephone, Drax had paused for a moment and then said, 'Oh yes. I know the fellow. Didn't know he was mixed up in that racket. I'd be interested to have another look at him. Send him along. I'll expect him in time for dinner.' Then he had rung off.

The people at the Ministry had their own view of Drax. In their dealings with him they had found him a dedicated man, completely bound up in the Moonraker, living for nothing but its success, driving his men to the limit, fighting for priorities in material with other departments, goading the Ministry of Supply into clearing his requirements at Cabinet level. They disliked his hectoring manners but they respected him for his know-how and his drive and his dedication. And, like the rest of England, they considered him a possible saviour of the country.

Well, thought Bond, accelerating down the straight stretch of road past Chilham Castle, he could see that picture too and if he was going to work with the man he must adjust himself to the heroic version. If Drax was willing, he would put the whole affair at Blades out of his mind and concentrate on protecting Drax and his wonderful project from their country's enemies. There were only about three days to go. The security precautions were already minute and Drax might resent suggestions for increasing them. It was not going to be easy and a great deal of tact would have to be used. Tact. Not Bond's long suit and not, he reflected, connected in any way with what he knew of Drax's character.

Bond took the short cut out of Canterbury by the Old Dover road and looked at his watch. It was six-thirty. Another fifteen minutes to Dover and then another ten minutes along the Deal road. Were there any other plans to be made? The double killing was out of his hands, thank heaven. 'Murder and suicide while of unsound mind' had been the coroner's verdict. The girl had not even been called. He would stop for a drink at the 'World Without Want' and have a quick word with the innkeeper. The next day he would have to try and smell out the 'something fishy' that Tallon had wanted to see the Minister about. No clue about that. Nothing had been found in Tallon's room, which presumably he would now be taking over. Well, at any rate that would give him plenty of leisure to go through Tallon's papers.

Bond concentrated on his driving as he coasted down into Dover. He kept left and was soon climbing out of the town again past the wonderful cardboard castle.

There was a patch of low cloud on top of the hill and a spit of rain on his windshield. There was a cold breeze coming in from the sea. The visibility was bad and he switched on his lights as he motored slowly along the coast-road, the ruby-spangled masts of the Swingate radar station rising like petrified Roman candles on his right.

The girl? He would have to be careful how he contacted her and careful not to upset her. He wondered if she would be any use to him. After a year on the site she would have had all the opportunities of a private secretary to 'The Chief' to get under the skin of the whole project – and of Drax. And she had a mind trained to his own particular craft. But he would have to be prepared for her to be suspicious of the new broom and perhaps resentful. He wondered what she was really like. The photograph on her record-sheet at the Yard had shown an attractive but rather severe girl and any hint of seductiveness had been abstracted by the cheerless jacket of her policewoman's uniform.

Hair: Auburn. Eyes: Blue. Height: 5 ft 7. Weight: 9 stone. Hips: 38. Waist: 26. Bust: 38. Distinguishing marks: Mole on upper curvature of right breast.

Hm! thought Bond.

He put the statistics out of his mind as he came to the turning to the right. There was a signpost that said Kingsdown, and the lights of a small inn.

He pulled up and switched off the engine. Above his head a sign which said 'World Without Want' in faded gold lettering groaned in the salt breeze that came over the cliffs half a mile away. He got out, stretched and walked over to the door of the public bar. It was locked. Closed for cleaning? He tried the next door, which opened and gave access to the small private bar. Behind the bar a stolid-looking man in shirt-sleeves was reading an evening paper.

He looked up as Bond entered, and put his paper down. 'Evening, sir,' he said, evidently relieved to see a customer.

'Evening,' said Bond. 'Large whisky and soda, please.' He sat up at the bar and waited while the man poured two measures of Black and White and put the glass in front of him with a syphon of soda.

Bond filled the glass with soda and drank. 'Bad business you had here last night,' he said, putting the glass down.

'Terrible, sir,' said the man. 'And bad for trade. Would you be from the Press, sir? Had nothing but reporters and policemen in and out of the house all day long.'

'No,' said Bond. 'I've come to take over the job of the fellow who got shot. Major Tallon. Was he one of your regular customers?'

'Never came here but the once, sir, and that was the end of him. Now I've been put out of bounds for a week and the public has got to be painted from top to bottom. But I will say that Sir Hugo has been very decent about it. Sent me fifty quid this afternoon to pay for the damage. He must be a fine gentleman that. Made himself well liked in these parts. Always very generous and a cheery word for all.'

'Yes. Fine man,' said Bond. 'Did you see it all happen?'

'Didn't see the first shot, sir. Serving a pint at the time. Then of course I looked up. Dropped the ruddy pint on the floor.'

'What happened then?'

'Well, everybody's standing back of course. Nothing but Germans in the place. About a dozen of them. There's the body on the floor and the chap with the gun looking down at him. Then suddenly he stands to attention and sticks his left arm up in the air. "Eil!" he shouts like the silly bastards used to do during the war. Then he puts the end of the gun in his mouth. Next thing,' the man made a grimace, 'he's all over my ruddy ceiling.'

'That was all he said after the shot?' asked Bond. 'Just "*Heil*"?'

'That's all, sir. Don't seem to be able to forget the bloody word, do they?'

'No,' said Bond thoughtfully, 'they certainly don't.'

11 Policewoman Brand

Five minutes later Bond was showing his Ministry pass to the uniformed guard on duty at the gate in the high wire fence.

The RAF sergeant handed it back to him and saluted. 'Sir Hugo's expecting you, sir. It's the big house up in the woods there.' He pointed to some lights a hundred yards further on towards the cliffs.

Bond heard him telephoning to the next guard point. He motored slowly along the new tarmac road that had been laid across the fields behind Kingsdown. He could hear the distant boom of the sea at the foot of the tall cliffs and from somewhere close at hand there was a high-pitched whine of machinery which grew louder as he approached the trees.

He was stopped again by a plain-clothes guard at a second wire fence through which a five-bar gate gave access to the interior of the wood, and as he was waved through he heard the distant baying of police dogs which suggested some form of night patrol. All these precautions seemed efficient. Bond decided that he wouldn't have to worry himself with problems of external security.

Once through the trees the car was running over a flat concrete apron the limits of which, in the bad light, were out of range even of the huge twin beams of his Marchal headlamps. A hundred yards to his left, on the edge of the trees, there were the lights of a large house half-hidden behind a wall six feet thick, that rose straight up off the surface of the concrete almost to the height of the house. Bond slowed the car down to walking pace and turned its bonnet away from the house towards the sea and towards a dark shape that suddenly glinted white in the revolving beams of the South Goodwin Lightship far out in the Channel. His lights cut a path down the apron to where, almost on the edge of the cliff and at least half a mile away, a squat dome surged up about fifty feet out of the concrete. It looked like the top of an observatory and Bond could distinguish the flange of a joint running east and west across the surface of the dome.

He turned the car back and slowly ran it up between what he now assumed to be a blast-wall and the front of the house. As he pulled up outside the house the door opened and a manservant in a white jacket came out. He smartly opened the door of the car.

'Good evening, sir. This way please.'

He spoke woodenly and with a trace of accent. Bond followed him into the house and across a comfortable hall to a door on which the butler knocked.

'In.'

Bond smiled to himself at the harsh tone of the well-remembered voice and at the note of command in the single monosyllable.

At the far end of the long, bright, chintzy living-room Drax was standing with his back to an empty grate, a huge figure in a plum-coloured velvet smoking-jacket that clashed with the reddish hair on his face. There were three other people standing near him, two men and a woman.

'Ah, my dear fellow,' said Drax boisterously, striding forward to meet him and shaking him cordially by the hand.

'So we meet again. And so soon. Didn't realize you were a ruddy spy for my Ministry or I'd have been more careful about playing cards against you. Spent that money yet?' he asked, leading him towards the fire.

'Not yet,' smiled Bond. 'Haven't seen the colour of it.'

'Of course. Settlement on Saturday. Probably get the cheque just in time to celebrate our little firework display, what? Now let's see.' He led Bond up to the woman. 'This is my secretary, Miss Brand.'

Bond looked into a pair of very level blue eyes.

'Good evening.' He gave her a friendly smile.

There was no answering smile in the eyes which looked calmly into his. No answering pressure of her hand. 'How do you do,' she said indifferently, almost, Bond sensed, with hostility.

It crossed Bond's mind that she had been well-chosen. Another Loelia Ponsonby. Reserved, efficient, loyal, virginal. Thank heavens, he thought. A professional.

'My right-hand man, Dr Walter.' The thin elderly man with a pair of angry eyes under the shock of black hair seemed not to notice Bond's outstretched hand. He sprang to attention and gave a quick nod of the head. 'Valter,' said the thin mouth above the black imperial, correcting Drax's pronunciation.

'And my – what shall I say – my dogsbody. What you might call my ADC, Willy Krebs.' There was the touch of a slightly damp hand. 'Ferry pleased to meet you,' said an ingratiating voice and Bond looked into a pale round unhealthy face now split in a stage smile which died almost as Bond noticed it. Bond looked into his eyes. They were like two restless black buttons and they twisted away from Bond's gaze.

Both men wore spotless white overalls with plastic zip fasteners at the sleeves and ankles and down the back. Their hair was close-cropped so that the skin shone through and they would have looked like people from another planet but for the untidy black moustache and imperial of Dr Walter and the pale wispy moustache of Krebs. They were both caricatures – a mad scientist and a youthful version of Peter Lorre.

The colourful ogreish figure of Drax was a pleasant contrast in this chilly company and Bond was grateful to him for the cheerful roughness of his welcome and for his apparent wish to bury the hatchet and make the best of his new security officer.

Drax was very much the host. He rubbed his hands together. 'Now, Willy,' he said, 'how about making one of your excellent dry Martinis for us? Except, of course, for the Doctor. Doesn't drink or smoke,' he explained to Bond, returning to his place by the mantelpiece. 'Hardly breathes.' He barked out a short laugh. 'Thinks of nothing but the rocket. Do you, my friend?'

The Doctor looked stonily in front of him. 'You are pleased to joke,' he said.

'Now, now,' said Drax, as if to a child. 'We will go back to those leading edges later. Everybody's quite happy about them except you.' He turned to Bond. 'The good Doctor is always frightening us,' he explained indulgently. 'He's always having nightmares about something. Now it's the leading edges of the fins. They're already as sharp as razor blades – hardly any wind resistance at all. And he suddenly gets it into his head that they're going to melt. Friction of the air. Of course everything's possible, but they've been tested at over 3000 degrees and, as I tell him, if they're going to melt then the whole rocket will melt. And that's just not going to happen,' he added with a grim smile.

Krebs came up with a silver tray with four full glasses and a frosted shaker. The Martini was excellent and Bond said so.

'You are ferry kind,' said Krebs with a smirk of satisfaction. 'Sir Hugo is ferry exacting.'

'Fill up his glass,' said Drax, 'and then perhaps our friend would like to wash. We dine at eight sharp.'

As he spoke there came the muffled wail of a siren and almost immediately the sound of a body of men running in strict unison across the concrete apron outside.

'That's the first night shift,' explained Drax. 'Barracks are just behind the house. Must be eight o'clock. We do everything at the double here,' he added with a gleam of satisfaction in his eye. 'Precision. Lot of scientists about, but we try to run the place like a military establishment. Willy, look after the Commander. We'll go ahead. Come along, my dear.'

As Bond followed Krebs to the door through which he had entered, he saw the other two with Drax in the lead make for the double doors at the end of the room which had opened as Drax finished speaking. The manservant in the white coat stood in the entrance. As Bond went out into the hall it crossed his mind that Drax would certainly go into the dining-room ahead of Miss Brand. Forceful personality. Treated his staff like children. Obviously a born leader. Where had he got it from? The Army? Or did it grow on one with millions of money? Bond followed the slug-like neck of Krebs and wondered.

The dinner was excellent. Drax was a genial host and at his own table his manners were faultless. Most of his conversation consisted in drawing out Dr Walter for the benefit of Bond, and it covered a wide range of technical matters which Drax took pains to explain briefly after each topic had been exhausted. Bond was impressed by the confidence with which Drax handled each abstruse problem as it was raised, and by his immense grasp of detail. A genuine admiration for the man gradually developed in him and overshadowed much of his previous dislike. He felt more than ever inclined to forget the Blades affair now that he was faced with the other Drax, the creator and inspired leader of a remarkable enterprise.

Bond sat between his host and Miss Brand. He made several attempts to engage her in conversation. He failed completely. She answered with polite monosyllables and would hardly meet his eye. Bond became mildly irritated. He found her physically very attractive and it annoyed him to be unable to extract the smallest response. He felt that her frigid indifference was overacted and that security would have been far better met with an easy, friendly approach instead of this exaggerated reticence. He felt a strong urge to give her a sharp kick on the ankle. The idea entertained him and he found himself observing her with a fresh eye – as a girl and not as an official colleague. As a start, and under cover of a long argument between Drax and Walter, in which she was required to join, about the collation of weather reports from the Air Ministry and from Europe, he began to add up his impressions of her.

She was far more attractive than her photograph had suggested and it was difficult to see traces of the severe competence of a police-woman in the seductive girl beside him. There was authority in the definite line of the profile, but the long black eyelashes over the dark blue eyes and the rather wide mouth might have been painted by Marie Laurencin. Yet the lips were too full for a Laurencin and the dark brown hair that curved inwards at the base of the neck was of a different fashion. There was a hint of northern blood in the high cheekbones and in the very slight upward slant of the eyes, but the warmth of her skin was entirely English. There was too much poise and authority in her gestures and in the carriage of her head for her to be a very convincing portrait of a secretary. In fact she seemed almost a member of Drax's team, and Bond noticed that the men listened with attention as she answered Drax's questions.

Her rather severe evening dress was in charcoal black grosgrain with full sleeves that came below the elbow. The wrap-over bodice just showed the swell of her breasts, which were as splendid as Bond had guessed from the measurements on her record sheet. At the point of the vee there was a bright blue cameo brooch, a Tassie intaglio, Bond guessed, cheap but imaginative. She wore no other jewellery except a half-hoop of small diamonds on her engagement finger. Apart from the warm rouge on her lips, she wore no make-up and her nails were square-cut with a natural polish.

Altogether, Bond decided, she was a very lovely girl and beneath her reserve, a very passionate one. And, he reflected, she might be a policewoman and an expert at jujitsu, but she also had a mole on her right breast.

With this comforting thought Bond turned the whole of his attention to the conversation between Drax and Walter and made no further attempts to make friends with the girl.

Dinner ended at nine. 'Now we will go over and introduce you to the Moonraker,' said Drax, rising abruptly from the table. 'Walter will accompany us. He has much to do. Come along, my dear Bond.'

Without a word to Krebs or the girl he strode out of the room. Bond and Walter followed him.

They left the house and walked across the concrete towards the distant shape on the edge of the cliff. The moon had risen and in the distance the squat dome shone palely in its light.

A hundred yards from the site Drax stopped. 'I will explain the geography,' he said. 'Walter, you go ahead. They will be waiting for you to have another look at those fins. Don't worry about them, my dear fellow. Those people at High Duty Alloys know what they're doing. Now,' he turned to Bond and gestured towards the milk-white dome, 'in there is the Moonraker. What you see is the lid of a wide shaft that has been cut about forty foot down into the chalk. The two halves of the dome are opened hydraulically and folded back flush with that twenty-foot wall. If they were open now, you would see the nose of the Moonraker just protruding above the level of the wall. Over there,' he pointed to a square shape that was almost out of sight in the direction of Deal, 'is the firing point. Concrete block-house. Full of radar tracking gadgets – Doppler velocity radar and flightpath radar, for instance. Information is fed to them by twenty telemetering channels in the nose of the rocket. There's a big television screen in there too so that you can watch the behaviour of the rocket inside the shaft after the pumps have been started. Another television set to follow the beginning of its climb. Alongside the blockhouse there's a hoist down the face of the cliff. Quite a lot of gear has been brought to the site by sea and then sent up on the hoist. That whine you hear is from the power house over there,' he gestured vaguely in the direction of Dover. 'The men's barracks and the house are protected by the blast-wall, but when we fire there won't be anyone within a mile of the site, except the Ministry experts and the BBC team who are going to be in the firing point. Hope it'll stand up to the blast. Walter says that the site and a lot of the concrete apron will be melted by the heat. That's all. Nothing else you need to know about until we get inside. Come along.'

Bond noted again the abrupt tone of command. He followed in silence across the moonlit expanse until they came to the supporting wall of the dome. A naked red bulb glowed over a steel-plated door in the wall. It illuminated a bold sign which said in English and German: MORTAL DANGER. ENTRY FORBIDDEN WHEN RED LAMP SHOWS. RING AND WAIT.

Drax pressed the button beneath the notice and there was the muffled clang of an alarm bell. 'Might be somebody working with oxy-acetylene or doing some other delicate job,' he explained. 'Take his mind off his job for a split second as somebody comes in and you could have an expensive mistake. Everybody downs tools when the bell rings and then starts up again when they see what it is.' Drax stood away from the door and pointed upwards to a row of four-foot wide gratings just below the top of the wall. 'Ventilator shafts,' he explained. 'Air-conditioned inside to 70 degrees.'

The door was opened by a man with a truncheon in his hand and a revolver at his hip. Bond followed Drax through into a small anteroom. It contained nothing but a bench and a neat row of felt slippers.

'Have to put these on,' said Drax sitting down and kicking off his shoes. 'Might slip up and knock into someone. Better leave your coat here, too. Seventy degrees is quite warm.'

'Thanks,' said Bond remembering the Beretta at his armpit. 'As a matter of fact I don't feel the heat.'

Feeling like a visitor to an operating theatre, Bond followed Drax through a communicating door out on to an iron catwalk and into a blaze of spotlights that made him automatically put a hand up to his eyes as he grasped the guard-rail in front of him.

When he took his hand away he was greeted by a scene of such splendour that for several minutes he stood speechless, his eyes dazzled by the terrible beauty of the greatest weapon on earth.

12 *The Moonraker*

It was like being inside the polished barrel of a huge gun. From the floor, forty feet below, rose circular walls of polished metal near the top of which he and Drax clung like two flies. Up through the centre of the shaft, which was about thirty feet wide, soared a pencil of glistening chromium, whose point, tapering to a needle-sharp antenna, seemed to graze the roof twenty feet above their heads.

The shimmering projectile rested on a blunt cone of latticed steel which rose from the floor between the tips of three severely back-swept delta fins that looked as sharp as surgeons' scalpels. But otherwise nothing marred the silken sheen of the fifty feet of polished chrome steel except the spidery fingers of two light gantries which stood out from the walls and clasped the waist of the rocket between thick pads of foam rubber.

Where they touched the rocket, small access doors stood open in the steel skin and, as Bond looked down, a man crawled out of one door on to the narrow platform of the gantry and closed the door behind him with a gloved hand. He walked gingerly along the narrow bridge to the wall and turned a handle. There was a sharp whine of machinery and the gantry took its padded hand off the rocket and held it poised in the air like the forelegs of a praying mantis. The whine altered to a deeper tone and the gantry slowly telescoped in on itself. Then it reached out again and seized the rocket ten feet lower down. Its operator crawled out along its arm and opened another small access door and disappeared inside.

'Probably checking the fuel-feed from the after tanks,' said Drax. 'Gravity feed. Tricky bit of design What do you think of her?' He looked with pleasure at Bond's rapt expression.

'One of the most beautiful things I've ever seen,' said Bond. It was easy to talk. There was hardly a sound in the great steel shaft and the voices of the men clustered below under the tail of the rocket were no more than a murmur.

Drax pointed upwards. 'Warhead,' he explained. 'Experimental one now. Full of instruments. Telemeters and so forth. Then the gyros just opposite us here. Then mostly fuel tanks all the way down until you get to the turbines near the tail. Driven by superheated steam, made by decomposing hydrogen peroxide. The fuel, fluorine and hydrogen' (he glanced sharply at Bond. 'That's top-secret by the way') 'falls down the feed tubes and gets ignited as soon as it's forced into the motor. Sort of controlled explosion which shoots the rocket into the air. That steel floor under the rocket slides away. There's a big exhaust pit underneath. Comes out at the base of the cliff. You'll see it tomorrow. Looks like a huge cave. When we ran a static test the other day the chalk melted and ran out into the sea like water. Hope we don't burn down the famous white cliffs when we come to the real thing. Like to come and have a look at the works?'

Bond followed silently as Drax led the way down the steep iron ladder that curved down the side of the steel wall. He felt a glow of admiration and almost of reverence for this man and his majestic achievement. How could he ever have been put off by Drax's childish behaviour at the card-table? Even the greatest men have their weaknesses. Drax must have an outlet for the tension of the fantastic responsibility he was carrying. It was clear from the conversation at dinner that he couldn't shed much on to the shoulders of his highly strung deputy. From him alone had to spring the vitality and confidence to buoy up his whole team. Even in such a small thing as winning at cards it must be important to him to be constantly reassuring himself, constantly searching out omens of good fortune and success, even to the point of creating these omens for himself. Who, Bond asked himself, wouldn't sweat and bite his nails when so much had been dared, when so much was at stake?

As they filed down the long curve of the stairway, their figures grotesquely reflected back at them by the mirror of the rocket's chromium skin, Bond almost felt the man-in-the-street's affection for the man whom, only a few hours previously, he had been dissecting without pity, almost with loathing.

When they reached the steel-plated floor of the shaft, Drax paused and looked up. Bond followed his eyes. Seen from that angle it seemed as if they were gazing up a thin straight shaft of light into the blazing heaven of the arcs, a shaft of light that was not pure white but a shot mother-of-pearl satin. There were shimmers of red in it picked up from the crimson canisters of a giant foam fire-extinguisher that stood near them, a man in an asbestos suit beside it aiming its nozzle at the base of the rocket. There was a streak of violet whose origin was a violet bulb on the board of an instrument panel in the wall, which controlled the steel cover over the exhaust pit. And there was a whisper of emerald green from the shaded light over a plain deal table at which a man sat and wrote down figures as they were called to him from the group gathered directly beneath the Moonraker's tail.

Gazing up this pastel column, so incredibly slim and graceful, it seemed unthinkable that anything so delicate could withstand the pressures which it had been designed to meet on Friday – the howling stream of the most powerful controlled explosion that had ever been attempted; the impact of the sound barrier; the unknown pressures of the atmosphere at 15,000 miles an hour; the terrible shock as it plunged back from a thousand miles up and hit the atmospheric envelope of the earth.

Drax seemed to read his thoughts. He turned to Bond. 'It will be like committing murder,' he said. Then surprisingly, he burst into a braying laugh. 'Walter,' he called to the group of men. 'Come here.' Walter detached himself and came over. 'Walter, I was saying to our friend the Commander that when we fire the Moonraker it will be like committing murder.'

Bond was not surprised to see a look of puzzled incredulity come over the Doctor's face.

Drax said irritably, 'Child murder. Murder of our child,' he gestured at the rocket. 'Wake up. Wake up. What's the matter with you?'

Walter's face cleared. Frostily he beamed his appreciation of the simile. 'Murder. Yes, that is good. Ha! ha! And now, Sir Hugo. The graphite slats in the exhaust vent. The Ministry is quite happy about their melting-point? They do not feel that . . .' Still talking, Walter led Drax under the tail of the rocket. Bond followed.

The faces of the ten men were turned towards them as they came up. Drax introduced him with a wave of the hand. 'Commander Bond, our new security officer,' he said briefly.

The group eyed Bond in silence. There was no move to greet him and the ten pairs of eyes were incurious.

'Now then, what's all this fuss about the graphite? . . .' The group closed round Drax and Walter. Bond was left standing alone.

He was not surprised by the coolness of his reception. He would have regarded the intrusion of an amateur into the secrets of his own department with much the same indifference mixed with resentment. And he sympathized with these hand-picked technicians who had lived for months among the highest realms of astronautics, and were now on the threshold of the final arbitration. And yet, he reminded himself, the innocent among them must know that Bond had his own duty to perform, his own vital part in this project. Supposing one pair of those uncommunicative eyes concealed a man within a man, an enemy, perhaps at this very moment exulting in his knowledge that the graphite which Walter seemed to mistrust was indeed under-strength. It was true that they had the look of a well-knit team, almost of a brotherhood, as they stood round Drax and Walter, hanging on their words, their eyes intent on the mouths of the two men. But was part of one brain moving within the privacy of some secret orbit, ticking off its hidden calculus like the stealthy mechanism of an infernal machine?

Bond moved casually up and down the triangle made by the three points of the fins as they rested in their rubber-lined cavities in the steel floor, interesting himself in whatever met his eyes, but every now and then focusing the group of men from a new angle.

With the exception of Drax they all wore the same tight nylon overalls fastened with plastic zips. There was nowhere a hint of metal and none wore spectacles. As in the case of Walter and Krebs their heads were close-shaved, presumably, Bond would have thought, to prevent a loose hair falling into the mechanism. And yet, and this struck Bond as a most bizarre characteristic of the team, each man sported a luxuriant moustache to whose culture it was clear that a great deal of attention had been devoted. They were in all shapes and tints: fair or mousy or dark; handlebar, walrus, Kaiser, Hitler – each face bore its own hairy badge, amongst which the rank, reddish growth of Drax's facial hair blazed like the official stamp of their paramount chief.

Why, wondered Bond, should every man on the site wear a moustache? He had never liked the things, but combined with these shaven heads, there was something positively obscene about this crop of hairy tufts. It would have been just bearable if they had all been cut to the same pattern, but this range of individual fashions, this riot of personalized growth, had something particularly horrible about it against the background of naked round heads.

There was nothing else to notice; the men were of average height and they were all on the slim side – tailored, Bond supposed, more or less to the requirements of their work. Agility would be needed on the gantries, and compactness for manoeuvring through the access doors and around the tiny compartments in the rocket. Their hands looked relaxed and spotlessly clean, and their feet in the felt slippers were motionless with concentration. He never once caught any of them glancing in his direction and, as for penetrating their minds or weighing up their loyalties, he admitted to himself that the task of unmasking the thoughts of fifty of these robot-like Germans in three days was quite hopeless. Then he remembered. It was fifty no longer. Only forty-nine. One of these robots had blown his top (apt expression, reflected Bond). And what had come out of Bartsch's secret thoughts? Lust for a woman and a Heil Hitler. Would he be far wrong, wondered Bond, if he guessed that, forgetting the Moon-raker, those were also the dominant thoughts inside forty-nine other heads?

'Doctor Walter! That is an order.' Drax's voice of controlled anger broke in on Bond's thoughts as he stood fingering the sharp leading edge of the tail of one of the Columbite fins. 'Back to work. We have wasted enough time.'

The men scattered smartly about their duties and Drax came up to where Bond was standing, leaving Walter hanging about indecisively beneath the exhaust vent of the rocket.

Drax's face was thunderous. 'Damn fool. Always seeing trouble,' he muttered. And then abruptly, as if he wanted to clear his deputy out of his mind, 'Come along to my office. Show you the flight plan. Then we'll go off to bed.'

Bond followed him across the floor. Drax turned a small handle flush with the steel wall and a narrow door opened with a soft hiss. Three feet inside there was another steel door and Bond noticed that they were both edged with rubber. Air-lock. Before closing the outer door Drax paused on the threshold and pointed along the circular wall to a number of similar inconspicuous flat knobs in the wall. 'Workshops,' he said. 'Electricians, generators, fuelling control, wash-rooms, stores.' He pointed to the adjoining door. 'My secretary's room.' He closed the outer door before he opened the second and walked into his office and shut the inner door behind Bond.

It was a severe room painted pale grey, containing a broad desk and several chairs of tubular metal and dark blue canvas. The floor was carpeted in grey. There were two green filing cabinets and a large metal radio set. A half-open door showed part of a tiled bathroom. The desk faced a wide blank wall which seemed to be made of opaque glass. Drax walked up to the wall and snapped down two switches on its extreme right. The whole wall lit up and Bond was faced with two maps each about six feet square traced on the back of the glass.

The left-hand map showed the eastern quarter of England from Portsmouth to Hull and the adjoining waters from Latitude 50 to 55. From the red dot near Dover which was the site of the Moonraker, arcs showing the range in ten-mile intervals had been drawn up the map. At a point eighty miles from the site, between the Friesian Islands and Hull, there was a red diamond in the middle of the ocean.

Drax waved towards the dense mathematical tables and columns of compass readings which filled the right-hand side of the map. 'Wind velocities, atmospheric pressure, ready-reckoner for the gyro settings,' he said. 'All worked out using the rocket's velocity and range as constants. We get the weather every day from the Air Ministry and readings from the upper atmosphere every time the RAF jet can get up there. When he's at maximum altitude he releases helium balloons that can get up still further. The earth's atmosphere reaches about fifty miles up. After twenty there's hardly any density to affect the Moonraker. It'll coast up almost in a vacuum. Getting through the first twenty miles is the problem. The gravity pull's another worry. Walter can explain all those things if you're interested. There'll be continuous weather reports during the last few hours on Friday. And we'll set the gryos just before the take-off. For the time being, Miss Brand gets together the data every morning and keeps a table of gyro settings in case they're wanted.'

Drax pointed at the second of the two maps. This was a diagram of the rocket's flight ellipse from firing point to target. There were more columns of figures. 'Speed of the earth and its effect on the rocket's trajectory,' explained Drax. 'The earth will be turning to the east while the rocket's in flight. That factor has to be married in with the figures on the other map. Complicated business. Fortunately you don't have to understand it. Leave it to Miss Brand. Now then,' he switched off the lights and the wall went blank, 'any particular questions about your job? Don't think there'll be much for you to do. You can see that the place is already riddled with security. The Ministry's insisted on it from the beginning.'

'Everything looks all right,' said Bond. He examined Drax's face. The good eye was looking at him sharply. Bond paused. 'Do you think there was anything between your secretary and Major Tallon?' he asked. It was an obvious question and he might just as well ask it now.

'Could have been,' said Drax easily. 'Attractive girl. They were thrown together a lot down here. At any rate she seems to have got under Bartsch's skin.'

'I hear Bartsch saluted and shouted "Heil Hitler" before he put the gun in his mouth,' said Bond.

'So they tell me,' said Drax evenly. 'What of it?'

'Why do all the men wear moustaches?' asked Bond, ignoring Drax's question. Again he had the impression that his question had nettled the other man.

Drax gave one of his short barking laughs. 'My idea,' he said. 'They're difficult to recognize in those white overalls and with their heads shaved. So I told them all to grow moustaches. The thing's become quite a fetish. Like in the RAF during the war. See anything wrong with it?'

'Of course not,' said Bond. 'Rather startling at first. I would have thought that large numbers on their suits with a different colour for each shift would have been more effective.'

'Well,' said Drax, turning away towards the door as if to end the conversation, 'I decided on moustaches.'

13 Dead Reckoning

On Wednesday morning Bond woke early in the dead man's bed.

He had slept little. Drax had said nothing on their way back to the house and had bidden him a curt good-night at the foot of the stairs. Bond had walked along the carpeted corridor to where light shone from an open door and had found his things neatly laid out in a comfortable bedroom.

The room was furnished in the same expensive taste as the ground floor and there were biscuits and a bottle of Vichy (not a Vichy bottle of tap-water, Bond established) beside the Heal bed.

There were no signs of the previous occupant except a leather case containing binoculars on the dressing-table and a metal filing cabinet which was locked. Bond knew about filing cabinets. He tilted it against the wall, reached underneath, and found the bottom end of the bar-lock which protrudes downwards when the top section has been locked. Upwards pressure released the drawers one by one and he softly lowered the edge of the cabinet back on to the floor with the unkind reflection that Major Tallon would not have survived very long in the Secret Service.

The top drawer contained scale maps of the site and its component buildings and Admiralty Chart No. 1895 of the Straits of Dover. Bond laid each sheet on the bed and examined them minutely. There were traces of cigarette ash in the folds of the Admiralty chart.

Bond fetched his tool-box – a square leather case that stood beside the dressing-table. He examined the numbers on the wheels of the combination lock and, satisfied that they had not been disturbed, turned them to the code number. The box was closely fitted with instruments. Bond selected a fingerprint powder-spray and a large magnifying glass. He puffed the fine greyish powder foot by foot over the whole expanse of the chart. A forest of fingerprints showed.

By going over these with the magnifying glass he established that they belonged to two people. He isolated two of the best sets, took a Leica with a flashbulb attachment out of the leather case and photographed them. Then he carefully examined through his glass the two minute furrows in the paper which the powder had brought to light.

These appeared to be two lines drawn out from the coast to form a cross-bearing in the sea. It was a very narrow bearing, and both lines seemed to originate from the house where Bond was. In fact, thought Bond, they might indicate observations of some object in the sea made from each wing of the house.

The two lines were drawn not with a pencil, but, presumably to avoid detection, with a stylus which had barely furrowed the paper.

At the point where they met there was the trace of a question mark, and this point was on the twelve-fathom line about fifty yards from the cliff on a direct bearing from the house to the South Goodwin Lightship.

There was nothing else to be gathered from the chart. Bond glanced at his watch. Twenty minutes to one. He heard distant footsteps in the hall and the click of a light being extinguished. On an impulse he rose and softly switched off the lights in his room, leaving only the shaded reading-light beside the bed.

He heard the heavy footsteps of Drax approaching up the stairs. There was the click of another switch and then silence. Bond could imagine the great hairy face turned down the corridor, looking, listening. Then there was a creak and the sound of a door being softly opened and as softly closed. Bond waited, visualizing the motions of the man as he prepared for bed. There was the muffled sound of a window being thrown open and the distant trumpet of a nose being blown. Then silence.

Bond gave Drax another five minutes then he went over to the filing cabinet and softly pulled out the other drawers. There was nothing in the second and third, but the bottom one was solid with files arranged under index letters. They were the dossiers of all the men working on the site. Bond pulled out the 'A' section and went back to the bed and started to read.

In each case the formula was the same: full name, address, date of birth, description, distinguishing marks, profession or trade since the war, war record, political record and present sympathies, criminal record, health, next of kin. Some of the men had wives and children whose particulars were noted, and with each dossier there were photographs, full face and profile, and the fingerprints of both hands.

Two hours and ten cigarettes later he had worked through all of them and had discovered two points of general interest. First, that every one of the fifty men appeared to have led a blameless life without a breath of political or criminal odium. This seemed so unlikely that he decided to refer every single dossier back to Station D for a thorough recheck at the first opportunity.

The second point was that none of the faces in the photographs bore a moustache. Despite Drax's explanations, this fact raised a second tiny question mark in Bond's mind.

Bond got up from the bed and locked everything away, putting the Admiralty Chart and one of the files in his leather case. He turned the wheels of the combination lock and thrust the case far under his bed so that it rested directly beneath his pillow at the inside angle of the wall. Then he quietly washed and cleaned his teeth in the adjoining bathroom and eased the window wide open.

The moon was still shining: as it must have shone, Bond thought, when, aroused perhaps by some unusual noise, Tallon had climbed up to the roof, maybe only a couple of nights before, and had seen, out at sea, what he had seen. He would have had his glasses with him and Bond, remembering, turned back from the window and picked them up. They were a very powerful German pair, booty perhaps from the war, and the 7 × 50 on the top plates told Bond that they were night glasses. And then the careful Tallon must have walked softly (but not softly enough?) to the other end of the roof and had raised his glasses again, estimating the distance from the edge of the cliff to the object in the sea, and from the object to the Goodwin Lightship. Then he would have come back the way he had gone and softly re-entered his room.

Bond saw Tallon, perhaps for the first time since he had been in the house, carefully lock the door and walk over to the filing cabinet and take out the chart which he had hardly glanced at till then and on it softly mark the lines of his rough bearing. Perhaps he looked at it for a long while before putting the minute question mark beside it.

And what had the unknown object been? Impossible to say. A boat? A light? A noise?

Whatever it was Tallon had not been supposed to see it. And somebody had heard him. Somebody had guessed he had seen it and had waited until Tallon had left his room next morning. Then that man had come into his room and had searched it. Probably the chart had revealed nothing, but there were the night glasses by the window.

That had been enough. And that night Tallon had died.

Bond pulled himself up. He was going too fast, building up a case on the flimsiest evidence. Bartsch had killed Tallon and Bartsch was not the man who had heard the noise, the man who had left finger-prints on the chart, the man whose dossier Bond had put away in his leather case.

That man had been the oily ADC, Krebs, the man with the neck like a white slug. They were his prints on the chart. For a quarter of an hour Bond had compared the impressions on the chart with the prints on Krebs's dossier. But who said Krebs had heard a noise or done anything about it if he had? Well, to begin with, he looked like a natural snooper. He had the eyes of a petty thief. And those prints

413

of his had definitely been made on the chart after Tallon had studied it. Krebs's fingers overlaid Tallon's at several points.

But how could Krebs possibly be involved, with Drax's eye constantly on him? The confidential assistant. But what about Cicero, the trusted valet of the British Ambassador in Ankara during the war? The hand in the pocket of the striped trousers hanging over the back of the chair. The Ambassador's keys. The safe. The secrets. This picture looked very much the same.

Bond shivered. He suddenly realized that he had been standing for a long time in front of the open windows and that it was time to get some sleep.

Before he got into bed he took his shoulder-holster from the chair where it hung beside his discarded clothes and removed the Beretta with the skeleton grip and slipped it under his pillow. As a defence against whom? Bond didn't know, but his intuition told him quite definitely that there was danger about. The smell of it was insistent although it was still imprecise and lingered only on the threshold of his subconscious. In fact he knew his feelings were based on a number of tiny question-marks which had materialized during the past twenty-four hours – the riddle of Drax; Bartsch's 'Heil Hitler'; the bizarre moustaches; the fifty worthy Germans; the chart; the night glasses; Krebs.

First he must pass on his suspicions to Vallance. Then explore the possibilities of Krebs. Then look to the defences of the Moonraker – the seaward side for instance. And then get together with this Brand girl and agree on a plan for the next two days. There wasn't much time to lose.

While he forced sleep to come into his teeming mind, Bond visualized the figure seven on the dial of a clock and left it to the hidden cells of his memory to wake him. He wanted to be out of the house and on the telephone to Vallance as early as possible. If his actions aroused suspicion he would not be dismayed. One of his objects was to attract into his orbit the same forces that had concerned themselves with Tallon, for of one thing he felt reasonably certain, Major Tallon had not died because he loved Gala Brand.

The extra-sensory alarm clock did not fail him. Punctually at seven, his mouth dry with too many cigarettes the night before, he forced himself out of bed and into a cold bath. He had shaved, gargled with a sharp mouth-wash, and now, in a battered black and white dogtooth suit, dark blue Sea Island cotton shirt and black silk knitted tie, he was walking softly, but not surreptitiously, along the corridor to the head of the stairs, the square leather case in his left hand.

He found the garage at the back of the house and the big engine of the Bentley answered with the first pressure on the starter. He motored slowly across the concrete apron beneath the indifferent gaze of the curtained windows of the house and pulled up, the engine idling in neutral, at the edge of the trees. His eyes travelled back to the house and confirmed his calculation that a man standing on its roof would be able to see over the top of the blast-wall and get a view of the edge of the cliff and of the sea beyond.

There was no sign of life round the domed emplacement of the Moonraker, and the concrete, already beginning to shimmer in the early morning sun, stretched emptily away towards Deal. It looked like a newly laid aerodrome or rather, he thought, with its three disparate concrete 'things', the beehive dome, the flat-iron blast-wall, and the distant cube of the firing point, each casting black pools of shadow towards him in the early sun, like a Dali desert landscape in which three *objets trouvés* reposed at carefully calculated random.

Out at sea, in the early mist that promised a hot day, the South Goodwin Lightship could just be seen, a dim red barque married for ever to the same compass point and condemned, like a property ship on the stage of Drury Lane, to watch the diorama of the waves and clouds sail busily into the wings while, without papers or passengers or cargo, it lay anchored for ever to the departure point which was also its destination.

At thirty seconds' interval it blared its sad complaint into the mist, a long double trumpet note on a falling cadence. A siren song, Bond reflected, to repel instead of to seduce. He wondered how the seven men of its crew were now supporting the noise as they munched their pork and beans. Did they flinch as it punctuated the Housewife's Choice coming at full strength from the radio in the narrow mess?

But a secure life,* Bond decided, although anchored to the gates of a graveyard.

He made a mental note to find out if those seven men had seen or heard the thing that Tallon had marked on the chart, then he drove quickly on through the guard posts.

In Dover, Bond pulled up at the Café Royal, a modest little restaurant with a modest kitchen but capable, as he knew of old, of turning out excellent fish and egg dishes. The Italian-Swiss mother and son who ran it welcomed him as an old friend and he asked for a plate of scrambled eggs and bacon and plenty of coffee to be ready in half an hour. Then he drove on to the police station and put a call in to Vallance through the Scotland Yard switchboard. Vallance was at home having breakfast. He listened without comment to Bond's guarded talk, but he expressed surprise that Bond had not had an opportunity to have a talk with Gala Brand. 'She's a bright girl, that,' he said. 'If Mr K. is up to something she's sure to have an idea what it is. And if T. heard a noise on Sunday night, she may have heard it too. Though I'll admit she's said nothing about it.'

Bond said nothing about the reception he had had from Vallance's agent. 'Going to talk to her this morning,' he said, 'and I'll send up the chart and the Leica film for you to have a look at. I'll give them to the Inspector. Perhaps one of the road patrols could bring them up. By the way, where did T. telephone from when he rang up his employer on Monday?'

'I'll have the call traced and let you know,' said Vallance. 'And I'll have Trinity House ask the South Goodwins and the Coastguards if they can help. Anything else?'

'No,' said Bond. The line went through too many switchboards. Perhaps if it had been M he would have hinted more. It seemed ridiculous to talk to Vallance about moustaches and the creep of danger he had felt the night before and which the daylight had dissipated. These policemen wanted hard facts. They were better, he decided, at solving crimes than at anticipating them. 'No. That's all.' He hung up.

* Bond was wrong: Friday 26 November 1954. R.I.P.

He felt more cheerful after an excellent breakfast. He read the *Express* and *The Times* and found a bare report of the inquest on Tallon. The *Express* had made a big play with the girl's photograph and he was amused to see what a neutral likeness Vallance had managed to produce. He decided that he must try and work with her. He would take her completely into his confidence whether she was receptive or not. Perhaps she also had her suspicions and intuitions which were so vague that she was keeping them to herself.

Bond drove back fast to the house. It was just nine o'clock and as he came through the trees on to the concrete there was the wail of a siren and from the woods behind the house a double file of twelve men appeared running, in purposeful unison, towards the launching dome. They marked time while one of their number rang the bell, then the door opened and they filed through and out of sight.

Scratch a German and you find precision, thought Bond.

14 *Itching Fingers*

Half an hour before, Gala Brand had stubbed out her breakfast cigarette, swallowed the remains of her coffee, left her bedroom and walked across to the site, looking very much the private secretary in a spotless white shirt and dark blue pleated skirt.

Punctually at eight-thirty she was in her office. There was a sheaf of Air Ministry teleprints on her desk and her first action was to transfer a digest of their contents on to a weather map and walk through the communicating door into Drax's office and pin the map to the board that hung in the angle of the wall beside the blank glass wall. Then she pressed the switch that illuminated the wall map, made some calculations based on the columns of figures revealed by the light, and entered the results on the diagram she had pinned to the board.

She had done this, with Air Ministry figures that became more and more precise as the practice shoot drew nearer, every day since the site was completed and the building of the rocket that had begun inside it, and she had become so expert that she now carried in her head the gyro settings for almost every variation in the weather at the different altitudes.

So it irritated her all the more that Drax did not seem to accept her figures. Every day when, punctually at nine, the warning bells clanged and he came down the steep iron stairway and into his office, his first action was to call for the insufferable Dr Walter and together they would work out all her figures afresh and transfer the results to the thin black notebook that Drax always carried in the hip pocket of his trousers. She knew that this was an invariable routine and she had become tired of watching it through an inconspicuous hole she had drilled, so as to be able to send Vallance a weekly record of Drax's visitors, in the thin wall between the two offices. The method was amateurish but effective and she had slowly built up a complete picture of the daily routine she came to find so irritating. It was irritating for two reasons. It meant that Drax didn't trust her figures, and it undermined her chance of having some part, however modest, in the final launching of the rocket.

It was natural that over the months she should have become as immersed in her disguise as she was in her real profession. It was fundamental to the thoroughness of her cover that her personality should be as truly split as possible. And now, while she spied and probed and sniffed the wind around Drax for her Chief in London, she was passionately concerned with the success of the Moonraker and had become as dedicated to its service as anyone else on the site.

And the rest of her duties as Drax's private secretary were insufferably dull. Every day there was a big post addressed to Drax in London and forwarded down by the Ministry, and that morning she had found the usual batch of about fifty letters waiting on her desk. They would be of three kinds. Begging letters, letters from rocket cranks, and business letters from Drax's stockbroker and from other commercial agents. To these Drax would dictate brief replies and the rest of her day would be occupied with typing and filing.

So it was natural that her one duty connected with the operation of the rocket should bulk very large in the dull round, and that morning, as she checked and rechecked her flight-plan, she was more than ever determined that her figures should be accepted on The Day.

And yet, as she often reminded herself, perhaps there was no question but that they would be. Perhaps the daily calculations of Drax and Walter for entry in the little black book were nothing but a recheck of her own figures. Certainly Drax had never queried either her weather plan or the gyro settings she calculated from them. And when one day she had asked straight out whether her figures were correct he had replied with evident sincerity, 'Excellent, my dear. Most valuable. Couldn't manage without them.'

Gala Brand walked back into her own office and started slitting open the letters. Only two more flight plans, for Thursday and Friday and then, on her figures or on a different set, the set in Drax's pocket, the gyros would be finally adjusted and the switch would be pulled in the firing point.

She absentmindedly looked at her finger-nails and then stretched her two hands out with their backs towards her. How often in the course of her training at the Police College had she been sent out among the other pupils and told not to come back without a pocket-book, a vanity case, a fountain pen, even a wrist-watch? How often during the courses had the instructor whipped round and caught her wrist with a 'Now, now, Miss. That won't do at all. Might have been an elephant looking for sugar in the keeper's pocket. Try again.'

Coolly she flexed her fingers and then, her mind made up, turned back to the pile of letters.

At a few minutes to nine the alarm bells rang and she heard Drax arrive in the office. A moment later she heard him open the double doors again and call for Walter. Then came the usual mumble of voices whose words were drowned by the soft whirr of the ventilators.

She arranged the letters in their three piles and sat forward relaxed, her elbows resting on the desk and her chin in her left hand.

Commander Bond. James Bond. Clearly a conceited young man like so many of them in the Secret Service. And why had he been sent down instead of somebody she could work with, one of her friends from the Special Branch, or even somebody from MI5? The message from the Assistant Commissioner had said that there was no one else available at short notice, that this was one of the stars of the Secret Service who had the complete confidence of the Special Branch and the blessings of MI5. Even the Prime Minister had had to give permission for him to operate, for just this one assignment, inside England. But what use could he be in the short time that was left? He could probably shoot all right and talk foreign languages and do a lot of tricks that might be useful abroad. But what good could he do down here without any beautiful spies to make love to. Because he was certainly good-looking. (Gala Brand automatically reached into her bag for her vanity case. She examined herself in the little mirror and dabbed at her nose with a powder puff.) Rather like Hoagy Carmichael in a way. That black hair falling down over the right eyebrow. Much the same bones. But there was something a bit cruel in the mouth, and the eyes were cold. Were they grey or blue? It had been difficult to say last night. Well, at any rate she had put him in his place and shown him that she wasn't impressed by dashing young men from the Secret Service, however romantic they might look. There were just as good-looking men in the Special Branch, and they were real detectives, not just people that Phillips Oppenheim had dreamed up with fast cars and special cigarettes with gold bands on them and shoulder-holsters. Oh, she had spotted that all right and had even brushed against him to make sure. Ah well, she supposed she would have to make some sort of show of working along with him, though in what direction heaven only knew. If she had been down there ever since the place had been built without spotting anything, what could this Bond man hope to discover in a couple of days? And what was there to find out? Of course there were one or two things she couldn't understand. Should she tell him about Krebs, for instance? The first thing was to see that he didn't blow her cover by doing something stupid. She would have to be cool and firm and extremely careful. But that didn't mean, she decided, as the buzzer went and she collected her letters and her shorthand book, that she couldn't be friendly. Entirely on her own terms, of course.

Her second decision made, she opened the communicating door and walked into the office of Sir Hugo Drax.

When she came back into her room half an hour later she found Bond sitting back in her chair with *Whitaker's Almanack* open on the desk in front of him. She pursed her lips as Bond got up and wished her a cheerful good morning. She nodded briefly and walked round her desk and sat down. She moved the *Whitaker's* carefully aside and put her letters and notebook in its place.

'You might have a spare chair for visitors,' said Bond with a grin which she defined as impertinent, 'and something better to read than reference books.'

She ignored him. 'Sir Hugo wants you,' she said. 'I was just going to see if you had got up yet.'

'Liar,' said Bond. 'You heard me go by at half-past seven. I saw you peering out between the curtains.'

'I did nothing of the sort,' she said indignantly. 'Why should I be interested in a car going by?'

'I told you you heard the car,' said Bond. He pressed home his advantage. 'And by the way,' he said, 'you shouldn't scratch your head with the blunt end of the pencil when you're taking dictation. None of the best private secretaries do.'

Bond glanced significantly at a point against the jamb of the communicating door. He shrugged his shoulders.

Gala's defences dropped. Damn the man, she thought. She gave him a reluctant smile. 'Oh, well,' she said. 'Come on. I can't spend all the morning playing guessing games. He wants both of us and he doesn't like being kept waiting.' She rose and walked over to the communicating door and opened it. Bond followed her through and shut the door behind him.

Drax was standing looking at the illuminated wall map. He turned as they came in. 'Ah, there you are,' he said with a sharp glance at Bond. 'Thought you might have left us. Guards reported you out at seven thirty this morning.'

'I had to make a telephone call,' said Bond. 'I hope I didn't disturb anyone.'

'There's a telephone in my study,' Drax said curtly. 'Tallon found it good enough.'

'Ah, poor Tallon,' said Bond non-committally. There was a hectoring note in Drax's voice that he particularly disliked and that made him instinctively want to deflate the man. On this occasion he was successful.

421

Drax shot him a hard glance which he covered up with a short barking laugh and a shrug of the shoulders. 'Do as you please,' he said. 'You've got your job to do. So long as you don't upset the routines down here. You must remember,' he added more reasonably, 'all my men are nervous as kittens just now and I can't have them upset by mysterious goings-on. I hope you're not wanting to ask them a lot of questions today. I'd rather they didn't have anything more to worry about. They haven't recovered from Monday yet. Miss Brand here can tell you all about them, and I believe all their files are in Tallon's room. Have you had a look at them yet?'

'No key to the filing cabinet,' said Bond truthfully.

'Sorry, my fault,' said Drax. He went to the desk and opened a drawer from which he took a small bunch of keys and handed them to Bond. 'Should have given you these last night. The Inspector chap on the case asked me to hand them over to you. Sorry.'

'Thanks very much,' said Bond. He paused. 'By the way, how long have you had Krebs?' He asked the question on an impulse. There was a moment's quiet in the room.

'Krebs?' repeated Drax thoughtfully. He walked over to his desk and sat down. He reached into his trouser pocket and pulled out a packet of his cork-tipped cigarettes. His blunt fingers scrabbled with its cellophane wrapping. He extracted a cigarette and stuffed it into his mouth under the fringe of his reddish moustache and lit it.

Bond was surprised. 'I didn't realize one could smoke down here,' he said, taking out his own case.

Drax's cigarette, a tiny white faggot in the middle of the big red face, waggled up and down as he answered without taking it out of his mouth. 'Quite all right in here,' he said. 'These rooms are air-tight. Doors lined with rubber. Separate ventilation. Have to keep the workshops and generators separate from the shaft and anyway,' his lips grinned round the cigarette, 'I have to be able to smoke.'

Drax took the cigarette out of his mouth and looked at it. He seemed to make up his mind. 'You were asking about Krebs,' he said. 'Well,' he looked meaningly up at Bond, 'just between ourselves I don't entirely trust the fellow.' He held up an admonitory hand. 'Nothing definite, of course, or I'd have had him put away, but I've found him snooping about the house and once I caught him in my study going through my private papers. He had a perfectly good explanation and I let him off with a warning. But quite honestly I have my suspicions of the man. Of course, he can't do any harm. He's part of the household staff and none of them are allowed in here but,' he looked candidly into Bond's eyes, 'I would have said you ought to concentrate on him. Bright of you to have bowled him out so quickly,' he added with respect.

'What put you on to him?'

'Oh, nothing much,' said Bond. 'He's got a shifty look. But what you say's interesting and I'll certainly keep an eye on him.'

He turned to Gala Brand who had remained silent ever since they had entered the room.

'And what do you think of Krebs, Miss Brand?' he asked politely.

The girl spoke to Drax. 'I don't know much about these things, Sir Hugo,' she said with a modesty and a touch of impulsiveness which Bond admired. 'But I don't trust the man at all. I hadn't meant to tell you, but he's been poking around my room, opening letters and so forth. I know he has.'

Drax was shocked. 'Has he indeed?' he said. He bashed his cigarette out in the ashtray and killed the glowing fragments one by one. 'So much for Krebs,' he said, without looking up.

15 Rough Justice

There was a moment's silence in the room during which Bond reflected how odd it was that suspicions should have fallen so suddenly and so unanimously on one man. And did that automatically clear all the others? Might not Krebs be the inside man of a gang? Or was he working on his own and, if so, with what object? And what did his snooping have to do with the death of Tallon and Bartsch?

Drax broke the silence. 'Well, that seems to settle it,' he said, looking to Bond for confirmation. Bond gave a non-committal nod. 'Just have to leave him to you. At all events, we must see he is kept well away from the site. As a matter of fact I shall be taking him to London tomorrow. Last-minute details to be settled with the Ministry and Walter can't be spared. Krebs is the only man I've got who can do the work of an ADC. That'll keep him out of trouble. We'll all have to keep an eye on him until then. Unless of course you want to put him under lock and key straight away. I'd prefer not,' he said candidly. 'Don't want to upset the team any more.'

'It shouldn't be necessary,' said Bond. 'Has he got any particular friends among the other men?'

'Never seen him speak to any of them except Walter and the household,' said Drax. 'Daresay he considers himself a cut above the others. Personally, I don't believe there's much harm in the chap or I wouldn't have kept him. He's left alone in that house all day long and I expect he's one of those people who like playing the detective and prying into other people's affairs. What do you say? Perhaps we could leave it like that?'

Bond nodded, keeping his thoughts to himself.

'Well, then,' said Drax, obviously glad to leave a distasteful subject and get back to business, 'we've got other things to talk about. Two more days to go and I'd better tell you the programme.' He got up from his chair and paced heavily up and down the room behind his desk. 'Today is Wednesday,' he said. 'At one o'clock the site will be closed for fuelling. This will be supervised by Dr Walter and myself and two men from the Ministry. Just in case anything goes wrong a television camera will record everything we do. Then, if there is an explosion, our successors will know better next time,' he barked a short laugh. 'Weather permitting, the roof will be opened tonight to allow the fumes to clear. My men will stand guard in watches at ten-yard intervals a hundred yards from the site. There will be three armed men on the beach opposite the exhaust hole in the cliff. Tomorrow morning the site will be opened again until midday for a final check and from that moment, except for the gyro settings, the Moonraker will be ready to go. The guards will be permanently on duty round the site. On Friday morning I shall personally supervise the gyro settings. The men from the Ministry will take over the firing point and the RAF will man the radar. The BBC will set up their vans behind the firing point and will begin their running commentary at eleven-forty-five. At midday exactly I shall press the plunger, a radio beam will break an electric circuit and,' he smiled broadly, 'we shall see what we shall see.' He paused, fingering his chin. 'Now what else? Well now. Shipping will be cleared from the target area from midnight on Thursday. The Navy will provide a patrol of the boundaries of the area all through the morning. There will be a BBC commentator in one of the ships. The Ministry of Supply experts will be in a salvage ship with deep-sea television and after the rocket has landed they will try to bring up the remains. You may be interested to know,' continued Drax, rubbing his hands with almost childish pleasure, 'that a messenger from the Prime Minister has brought me the very welcome news that not only will there be a special Cabinet Meeting to listen to the broadcast, but the Palace will also be listening in to the launching.'

'Splendid,' said Bond, pleased for the man's sake.

'Thank you,' said Drax. 'Now I want to be quite certain that you are satisfied with my security arrangements on the site itself. I don't think we need worry about what goes on outside. The RAF and the police seem to be doing a very thorough job.'

'Everything seems to have been taken care of,' said Bond. 'There doesn't seem to be very much for me to do in the time that's left.'

'Nothing that I can think of,' agreed Drax, 'except our friend Krebs. This afternoon he will be in the television van taking notes, so he will be out of trouble. Why don't you have a look at the beach and the bottom of the cliff while he's out of action? That's the only weak spot I can think of. I've often thought that if someone wanted to get into the site he would try the exhaust pit. Take Miss Brand with you. Two pairs of eyes, and so forth, and she won't be able to use her office until tomorrow morning.'

'Good,' said Bond. 'I'd certainly like to have a look at the seaward side after lunch, and if Miss Brand's got nothing better to do . . .' He turned towards her with his eyebrows raised.

Gala Brand looked down her nose. 'Certainly, if Sir Hugo wishes,' she said without enthusiasm.

Drax rubbed his hands together. 'Then that's settled,' he said. 'And now I must get down to work. Miss Brand, would you ask Dr Walter

425

to come along if he's free. See you at lunch,' he said to Bond, on a note of dismissal.

Bond nodded. 'I think I'll walk over and have a look at the firing point,' he said, not quite knowing why he lied. He turned and followed Gala Brand out through the double doors into the base of the shaft.

A huge black snake of rubber piping meandered over the shining steel floor and Bond watched the girl pick her way among its coils to where Walter was standing alone. He was gazing up at the mouth of the fuel pipe being hoist to where a gantry, outstretched to the threshold of an access door halfway up the rocket, indicated the main fuel tanks.

She said something to Walter and then stood beside him looking upwards as the pipe was delicately manhandled through into the interior of the rocket.

Bond thought she looked very innocent standing there with her brown hair falling back from her head and the curve of her ivory throat sweeping down into the plain white shirt. With her hands clasped behind her back, gazing raptly upwards at the glittering fifty feet of the Moonraker, she might have been a schoolgirl looking up at a Christmas tree – except for the impudent pride of the jutting breasts, swept up by the thrown-back head and shoulders.

Bond smiled to himself as he walked to the foot of the iron stairway and started to climb. That innocent, desirable girl, he reminded himself, is an extremely efficient policewoman. She knows how to kick, and where; she can break my arm probably more easily and quickly than I can break hers, and at least half of her belongs to the Special Branch of Scotland Yard. Of course, he reflected, looking down just in time to see her follow Dr Walters into Drax's office, there is always the other half.

Outside, the brilliant May sunshine seemed particularly golden after the blue-white of the arcs and Bond could feel it hot on his back as he walked purposefully across the concrete towards the house. The foghorn from the Goodwins was silent and the morning was so quiet that he could hear the rhythmic thump of a ship's engines as a coaster negotiated the Inner Leads, between the Goodwins and the shore, on its way northwards.

He approached the house under cover of the wide blast-wall and then quickly crossed the few yards to the front door, the crêpe rubber soles of his shoes making no noise. He eased open the door and left it ajar and walked softly into the hall and stood listening. There was the early summer noise of a bumble-bee fussing against the pane of one of the windows and a distant clatter from the barracks behind the house. Otherwise the silence was deep and warm and reassuring.

Bond walked carefully across the hall and up the stairs, placing his feet flat on the ground and using the extreme edges of the steps where the boards would be less likely to creak. There was no noise in the corridor but Bond saw that his door at the far end was open. He took his gun from under his armpit and walked swiftly down the carpeted passage.

Krebs had his back to him. He was kneeling forward in the middle of the floor with his elbows on the ground. His hands were at the wheels of the combination lock of Bond's leather case. His whole attention was focused on the click of the tumblers in the lock.

The target was tempting and Bond didn't hesitate. His teeth showed in a hard smile, he took two quick paces into the room and his foot lashed out.

All his force was behind the point of his shoe and his balance and timing were perfect.

The scream of a jay was driven out of Krebs as, like the caricature of a leaping frog, he hurtled over Bond's case, across a yard or so of carpet, and into the front of the mahogany dressing-table. His head hit the middle of it so hard that the heavy piece of furniture rocked on its base. The scream was abruptly cut off and he crashed in an inert spreadeagle on the floor and lay still.

Bond stood looking at him and listening for the sound of hurrying footsteps, but there was still silence in the house. He walked over to the sprawling figure and bent down and heaved it over on its back. The face around the smudge of yellow moustache was pale and some blood had oozed down over the forehead from a cut in the top of the skull. The eyes were closed and the breathing was laboured.

Bond knelt down on one knee and went carefully through every pocket of Krebs's neat grey pinstripe suit, laying the disappointingly

427

meagre contents on the carpet beside the body. There was no pocket-book and no papers. The only objects of interest were a bunch of skeleton keys, a spring knife with a well-sharpened stiletto blade, and an obscene little truss-shaped black leather cosh. Bond pocketed these and then went to his bedside table and fetched the untouched bottle of Vichy water.

It took five minutes to revive Krebs and get him into a sitting position with his back to the dressing-table and another five for him to be capable of speaking. Gradually the colour came back to his face and the craftiness to his eyes.

'I answer no questions except to Sir Hugo,' he said as Bond started the interrogation. 'You have no right to question me. I was doing my duty.' His voice was surly and assured.

Bond took the empty Vichy bottle by the neck. 'Think again,' he said. 'Or I'll beat the daylight out of you until this breaks and then use the neck for some plastic surgery. Who told you to go over my room?'

'*Leck mich am Arsch.*' Krebs spat the obscene insult at him.

Bond bent down and cracked him sharply across the shins. Krebs's body cringed, but, as Bond raised his arm again, he suddenly shot up from the floor and dived under the descending bottle. The blow caught him hard on the shoulder, but it didn't check his momentum and he was out of the door and halfway down the corridor before Bond started in pursuit.

Bond stopped outside the door and watched the flying figure swerve down the stairs and out of sight. Then, as he heard the scurrying squeak of the rubber-soled shoes as they fled down the stairs and across the hall, he laughed abruptly to himself and went back into his room and locked the door. Short of beating the man's brains out it hadn't looked as if he would get much out of Krebs. He had given him something to think about. Crafty little brute. His injuries couldn't have been so bad after all. Well, it would be up to Drax to punish him. Unless, of course, Krebs had been carrying out Drax's orders.

Bond cleaned up the mess in his room and sat down on his bed and gazed at the opposite wall with unseeing eyes. It had not been only instinct that had made him tell Drax he was going to the firing point instead of to the house. It had seriously crossed his mind that the snooping of Krebs was on Drax's orders, and that Drax ran his own security system. And yet how did that tally with the deaths of Tallon and Bartsch? Or had the double killing been a coincidence unrelated to the marks on the chart and the fingerprints of Krebs?

As if summoned by his thoughts, there came a knock on the door and the butler came in. He was followed by a police sergeant in road patrol uniform who saluted and handed Bond a telegram. Bond took it over to the window. It was signed Baxter, which meant Vallance, and it read:

FIRSTLY CALL WAS FROM HOUSE SECONDLY FOG REQUIRED OPERATION OF FOGHORN SO SHIP HEARD COMMA OBSERVED NOTHING THIRDLY YOUR COMPASS RECKONING TOO NEAR SHORE THUS OUT OF SIGHT OF SAINT MARGARETS OR DEAL COASTGUARD ENDS.

'Thank you,' said Bond. 'No answer.'

When the door was closed Bond put his lighter to the telegram and dropped it in the fireplace, scuffing the charred remains into powder with the sole of his shoe.

Nothing much there except that Tallon's call to the Ministry might indeed have been heard by someone in the house, which might have resulted in the search of his room, which might have resulted in his death. But what about Bartsch? If all this was part of something much bigger how could it be linked up with an attempt to sabotage the rocket? Wasn't it much simpler to conclude that Krebs was a natural snooper, or more likely that he was operating for Drax, who seemed to be meticulously security-conscious and who might want to be sure of the loyalty of his secretary, of Tallon, and certainly, after their encounter at Blades, of Bond? Wasn't it just acting like the chief (and Bond had known many of them who would fit the picture) of some super-secret project during the war who had reinforced official security with his own private spy system?

If that theory was correct there only remained the double killing. Now that Bond had caught the magic and the tension of the Moonraker the facts of the hysterical shooting seemed more reasonable. As for the mark on the chart, that might have been made any day in the past year; the night-glasses were just night-glasses and the moustaches on the men were just a lot of moustaches.

Bond sat on in the silent room, shifting the pieces in the jigsaw so that two entirely different pictures alternated in his mind. In one the sun shone and all was clear and innocent as the day. The other was a dark confusion of guilty motives, obscure suspicions, and nightmare queries.

When the gong sounded for lunch he still did not know which picture to choose. To shelve a decision he cleared his mind of everything but the prospect of his afternoon alone with Gala Brand.

16 A Golden Day

It was wonderful afternoon of blue and green and gold. When they left the concrete apron through the guard-gate near the empty firing point, now connected by a thick cable with the launching site, they stopped for a moment on the edge of the great chalk cliff and stood gazing over the whole corner of England where Caesar had first landed two thousand years before.

To their left the carpet of green turf, bright with small wildflowers, sloped gradually down to the long pebble beaches of Walmer and Deal, which curved off towards Sandwich and the bay. Beyond, the cliffs of Margate, showing white through the distant haze that hid the North Foreland, guarded the grey scar of Manston aerodrome above which American Thunderjets wrote their white scribbles in the sky. Then came the Isle of Thanet and, out of sight, the mouth of the Thames.

It was low tide and the Goodwins were golden and tender in the sparkling blue of the Straits with only the smattering of masts and spars that stretched along their length to tell the true story. The white lettering on the South Goodwins Lightship was easy to read and even the name of her sister ship to the north showed white against the red of her hull.

Between the sands of the coast, along the twelve-fathom channel of the Inner Leads, there were half a dozen ships beating up through the Downs, the thud of their engines coming clearly off the quiet sea, and between the evil sands and the sharp outline of the French coast there were ships of all registries going about their business – liners, merchantmen, ungainly Dutch schuyts, and even a slim corvette hastening down south, perhaps to Portsmouth. As far as the eye could reach the Eastern Approaches of England were dotted with traffic plying towards near or distant horizons, towards a home port, or towards the other side of the world. It was a panorama full of colour and excitement and romance and the two people on the edge of the cliff were silent as they stood for a time and watched it all.

The peace was broken by two blasts on the siren from the house and they turned to gaze back at the ugly concrete world that had been cleaned out of their minds. As they watched, a red flag was broken out above the dome of the launching site and two RAF crash-wagons with red crosses on their sides rolled out of the trees to the edge of the blast-wall and pulled up.

'Fuelling's going to begin,' said Bond. 'Let's get on with our walk. There'll be nothing to see and if there happened to be something we probably wouldn't survive it at this range.'

She smiled at him. 'Yes,' she said. 'And I'm sick of the sight of all this concrete.'

They walked on down the gentle slope and were soon out of sight of the firing point and the high wire fence.

The ice of Gala's reserve melted quickly in the sunshine.

The exotic gaiety of her clothes, a black and white striped cotton shirt tucked into a wide hand-stitched black leather belt above a medium-length skirt in shocking pink, seemed to have infected her, and it was impossible for Bond to recognize the chill woman of the night before in the girl who now walked beside him and laughed happily at his ignorance of the names of the wildflowers, the samphire, Viper's bugloss, and fumitory round their feet.

Triumphantly she found a bee orchis and picked it.

'You wouldn't do that if you knew that flowers scream when they are picked,' said Bond.

Gala looked at him. 'What do you mean?' she asked, suspecting a joke.

'Didn't you know?' He smiled at her reaction. 'There's an Indian called Professor Bhose, who's written a treatise on the nervous system of flowers. He measured their reaction to pain. He even recorded the scream of a rose being picked. It must be one of the most heart-rending sounds in the world. I heard something like it as you picked that flower.'

'I don't believe it,' she said, looking suspiciously at the torn root. 'Anyway,' she said maliciously, 'I wouldn't have thought you were a person to get sentimental. Don't people in your section of the Service make a business of killing? And not just flowers either. People.'

'Flowers can't shoot back,' said Bond.

She looked at the orchis. 'Now you've made me feel like a murderer. It's very unkind of you. But,' she admitted reluctantly, 'I shall have to find out about this Indian and if you're right I shall never pick a flower again as long as I live. What am I to going to do with this one? You make me feel it's bleeding all over my hands.'

'Give it to me,' said Bond. 'According to you, my hands are dripping with blood already. A little more won't hurt.'

She handed it to him and their hands touched. 'You can stick it in the muzzle of your revolver,' she said to cover the flash of contact.

Bond laughed. 'So the eyes aren't only for decoration,' he said. 'Anyway it's an automatic and I left it in my room.' He drew the stalk of the flower through one of the button holes in his blue cotton shirt. 'I thought a shoulder-holster would look a bit conspicuous without a coat to cover it. And I don't think anyone will be going over my room this afternoon.'

By tacit agreement they edged away from the moment of warmth. Bond told her of his discovery of Krebs and of the scene in his bedroom.

'Serves him right,' she said. 'I've never trusted him. But what did Sir Hugo say?'

'I had a word with him before lunch,' said Bond. 'Gave him Krebs's knife and keys as proof. He was furious and went straight off to see the man, muttering with rage. When he came back he said that Krebs seemed to be in a pretty bad way and was I satisfied that he'd been punished enough? All that business about not wanting to upset the team at the last moment and so forth. So I agreed that he'd be sent back to Germany next week and that meanwhile he would consider himself under open arrest – only allowed out of his room under surveillance.'

They scrambled down a steep cliff-path to the beach and turned to the right beside the deserted small-arms range of the Royal Marine Garrison at Deal. They walked along in silence until they came to the two-mile stretch of shingle that runs at low tide beneath the towering white cliffs to St Margaret's Bay.

As they trudged slowly through the deep smooth pebbles Bond told her of all that had gone through his mind since the previous day. He held nothing back and he showed each false hare as it had been started and finally run to earth, leaving nothing but a thin scent of ill-founded suspicions and a muddle of clues that all ended in the same question mark . . . where was a pattern? Where was a plan into which the clues would fit? And always the same answer, that nothing Bond knew or suspected seemed to have any conceivable bearing on the security from sabotage of the Moonraker. And that, when all was said and done, was the only matter with which he and the girl were concerned. Not with the death of Tallon and Bartsch, not with the egregious Krebs, but only with the protection of the whole Moonraker project from its possible enemies.

'Isn't that so?' Bond concluded.

Gala stopped and stood for a moment looking out across the tumbled rocks and seaweed towards the quiet glimmering swell of the sea. She was hot and out of breath from the hard going through the shingle and she thought how wonderful it would be to bathe – to step back for a moment into those childish days beside the sea before her life had been caught up in this strange cold profession with its tensions and hollow thrills. She glanced at the ruthless brown face of the man beside her. Did he have moments of longing for the peaceful simple things of life? Of course not. He liked Paris and Berlin and New York and trains and aeroplanes and expensive food, and, yes certainly, expensive women.

'Well?' said Bond, wondering if she was going to come out with some piece of evidence that he had overlooked.

'What do you think?'

'I'm sorry,' said Gala. 'I was dreaming. No,' she answered his question. 'I think you're right. I've been down here since the beginning and although there've been odd little things from time to time, and of course the shooting, I've seen absolutely nothing wrong. Every one of the team, from Sir Hugo down, is heart and soul behind the rocket. It's all they live for and it's been wonderful to see the whole thing grow. The Germans are terrific workers – and I can quite believe that Bartsch broke under the strain – and they love being driven by Sir Hugo and he loves driving them. They worship him. And as for security, the place is solid with it and I'm sure that anyone who tried to get near the Moonraker would be torn to pieces. I agree with you about Krebs and that he was probably working under Drax's orders. It was because I believed that, that I didn't bother to report him when he went through my things. There was nothing for him to find, of course. Just private letters and so on. It would be typical of Sir Hugo to make absolutely sure. And I must say,' she said candidly, 'that I admire him for it. He's a ruthless man with deplorable manners and not a very nice face under all that red hair, but I love working for him and I'm longing for the Moonraker to be a success. Living with it for so long has made me feel just like his men do about it.'

She looked up to see his reactions.

He nodded. 'After only a day I can understand that,' he said. 'And I suppose I agree with you. There's nothing to go on except my intuition and that will have to look after itself. The main thing is that the Moonraker looks as safe as the Crown Jewels, and probably safer.' He shrugged his shoulders impatiently, dissatisfied with himself for disowning the intuitions that were so much of his trade. 'Come on,' he said, almost roughly. 'We're wasting time.'

Understanding, she smiled to herself and followed.

Round the next bend of the cliff they came up with the base of the hoist, encrusted with seaweed and barnacles. Fifty yards further on they reached the jetty, a strong tubular iron frame paved with latticed iron strips that ran out over the rocks and beyond.

Between the two, and perhaps twenty feet up the cliff face, yawned the wide black mouth of the exhaust tunnel which slanted up inside the cliff to the steel floor beneath the stern of the rocket. From the under-lip of the cave melted chalk drooled like lava and there were splashes of the stuff all over the pebbles and rocks below. In his mind's eye Bond could see the blazing white shaft of flame come howling out of the face of the cliff and he could hear the sea hiss and bubble as the liquid chalk poured into the water.

He looked up at the narrow section of the launching dome that showed above the edge of the cliff two hundred feet up in the sky, and imagined the four men in their gas-masks and asbestos suits watching the gauges as the terrible liquid explosive pulsed down the black rubber tube into the stomach of the rocket. He suddenly realized that they were in range if anything went wrong with the fuelling.

'Let's get away from here,' he said to the girl.

When they had put a hundred yards between themselves and the cave Bond stopped and looked back. He imagined himself with six tough men and all the right gear, and he wondered how he would set about attacking the site from the sea – kayaks to the jetty at low tide; a ladder to the lip of the cave? and then what? Impossible to climb the polished steel walls of the exhaust tunnel. It would be a question of firing an anti-tank weapon through the steel floor beneath the rocket, following up with some phosphorus shells and hoping that something would catch fire. Untidy business, but it might be effective. Getting away afterwards would be nasty. Sitting targets from the top of the cliff. But that wouldn't worry a Russian suicide squad. It was all quite feasible.

Gala had been standing beside him watching the eyes that measured and speculated. 'It's not as easy as you might think,' she said, seeing the frown on his face. 'Even when it's high tide and very rough they have guards along the top of the cliff at night. And they've got searchlights and Brens and grenades. Their orders are to shoot and ask questions afterwards. Of course it would be better to floodlight the cliff at night. But that would only pinpoint the site. I really believe they've thought of everything.'

Bond was still frowning. 'If they had covering fire from a submarine or an X-craft, a good team could still do it,' he said. 'It'll be hell, but I'm going for a swim. The Admiralty chart says there's a twelve-fathom channel out there, but I'd like to have a look. There must be plenty of water at the end of the jetty but I'll be happier when I've seen for myself.' He smiled at her. 'Why don't you have a bathe too? It's going to be dam' cold, but it would do you good after stewing inside that concrete dome all the morning.'

Gala's eyes lit up. 'Do you think I could?' she asked doubtfully. 'I'm frightfully hot. But what are we going to wear?' She blushed at the thought of her brief and almost transparent nylon pants and brassière.

'To hell with that,' said Bond airily. 'You must have got some bits and pieces on underneath and I've got pants on. We shall be perfectly respectable and there's no one to see, and I promise not to look,' he lied cheerfully, leading the way round the next bend in the cliff. 'You undress behind that rock and I'll use this one,' he said. 'Come on. Don't be a goose. It's all in the line of duty.'

Without waiting for her to answer he moved behind the tall rock, taking off his shirt as he did so.

'Oh, well,' said Gala, relieved to have the decision taken out of her hands. She went behind her rock and slowly unbuttoned her skirt.

When she peered nervously out, Bond was already halfway down the strip of coarse brown sand that led out among the pools to where the incoming tide eddied through the green and black moraine of the rocks. He looked lithe and brown. The blue pants were reassuring.

Gingerly she followed him, and then suddenly she was in the water. At once nothing else mattered but the velvet ice of the sea and the beauty of the patches of sand between the waving hair of the seaweed that she could see in the clear green depths below her as she buried her head and swam along parallel with the shore in a fast crawl.

When she was level with the jetty she stopped for a moment to get her breath. There was no sign of Bond whom she had last seen streaking along a hundred yards ahead of her. She trod water hard to keep up her circulation and then started back again, unwillingly thinking of him, thinking of the hard brown body that must be somewhere near her, among the rocks, perhaps, or diving to the sand to gauge the depth of water that would be available to an enemy.

She turned back to look for him again and it was then that he suddenly surged up from the sea beneath her. She felt the quick tight clasp of his arms round her and the swift hard impact of his lips on hers.

'Damn you,' she said furiously, but already he had dived again and by the time she had spat out a mouthful of seawater and got her bearings he was swimming blithely twenty yards away.

She turned and swam aloofly out to sea, feeling rather ridiculous but determined to snub him. It was just as she had thought. These Secret Service people always seemed to have time for sex however important their jobs might be.

But her body obstinately tingled with the shock of the kiss and the golden day seemed to have taken on a new beauty. As she swam further out to sea and then turned back and looked along the snarling milk-white teeth of England to the distant arm of Dover and at the black and white confetti of the ravens and gulls tossed against the vivid backcloth of green fields, she decided that anything was permissible on such a day and that, just this once, she would forgive him.

Half an hour later they were lying, waiting for the sun to dry them, separated by a respectable yard of sand at the foot of the cliff.

The kiss had not been mentioned, but Gala's efforts to preserve an atmosphere of aloofness had collapsed under the excitement of examining a lobster that Bond had dived for and caught with his hands. Reluctantly they put it back into one of the rockpools and watched it scuttle backwards into the shelter of the seaweed. And now they lay, tired and exhilarated by their icy swim, and prayed that the sun would not slip behind the clifftop high above their heads before they were warm and dry enough to get back into their clothes.

But those were not Bond's only thoughts. The beautiful strapping body of the girl beside him, incredibly erotic in the tight emphasis of the clinging brassière and pants, came between him and his concern about the Moonraker. And anyway there was nothing he could do about the Moonraker for another hour. It was not yet five o'clock and the fuelling would not be finished until after six. It would only be then that he could get hold of Drax and make certain that for the next two nights the guards were strengthened on the cliff and that they had the right weapons. For he had seen for himself that there was plenty of water, even at low tide, for a submarine.

So there was at least a quarter of an hour to spare before they would have to start back.

Meanwhile this girl. The half-stripped body splayed above him on the surface as he swam up from below; the soft-hard quick kiss with his arms about her; the pointed hillocks of her breasts, so close to him, and the soft flat stomach descending to the mystery of her tightly closed thighs.

To hell with it.

He wrenched his mind out of its fever and gazed straight up into the endless blue of the sky, forcing himself to watch the soaring beauty of the herring gulls as they ranged effortlessly among the air currents that fountained up over the high clifftop above them. But the soft down of the birds' white underbellies seduced his thoughts back to her and gave him no rest.

'Why are you called Gala?' he said to break his hot crouching thoughts.

She laughed. 'I was teased about it all through school,' she said, and Bond was impatient at the easy, clear voice, 'and then through the Wrens and then by half the police force of London. But my real name's even worse. It's Galatea. She was a cruiser my father was serving in when I was born. I suppose Gala's not too bad. I've almost forgotten what I'm called. I'm always having to change my name now that I'm in the Special Branch.'

'In the Special Branch.' 'In the Special Branch.' 'In the . . .'

When the bomb falls. When the pilot miscalculates and the plane hits short of the runway. When the blood leaves the heart and consciousness goes, there are thoughts in the mind, or words, or perhaps a phrase of music, which ring on for the few seconds before death like the dying clang of a bell.

Bond wasn't killed, but the words were still in his mind, several seconds later, after it had all happened.

Ever since they had lain down on the sand up against the cliff, while his thoughts had been of Gala, his eyes had been carelessly watching two gulls playing around a wisp of straw that was the edge of their nest on a small ledge about ten feet below the distant top of the cliff. They would crane and bow in their love-play, with only their heads visible to Bond against the dazzling white of the chalk, and then the male would soar out and away and at once back to the ledge to take up his love-making again.

Bond was dreamily watching them as he listened to the girl, when suddenly both gulls dashed away from the ledge with a single shrill scream of fear. At the same moment there was a puff of black smoke and a soft boom from the top of the cliff and a great section of the white chalk directly above Bond and Gala seemed to sway outwards, zigzag cracks snaking down its face.

The next thing Bond knew was that he was lying on top of Gala, his face pressed into her cheek, that the air was full of thunder, that his breath was stifled and that the sun had gone out. His back was numb and aching under a great weight and in his left ear, besides the echo of the thunder, there was the end of a choking scream.

He was barely conscious and he had to wait until his senses came halfway back to life.

The Special Branch. What was it she had said about the Special Branch?

He made frantic efforts to move. Only in his right arm, the arm nearest to the cliff, was there any play at all, but as he jerked his shoulder the arm became freer until at last, with a great backward heave, light and air reached down to them. Retching in the fog of chalk-dust, he widened the hole until his head could take its crushing weight off Gala. He felt the feeble movement as she turned her head sideways towards the light and air. A growing trickle of dust and stones into the hole he had cleared made him dig fiercely again. Gradually he enlarged the space until he could get a purchase on his right elbow and then, coughing so that he thought his lungs would burst, he heaved his right shoulder up until suddenly it and his head were free.

His first thought was that there had been an explosion in the Moonraker. He looked up at the cliff and then along the shore. No. They were a hundred yards from the site. It was only in the skyline directly above them that a great mouthful had been bitten out of the cliff.

Then he thought of their immediate danger. Gala moaned and he could feel the frantic thud of her heart against his chest, but the ghastly white mask of her face was now free to the air and he wrenched his body from side to side on top of her to try and ease the pressure on her lungs and stomach. Slowly, inch by inch, his muscles cracking under the strain, he worked his way under the pile of dust and rubble towards the cliff face where he knew the weight would be less.

And then at last his chest was free and he could snake his body into a kneeling position beside her. Blood dripped from his cut back and arms and mingled with the chalk dust that continually poured down the sides of the hole he had made, but he could feel that no bones were broken and, in the rage of the rescue work, he felt no pain.

Grunting and coughing and without a pause to take breath he heaved her up into a sitting position and with a bleeding hand wiped some of the chalk dust from her face. Then, freeing his legs from the tomb of chalk, he somehow manhandled her up on to the top of the mound with her back against the cliff.

He knelt and looked at her, at the terrible white scarecrow that minutes before had been one of the most beautiful girls he had ever seen, and as he looked at her and at the streaks of his blood down her face he prayed that her eyes would open.

When, seconds later, they did, the relief was so great that Bond turned away and was rackingly sick.

17 Wild Surmises

When the paroxysm was over he felt Gala's hand in his hair. He looked round and saw her wince at the sight of him. She tugged at his hair and pointed up the cliffs. As she did so a shower of small pieces of chalk rattled down beside them.

Weakly he got to his knees and then to his feet and together they scrambled and slid down off the mountain of chalk and away from the crater against the cliff from which they had escaped.

The harsh sand under their feet was like velvet. They both collapsed full length and lay clutching at it with their horrible white hands as if its rough gold would wash the filthy whiteness away. Then Gala too was mercifully sick and Bond crawled a few paces away to leave her alone. He hauled himself to his feet against a single lump of chalk as big as a small motor-car, and at last his bloodshot eyes took in the hell that had almost engulfed them.

Down to the beginning of the rocks, now lapped by the incoming tide, sprawled the debris of the cliff face, an avalanche of chalk blocks and shapes. The white dust of its collapse covered nearly an acre. Above it a jagged rent had appeared in the cliff and a wedge of blue sky had been bitten out of the distant top where before the line of the horizon had been almost straight. There were no longer any seabirds near them and Bond guessed that the smell of disaster would keep them away from the place for days.

The nearness of their bodies to the cliff was what had saved them, that and the slight protection of the overhang below which the sea had bitten into the base of the cliff. They had been buried by the deluge of smaller stuff. The heavier chunks, any one of which would have crushed them, had fallen outwards, the nearest missing them by a few feet. And their nearness to the cliff was the reason for Bond's right arm having been comparatively free so that they had been able to burrow out of the mound before they were stifled. Bond realized that if some reflex had not hurled him on top of Gala at the moment of the avalanche they would now both be dead.

He felt her hand on his shoulder. Without looking at her he put his arm round her waist and together they got down to the blessed sea and let their bodies fall weakly, thankfully into the shallows.

Ten minutes later it was two comparatively human beings who walked back up the sand to the rocks where their clothes lay, a few yards away from the cliff-fall. They were both completely naked. The rags of their underclothing lay somewhere under the pile of chalk dust, torn off in their struggle to escape. But, like survivors from a shipwreck, their nakedness meant nothing. Washed clean of the cloying gritty chalk dust and with their hair and mouths scoured with the salt water, they felt weak and bedraggled, but by the time they had got

441

their clothes on and had shared Gala's comb there was little to show what they had been through.

They sat with their backs to a rock and Bond lit a first delicious cigarette, drinking the smoke deeply into his lungs and expelling it slowly through his nostrils. When Gala had done the best she could with her powder and lipstick he lit a cigarette for her and, as he handed it to her, for the first time they looked into each other's eyes and smiled. Then they sat and looked silently out to sea, at the golden panorama that was the same and yet entirely new.

Bond broke the silence.

'Well, by God,' he said. 'That was close.'

'I still don't know what happened,' said Gala. 'Except that you saved my life.' She put her hand on his and then took it away.

'If you hadn't been there I should be dead,' said Bond. 'If I'd stayed where I was −' He shrugged his shoulders.

Then he turned and looked at her. 'I suppose you realize,' he said flatly, 'that someone pushed the cliff down on us?' She looked back at him with wide eyes. 'If we searched around in all that,' he gestured towards the avalanche of chalk, 'we would find the marks of two or three drill-holes and traces of dynamite. I saw the smoke and I heard the bang of the explosion a split second before the cliff came down. And so did the gulls,' he added.

'And what's more,' continued Bond after a pause, 'it can't have been only Krebs. It was done in full view of the site. And it was done by several people, well organized, with spies on us from the moment we went down the cliff path to the beach.'

There was comprehension in Gala's eyes and a flash of fear. 'What are we to do?' she asked anxiously. 'What's it all about?'

'They want us dead,' said Bond calmly. 'So we have to stay alive. As to what it's all about, we'll just have to find that out.

'You see,' he went on, 'I'm afraid even Vallance isn't going to be much help. When they made up their minds we were properly buried, they'll have got away from the top of the cliff as fast as they could. They'd know that even if someone saw the cliff-fall, or heard it, they wouldn't get very excited. There are twenty miles of these cliffs and not many people come here until the summer. If the coastguards heard it they may have made a note in the log. But in the spring I expect they get plenty of falls. The winter frosts thaw out in cracks that may be hundreds of years old. So our friends would wait until we didn't turn up tonight and then get the police and coastguards to search for us. They'd keep quiet until the high tide had made porridge out of a good deal of this.' He gestured towards the shambles of fallen chalk. 'The whole scheme is admirable. And even if Vallance believes us, there's not enough evidence to make the Prime Minister interfere with the Moonraker. The damn thing's so infernally important. All the world's waiting to see if it'll work or not. And anyway, what's our story? What the hell's it all about? Some of those bloody Germans up there seem to want us dead before Friday. But what for?' He paused. 'It's up to us, Gala. It's a lousy business but we've simply got to solve it ourselves.'

He looked into her eyes. 'What about it?'

Gala laughed abruptly. 'Don't be ridiculous,' she said. 'It's what we're paid for. Of course we'll take them on. And I agree we'd get nowhere with London. We'd look absolutely ridiculous telephoning reports about cliffs falling on our heads. What are we doing down here anyway, fooling around without any clothes on instead of getting on with our jobs?'

Bond grinned. 'We only lay down for ten minutes to get dry,' he protested mildly. 'How do you think we ought to have spent the afternoon? Taking everybody's fingerprints all over again? That's about all you police think about.' He felt ashamed when he saw her stiffen. He held his hand up. 'I didn't really mean that,' he said. 'But can't you see what we've done this afternoon? Just what had to be done. We've made the enemy show his hand. Now we've got to take the next step and find out who the enemy is and why he wanted us out of the way. And then if we've got enough evidence that someone's trying to sabotage the Moonraker we'll have the whole place turned inside out, the practice shoot postponed, and to hell with politics.'

She jumped to her feet. 'Oh, of course you're right,' she said impatiently. 'It's just that I want to do something about it in a hurry.' She looked for a moment out to sea, away from Bond. 'You've only just come into the picture. I've been living with this rocket for more than a year and I can't bear the idea that something may happen to it. So much seems to depend on it. For all of us. I want to get back there quickly and to find out who wanted to kill us. It may be nothing to do with the Moonraker, but I want to make sure.'

Bond stood up, showing nothing of the pain from the cuts and bruises on his back and legs. 'Come on,' he said, 'it's nearly six o'clock. The tide's coming in fast but we can get to St Margaret's before it catches us. We'll clean up at the Granville there and have a drink and some food and then we'll go back to the house in the middle of dinner. I shall be interested to see what sort of a reception we get. After that we'll have to concentrate on staying alive and seeing what we can see. Can you make it to St Margaret's?'

'Don't be silly,' said Gala. 'Policewomen aren't made of gossamer.' She gave a reluctant smile at Bond's ironically respectful 'Of course not', and they turned towards the distant tower of the South Foreland lighthouse and set off through the shingle.

At half-past eight the taxi from St Margaret's dropped them at the second guard gate and they showed their passes and walked quietly up through the trees on to the expanse of concrete. They both felt keyed up and in high spirits. A hot bath and an hour's rest at the accommodating Granville had been followed by two stiff brandies-and-sodas for Gala and three for Bond followed by delicious fried soles and Welsh rarebits and coffee. And now, as they confidently approached the house, it would have needed second sight to tell that they were both dead tired and that they were naked and bruised under their walking clothes.

They let themselves quietly in through the front door and stood for a moment in the lighted hall. A cheerful mumble of voices came from the dining-room. There was a pause followed by a burst of laughter which was dominated by the harsh bark of Sir Hugo Drax.

Bond's mouth twisted wryly as he led the way across the hall to the door of the dining-room. Then he fixed a cheerful smile on his face and opened the door for Gala to pass through.

Drax sat at the head of the table, festive in his plum-coloured smoking-jacket. A forkful of food, halfway to his open mouth, had stopped in mid-air as they appeared in the doorway. Unnoticed, the food slid off the fork and fell with a soft, distinct 'plep' on to the edge of the table.

Krebs had been in the act of drinking a glass of red wine and the glass, frozen against his mouth, poured a thin trickle down his chin and thence on to his brown satin tie and yellow shirt.

Dr Walter had had his back to the door and it was not until he observed the unusual behaviour of the others, the bulging eyes, the gape of the mouths, and the blood-drained faces, that he whipped his head round towards the door. His reactions, thought Bond, were slower than the others, or else his nerves were steadier. 'Ach so,' he said softly. 'Die Engländer.'

Drax was on his feet. 'My dear chap,' he said thickly. 'My dear chap. We were really very worried. Just wondering whether to send out a search party. Few minutes ago one of the guards came in and reported there seemed to have been a cliff-fall.' He came round towards them, his napkin in one hand and the fork still erect in the other.

With the movement the blood surged back into his face, which became first mottled and then its usual red. 'You really might have let me know,' he spoke to the girl, anger rising in his voice. 'Most extraordinary behaviour.'

'It was my fault,' said Bond, moving forward into the room so that he could keep them all in view. 'The walk was longer than I expected. I thought we might get caught by the tide so we went on to St Margaret's and had something to eat there and took a taxi. Miss Brand wanted to telephone but I thought we would be back before eight. You must put the blame on me. But please go ahead with your dinner. Perhaps I might join you for coffee and dessert. I expect Miss Brand would prefer to go to her room. She must be tired after her long day.'

Bond walked deliberately round the table and took the chair next to Krebs. Those pale eyes, he noticed, after the first shock, had been fixed firmly on his plate. As Bond came up behind him he was delighted to see a large mound of Elastoplast on the crown of Krebs's head.

'Yes, go to bed, Miss Brand, I will talk to you in the morning,' said Drax testily. Gala obediently left the room and Drax went to his chair and sat heavily down.

'Most remarkable those cliffs,' said Bond blithely. 'Quite awe-inspiring walking along wondering if they're going to choose just that moment to collapse on one. Reminded me of Russian roulette. And yet one never reads of people being killed by cliffs falling on them. The odds against getting hurt must be terrific.' He paused. 'By the way, what was that you were saying about a cliff-fall just now?'

There was a faint groan on Bond's right, followed by a crash of glass and china as Krebs's head fell forward on to the table.

Bond looked at him with polite curiosity.

'Walter,' said Drax sharply. 'Can't you see that Krebs is ill? Take the man out and put him to bed. And don't be too soft with him. The man drinks too much. Hurry up.'

Walter, his face crumpled and angry, strode round the table and jerked Krebs's head out of the debris. He took him by his coat collar and hauled him to his feet and away from his chair.

'*Du Scheisskerl,*' hissed Walter at the mottled, vacant face. '*Marsch!*' He turned him round and hustled him to the swing door into the pantry and rammed him through. There were muffled sounds of stumbling and cursing and then a door banged and there was silence.

'He must have had a heavy day,' said Bond looking at Drax.

The big man was sweating freely. He wiped his face with a circular sweep of his napkin. 'Nonsense,' he said shortly. 'He drinks.'

The butler, erect and unperturbed by the apparition of Krebs and Walter in his pantry, brought in the coffee. Bond took some and sipped it. He waited for the pantry door to close again. Another German, he thought. He'll already have passed the news back to the barracks. Or perhaps all the team weren't involved. Perhaps there was a team within a team. And if so, did Drax know about it? His behaviour when Bond and Gala had come through the door had been inconclusive. Had part of his astonishment been affronted dignity, the shock of a vain man whose programme had been upset by a chit of a secretary? He had certainly covered up well. And all the afternoon he had been down the shaft supervising the fuelling. Bond decided to probe a little.

'How did the fuelling go?' he asked, his eyes fixed on the other man.

Drax was lighting a long cigar. He glanced up at Bond through the smoke and the flame of his match.

'Excellently.' He puffed at the cigar to get it going. 'Everything is ready now. The guards are out. An hour or two clearing up down there in the morning and then the site will be closed. By the way,' he added. 'I shall be taking Miss Brand up to London in the car tomorrow afternoon. I shall need a secretary as well as Krebs. Have you got any plans?'

'I have to go to London too,' said Bond on an impulse. 'I have my final report to make to the Ministry.'

'Oh, really?' said Drax casually. 'What about? I thought you were satisfied with the arrangements.'

'Yes,' said Bond non-committally.

'That's all right then,' said Drax breezily. 'And now if you don't mind,' he got up from the table, 'I've got some papers waiting for me in my study. So I'll say good-night.'

'Good-night,' said Bond to the already retreating back.

Bond finished his coffee and went out into the hall and up to his bedroom. It was obvious that it had been searched again. He shrugged his shoulders. There was only the leather case. Its contents would show nothing except that he had come equipped with the tools of his trade.

His Beretta in its shoulder-holster was still where he had hidden it, in the empty leather case that belonged to Tallon's night-glasses. He took the gun out and slipped it under his pillow.

He took a hot bath and used half a bottle of iodine on the cuts and bruises he could reach. Then he got into bed and turned out the light. His body hurt and he was exhausted.

For a moment he thought of Gala. He had told her to take a sleeping pill and lock her door, but otherwise not to worry about anything until the morning.

Before he emptied his mind for sleep he wondered uneasily about her trip with Drax the next day to London.

Uneasily, but not desperately. In due course many questions would have to be answered and many mysteries probed, but the basic facts seemed solid and unanswerable. This extraordinary millionaire had built this great weapon. The Ministry of Supply were pleased with it and considered it sound. The Prime Minister and Parliament thought so too. The rocket was to be fired in less than thirty-six hours under full supervision and the security arrangements were as strict as they could possibly be. Somebody, and probably several people, wanted him and the girl out of the way. Nerves were stretched down here. There was a lot of tension about. Perhaps there was jealousy. Perhaps some people actually suspected them of being saboteurs. But what would that matter so long as he and Gala kept their eyes open? Not much more than a day to go. They were right out in the open here, in May, in England, in peacetime. It was crazy to worry about a few lunatics so long as the Moonraker was out of danger.

And as for tomorrow, reflected Bond as sleep reached out for him, he would arrange to meet Gala in London and bring her back with him. Or she could even stay up in London for the night. Either way he would look after her until the Moonraker was safely fired and then, before work began on the Mark II weapon, there would have to be a very thorough clean-up indeed.

But these were treacherously comforting thoughts. There was danger about and Bond knew it.

He finally drifted into sleep with one small scene firmly fixed in his mind.

There had been something very disquieting about the dinner-table downstairs. It had been laid for only three people.

Part 3: Thursday, Friday

18 Beneath the Flat Stone

The Mercedes was a beautiful thing. Bond pulled his battered grey Bentley up alongside it and inspected it.

It was a Type 300 S, the sports model with a disappearing hood – one of only half a dozen in England, he reflected. Left-hand drive. Probably bought in Germany. He had seen a few of them over there. One had hissed by him on the Munich Autobahn the year before when he was doing a solid ninety in the Bentley. The body, too short and heavy to be graceful, was painted white, with red leather upholstery. Garish for England, but Bond guessed that Drax had chosen white in honour of the famous Mercedes-Benz racing colours that had already swept the board again since the war at Le Mans and the Nurburgring.

Typical of Drax to buy a Mercedes. There was something ruthless and majestic about the cars, he decided, remembering the years from 1934 to 1939 when they had completely dominated the Grand Prix scene, children of the famous Blitzen Benz that had captured the world's speed record at 142 m.p.h. back in 1911. Bond recalled some of their famous drivers, Caracciola, Lang, Seaman, Brauchitsch, and the days when he had seen them drifting the fast sweeping bends of Tripoli at 190, or screaming along the tree-lined straight at Berne with the Auto Unions on their tails.

And yet, Bond looked across at his supercharged Bentley, nearly twenty-five years older than Drax's car and still capable of beating 100, and yet when Bentleys were racing, before Rolls had tamed them into sedate town carriages, they had whipped the blown SS-K's almost as they wished.

Bond had once dabbled on the fringe of the racing world and he was lost in his memories, hearing again the harsh scream of

Caracciola's great white beast of a car as it howled past the grandstands at Le Mans, when Drax came out of the house followed by Gala Brand and Krebs.

'Fast car,' said Drax, pleased with Bond's look of admiration. He gestured towards the Bentley. 'They used to be good in the old days,' he added with a touch of patronage.

'Now they're only built for going to the theatre. Too well-mannered. Even the Continental. Now then you, get in the back.'

Krebs obediently climbed into the narrow back seat behind the driver. He sat sideways, his mackintosh up round his ears, his eyes fixed enigmatically on Bond.

Gala Brand, smart in a dark grey tailor-made and black beret and carrying a lightweight black raincoat and gloves, climbed into the right half of the divided front seat. The wide door closed with the rich double click of a Fabergé box.

No sign passed between Bond and Gala. They had made their plans at a whispered meeting in his room before lunch – dinner in London at half-past seven and then back to the house in Bond's car. She sat demurely, her hands in her lap and her eyes to the front, as Drax climbed in, pressed the starter, and pulled the gleaming lever on the steering wheel back into third. The car surged away with hardly a purr from the exhaust and Bond watched it disappear into the trees before he climbed into the Bentley and moved off in leisurely pursuit.

In the hastening Mercedes, Gala busied herself with her thoughts. The night had been uneventful and the morning had been devoted to clearing the launching site of everything that might possibly burn when the Moonraker was fired. Drax had not referred to the events of the previous day and there had been no change in his usual manner. She had prepared her last firing plan (Drax himself was to do it on the morrow) and as usual Walter had been sent for and through her spy-hole she had seen the figures being entered in Drax's black book.

It was a hot, sunny day and Drax was driving in his shirtsleeves. She glanced down and to the left at the top of the little book protruding from his hip-pocket. This drive might be her last chance. Since the evening before she had felt a different person. Perhaps Bond had aroused her competitive spirit, perhaps it was revulsion from playing the secretary too long, perhaps it was the shock of the cliff-fall and the zest of realizing after so many quiet months that she was playing a dangerous game. But now she felt the time had come to take risks. Discovery of the Moonraker's flight-plan was a routine affair and it would give her personal satisfaction to find out the secret of the black notebook. It would be easy.

Casually she laid her folded coat over the space between herself and Drax. At the same time she made a show of arranging herself comfortably, during the course of which she drew an inch or two nearer Drax and her hand came to rest in the folds of the coat between them. Then she settled herself to wait.

Her chance came, as she had thought it might, in the congested traffic of Maidstone. Drax, intent, was trying to beat the traffic lights at the corner of King Street and Gabriel's Hill, but the line of traffic was too slow and he was checked behind a battered family saloon. Gala could see that when the lights changed he was determined to cut in front of the car in front and teach it a lesson. He was a brilliant driver, but a vindictive and impatient one who was always anxious for any car that held him up to be given something to remember.

As the lights went green he gave a blast on his triple horns, pulled out to the right at the intersection, accelerated brutally and got by, shaking his head angrily at the driver of the saloon as he passed it.

In the middle of this harsh manoeuvre it was natural for Gala to allow herself to be thrown towards him. At the same time her left hand dived under the coat and her fingers touched, felt, and extracted the book in one flow of motion. Then the hand was back in the folds of the coat again and Drax, all his feeling in his feet and hands, was seeing nothing but the traffic ahead and the chances of getting across the zebra outside the Royal Star without hitting two women and a boy who were nearly halfway across it.

Now it was a question of facing Drax's growl of rage as with a maidenly but urgent voice she asked if she could possibly stop for a moment to powder her nose.

A garage would be dangerous. He might decide to fill up with petrol. And perhaps he also carried his money in his hip-pocket. But was there an hotel? Yes, she remembered, the Thomas Wyatt just outside Maidstone. And it had no petrol pumps. She started to fidget slightly. She pulled the coat back on to her lap. She cleared her throat.

'Oh, excuse me, Sir Hugo,' she said in a strangled voice.

'Yes. What is it?'

'I'm terribly sorry, Sir Hugo. But could you possibly stop for just a moment. I want, I mean, I'm terribly sorry but I'd like to powder my nose. It's terribly stupid of me. I'm so sorry.'

'Christ,' said Drax. 'Why the hell didn't you . . . Oh, yes. Well, all right. Find a place.' He grumbled on into his moustache, but brought the big car down into the fifties.

'There's a hotel just around this bend,' said Gala nervously. 'Thank you so much, Sir Hugo. It was stupid of me. I won't be a moment. Yes, here it is.'

The car swerved up to the front of the inn and stopped with a jerk. 'Hurry up. Hurry up,' said Drax as Gala, leaving the door of the car open, sped obediently across the gravel, her coat with its precious secret held tightly in front of her body.

She locked the door of the lavatory and snatched open the notebook.

There they were, just as she had thought. On each page, under the date, the neat columns of figures, the atmospheric pressure, the wind velocity, the temperature, just as she had recorded them from the Air Ministry figures. And at the foot of each page the estimated settings for the gyro compasses.

Gala frowned. At a glance she could see that they were entirely different from hers. Drax's figures simply bore no relation to hers whatsoever.

She turned to the last completed page containing the figures for that day. Why, she was wrong by nearly ninety degrees on the estimated course. If the rocket were fired on her flight plan it would land somewhere in France. She looked wildly at her face in the mirror over the washbasin. How could she have gone so monstrously wrong? And why hadn't Drax ever told her? Why, she ran quickly through the book again, every day she had been ninety degrees out, firing the Moonraker at right angles to its true course. And yet she simply couldn't have made such a mistake. Did the Ministry know these secret figures? And why should they be secret?

Suddenly her bewilderment turned to fright. She must somehow get safely, quietly to London and tell somebody. Even though she might be called a fool and a meddler.

Coldly she turned back several pages in the book, took her nail file out of the bag and, as neatly as she could, cut out a specimen page, rolled it up into a tight ball and stuffed it into the tip of a finger of one of her gloves.

She glanced at her face in the mirror. It was pale and she quickly rubbed her cheeks to bring back the colour. Then she put back the look of an apologetic secretary and hurried out and ran across the gravel to the car, clutching the notebook among the folds of her coat.

The engine of the Mercedes was turning over. Drax glowered at her impatiently as she scrambled back into her seat.

'Come on. Come on,' he said, putting the car into third and taking his foot off the clutch so that she nearly caught her ankle in the heavy door. The tyres churned up the gravel as he accelerated out of the parking place and dry-skidded into the London road.

Gala was jerked back, but she remembered to let the coat with her guilty hand in its folds fall on the seat between her and the driver.

And now the book back into the hip-pocket.

She watched the speedometer hovering in the seventies as Drax flung the heavy car along the crown of the road.

She tried to remember her lessons. Distracting pressure on some other part of the body. Distracting the attention. Distraction. The victim must not be at ease. His senses must be focused away. He must be unaware of the touch on his body. Anaesthetized by a stronger stimulus.

Like now, for instance. Drax, bent forward over the wheel, was fighting for a chance to get past a sixty-foot RAF trailer, but the oncoming traffic was leaving no room on the crown of the road. There was a gap and Drax rammed the lever into second and took it, his horns braying imperiously.

Gala's hand reached to the left under the coat.

But another hand struck like a snake.

'Got you.'

Krebs was leaning half over the back of the driving seat. His hand was crushing hers into the slippery cover of the notebook under the folds of the coat.

Gala sat frozen into black ice. With all her strength she wrenched at her hand. It was no good. Krebs had all his weight on it now.

Drax had got past the trailer and the road was empty. Krebs said urgently in German, 'Please stop the car, *mein Kapitän*. Miss Brand is a spy.'

Drax gave a startled glance to his right. What he saw was enough. He put his hand quickly down to his hip-pocket, and then, slowly, deliberately, put it back on the wheel. The sharp turning to Mereworth was just coming up on his left. 'Hold her,' said Drax. He braked so that the tyres screamed, changed down and wrenched the car into the side-road. A few hundred yards down it he pulled the car into the side and stopped.

Drax looked up and down the road. It was empty. He reached over one gloved hand and wrenched Gala's face towards him.

'What is this?'

'I can explain it, Sir Hugo.' Gala tried to bluff against the horror and desperation she knew was in her face. 'It's a mistake. I didn't mean . . .'

Under cover of an angry shrug of the shoulders, her right hand moved softly behind her and the guilty pair of gloves were thrust behind the leather cushion.

'*Sehen sie her, mein Kapitän*. I saw her edging up close to you. It seemed to me strange.'

With his other hand Krebs had whipped the coat away and there were the bent white fingers of her left hand crushed into the cover of the notebook still a foot away from Drax's hip-pocket.

'So.'

The word was deadly cold and with a shivering finality.

Drax let go her chin, but her horrified eyes remained locked into his.

A kind of frozen cruelty was showing through the jolly façade of red skin and whiskers. It was a different man. The man behind the mask. The creature beneath the flat stone that Gala Brand had lifted.

Drax glanced again up and down the empty road.

Then, looking carefully into the suddenly aware blue eyes, he drew the leather driving gauntlet off his left hand and with his right whipped her as hard as he could across the face with it.

Only a short cry was forced out of Gala's constricted throat, but tears of pain ran down her cheeks. Suddenly she began to fight like a madwoman.

With all her strength she heaved and fought against the two iron arms that held her. With her free right hand she tried to reach the face that leant over her hand and get at the eyes. But Krebs easily moved his head out of her reach and quietly increased the pressure across her throat, hissing murderously to himself as her nails tore strips of skin off the backs of his hands, but noting with a scientist's eye as her struggles became weaker.

Drax watched carefully, with one eye on the road, as Krebs brought her under control and then he started the car and drove cautiously on along the wooded road. He grunted with satisfaction as he came upon a cart-track into the woods and he turned up it and only stopped when he was well out of sight of the road.

Gala had just realized that there were no noises from the engine when she heard Drax say 'there'. A finger touched her skull behind the left ear. Krebs' arm came away from her throat and she slumped gratefully forward, gasping for air. Then something crashed into the back of her head where the finger had touched it, and there was a flash of wonderfully releasing pain and blackness.

An hour later passers-by saw a white Mercedes draw up outside a small house at the Buckingham Palace end of Ebury Street and two kind gentlemen help a sick girl out and through the front door. Those who were near could see that the poor girl's face was very pale and that her eyes were shut and that the kind gentlemen almost had to carry her up the steps. The big gentleman with the red face and whiskers was heard to say quite distinctly to the other man that poor Mildred had promised she wouldn't go out until she was quite well again. Very sad.

Gala came to herself in a large top-floor room that seemed to be full of machinery. She was tied very securely to a chair and apart from the searing pain in her head she could feel that her lips and cheek were bruised and swollen.

Heavy curtains were drawn across the window and there was a musty smell in the room as if it was rarely used. There was dust on the few pieces of conventional furniture and only the chromium and ebonite dials on the machines looked clean and new. She thought that she was probably in hospital. She closed her eyes and wondered. It was not long before she remembered. She spent several minutes controlling herself and then she opened her eyes again.

Drax, his back to her, was watching the dials on a machine that looked like a very large radio set. There were three more similar machines in her line of sight and from one of them a thin steel aerial reached up to a rough hole that had been cut for it in the plaster of the ceiling. The room was brightly lit by several tall standard lamps, each of which held a naked high wattage bulb.

To her left there was a noise of tinkering and by swivelling her half-closed eyes in their sockets, which made the pain in her head much worse, she saw the figure of Krebs bent over an electric generator on the floor. Beside it there was a small petrol engine and it was this that was giving trouble. Every now and then Krebs would grasp the starting-handle and crank it hard and a feeble stutter would come from the engine before he went back to his tinkering.

'You dam' fool,' said Drax in German, 'hurry up. I've got to go and see those bloody oafs at the Ministry.'

'At once, *mein Kapitän*,' said Krebs dutifully. He seized the handle again. This time after two or three coughs the engine started up and began to purr.

'It won't make too much noise?' asked Drax.

'No, *mein Kapitän*. The room has been sound-proofed,' answered Krebs. 'Dr Walter assures me that nothing will be heard outside.'

Gala closed her eyes and decided that her only hope was to feign unconsciousness for as long as possible. Did they intend to kill her? Here in this room? And what was all this machinery? It looked like wireless, or perhaps radar. That curved glass screen above Drax's head that had given an occasional flicker as Drax fiddled with the knobs below the dials.

Slowly her mind started to work again. Why, for instance, was Drax suddenly talking perfect German? And why did Krebs address him as

Herr Kapitän? And the figures in the black book. Why did they nearly kill her because she had seen them? What did they mean?

Ninety degrees, ninety degrees.

Lazily her mind turned the problem over.

Ninety degrees difference. Supposing her figures had been right all the time for the target eighty miles away in the North Sea. Just supposing she had been right. Then she wouldn't have been aiming the rocket into the middle of France after all. But Drax's figures. Ninety degrees to the left of her North Sea target? Somewhere in England presumably. Eighty miles from Dover. Yes, of course. That was it. Drax's figures. The firing plan in the little black book. They would drop the Moonraker just about in the middle of London.

But on London! On London!!

So one's heart really does go into one's throat. How extraordinary. Such a commonplace and yet there it is and it really does almost stop one breathing.

And now, let me see, so this is a radar homing device. How ingenious. The same as there would be on the raft in the North Sea. This would bring the rocket down within a hundred yards of Buckingham Palace. But would that matter with a warhead full of instruments?

It was probably the cruelty of Drax's blow across her face that settled it, but suddenly she *knew* that somehow it would be a real warhead, an atomic warhead, and that Drax was an enemy of England and that tomorrow at noon he was going to destroy London.

Gala made a last effort to understand.

Through this ceiling, through this chair, into the ground.

The thin needle of the rocket. Dropping fast as light out of a clear sky. The crowds in the streets. The Palace. The nursemaids in the park. The birds in the trees. The great bloom of flame a mile wide. And then the mushroom cloud. And nothing left. Nothing. Nothing. Nothing.

'No. Oh, *no!*'

But the scream was only in her mind and Gala, her body a twisted black potato crisp amongst a million others, had already fainted.

19 Missing Person

Bond sat at his favourite restaurant table in London, the right-hand corner table for two on the first floor, and watched the people and the traffic in Piccadilly and down the Haymarket.

It was 7.45 and his second Vodka dry Martini with a large slice of lemon peel had just been brought to him by Baker, the head waiter. He sipped it, wondering idly why Gala was late. It was not like her. She was the sort of girl who would telephone if she had been kept at the Yard. Vallance, whom he had visited at five, had said that Gala was due with him at six.

Vallance had been very anxious to see her. He was a worried man and when Bond reported briefly on the security of the Moonraker, Vallance seemed to be listening with only half his mind.

It appeared that all that day there had been heavy selling of sterling. It had started in Tangier and quickly spread to Zurich and New York. The pound had been fluctuating wildly in the money markets of the world and the arbitrage dealers had made a killing. The net result was that the pound was a whole three cents down on the day and the forward rates were still weaker. It was front-page news in the evening papers and at the close of business the Treasury had got on to Vallance and told him the extraordinary news that the selling wave had been started by Drax Metals Ltd. in Tangier. The operation had begun that morning and by close of business the firm had managed to sell British currency short to the tune of twenty million pounds. This had been too much for the markets, and the Bank of England had had to step in and buy in order to stop a still sharper run. It was then that Drax Metals had come to light as the seller.

Now the Treasury wanted to know what it was all about – whether it was Drax himself selling or one of the big commodify interests who were clients of his firm. The first thing they did was to tackle Vallance. Vallance could only think that in some way the Moonraker was to be a failure and that Drax knew it and wanted to profit by his knowledge. He at once spoke to the Ministry of Supply, but they pooh-poohed the idea. There was no reason to think the Moonraker would be a failure and even if its practice flight was not successful the fact would be covered up with talk of technical hitches and so forth. In any case, whether the rocket was a success or not, there could be no possible reaction on British financial credit. No, they certainly wouldn't think of mentioning the matter to the Prime Minister. Drax Metals was a big trading organization. They were probably acting for some foreign government. The Argentine. Perhaps even Russia. Someone with big sterling balances. Anyway it was nothing to do with the Ministry, or with the Moonraker, which would be launched punctually at noon the next day.

This had made sense to Vallance, but he was still worried. He didn't like mysteries and he was glad to share his concern with Bond. Above all he wanted to ask Gala if she had seen any Tangier cables and if so whether Drax had made any comment on them.

Bond was sure Gala would have mentioned anything of the sort to him, and he said so to Vallance. They had talked some more and then Bond had left for his headquarters where M was expecting him.

M had been interested in everything, even the shaven heads and moustaches of the men. He questioned Bond minutely and when Bond finished his story with the gist of his last conversation with Vallance M sat for a long time lost in thought.

'007,' he said at last, 'I don't like any part of this. There's something going on down there but I can't for the life of me make any sense out of it. And I don't see where I can possibly interfere. All the facts are known to the Special Branch and to the Ministry and, God knows, I've got nothing to add to them. Even if I had a word with the PM, which would be damned unfair on Vallance, what am I to tell him? What facts? What's it all about? There's nothing but the smell of it all. And it's a bad smell. And,' he added, 'a very big one, if I'm not mistaken.

'No,' he looked across at Bond and his eyes held an unusual note of urgency. 'It looks as if it's all up to you. And that girl. You're lucky she's a good one. Anything you want? Anything I can do to help?'

'No, thank you, sir,' Bond had said and he had walked out through the familiar corridors and down in the lift to his own office where he had terrified Loelia Ponsonby by giving her a kiss as he said good night. The only times he ever did that were at Christmas, on her birthday, and just before there was something dangerous to be done.

Bond drank down the rest of his Martini and looked at his watch. Now it was eight o'clock and suddenly he shivered.

He got straight up from his table and walked out to the telephone.

The switchboard at the Yard said that the Assistant Commissioner had been trying to reach him. He had had to go to a dinner at the Mansion House. Could Commander Bond please stay by the telephone? Bond waited impatiently. All his fears surged up at him from the chunk of black bakelite. He could see the rows of polite faces. The uniformed waiter slowly edging his way round to Vallance. The quickly pulled-back chair. The unobtrusive exit. Those echoing stone lobbies. The discreet booth.

The telephone screamed at him. 'That you, Bond? Vallance here. Seen anything of Miss Brand?'

Bond's heart went cold. 'No,' he said sharply. 'She's half an hour late for dinner. Didn't she turn up at six?'

'No, and I've had a "trace" sent out and there's no sign of her at the usual address she stays at when she comes to London. None of her friends have seen her. If she left in Drax's car at two-thirty she should have been in London by half-past four. There's been no crash on the Dover road during the afternoon and the AA and the RAC are negative.' There was a pause. 'Now listen.' There was urgent appeal in Vallance's voice. 'She's a good girl that, and I don't want anything to happen to her. Can you handle it for me? I can't put out a general call for her. The killing down there has made her news and we'd have the whole Press round our ears. It will be even worse after ten tonight. Downing Street are issuing a communiqué about the practice shoot and tomorrow's papers are going to be nothing but Moonraker. The PM's going to broadcast. Her disappearance would turn the whole thing into a crime story. Tomorrow's too important for that and anyway the girl may have had a fainting fit or something. But I want her found. Well? What do you say? Can you handle it? You can have all the help you want. I'll tell the Duty Officer that he's to accept your orders.'

'Don't worry,' said Bond. 'Of course I'll look after it.' He paused, his mind racing. 'Just tell me something. What do you know about Drax's movements?'

'He wasn't expected at the Ministry until seven,' said Vallance. 'I left word . . .' There was a confused noise on the line and Bond heard Vallance say 'Thanks.' He came back on the line. 'Just got a report passed on by the City police,' he said. 'The Yard couldn't get me on the 'phone. Talking to you. Let's see,' he read, ' "Sir Hugo Drax arrived Ministry 1900 left at 2000. Left message dining at Blades if wanted. Back at site 2300." ' Vallance commented: 'That means he'll be leaving London about nine. Just a moment.' He read on: ' "Sir Hugo stated Miss Brand felt unwell on arrival in London but at her request he left her at Victoria Station bus terminal at 16.45. Miss Brand stated she would rest with some friends, address unknown, and contact Sir Hugo at Ministry at 1900. She had not done so." And that's all,' said Vallance. 'Oh, by the way, we made the inquiry about Miss Brand on your behalf. Said you had arranged to meet her at six and she hadn't turned up.'

'Yes,' said Bond, his thoughts elsewhere. 'That doesn't seem to get us anywhere. I'll have to get busy. Just one more thing. Has Drax got a place in London, flat or anything like that?'

'He always stays at the Ritz nowadays,' said Vallance. 'Sold his house in Grosvenor Square when he moved down to Dover. But we happen to know he's got some sort of an establishment in Ebury Street. We checked there. But there was no answer to the bell and my man said the house looked unoccupied. Just behind Buckingham Palace. Some sort of hideout of his. Keeps it very quiet. Probably takes his women there. Anything else? I ought to be getting back or all this big brass will think the Crown Jewels have been stolen.'

'You go ahead,' said Bond. 'I'll do my best and if I get stuck I'll call on your men to help. Don't worry if you don't hear from me. So long.'

'So long,' said Vallance with a note of relief in his voice. 'And thanks. Best of luck.'

Bond rang off.

He picked up the receiver again and called Blades.

'This is the Ministry of Supply,' he said. 'Is Sir Hugo Drax in the club?'

'Yes, sir,' it was the friendly voice of Brevett. 'He's in the dining-room. Do you wish to speak to him?'

'No, it's all right,' said Bond. 'I just wanted to make certain he hadn't left yet.'

Without noticing what he was eating Bond wolfed down some food and left the restaurant at 8.45. His car was outside waiting for him and he said good-night to the driver from Headquarters and drove to St James's Street. He parked under cover of the central row of taxis outside Boodle's and settled himself behind an evening paper over which he could keep his eyes on a section of Drax's Mercedes which he was relieved to see standing in Park Street, unattended.

He had not long to wait. Suddenly a broad shaft of yellow light shone out from the doorway of Blades and the big figure of Drax appeared. He wore a heavy ulster up round his ears and a cap pulled down over his eyes. He walked quickly to the white Mercedes, slammed the door, and was away across to the left-hand side of St James's Street and braking to turn opposite St James's Palace while Bond was still in third.

God, the man moves quickly, thought Bond, doing a racing change round the island in The Mall with Drax already passing the statue in front of the Palace. He kept the Bentley in third and thundered in pursuit. Buckingham Palace Gate. So it looked like Ebury Street. Keeping the white car just in view, Bond made hurried plans. The lights at the corner of Lower Grosvenor Place were green for Drax and red for Bond. Bond jumped them and was just in time to see Drax swing left into the beginning of Ebury Street. Gambling on Drax making a stop at his house, Bond accelerated to the corner and pulled up just short of it. As he jumped out of the Bentley, leaving the engine ticking over, and took the few steps towards Ebury Street, he heard two short blasts on the Mercedes' horn and as he carefully edged round the corner he was in time to see Krebs helping the muffled figure of a girl across the pavement. Then the door of the Mercedes slammed and Drax was off again.

Bond raced back to his car, whipped into third, and went after him.

Thank God the Mercedes was white. There it went, its stop-lights blazing briefly at the intersections, the headlamps full on and the horn blaring at any hint of a check in the sparse traffic.

Bond set his teeth and rode his car as if she was a Lipizaner at the Spanish Riding School in Vienna. He could not use headlights or horn for fear of betraying his presence to the car in front. He just had to play on his brakes and gears and hope for the best.

The deep note of his two-inch exhaust thundered back at him from the houses on either side and his tyres screamed on the tarmac. He thanked heavens for the new set of racing Michelins that were only a week old. If only the lights would be kind. He seemed to be getting nothing but amber and red while Drax was always being swept on by the green. Chelsea Bridge. So it did look like the Dover road by the South Circular! Could he hope to keep up with the Mercedes on A20? Drax had two passengers. His car might not be tuned. But with that independent springing he could corner better than Bond. The old Bentley was a bit high off the ground for this sort of work. Bond stamped on his brakes and risked a howl on his triple klaxons as a homeward-bound taxi started to weave over to the right. It jerked back to the left and Bond heard a four-letter yell as he shot past.

Clapham Common and the flicker of the white car through the trees. Bond ran the Bentley up to eighty along the safe bit of road and saw the lights go red just in time to stop Drax at the end of it. He put the Bentley into neutral and coasted up silently. Fifty yards away. Forty, thirty, twenty. The lights changed and Drax was over the crossing and away again, but not before Bond had seen that Krebs was beside the driver and there was no sign of Gala except the hump of a rug over the narrow back seat.

So there was no question. You don't take a sick girl for a drive like a sack of potatoes. Not at that speed for the matter of that. So she was a prisoner. Why? What had she done? What had she discovered? What the hell, in fact, was all this about?

Each dark conjecture came and for a moment settled like a vulture on Bond's shoulder and croaked into his ear that he had been a blind fool. Blind, blind, blind. From the moment he had sat in his office after the night at Blades and made his mind up about Drax being a dangerous man he should have been on his toes. At the first smell of trouble, the marks on the chart for instance, he should have taken action. But what action? He had passed on each clue, each fear. What could he have done except kill Drax? And get hanged for his pains? Well, then. What about the present? Should he stop and telephone the Yard? And let the car get away? For all he knew Gala was being taken for a ride and Drax planned to get rid of her on the way to Dover. And that Bond might conceivably prevent if only his car could take it.

As if to echo his thoughts the tortured rubber screamed as he left the South Circular road into the A20 and took the roundabout at forty. No. He had told M that he would stay with it. He had told Vallance the same. The case had been dumped firmly into his lap and he must do what he could. At least if he kept up with the Mercedes he might shoot up its tyres and apologize afterwards. To let it get away would be criminal.

So be it, said Bond to himself.

He had to slow for some lights and he used the pause to pull a pair of goggles out of the dashboard compartment and cover his eyes with them. Then he leant over to the left and twisted the big screw on the windscreen and then eased the one beside his right hand. He pressed the narrow screen flat down on the bonnet and tightened the screws again.

Then he accelerated away from Swanley Junction and was soon doing ninety astride the cats' eyes down the Farningham by-pass, the wind howling past his ears and the shrill scream of his supercharger riding with him for company.

A mile ahead the great eyes of the Mercedes hooded themselves as they went over the crest of Wrotham Hill and disappeared down into the moonlit panorama of the Weald of Kent.

20 Drax's Gambit

There were three separate sources of pain in Gala's body. The throbbing ache behind her left ear, the bite of the flex at her wrists, and the chafing of the strap round her ankles.

Every bump in the road, every swerve, every sudden pressure of Drax's foot on the brakes or the accelerator awoke one or another of these pains and rasped at her nerves. If only she had been wedged into the back seat more tightly. But there was just room enough for her body to roll a few inches on the occasional seat so that she was constantly having to twist her bruised face away from contact with the walls of shiny pigskin.

The air she breathed was stuffy with a smell of new leather upholstery, exhaust fumes, and the occasional sharp stench of burning rubber as Drax flayed the tyres on a sharp corner.

And yet the discomfort and pain were nothing.

Krebs! Curiously enough her fear and loathing of Krebs tormented her most. The other things were too big. The mystery of Drax and his hatred of England. The riddle of his perfect command of German. The Moonraker. The secret of the atomic warhead. How to save London. These were matters which she had long ago put away in the back of her mind as insoluble.

But the afternoon alone with Krebs was present and dreadful and her mind went back and back to the details of it like a tongue to an aching tooth.

Long after Drax had gone she had kept up her pretence of unconsciousness. At first Krebs had occupied himself with the machines, talking to them in German in a cooing baby-talk. 'There, my *Liebchen*. That's better now, isn't it? A drop of oil for you, my *Pupperl*? But certainly. Coming up at once. No, no, lazybones. I said a thousand revolutions. Not nine hundred. Come along now. We can do better than that, can't we. Yes, my *Schatz*. That's it. Round and round we go. Up and down. Round and round. Let me wipe your pretty face for you so that we can see what the little dial is saying. *Jesu Maria, bist du ein braves Kind!*'

And so it had gone on with intervals of standing in front of Gala, picking his nose and sucking his teeth in a horribly ruminative way. Until he stayed longer and longer in front of her, forgetting the machines, wondering, making up his mind.

And then she had felt his hand undo the top button of her dress and the automatic recoil of her body had had to be covered by a realistic groan and a pantomime of consciousness returning.

She had asked for water and he had gone into a bathroom and

fetched some for her in a toothglass. Then he had pulled a kitchen chair up in front of her and had sat down astride it, his chin resting on the top rail of its back, and had gazed at her speculatively from under his pale drooping lids.

She had been the first to break the silence. 'Why have I been brought here?' she asked. 'What are all those machines?'

He licked his lips and the little pouting red mouth opened under the smudge of yellow moustache and formed itself slowly into a rhomboid-shaped smile. 'That is a lure for little birds,' he said. 'Soon it will lure a little bird into this warm nest. Then the little bird will lay an egg. Oh, such a big round egg! Such a beautiful fat egg.' The lower half of his face giggled with delight while his eyes mooned. 'And the pretty girl is here because otherwise she might frighten the little bird away. And that would be so sad, wouldn't it,' he spat out the next three words, 'filthy English bitch?'

His eyes became intent and purposeful. He hitched his chair nearer so that his face was only a foot away from hers and she was enveloped in the miasma of his breath. 'Now, English bitch. Who are you working for?' He waited. 'You must answer me, you know,' he said softly. 'We are all alone here. There is no one to hear you scream.'

'Don't be stupid,' said Gala desperately. 'How could I be working for anyone except Sir Hugo?' (Krebs smiled at the name.) 'I was just curious about the flight plan . . .' She went into a rambling explanation about her figures and Drax's figures and how she had wanted to share in the success of the Moonraker.

'Try again,' whispered Krebs when she had finished. 'You must do better than that,' and suddenly his eyes had turned hot with cruelty and his hands had reached towards her from behind the back of his chair . . .

In the rear of the hurtling Mercedes Gala ground her teeth together and whimpered at the memory of the soft crawling fingers on her body, probing, pinching, pulling, while all the time the hot vacant eyes gazed curiously into hers until finally she gathered the saliva in her mouth and spat full in his face.

He hadn't even paused to wipe his face, but suddenly he had really hurt her and she had screamed once and then mercifully fainted.

466

And then she had found herself being pushed into the back of the car, a rug was thrown over her, and they were hurtling through the streets of London and she could hear other cars near them, the frantic ringing of a bicycle bell, an occasional shout, the animal growl of an old klaxon, the whirring putter of a motor-scooter, a scream of brakes, and she had realized that she was back in the real world, that English people, friends, were all around her. She had struggled to get to her knees and scream, but Krebs must have felt her movement because his hands were suddenly at her ankles, strapping them to the foot-rail along the floor, and she knew that she was lost and suddenly the tears were pouring down her cheeks and she was praying that somehow, somebody would be in time.

That had been less than an hour ago and now she could tell from the slow pace of the car and the noise of other traffic that they had reached a large town – Maidstone if she was being taken back to the site.

In the comparative silence of their progress through the town she suddenly heard Krebs's voice. There was a note of urgency in it.

'*Mein Kapitän*,' he said. 'I have been watching a car for some time. It is certainly following us. It has seldom been using its lights. It is only a hundred metres behind us now. I think it is the car of Commander Bond.'

Drax grunted with surprise and she could hear his big body shift round to get a quick look.

He swore sharply and then there was silence and she could feel the big car weaving and straining in the thin traffic. '*Ja, sowas!*' said Drax finally. His voice was thoughtful. 'So that old museum-piece of his can still move. So much the better, my dear Krebs. He seems to be alone.' He laughed harshly. 'So we will give him a run for his money and if he survives it we will get him in the bag with the woman. Turn on the radio. Home Service. We will soon find out if there is a hitch.'

There was a short crackle of static and then Gala could hear the voice of the Prime Minister, the voice of all the great occasions in her life, coming through in broken fragments as Drax put the car into third and accelerated out of the town, '. . . weapon devised by the ingenuity of man . . . a thousand miles into the firmament . . . area

467

patrolled by Her Majesty's ships ... designed exclusively for the defence of our beloved island ... a long era of peace ... development for Man's great journey away from the confines of this planet ... Sir Hugo Drax, that great patriot and benefactor of our country ...'

Gala heard Drax's roar of laughter above the howling of the wind, a great scornful bray of triumph, and then the set was switched off.

'James,' whispered Gala to herself. 'There's only you left. Be careful. But make haste.'

Bond's face was a mask of dust and filthy with the blood of flies and moths that had smashed against it. Often he had had to take a cramped hand off the wheel to clear his goggles but the Bentley was going beautifully and he felt sure of holding the Mercedes.

He was touching ninety-five on the straight just before the entrance to Leeds Castle when great lights were suddenly switched on behind him and a four-tone windhorn sounded its impudent 'pom-pim-pom-pam' almost in his ear.

The apparition of a third car in the race was almost unbelievable. Bond had hardly troubled to look in his driving-mirror since he left London. No one but a racing-driver or a desperate man could have kept up with them, and his mind was in a turmoil as he automatically pulled over to the left and saw out of the corner of his eye a low, fire-engine-red car come up level with him and draw away with a good ten miles an hour extra on its clock.

He caught a glimpse of the famous Alfa radiator and along the edge of the bonnet in bold white script the words *Attaboy II*. Then there was the grinning face of a youth in shirtsleeves who stuck two rude fingers in the air before he pulled away in the welter of sound which an Alfa at speed compounds from the whine of its supercharger, the Gatling crackle of its exhaust, and the thunderous howl of its transmission.

Bond grinned in admiration as he raised a hand to the driver. Alfa-Romeo supercharged straight-eight, he thought to himself. Must be nearly as old as mine. '32 or '33 probably. And only half my c.c. Targa Florio in 1931 and did well everywhere after that. Probably a hot-rod type from one of the RAF stations round here. Trying to get back from a party in time to sign in before he's put on the report. He watched affectionately as the Alfa wagged its tail in the S-bend abreast of Leeds Castle and then howled off on the long wide road towards the distant Charing-fork.

Bond could imagine the grin of delight as the boy came up with Drax. 'Oh, boy. It's a Merc!' And the rage of Drax at the impudent music of the windhorn. Must be doing 105, reflected Bond. Hope the damn fool doesn't run out of road. He watched the two sets of tail lights closing up, the boy in the Alfa preparing for his trick of coming up behind and suddenly switching everything on when he could see a chance to get by.

There. Four hundred yards away the Mercedes showed white in the sudden twin shafts from the Alfa. There was a mile of clear road ahead, straight as a die. Bond could almost feel the boy's feet stamping the pedal still further into the floorboards. Attaboy!

Up front in the Mercedes Krebs had his mouth close to Drax's ear. 'Another of them,' he shouted urgently. 'Can't see his face. Coming up to pass now.'

Drax let out a harsh obscenity. His bared teeth showed white in the pale glimmer from the dashboard. 'Teach the swine a lesson,' he said, setting his shoulders and gripping the wheel tightly in the great leather gauntlets. Out of the corner of his eye he watched the nose of the Alfa creep up to starboard. 'Pom-pim-pom-pam' chirped the windhorn. Softly, delicately, Drax inched the wheel of the Mercedes to the right and, at the horrible crash of metal, whipped it back again to correct the slew of his tail.

'Bravo! Bravo!' screamed Krebs, beside himself with excitement as he knelt on the seat and looked back. 'Double somersault. Jumped the hedge upside down. I think he's burning already. Yes. There are flames.'

'That'll give our fine Mister Bond something to think about,' snarled Drax, breathing heavily.

But Bond, his face a tight mask, had hardly checked his speed and there was nothing but revenge in his mind as he hurtled on after the flying Mercedes.

He had seen it all. The grotesque flight of the red car as it turned over and over, the flying figure of the driver, his arms and legs spreadeagled as he soared out of the driving seat, and the final thunder as the car hurdled the hedge upside down and crashed into the field.

As he flashed by, noting the horrible graffiti of the black skid-marks across the tarmac, his mind recorded one final macabre touch. Somehow undamaged in the holocaust, the windhorn was still making contact and its ululations were going on up to the sky, stridently clearing imaginary roads for the passage of *Attaboy II* – 'Pom-pim-pom-pam.' 'Pom-pim-pom-pam . . .'

So a murder had taken place in front of his eyes. Or at any rate an attempted murder. So, whatever his motives, Sir Hugo Drax had declared war and didn't mind Bond knowing it. This made a lot of things easier. It meant that Drax was a criminal and probably a maniac. Above all it meant certain danger for the Moonraker. That was enough for Bond. He reached under the dashboard and from its concealed holster drew out the long-barrelled .45 Colt Army Special and laid it on the seat beside him. The battle was now in the open and somehow the Mercedes must be stopped.

Using the road as if it was Donington, Bond rammed his foot down and kept it there. Gradually, with the needle twitching either side of the hundred mark he began to narrow the gap.

Drax took the left-hand fork at Charing and hissed up the long hill. Ahead, in the giant beam of his headlights, one of Bowaters' huge eight-wheeled AEC Diesel carriers was just grinding into the first bend of the hairpin, labouring under the fourteen tons of newsprint it was taking on a night run to one of the East Kent newspapers.

Drax cursed under his breath as he saw the long carrier with the twenty gigantic rolls, each containing five miles of newsprint, roped to its platform. Right in the middle of the tricky S-bend at the top of the hill.

He looked in the driving mirror and saw the Bentley coming into the fork.

And then Drax had his idea.

'Krebs,' the word was a pistol shot. 'Get out your knife.'

There was a sharp click and the stiletto was in Krebs's hand. One didn't dawdle when there was that note in the master's voice.

'I am going to slow down behind this lorry. Take your shoes and socks off and climb out on to the bonnet and when I come up behind the lorry jump on to it. I shall be going at walking-pace. It will be safe. Cut the ropes that hold the rolls of paper. The left ones first. Then the right. I shall have pulled up level with the lorry and when you have cut the second lot jump into the car. Be careful you are not swept off with the paper. *Verstanden? Also. Hals und Beinbruch!*'

Drax dowsed his headlights and swept round the bend at eighty. The lorry was twenty yards ahead and Drax had to brake hard to avoid crashing into its tail. The Mercedes executed a dry skid until its radiator was almost underneath the platform of the carrier.

Drax changed down to second. 'Now!' He held the car steady as a rock as Krebs, with bare feet, went over the windscreen and scrambled along the shining bonnet, his knife in his hand.

With a leap he was up and hacking at the left-hand ropes. Drax pulled away to the right and crawled up level with the rear wheels of the Diesel, the oily smoke from its exhaust in his eyes and nostrils.

Bond's lights were just showing round the bend.

There was a series of huge thuds as the left-hand rolls poured off the back of the lorry into the road and went hurtling off into the darkness. And more thuds as the right-hand ropes parted. One roll burst as it landed and Drax heard a tearing rattle as the unwinding paper crashed back down the one-in-ten gradient.

Released of its load the lorry almost bounded forward and Drax had to accelerate a little to catch the flying figure of Krebs who landed half across Gala's back and half in the front seat. Drax stamped his foot into the floor and sped off up the hill, ignoring a shout from the lorry-driver above the clatter of the Diesel pistons as he shot ahead.

As he hurtled round the next bend he saw the shaft of two headlights curve up into the sky above the tops of the trees until they were almost vertical. They wavered there for an instant and then the beams whirled away across the sky and went out.

A great barking laugh broke out of Drax as for a split second he took his eyes off the road and raised his face triumphantly towards the stars.

21 'The Persuader'

Krebs echoed the maniac laugh with a high giggle. 'A master-stroke, *mein Kapitän*. You should have seen them charge off down the hill. The one that burst. *Wunderschön!* Like the lavatory paper of a giant. That one will have made a pretty parcel of him. He was just coming round the bend. And the second salvo was as good as the first. Did you see the driver's face? *Zum Kotzen!* And the *Firma* Bowater! A fine paperchase they have got on their hands.'

'You did well,' said Drax briefly, his mind elsewhere. Suddenly he pulled into the side of the road with a scream of protest from the tyres.

'*Donnerwetter*,' he said angrily, as he started to turn the car. 'But we can't leave the man there. We must get him.' The car was already hissing back down the road. 'Gun,' ordered Drax briefly.

They passed the lorry at the top of the hill. It was stopped and there was no sign of the driver. Probably telephoning to the company, thought Drax, slowing up as they went round the first bend. There were lights on in the two or three houses and a group of people were standing round one of the rolls of newsprint that lay amongst the ruins of their front gate. There were more rolls in the hedge on the right side of the road. On the left a telegraph pole leant drunkenly, snapped in the middle. Then at the next bend was the beginning of a great confusion of paper stretching away down the long hill, festooning the hedges and the road like the sweepings of some elephantine fancy-dress ball.

The Bentley had nearly broken through the railings that fenced off the right of the bend from a steep bank. Amidst a puzzle of twisted iron stanchions it hung, nose down, with one wheel, still attached to the broken back axle, poised crookedly over its rump like a surrealist umbrella.

Drax pulled up and he and Krebs got out and stood quietly, listening.

There was no sound except the distant rumination of a car travelling fast on the Ashford road and the chirrup of a sleepless cricket.

With their guns out they walked cautiously over to the remains of the Bentley, their feet crunching the broken glass on the road. Deep furrows had been cut across the grass verge and there was a strong smell of petrol and burnt rubber in the air. The hot metal of the car ticked and crackled softly and steam was still fountaining from the shattered radiator.

Bond was lying face downwards at the bottom of the bank twenty feet away from the car. Krebs turned him over. His face was covered with blood but he was breathing. They searched him thoroughly and Drax pocketed the slim Beretta. Then together they hauled him across the road and wedged him into the back seat of the Mercedes, half on top of Gala.

When she realized who it was she gave a cry of horror.

'Halt's Maul,' snarled Drax. He got into the front seat and while he turned the car Krebs leant over from the front seat and busied himself with a long piece of flex. 'Make a good job of it,' said Drax. 'I don't want any mistakes.' He had an afterthought. 'And then go back to the wreck and get the number plates. Hurry. I will watch the road.'

Krebs pulled the rug over the two inert bodies and jumped out of the car. Using his knife as a screwdriver he was soon back with the plates, and the big car started to move just as a group of the local residents appeared walking nervously down the hill shining their torches over the scene of devastation.

Krebs grinned happily to himself at the thought of the stupid English having to clean up all this mess. He settled himself back to enjoy the part of the drive he had always liked best, the spring woods full of bluebells and celandines on the way to Chilham.

They had made him particularly happy at night. Lit up amongst the green torches of the young trees by the great headlamps of the Mercedes, they made him think of the beautiful forests of the Ardennes and of the devoted little band with which he had served, and of driving along in a captured American jeep with, just like tonight, his adored leader at the wheel. *Der Tag* had been a long time coming, but now it was here. With young Krebs in the van. At last the cheering crowds, the medals, the women, the flowers. He gazed out at the fleeting hosts of bluebells and felt warm and happy.

Gala could taste Bond's blood. His face was beside hers on the leather seat and she shifted to give him more room. His breathing was heavy and irregular and she wondered how badly he was hurt. Tentatively she whispered into his ear. And then louder. He groaned and his breath came faster.

'James,' she whispered urgently. 'James.'

He mumbled something and she pushed hard against him.

He uttered a string of obscenities and his body heaved.

He lay still again and she could almost feel him exploring his sensations.

'It's me, Gala.' She felt him stiffen.

'Christ,' he said. 'Hell of a mess.'

'Are you all right? Is anything broken?'

She felt him tense his arms and legs. 'Seems all right,' he said. 'Crack on the head. Am I talking sense?'

'Of course,' said Gala. 'Now listen.'

Hurriedly she told him all she knew, beginning with the notebook.

His body was as rigid as a board against her, and he hardly breathed as he listened to the incredible story.

Then they were running into Canterbury and Bond put his mouth to her ear. 'Going to try and chuck myself over the back,' he whispered. 'Get to a telephone. Only hope.'

He started to heave himself up on his knees, his weight almost grinding the breath out of the girl.

There was a sharp crack and he fell back on top of her.

'Another move out of you and you're dead,' said the voice of Krebs coming softly between the front seats.

Only another twenty minutes to the site! Gala gritted her teeth and set about bringing Bond back to consciousness again.

She had only just succeeded when the car drew up at the door of the launching-dome and Krebs, a gun in his hand, was undoing the bonds round their ankles.

They had a glimpse of the familiar moonlit cement and of the semicircle of guards some distance away before they were hustled through the door and, when their shoes had been torn off by Krebs, out on to the iron catwalk inside the launching-dome.

There the gleaming rocket stood, beautiful, innocent, like a new toy for Cyclops.

But there was a horrible smell of chemicals in the air and to Bond the Moonraker was a giant hypodermic needle ready to be plunged into the heart of England. Despite a growl from Krebs he paused on the stairway and looked up at its glittering nose. A million deaths. A million. A million. A million.

On his hands? For God's sake! On *his* hands?

With Krebs's gun prodding him, he went slowly down the steps on the heels of Gala.

As he turned through the doors of Drax's office, he pulled himself together. Suddenly his mind was clear and all the lethargy and pain had left his body. Something, anything, must be done. Somehow he would find a way. His whole body and mind became focused and sharp as a blade. His eyes were alive again and defeat sloughed off him like the skin of a snake.

Drax had gone ahead and was sitting at his desk. He had a Luger in his hand. It was pointing at a spot halfway between Bond and Gala and it was steady as a rock.

Behind him, Bond heard the double doors thud shut.

'I was one of the best shots in the Brandenburg Division,' said Drax conversationally. 'Tie her to that chair, Krebs. Then the man.'

Gala looked desperately at Bond.

'You won't shoot,' said Bond. 'You'd be afraid of touching off the fuel.' He walked slowly towards the desk.

Drax smiled cheerfully and looked along the barrel at Bond's stomach. 'Your memory is bad, Englishman,' he said flatly. 'I told you this room is cut off from the shaft by the double doors. Another step and you will have no stomach.'

Bond looked at the confident, narrowed eyes and stopped.

'Go ahead, Krebs.'

When they were both tied securely and painfully to the arms and legs of two tubular steel chairs a few feet apart beneath the glass wall-map, Krebs left the room. He came back in a moment with a mechanic's blowtorch.

He set the ugly machine on the desk, pumped air into it with a few brisk strokes of the plunger, and set a match to it. A blue flame hissed out a couple of inches into the room. He picked up the instrument and walked towards Gala. He stopped a few feet to one side of her.

'Now then,' said Drax grimly. 'Let's get this over without any fuss. The good Krebs is an artist with one of those things. We used to call him *Der Zwangsmann* – The Persuader. I shall never forget the way he went over the last spy we caught together. Just south of the Rhine, wasn't it, Krebs?'

Bond pricked up his ears.

'Yes, *mein Kapitän.*' Krebs chuckled reminiscently. 'It was a pig of a Belgian.'

'All right then,' said Drax. 'Just remember, you two. There's no fair play down here. No jolly good sports and all that. This is business.' The voice cracked like a whip on the word. 'You,' he looked at Gala Brand, 'who are you working for?'

Gala was silent.

'Anywhere you like, Krebs.'

Krebs's mouth was half open. His tongue ran up and down his lower lip. He seemed to be having difficulty with his breathing as he took a step towards the girl.

The little flame roared greedily.

'Stop,' said Bond coldly. 'She works for Scotland Yard. So do I.' These things were pointless now. They were of no conceivable use to Drax. In any case, by tomorrow afternoon there might be no Scotland Yard.

'That's better,' said Drax. 'Now, does anybody know you are prisoners? Did you stop and telephone anyone?'

If I say yes, thought Bond, he will shoot us both and get rid of the bodies and the last chance of stopping the Moonraker will be gone. And if the Yard knows, why aren't they here already? No. Our chance may come. The Bentley will be found. Vallance may get worried when he doesn't hear from me.

'No,' he said. 'If I had, they'd be here by now.'

'True,' said Drax reflectively. 'In that case I am no longer interested in you and I congratulate you on making the interview so harmonious. It might have been more difficult if you had been alone. A girl is always useful on these occasions. Krebs, put that down. You may go. Tell the others what is necessary. They will be wondering. I shall entertain our guests for a while and then I shall come up to the house. See the car gets properly washed down. The back seat. And get rid of the marks on the right-hand side. Tell them to take the whole panel off if necessary. Or they can set fire to the dam' thing. We shan't be needing it any more,' he laughed abruptly. '*Verstanden?*'

'Yes, *mein Kapitän.*' Krebs reluctantly placed the softly roaring blowtorch on the desk beside Drax. 'In case you need it,' he said, looking hopefully at Gala and Bond. He went out through the double doors.

Drax put the Luger down on the desk in front of him. He opened a drawer and took out a cigar and lit it from a Ronson desk lighter. Then he settled himself comfortably. There was silence in the room for several minutes while Drax puffed contentedly at his cigar. Then he seemed to make up his mind. He looked benevolently at Bond.

'You don't know how I have longed for an English audience,' he said as if he was addressing a Press conference.

'You don't know how I have longed to tell my story. As a matter of fact, a full account of my operations is now in the hands of a very respectable firm of Edinburgh solicitors. I beg their pardon – Writers to the Signet. Well out of danger.' He beamed from one to the other. 'And these good folk have instructions to open the envelope on the completion of the first successful flight of the Moonraker. But you lucky people shall have a preview of what I have written and then, when tomorrow at noon you see through those open doors,' he gestured to his right, 'the first wisp of steam from the turbines and know that you are to be burnt alive in about half a second, you will have the momentary satisfaction of knowing what it is all in aid of, as,' he grinned wolfishly, 'we English men say.'

'You can spare us the jokes,' said Bond roughly. 'Get on with your story, Kraut.'

Drax's eyes blazed momentarily. 'A Kraut. Yes, I am indeed a *Reichsdeutscher*' – the mouth beneath the red moustache savoured the fine word – 'and even England will soon agree that they have been licked by just one single German. And then perhaps they'll stop calling us Krauts – BY ORDER!' The words were yelled out and the whole of Prussian militarism was in the parade-ground bellow.

Drax glowered across the desk at Bond, the great splayed teeth under the red moustache tearing nervously at one fingernail after another. Then, with an effort, he crammed his right hand into his trouser pocket, as if to put it out of temptation, and picked up his cigar with his left. He puffed at it for a moment and then, his voice still taut, he began.

22 Pandora's Box

'My real name,' said Drax, addressing himself to Bond, 'is Graf Hugo von der Drache. My mother was English and because of her I was educated in England until I was twelve. Then I could stand this filthy country no longer and I completed my education in Berlin and Leipzig.'

Bond could imagine that the hulking body with the ogre's teeth had not been very welcome at an English private school. And being a foreign count with a mouthful of names would not have helped much.

'When I was twenty,' Drax's eyes glowed reminiscently, 'I went to work in the family business. It was a subsidiary of the great steel combine *Rheinmetall Borsig*. Never heard of it, I suppose. Well, if you'd been hit by an 88 mm shell during the war it would probably have been one of theirs. Our subsidiary were experts in special steels and I learned all about them and a lot about the aircraft industry. Our most exacting customers. That's when I first heard about Columbite. Worth diamonds in those days. Then I joined the party and almost immediately we were at war. A wonderful time. I was twenty-eight and a lieutenant in the 140th Panzer Regiment. And we ran through the British Army in France like a knife through butter. Intoxicating.'

For a moment Drax puffed luxuriously at his cigar and Bond guessed that he was seeing the burning villages of Belgium in the smoke.

'Those were great days, my dear Bond.' Drax reached out a long arm and tapped the ash of his cigar off on to the floor. 'But then I was picked out for the Brandenburg Division and I had to leave the girls and the champagne and go back to Germany and start training for the big water-jump to England. My English was needed in the Division. We were all going to be in English uniforms. It would have been fun, but the damned generals said it couldn't be done and I was transferred to the Foreign Intelligence Service of the SS. The RSHA it was called, and SS *Obergruppenführer* Kaltenbrunner had just taken over the command after Heydrich was assassinated in '42. He was a good man and I was under the direct orders of a still better one, *Obersturmbannführer*,' he rolled out the delicious title with relish, 'Otto Skorzeny. His job in the RSHA was terrorism and sabotage. A pleasant interlude, my dear Bond, during which I was able to bring many an Englishman to book which,' Drax beamed coldly at Bond, 'gave me much pleasure. But then,' Drax's fist crashed down on the desk, 'Hitler was betrayed again by those swinish generals and the English and Americans were allowed to land in France.'

'Too bad,' said Bond drily.

'Yes, my dear Bond, it was indeed too bad.' Drax chose to ignore the irony. 'But for me it was the high-spot of the whole war. Skorzeny turned all his saboteurs and terrorists into *SS Jagdverbände* for use behind the enemy lines. Each *Jagdverband* was divided into *Streifkorps* and then into *Kommandos*, each carrying the names of its commanding officer. With the rank of *Oberleutnant*,' Drax swelled visibly, 'at the head of *Kommando* "Drache" I went right through the American lines with the famous 150 Panzer Brigade in the Ardennes breakthrough in December '44. No doubt you will remember the effect of this Brigade in its American uniforms and with its captured American tanks and vehicles. *Kolossal!* When the Brigade had to withdraw I stayed where I was and went to ground in the Forests of Ardennes, fifty miles behind the Allied lines. There were twenty of us, ten good men and ten Hitlerjugend Werewolves. In their teens, but good lads all of them. And, by a coincidence, in charge of them was a young man called Krebs who turned out to have certain gifts which qualified him for the post of executioner and "persuader" to our merry little band.' Drax chuckled pleasantly.

Bond licked his lips as he remembered the crack Krebs's head had made against the dressing-table. Had he kicked him as hard as he possibly could? Yes, his memory reassured him, with every ounce of strength he could put into his shoe.

'We stayed in those woods for six months,' continued Drax proudly, 'and all the time we reported back to the Fatherland by radio. The location vans never spotted us. Then one day disaster came.' Drax shook his head at the memory. 'There was a big farmhouse a mile away from our hideout in the forest. A lot of Nissen huts had been built round it and it was used as a rear headquarters for some sort of liaison group. English and Americans. A hopeless place. No discipline, no security, and full of hangers-on and shirkers from all over the place. We had kept an eye on it for some time and one day I decided to blow it up. It was a simple plan. In the evening, two of my men, one in American uniform and one in British, were to drive up in a captured scout car containing two tons of explosive. There was a car park – no sentries of course – near the mess hall and they were to run the car in as close to the mess hall as possible, time the fuse for the seven o'clock dinner hour, and then get away. All quite easy and I went off that morning on my own business and left the job to my second in command. I was dressed in the uniform of your Signal Corps and I set off on a captured British motor-cycle to shoot a dispatch rider from the same unit who made a daily run along a nearby road. Sure enough he came along dead on time and I went after him out of a side road. I caught up with him,' said Drax conversationally, 'and shot him in the back, took his papers and put him on top of his machine in the woods and set fire to him.'

Drax saw the fury in Bond's eyes and held up his hand. 'Not very sporting? My dear chap, the man was already dead. However, to continue. I went on my way and then what should happen? One of our own planes coming back from a reconnaissance came after me down the road with his cannon. One of our own planes! Blasted me right off the road. God knows how long I lay in the ditch. Some time in the afternoon I came to for a bit and had the sense to hide my cap and jacket and the dispatches. In the hedge. They're probably still there. I must go and collect them one day. Interesting souvenirs. Then

I set fire to the remains of the motorcycle and I must have fainted again because the next thing I knew I had been picked up by a British vehicle and we were driving into that damned liaison headquarters! Believe it or not! And there was the scout car, right up alongside the mess hall! It was too much for me. I was full of shell splinters and my leg was broken. Well, I fainted and when I came round there was half the hospital on top of me and I only had half a face.' He put up his hand and stroked the shiny skin on his left temple and cheek. 'After that it was just a question of acting a part. They had no idea who I was. The car that had picked me up had gone or been blown to pieces. I was just an Englishman in an English shirt and trousers who was nearly dead.'

Drax paused and took out another cigar and lit it. There was silence in the room save for the soft diminished roar of the blowtorch. Its threatening voice was quieter. Pressure running out, reflected Bond.

He turned his head and looked at Gala. For the first time he saw the ugly bruise behind her left ear. He gave her a smile of encouragement and she smiled wryly back.

Drax spoke through the cigar smoke: 'There is not much more to tell,' he said. 'During the year that I was being pushed from one hospital to the next I made my plans down to the smallest detail. They consisted quite simply of revenge on England for what she had done to me and to my country. It gradually became an obsession, I admit it. Every day during the year of the rape and destruction of my country, my hatred and scorn for the English grew more bitter.' The veins on Drax's face started to swell and suddenly he pounded on the desk and shouted across at them, looking with bulging eyes from one to the other. 'I loathe and despise you all. You swine! Useless, idle, decadent fools, hiding behind your bloody white cliffs while other people fight your battles. Too weak to defend your colonies, toadying to America with your hats in your hands. Stinking snobs who'll do anything for money. Hah!' he was triumphant. 'I knew that all I needed was money and the façade of a gentleman. Gentleman! *Pfui Teufel!* To me a gentleman is just someone I can take advantage of. Those bloody fools in Blades for instance. Moneyed oafs. For months I took thousands of pounds off them, swindled them right under their noses until you came along and upset the apple-cart.'

Drax's eyes narrowed. 'What put you on to the cigarette case?' he asked sharply.

Bond shrugged his shoulders. 'My eyes,' he said indifferently.

'Ah well,' said Drax, 'perhaps I was a bit careless that night. But where was I? Ah yes, in hospital. And the good doctors were so anxious to help me find out who I really was.' He let out a roar of laughter. 'It was easy. So easy.' His eyes became cunning. 'From the identities they offered me so helpfully I came upon the name of Hugo Drax. What a coincidence! From Drache to Drax! Tentatively I thought it *might* be me. They were very proud. Yes, they said, *of course* it is you. The doctors triumphantly forced me into his shoes. I put them on and walked out of the hospital in them and I walked round London looking for someone to kill and rob. And one day, in a little office high above Piccadilly, a Jewish moneylender.' (Now Drax was talking faster. The words poured excitedly from his lips. Bond watched a fleck of foam gather at one corner of his mouth and grow.) 'Ha. It was easy. Crack on his bald skull. £15,000 in the safe. And then away and out of the country, Tangier – where you could do anything, buy anything, fix anything. Columbite. Rarer than platinum and everyone would want it. The Jet Age. I knew about these things. I had not forgotten my own profession. And then by God I worked. For five years I lived for money. And I was brave as a lion. I took terrible risks. And suddenly the first million was there. Then the second. Then the fifth. Then the twentieth. I came back to England. I spent a million of it and London was in my pocket. And then I went back to Germany. I found Krebs. I found fifty of them. Loyal Germans. Brilliant technicians. All living under false names like so many others of my old comrades. I gave them their orders and they waited, peacefully, innocently. And where was I?' Drax stared across at Bond, his eyes wide. 'I was in Moscow. Moscow! A man with Columbite to sell can go anywhere. I got to the right people. They listened to my plans. They gave me Walter, the new genius of their guided missile station at Peenemunde, and the good Russians started to build the atomic warhead,' he gestured up to the ceiling, 'that is now waiting up there.

Then I came back to London.' A pause. 'The Coronation. My letter to the Palace. Triumph. Hooray for Drax,' he burst into a roar of laughter. 'England at my feet. Every bloody fool in the country! And then my men come over and we start. Under the very skirts of Britannia. On top of her famous cliffs. We work like devils. We built a jetty into your English Channel. For supplies! For supplies from my good friends the Russians that came in dead on time last Monday night. But then Tallon had to hear something. The old fool. He talks to the Ministry. But Krebs is listening. There were fifty volunteers to kill the man. Lots are drawn and Bartsch dies a hero's death.' Drax paused. 'He will not be forgotten.' Then he went on. 'The new warhead is hoisted into place. It fits. A perfect piece of design. The same weight. Everything perfect, and the old one, the tin can full of the Ministry's cherished instruments, is now in Stettin – behind the Iron Curtain. And the faithful submarine is on her way back here and will soon,' he looked at his watch, 'be creeping under the waters of the English Channel to take us all off at one minute past midday tomorrow.'

Drax wiped his mouth with the back of his hand and lay back in his chair gazing up at the ceiling, his eyes full of visions. Suddenly he chuckled and squinted quizzically down his nose at Bond.

'And do you know what we shall do first when we go on board? We shall shave off those famous moustaches you were so interested in. You smelt a mouse, my dear Bond, where you ought to have smelt a rat. Those shaven heads and those moustaches we all cultivated so assiduously. Just a precaution, my dear fellow. Try shaving your own head and growing a big black moustache. Even your mother wouldn't recognize you. It's the combination that counts. Just a tiny refinement. Precision, my dear fellow. Precision in every detail. That has been my watchword.' He chuckled fatly and puffed away at his cigar.

Suddenly he looked sharply, suspiciously up at Bond. 'Well. Say something. Don't sit there like a dummy. What do you think of my story? Don't you think it's extraordinary, remarkable? For one man to have done all that? Come on, come on.' A hand came up to his mouth and he started tearing furiously at his nails. Then it was plunged back into his pocket and his eyes became cruel and cold. 'Or do you want me to have to send for Krebs,' he made a gesture towards the house telephone on his desk. 'The Persuader. Poor Krebs. He's like a child who's had his toys taken away from him. Or perhaps Walter. He would give you both something to remember. There's no softness in that one. Well?'

'Yes,' said Bond. He looked levelly at the great red face across the desk. 'It's a remarkable case-history. Galloping paranoia. Delusions of jealousy and persecution. Megalomaniac hatred and desire for revenge. Curiously enough,' he went on conversationally, 'it may have something to do with your teeth. Diastema, they call it. Comes from sucking your thumb when you're a child. Yes. I expect that's what the psychologists will say when they get you into the lunatic asylum. "Ogre's teeth." Being bullied at school and so on. Extraordinary the effect it has on a child. Then Nazism helped to fan the flames and then came the crack on your ugly head. The crack you engineered yourself. I expect that settled it. From then on you were really mad. Same sort of thing as people who think they're God. Extraordinary what tenacity they have. Absolute fanatics. You're almost a genius. Lombroso would have been delighted with you. As it is you're just a mad dog that'll have to be shot. Or else you'll commit suicide. Paranoiacs generally do. Too bad. Sad business.'

Bond paused and put all the scorn he could summon into his voice. 'And now let's get on with this farce, you great hairy-faced lunatic.'

It worked. With every word Drax's face had become more contorted with rage, his eyes were red with it, the sweat of fury was dripping off his jowls on to his shirt, the lips were drawn back from the gaping teeth and a string of saliva had crept out of his mouth and was hanging down from his chin. Now, at the last private-school insult that must have awoken God knows what stinging memories, he leapt up from his chair and lunged round the desk at Bond, his hairy fists flailing.

Bond gritted his teeth and took it.

When Drax had twice had to pick the chair up with Bond in it, the tornado of rage suddenly passed. He took out his silk handkerchief and wiped his face and hands. Then he walked quietly to the door and spoke across the lolling head of Bond to the girl.

'I don't think you two will give me any more trouble,' he said, and his voice was quite calm and certain. 'Krebs never makes a mistake with his knots.' He gesticulated towards the bloody figure in the other chair. 'When he wakes up,' he said, 'you can tell him that these doors will open once more, just before noon tomorrow. A few minutes later there will be nothing left of either of you. Not even,' he added as he wrenched open the inner door, 'the stoppings in your teeth.' The outer door slammed.

Bond slowly raised his head and grinned painfully at the girl with his bloodstained lips.

'Had to get him mad,' he said with difficulty. 'Didn't want to give him time to think. Had to work up a brainstorm.' Gala looked at him uncomprehendingly, her eyes wide at the terrible mask of his face.

''S'all right,' said Bond thickly. 'Don't worry. London's okay. Got a plan.'

Over on the desk the blowtorch gave a quiet 'plop' and went out.

23 Zero Minus

Through half-closed eyes Bond looked intently at the torch while for a few precious seconds he sat and let life creep back into his body. His head felt as if it had been used as a football, but there was nothing broken. Drax had hit him unscientifically and with the welter of blows of a drunken man.

Gala watched him anxiously. The eyes in the bloody face were almost shut, but the line of the jaw was taut with concentration and she could feel the effort of will he was making.

He gave his head a shake and when he turned towards her she could see that his eyes were feverish with triumph.

He nodded towards the desk. 'The lighter,' he said urgently. 'I had to try and make him forget it. Follow me. I'll show you.' He started to rock the light steel chair inch by inch towards the desk. 'For God's sake don't tip over or we've had it. But make it fast or the blowlamp'll get cold.'

Uncomprehendingly, and feeling almost as if they were playing some ghastly children's game, Gala carefully rocked her way across the floor in his wake.

Seconds later Bond told her to stop beside the desk while he went rocking on round to Drax's chair. Then he manoeuvred himself into position opposite his target and with a sudden lurch heaved himself and the chair forward so that his head came down.

There was a painful crack as the Ronson desk lighter connected with his teeth, but his lips held it and the top of it was in his mouth as he heaved the chair back with just enough force to prevent it spilling over. Then he started his patient journey back to where Gala was sitting at the corner of the desk on which Krebs had left the blowlamp.

He rested until his breath was steady again. 'Now we come to the difficult part,' he said grimly. 'While I try to get this torch going, you get your chair round so that your right arm is as close in front of me as possible.'

Obediently she edged herself round while Bond swayed his chair so that it leant against the edge of the desk and allowed his mouth to reach forward and grip the handle of the blowtorch between his teeth.

Then he eased the torch towards him and after minutes of patient work he had the torch and the lighter arranged to his liking at the edge of the desk.

After another rest he bent down, closed the valve of the torch with his teeth, and proceeded to get pressure back by slowly and repeatedly pulling up the plunger with his lips and pressing it back with his chin. His face could feel the warmth in the pre-heater and he could smell the remnants of gas in it. If only it hadn't cooled off too much.

He straightened up.

'Last lap, Gala,' he said, smiling crookedly at her. 'I may have to hurt you a bit. All right?'

'Of course,' said Gala.

'Then here goes,' said Bond, and he bent forward and released the safety valve on the left of the canister.

Then he quickly bent forward over the Ronson, which was standing at right angles and just below the neck of the torch, and with his two front teeth pressed down sharply on the ignition lever.

It was a horrible manoeuvre and though he whipped back his head with the speed of a snake he let out a gasp of pain as the jet of blue fire from the torch seared across his bruised cheek and the bridge of his nose.

But the vaporized paraffin was hissing out its vital tongue of flame and he shook the water out of his streaming eyes and bent his head almost at right angles and again got his teeth to the handle of the blowtorch.

He thought his jaw would break with the weight of the thing and the nerves of his front teeth screamed at him, but he swayed his chair carefully upright away from the desk and then strained his bent neck forward until the tip of blue fire from the torch was biting into the flex that bound Gala's right wrist to the arm of her chair.

He tried desperately to keep the flame steady but the breath rasped through the girl's teeth as the handle shifted between his jaws and the flame of the torch brushed her forearm.

But then it was over. Melted by the fierce heat, the copper strands parted one by one and suddenly Gala's right arm was free and she was reaching to take the torch out of Bond's mouth.

Bond's head fell back on to his shoulders and he twisted his neck luxuriously to get the blood moving in the aching muscles.

Almost before he knew it, Gala was bending over his arms and legs and he too was free.

As he sat still for a moment, his eyes closed, waiting for the life to come back into his body, he suddenly, delightedly felt Gala's soft lips on his mouth.

He opened his eyes. She was standing in front of him, her eyes shining. 'That's for what you did,' she said seriously.

'You're a wonderful girl,' he said simply.

But then, knowing what he was going to have to do, knowing that while she might conceivably survive, he had only another few minutes to live, he closed his eyes so that she should not see the hopelessness in them.

Gala saw the expression on his face and she turned away. She thought it was only exhaustion and the cumulative effect of what his body had suffered, and she suddenly remembered the peroxide in the washroom next to her office.

She went through the communicating door. How extraordinary it was to see her familiar things again. It must be someone else who had sat at that desk and typed letters and powdered her nose. She shrugged her shoulders and went into the little washroom. God what a sight and God how tired she felt! But first she took a wet towel and some peroxide and went back and spent ten minutes attending to the battlefield which was Bond's face.

He sat silent, a hand resting on her waist, and watched her gratefully. Then when she had gone back into her room and he heard her shut the door of the washroom behind her he got up, turned off the still hissing blowtorch, and walked into Drax's shower, stripped and stood for five minutes under the icy water. 'Preparing the corpse!' he reflected ruefully as he surveyed his battered face in the mirror.

He put on his clothes and went back to Drax's desk which he searched methodically. It yielded only one prize, the 'office bottle', a half-full bottle of Haig and Haig. He fetched two glasses and some water and called to Gala.

He heard the door of the washroom open. 'What is it?'

'Whisky.'

'You drink. I'll be ready in a minute.'

Bond looked at the bottle and poured himself three quarters of a toothglass and drank it straight down in two gulps. Then he gingerly lit a blessed cigarette and sat on the edge of the desk and felt the liquor burn down through his stomach into his legs.

He picked up the bottle again and looked at it. Plenty for Gala and a whole full glass for himself before he walked out through the door. Better than nothing. It wouldn't be too bad with that inside him so long as he walked quickly out and shut the doors behind him. No looking back.

Gala came in, a transformed Gala, looking as beautiful as the night he had first seen her, except for the lines of exhaustion under the eyes that the powder could not quite conceal and the angry welts at her wrists and ankles.

Bond gave her a drink and took another one himself and their eyes smiled at each other over the rims of their glasses.

Then Bond stood up.

'Listen, Gala,' he said in a matter-of-fact voice. 'We've got to face it and get it over so I'll make it short and then we'll have another drink.' He heard her catch her breath, but he went on. 'In ten minutes or so I'm going to shut you into Drax's bathroom and put you under the shower and turn it full on.'

'James,' she cried. She stepped close to him. 'Don't go on. I know you're going to say something dreadful. Please stop, James.'

'Come on, Gala,' said Bond roughly. 'What the hell does it matter. It's a bloody miracle we have got the chance.' He moved away from her. He walked to the doors leading out into the shaft.

'And then,' he said, and he held up the precious lighter in his right hand, 'I shall walk out of here and shut the doors and go and light a last cigarette under the tail of the Moonraker.'

'God,' she whispered. 'What are you saying? You're mad.' She looked at him through eyes wide with horror.

'Don't be ridiculous,' said Bond impatiently. 'What the hell is there else to do? The explosion will be so terrific that one won't feel anything. And it's bound to work with all that fuel vapour hanging around. It's me or a million people in London. The warhead won't go off. Atom bombs don't explode like that. It'll be melted probably. There's just a chance you may get away. Most of the explosion will take the line of least resistance through the roof – and down the exhaust pit, if I can work the machinery that opens up the floor.' He smiled. 'Cheer up,' he said, walking over to her and taking one of her hands. 'The boy stood on the burning deck. I've wanted to copy him since I was five.'

Gala pulled her hand away. 'I don't care what you say,' said angrily. 'We've got to think of something else. You don't trust me to have any ideas. You just tell me what you think we've got to do.' She walked over to the wall map and pressed down the switch. 'Of course if we have to use the lighter we have to.' She gazed at the map of the false flight plan, barely seeing it. 'But the idea of you walking in there alone and standing in the middle of all those ghastly fumes from the fuel and calmly flicking that thing and then being blown to dust . . . And anyway, if we have to do it, we'll do it together. I'd rather that than be burnt to death in here. And anyway,' she paused, 'I'd like to go with you. We're in this together.'

Bond's eyes were tender as he walked towards her and put an arm round her waist and hugged her to him. 'Gala, you're a darling,' he said simply. 'And if there's any other way we'll take it. But,' he looked at his watch, 'it's past midnight and we've to decide quickly. At any moment it may occur to Drax to send guards down to see that we're all right, and God knows what time he'll be coming down to set the gyros.'

Gala twisted her body round like a cat. She gazed at him with her mouth open, her face taut with excitement. 'The gyros,' she whispered, 'to set the gyros.' She leant weakly back against the wall, her eyes searching Bond's face. 'Don't you *see*?' her voice was on the edge of hysteria. 'After he's gone, we could alter the gyros back, back to the old flight plan, then the rocket will simply fall into the North Sea where it's supposed to go.'

She stepped away from the wall and seized his shirt in both hands and looked imploringly at him. 'Can't we?' she said. 'Can't we?'

'Do you know the other settings?' asked Bond sharply.

'Of course I do,' she said urgently. 'I've been living with them for a year. We won't have a weather report but we'll just have to chance that. The forecast this morning said we would have the same conditions as today.'

'By God,' said Bond. 'We might do it. If only we can hide somewhere and make Drax think we've escaped. What about the exhaust pit? If I can work the machine to open the floor.'

'It's a straight hundred-foot drop,' said Gala, shaking her head. 'And the walls are polished steel. Just like glass. And there's no rope or anything down here. They cleared everything out of the workshop yesterday. And anyway there are guards on the beach.'

Bond reflected. Then his eyes brightened. 'I've got an idea,' he said. 'But first of all what about the radar, the homing device in London? Won't that pull the rocket off its course and back on to London?'

Gala shook her head. 'It's only got a range of about a hundred miles,' she said. 'The rocket won't even pick up its signal. If it's aimed into the North Sea it will get into the orbit of the transmitter on the raft. There's absolutely nothing wrong with my plans. But where can we hide?'

'One of the ventilator shafts,' said Bond. 'Come on.' He gave a last look round the room. The lighter was in his pocket. That would still be the last resort. There was nothing else they would want. He followed Gala out into the gleaming shaft and made for the instrument panel which controlled the steel cover to the exhaust pit.

After a quick examination he threw over a heavy lever from 'Zu' to 'Auf'. There was a soft hiss from the hydraulic machinery behind the wall and the two semicircles of steel opened beneath the tail of the rocket and slid back into their grooves. He walked over and looked down.

The arcs in the roof above glinted back at him from the polished walls of the wide steel funnel until they curved away out of sight towards the distant hollow boom of the sea.

Bond went back into Drax's office and pulled down the shower curtain in the bathroom. Then Gala and he tore it into strips and tied them together. He made a jagged rent at the end of the last strip so as to give an impression that the escape rope had broken. Then he tied the other end firmly round the pointed tip of one of the Moonraker's three fins and dropped the rest so that it hung down the shaft.

It was not much of a false scent, but it might gain some time.

The big round mouths of the ventilator shafts were spaced about ten yards apart and about four feet off the floor. Bond counted. There were fifty of them. He carefully opened the hinged grating that covered one of them and looked up. Forty feet away there was a faint glimmer from the moonlight outside. He decided that they were tunnelled straight up inside the wall of the site until they turned at right angles towards the gratings in the outside walls.

Bond reached up and ran his hand along the surface. It was unfinished roughcast concrete and he grunted with satisfaction as he felt first one sharp protuberance and then another. They were the jagged ends of the steel rods reinforcing the walls, cut off where the shafts had been bored.

It was going to be a painful business, but there was no doubt they could inch their way up one of these shafts, like mountaineers up a rock chimney, and, in the turn at the top, lie hidden from anything but the sort of painstaking search that would be difficult in the morning with all the officials from London round the site.

Bond knelt down and the girl climbed on to his back and started up.

An hour later, their feet and shoulders bruised and cut, they lay exhausted, squeezed tight in each other's arms, their heads inches away from the circular grating directly above the outside door, and listened to the guards restlessly shifting their feet in the darkness a hundred yards away.

Five o'clock, six, seven.

Slowly the sun came up behind the dome and the seagulls started to call in the cliffs and then suddenly there were the three figures walking towards them in the distance, passed by a fresh platoon of guards doubling, chins up, knees up, to relieve the night watch.

The figures came nearer and the squinting, exhausted eyes of the hidden couple could see every detail of Drax's blood-orange face, the lean, pale foxiness of Dr Walter, the suety, overslept puffiness of Krebs.

The three men walked like executioners, saying nothing. Drax took out his key and they silently filed through the door a few feet below the taut bodies of Bond and Gala.

Then for ten minutes there was silence except for the occasional boom of voices up the ventilator shaft as the three men moved about down on the steel floor round the exhaust pit. Bond smiled to himself at the thought of the rage and consternation on Drax's face; the miserable Krebs wilting under the lash of Drax's tongue; the bitter accusation in Walter's eyes. Then the door burst open beneath him and Krebs was calling urgently to the leader of the guards. A man detached himself from the semicircle and ran up.

'*Die Engländer*,' Kreb's voice was almost hysterical. 'Escaped. The *Herr Kapitän* thinks they may be in one of the ventilator shafts. We are going to take a chance. The dome will be opened again and we will clear out the fumes from the fuel. And then the *Herr Doktor* will put the steam hose up each shaft. If they're there it will finish them. Choose four men. The rubber gloves and firesuits are down there. We'll take the pressure off the heating. Tell the others to listen for the screams. *Verstanden?*'

'*Zu Befehl!*' The man doubled smartly back to his troop and Krebs, the sweat of anxiety on his face, turned and disappeared back through the door.

For a moment Bond lay motionless.

There was a heavy rumble above their heads as the dome divided and swung open.

The steam hose!

He had heard of mutinies in ships being fought with it. Rioters in factories. Would it reach forty feet? Would the pressure last? How many boilers fed the heating? Among the fifty ventilator shafts, where would they choose to begin? Had Bond or Gala left any clue to the one they had climbed?

He felt that Gala was waiting for him to explain. To do something. To protect them.

Five men came doubling from the semicircle of guards. They passed underneath and disappeared.

Bond put his mouth to Gala's ear. 'This may hurt,' he said. 'Can't say how much. Can't be helped. Just have to take it. No noise.' He felt the answering tentative pressure from her arms. 'Bring your knees up. Don't be shy. This is no time to be maidenly.'

'Shut up,' whispered Gala angrily. He felt one knee creep up until it was locked between his thighs. His own knee followed suit until it would go no further. She squirmed furiously. 'Don't be a bloody fool,' whispered Bond, pulling her head in close to his chest so that it was half covered by his open shirt.

He overlay her as much as possible. There was nothing to be done about their ankles or his hands. He pulled his shirt collar up as far over their heads as possible. They held tightly to each other.

Hot, cramped, breathless. Waiting, it suddenly occurred to Bond, like two lovers in the undergrowth. Waiting for the footsteps to go by so that they could start again. He smiled grimly to himself and listened.

There was silence down the shaft. They must be in the engine room. Walter would be watching the hose being coupled to the outlet valve. Now there were distant noises. Where would they start?

Somewhere, not far away, there was a soft, long-drawn-out whisper, like the inefficient whistle of a distant train.

He drew his shirt collar back and stole a look out through the grating at the guards. Those he could see were looking straight at the launching-dome, somewhere to his left.

Again the long harsh whisper. And again.

It was getting louder. He could see the heads of the guards pivoting towards the grating in the wall which hid him and Gala. They must be watching, fascinated, as the thick white jets of steam shot out through the gratings high up in the cement wall, wondering if this one, or that one, or that one, would be accompanied by a double scream.

He could feel Gala's heart beating against his. She didn't know what was coming. She trusted him.

'It may hurt,' he whispered to her again. 'It may burn. It won't kill us. Be brave. Don't make a sound.'

'I'm all right,' she whispered angrily. But he could feel her body press closer in to his.

Whoosh. It was getting closer.

Whoosh! Two away.

WHOOSH!! Next door. A suspicion of the wet smell of steam came to him.

Hold tight, Bond said to himself. He smothered her in towards him and held his breath.

Now. Quick. Get it over, damn you.

And suddenly there was a great pressure and heat and a roaring in the ears and a moment of blazing pain.

Then dead silence, a mixture of sharp cold and fire on the ankles and hands, a feeling of soaking wet and a desperate, choking effort to get pure air into the lungs.

Their bodies automatically fought to withdraw from each other, to capture some inches of space and air for the areas of skin that were already blistering. The breath rattled in their throats and the water poured off the cement into their open mouths until they bent sideways and choked the water out to join the trickle that was oozing under their soaking bodies and along past their scalded ankles and then down the vertical walls of the shaft up which they had come.

And the howl of the steam pipe drew away from them until it became a whisper and finally stopped, and there was silence in their narrow cement prison except for their stubborn breathing and the ticking of Bond's watch.

And the two bodies lay and waited, nursing their pain.

Half an hour – half a year – later, Walter and Krebs and Drax filed out below them.

But, as a precaution, the guards had been left behind in the launching dome.

24 Zero

'Then we're all agreed?'

'Yes, Sir Hugo,' it was the Minister of Supply speaking. Bond recognized the dapper, assured figure. 'Those are the settings. My people have checked them independently with the Air Ministry this morning.'

'Then if you'll allow me the privilage,' Drax held up the slip of paper and made to turn towards the launching-dome.

'Hold it, Sir Hugo. Just like that, please. Arm in the air.' The bulbs flashed and the bank of cameras whirred and clicked for the last time and Drax turned and walked the few yards towards the dome, almost, it seemed to Bond, looking him straight in the eye through the grating above the door of the site.

The small crowd of reporters and cameramen dissolved and straggled off across the concrete apron, leaving only a nervously chatting group of officials to wait for Drax to emerge.

Bond looked at his watch. 11.45. Hurry up, damn you, he thought.

For the hundredth time he repeated to himself the figures Gala had taught him during the hours of cramped pain that had followed their ordeal by steam, and for the hundredth time he shifted his limbs to keep the circulation going.

'Get ready,' he whispered into Gala's ear. 'Are you all right?'

He could feel the girl smile. 'Fine.' She shut her mind to the thought of her blistered legs and the quick rasping descent back down the ventilator shaft.

The door clanged shut beneath them followed by the click of the lock and, preceded by the five guards, the figure of Drax appeared below striding masterfully towards the group of officials, the slip of lying figures in his hand.

Bond looked at his watch. 11.47. 'Now,' he whispered.

'Good luck,' she whispered back.

Slither, scrape, rip. His shoulders carefully expanding and contracting; blistered, bloodstained feet scrabbling for the sharp knobs of iron, Bond, his lacerated body tearing its way down the forty feet of shaft, prayed that the girl would have strength to stand it when she followed.

A last ten-foot drop that jarred his spine, a kick at the grating and he was out on the steel floor and running for the stairs, leaving a trail of red footprints and a spray of blood-drops from his raw shoulders.

The arcs had been extinguished, but the daylight streamed down through the open roof and the blue from the sky mingling with the fierce glitter of the sunshine gave Bond the impression that he was running up inside a huge sapphire.

The great deadly needle in the centre might have been made of glass. Looking above him as he sweated and panted up the endless sweep of the iron stairway, it was difficult for him to see where its tapering nose ended and the sky began.

Behind the crouching silence that enveloped the shimmering bullet, Bond could hear a quick, deadly ticking, the hasty tripping of tiny metal feet somewhere in the body of the Moonraker. It filled the great steel chamber like the beating heart in Poe's story and Bond knew that directly Drax at the firing point pressed the switch that sent the radio beam zinging over two hundred yards to the waiting rocket, the ticking would suddenly cease, there would be the soft whine of the lighted pinwheel, a wisp of steam from the turbines, and then the howling jet of flame on which the rocket would slowly rise and sweep majestically out on the start of its gigantic acceleration curve.

And then in front of him there was the spidery arm of the gantry folded back against the wall and Bond's hand was at the lever and the arm was slowly stretching down and out towards the square hairline on the glittering skin of the rocket that was the door of the gyro chamber.

Bond, on hands and knees, was along it even before the rubber pads came to rest against the polished chrome. There was the flush disc the size of a shilling, just as Gala had described. Press, click, and the tiny door had flicked open on its hard spring. Inside. Careful not to cut your head. The gleaming handles beneath the staring compass-roses. Turn. Twist. Steady. That's for the roll. Now the pitch and yaw. Turn. Twist. Ever so gently. And steady. A last look. A glance at his watch. Four minutes to go. Don't panic. Back out. Door click. A cat-like scurry. Don't look down. Gantry up. Clang against the wall. And now for the stairs.

Tick-tick-tick-tick.

As Bond shot down he caught a glimpse of Gala's tense, white face as she stood holding open the outer door of Drax's office. God, how his body hurt! A final leap and a clumsy swerve to the right. Clang as Gala slammed the outer door. Another clang and they were across the room and into the shower and the water was hissing down on their clinging, panting bodies.

Through the noise of it all, above the beating of his heart, Bond heard the sudden crackle of static and then the voice of the BBC announcer coming from the big set in Drax's room a few inches away through the thin wall of the bathroom. It had been Gala again who had remembered Drax's wireless and who had found time to throw the switches while Bond was working on the gyros.

'. . . be five minutes' delay,' said the breezy, excited voice. 'Sir Hugo has been persuaded to say a few words into the microphone.' Bond turned off the shower and the voice came to them more clearly. 'He looks very confident. Just saying something into the Minister's ear. They're both laughing. Wonder what it was? Ah, here's my colleague with the latest weather report from the Air Ministry. What's that? Perfect at all altitudes. Good show. It certainly is a wonderful day down below here. Haha. Those crowds in the distance by the coast-guard station will be getting quite a sunburn. There must be thousands. What's that you say? Twenty thousand? Well, it certainly looks like it. And Walmer Beach is black with them too. The whole of Kent seems to be out. Terrible crick in the neck we're all going to get, I'm afraid. Worse than Wimbledon. Haha. Hullo, what's going on down there by the jetty? By jove, there's a submarine just surfaced alongside. I say, what a sight. One of our biggest I should say. And Sir Hugo's team is down there too. Lined up on the jetty as if they were on parade. Magnificent body of men. Now they're filing on board. Perfect discipline. Must be an idea of the Admiralty's. Give them a special grandstand out in the Channel. Splendid show. Wish you could be here to see it. Now Sir Hugo is coming towards us. In a moment he'll be speaking to you. Fine figure of a man. Everyone in the firing point is giving him a cheer. I'm sure we all feel like cheering him today. He's coming into the firing point. I can see the sun glinting on the nose of the Moonraker way over there behind him. Just showing out of the top of the launching-dome. Hope somebody's got a camera. Now here he is,' a pause. 'Sir Hugo Drax.'

Bond looked into Gala's dripping face. Soaked and bleeding they stood in each other's arms, speechless and trembling slightly with the storm of their emotions. Their eyes were blank and fathomless as they met and held each other's gaze.

'Your majesty, men and women of England,' the voice was a velvet snarl. 'I am about to change the course of England's history.' A pause. 'In a few minutes' time the lives of all of you will be altered, in some cases, ahem, drastically, by the, er, impact of the Moonraker. I am very proud and pleased that fate has singled me out, from amongst all my fellow countrymen, to fire this great arrow of vengeance into the skies and thus to proclaim for all time, and for all the world to witness, the might of my fatherland. I hope that this occasion will be forever a warning that the fate of my country's enemies will be written in dust, in ashes, in tears, and,' a pause, 'in blood. And now thank you all for listening and I sincerely hope that those of you who are able will repeat my words to your children, if you have any, tonight.'

A rattle of rather hesitant applause sounded out of the machine and then came the breezy voice of the announcer. 'And that was Sir Hugo Drax saying a few words to you before he walks across the floor of the firing point to the switch on the wall which will fire the Moonraker. The first time he has spoken in public. Very, ahem, forthright. Doesn't mince his words. However, a lot of us will say there's no harm in that. And now it's time for me to hand over to the expert, Group Captain Tandy of the Ministry of Supply, who will describe to you the actual firing of the Moonraker. After that you will hear Peter Trimble in one of the naval security patrol, HMS *Merganzer*, describe the scene in the target area. Group Captain Tandy.'

Bond glanced at his watch. 'Only a minute more,' he said to Gala. 'God, I'd like to get my hands on Drax. Here,' he reached for the cake of soap and gouged some pieces off it. 'Stuff this in your ears when the time comes. The noise is going to be terrific, I don't know about the heat. It won't last long and the steel walls may stand up to it.'

Gala looked at him. She smiled. 'If you hold me it won't be too bad,' she said.

'. . . and now Sir Hugo has his hand on the switch and he's watching the chronometer.'

'TEN,' broke in another voice, heavy and sonorous as the toll of a bell.

Bond turned on the shower and the water hissed down on their clinging bodies.

'NINE,' tolled the voice of the time-keeper.

'. . . the radar operators are watching the screens. Nothing but a mass of wavy lines . . .'

'EIGHT.'

'. . . all wearing ear-plugs. Blockhouse should be indestructible. Concrete walls are twelve feet thick. Pyramid roof, twenty-seven feet thick at the point . . .'

'SEVEN.'

'. . . first the radio beam will stop the time mechanism alongside the turbines. Set the pinwheel going. Flaming thing like a catherine wheel . . .'

'SIX.'

'. . . valves will open. Liquid fuel. Secret formula. Terrific stuff. Dynamite. Pours down from the fuel tanks . . .'

'FIVE.'

'. . . ignited by the pinwheel when the fuel gets to the rocket motor . . .'

'FOUR.'

'. . . meanwhile the peroxide and permanganate have mixed, made steam and the turbine pumps begin to turn . . .'

'THREE.'

'. . . pumping the flaming fuel through the motor out of the stern of the rocket into the exhaust pit. Gigantic heat . . . 3500 degrees . . .'

'TWO.'

'. . . Sir Hugo is about to press the switch. He's staring out through the slit. Perspiration on his forehead. Absolute silence in here. Terrific tension.'

'ONE.'

Nothing but the noise of the water, steadily pouring down on the two clinging bodies.

FIRE!

Bond's heart jumped into his throat at the shout. He felt Gala shudder. Silence. Nothing but the hissing of the water . . .

'. . . Sir Hugo's left the firing point. Walking calmly over to the edge of the cliff. So confident. He's stepped on to the hoist. He's going down. Of course. He must be going out to the submarine. Television screen shows a little steam coming out of the tail of the rocket. A few more seconds. Yes, he's out on the jetty. He looked back and raised his arm in the air. Good old Sir Hu . . .'

A soft thunder came to Bond and Gala. Louder. Louder. The tiled floor began to tremble under their feet. A hurricane scream. They were being pulverized by it. The walls were quaking, steaming. Their legs began going out of control under their teetering bodies. Hold her up. Hold her up. Stop it! Stop it!! STOP THAT NOISE!!!

Christ, he was going to faint. The water was boiling. Must turn it off. Got it. No. Pipe's burst. Steam, smell, iron, paint.

Get her out! Get her out!! Get her out!!!

And then there was silence. Silence you could feel, hold, squeeze. And they were on the floor of Drax's office. Only the light in the bathroom still shining out. And the smoke's clearing. And the filthy smell of burning iron and paint. Being sucked out by the air-conditioner. And the steel wall is bent towards them like a huge blister. Gala's eyes are open and she's smiling. But the rocket. What happened?

London? North Sea? The radio. Looks all right. He shook his head and the deafness slowly cleared. He remembered the soap. Gouged it out.

'. . . through the sound barrier. Travelling perfectly right in the centre of the radar screen. A perfect launching. Afraid you couldn't hear anything because of the noise. Terrific. First of all the great sheet of flame coming out of the cliff from the exhaust pit and then you should have seen the nose slowly creep up out of the dome. And there she was like a great silver pencil. Standing upright on this huge column of flame and slowly climbing into the air and the flame splashing for hundreds of yards over the concrete. The howl of the thing must have nearly burst our microphones. Great bits have fallen off the cliff and the concrete looks like a spider's web. Terrible vibration. And then she was climbing faster and faster. A hundred miles an hour. A thousand. And,' he broke off, 'what's that you say? Really! And now she's travelling at over ten thousand miles an hour! She's three hundred miles up. Can't hear her any more, of course. We could only see her flame for a few seconds. Like a star. Sir Hugo must be a proud man. He's out there in the Channel now. The submarine went off like a rocket, haha, must be doing more than thirty knots. Throwing up a huge wake. Off the East Goodwins now. Travelling north. She'll soon be up with the patrol ships. They'll have a view of the launching and of the landing. Quite a surprise trip that. No one here had an inkling. Even the naval authorities seem a bit mystified. C-in-C Nore has been on the telephone. But now that's all I can tell you from here and I'll hand you over to Peter Trimble on board HMS *Merganzer* somewhere off the East Coast.'

Nothing but the pumping lungs showed that the two limp bodies in the creeping pool of water on the floor were still alive, but their battered ear-drums were desperately clinging to the crackle of static that came briefly from the blistered metal cabinet. Now for the verdict on their work.

'And this is Peter Trimble speaking. It's a beautiful morning, I mean – er – afternoon here. Just north of the Goodwin Sands. Calm as a millpond. No wind. Bright sunshine. And the target area is reported clear of shipping. Is that right, Commander Edwards? Yes, the Captain says it's quite clear. Nothing on the radar screens yet. I'm not allowed to tell you the range we shall pick her up at. Security and all that. But we shall only catch the rocket for a split second. Isn't that right, Captain? But the target's just showing on the screen. Out of sight from the bridge, of course. Must be seventy miles north of here. We could see the Moonraker going up. Terrific sight. Noise like thunder. Long flame coming out of the tail. Must have been ten miles away but you couldn't miss the light. Yes, Captain? Oh yes, I see. Well, that's very interesting. Big submarine coming up fast. Only about a mile away. Suppose it's the one they say Sir Hugo's aboard with his men. None of us here were told anything about her. Captain Edwards says she doesn't answer the Aldis lamp. Not flying colours. Very mysterious. I've got her now. Quite clear in my glasses. We've changed course to intercept her. Captain says she isn't one of ours. Thinks she must be a foreigner. Hullo! She's broken out her colours. *What's* that? Good heavens. The Captain says she's a Russian. I say! And now she's hauled down her colours and she's submerging. Bang. Did you hear that? We fired a shot across her bows. But she's disappeared. What's that? The asdic operator says she's going even faster under water. Twenty-five knots. Terrific. Well, she can't see much under water. But she's right in the target area now. Twelve minutes past noon. The Moonraker must have turned and be on her way down. A thousand miles up. Coming down at ten thousand miles an hour. She'll be here any second now. Hope there's not going to be a tragedy. The Russian's well inside the danger zone. The radar operator's holding up his hand. That means she's due. She's coming. She's COMING . . . Whew! Not even a whisper. GOD! What's that? Look out! Look out! Terrific explosion. Black cloud going up into the air. There's a tidal wave coming at us. Great wall of water tearing down. There goes the submarine. God! Thrown out of the water upside down. It's coming. It's COMING . . .'

25 *Zero Plus*

'. . . Two hundred dead so far and about the same number missing,' said M. 'Reports still coming in from the East Coast and there's bad news from Holland. Breached miles of their sea defences. Most of our losses were among the patrol craft. Two of them capsized, including the *Merganzer*. Commanding Officer missing. And that BBC chap. Goodwin Lightships broke their moorings. No news from Belgium or France yet. There are going to be some pretty heavy bills to pay when everything gets sorted out.'

It was the next afternoon and Bond, a rubber-tipped stick beside his chair, was back where he had started – across the desk from the quiet man with the cold grey eyes who had invited him to dinner and a game of cards a hundred years ago.

Under his clothes Bond was latticed with surgical tape. Pain burned up his legs whenever he moved his feet. There was a vivid red streak across his left cheek and the bridge of his nose, and the tannic ointment dressing glinted in the light from the window. He held a cigarette clumsily in one gloved hand. Incredibly M had invited him to smoke.

'Any news of the submarine, sir?' he asked.

'They've located her,' said M with satisfaction. 'Lying on her side in about thirty fathoms. The salvage ship that was to look after the remains of the rocket is over her now. The divers have been down and there's no answer to signals against her hull. The Soviet Ambassador has been round at the Foreign Office this morning. I gather he says a salvage ship is on her way down from the Baltic, but we've said that we can't wait as the wreck's a danger to navigation.' M chuckled. 'So she would be I dare say if anyone happened to be navigating at thirty fathoms in the Channel. But I'm glad I'm not a member of the Cabinet,' he added drily. 'They've been in session on and off since the end of the broadcast. Vallance got hold of those Edinburgh solicitors before they'd opened Drax's message to the world. I gather it's a terrific document. Reads as if it had been written by Jehovah. Vallance took it to the Cabinet last night and stayed at No. 10 to fill in the blanks.'

'I know,' said Bond. 'He kept on telephoning me at the hospital for details until after midnight. I could hardly think straight for all the dope they'd pushed into me. What's going to happen?'

'They're going to try the biggest cover-up job in history,' said M. 'A lot of scientific twaddle about the fuel having been only half used up. Unexpectedly powerful explosion on impact. Full compensation will be paid. Tragic loss of Sir Hugo Drax and his team. Great patriot. Tragic loss of one of HM submarines. Latest experimental model. Orders misunderstood. Very sad. Fortunately only a skeleton crew. Next of kin will be informed. Tragic loss of BBC man. Unaccountable error in mistaking White Ensign for Soviet naval colours. Very similar design. White Ensign recovered from the wreck.'

'But what about the atomic explosion?' asked Bond. 'Radiation and atomic dust and all that. The famous mushroom-shaped cloud. Surely that's going to be a bit of a problem.'

'Apparently it's not worrying them too much,' said M. 'The cloud is going to be passed off as the normal formation after an explosion of that size. The Ministry of Supply know the whole story. Had to be told. Their men were down on the East Coast all last night with Geiger counters and there's not been a positive report yet.' M smiled coldly. 'The cloud's got to come down somewhere, of course, but by a happy chance such wind as there is is drifting it up north. Back home, as you might say.'

Bond smiled painfully. 'I see,' he said. 'How very appropriate.'

'Of course,' continued M, picking up his pipe and starting to fill it, 'there are going to be some nasty rumours. They've begun already. A lot of people saw you and Miss Brand being brought out of the site on stretchers. Then there's the Bowaters' case against Drax for the loss of all that newsprint. There'll be the inquest on the young man who was killed in the Alfa Romeo. And somebody's got to explain away the remains of your car, amongst which,' he looked accusingly at Bond, 'a long-barrel Colt was found. And then there's the Ministry of Supply. Vallance had to call some of their men yesterday to help clean out that house in Ebury Street. But those people are trained to keep secrets. You won't get a leak there. Naturally it's going to be a risky business. The big lie always is. But what's the alternative? Trouble with

Germany? War with Russia? Lots of people on both sides of the Atlantic would be only too glad of an excuse.'

M paused and put a match to his pipe. 'If the story holds,' he continued reflectively, 'we shan't come out of this too badly. We've wanted one of their high-speed U-boats and we'll be glad of the clues we can pick up about their atom bombs. The Russians know that we know that their gamble failed. Malenkov's none too firmly in the saddle and this may mean another Kremlin revolt. As for the Germans. Well, we all knew there was plenty of Nazism left and this will make the Cabinet go just a bit more carefully on German rearmament. And, as a very minor consequence,' he gave a wry smile, 'it will make Vallance's security job, and mine for the matter of that, just a little bit easier in the future. These politicians can't see that the atomic age has created the most deadly saboteur in the history of the world – the little man with the heavy suitcase.'

'Will the Press wear the story?' asked Bond dubiously.

M shrugged his shoulders. 'The Prime Minister saw the editors this morning,' he said, putting another match to his pipe, 'and I gather he's got away with it so far. If the rumours get bad later on, he'll probably have to see them again and tell them some of the truth. Then they'll play all right. They always do when it's important enough. The main thing is to gain time and stave off the firebrands. For the moment everyone's so proud of the Moonraker that they're not inquiring too closely into what went wrong.'

There was a soft burr from the intercom. on M's desk and a ruby light winked on and off. M picked up the single earphone and leant towards it. 'Yes?' he said. There was a pause. 'I'll take it on the Cabinet line.' He picked up the white receiver from the bank of four telephones.

'Yes,' said M. 'Speaking.' There was a pause. 'Yes, sir? Over.' M pressed down the button of his scrambler. He held the receiver close to his ear and not a sound from it reached Bond. There was a long pause during which M puffed occasionally at the pipe in his left hand. He took it out of his mouth. 'I agree, sir.' Another pause. 'I know my man would have been very proud, sir. But of course it's a rule here.' M frowned. 'If you will allow me to say so, sir, I think it would be very unwise.' A pause, then M's face cleared. 'Thank you, sir. And of course

Vallance has not got the same problem. And it would be the least she deserves.' Another pause. 'I understand. That will be done.' Another pause. 'That's very kind of you, sir.'

M put the white receiver back on its cradle and the scrambler button clicked back to the *en clair* position.

For a moment M continued to look at the telephone as if in doubt about what had been said. Then he twisted his chair away from the desk and gazed thoughtfully out of the window.

There was silence in the room and Bond shifted in his chair to ease the pain that was creeping back into his body.

The same pigeon as on Monday, or perhaps another one, came to rest on the window-sill with the same clatter of wings. It walked up and down, nodding and cooing, and then planed off towards the trees in the park. The traffic murmured sleepily in the distance.

How nearly it had come, thought Bond, to being stilled. How nearly there might be nothing now but the distant clang of the ambulance bells beneath a lurid black and orange sky, the stench of burning, the screams of people still trapped in the buildings. The softly beating heart of London silenced for a generation. And a whole generation of her people dead in the streets amongst the ruins of a civilization that might not rise again for centuries.

All that would have come about but for a man who scornfully cheated at cards to feed the fires of his maniac ego; but for the stuffy chairman of Blades who detected him; but for M who agreed to help an old friend; but for Bond's half-remembered lessons from a card-sharper; but for Vallance's precautions; but for Gala's head for figures; but for a whole pattern of tiny circumstances, a whole pattern of chance.

Whose pattern?

There was a shrill squeak as M's chair swivelled round. Bond carefully focused again on the grey eyes across the desk.

'That was the Prime Minister,' M said gruffly. 'Says he wants you and Miss Brand out of the country.' M lowered his eyes and looked stolidly into the bowl of his pipe. 'You're both to be out by tomorrow afternoon. There are too many people in this case who know your faces. Might put two and two together, when they see the shape you're both in. Go anywhere you like. Unlimited expenses for both of you. Any currency you like. I'll tell the Paymaster. Stay away for a month. But keep out of circulation. You'd both be gone this afternoon only the girl's got an appointment at eleven tomorrow morning. At the Palace. Immediate award of the George Cross. Won't be gazetted until the New Year of course. Like to meet her one day. Must be a good girl. As a matter of fact,' M's expression as he looked up was unreadable, 'the Prime Minister had something in mind for you. Forgotten that we don't go in for those sort of things here. So he asked me to thank you for him. Said some nice things about the Service. Very kind of him.'

M gave one of the rare smiles that lit up his face with quick brightness and warmth. Bond smiled back. They understood the things that had to be left unsaid.

Bond knew it was time to go. He got up. 'Thank you very much, sir,' he said. 'And I'm glad about the girl.'

'All right then,' said M on a note of dismissal. 'Well, that's the lot. See you in a month. Oh and by the way,' he added casually. 'Call in at your office. You'll find something there from me. Little memento.'

James Bond went down in the lift and limped along the familiar corridor to his office. When he walked through the inner door he found his secretary arranging some papers on the next desk to his.

'008 coming back?' he asked.

'Yes,' she smiled happily. 'He's being flown out tonight.'

'Well, I'm glad you'll have company,' said Bond. 'I'm going off again.'

'Oh,' she said. She looked quickly at his face and then away. 'You look as if you needed a bit of a rest.'

'I'm going to get one,' said Bond. 'A month's exile.' He thought of Gala. 'It's going to be pure holiday. Anything for me?'

'Your new car's downstairs. I've inspected it. The man said you'd ordered it on trial this morning. It looks lovely. Oh, and there's a parcel from M's office. Shall I unpack it?'

'Yes, do,' said Bond.

He sat down at his desk and looked at his watch. Five o'clock. He was feeling tired. He knew he was going to feel tired for several days.

He always got these reactions at the end of an ugly assignment, the aftermath of days of taut nerves, tension, fear.

His secretary came back into the room with two heavy-looking cardboard boxes. She put them on his desk and he opened the top one. When he saw the grease-paper he knew what to expect.

There was a card in the box. He took it out and read it. In M's green ink it said: 'You may be needing these.' There was no signature.

Bond unwrapped the grease-paper and cradled the shining new Beretta in his hand. A memento. No. A reminder. He shrugged his shoulders and slipped the gun under his coat into the empty holster. He got clumsily to his feet.

'There'll be a long-barrel Colt in the other box,' he said to his secretary. 'Keep it until I get back. Then I'll take it down to the range and fire it in.'

He walked to the door. 'So long, Lil,' he said, 'regards to 008 and tell him to be careful of you. I'll be in France. Station F will have the address. But only in an emergency.'

She smiled at him. 'How much of an emergency?' she asked.

Bond gave a short laugh. 'Any invitation to a quiet game of bridge,' he said.

He limped out and shut the door behind him.

The 1953 Mark VI had an open touring body. It was battleship grey like the old 4½ litre that had gone to its grave in a Maidstone garage, and the dark blue leather upholstery gave a luxurious hiss as he climbed awkwardly in beside the test driver.

Half an hour later the driver helped him out at the corner of Birdcage Walk and Queen Anne's Gate. 'We could get more speed out of her if you want it, sir,' he said. 'If we could have her back for a fortnight we could tune her to do well over the hundred.'

'Later,' said Bond. 'She's sold. On one condition. That you get her over to the ferry terminal at Calais by tomorrow evening.'

The test driver grinned. 'Roger,' he said. 'I'll take her over myself. See you on the pier, sir.'

'Fine,' said Bond. 'Go easy on A20. The Dover road's a dangerous place these days.'

'Don't worry, sir,' said the driver, thinking that this man must be a bit of a cissy for all that he seemed to know plenty about motor-cars. 'Piece of cake.'

'Not every day,' said Bond with a smile. 'See you at Calais.'

Without waiting for a reply, he limped off with his stick through the dusty bars of evening sunlight that filtered down through the trees in the park.

Bond sat down on one of the seats opposite the island in the lake and took out his cigarette-case and lit a cigarette. He looked at his watch. Five minutes to six. He reminded himself that she was the sort of girl who would be punctual. He had reserved the corner table for dinner. And then? But first there would be the long luxurious planning. What would she like? Where would she like to go? Where had she ever been? Germany, of course. France? Miss out Paris. They could do that on their way back. Get as far as they could the first night, away from the Pas de Calais. There was that farmhouse with the wonderful food between Montreuil and Etaples. Then the fast sweep down to the Loire. The little places near the river for a few days. Not the château towns. Places like Beaugency, for instance. Then slowly south, always keeping to the western roads, avoiding the five-star life. Slowly exploring. Bond pulled himself up. Exploring what? Each other? Was he getting serious about this girl?

'James.'

It was a clear, high, rather nervous voice. Not the voice he had expected.

He looked up. She was standing a few feet away from him. He noticed that she was wearing a black beret at a rakish angle and that she looked exciting and mysterious like someone you see driving by abroad, alone in an open car, someone unattainable and more desirable than anyone you have ever known. Someone who is on her way to make love to somebody else. Someone who is not for you.

He got up and they took each other's hands.

It was she who released herself. She didn't sit down.

'I wish you were going to be there tomorrow, James.' Her eyes were soft as she looked at him. Soft, but, he thought, somehow evasive.

He smiled. 'Tomorrow morning or tomorrow night?'

'Don't be ridiculous,' she laughed, blushing. 'I meant at the Palace.'

'What are you going to do afterwards?' asked Bond.

She looked at him carefully. What did the look remind him of? The Morphy look? The look he had given Drax on that last hand at Blades? No. Not quite. There was something else there. Tenderness? Regret?

She looked over his shoulder.

Bond turned round. A hundred yards away there was the tall figure of a young man with fair hair trimmed short. His back was towards them and he was idling along, killing time.

Bond turned back and Gala's eyes met his squarely.

'I'm going to marry that man,' she said quietly. 'Tomorrow afternoon.' And then, as if no other explanation was needed, 'His name's Detective-Inspector Vivian.'

'Oh,' said Bond. He smiled stiffly. 'I see.'

There was a moment of silence during which their eyes slid away from each other.

And yet why should he have expected anything else? A kiss. The contact of two frightened bodies clinging together in the midst of danger. There had been nothing more. And there had been the engagement ring to tell him. Why had he automatically assumed that it had only been worn to keep Drax at bay? Why had he imagined that she shared his desires, his plans?

And now what? wondered Bond. He shrugged his shoulders to shift the pain of failure – the pain of failure that is so much greater than the pleasure of success. The exit line. He must get out of these two young lives and take his cold heart elsewhere. There must be no regrets. No false sentiment. He must play the role which she expected of him. The tough man of the world. The Secret Agent. The man who was only a silhouette.

She was looking at him rather nervously, waiting to be relieved of the stranger who had tried to get his foot in the door of her heart.

Bond smiled warmly at her. 'I'm jealous,' he said. 'I had other plans for you tomorrow night.'

She smiled back at him, grateful that the silence had been broken. 'What were they?' she asked.

'I was going to take you off to a farmhouse in France,' he said. 'And after a wonderful dinner I was going to see if it's true what they say about the scream of a rose.'

She laughed. 'I'm sorry I can't oblige. But there are plenty of others waiting to be picked.'

'Yes, I suppose so,' said Bond. 'Well, goodbye, Gala.' He held out his hand.

'Goodbye, James.'

He touched her for the last time and then they turned away from each other and walked off into their different lives.

PENGUIN MODERN CLASSICS

FROM RUSSIA WITH LOVE, DR NO, GOLDFINGER
IAN FLEMING

'Fleming is splendid; he stops at nothing' *New Statesman*

With the creation of suave secret agent James Bond, Ian Fleming invented one of
the most iconic heroes ever to appear in print or on film. This volume contains
three of the greatest Bond novels, full of the dazzling plots and arch-villains that
made 007 a phenomenon. Here Bond encounters ravishing agent Tatiana
Romanova and fiendish Rosa Klebb in Russia; becomes trapped in Dr No's
tropical lair with beautiful Honey Rider; and confronts ruthless criminal Auric
Goldfinger, whose lethal schemes involve fifteen billion dollars' worth of gold ...

'Possibly the best Ian Fleming thriller ... Rosa Klebb is a female unparalleled for
awfulness. From beginning to end here's magnificent writing' Elizabeth Bowen
on *From Russia with Love*

With an Introduction by Christopher Hitchens

PENGUIN MODERN CLASSICS

ON HER MAJESTY'S SECRET SERVICE
IAN FLEMING

'Fleming is in a class by himself' *Daily Mail*

'If there was one thing that set James Bond really moving, it was being passed at speed by a pretty girl ...'

From the moment he first meets Teresa di Vicenzo – a reckless playgirl with a love of fast cars and danger – Bond is fascinated. She also leads him to new information on one of the most dangerous criminals in the world, Ernst Stavro Blofeld. In his Alpine mountain base, Blofeld is developing weapons that could threaten the whole world. Only 007 – with the help of someone who can handle herself at speed – can stop the evil genius. Filled with ski chases, schnapps and snow-bound lairs, *On Her Majesty's Secret Service* also shows confirmed bachelor Bond's icy reserve finally melting ...

PENGUIN MODERN CLASSICS

A CAPOTE READER
TRUMAN CAPOTE

'Vintage Capote … There is a depth and clarity to his writing that captivates the reader' *Sunday Times*

Truman Capote began writing when he was eight and became one of America's most versatile and gifted authors. *A Capote Reader* contains much of his published work: his dazzling fiction, including *Breakfast at Tiffany's*, as well as his prolific output of short stories, travel sketches in which he evokes places from Tangiers to Brooklyn, portraits of his contemporaries such as Marlon Brando, Marilyn Monroe and Cecil Beaton, and his brilliant reportage and essays. His piece entitled 'The Muses are Heard', which recounts a trip to Communist Europe with the cast of *Porgy and Bess*, shows the chameleon-like talents of a literary legend.

'Demonstrates the unvaryingly high quality of Capote's writing and the exquisite, fairy-tale aspect of his talent' Edmund White

Contemporary ... Provocative ... Outrageous ...
Prophetic ... Groundbreaking ... Funny ... Disturbing ...
Different ... Moving ... Revolutionary ... Inspiring ...
Subversive ... Life-changing ...

What makes a modern classic?

At Penguin Classics our mission has always been to make the best books ever written available to everyone. And that also means constantly redefining and refreshing exactly what makes a 'classic'. That's where Modern Classics come in. Since 1961 they have been an organic, ever-growing and ever-evolving list of books from the last hundred (or so) years that we believe will continue to be read over and over again.

They could be books that have inspired political dissent, such as *Animal Farm*. Some, like *Lolita* or *A Clockwork Orange*, may have caused shock and outrage. Many have led to great films, from *In Cold Blood* to *One Flew Over the Cuckoo's Nest*. They have broken down barriers – whether social, sexual, or, in the case of *Ulysses*, the boundaries of language itself. And they might – like *Goldfinger* or *Scoop* – just be pure classic escapism. Whatever the reason, Penguin Modern Classics continue to inspire, entertain and enlighten millions of readers everywhere.

'No publisher has had more influence on reading habits than Penguin'
Independent

'Penguins provided a crash course in world literature'
Guardian

The best books ever written

PENGUIN 🐧 CLASSICS

SINCE 1946

Find out more at www.penguinclassics.com